PRIVATEER

Books by MARGARET WEIS and ROBERT KRAMMES

Dragon Brigade

Shadow Raiders
*Storm Riders**
*The Seventh Sigil**

Dragon Corsairs

*Spymaster**
*Privateer**

*A TOR BOOK

PRIVATEER

Margaret Weis
and Robert Krammes

TOR

A TOM DOHERTY ASSOCIATES BOOK / NEW YORK

PRIVATEER

Copyright © 2018 by Margaret Weis and Robert Krammes

Dragon ornament © 2014 by Jeff Easley

Map and family tree by Ellisa Mitchell

A Tor Book
Published by Tom Doherty Associates
175 Fifth Avenue
New York, NY 10010

www.tor-forge.com

Tor® is a registered trademark of Macmillan Publishing Group, LLC.

The Library of Congress Cataloging-in-Publication Data is available upon request.

ISBN 978-0-7653-8109-5 (hardcover)
ISBN 978-1-4668-7796-2 (ebook)

Our books may be purchased in bulk for promotional, educational, or business use. Please contact your local bookseller or the Macmillan Corporate and Premium Sales Department at 1-800-221-7945, extension 5442, or by email at MacmillanSpecialMarkets@macmillan.com.

First Edition: August 2018

Printed in the United States of America

0 9 8 7 6 5 4 3 2 1

Thank you to my friends in the Middle Kingdom of the SCA, for your expertise, your support, and often, your names. A special thanks to Frank Sloan, Randy Baker, Paul Koontz, Tim Miller, Jeffrey Skevington, Leonard Albright, Richard Craig, and Jim Hart.

Robert Krammes

To my mom, who didn't really get fantasy, but tried very hard. She would proudly refer to herself as Tasslehoff's grandmother.

Margaret Weis

King Lionel II

Ester of Travia (M) — (D)   Blanche Hunsman (M)

Osric (D)   Frederick (M) Elizabeth   Oswald I (M) Caroline
Died with
Queen Ester

Victoria (M) Michael   Bridgett   Oswald II (M) Ann

Richard (M) Margaret   Mary (M) Oswald III   Phillip (M) Martha
                               (K)

Lucia (M) James I (K)   Oswald   Mortimer   Alfred I (M) Susan
                         (K)   (K)

Vincent (M) Evelyn   Margaret   Thomas   Marjorie (M) William I   Jonathan   Richard
                            Died   (D)
                            as a Baby (D)

Elanora (M) Henry   George I (M) Caroline

Giovana (M) Joseph   Anne (M) George II   **Bastard Line**

Constanza (M) Alistair Oberlein   Godfrey I (M) Jane   Godfrey (M) Honoria

                                             Elise (M) Hugh

Thomas Stanford   Michael Owens (M) Mary I   Elinor   Martha   Claire (M) Jeffrey
(Prince Tom)   Susan

                          (D) Osric   Jonathan   Henry F. (M) Ann

                                           Henry E.

House Stanford   **House Chessington**

(M)	Married
(D)	Died
(K)	Killed

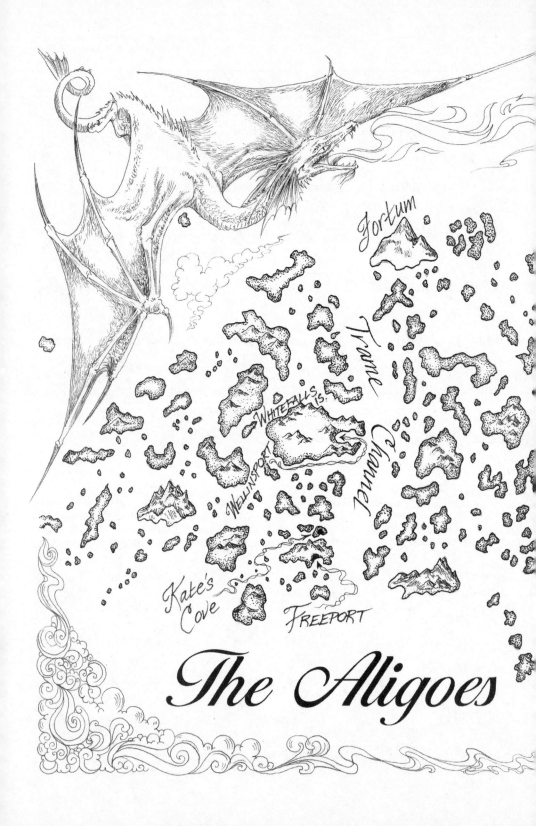

Jortum

Trame Channel

WHITEFALLS IS.

WELLINSPORT

Kate's
Cove

FREEPORT

The Aligoes

Maribeau

Imperial Channel

Sornhagen

100 Miles

PRIVATEER

BOOK 1

ONE

His Highness Thomas Stanford, known fondly as "Prince Tom" to some in Freya and not so fondly as the "Pretender" to others, was to dine today with the admiral of the Rosian navy on board his flagship, *Vent d'Argent,* anchored in Maribeau's harbor.

Phillip Masterson, Duke of Upper and Lower Milton in Freya, accompanied his friend Prince Tom. King Renaud of Rosia had invited the prince to observe the workings of the Rosian Royal Navy as their ships and the famed Dragon Brigade were engaged in clearing the Aligoes of pirates, smugglers, and other miscreants.

King Renaud knew that the presence of a Freyan prince on board a Rosian ship would cause consternation among his officers, for Thomas could well be the future ruler of Rosia's most implacable foe. The king let it be known, however, that his officers had no choice in the matter. Thomas was engaged to be married to the king's sister, Princess Sophia. Renaud believed that once Thomas became king of Freya, he would usher in a new era of peace between the two warring nations.

"In other words," Thomas remarked caustically to Phillip as they were being ferried to the *Vent d'Argent,* "if I become king, Renaud expects me to become Rosia's vassal."

Thomas gestured at the assembled ships of the Rosian navy, floating at anchor on the mists of the Breath: the two massive seventy-fours, frigates, and brigs, watched over by three dragons of the Dragon Brigade circling overhead.

"Renaud invited me to view this show of force in order to impress me with Rosian might," Thomas continued. "He wants to frighten me into good behavior."

"I think you are making too much of this," Phillip said. "You forget that I used to live in the Aligoes. I believe Rosia is doing the world a favor. The pirates were growing increasingly bold and powerful. No ship was safe, and that includes Freyan merchant shipping."

"The Freyans dispatched strongly worded communiqués protesting the Rosian naval blockade of the Trame Channel," said Thomas.

"But all they have done is talk," said Phillip. "Freya is secretly happy to see the end of the pirate scourge in the Aligoes and extremely glad that they don't have to pay for it."

Thomas grinned at his friend. "This spoken by a former pirate. I suppose I should not mention over the soup course that His Grace, the Duke of Upper and Lower Milton, was one of the notorious Rose Hawks who once preyed upon Rosian ships in the Aligoes."

"I fear such a statement would land me *in* the soup, not dining on it," said Phillip, laughing.

The shore boat ferrying the two friends arrived at the *Vent d'Argent* just as the ship's bells struck two times, one of the clock in the afternoon. The prince was accorded the honors due to him: the twittering of pipes, marines standing at attention, sailors in their best uniforms. A flag lieutenant was on hand to greet them.

He made introductions to the captain and lieutenants, then ushered them into the admiral's elegantly appointed cabin.

Silver lamps hung from overhead. A beautiful rosewood table was set for twelve with white tablecloth, silver and gold place settings, and crystal stemware. Flowers filled the room, where sailors in white gloves handed around the dishes.

The admiral had invited the other captains and commanders of the ships of the Rum Fleet, as it was called, to dine with them. Thomas and Phillip already knew many of them. They were currently living aboard the seventy-four-gun *Belle Fleur,* and they had visited other ships during their time in the Aligoes and met many of the other captains. Thomas liked all of them with the exception of Captain Favager, commander of a frigate.

Favager had the reputation among the fleet as a bully and a tyrant, faults that might have been overlooked if he had been a good officer and sailor. He was neither, however. He was the kind of man who built himself up by publicly tearing down others. He took pride in "speaking his mind," which meant being rude and offensive.

"Favager is fortunate that dueling is forbidden, or he would spend half his time on the field of honor," one captain had confided to Thomas.

Favager's fellow captains disliked him not only for his sneering remarks, but also because he had obtained his posting solely due to his wife's connections; she was sister to one of the Lords of the Divinebrises Gardiens, the Rosian equivalent of the Freyan Lords of the Admiralty.

Thus it was with extreme displeasure that Thomas found himself seated across from Favager, with Phillip opposite him. Captain Dag Thorgrimson, of the Dragon Brigade, was seated at Thomas's right. The captain grimaced as Captain Favager settled himself.

"Bad luck for us, Your Highness," said Captain Thorgrimson in a low voice. "Favey will be in rare form today. He fought a battle yesterday and actually won. Although from what my dragons tell me, it was a bad business."

Thomas was surprised to hear the man speak so forthrightly. He did not know Captain Thorgrimson well, but from what he had seen and heard of him, he liked him. A former mercenary from the nation of Guundar, Thorgrimson was now the commander of the Dragon Brigade. He had been recommended to his post by the Brigade's previous commander, Stephano de Guichen, and had received his promotion from King Renaud himself. He had been unanimously approved by the Dragon Brigade's Council of Arms.

Thorgrimson was well liked and highly respected both by his fellow officers and by the dragons who served under him. Thomas was interested to hear more, but their conversation was interrupted by the arrival of the soup. The captain on Thomas's left asked him a question about the Estaran navy. Thomas had served in the Estaran army, but he knew enough about the navy to reply. Then another captain wanted to know details about the battle of San Estavan in which Thomas had fought during the war with the Bottom Dwellers. Discussion of the battle carried them through the soup course.

The sailors served the fish course and the talk turned to the scourge of yellow jack, the virulent fever that was the curse of these islands. The disease was often fatal and could ravage a ship. Yellow jack ended when the meat course was being served. As Thorgrimson had predicted, Favager took the opportunity of a momentary lull in the conversation to brag about the battle he had fought.

"I fired a broadside that knocked down the pirates' mizzenmast—" Favager began.

"*After* the ship had struck her colors," Thorgrimson interjected. "You fired on a ship that had surrendered."

His voice was deep and resonant, and carried well. Everyone heard his accusation and a hush descended, save for the head of the table where their host, Admiral Charbonneau, was bitterly complaining about the difficulties of storing his best claret in the Aligoes heat.

"Pirates deserve no such consideration, sir," Favager stated. He was lean, tall, and rawboned with an underslung jaw. He drank heavily, but always appeared perfectly sober.

"The men you sent to the bottom were not pirates," said Thorgrimson. "They were privateers—men holding letters of marque from Freya."

"One and the same," Favager said with a sneer. He added with a shrug, "We make allowances for you, Thorgrimson. We would not expect a man of low birth such as yourself to understand the complexities of naval warfare."

Thomas was shocked by the insult and waited for Thorgrimson to challenge the man on the spot, dueling laws be damned. Several of the others looked shocked as well. There were a few mutterings, but everyone waited to see how Thorgrimson reacted.

Laying down his knife and fork, he wiped his lips with his napkin, then said calmly, "Even a man of low birth knows the meaning of honor, sir. Or more particularly, the lack of honor."

His fellow officers smiled, and several nodded. Phillip looked across at Thomas and mouthed the word "Touché!"

Favager flushed an ugly red. Throwing down his napkin, he started to rise from his chair. He was interrupted by Admiral Charbonneau. Notoriously obtuse, the admiral only now was aware of the conversation.

"Eh? What's that you are saying, Captain Favager?" Charbonneau called out. "Talking about that pirate you sank? Damned good work. I read your report. The fiends put up a vicious fight. Give us the details, Captain."

The officer to Thomas's left choked on his beef and several more were forced to hide their laughter in their napkins.

Captain Favager couldn't very well describe a fight that had not taken place—except, it seemed, in his report to the admiral. He cast a hate-filled look at Dag, then resumed his seat.

"The bitch was a damned pirate," he said. "I sank her ship and captured her and now the notorious 'Captain Kate,' as the rabble call her, is going to hang."

Captain Kate. Thomas heard her name and he could feel the blood drain from his face. He must be as white as the tablecloth and he could see by Phillip's alarmed expression that others would soon notice and start to wonder.

Thomas should say something to explain his dramatic change of countenance, but he seemed paralyzed. He couldn't think, move, or even breathe.

Phillip gestured to a sailor.

"I will have more of that gravy," he said.

The sailor hurried over to ladle the gravy from its tureen, and that's when the mishap occurred.

Phillip was raising a glass of wine to his lips just as the sailor was bending to ladle out the gravy. The two of them collided.

The sailor upset the tureen and dumped steaming hot beef gravy down the front of Phillip's jacket, causing Phillip to jump to his feet in shock and pain. As he did so, he jerked his arm and flung claret directly into Thomas's face.

Confusion reigned as the other officers pushed back their chairs to try to avoid the gravy spill, which was spreading. Thomas gasped and blinked. The wine stung his eyes as he fumbled blindly for something to wipe them with.

Thorgrimson thrust a napkin into Thomas's hand and he mopped his face. A lieutenant hustled the unfortunate sailor away.

"Entirely my fault," Phillip was saying. "I hope the sailor will not be punished. I barged into him, poor devil. My apologies, Admiral, gentlemen."

The flag lieutenant hurried over. "If you gentlemen would care to retire to clean up, I can take you to my cabin and provide you with towels and fresh water."

He led the way. Thomas and Phillip both bowed their excuses and left.

"Quick thinking!" Thomas said in a low voice as they followed the lieutenant.

"Now at least you have some color in your face," Phillip said. He added more somberly, "What are we going to do about Kate? Can they be serious about hanging her? This is terrible!"

"We must find out where they are holding her," Thomas said.

Phillip nodded and accosted the flag lieutenant.

"I am fond of a good hanging, sir," Phillip said. "When and where is this female pirate to be strung up? That is a spectacle I would not want to miss."

"They are holding her in Fort Saint-Jean, Your Grace," the flag lieutenant replied. "You can see the fortress from here if you look off the port bow. I understand she is to be executed at dawn. The Admiralty wants her dispatched swiftly and quietly, for they fear she has influential friends who might try to save her. She was part of a gang of Freyan thugs who called themselves the 'Rose Hawks.'"

"I've heard stories of these Rose Hawks," Phillip said. "They say they were all extremely handsome men of rare courage—"

The flag lieutenant was staring at him. Thomas hastily intervened. "Thank you for the offer of a cabin, Lieutenant, but I believe we will return to our ship. Phillip has done damage enough for one day. Please make our excuses to the admiral and extend our thanks for his hospitality."

The flag lieutenant politely tried to convince them to stay. Thomas was insistent, however, and the lieutenant sent one midshipman to fetch their hats and another to summon their boat.

The Breath was calm today. The ship floated on a cool autumn breeze and the orange mists. The Rosian fleet relied on the magical crystals known as the Tears of God and magic to keep afloat. The helmsman controlled the flow of the magic to the lift tanks from the magical constructs on the brass helm. The large seventy-four, so called because of her seventy-four cannons, was propelled by six airscrews that were also controlled from the helm. The airscrews were barely moving, and the ship's forward motion had nearly slowed to a crawl, so as not to disturb the dinner guests.

While Thomas and Phillip waited for their boat, they strolled over to the port bow to take a look at the fort.

"The last we heard of Kate, she was in Freya working for Sir Henry Wallace," Phillip said. "What the devil do you suppose caused her to return to the Aligoes? Everyone in the islands knew the Rosians were coming to wage war on the pirates. Perhaps Wallace sent her here on some mission."

"Your spymaster friend Wallace is up to his eyeballs in trouble these days," Thomas said. "He's forced to deal with Freya's failing economy, rioting in the streets, and now the mysterious death of this dragon, Lady Odila. The *Haever Gazette* talks of nothing else. I doubt if he has time for a secret mission."

"Kate must have understood the danger she would face if she returned to the Aligoes," said Phillip. "The Rosians hate her and small wonder. They read the stories about her in the *Gazette* wherein the fictional Captain Kate always outwits the Rosian navy. Maybe she thought she could do so in real life."

They stood at the rail, somberly studying the fort where Kate was being held prisoner.

Fort Saint-Jean was a solid, no-nonsense structure, constructed to serve, not to adorn. Standing atop Point La Fierté du Roi, the fort consisted of three squat stone towers connected by walls and bristling with cannons. The fort was one of three guarding the entrance to the harbor and the Rosian city of Maribeau.

Phillip gave a low whistle. "That's rather formidable, isn't it? How do you propose to get inside?"

"Getting inside won't be a problem," said Thomas. "Getting out will."

TWO

"You can drop us off at the wharf," Thomas told the coxswain, who was ferrying them to Maribeau in the ship's pinnace. "Inform Captain Stanzi that we will be spending several days on shore. I have pressing matters of state to which I must attend, so I am not certain when we will be able to return to the ship."

The coxswain promised he would relay the message, dropped them off at the wharf, then sailed back to his ship.

"Stanzi will find it odd that you didn't mention these pressing matters of state earlier," Phillip remarked.

"He'll think that we are too embarrassed by your appalling gaffe at dinner to return to the ship and I'm using that as an excuse," said Thomas.

He could see Fort Saint-Jean more clearly now, perched on the cliff, practically on top of them. Phillip followed his gaze and shook his head. "It looks worse close-up."

"How many soldiers man it?" Thomas asked.

"Four thousand during the Bottom Dweller war," said Phillip. "Now probably about a thousand. Steep odds, even for us."

"With luck, it won't matter. We will be in and out before they know it," Thomas said. He looked at his watch. "Three of the clock. We need to go to our lodgings and change clothes. I look as though I have been on an all-night debauch and you smell like pot roast."

Phillip fell into step beside him. "After that, where are we bound?"

"To the cathedral. I want to be there in time for Vespers at four, so we must hurry."

"The cathedral?" Phillip repeated, startled. "I know we need all the help we can get, but I am not certain God would side with us in any attempt to free Kate. I hate to say that Favager is right about anything, but he does have a point. Kate is far more pirate than she is privateer. I take it you have formed a plan?"

"We are going to the cathedral to secure disguises," said Thomas. "After that, we will need to hire griffins, have them ready and waiting to fly us off Maribeau. I was thinking we could take Kate to Wellinsport and put her on a merchant ship bound for Freya. The Rosians are not stopping merchant ships."

"They are not stopping them *now*," said Phillip. "They will once they find out Kate has escaped."

"Damn! You are right," said Thomas, discouraged.

They continued to discuss the matter as they entered their lodgings and hurriedly put on more somber attire, suitable to attending holy services.

"We will need cloaks," said Thomas, picking up his as they started to leave.

"It is hot as blazes! We will look ridiculous," Phillip protested.

"If anyone asks, we can always say it might rain," said Thomas.

Phillip sighed and picked up his cloak. They turned their steps toward the cathedral, which was located in the middle of Maribeau. Designed to be the center of attention, the single spire was visible from every part of the city. Phillip was intimately familiar with Maribeau, for he had visited the city on numerous occasions during his time as a Rose Hawk, and he led the way.

"I'm not really accustomed to walking about in broad daylight," Phillip said. "Most of my work here took place at night. So what is the plan?"

"Consider this, Pip. If a person is going to be executed, who is the one person the guards will allow into the cell, permit to be alone with the prisoner?"

Phillip stared, aghast, at Thomas. "Oh, no! You are not thinking what I think you are thinking!"

"I think I probably am," Thomas admitted.

"I draw the line at assaulting a priest to steal his robes."

Thomas gripped his friend by the arm, digging his fingers in. "Pip, they are going to hang Kate! Have you ever seen a man hanged? During the war, I saw a soldier hanged for striking a superior officer. We officers had to be there to witness it. The executioner put the noose around the man's neck, then released the trapdoor. If the victim is lucky, the fall snaps his neck. This poor bastard was not lucky. He hung there, kicking and writhing in agony, as the noose slowly choked off his life. I can't bear to think of her—"

Thomas shook his head, unable to go on.

"We will save her," Phillip said. "You can count on me."

"I know I can," said Thomas with a faint smile. "And if my plan works, we won't have to assault anyone. Now, hurry. I want to be there when the service starts."

The two quickened their pace.

Maribeau had been founded over one hundred years ago by Rosian settlers worried about Freyan expansion into the Aligoes with the establishment of Wellinsport. Now, Maribeau was the largest city in the islands, the cathedral the most imposing structure.

The original church building had been made of timber with a thatched roof. The burgeoning population soon outgrew the small church and when the Freyans in Wellinsport constructed a church made of stone, the Rosians would not rest until they had built a more impressive one.

Blessed with an energetic archbishop and an equally energetic order of monks intent on bringing God to the pirates, they used money derived from the manufacture and sale of gunpowder to the same pirates and paid vast sums to have marble shipped all the way from Rosia. The story goes that the towns-people came together to haul the marble blocks from the docks to the building site.

The cathedral was not as large as the grandest ones on the continent of Rosia, but with its simple and elegant design, white marble and dark cedar timbers, it was considered by many to have its own unique beauty.

Cathedral Square was a popular meeting place for the city's inhabitants. Farmers came from all over the island to sell their goods in the market that was held in the middle of the square. The farmers were packing up for the day by the time Phillip and Thomas arrived and the two men had to navigate their way among the colorful stalls and dodge flocks of geese and chickens, children and handcarts.

The cathedral bell sounded the call to Vespers. The church doors stood open. People began leisurely making their way toward the church.

Thomas did not enter the cathedral, but continued past the main building to the rear where the monks of the order of the martyr Saint Guillaume had built their monastery. They ran a school for the teaching of crafting, and the school building was also behind the church. A high stone wall enclosed the monastery grounds and the school.

The wall was not meant to keep out intruders so much as to shut out the noise of the city and provide the monks a peaceful sanctuary to live and worship. It was an old wall, covered with trailing vines adorned with colorful flowers.

They passed a monk holding open a wicket gate as a stream of excited children flooded out into the square, glad to be released from school. The monk gave Thomas and Phillip a friendly nod as they passed. Several of the older female students gave them friendly nods, too, adding friendly smiles as well, for the two young men were clearly gentlemen, comely and well dressed.

Thomas received most of their attention. He was strikingly handsome, with black curly hair and blue eyes, a trait his mother claimed was part of the Stanford heritage. A scar on his cheek from the battle of San Estavan added a touch of romance.

Phillip was not as handsome as Thomas, nor was he as tall. He had a shock of blond hair bleached almost white by the sun and one blue eye and one green. His mouth was too wide, but that gave him a generous smile and made people want to smile back. He and Thomas smiled at the girls, who giggled and ran off.

Thomas eyed the wall. "I need to climb over that, sneak onto the grounds."

"And what will you say when you are caught?" Phillip asked. "That you felt a sudden urge to become a priest?"

"I won't get caught," said Thomas. "The monks will all be attending Vespers."

The two continued to follow the wall around to the back until they found a likely looking place to scale the wall. The vines were thick and tough and this portion of the wall was in deep shadow cast by the leafy branches of a nearby tree. Thomas removed his hat and his jacket and took hold of a vine with both hands. He immediately let go, winced, swore.

"Damn! Thorns!" He looked at his scratched hands, eyed the vines, then said, "Take off your cravat."

Phillip understood his intention. He removed the cravat and handed the wide strip of cloth to Thomas, who took off his own cravat and wrapped them both around his palms.

"I'll go. You stay here," said Thomas.

"What do I do if someone comes? I look very suspicious, loitering around the wall," said Phillip.

"Say you're a botanist, studying the flora," said Thomas. He took off his jacket and handed it to his friend. "Besides, no one will come. Everyone will be in church."

He once more grasped hold of the vine and began to climb it. The climb was not easy. The thorns were tiny but wicked, and though his hands were somewhat protected, the thorns snagged his stockings and his shirt, and tugged at his hair. Small branches cracked and snapped underfoot, sounding as loud as gunshots. Fortunately the bell was still ringing and he hoped no one would hear.

Thomas reached the top and looked back down. Phillip stood below, anxiously watching. Thomas gave him a reassuring wave and looked from his perch into the compound. The monks kept a vegetable garden here, as well as pigs, to judge by the smell. From here he could see the monks filing into the church.

He located the *dortoir* where the monks lived, and fixed the position in his mind. Thanking Providence that the vine also covered the inside of the wall he'd climbed, he carefully shinnied partway down the vine, then dropped the rest of the way, landing in a tangle of undergrowth. He took a moment to locate a landmark that would guide him back to this section of the wall. A tree laden with sweet-smelling purple flowers stood not far from where he had landed.

He set out, circling around the garden and the pigs, keeping to the shadows as much as possible. While most of the monks and lay brothers would be attending Vespers, the infirm and the elderly would be excused from going, and Thomas did not want to take the chance of being seen.

He made his way swiftly past the abbot's house, the bakery, and kitchen. He passed the stables and came at last to the rear of the compound. Here he found what he was seeking: a stream of fresh water.

The stream led him to the bathhouse and the laundry area, marked by large washtubs and poles strung with rope on which to hang the wet clothes.

Thomas hoped he would find robes hanging on the line and that he would not be forced to sneak inside the *dortoir* to pilfer them from the monks' cells. He breathed a sigh of relief. Robes were neatly pinned to the lines, gently waving in the soft breeze. He selected two woolen tunics and two scapulars— the aprons with attached cowls that covered the tunics. Removing them from the line, he hurriedly folded them and tucked them underneath his arm, then made his way back through the garden.

He found the wall and spent a few tense moments searching for the tree with the purple flowers. Just when he was starting to panic, thinking he was completely lost, he found the tree. Hoping it was the right tree, he gave a low whistle.

Phillip whistled back.

"All clear!" he added, keeping his voice as soft as possible. "Did you find robes?"

"I did. Be ready! I'm tossing them over the wall."

Thomas tied the two cravats he'd worn around his hands together, tightly knotted the makeshift rope around the monks' tunics and scapular, then tried throwing them over the wall.

He missed the first time. The bundle struck the wall and tumbled down, nearly hitting him in the face. His aim was better the second time. The bundle sailed over the wall and disappeared.

"Got it!" Phillip called.

Thomas eyed the thorns on the vines, looked at the limbs of the purple flowering tree and decided for the tree. He broke one of the limbs about halfway up, causing his foot to slip, but he managed to hang on and hoisted himself onto the top of the wall.

Phillip stood below, watching anxiously. "Hurry up! Someone's coming!"

Thomas dropped off the wall and landed with a jarring thud on the ground. He could hear voices drawing closer. A young man and a young woman came into sight, holding hands. They had eyes only for each other. Thomas hurriedly snatched up his hat and put it on, then struggled into his jacket. Phillip tucked the bundle beneath his cloak and pointed to the tree.

"A fine specimen of jacaranda," he said loudly. "From which we derive logwood, used in dyes and for various medicinal purposes."

"I don't believe I have ever seen one with flowers quite that delicate shade of purple," Thomas remarked.

The young man and the young woman realized they were not alone. The young woman blushed and quickly dropped the young man's hand. Phillip and Thomas regarded them with vague smiles and went back to discussing the tree.

The young man doffed his cap, the young woman curtsied, and they continued down the path.

"I believe we interrupted a lover's tryst," Phillip said.

Thomas was watching the young couple. He guessed, by the ink stain on the young man's index finger, that he was probably a clerk. The young woman was neatly dressed and wore a frilly cap; perhaps she was a maid. The two walked on, once again holding hands. For them, no one else existed, certainly not two men discussing logwood.

"I wonder if they know how lucky they are," Thomas said. "I would give anything just to walk together in a garden with Kate, holding hands."

"Kate is not the kind of woman who would walk demurely by your side, holding your hand," Phillip commented. "She's the kind of woman about to be hanged as a pirate unless we can stop it. You have twigs stuck in your hair."

Thomas pulled out the twigs and the two left the monastery, heading back to their lodgings. Once they were out in the open in Cathedral Square, Thomas's gaze was drawn to Fort Saint-Jean. The enormity of the task he had set for himself suddenly appeared insurmountable.

"What the hell am I thinking, Pip?" he said, discouraged. "We don't know the guards' routine. We don't know where Kate is being held. We don't even know where the prison is located! I don't suppose you were ever inside?"

"Only in my nightmares," said Phillip. "I came a bit too close to being locked up once. I do, though, know someone who might be able to help us."

"That would be a godsend!" Thomas exclaimed.

"We will pay a visit to Louie. He was one of my contacts during the Rose Hawks days," said Phillip. "He will have closed up his shop at this hour, but he lives behind it, so we should find him there—provided he hasn't been arrested again."

"Is that likely?" Thomas asked, startled.

"Unfortunately, yes," said Phillip. "Poor Louie always found it hard to resist temptation. But perhaps he has reformed. You will need your purse. Louie's services do not come cheap."

Phillip led Thomas to a narrow, dirty street in an old part of the city a few blocks from the wharf. The shops in this part of Maribeau were small and dingy with an air of resignation about them, for they had long ago given up any ambitions of being prosperous and now seemed resigned to simply eking out a living.

The odor of boot blacking wafted from the workshop of a cobbler, who was out in the street in his leather apron, hanging up his shutters. He gave Thomas's fine leather boots a wistful, admiring glance, then turned back to his work.

"Here is our destination," Phillip said, stopping before a shop located at the end of the block.

A sign in the shape of an enormous key hung over the door. LOUIE'S LOCKS: MAGICAL AND MECHANICAL.

"Louie is a locksmith," said Thomas.

"One of the best," said Phillip.

Louie had already closed for the day, apparently, for the windows were shuttered and no one answered when Phillip knocked. They circled around to a side door where Phillip knocked again. A hatch popped open and an eye, remarkable for its shrewdness, peered out at them.

Phillip smiled. "It's me, Louie."

The eye narrowed, as though trying to remember, then suddenly vanished. The hatch shut and the door opened to reveal a short, slender, dapper man with sleek black hair. He ushered them inside. After a last glance outside, he shut the door again.

Louie opened his arms wide and embraced Phillip. "Master Pip! My dear friend! I am delighted to see you again, sir. Delighted."

Louie shifted his shrewd eyes to Thomas. "And you have brought a friend.

I do not recall meeting this gentleman before. Was he one of the . . ." Louie gave a delicate cough.

"A Rose Hawk? No, he was not. You may call him Master Tom," Phillip replied, adding for Thomas's benefit, "Louie and I do not stand on formality. We are on a first-name basis. We consider surnames to be superfluous."

"I understand and approve," said Thomas.

Louie made a bobbing bow and extended a hand that was so remarkable Thomas could hardly keep from staring. The locksmith's hand was fine-boned and slender; its long, tapering fingers moved with delicate grace. Thomas had known ladies of the court who would have given half their wealth for such elegant hands.

After introductions, Louie politely asked if they would take tea with him.

"Thank you, but we are here on business, and as fate would have it, time is of the essence," said Phillip. "Louie is the best locksmith in all of the Aligoes and perhaps all the world."

"'Locks mechanical and magical,'" said Louie, quoting the sign over the door.

"Louie is also renowned for his lock-picking skills. He put them to good use for the Rose Hawks when we needed to acquire information from Rosian officials who were so disobliging as to lock it away."

"Those were exciting times, sir," said Louie, sighing wistfully.

"A little too exciting on occasion," said Phillip with a wry smile. "Unfortunately, Louie's passion for locks tends to land him in trouble with the constables."

"I cannot resist a lock, Master Tom," said Louie. His eyes glistened at the thought. "Whenever a new lock is advertised as being 'proof against housebreakers,' I cannot rest until I have defeated it."

Seeing Thomas look dubious, Phillip was quick to reassure him. "Louie is no common thief."

"Indeed, I am not, sir!" said Louie, indignant at the mere suggestion. "I confess that once I have picked the lock, I do break into the house, but only to leave the housekeeper a note, along with my card, advising them that they have been defrauded by purchasing a worthless lock. I suggest that they come to me for a lock that I guarantee will resist all attempts to break it."

"Except your own," said Thomas.

Louie gave a modest smile and bowed.

Phillip said, "Unfortunately the constabulary cannot be made to see that Louie is performing a public service and they persist in arresting him for housebreaking."

"I have my own special cell in Fort Saint-Jean overlooking the harbor," said Louie with a certain amount of pride. "The warden and I have developed a friendship over the years. Often while I am serving my time, I perform various services around the prison for him."

"Louie repairs broken locks, replaces warding constructs, and makes certain the magical damping magic is working," said Phillip.

"Magical damping magic?" Thomas asked curiously.

"Certain cells are specially designed for prisoners who are crafters who could use their magic to effect an escape," Louie explained. "The walls and the cell doors are covered with magical constructs intended to disrupt or dissipate any new constructs. Let us say that a prisoner wants to set the door to his cell on fire. If he tries, not only will the magic prevent him, it will rebound on him, causing him to burn himself in the process."

"As you see, Louie is extremely familiar with the prison in Fort Saint-Jean," said Phillip. "One might say he knows it inside out."

Louie gave another of his bobbing bows, then shifted his shrewd gaze from one man to the other. "How may I be of assistance to you, gentlemen?"

"A friend from the old days is being held in the fort's prison," Phillip explained. "She is going to be hanged in the morning unless we can break her out. We already have a plan in mind. What we need from you is the layout of the prison and any information you can give us, such as when the guards change shifts and where her cell might be located."

"I am glad to help," said Louie.

"The usual fee?" Phillip asked.

"That will suffice, sir," said Louie.

"Two hundred silver rosuns," Phillip told Thomas, who drew out his purse, counted the rosuns and handed them over. "We also need to hire three griffins. Is Big Dimitri still in business?"

"Alas, Big Dimitri is dead, Master Pip," said Louie. "A wyvern bite turned gangrenous. His son, Little Dimitri, has taken over."

Louie placed the silver coins in a cloth bag. Excusing himself, he carried the bag into his shop and presumably locked them away, for he returned without them. He then led them into a neat, tidy kitchen and indicated they were to sit down at the table. Disappearing again, he returned with paper, pen, and ink. As they watched, he swiftly sketched a layout of the prison.

"Is your friend a crafter?" he asked.

"She is," said Phillip.

"Then she will be in one of these magic-damping cells," said Louie, indicating a row of cells on the second floor. "Since she is going to be hanged, the guards will put her in a cell overlooking the courtyard, so that she can easily hear them building the scaffold, and if she looks out her window, she'll be forced to see it."

Thomas shuddered. Louie, absorbed in his drawing, did not appear to notice.

"They will put her in one of these three cells," he was saying, noting each with a neat check mark. "You should not have trouble finding the correct one. Since she is to be executed, they will place a guard directly outside her cell door."

"When do the guards change shifts?" Phillip asked.

"The night guard remains on duty until morning." Louie looked up from his work. "Do you need lock picks, Master Pip? The padlocks on the cells are somewhat difficult, but you were always a quick study, sir."

"No, thank you, not this time, Louie," said Phillip, smiling. He glanced at Thomas, by way of asking if he should tell Louie their plan. Thomas nodded, and Phillip continued. "We could use information on the priests that come to sit with those about to be executed."

Louie understood at once, and quirked an eyebrow in admiration. "I believe that could work, Master Pip. But only one priest visits and he generally arrives an hour prior to the execution to spend his time in prayer with the prisoner."

Phillip and Thomas again exchanged glances, this time in dismay.

"An hour won't give us enough time, Louie," said Phillip. "And we both need to be there."

"And we don't want to risk bumping into the real priest," Thomas added.

While Louie sat mulling over their problem, Thomas and Phillip discussed the man who had put Kate in such danger.

"I believe I will mention Favager's name to the Countess de Marjolaine," Thomas said. "She is friends with the king. A word from her, and Favager will not be attending any more dinner parties. He will be swabbing decks. . . ."

Thomas stopped talking. Recalling the conversation among the officers attending the dinner party, he rolled up Louie's map and tucked it into an inner pocket of his jacket.

"I have an idea. Thank you, Louie, you have been an immense help," he said, gratefully shaking hands. "Forgive me if I don't explain further, but the less you know the better."

"Such has always been my motto, sir," said Louie. "One moment."

He disappeared, going through a door into an interior room. They heard him rummaging about. He returned, carrying a leather pouch. He handed it to Thomas.

"Similar to the scrips carried by the priests," said Louie. "They bring in all manner of potions and herbal concoctions. You could take that into the prison without causing comment."

"Will the guards search it?" Thomas asked.

"They might," said Louie. "And thus, we have this."

He opened the scrip, spoke a word, and drew his finger across the leather to reveal a secret pocket.

"From the old days," he said wistfully. "I regret to say you could not conceal a pistol, for they would see the bulge. You could conceal banknotes, however. Money is always useful."

He escorted them to the door and once more embraced Phillip.

"Seeing you again has taken me back to those old days, Master Pip. What glorious times we had then!" Louie wiped a little moisture from his eyes. "How is Captain Northrop? I hear he has turned respectable."

Judging by his sorrowful tone, Louie appeared to take the captain's downfall very much to heart.

Phillip laughed. "Do not worry about Captain Northrop, Louie. Alan does have his commission in the navy now, but no one would ever accuse him of being respectable. Good-bye, my friend, and thank you again."

"Indeed, I cannot thank you enough, Louie," said Thomas.

"If you ever require a lock, Master Tom, please call upon me," said Louie with another of his bobbing bows. "Remember: magical *and* mechanical."

He opened the door, cast a sweeping look up and down the street, told them it was safe to leave, and shut the door behind them.

"What is your idea?" Phillip asked, mystified.

"Think back to the conversation during the fish course," said Thomas. "If you will lead the way to Little Dimitri, I will explain as we go along."

THREE

"Big Dimitri was a big man with a heart to match," said Phillip, once again leading Thomas through the streets of Maribeau. "I am sorry to hear he has died. I knew his son from back in the old days. Little Dimitri is bigger than his father and will be a worthy successor."

Cobblestone streets gave way to dirt roads. They passed a blacksmith's shop, a tannery, and a brewery. The odors of hops and tanned hides seemed to be trying to outdo one another to see which was the most vile.

Evening was coming on by the time Phillip turned down a narrow side street. Thomas could smell the stable yards before he saw them. He waited while Phillip went up to a small house, knocked on the door, and spoke briefly to the woman who answered. She directed them to stables in back of the house, and sent one of her children running to find her husband and tell him he had customers.

"Say Master Pip needs him," Phillip added.

Little Dimitri came out from one of the horse stalls, wiping his hands on a rag. He was large and broad-shouldered, with long, black hair and a full beard. Thomas could picture him wrestling wyverns into their harnesses with ease.

"Master Pip!" Little Dimitri said in a booming baritone. "Good to see you, sir!"

"I am sorry to hear about your father," said Phillip, shaking hands. "He was a great man."

"Thank you, sir," said Little Dimitri. "He was that. How can I help you?"

"We need three griffins, saddled and ready to ride this night," said Phillip.

"You will have my three best, provided they agree, of course," said Little Dimitri.

Griffins were proud beasts who considered themselves the equal of humans, and nothing infuriated them more than being compared to wyverns or horses. They would agree to carry human riders, but only on their own terms.

"As you probably know, the griffins don't work for me," said Little Dimitri. "To their way of thinking, I work for them. I accept payment on their behalf in coin and provide them with sheep and goats, which they carry to their eyries in the mountains."

Little Dimitri took them to the griffin stables and introduced them. Thomas and Phillip were both familiar with griffins. They expressed their pleasure in meeting them and took time to make polite conversation, as one might at afternoon tea, asking after the health of their families and discussing whether or not they might encounter rain. Once the formalities had been concluded, they asked if the griffins would deign to carry them and a companion on a journey this night.

The griffins were extremely pleased with the courtly manners of both humans. As Little Dimitri later confided to Phillip, his griffins were accustomed to a rougher sort of clientele. The griffins grumbled some about having to fly on such short notice, but at last agreed, on the condition that Thomas pay double. Finally they wanted to know their destination.

"We are flying to Wellinsport," said Phillip. "I know it's a long flight. I hope that won't be a problem."

The griffins were amenable.

Phillip turned to Little Dimitri. "That's settled. Will you see to the stealing of the boat?"

Little Dimitri's expression softened. "By God, Master Pip, I had forgotten about the stolen-boat ruse! Ah, that does take me back to the old days. I will steal Pa's for you. He would have wanted that."

Phillip thanked him. Thomas paid him and the two departed.

"Steal a boat?" Thomas asked. "We're traveling by griffin. Why does Little Dimitri need to steal his father's boat?"

"To throw off pursuit," Phillip explained. "Big Dimitri came up with the idea. If any of us needed to flee Maribeau in a hurry, he would steal a boat—either his own, or one belonging to a crony. He would report the theft of the boat to the authorities, and while the constables were searching for a boat, we would fly out on griffins. Big Dimitri would hide the boat away until the hunt died down, then miraculously discover it."

Thomas regarded his friend with admiration. "You have hidden depths, Pip."

They went back to their lodgings to eat a late supper and commit Louie's map to memory. After that, they pulled the monks' homespun wool tunics over their breeches and shirts and covered the tunics with the scapulars. Phillip cut lengths of rope to tie around their waists. Only then did they realize they had a problem. The tunics stopped short at their ankles, revealing their boots, which were far too expensive and elegant to be worn by monks.

"We should have thought of that," said Thomas.

"No help for it," said Phillip. "We can't go barefoot. The light will be dim and there's no reason anyone would be staring at our feet. They're covered with muck from the stable and we can muddy them up some more on the way."

They hung bull's-eye lanterns around their necks, concealed by the robes, and tucked pocket pistols into their boots. Taking Louie's advice, they stuffed the scrip's secret pocket with currency, then filled it with some potions they had picked up at an apothecary's.

After that, they had nothing to do but wait.

Time had never passed so slowly. Thomas checked his watch repeatedly, convinced that every clock in the city had quit working. At last the clocks chimed eleven times and Phillip said they should go.

They made their way up the hill to the fort, avoiding the well-lighted main streets, instead taking dark side streets and alleys. They walked with their hands in their sleeves and their heads bowed, their cowls pulled low.

Monks were often called upon at night to tend the sick or minister to the dying, and the few people they met paid no attention to them. A night watchman, walking his rounds, asked if they needed any help. Phillip thanked him, said they knew the way, and gave him his blessing.

Finally, the city streets were at an end, and they were forced to take the wide, paved road that led up the side of the cliff at a steep angle. A beacon light flashed from a lighthouse tower on the shore near the fort, serving as a guide to friendly ships and a warning to those that were not so friendly.

The fort walls were constructed of granite and were sheer and steep, long and low. The front of the fort facing the harbor had no windows, while the back of the fort, overlooking the city, had a few windows and those, according to Louie, were covered with iron grates. Each tower was topped by a battery of cannons, and more cannons stood on a rock platform facing the harbor.

All the cannons were mounted on wheels and could be moved if need arose in order to repel an attack either from the land or the Breath.

The night was clear, the sky filled with stars, and a half-moon seemed to shine as bright as the sun. The walls of the fort glimmered a cold, pale gray in the moonlight.

Thomas peered out from beneath his cowl, unable to take his eyes from the fort as they trudged up the empty street. He was oppressed by the sight of the massive walls, the black-barred windows, and the narrow, walled ramp, bathed in moonlight, that led from the street to the gatehouse.

"A mouse crawling along that ramp would be visible to the naked eye at thirty paces," he muttered. "Isn't there another way inside?"

"The only other way is through that large portcullis, which is always closed and locked. Now you see why Fort Saint-Jean has never fallen to an enemy," Phillip replied. "The Bottom Dwellers attacked it with three of their black ships and lost all three of them. That ended their attempt to seize Maribeau, which they had hoped to make a base of operations."

"I begin to think we are fools," Thomas said.

"I have heard it said that the definition of a hero is a fool who won't take no for an answer," Phillip returned with a smile.

"Good old Pip," said Thomas. "You can pick locks, you know giant griffin keepers named 'Little Dimitri,' and you never say things such as 'We can always turn back' or 'Perhaps we should reconsider.'"

"Because I know I would be wasting my breath," said Phillip wryly. "Seriously, Tom, Kate is my friend, too. I have known her for years and I could not live with myself if I did not do everything in my power to save her."

They came to the narrow stone walkway that led to the guardhouse. The walkway had waist-high walls and was only wide enough for two men to walk side by side.

Thomas peered over the wall on his left to see the mists of the Breath, ghostly in the moonlight, drifting below. To the right stood the first of the three towers, its wall pierced by arrow-slit windows. When the fort had first been built, archers standing at those windows could, at their leisure, pick off an enemy attempting to storm the fort.

The days of the archer had long passed, but riflemen would have an even easier time. Thomas glanced at the windows. Fortunately, Maribeau was not at war. Soldiers were not at their posts. The riflemen would have to be roused from their beds, and by the time they were awake, he and Phillip and Kate would be far from this grim place.

They walked across the ramp in silence. At the thought of the coming action, Thomas felt his pulse quicken, his heart beat faster. The oppressive clouds of doubt and misgiving lifted, and his senses heightened. Despite the late hour, he could see, hear, and think with extraordinary clarity.

The guards in the gatehouse were chatting as they approached. They broke off their conversation when they saw they had visitors. They were not alarmed. Monks often came and went from the prison.

"Good evening, Brothers," said one of the guards, emerging from the gatehouse with a lantern. "What brings you here at this time of night?"

Thomas and Phillip cast troubled glances at each other.

"Did no one tell you to expect us?" Phillip asked. "We are healers, summoned to treat a prisoner said to be suffering from a virulent fever."

"We fear it could be yellow jack," Thomas added.

"Yellow jack!" one of the guards gasped.

"Do not be an alarmist, Brother Sebastian," Phillip chided. "We do not know that for certain until we have examined the poor man. We don't want to start a panic."

The panic had already started. The guards hurriedly conferred in agitated voices, then hurried out to open the gate. Prisoners lived in crowded conditions. An outbreak of yellow jack in a prison could be dire, taking its toll on both prisoners and those who guarded them.

"I assume you know the way to the cellblock, Brothers," said the guard, clearly not eager to escort them.

"We have been here before," Phillip replied. "Come along, Brother Sebastian. And mind that gossiping tongue of yours. You know what Father Abbot is always telling you."

"I am sorry, Brother Gregory," said Thomas, chastened.

He bowed his head and followed Phillip. They could hear the guards commiserating in frightened tones.

They proceeded down a narrow corridor, carrying Louie's map in their heads. The fort's architect must have been a military man not much given to flights of fancy, eschewing the romantic and picturesque labyrinthine corridors of novels in favor of wide, straight hallways that took soldiers straight to where they needed to go.

Lanterns hung from the walls at intervals, and the staircases were broad and easy to climb. Thomas could picture a flood of soldiers running down the stairs in pursuit of jail breakers. He immediately banished the thought from his mind.

"Right turn, walk to the end, right turn, up the stairs," Phillip was murmuring as they went along. "Down the corridor, right turn, left turn."

He stopped to look around. "We should be close to the cellblock."

"Judging by the stench, we are," said Thomas.

The hall stank of chamber pots, unwashed bodies, sickness, and vomit.

Thomas thought of Kate, imagined her terror, loneliness, and fear. He could not bear that another minute should pass for her in this horrible place, and he had to exert all his self-control to keep from rushing down the corridor in search of her.

He marveled at Phillip, who seemed as calm and cool as though they were entering a ballroom, not breaking into a prison which, if they were discovered, could turn into their permanent residence. Phillip seemed to have transformed into the monk he was impersonating. Sighting the jailer, he approached him with brisk confidence and an air of authority that came from God.

The night jailer was seated at a small desk beneath an overhanging lantern, munching on bread and cold meat and engaged in writing something in a large book.

"God be with you this night, sir," Phillip said, walking up to the desk.

The jailer gave a violent start and dropped his sandwich. He was clearly not expecting visitors at this hour and he stared at the monks in astonishment.

"Brothers! What are you doing here?"

"We received a message that a prisoner is exhibiting symptoms of yellow jack," said Phillip.

The jailer blanched.

"I know nothing about this," he said.

"We received the message from the commander late this afternoon," said Phillip.

The jailer was perplexed. "Colonel Sartoine? He said nothing to me!"

Thomas and Phillip exchanged glances.

"There might be a reason he did not tell you, sir," Thomas said gently.

The jailer frowned. "I don't understand."

"I am certain that *you* would never refuse to go on duty in a cellblock infected with yellow jack, sir," said Phillip. "Others would not be so courageous."

The jailer gulped. "Which prisoner?"

"A female condemned for piracy," said Phillip. "We were told she comes from Freeport, where there has been a recent outbreak."

"So many dead," Thomas remarked in sorrow. "They say the bodies are piling up in the streets."

The jailer looked nervous, but he was not to be cheated of his hanging.

"She is condemned to die this very morning," he said. "Not long to wait. Let us leave her to God."

Phillip shrugged. "That is your decision, sir. I would, however, recommend that those who escort her to the gallows keep as far from her as possible."

The jailer stirred uneasily; perhaps he was an escort. Still, he didn't budge. Thomas could have throttled him.

Phillip leaned close to his friend and spoke in a low, ominous tone that was meant to be confidential, but which carried remarkably well.

"The jailer is sweating profusely, Brother Sebastian."

"So he is, Brother Gregory," said Thomas, alarmed. He regarded the jailer with grave concern. "He is red in the face."

"Have you felt dizzy or nauseous, sir?" Phillip asked. "Were you in contact with this prisoner?"

"Not me! I have scarcely set eyes on her!" The jailer shuddered. "You will find her in one of the cells for the condemned. Down that corridor. Number sixteen. Take this lantern. Magic won't work down there."

Thomas picked up the lantern that was filled with oil, not magic, and accompanied Phillip down the darkened corridor.

"If that bastard jailer wasn't sweating before, he is now," Thomas muttered.

"He might send for the colonel," said Phillip. "We need to hurry."

According to Louie's map, cell number sixteen was at the very end of the cellblock, several hundred feet from the entrance. Thomas was grateful that the jailer had not accompanied them, for they were going to have to change their story. He could feel the man's eyes staring after him as it was.

The corridor was dark. The wooden doors on the cells they passed were closed. Thomas was grateful. He could not see inside, but he could hear, and the sounds of the misery coming from behind the locked doors were bad enough.

They knew Kate's cell by the soldier seated on a camp stool in front of the door, his rifle resting in his arms, his head on his chest.

"He's asleep on duty," Thomas whispered.

"He'll be the one who is hanged if someone catches him," Phillip said. "God be with you, sir," he called loudly, kindly giving the soldier advance notice of their coming.

The soldier sat bolt upright, fumbling at his rifle as he scrambled to his feet. He was young and gangly, probably no more than eighteen. He squinted at them in the bright lantern light.

"Who is there?" he asked uneasily, undoubtedly fearing it was the jailer.

"I am Brother Gregory and this is Brother Sebastian," said Phillip. "We have come to sit with the condemned and pray for her soul."

Either the guard was new and had no idea that the priest was not supposed to arrive until dawn, or he didn't want to question a priest, especially not one who had just caught him napping. He brought out his key ring, sorted through the keys, and inserted one into the lock.

"The priest is here," he said to the prisoner.

"Tell him to go away!" a woman's voice called.

Thomas remembered her voice, rich and mellow, laced with spice and fire, and now, ragged with fear.

"I am not a believer," Kate added. "I don't want a priest."

Thomas was stirred to his soul. Kate was trying very hard to sound brave, but her voice betrayed her. She was frightened and alone, condemned to die, without hope. Thomas longed to embrace her and comfort her, hold her in his arms. He restrained himself, however, and followed their plan.

Phillip opened the cell door and raised the lantern to shine the light on Kate. She was sitting on the bed, her back against the wall, facing them in defiance.

Thomas was thankful his friend was carrying the lantern, for he might have dropped it. Kate was so altered he would not have recognized her.

They had shaved her head, her blond curls gone. A surgeon had sewed up an ugly gash on her scalp. Her face was bruised and bloody, her lips swollen. Her eyes, red from crying, seemed huge in her pallid face. Her tears had left tracks in the blood. She was dressed in a long white shift, her legs and ankles bare.

Mindful of the corporal standing outside the cell door, Phillip was saying something to Kate about praying for her soul. Thomas could scarcely hear his friend for the rushing of blood in his ears.

"I don't want your prayers!" Kate retorted. "Just leave me alone to die in peace."

"Go in to the poor girl, Brother Sebastian," said Phillip. "I will keep the corporal company, if that is permitted. Take the lantern, Brother."

He handed Thomas the lantern and stood aside to allow him to enter, then shut the cell door. Thomas had difficulty with the lantern, for his hands were shaking, and the lantern light flared about the cell, half blinding Kate, who shielded her eyes and averted her face.

"I said go away!" she mumbled.

Thomas set the lantern on the floor. He drew near to her and pulled back the cowl so that she could see his face.

"But I have come to save you, my child," he said softly.

FOUR

Thomas worried that she might not recognize him, and at first, she didn't. She stared at him, frowning, probably wondering why a priest should speak with such a thrill in his voice. Her eyes widened, and she gave a little gasp. Thomas gently rested his hand over her bruised mouth.

"Not a word!" he whispered. "Pip is dealing with the guard."

They heard the sounds of a brief scuffle outside the cell door and then it swung open and Phillip came in, dragging the unconscious corporal into the cell by the shoulders. He stretched the corporal out on the floor, then shut the cell door.

Kate stared, not moving. "Am I dreaming?" She spoke in a low voice, as if she didn't want to wake herself.

"You are not dreaming, Kate," Phillip replied with a deliberately cheerful grin. "We are quite real, I assure you. Tom, I need your help," he added sternly, for Thomas could do nothing except gaze at Kate. "We have to move fast and we need to relieve this poor devil of his uniform."

"Yes, of course," said Thomas, seeming to come out of a daze.

He set the scrip on the floor, then he and Phillip pulled off the soldier's boots and stripped off his jacket and breeches. Kate did not move. She sat on the bed, watching them work, perhaps still trying to convince herself there was hope. Suddenly she lunged off the bed and flung one arm around Thomas and her other arm around Phillip.

"Thank you!" Kate whispered fiercely, hugging them. "Thank you both so much!"

Thomas put his arm around her and she clung to him for a moment, half sobbing and half laughing. Thomas tightened his grip on her.

"You are safe now, Kate," he said, his heart wrung with love and pity.

"No! She isn't," said Phillip sharply. "Not yet. She is going to be hanged and they'll hang us with her unless we get out of here! The jailer could come at any moment, so get to work! Remove his other boot. Kate, take off that wretched thing you are wearing and put on the guard's clothes while we get him into bed."

"What's the plan?" Kate asked. Seeing Phillip's grim look, she added hurriedly, "Hand me his stockings."

She sat down on the bed, hiked up her shift, and pulled the stockings on over her bare legs. Phillip tossed her the breeches and Thomas handed her the shirt. Kate retreated into a corner of the cell.

"Turn around," she ordered, taking off her shift.

"Help me get him onto the bed," said Phillip to Thomas.

Thomas picked up the man's shoulders, Phillip lifted his feet, and they hauled him onto the bed. Phillip laid him out as one would a corpse, folding his hands over his chest. Thomas covered him from head to toe with the bedsheet.

By that time, Kate had put on the shirt and the breeches and was buttoning the guard's jacket. She was taller than average and the guard's clothing almost fit her. Then she put on his boots and shook her head.

"These are way too big. I won't be able to walk in them. And what about my head? *He* has hair," she said bitterly.

Phillip picked up the blanket. "Drape this over your head. Tom and I will carry you—"

"Brothers!" the jailer bellowed. "What is going on?"

"Sounds as though he's standing at the end of the corridor," Thomas said. "At least he's keeping his distance."

Kate enveloped herself in the blanket. Thomas and Phillip put their arms around her.

"Hang your head," Phillip admonished her. "You are sick with the yellow jack, so it would be appropriate if you moaned now and then. Brother Sebastian, the scrip and your cowl."

Thomas had forgotten about the damn cowl, which he had lowered to talk to Kate. He hurriedly pulled it up over his head and draped the leather pouch with the money over his shoulder.

"Everyone ready?" Phillip asked. He drew in a breath. "God be with us!"

Thomas grasped hold of Kate around her waist. Phillip opened the cell door with one hand, supporting Kate with the other. She went limp, her head down, her feet in the overlarge boots dragging along the floor.

Thomas and Phillip emerged from the cell carrying Kate between them. The jailer had ventured as far as the end of the cellblock. He stared at them in alarm. All he could see in the dim light was a man in uniform, his head covered with a blanket.

"Who do you have there, Brothers?" the jailer asked. "What is the matter with him? What about the prisoner? How is she?"

"She is dead, God rest her," said Phillip. "She died of the yellow jack. Her guard now has the dread disease."

"For God's sake, keep your voice down, Brother," said the jailer, going pale. "You will start a riot!"

"You need to do something to contain the fever, sir," Phillip added, just in case someone hadn't heard him the first time. "Yellow jack spreads quickly, you know."

The words were apparently as contagious as the disease, for they began spreading rapidly from cell to cell.

"Yellow jack! Did you hear that, lads!" one of the prisoners shouted.

"We're all going to die in this stinking hellhole!" cried another.

"Let us out!" The prisoners yelled and began banging on the cell doors.

Kate moaned from beneath the blanket. Thomas and Phillip kept walking, hauling her between them.

"Perhaps I should go view the body . . ." said the jailer.

Thomas cast Phillip an alarmed glance. "I do not think that would be wise, do you, Brother?"

"I applaud your courage, sir," Phillip told the jailer in admiring tones. "Most people would not go anywhere near that cell. I do caution you not to touch the corpse. Some of the brethren will be back to remove it for burial."

The jailer cast an uncertain glance down the corridor.

The prisoners were in an uproar, demanding to be set free. Thomas and Phillip, dragging Kate along with them, were only steps from the exit. The jailer took out his handkerchief to mop his sweating face.

"Are you feeling unwell, sir?" Thomas asked solicitously.

The jailer shuddered and thrust the handkerchief into his pocket.

"You really should inform the colonel that there is yellow jack in the cellblock," Phillip advised him, just as another guard came running from a different part of the jail.

"Yellow jack!" the guard cried. He turned on his heel and bolted.

The jailer watched him leave. "You are right, Brother. I should go tell the colonel."

He ran out the door. The prisoners heard him go and howled in outrage. They hurled themselves against the cell doors, trying to break them down.

Thomas and Phillip hurried out of the cellblock, into the corridor, and headed for the stairs that led to the ground floor and freedom.

"If he does tell the colonel, he will likely know that yellow jack could not possibly spread this fast," Thomas said.

"True," said Phillip. "Keep moving!"

They hurried down the stairs. Kate's moans were starting to sound a little too real. Thomas and Phillip had hold of her with bruising force and her arms must be aching from the strain.

"Just a little farther," Thomas told her, doing what he could to brace her, ease the strain. "Do you need to stop to rest?"

"No!" Kate gasped, her voice muffled by the blanket. "Keep going!"

They reached the bottom of the stairs and Phillip slowed.

"Do we go left here?"

"I think so," Thomas said, grateful for the chance to catch his breath. "I remember that crack in the wall."

At least he hoped he remembered that crack in the wall. He began to doubt himself. Perhaps he was thinking of another crack in a different wall. He did not remember the corridor being this long and he was positive he had not seen that pile of refuse in the corner. Just when he had convinced himself that they were hopelessly lost, he smelled fresh air and knew with relief they had come the right way.

"Almost there," he told Kate. "Two more guards and we're home free."

The guards had been watching for them. Seeing two monks dragging a soldier wrapped in a blanket coming toward them at a fast pace, the guards flung the gates open wide and then retreated into the gatehouse. Phillip and Thomas hurried by, dragging Kate.

"Is it yellow jack, Brother?" one of the guards called.

"Yes, one poor soul is dead already and I fear this man is not long for the world," Phillip replied. "Lock the gate after us. Do not permit anyone to go inside and, for God's sake, do not let anyone out! We do not want contagion to spread through the city!"

The guards watched them pass as they exited the fortress and began crossing the walled walkway.

"Keep moving at a normal pace," Phillip counseled. "They can still see us."

Thomas heard the gate clank shut behind them and he started to relax.

Then he heard the sound of booted feet pounding along the walkway. He looked over his shoulder.

"What is it?" Phillip asked, alarmed.

"The guards," said Thomas. "They are after us."

"Let go of me!" Kate gasped, struggling in his grasp. "I can fight! I said let go!"

She lashed out at them, kicking them. "I won't hang!"

"We won't let them take you, Kate," Thomas promised.

The booted feet were coming closer. The guards were closing fast. Thomas and Phillip stopped, bracing for a fight.

The guards ran past them with frightened glances. The last Thomas saw of them, they were pounding down the street, running for their lives.

Thomas and Phillip looked at each other and sighed in relief.

"What's happening?" Kate cried. "I can't see!"

"The guards are gone," said Thomas. "No, Kate, don't stop. We have to keep going. We're still within sight of the fort."

"There's an alley off to the right," Phillip said. "We can rest in there."

When they reached the alley, Thomas listened behind them for sounds that their ruse had been discovered and that the colonel was turning out the guard. He heard only muffled howls coming from the cellblock.

"We can rest a little while," said Phillip.

"Thank goodness!" Kate breathed.

She threw off the blanket and stood upright, flexing and rubbing her sore arms. Phillip released his hold on her, but Thomas was reluctant to let go.

"Are you sure you're all right, Kate?" he asked.

She pulled free of his grasp.

"I am not one of your delicate princesses, Your Highness. So don't treat me like one. You lied to me!" she added with an accusing glance. "You should have told me you were a prince."

Thomas regarded her, perplexed. "Forgive me for not properly introducing myself, but the first time we met you were holding me at gunpoint, the damn boat was sinking underneath us, and Guundaran marines were shooting at us!"

"It doesn't matter," said Kate. "I don't care what you are." Dragging off the boots that were too large, she tossed them aside.

Thomas couldn't imagine why she was so upset. He looked to Phillip for an explanation, but his friend only shook his head.

"We should be going," he advised. "That wretched corpse will wake up anytime now and start yelling. They will discover you've escaped and all hell will break loose."

"You are right," said Kate.

She looked from Thomas to Phillip and back to Thomas. Her face was a pale glimmer in the moonlight, her eyes large and shimmering.

"You both risked your lives and more to save me. I cannot thank you enough. I will always be grateful."

She kissed Phillip on the cheek. "Good-bye, Pip. Take care of yourself."

She gently kissed Thomas. "Thank you, Your Highness."

She gave them both a tremulous smile, then she turned and ran, barefoot, down the alley.

FIVE

Thomas and Phillip gazed after Kate in blank astonishment. Her sudden mad dash had taken them completely by surprise.

"We have to stop her!" Phillip said, coming to his senses.

"She's not thinking. Kate!" Thomas called and ran after her.

She had a head start, but she was running barefoot and he caught up to her. He seized hold of her wrist.

"Kate! You need to stay with us!"

"I can't," said Kate, trying to free herself from his grasp. "I know you mean well, but you don't understand—"

"Listen to me, Kate!" Thomas gave her a little shake to force her to look at him. "When the guards find out you've escaped, they will turn out the entire garrison. They will search every house until they find you."

"I can fend for myself—" Kate began.

"I know you can. You held me at gunpoint, remember? But give Pip and me a little credit for planning a good escape," Thomas said. "Would we bring you this far and then abandon you? We hired griffins—"

"Griffins!" Kate exclaimed. "Why didn't you say so in the first place?"

She broke free of his hold and hurried back into the alley, where Phillip was waiting.

"Where are the griffins?" Kate demanded. "Are they close?"

"I hired them from a friend who lives on the outskirts of the city. We'll take you there," said Phillip.

"We should get rid of these first." Thomas removed the scapular and then dragged the priest's robe off over his head. "They'll be searching for two monks."

"Good thought," said Phillip, doing the same. He made a bundle of the robes and tucked them under his arm.

"Just dump them," said Kate, fidgeting with impatience.

"I have a better use for them," Phillip said.

The alley was narrow and crooked, dark and filthy. Phillip switched on the bull's-eye lantern he had been wearing under his robes.

"Watch where you walk, Kate," he cautioned, shining the light on broken glass.

Kate shrugged off the warning. She was more interested in escape. "Where did you tell the griffins to take us?"

"We were thinking of flying to Wellinsport," Thomas explained. "From there, you can catch a boat to Freya."

Kate shook her head. "I'm not going to Freya. I have to go to Freeport to save my crew."

Thomas and Phillip exchanged troubled glances.

"We heard the Rosians sank your ship, Kate," said Phillip gently. "I hate to say this, but you have to face facts. Your ship and your crew are lost."

"The Rosians *thought* they sank her," Kate said. "I know *Victorie* survived. The Deep Breath is filled with countless small islands. I heard the sound of wood snapping right after *Victorie* sank. My ship came down on one of those islands. I begged that bloody captain to send a rescue boat, but he refused. Now my crew is marooned. I have to go back to Freeport!"

Phillip continued to argue. "The Rosians know that was your home, Kate. They know that you still have friends there. That's the first place they will look for you."

"Kate, you need to be realistic," Thomas added. "Two days have passed. The cold can kill a man in one and it will be another day or two before you can reach them. Your crew could not survive—"

"Yes they can. Akiel's magic will keep them alive," said Kate.

She faced Phillip and Thomas, her hands on her hips. Her jaw set. Her face was drawn and gray with fatigue and exhaustion. But her voice was firm with resolve.

"They are my crew. I am their captain. I am responsible. I will not abandon them."

Thomas regarded her with admiration. He had known many beautiful, charming women in his life and Kate—with her shaved head, bruised face, swollen eyes, and prison stench—was certainly not one of them. But she was the only one he had ever met who touched his heart.

"We will go to Freeport with you," he said.

"We will?" Phillip asked, startled. "Thomas, think about what you are saying. Your absence will be noticed. The Rosian navy will institute a search for you—"

Thomas flashed his friend a warning glance, but it was too late.

"Rosian navy!" Kate demanded, rounding on them. She regarded Thomas with suspicion. "What do you have to do with the Rosian navy? Maybe you're planning to collect the bounty on me yourself!"

"Kate, you're not thinking," said Phillip. "You know Alan would skin me alive if I let anything happen—"

A cannon fired. The echoes bounced off the buildings and rolled through the alley, sounding like thunder in the still night.

"They've discovered that Kate is gone," Phillip stated. "The fort fires a cannon to warn the citizens that a prisoner has escaped. This place will soon be swarming with soldiers."

"You can trust us, Kate," Thomas assured her. "We've brought you this far, haven't we?"

Kate sighed and wiped her hand across her face, smearing the sweat and the blood and the grime. She was exhausted. Adrenaline and fear had carried her along, but the adrenaline, at least, must be starting to seep away.

"I'm sorry, Pip," she said. "All I can think about is Olaf. He is waiting for me to find him. He knows I'll come . . ."

Thomas cast a puzzled glance at Phillip, asking if he knew what Kate was talking about.

Phillip shook his head. "We should go. We're not safe here. Or anywhere, for that matter."

They switched off the bull's-eye lanterns and continued down the alley in the darkness until they reached the end. Phillip did not pause. He led them from one street to another, from one alley to another. Thomas was soon hopelessly turned around, but Phillip moved with unwavering confidence.

"I begin to think you've dodged soldiers before," Thomas said to his friend.

"Once or twice," Phillip admitted with a grin.

The cannon woke the city. Lights flared. People clad in their nightclothes flung open their shutters or rushed into the street to find out what was going on, while others locked their doors and bolted their windows.

Ducking into another alley, Phillip called a halt to let them catch their breath.

"I think we're safe so far," Thomas ventured, hazarding a guess. "I don't hear anything."

Phillip nodded. "If the colonel follows standard procedure, he will order a contingent of soldiers to head for the harbor to shut it down, prevent any ships from leaving. The rest will conduct a house-to-house search, starting at the center of town and spreading outward. My biggest fear is that we will be shot by some overzealous citizen."

He pointed to an elderly man, armed with an ancient blunderbuss, prowling about the end of the alley, and led them in the opposite direction.

"Pip, wait!" Thomas said. "Kate is hurt. She's limping."

"I'm fine," Kate protested. "We need to keep going!"

"We are not far from where my friend lives," said Phillip, regarding her with concern. "Can you manage?"

"I said I was fine," Kate returned.

"Then put weight on your foot," said Thomas.

She glared at him. "It's just a bruise. I've had worse. Let's go."

Kate walked on, clearly trying not to favor her injured foot. Thomas saw her wince, and he almost said something, but she flashed him an angry glance and he kept quiet.

They kept to alleys as much as possible. When they had to resort to streets, they slipped from shadow to shadow, avoiding the pools of light cast by the street lamps. The cobblestones gave way to dirt roads and Thomas now recognized his surroundings. He knew they had arrived when he smelled the foul odor of the tannery and saw the silhouettes of stables and barns black against the starlight.

Phillip went on ahead, motioning for Thomas and Kate to keep behind him. He was approaching the house when Little Dimitri stepped out of the shadows.

"Who's there?" he called.

"Rose Hawks," Phillip answered.

Little Dimitri grunted. "Ah, I thought that might be you, Master Pip. I heard the cannon."

He lifted the cover from a dark lantern, flashed it around, cast a swift, curious glance at Kate, and turned back to Phillip.

"The griffins are saddled and ready. I've brought peacoats and helms for the flight. Do you need anything else?"

"You might want to put these into the stolen boat," Phillip suggested, handing over the monks' robes.

"Good idea," Little Dimitri said, grinning.

"Our friend hurt her foot. She needs shoes," Thomas said.

"I don't need shoes," Kate protested. "I'm used to going barefoot."

"You will need them for the flight," said Little Dimitri. "My wife has some old shoes that might fit."

"We don't have time—" Kate argued.

"Actually we do," said Phillip. "I'm going to have to explain to the griffins that there's been a change of plans. We're flying to Freeport instead of Wellinsport."

"They'll grumble and probably demand more money," said Little Dimitri. "But that shouldn't be a problem. You wait with your friend, Master Tom. I'll be back with shoes and something for that foot."

He aimed the beam of the dark lantern at Kate's foot. She tried to avoid the light, but not before Thomas could see that her stockings were filthy and torn and one was dark with blood.

Little Dimitri and Phillip hurried off, leaving Kate and Thomas alone in the stable yard. Thomas didn't want to open the dark lantern, fearing it might draw unwanted attention. He could see well enough by the moonlight and he searched the yard until he found a crate. He dragged it over and tossed it down in front of Kate.

"You should sit," he told Kate. "Rest your foot."

"I keep telling you I'm fine," she said, but she did sit down.

The stable yard was blessedly quiet. The only sounds came from the barn and they were the usual sounds of the night: horses snuffling, and a couple of wyverns snapping at each other. Thomas paced restlessly back and forth, wondering what was keeping Pip.

"So why *are* you serving with the Rosian navy?" Kate asked.

Thomas stopped pacing and walked over to confront her. "And why are you so suspicious? Do you think I would risk my life to break you out of prison only to send you back again?"

Kate shrugged. "You are a prince. God knows why your lot does anything. So why did you help me? Pip has been my friend for a long time, but you don't even know me."

"I know you are the legendary Captain Kate, celebrated in story and song and the *Haever Gazette*," said Thomas archly. He added more seriously, "And because ever since I met you, I haven't been able to stop thinking about you."

Kate was startled into silence. She stared at him, nonplussed, as a flush crept into her cheeks, visible even in the starlight.

"Well, stop thinking about me," she said. "You are engaged to be married to another woman, Your Highness. I read *that* in the *Haever Gazette*."

Now it was Thomas's turn to flush. "I am not in love with her. I barely know her."

"But you are engaged to her," said Kate.

"Not by choice," Thomas said.

He fell grimly silent. Kate seemed about to say something, glanced at his face, and changed her mind. She, too, lapsed into silence. Both were relieved to see the hulking figure of Little Dimitri coming toward them at a jog trot.

"Sorry I took so long," he said, puffing from the exertion. "A couple of soldiers came to the door."

"Soldiers!" Kate gasped in alarm.

Little Dimitri waved his hand in reassurance. "They just asked routine questions. Wanted to know if I'd seen anything or if I was missing any horses. I told them the night had been quiet and they went on their way."

He held out a pair of leather boots. "My wife sent these for you, along with clean stockings, bandages, and her own special ointment. There's water in the horse trough and some rags. You tend to your hurt and I'll go see what's keeping Master Pip."

Little Dimitri handed Kate the boots and the stockings, gave Thomas the bandages, and hurried off before they could thank him. Kate pulled off the corporal's stocking.

"I'll fetch water," Thomas said.

"It's just a cut," Kate said impatiently. "We need to leave. The soldiers are here."

She started to pull on one of the boots. Thomas snatched it out of her hand.

"You have a cut on your foot. You've been walking about in muck and filth. If the cut turns grangrenous, I will have to cut off your foot and then how will you dance with me?"

He smiled at her. Kate glowered at him, but then her lips twitched and she gave him a grudging smile.

"Go ahead, if you must," she told him.

Thomas brought back a bucket of water. Kate made a scoop of her hands and dipped them in the water. She splashed the water over her face and head.

Thomas was shining the light on a jagged gash on her instep.

"You stepped on broken glass. There's a piece imbedded in the wound. I need to dig it out." Thomas looked up at her. "It's going to hurt like hell."

"Just get it done," said Kate, bracing herself.

"Hold the lantern for me," Thomas said.

Kate shone the light on her foot while he probed the wound with his fingers. She winced and bit down on her lip.

"What makes you think I would dance with you anyway?" she asked.

"According to the rules of etiquette, a lady may not refuse a gentleman's invitation to dance," Thomas replied. "Hold the light steady."

"My mother was a lady. I know the rules of etiquette. I may refuse you if I previously agreed to dance with someone else," Kate said, sucking in a breath. "Ouch! Bloody hell!"

She jerked her foot out of his grasp.

"I'm sorry," Thomas said. "I almost had it."

Kate grimaced and allowed him take hold of her foot again.

"My dance card is full. Does your princess dance well?" she asked.

"She does," said Thomas. "But that is all she and I have in common."

"Whereas you and I almost shot each other," said Kate.

Thomas smiled, plucked out the piece of bloody glass, and held it up to the light for Kate to see.

"Your foot should feel better now."

He spread the ointment on the wound, then wrapped the bandage around her foot.

"Try that," he said, standing up.

Kate pulled on the stockings, slid her feet into the boots and tied the leather laces. She stood up slowly, gingerly testing her foot.

"I guess it does feel better," she admitted.

"Good," said Thomas. "You wait here. I will go see what is taking Pip so long."

He was startled to feel her hand on his shoulder. He turned around.

"I need to apologize," said Kate. "You saved my life and I've been horrid—"

A sudden crackle of gunfire made them both jump and move closer together, hands touching, but not clasping.

"That was close," Thomas said worriedly. "Where the devil is Pip—"

"Here," said Phillip, coming out of the darkness. "We have a problem."

Kate hurriedly backed away from Thomas and turned to Phillip. "What is wrong?"

"The griffins refuse to fly us to Freeport. They claim a dragon lives there and they won't go near the place. I was thinking, Kate, that they could be talking about your dragon friend, Dalgren. If that's the case, you could explain to them that he won't harm them."

"The griffins don't have to worry," Kate said. "Dalgren was in Freeport, but he's not anymore. I'll talk to the griffins. Where are they?"

"In the yard by that large barn over there," said Phillip, pointing.

"You two wait here for your friend," Kate said, and she limped off.

"So Dalgren left Freeport," Phillip remarked, frowning after Kate. "You know, I wondered why the dragon wasn't with her when Favager attacked her ship. Dalgren would have made short work of that bastard. By the way, did I hear gunfire?"

"You did," said Thomas. "I hope the soldiers didn't kill some poor devil, mistaking him for us."

"If their aim has not improved since I was here, I think the public is safe," said Phillip. "But we do need to leave. The griffins are saddled and ready to fly if only they can be convinced to do so."

"If they can't?" Thomas asked.

"Then we may need to steal Big Dimitri's boat for real," said Phillip.

He and Thomas set out to find Little Dimitri, only to meet him coming to find them.

"That was gunfire," he said worriedly. "You should be gone by now. What is the problem?"

Phillip explained about Freeport and the dragon. Little Dimitri shook his head in exasperation and set out to talk to the griffins himself. Thomas and Phillip followed him.

Stars shone above them. A few thin, high clouds trailed across the sky. The moon was noticeably lower. The griffins were preening their feathers and talking in low croaks. One rubbed its beak with a talon.

"The griffins have agreed to fly us to Freeport," Kate reported. "They want to be paid extra, however."

"Give me your purse. I will settle matters with Little Dimitri," said Phillip. "You two go on ahead."

Thomas handed over the scrip and Phillip and Little Dimitri discussed payment. Thomas and Kate put on the heavy peacoats they would need for the flight and prepared to mount the griffins. Thomas inspected the saddles on both beasts, tugging at straps, making certain they were secure. Kate watched with interest.

"I have never flown on griffinback before. The saddle is different from a dragon saddle. How do you mount?"

"I will show you," said Thomas, and before she could say a word, he coolly put his hands around her waist, picked her up, and lifted her onto the griffin's back.

As he settled her into the saddle Kate gave a little gasp and glowered at him. She seemed about to say something sharp, but perhaps she thought of their earlier conversation.

"Thank you," she said grudgingly. "Now tell me how all the straps work."

"A dragon saddle is constructed with a high front and a back that is similar to a chair for the rider to lean against," said Thomas. "A griffin saddle has a lower profile, closer to a horse saddle. The tall cantle prevents you from being blown off the back of the seat. The swell has deep undercuts that allow the thighs of the rider to grip under the pommel."

"You know a lot about griffin saddles for a prince," said Kate. "I would think you would travel by royal yacht."

"I have flown griffins many times before. I was officer in the Estaran army," said Thomas.

"Why Estara? You are Freyan," Kate said.

Thomas reached across her shoulders and began to sort the straps. "Put these over your shoulders and attach them here in the center of your chest. These go around your legs." He cinched the straps tight.

"To answer your question, my mother is Estaran. I was raised in that country," Thomas continued. "She believes a king should have military training, and through her influence, I obtained a commission in the Royal Estaran Army. I have never set foot in Freya."

"Then why do you want to be king?" Kate asked.

"Who says I do?" Thomas returned.

Kate stared at him. "Don't you?"

Thomas handed her the helm. "Put this on. Make sure it's fastened tightly."

"We're ready to go," Phillip said, hurrying over. "I have arranged to keep the griffins as long as we need them."

He tossed the scrip to Thomas, who deftly caught it and placed it in the griffin's saddlebags.

"Do we have any money left?" Thomas asked.

"A little," Phillip said, grinning.

Thomas strapped himself into his saddle and waited for Phillip to mount and secure himself to his own saddle. Phillip put on his helm and raised his hand to indicate he was ready. Thomas looked over at Kate, who nodded and raised her hand.

Thomas leaned forward, patted the griffin on the neck.

"We are ready when you are," Thomas said.

The griffins carried them to a large empty field, cleared of trees and rocks, specially designed for the use of the griffins for taking off and landing.

The griffin on which Thomas was riding took the lead. The beast glanced back at him. Thomas braced himself. The griffin crouched down, then sprang off the hard-packed ground, propelling itself upward with its powerful leonine hind legs. The enormous wings caught the air and the griffin soared low across the field, circled, and started to rise.

The other two griffins followed the first, while Little Dimitri watched to make certain they got away safely, before hurrying back to his house.

The griffins continued to circle, gaining altitude, before flying off to the southwest, heading for Freeport. Thomas looked down to see the fort ablaze with light. He caught a glimpse of the stark, skeletal black shadow cast by the gallows in the middle of the courtyard, and then the fort and the gallows were behind him. He and his friends were flying over the inky blackness of the harbor into the Breath.

Thomas looked back at Kate, silhouetted against the stars. Most first-time griffin riders hunched over the beast's neck, clutching its feathers in terror, but Kate was accustomed to flight. She sat upright and faced forward, with nary a glance back at the fort or the gallows. She is putting the horror behind her, he thought, concentrating on her crew, going to save Olaf, who was waiting for her.

She is a remarkable woman, Thomas thought. Not like any woman I have ever known.

Of course, no other woman he knew had threatened to shoot him. But that was not all that made Kate different. Most women were attracted to him because he was a prince. Whereas Kate seemed to feel that being a prince was a blot upon his character.

He remembered her blunt question. "Why do you want to be king?"

Despite his glib answer, he had been giving the matter serious thought. He owed that to Phillip, who had made him realize that his country, Freya, was in trouble. The crown prince had been killed in a tragic accident; his only child had died. The queen was past the age to bear more children. Only two heirs were currently in the running.

"The queen favors her sister, Elinor," Phillip had said. "The Freyan people can't stand her. She is married to a Rosian merchant, lives in Rosia, and is a devout follower of the detested Rosian church. The other candidate is the queen's bastard half brother, Hugh. Sir Henry is urging her to choose Hugh, but that will be a long slog, for the queen hates him."

Thomas had the best claim to the throne dating back almost two hundred years to King Frederick, who had been deposed by his brother, King Alfred, who had died on the field of battle. His wife and his children had fled to Estara where the Stanford family had remained in exile until Thomas's mother gave birth to a son. Since that day, Constanza had schemed and plotted to restore the Stanford family to the Freyan throne.

The Freyan newspaper loved him, affectionately calling him "Prince Tom."

"But Sir Henry refers to you only as the 'Pretender,'" Phillip had said dryly.

The queen's spymaster, Henry Wallace, had sent Phillip to spy on Thomas, but Phillip had since come to believe that Thomas was the true and rightful king. He had confessed the truth to Thomas and now the two were firm friends. And Phillip's faith in Thomas had begun to awaken Thomas's faith in himself.

Phillip knew a great deal about the sad state of his country, especially the economic problems Freya faced following the war. He and Thomas had spent much of their time devising plans for reform that sounded very good, especially after the fourth glass of port.

But those plans were based on some far distant future. What would happen if Queen Mary were to suddenly drop dead tomorrow? Thomas would face a daunting challenge if he wanted to press his claim to the throne. He might be "Prince Tom" to the Freyan people, but neither Hugh nor Elinor would give up without a fight.

Hugh had long wanted the throne, according to Phillip, and he had the backing of Sir Henry and his faction. The queen and her faction supported the queen's sister, Elinor.

King Renaud of Rosia was currently backing Thomas, due to the influence of the Countess de Marjolaine. But there were those in the Rosian court who were urging Renaud to side with Elinor.

Then there was his mother, Constanza, and her plots and schemes. She spoke of armies marching into the Freyan capital to seize the throne by force. Thomas did not often argue with his intrigue-loving, volatile mother, for he did not want to have to endure tears, recriminations, and thrown crockery. He had made it clear to her, however, that he would not be party to overthrowing the queen.

The death of Queen Mary could draw the largest two kingdoms in Aeronne into war, for Rosia would be quick to take advantage of a perceived weakness in Freya. Thomas had heard captains in the Rosian navy talking about it when they thought he wasn't within earshot. Freya would be plunged into civil war, torn apart by competing factions.

Why did he want to be king?

The truth was, he didn't, and who could blame him?

Thomas sighed. He'd much rather run away with Kate and be a pirate.

SIX

Securely strapped into the saddle on the griffin's broad leonine back, Kate was grateful for the chance to rest and try to recover from the shock of her ordeal. She was in the state of exhaustion in which reality seemed unreal and dreams the only reality. Her eyes closed of their own volition, and once more she was back in that bleak jail cell waiting with dread for the hangman.

She woke, sweating and shivering, to find herself safe and free, on griffin-back, flying through the starlit night to save her crew.

As she had told Thomas, she was their captain. She was responsible.

She had made the decision to remain in the Aligoes even after she saw the Dragon Brigade and the Rosian "Rum Fleet" blockading the Trame Channel. She had put her ship and her crew in harm's way. She had fled Freya because she had feared she would be implicated in the murder of the dragon, Lady Odila. Kate had returned to the Aligoes to prove her innocence to Dalgren, who had parted with her in anger, believing her to be guilty.

The men who had signed on with her as privateer's-men had known the risks involved. She believed she had done everything possible to save her ship. The only reason she had not gone down with *Victorie* was because she had been on shore, desperately trying to free the fouled anchor. She had tried to rejoin her ship, to sink with her crew if she couldn't save them, but she had been captured and forced to watch *Victorie* vanish into the Deep Breath.

She had heard what sounded like the ship crash-landing on one of the many islands. She had reason to think some of the crew had survived. If so, they would be waiting for her to save them.

"I am coming for you," Kate promised Olaf and Akiel and the others. "Please, just hold on a little longer."

And suppose I do save Olaf and Akiel and the others, Kate thought to herself. What will we do then? She was destitute, had no warship and there-fore no letters of marque, and no patron. Sir Henry suspected her of murder and had probably put out a warrant for her arrest. She had even lost Dalgren, who had gone back to Rosia to face charges of desertion.

Fight for your dreams, Stephano de Guichen had told her.

"What's the use?" Kate asked dispiritedly.

She dozed off again. This time her dreams were not of war or prison. She was a child on her father's ship, the dear old *Barwich Rose*. She was stand-ing at the rail, moodily tearing up a hunk of bread that should have been her breakfast and throwing the pieces into the murky depths of the Breath.

Her father had lost everything last night. He had gambled away a month's worth of savings, a month's worth of work. In that moment she hated him, detested him. She decided that at the next port of call, she would run away. She would go back to her beloved Barwich Manor. She would live in the abandoned house, eating rabbits and squirrels. No one would find her. Ever.

A hand clapped Kate on the shoulder. She looked up to see her father, giving her his usual cheerful, disarming smile.

"Here now, girl," said Morgan. "Why the glum face? So I lost money at the gaming tables last night. There's always more where that came from. Like they say, the world floats on money as a ship floats on the Breath. If there's no money in my purse now, what does it matter? There soon will be."

Morgan rested his arms on the rail and gazed out into the Breath. "In the meantime, we have blue sky and a lovely day for sailing. We have our ship. We have our friends. We have the horizon, and beyond that, our fortune awaits."

The griffin made a sudden banking turn and Kate jerked awake. The dream had been very real. She could almost feel the touch of her father's hand and see his smile. He had come to her for a reason.

"The *Barwich Rose,*" Kate said, speaking the words aloud, feeling the warm moisture of her breath on the inside of the leather helm. "I still have the *Barwich Rose!*"

She and her crew had hidden the old ship from the Rosians in the jungle, hauling her ashore and hiding her in the thick vegetation. Her only worry was that the Rosians had discovered the ship and destroyed it. She tried to remember everything that horrible captain had said to her. He had not spoken of having destroyed her other ship and he was the type to have gloated over it.

As Morgan would say, *I am alive,* she reflected, and that, she realized, was more than she had reason to expect only a few hours ago. She had friends: Pip and Thomas. And even though Thomas was a prince, he did seem to have some sense.

Kate glanced at the two men, flying alongside her. Phillip was slumped forward in the saddle, asleep. Thomas was awake, enjoying the flight. He sat a griffin well, tall and upright, one hand lightly grasping the reins, the other on his hip. He rode the way Kate imagined he did everything: with confidence and an easy grace.

She could not see his face, hidden behind the helm, but she could picture his smile, his lips slightly parted as though to drink in the night, his blue eyes alight with the thrill of the adventure.

She remembered the look in those blue eyes when he had found her in that prison cell, seen her wretched and frightened, bald, bruised, and bloodied. She had seen pity and horror in the blue eyes, followed by anger and determination.

"I have come to save you."

He had risked his life to save her, and she had repaid him by being offensive and insulting.

I was shocked to see him, that's all, Kate rationalized. When they had said good-bye, she had never expected to see him again. Why would she?

She and Thomas had met by chance when he and Phillip had tried to steal the lucrative cargo she had just stolen from the Braffans—a fiasco that had almost ended in disaster. They had survived, said good-bye, and parted.

But she had found herself thinking about him often after that, particularly his striking blue eyes, black curly hair, and bold smile. Kate had no idea who he was, for he had refused to tell her his name. She had fondly pictured him as a daring vagabond, roaming the world in search of adventure.

She had discovered the truth from Sir Henry. Thomas was not a vagabond. He was a descendant of King James I of Freya with a claim to the Freyan throne. And he was engaged to be married to a Rosian princess.

Kate had been outraged, vexed, and disappointed. She had been vexed at Thomas for being a prince. Vagabonds were at least hardworking, while princes were arrogant, indolent, puffed-up dandies who did nothing useful. She was outraged at him for being engaged to a princess at the same time he had looked at her with admiration and warmth. And she was disappointed in herself, for having let herself daydream about his striking blue eyes.

Kate had resolved to forget him after that, and she had almost succeeded, mainly due to the fact that she had more urgent matters on her mind, such as being framed for a murder, losing her ship, captured by the Rosians, and almost hanged as a pirate.

But then, in her moment of despair, Thomas appeared in her jail cell to save her from death, just like some prince in a fairy tale.

And Kate was vexed and outraged and disappointed all over again.

She was thinking about him, absently gazing at him, when he suddenly turned his head to look at her, as though he had been thinking of her.

Kate flushed in annoyance and hurriedly turned her head away. She was sweating in the leather helm and she took it off so she could run her hands through her hair, only to feel her bare scalp, a cruel reminder, she thought with a pang, that she didn't have any hair.

She had always mockingly disparaged her own hair. Her mother, whose hair had been spun gold, had termed the color of Kate's hair "dishwater blond" and Kate had laughingly called it "dirty dishwater." She realized now she had been secretly vain of the luxuriant blond and mahogany curls that had once framed her face.

The surgeon had shaved off the curls to sew up the cut on her head. She had watched in a daze as they dropped onto the deck, where they lay soaking up the blood and the muck. The daring, reckless Kate of the dirty dishwater curls had lost her ship and her crew and had nearly gotten herself hanged. She was now Kate of the shorn head and she had been given a chance to redeem herself.

All very well, but she writhed inside when she remembered Thomas entering the cell and seeing her bald and bloodied.

True, he had held her tightly in his arms moments later, but she could well imagine that he had embraced her out of pity, as well. She couldn't think of any other reason. He was, after all, engaged to be married to someone else.

The rushing wind felt good. Kate closed her eyes to enjoy the sensation.

"Are you all right?" Thomas called, raising his visor.

Kate opened her eyes and saw him looking worried.

"Fine," she returned, irritated.

She put the helm back on her head so she didn't have to look at him—and he could not look at her.

The stars were starting to pale, and the Breath was brightening from gray-black to rose-orange. Kate could view her surroundings. The griffins were flying over the Trame Channel, a narrow stretch of empty sky that flowed like a river between the myriad islands of the Aligoes, cutting a wide swath that was easy to see from the air. Kate realized with excitement that they were close to Freeport, and home.

She searched the sky for the dragons of the Dragon Brigade. They would have no reason to suspect three people riding griffins. Travelers were common in the Aligoes, and news of her escape could not have reached the naval fleet this fast.

Still, she kept close watch, both for dragons and the Rosian ships that had been patrolling the channel. Thomas and Phillip had said they had been with the Rum Fleet in Maribeau. Kate figured that the Rosians might leave a frigate or two behind, just to keep watch. She saw a merchant ship and several island hoppers, making early-morning runs, but that was all.

The griffins started their descent.

Kate recognized the jagged peak of Mount Invicto in the distance and knew precisely where she was now. She and Dalgren had often flown this route in the early morning, practicing when they thought no one would see them. Dalgren had lived in a cave near the summit of the mountain. The dragon Coreg had his dwelling underneath.

Kate had forgotten about Coreg when she had confidently assured the griffins that there were no dragons on Freeport. If the griffins caught sight of him, they would refuse to land. They might be angry and carry her back to Maribeau in a huff. Kate wondered if she should mention him and decided to keep quiet. Coreg never ventured out during the day. Indeed, she was one of the few who knew that a dragon had been living on the island for about ten years.

Kate looked from Mount Invicto to the vast expanse of the Breath that was Freeport Bay and kept eager watch for the small town of Freeport, whose bright-colored stucco houses and shops lined a single dirt street facing the bay. Her eyes dimmed when Freeport came into view. She had never thought to see it again.

As the griffins descended, they started peering about for a safe place to land. Kate raised the visor on her helm and leaned over to speak to her mount, who swiveled its head to fix her with a beady eye.

"Keep flying due south until you reach a lighthouse," she instructed. "There you will head west. About three miles inland is a large open field where you can land. I can guide you."

The griffin relayed her instructions to the other two griffins and they continued south and eventually soared over the town. Only a few people were in the streets this early, going to their farms or opening up their shops. No one paid much attention to them. Griffin riders often visited Freeport to conduct business with Greenstreet and Coreg.

The harbor was almost empty. Business must have slowed considerably since the arrival of the Rum Fleet and the subsequent departure of smugglers and pirates. Kate suddenly wondered uneasily if Coreg and Greenstreet had also left town. If so, she would have no way to prove her innocence.

Kate sighed. One more damn thing to worry about.

The griffins flew over the Perky Parrot. No one was about. The Parrot would not open until the noon hour—if it opened at all now that Olaf was gone.

Kate almost fell off her griffin trying to get a good view of the tavern. She gazed down on it with tears in her eyes. She would give anything to be back down in the Parrot now, going about her daily chores, grinning at Olaf when he scolded her for trying to hide the dust by sweeping it into a dark corner.

She blinked her tears away, but not before they had fogged up the glass on her helm. She had to take it off to watch for the abandoned lighthouse.

When it came into view, the griffins headed west and soon found the open field where she and Dalgren had trained. The griffins started to land, then something alarmed them and they pulled up so fast that Kate had to hold on to the saddle to keep from sliding off.

The griffins rose into the air, then circled the field, squawking to each other.

"The griffins think there's a dragon down there!" Phillip reported. "I told them Dalgren isn't here, but they don't believe me. The place probably reeks of dragon."

"I told you before," Kate said to her griffin. "The dragon *was* here, but he's gone! You can see for yourselves! There's no dragon down there!"

Her griffin eyed her, then it eyed the field, and then said something to the others. After more circling and cawing, the griffins finally agreed to land. They came in one at a time, settling on all fours like a cat jumping from a tree.

Kate knew Thomas would come to assist her from the saddle, as though she were some fine lady alighting from her carriage, and she quickly unstrapped herself and dismounted before he could. She looked around the field where she and Dalgren had spent so many happy hours and realized he was gone. Truly gone.

Her stupid tears came again. She didn't want Thomas and Phillip to see that she had been crying. Fortunately the two men were engaged in some sort of altercation with the griffins, who were gnashing their beaks and digging up the dirt with their talons. Kate hurried over to a rain barrel she kept near the equipment shed. She drank thirstily and splashed water on her face and felt better.

After a great deal of groveling on the part of Phillip and Thomas and lots of cawing and gnashing on the part of the griffins, Phillip came over to share the water and report.

"The griffins have finally agreed to return here to pick us up, but they refuse to remain anywhere around Freeport or to check back in with us. We have arranged for them to come back in a week. Do you think that will give us time to rescue your crew?"

"A week should be enough time," said Kate.

She didn't add that if they couldn't find her crew in a week, it wouldn't matter. Olaf and Akiel and the others would all be dead from the cold.

"How is your foot?" Thomas asked Kate as he came over to share the water.

"Don't fuss over me," Kate began, then realized she was once again being rude. She put on her mother's courtly manners. "My foot is feeling better, kind sir. Thank you for asking."

Thomas grinned at her. "You can tell me not to fuss over you all you want, Kate, but I intend to keep fussing. You look exhausted. Sit down and rest. Phillip and I will unload the saddlebags."

He probably expected her to argue with him, but Kate was too tired to give him the satisfaction. She meekly sat down on the log where she had used to sit to talk with Dalgren and laughed inwardly to see Thomas look surprised.

"You don't know me as well as you think you do," she told him under her breath.

The griffins kept watch for dragons as the two men worked, removing the saddlebags Little Dmitri had packed for them. Kate worried that Coreg might be out there somewhere searching for her. She planned to confront the dragon, but now was not the time. She had to rescue her crew first.

The griffins left the moment the men had removed the last saddlebag, flying back to Maribeau.

"I hope they remember to come back," Thomas said, watching them wing out of sight.

"Little Dimitri will see to that. He thinks of everything," Phillip reported, peering into the saddlebags. "He packed pistols and powder and ammunition."

"Any sign of rations?" said Thomas. "I can't eat bullets."

Phillip rummaged around. "Bread and cheese!"

Kate realized she was ravenously hungry. Fear had kept her from eating the prison food, even if she been able to stomach it. Thomas and Phillip joined her on her log and did justice to the bread and cheese.

Once Kate had finished eating, she was eager to be on their way. The morning was already halfway gone and they still had to sail to the cove where she had hidden the *Barwich Rose*.

The *Rose* will be there, just as good as when we left her, Kate reassured herself. She couldn't help but feel a chill undercurrent of doubt, however, and she was grateful when Thomas broke in on her worried musings.

"I am sorry Dalgren is gone," he said as they ate. "He saved our lives in Braffa and I did not have a chance to properly thank him."

"Too bad he wasn't there to turn that bastard Favager into a living torch," said Phillip. "Where did the dragon go?"

"He went back to the Dragon Duchies. He has family there," said Kate.

She hadn't lied, well, not exactly. Dalgren did have family in the Dragon

Duchies, though his family had disowned him after he deserted from the Dragon Brigade. These two didn't need to know that.

Seeing Phillip exchange glances with Thomas, she realized that they knew there was more to the story; previously, Dalgren would never have left her to face danger alone. Fearing Phillip was about to ask another question; she changed the subject.

"So here's the plan. I have a ship, the *Barwich Rose,* hidden in a cove about twenty miles from here. The only way to reach the cove is by boat. I don't have one and I can't go into Freeport, lest someone recognize me."

Someone being Greenstreet or his men. Greenstreet had betrayed her to the Rosians once. Kate wasn't going to give him the chance to do it again.

"I remember the *Rose,*" said Phillip. "She's a two-master, as I recall. Can you sail her into the Deep Breath?"

"The trip won't be comfortable, but we'll manage," said Kate. "I was thinking you and Thomas could go into Freeport to talk to Old Benito. You remember him, don't you, Pip? He has an island hopper he will let you borrow."

"Old Benito!" Pip smiled. "He used to carry messages for us. He must be eighty if he's a day."

"He still talks about the Rose Hawks," said Kate. "He will be glad to see you."

"I haven't been in Freeport in years, Kate," said Phillip. "Old Benito and others will wonder why I've suddenly turned up. What do I tell people?"

"Say that you and your friend came to do business with Greenstreet," said Kate.

"Greenstreet. He's the fellow who tried to assassinate Sir Henry, isn't he?" said Phillip.

"Yes, he's the one," said Kate. "Greenstreet runs a criminal organization. He's involved in smuggling, arms sales, thieving, piracy. He was around during the Rose Hawks days, but he went to ground when Captain Northrop was in Freeport."

"Alan would not have dealt kindly with such a man," Phillip said.

Kate had once daydreamed about Alan Northrop. She had become a privateer to join his fleet and—it should be admitted—win his heart. She had not thought about him or his heart in a long time, however. She blamed Thomas for that, too.

"Greenstreet is the only reason anyone ever comes to Freeport," Kate added. "As for why you need a boat, tell Old Benito yours was damaged in a wizard storm."

"Old Benito, Greenstreet, wizard storm," Phillip repeated, committing them to memory. "Where will you be?"

"I'll wait for you at the lighthouse we passed on the way here. You can pick me up there."

Thomas frowned. "I don't like leaving you alone—"

"I can take care of myself!" Kate said, flashing anger.

"I was about to say that I don't like leaving you alone *without any means of protecting yourself,*" Thomas stated, laying emphasis on the end of the sentence. He handed over a pistol he had just finishing loading, adding with a cool smile, "I know you know how to use it."

Kate remembered vividly the time she had held him at gunpoint; that was the first time she had noticed his remarkable eyes. She muttered her thanks, accepted the pistol, and thrust it into the waistband of the corporal's trousers.

"We should be going—" she said, and started to stand, forgetting about her injured foot.

She staggered and nearly fell, and Thomas was quickly by her side, his hand on her elbow.

"You're hurt and you're tired," he admonished. "You should rest—"

"I will have plenty of time to rest once I've saved my crew!" Kate rounded on him. "Stop coddling me! I am not one of your fine court ladies in perfume and lace. I am plain Kate with no hair and stinking of prison. I am grateful to you for saving my life. I will find a way to repay my debt—"

"Don't speak of debt!" Thomas said angrily. "We did what we did because we care about you!"

Phillip regarded her, troubled. "We are here because you're our friend, Kate."

Kate looked from one to the other and sighed. Two such wealthy, powerful young men could never understand her or her life. But she needed to make them try.

"The truth is, I can't allow myself to care. I can't start depending on you. I might get used to using you as a crutch, and when this is over, you will leave and I will be alone. I have to stand on my own two feet—even if one hurts."

She looked at Thomas as she spoke.

"Can you understand?" she asked him.

"No," he said.

Kate gave up. She started to turn away.

"But I will try," he promised. "I will not coddle if you will try to smooth your prickles."

Kate gave a rueful smile. "Deal."

"Deal," said Thomas.

They solemnly shook hands.

"But we will carry the saddlebags," he added, teasing.

"Of course, you will, sailor," said Kate in lofty tones. "I'm your captain."

She grinned and limped off down the trail.

Thomas and Phillip hefted the saddlebags, then followed Kate down the dirt trail she had worn through the jungle on her daily trips to visit Dalgren.

The sun was bright. The birds and animals were going about their business. The jungle was alive with twitterings and screeches and caws. They had shed the peacoats in the heat the moment they had landed. Kate had insisted that they bring the heavy woolen coats along, saying they would need them in the cold of the Deep Breath.

When they reached the lighthouse, Thomas and Phillip dropped off the saddlebags, which they would load into the island hopper, and looked around.

"I remember this place," said Phillip. "Only the beacon light was working the last time I was here. As I recall, if I follow this road, it will lead me into town. Where will we find Old Benito?"

"He'll be in the Parrot the moment it opens," said Kate. "I'm sure he'll remember you. Just don't let him start reminiscing about his adventures with the Rose Hawks or you will be there for a week."

Thomas and Phillip started off down the dirt road. Kate watched them go. When the road rounded a bend, Thomas turned to wave at her. Kate waved back, sighed, and ran her hand over her shaved head.

"Hair will grow back," she admonished herself. "Be thankful you are alive."

She left the road and walked the short distance to the stone lighthouse, which stood on the edge of the cliff overlooking Freeport Bay. Kate had used the old signal flags to signal Dalgren. He could see the lighthouse from his cave, and when he saw the flags, he knew she needed him.

The day the Rosians had attacked her ship, she had been preparing to signal to him. The flags were still lying on the ground where she had dropped them when Akiel had told her Dalgren was gone. The dragon, for years her most steadfast friend, had surrendered himself to the Dragon Brigade and gone back to face trial for desertion.

The penalty for desertion from human armies was death. Dragons were more civilized. They did not kill their own kind, but his punishment would be severe. Kate realized she had no idea what the dragons might do to him.

She picked up the flags, smoothed them with her hand, then carried them inside the lighthouse and packed them back in their canvas storage bag, even though she doubted she would ever return to use them.

The lighthouse keeper had diverted water from a nearby stream for his own use, channeling the water into a pool not far from the lighthouse. Kate stripped off the corporal's clothes and dove into the pool, glad to wash away the blood and the prison stench.

She looked at the wound on her foot. Little Dimitri's healing ointment was working, the cut healing nicely. Kate smiled to herself. Thomas would not have to cut off her foot now. Feeling immeasurably better, she put the shirt and trousers back on and sat down to rest in the shade of the lighthouse. She leaned back against the cool stone wall, went over her plans for the rescue in her mind, and fell asleep.

SEVEN

Kate woke to someone shaking her by the shoulder. She had been deeply asleep and she had to take a moment to remember where she was. When she recognized Phillip, she flushed and jumped to her feet.

"I didn't mean to fall asleep," she said. "Did you find Old Benito?"

"We found him, and he was happy to loan us his hopper." Phillip gestured to the small vessel, known as an island hopper because it was mostly used for brief trips—"hops"—from island to island.

He and Thomas had tied up the boat to a small dock below the lighthouse, and Thomas was waiting in the hopper. He and Phillip had both acquired broad-brimmed straw hats to ward off the hot sun. Kate didn't wonder how they had come by those. Phillip had been a favorite with everyone in Freeport during the Rose Hawks days.

"You were gone a long time. Did you run into trouble?" Kate asked worriedly.

"No trouble," said Phillip. "Although something rather curious happened."

"What?" Kate asked, alarmed.

"Nothing to fret over. The story will keep," said Phillip. "I thought you might need these."

He held up a bundle of clothes and a pair of boots.

"Those are mine," said Kate, pleased. "How did you get them? Never mind. You can tell me later."

Kate carried the clothes into the lighthouse. Discarding the corporal's clothes, she pulled on her slops and one of Olaf's calico shirts she often borrowed; thus restored, she felt almost like her old self again. She even smiled, when she saw that Phillip had thought to bring along the red kerchief. Tying the kerchief around her bare head, she returned to the boat. Phillip threw off the lines, took his place in the boat, and they sailed into the bay.

Old Benito's island hopper was one of the smaller craft of its class, with two sails, a helm, and two lift tanks that used the gaseous form of the Breath. He used the boat to visit family on a neighboring island.

"I'll take the helm," Kate said. She steered the boat along the shoreline, heading for Freeport Bay. "Now tell me what happened that was so curious."

"First things first," said Phillip. "Gert is running the Parrot. Everyone was pleased to hear you had escaped the hangman."

"You didn't tell them I was here in Freeport, did you?" Kate asked.

Phillip gave her a reproachful glance. "Give me credit for having *some* sense, Kate. I told them we had just come from Maribeau where everyone was talking about your daring escape from prison. I mentioned that it was widely believed you had fled to Freya."

"Good," said Kate, relieved.

"Old Benito was in the Parrot, as were a few others who remembered me. While Thomas kept them talking about the old days, I made an excuse, slipped off, sneaked into your room, and stole your clothes. Gert sent rations: food and ale, brandy, and cider," said Phillip. "She said we'd likely need blankets, and she sent those, too."

"Smart thinking," said Kate. "So what happened?"

"That fellow, Greenstreet. Turns out he's gone," said Phillip.

"Gone!" Kate repeated in dismay. "Where did he go?"

"No one seems to know," said Phillip. "His house is deserted. Apparently there was some sort of falling-out between him and his hirelings, for they found one of them shot to death."

"You look upset, Kate," said Thomas. "What's the matter?"

"I had important business with Greenstreet. If he's gone . . ."

She shook her head. If Greenstreet was gone, then perhaps Coreg was gone, as well. The dragon was the only one who knew the identity of the man who had framed her for murder. She had no way now to prove her innocence.

She sighed and said, "Never mind Greenstreet. What else happened?"

"You know Sir Henry's secretary, Mr. Sloan," Phillip said.

"I have met him. Why?" Kate asked, and suddenly she knew the answer. "You saw Mr. Sloan in Freeport!"

"He was in the Parrot," Phillip said. "How did you know that?"

"Because *I* saw him the day the Rosians attacked my ship," Kate said. In the midst of all the turmoil, she had forgotten about Mr. Sloan. "I assumed he had come here looking for me on orders from Sir Henry."

The truth was, she had assumed Mr. Sloan had come to Freeport to arrest her for the murder of the dragon.

"But then I realized I was wrong," Kate continued. "He looked as shocked to see me as I was to see him. I wonder why he is still in Freeport? He must have heard that the Rosians sank my ship."

"Especially when he knew you were going to be hanged!" Thomas added, frowning. "You held letters of marque. You were in Freeport on Wallace's orders. This Mr. Sloan should have gone to Maribeau to try to save you."

"Sir Henry has his faults," Phillip added, "but he is loyal to those who serve him."

He was eyeing her askance. He didn't want to say anything, but he guessed she wasn't being honest about why she had come to Freeport.

"So tell me what happened with Mr. Sloan," Kate said. "Did he recognize you? Sir Henry was livid with rage when I gave him the message that you quit his service. He would have killed you on the spot if you had been there."

"Yes, he recognized me," said Phillip. "Here is what happened. After we arranged with Old Benito to borrow the hopper, Thomas went with him to the dock to fetch it, and I waited in the Parrot to pick up the supplies. I was leaning on the bar when the door opened and in walked Mr. Sloan.

"I was never so shocked in my life!" Phillip added, shaking his head. "Neither was he. He knew me at once. I was cornered, nowhere to run. He walked up to the bar and stood right beside me.

"He ordered ale. When Gert went to fetch the ale, Mr. Sloan spoke quietly, not looking at me, 'I regret that I am not at leisure to apprehend you for treason today, Your Grace. Another time, perhaps.' Gert brought Mr. Sloan his ale. He took it, turned from me without a glance, and walked away to sit down at a table. As you might imagine, the moment she handed me the supplies, I left in haste."

"Poor Pip looked as though he had seen a ghost," Thomas said.

"I wonder why Mr. Sloan pretended he didn't know you?" Kate said, puzzled.

"The answer is obvious," Phillip said. "Mr. Sloan is here on some sort of undercover mission and he was afraid I would expose him."

"But how would he know you would keep his secret?"

"Because, I am sure, he assumes that *I* am here on a secret mission of my own," said Phillip. "If I exposed him, I would end up exposing myself. Thus we each had to pretend that neither of us knew the other. What he didn't know, of course, is that I am here as myself."

"Spies lead very confusing lives," said Thomas.

"Which is why I have since given up the trade," said Phillip.

"So why would Mr. Sloan be in Freeport?" Thomas pondered the question. "Let's face it, this town is not the world's capital of international intrigue! It has one street and it's mostly mud. This man must be here because of you, Kate. Which means you could still be in danger."

Phillip shook his head. "Mr. Sloan had to know Kate was in prison in Maribeau. Everyone on the island knew."

Kate could guess the reason. She could explain everything to them and she probably should, for now Phillip was involved and, although he made light of it, he was in danger. Mr. Sloan might be here on other business, but he would not forget he had seen Phillip, and when he was free to act on that knowledge, he would find a way to track him down and take him into custody.

If Kate told them the truth, she would have to reveal unpleasant facts about herself. She had always avoided that, if possible, for she did not want to disappoint those who cared for her. Lies were so much easier, kept everyone happy. Sweep the dust into a corner and hope Olaf never saw it.

But she owed Thomas and Phillip her life. At the very least, they deserved to know what was really going on.

"I think I know why Mr. Sloan is here," she said.

Thomas and Phillip had been talking of something else. They turned to her, startled.

"It does have something to do with me," Kate admitted. "I did something bad, although I had good reason for doing it. But what I did wasn't nearly as bad as what Sir Henry thinks I did. You must believe me!"

She gave them a pleading look.

Thomas smiled. "Of course we believe you, Kate. How bad could it possibly be?"

"Sir Henry thinks I murdered the dragon Lady Odila."

"Good God!" Phillip exclaimed, stunned.

Thomas said nothing, but she saw a shadow darken his eyes. "Why would he think you were involved?"

"Because I was," said Kate simply. "Greenstreet was only a mouthpiece for a dragon called Coreg. The dragon was the true head of the criminal organization that operated out of Freeport. I know because I used to work for him."

She told them the whole story, leaving out only Trubgek—Coreg's servant. She didn't like to think about him, much less talk about him.

"Someone told Coreg that there existed a magical spell that could kill a dragon while it was asleep in its lair. Coreg hired me to steal the spell. I refused at first," said Kate, seeing Thomas and Phillip both looking troubled. "But his servant threatened to burn my ship and hurt Olaf if I didn't. I told Dalgren, who said he had heard rumors that such a spell existed. I told him I would never harm a dragon, but I was in a tight spot, because I owed a lot of money to Greenstreet, and thus to Coreg. Feeling I needed the advice of someone who could be objective about the situation, I turned to my friend Miss Amelia, who writes for the *Haever Gazette*."

"She's the one who writes the stories about you," Thomas said, interrupting.

Kate nodded. "She had heard that the spell existed, but that it didn't work. We decided that I should steal it, but instead of giving it to Coreg, she and I would take it to Sir Henry. I went to the house and found the spell."

She shivered. "It was horrible. I knew the moment I saw it that Miss Amelia was wrong. The spell *would* work. But before I could take it to Miss Amelia, a man came out of the shadows, attacked me, and drugged me into insensibility. When I next awoke, I was in Barwich Manor, covered in blood. And Lady Odila was dead, killed by that spell."

"So you were a cat's-paw," said Phillip. He frowned. "Does Sir Henry really think you were responsible? Such a powerful spell must be difficult to cast. You're a fair crafter, Kate, but something so powerful would require the skill of a savant."

"Miss Amelia said the same thing. She was going to tell Sir Henry the truth about Coreg. She said I would be safe, but I didn't dare take a chance. Sir Henry was in political trouble over this because of Freya's troubled relations with dragons. He needed to make an arrest, and I feared he wouldn't care very much who he arrested. So I fled.

"My plan was to sail to the Aligoes to talk to Coreg, convince him to tell me who had hired him. But then Dalgren . . ."

Kate couldn't finish the sentence. She couldn't bear to think about the last words he had said to her. *As Olaf is always saying, you are your father's daughter*. He hadn't meant it as a compliment.

"Dalgren thought you committed the murder," said Thomas.

"He did," said Kate, swallowing. "I had to talk to Coreg! I had to convince Dalgren of the truth. So I came to the Aligoes and . . . all my plans went horribly wrong. And now I've lost Dalgren and my ship and my crew."

"You have us, Kate," said Thomas.

She gave him a grateful look.

"I seem to be a bit lost," said Phillip. "How does the murder of Lady Odila and you being framed for it explain Mr. Sloan's presence in Freeport?"

"I think he came to do the same thing I was going to do," said Kate. "Sir Henry sent Mr. Sloan to learn the truth from Coreg."

"Ah, of course!" Phillip exclaimed. "He would not advertise to the world that he worked for Sir Henry."

Kate grew despondent. "But if Greenstreet is gone, then I fear Coreg may have left, as well. And if he is gone, too, then I have no proof to give Dalgren."

"Perhaps Mr. Sloan found out the truth," said Phillip. "If anyone could twist the arm of a dragon and convince him to spill what he knows, it would be Mr. Sloan."

Kate smiled. "I hope so. Thank you both. You make me feel better."

"Where did Dalgren go?" Thomas asked.

"He went back to the Dragon Duchies," Kate said.

She said nothing more, and she was glad Thomas didn't ask. Dalgren's dark secret wasn't hers to tell.

Kate steered the island hopper through the maze of narrow channels that wound among the islands. She had made the trip often and picked out landmarks to guide her: west at a particular large banyan tree, east after passing under an overhanging rock ledge, south at the waterfall.

The only problem with using landmarks was that the floating islands often shifted location, especially the smaller ones. Thus for guidance she also had to rely on her sense of direction, the position of the sun, and the wind on her cheek.

Even though Old Benito's boat was small, sailing through the narrow channels was not easy. The islands were uninhabited, overgrown with jungle trees and plants. Dangling vines and low-hanging tree limbs fouled the rigging. Floating chunks of rock could crash into the hull and sink a small boat. She gave Phillip and Thomas boat hooks to fend off the rocks.

The air was hot and humid, and filled with raucous noises. Monkeys gibbered at them; birds with bright-colored plumage flitted past; Dalgren's favorite meal—wild hogs—snorted at them from the underbrush. Rain showers drenched them one moment, the sun shone brightly the next.

Kate found her gaze straying to Thomas, who was at the prow, standing ready with a boat hook. His face, shaded by the broad brim of the hat, was now reddened by the sun, and his shoulder-length, curly black hair straggled about his face. He had opened his shirt collar and unbuttoned his shirt, which was soaked with rainwater. At Kate's suggestion, he and Phillip had shed their shoes and stockings. Bare feet found easier purchase on the wet deck.

He must have been a good officer, Kate thought, recalling his courage in Braffa. His was an indomitable spirit, buoyed by confidence and cheerfulness, anchored by honor. Kate's spirit was similar, except that hers was stubborn and energetic, "full of piss and vinegar," her father had often said with a laugh.

"You two can rest now," Kate told her crew. "We're through the worst of the rocks."

Thomas and Phillip were thankful for the respite; they dropped the boat hooks and wiped away the sweat with their shirtsleeves. Phillip had purchased a jug of cold cider from the Parrot, and while it was no longer cold, it tasted good and slaked their thirst.

"What I don't understand is how the Rosians ever found your ship," Thomas said, sitting next to her and passing her the jug.

"Greenstreet betrayed me for the bounty money," said Kate. "He told the Rosians where to look for the *Victorie*."

Kate drank and passed the jug to Phillip.

He, like Thomas, was red-faced from the sun, his shock of yellow hair damp and rumpled. He had removed the hat and now was using it as a fan.

"Tell us your plan to save your friends," he said. "Do you know where they went down?"

"I was onshore, trying to board the ship," Kate said. "*Victorie* was on fire. The powder magazine had blown up and she was sinking fast. I heard a crash not far from where I was standing. There are scores of islands in the Deep Breath. She must have landed on one of those."

"On fire," Phillip repeated, looking grave. "And no way to put it out."

"I've seen wrecks where the crew managed to escape a burning ship," said Kate.

"Then there's the cold—" Phillip began.

"They can use wood from the ship to build a fire," said Kate. "My friend Akiel knows magic that can warm the blood."

"But Kate . . ." Phillip began.

"Just tell us what we can do to help, Kate," Thomas said, giving his friend a frowning glance.

"My plan is to sail down below the Deep Breath in the *Barwich Rose*," said Kate. "Pip remembers her."

"The dear old *Rose* was a grand lady," said Phillip. "I am glad she is still among the living. Tom is right. He and I will help any way we can."

"You are right," Kate admitted. "The trip will be cold and perilous and it might all be for nothing. The *Rose* could be hit by rocks or get caught in magical tides. And if we crash, there will be no one to come to save us. I have to go, but I won't blame you if you back out."

Thomas took off his hat and ran his hand through his sweat-damp hair. "I cannot speak for Pip, but I am looking forward to being out of this blazing sun. I imagine the Deep Breath will feel quite cool and refreshing."

"I'll remind you of that when your teeth are chattering and you can no longer feel your feet," Phillip said to him, grinning.

Kate looked from one to the other with heartfelt gratitude.

"I do not know how I can ever thank you enough," she said. "First you save my life and now you are helping me save the lives of my crew. I am serious about repaying my debt to you. If I can ever do anything—"

Thomas leaned back against the gunwale and smiled at her. "Promise to dance with me."

"What?" said Kate, taken aback. "I am trying to be serious."

"So am I," said Thomas. "One dance, Kate. That is all I ask."

"Very well, sir," said Kate, teasing. "The next royal ball I attend, I will add Your Highness to my dance card."

"I look forward to it," said Thomas.

Kate eyed him. "You know I am making sport of you."

"All I know is that you have just promised to dance with me," said Thomas.

"What will your princess say?" Kate asked archly, hoping to ruffle his maddening calm.

Thomas merely smiled and cast a sidelong glance at Phillip, who flushed to the roots of his hair and shot his friend a warning look in return.

Kate wondered what this bit of byplay was about, but she couldn't take time to ask. The hopper had entered the winding, narrow straits near the cove and she had to concentrate on her sailing.

The hopper rounded a bend in the channel, and the cove came into view. Kate had braced herself to face what she knew would be a scene of destruction, but she had not braced herself to face the memories.

Flames blazed in her eyes, smoke filled her nostrils. Cannonballs crashed into the hull of her ship, tore through the rigging. The screams of the wounded and the dying dinned in her ears.

Kate lowered her head. Her vision blurred, and her hand trembled on the helm. A horrible warm sensation flooded her body, and a bad taste filled her mouth. Her ship was sinking and she was sinking with it . . .

The next thing she knew a strong arm was supporting her and someone was dabbing her lips with water.

Kate blinked and her head cleared. She was sitting on the deck with Thomas's arm around her. Pip had taken over at the helm, and they were both regarding her with sympathy and concern.

Kate gently pushed Thomas away. "What happened?"

"You fainted," said Thomas.

"I never faint!" Kate protested. She tried to sit up and failed. "I . . . passed out from the heat. That's all."

Thomas handed her a waterskin. She drank, and felt better. She forced herself to look at the cove, daring the memories to come for her again. When the magazine had exploded, the trees had caught fire. They were blackened and burned, their limbs dangling. The anchor lay on the ground. She remembered the desperate fight she had waged to free it from the bollards.

She steeled herself to look for the remains of the sailor who had died at her feet. The body wasn't there and the frequent rains had washed away the blood. Either the Rosians had tossed the body Below or some wild beast had carried it off.

"Sorry to disturb you, Kate, but where am I going?" Phillip asked from his place at the helm.

Kate shook herself, came back to business. "Head east toward that point. On the other side is an inlet. We hid the *Rose* in there."

Phillip sailed the boat in the direction indicated. Kate turned away from the burned trees and looked toward the point where the trees were still green and lush. Her spirits rose. If the Rosians had found her ship, they would have set fire to it and burned down the jungle.

They sailed into the small inlet. She and Olaf had tied the *Barwich Rose* to the trees, then lowered the sails, deflated the colorful balloons, and covered the deck with canvas to protect it from the wind and the rain.

"Are you certain the *Rose* is in there?" Pip asked.

"I'm certain," said Kate, and she was quite sure now.

As Phillip edged the boat closer to the shore, Kate caught glimpses of canvas and rigging and finally the bowsprit sticking out from among the brush.

"She's safe!" Kate breathed.

Her despondency lifted, blown away by a strong breath of hope, and her strength and energy returned. Ignoring Thomas's remonstrations, she climbed out of the hopper the moment Phillip landed on a sandy strip of beach.

Kate ran to the *Rose* and began tugging at one of the tarps that covered the hull.

"The dear old *Rose,*" she said, climbing onto the deck. "I grew up on this boat."

The *Barwich Rose* was ninety feet long with a wide beam, two full decks, two masts, two large balloons, four lift tanks, and four airscrews. She had no cannon, only a couple of swivel guns for defense. Morgan had chosen to forgo the weight of cannon in order to increase the Rose's speed. He would always choose to outrun trouble if he could.

Phillip was looking around, frowning. "The *Rose* had a crew of fifteen. Can three of us sail her?"

"If we were heading out into the open Breath, no," Kate said. "But we're not going far. We're mostly going straight down."

"In other words," said Phillip, "it's difficult to float, easy to sink."

"You're such a comfort," said Thomas.

EIGHT

Months had passed since Kate and Olaf had hidden the *Rose,* and had left for Freya in the *Victorie.* Kate went first to check the level of gas in the main lift tanks and the reserve. If the tanks had rusted and the gas leaked out, her hopes of setting sail would quickly be dashed. She would have to send Thomas and Pip back to Freeport to obtain more gas.

She was relieved to find that the tanks were still in relatively good condition, each about half full.

Kate then inspected the ship, making a mental list of what they needed to do to sail down into the Deep Breath. They had to haul the balloons out of storage and check the silk for rents and tears, then secure the balloons to the masts and inflate them. They then had to connect the control cables from the helm to each balloon, and finally, to grease the gears of the airscrews, and go over every inch of every cable to make certain the magic was still working.

She had hoped to make the descent today, before darkness fell. She soon had to admit that this goal was impossible to achieve. They had too much work to do, only three people to do it, and she was the sole crafter. Olaf and Akiel and the others would have to spend one more night in the Deep Breath.

Kate set Thomas and Phillip to work on the balloons while she inspected and repaired the ship's magic. Magical constructs were used in every part of the ship. Magic reinforced the hull, prevented the lift tanks from rusting, and turned the airscrews.

Olaf was a ship's crafter and had always kept the magic on the old *Rose* in good repair, even when she was no longer in use. Kate remembered chiding him for working on the old boat when he should have been working on *Victorie*.

"Someday you might find you need the old girl, Katydid," Olaf had said. "When you do, she'll be ready."

He had been prescient. She had reason to be grateful. All magic wears over time. Kate was relieved to see that the constructs had not broken down as much as she had feared. Still, she had work to do to repair it.

The sun sank down behind the trees to the west, and darkness crept through the jungle and onto the *Rose.* In the waning light, Kate couldn't tell one sigil from another and reluctantly had to admit it was time to quit.

She straightened from a stooping position and stretched to ease her aching muscles, then looked around at her "crew." She had assigned Thomas the task of checking every strand of braided leather cable for breaks that might impede the flow of magic. She had told Phillip to inflate the balloons, and he was currently wrestling with the heavy folds of the chambered silk, trying to stretch it out flat on the deck.

Kate had to give them credit. He and Thomas had worked hard, without complaint, doing whatever she asked of them. Both were filthy and suffering in the heat. They had long ago shed their shirts. Phillip was red in the face, his shock of blond hair standing up straight on his head. Thomas had tied back his hair with a length of rope and appeared completely unaware that his face was covered with grime.

As she watched, Phillip lost his grip on the balloon and tumbled over. The silk slithered to the deck and he sat down on his backside. Thomas laughed at him and Phillip made a rude gesture.

"You can both stop working," Kate told them, smiling. "We will finish in the morning."

"Are you sure?" Phillip asked.

"We can't sail the Deep Breath after dark," Kate said regretfully. "Besides, we're all exhausted."

Phillip gave a thankful sigh and flopped down flat on the deck, too tired to move.

Thomas continued to peer down at a length of leather braid, trying to see. Kate walked over to him.

"You are a hard worker for a prince," she said. "If you ever need an honest way to make a living, I might consider hiring you."

Thomas smiled. "I think you should look at this section of the braid."

The magical constructs were damaged. One of the strands had broken, and others were starting to unravel. Olaf had warned her the leather needed to be replaced.

"Magic and spit can do only so much to hold it together," he had grumbled.

At the time, Kate had ignored his warning. She couldn't afford to spend money on *Rose;* she had needed the money to repair *Victorie*.

"Can we fix it?" he asked.

"Ideally we should remove the entire length of leather braid, replace the leather, braid it again and then reattach it," Kate said, sighing. "But I don't have time or materials. I'll have to fuse it with magic. It won't work as well, but it will work.

"I need your help. Pull this strand tight, like this," she instructed, demonstrating. "Keep hold and don't let go while I cast the magic."

Thomas did as she ordered. Kate traced constructs on the leather braid, then murmured beneath her breath. The constructs glowed blue, and smoke and the smell of cooked meat filled the air.

"Hold still!" she scolded Thomas. "I won't burn you."

"I beg your pardon, Captain," he said.

A tremor in his voice made her look up at him. They were standing shoulder to shoulder, their bodies pressed close together, arms and hands touching.

Kate wished she could escape his touch, for his nearness was having an unsettling effect on her. She didn't dare move, however, for fear of disrupting the magic. Gritting her teeth, she concentrated on the spell. The blue glow strengthened, fusing the leather braid together.

"Hopefully that will work, at least for a little while," Kate said, taking several steps back away from him. "The patch will slow the flow of the magic, but as long as some reaches the lift tank we should be fine."

"Your use of the words 'hopefully' and 'should be' do not fill me with confidence," said Phillip, coming over to join them.

"I can nurse the magic along by hand, if I have to," said Kate. "Let's see what Gert packed for dinner."

Phillip brought out the food: a cold collation of smoked meats, plantains, and hardtack. The three ate supper by lantern light, sitting on the deck to take advantage of the evening breeze.

"I'm sorry we didn't finish our work today," said Thomas. "Your friends will have to spend another night down there."

"They will be starting to think I abandoned them," Kate said.

"I know Olaf," said Phillip. "He would never think that."

"You are right," Kate admitted. "Olaf always believes in me, even when I don't deserve it."

"I've been meaning to ask about Olaf," said Thomas. "You seem very close to him. Is he some relation to you?"

"Olaf was my father's friend, probably Morgan's only friend," Kate answered. "They were shipmates before the navy court-martialed my father. Olaf stood by Morgan when he didn't deserve it and he's done the same for me."

"You said you lived on this ship," Thomas said. "Seems an odd place to raise a child."

He seemed to realize what he was asking, for he flushed. "I'm sorry. I don't mean to pry."

Kate shrugged. "I don't mind talking about it. My mother died when I was six. She had no family and no money, and the bank seized the family estate. Morgan's family had disowned him, so he had no one to look after me. He didn't know what else to do with me, and he took me to live with him on board the *Rose*."

Kate smiled, thinking back. "It was a wonderful life for a child. My father was charming and handsome. He was good at lying, smuggling, and swindling people out of their money. He was bad at cards and at raising a daughter. He let me run wild on board ship. I spent my days climbing the rigging and running along the yardarms. We were rarely in the same place two days in a row and so by the time I was ten I had seen the world."

"Sounds wonderful," said Thomas. "My parents shipped me off to boarding school when I was six. I spent my days cooped up in classrooms that smelled of cabbage, conjugating verbs, while the other boys made me wear gilt paper crowns and called me 'His Minus.'"

He laughed, and Kate was going to make some cutting remark about the "poor little rich boy" until she saw the shadow of pain darken his eyes. Her father had loved her, kept her with him, given her a family of sorts. Thomas's parents had shipped him away from home to live among strangers.

"You should have known Kate when we first met her," Phillip was saying. "She was wild as a catamount. She could drink any man under the table and knew more swear words than any pirate in the Aligoes."

Kate laughed. "My poor father tried to turn me into a lady. When I was sixteen, he bought me a green silk dress and a book on deportment. I think he hoped they would magically transform me from hoyden to gracious gentlewoman."

"I'm glad he didn't," said Thomas. "I like you the way you are."

Phillip cleared his throat and shot his friend a warning glance from beneath lowered brows.

Thomas frowned. His brow darkened and he looked away.

Kate realized that she must have been the subject of conversation between these two, perhaps even of contention. She wondered if Thomas had expressed his admiration for her to his friend.

I haven't been able to stop thinking about you, he had told her.

Phillip would have probably told Thomas what Kate had already told him. That she was a convict, formerly a pirate, and that he was engaged to a princess.

She began to pack away the uneaten food, and snatched a piece of hardtack from Phillip just as he was starting to eat it.

"Hey!" he protested. "I'm not finished."

"Yes you are. We need to save some for Olaf and the others," said Kate. "It's time to go to bed. I plan to be up at first light."

"I could sleep for days," said Thomas, yawning. Catching Kate's baleful eye, he added hurriedly, "But I won't. Should one of us stand watch?"

"I vote no," said Phillip. "If some monster is going to crawl out of the jungle to devour me, I am willing to let it, so long as it doesn't wake me first."

"I agree," said Kate. She slapped at a mosquito. "Cabins are below."

They each took a lantern and she led the way below deck.

"You and Thomas can sleep here," said Kate.

She opened the door to the cabin Marco and Akiel had shared. Two hammocks hung suspended from hooks in the overhead. Phillip climbed into one and flung his arm over his eyes.

"Good night," he mumbled.

Kate dimmed the lantern light, so as not to disturb him, and waited for Thomas to join him. Instead he continued to stand in the corridor.

"Where do you sleep?" he asked.

"In the captain's cabin," said Kate. "It's down the hall, in the stern. Now go to bed, sailor." She smiled at him. "Thank you for helping me. I could never have done this work alone."

"So long as I am alive, you will never be alone," said Thomas.

He took hold of her in his arms, drew her close, and kissed her.

"Good night, Kate," he whispered, and before she could draw breath or push him or slap him, he had slipped into the cabin and shut the door.

Kate stood in the corridor, glaring at the door. She had a good mind to go in there and tell him what she thought of him.

Except that right now, her thoughts were of his kiss.

Thunder rumbled in the distance. A gentle rain began to fall, pattering on the deck above. Kate stalked off down the corridor to the stern.

She opened the door to her cabin, and stood looking about in dismay. The cabin was empty. She had moved all the furniture, the desk and the chairs, her books and maps and charts, onto the *Victorie.*

The only stick of furniture was the bed, which had been built into the bulwark. She had no mattress, only a blanket. She would have to sleep on the bare wood, but she was so exhausted that didn't matter. She lay down and listened to the rain. Thunder growled, far away.

She could still feel Thomas's arms around her.

"Bloody hell!" Kate muttered. She pulled the blanket up over her head.

NINE

Kate woke from a deep sleep to find bright sunlight streaming in through the small porthole in her cabin. Swearing, she flung off the blanket and sat up on the edge of the bed. She had not meant to sleep so late. She had told Thomas and Phillip she would be up before dawn.

She stretched and stifled a groan. She had spent the night without pillow or mattress and her neck was stiff, her back sore. She thought of Olaf and how he must have spent the night, freezing in the darkness of the Deep Breath, wondering why she hadn't come to rescue him. Remorseful, she rubbed the sleep from her eyes.

"Today," Kate promised him. "I'm coming today."

She had fallen asleep in her clothes, so there was no need to dress. She checked the cut on her foot and found it was still healing well, now hardly noticeable. She couldn't believe Thomas had made such a huge fuss over a small wound, though she also had to give credit to Little Dimitri's healing salve.

She left her cabin and walked barefoot down the corridor, moving quietly. She heard no sounds on the ship except the stirring of rodents and water dripping from the rigging and the yardarms. Pausing outside the cabin where Phillip and Thomas were sleeping, Kate quietly opened the door a crack and peeped inside.

A ray of sunlight crept in through a chink in the planks of the hull. Both men were still in their hammocks, still fast asleep. Phillip lay on his stomach, one arm dangling over the edge of the hammock. Thomas slept on his back, his arms at his sides. He slightly smiled, as though he was enjoying a pleasant dream.

He was probably thinking about kissing her.

"It would serve you right if I tipped you out of the hammock," she muttered.

Thomas stirred in his sleep as though he had heard her. He shifted with a sigh. Kate flushed, afraid he would catch her watching him, and hurriedly closed the door.

She considered waking them, but decided she wanted to be alone for a little while. A lot had happened; she needed to sort out her thoughts.

She climbed the stairs and walked out onto the deck, blinking in the sunlight. The rain had ended, leaving the world clean and fresh scrubbed. Kate picked up the waterskin, discovered it was empty, and went to fill it in a stream that flowed down the mountainside.

Every ship's captain's first concern was fresh water and she and Olaf had chosen this cove to work on *Victorie* because of the proximity of the stream, which provided a plentiful supply.

Olaf had rigged up what he termed a "cyclical" pump operated by the swift flow of the water. She reminded herself to check on the pump, make certain it was working, for they would have to fill the *Rose*'s water barrels before they descended to the Deep Breath.

The rain had caused the stream to swell. The water bubbled and gurgled over the rocks before vanishing into the jungle.

Kate cupped her hands and drank, then filled the waterskin and went to check the pump. Because it ran off the power of the water, Olaf had said it could work forever, long after the two of them were gone.

Thinking how close that pump recently had come to outliving her, she shivered in the cool morning air.

When she had worked on *Victorie*, she had found a place where an offshoot of the stream lost itself among the mangroves, forming a pool beneath the roots. She had often come here to rest and dangle her feet in the placid water, watch the fish and dream of how she would find her fortune.

She sat down on the bank and sighed. She had no more dreams left in her.

Remembering that the day was wasting, she removed the red kerchief from her head, preparing to use it to scrub her face. She reached down into the pool and, seeing her reflection, she stared, overcome by shock.

She had known she must look different. She had not known how different.

She would not have recognized herself. Her face was bronze from the sun, her shaved scalp, by contrast, white as a fish's belly. The jagged wound on her head was clearly visible, a purple streak held together by black, zigzag stitches. The bruises on her face were purple and puce. At least the swelling was going down on her lip.

Her large eyes were her one beauty: hazel with golden flecks. The curls that had framed her face had often fallen over her eyes. Now, without them, her eyes seemed huge.

"Good God!" Kate whispered.

She dunked the kerchief into the water, ruthlessly destroying her reflection.

She carried the waterskin back to the *Rose*, thinking about Thomas and his kiss. Having seen her reflection, she decided he must be toying with her for his own amusement. He couldn't truly be serious. Kate decided to make it clear to him that she didn't like his advances. He needed to stop.

She was disappointed on her return to discover that both men were still fast asleep. She supposed she should go down to wake them, but where was the fun in that?

She began the process of inflating the balloon, making as much noise as she could.

Since Phillip had spread out the balloon on deck, all she had to do was attach the first set of guylines that ran from the hull to each balloon, then connect the hoses from the reserve tank to the balloons and fill them with just enough lift gas to cause the balloons to float up into the air. That enabled her to then maneuver the balloon into position between the foremast and mizzenmast. She would fully inflate them when they were ready to sail.

As she worked, she stomped about the deck, dragged the hose, and banged on the lift tank a couple of times for good measure. Soon a rumpled-looking Phillip came up on deck. He cast her a bleary-eyed glance.

"I take the hint," he grumbled, and disappeared into the jungle.

Thomas appeared moments later. The stubble of a day's growth of beard was dark on his jaw and chin, and his black curly hair straggled about his face. He was carrying his shirt, and she could see that his bare chest and arms were red from the sun.

"Good morning," Kate said, nonchalant. "There's water if you're thirsty and food from yesterday. Oh, and don't ever kiss me again. I didn't like it."

Thomas smiled. "I was merely returning the favor. After all, you kissed me first."

"I did not!" Kate protested, thinking he meant last night.

Then she remembered, and blushed red. He was talking about the time she had kissed him in Braffa.

"That wasn't a kiss," said Kate, annoyed. "That was my way of letting you know that I had outsmarted you."

Thomas raised his eyebrows. "Your lips touching mine. Certainly seemed like a kiss to me."

He walked away, leaving the ship before she had time to think of a flattening rejoinder.

By the time he and Phillip returned to the *Rose,* Kate fed them what food she could spare, then put them to work. They finished with the balloons, then she sent them back to the stream with empty water barrels and instructions on how to operate the pump.

While they were gone, Kate made a final inspection of the *Rose* and was satisfied.

"We can set sail," she told them when they returned.

Phillip finished inflating the balloons, filling it not to capacity, but just enough to provide stability. Thomas released the ropes that tethered the *Rose* to the shore and jumped on board.

Kate put her hands on the helm.

"This is the critical moment," she told them. "If the magic doesn't work . . ."

They waited tensely, as Kate sent the magic flowing to the lift tanks and the airscrews. When the lift tanks started to glow a faint blue and the airscrews whirred to life, Phillip cheered and Kate breathed a sigh of relief. She carefully steered the *Barwich Rose* along the shoreline to where they had left the water barrels and loaded them onto the ship. From there they sailed into the channel. When the rigging and masts were clear of the trees, Thomas helped Phillip raise the sails and they returned to the cove, near where *Victorie* had gone down.

"I am going to reduce the flow of magic to the lift tanks and stop the airscrews," Kate told them. "Pip, I need you to keep watch on the port side. Tom, take the starboard. The mists will grow thicker as we start to descend, and that will make it difficult to see. Search for any sign of a shipwreck and watch for floating chunks of rock."

Phillip handed around the peacoats. They didn't need them now—the heat was stifling—but they kept them nearby. He took his place on the port side and Thomas went to the starboard. They both stood at the rail, peering intently into the murky depths of the Breath, and each held a boat hook to fend off rocks.

Kate carefully moved her hand over the magical constructs on the helm until the bright blue glow on the lift tanks began to dim. She stopped the flow of magic to the airscrews and they quit turning.

The *Rose* floated on the orange-tinged mists of the Breath, then slowly began to sink. The mists closed in, shimmering with sunlight at first and then darkening as the ship sank beneath them.

The air grew chill and dank as the mists closed around the ship. Phillip and Thomas were ghostly figures in the fog and then Kate lost sight of them altogether. She seemed alone on the boat. The sail above her hung limp, damp with mist. In the eerie silence, she could hear water dripping from the yard-arms with dull, plopping regularity.

Kate watched the blue glow on the lift tank slowly fade. She had to be careful not to reduce the flow of magic too much or they would sink too fast and end up below the Breath, where "not even God can breathe," as the sailors said. If that happened, the *Rose* wouldn't have enough lift gas to return to the surface.

She was concentrating so intently on her work that she didn't notice she was cold until she felt someone drape her peacoat over her shoulders.

"You're shivering," Thomas said.

"I am enjoying the 'cool, refreshing' air," Kate said caustically. "Aren't you?"

Thomas laughed, remembering his words from yesterday, and then vanished into the mist, returning to his post.

Kate thrust her arms into the peacoat, keeping one hand on the helm. They were now through the thickest part of the Breath, and the mists began to part, changing from woolly blankets to wispy scarves.

Suddenly the mists around them started to swirl. The ship rocked, forcing Kate to grab hold of the helm to keep from falling. Phillip lost his balance and fell flat. Thomas grabbed hold of the rigging.

"Damnation! We've hit a riptide!" Kate shouted. "Hang on!"

"A bit late with the warning!" Phillip grumbled, picking himself up.

"You've sailed the Deep Breath before," Kate told him.

"Yes, but I had forgotten the joys of being caught in a riptide," Phillip returned.

"What do you mean by a riptide?" Thomas asked. "I have been caught in those when swimming in an inland ocean, but we're not in an ocean."

"You remember when Captain Galvez told us about the phenomenon of magical 'tides' in the Aligoes, where the magic ebbs and flows," said Phillip.

"I was enjoying the captain's very fine port at the time, but I do seem to remember that he called these tides a 'quirk of the Aligoes,'" said Thomas. "They cause wizard storms and blow ships onto the rocks."

"And sometimes these same magical 'quirks' create turbulent waves known as riptides, particularly when the ship is in proximity to one of the Six Old Men," Phillip explained.

"Charming place, the Aligoes," said Thomas dryly, transferring his hold from the rigging to the gunwale as the ship rocked again. "I assume we are close to one of these terrible old men?"

"Most people think Freeport was built on an island, but it's actually located on the side of Mount Invicto, one of the Six Old Men," said Kate, clinging to the helm. "The mountain has its base at the bottom of the world. I thought *Victorie* might have crashed on a true island, but if the ship landed on the side of Mount Invicto, that would be better. The survivors can find streams and caves."

"And we could end up joining them," Phillip said grimly.

The *Rose* rolled and pitched, the boom swung wildly, the airscrews rattled, and the wooden hull creaked and groaned.

"These riptides come and go," Kate said. "We should be through the worst in a moment."

The shaking continued longer than she had ever known, however. Just as she was thinking the ship might start to come apart, the buffeting stopped. The *Rose* righted herself. Dim sunlight filtered down through the mists of the Breath. Looking down, they could see that the ship was floating above a vast expanse of gray rock marked by crevices, cracks, jagged hills, and shadowed valleys.

"Any sign of the wreck?" Kate called.

She longed to look for herself, but she had to keep her attention on the helm.

"Nothing on the port side," Phillip reported, peering over the rail.

"Nothing on the starboard," Thomas said.

Kate told herself not to start worrying yet, and reduced the magic to next to nothing, until the lift tanks barely glowed. She took time to button the peacoat and turn up the collar. She found a knit cap stuffed in the pocket and she pulled that over her shorn head.

"So this is the Deep Breath," said Thomas. "I read Captain Stephano de Guichen's account of descending to the land of the Bottom Dwellers. According to him, the farther he went the thicker the Breath. Here the air is relatively clear. I assume this is yet another quirk of the Aligoes?"

"Or just a quirk of the Breath," said Kate. "In Braffa, the Breath is so cold it congeals."

Seeing Thomas flash her a grin and a knowing look, Kate flushed and wished she had never brought up Braffa.

The *Rose* drifted above the mountainside, still slowly descending.

"Kate, I think I see something!" Thomas shouted. "Almost directly below us. Phillip, come look!"

"It does appear to be the wreckage of a ship," Phillip reported, hurrying over to join his friend. He added somberly "Or what is left of one."

"Pip, take the helm," Kate said. "I need to see for myself."

She went to the rail and leaned over to look.

The *Victorie* was down there—a charred and burned-out hulk.

When Kate had salvaged her she was already an old ship, built during the days when shipbuilders had constructed heavy vessels meant to survive wizard storms and broadsides. She had the distinctive broad sterncastle that was now out of fashion and a lower and wider forecastle.

The ship had survived the impact, but not the fire, which had left much of the hull blackened and charred. The flames had made cinders of the masts, rigging, and balloons. The fire had been so intense it had burned a wide swath of ground around the ship.

Phillip and Thomas exchanged grim glances, and Kate knew what they were thinking.

"My crew could have survived," she said defiantly. "Crafters always put magical constructs on the wooden planks to guard against fire. The magic would have slowed the flames and given the crew a chance to escape."

"Kate . . ." Thomas began gently.

"There!" Kate cried. "Look! Those spars over there on that flat rock. They form an *X*! Someone did that deliberately. It's a signal."

"I don't see anyone around," said Phillip.

"Sail closer," said Kate.

The ship lurched and the deck canted, almost sending Kate overboard. Thomas caught hold of her, grabbing the collar of her peacoat with one hand and hanging on to the rail with the other. Phillip adjusted the trim by using the airscrews, but the ship was caught in another riptide, and continued to rock and shudder.

"The *Rose* can't take much more of this, Kate," Phillip shouted. "We need to gain altitude, go back to where the air is calmer!"

Kate knew he was right, and she had to fight down her disappointment.

"I'm sorry, Kate," said Thomas.

"I'm not giving up," said Kate. "Now that I know where the wreck is, you and Phillip can lower me down there in the bosun's chair."

Thomas stared at her. "The bosun's chair! You can't be serious!"

Kate shrugged. "I'm used to it. When I made my living as a wrecker, I would dock the *Rose* on the surface of the Breath, and the crew would lower me down onto the wreck."

"But you could be caught in one of those riptides," Thomas protested. "The ropes could snap. You could fall out of the chair . . ."

"Or we could get hit by that chunk of rock coming toward us off the port bow," Phillip shouted. "You two need to stop arguing, and pay attention."

"He's right," said Kate, walking off.

"This isn't over," Thomas called after her, grabbing the boat hook. "I'm not letting you go down there."

"You don't have a say!" Kate returned. "I'm the captain."

She could see a small island floating in the mists above. They could tie off the ship up there. She took over the helm from Phillip.

"Can either of you throw a grappling hook?" she called, shifting the direction of the airscrews and increasing the flow of magic to the lift tank. "We're going to need to tether the ship to that island."

"I was in the army and therefore trained to throw grappling hooks over fortress walls, not onto floating chunks of rock," Thomas said. "But I will do my best."

"Good," said Kate. "Pip, let me know when we're close."

Phillip nodded and went to stand on the bow beside Thomas. They peered upward, both of them rubbing their hands and stamping their feet to keep warm.

"I would not term it an island so much as a glorified boulder," Phillip remarked. "It is adrift, but doesn't appear to be in any great hurry. I think we should be able to anchor the ship to it."

Kate steered the *Rose* as Phillip shouted directions and motioned with his hand. Thomas stood by, swinging the grappling hook.

"Stop!" Phillip yelled.

Kate cut the magic to the airscrews. Momentum continued to slowly carry the *Rose* toward the island, but the ship now moved at a crawl.

"See that spear of jagged rock?" Kate called, pointing. "Don't throw the grapple onto the rock. Toss the grapple so that the line will catch on the rock and cause the hook to swing around the rock before it catches."

Thomas hurled the grapple and missed. He reeled the grappling hook back in.

"I have my aim now," he said, seeing Kate frown.

He tried again and this time the grappling hook performed as planned, whipping around the rock formation and catching with a ringing clang.

Kate reduced the magic in the lift tanks, using just enough to keep them afloat. They were about thirty feet above the island. She could see the wreckage clearly. No one was down there, no one moving about. The only sign of life was that X.

The cold was insidious, creeping through the peacoats, chilling to the bone.

Even if the crew had found shelter and Akiel was still able use his spirit magic, their odds of surviving such brutal conditions were not good.

Kate had refused to let herself think that Olaf and the others might be dead. Now, gazing down at the charred and broken bones of her ship, she had to face the hard facts.

Thomas looked grave. He started to say something.

"You don't have to tell me," Kate interrupted him. "I know it looks hopeless. But I can't leave without trying."

"What I was about to say was that we could fire our pistols," said Thomas. "If your crew is sheltering in a cave, they might not have seen us."

"That's a good idea," said Kate, giving him a grateful glance.

"You don't have to sound so startled. I do have them occasionally. I still don't like the thought of you going down there," Thomas added.

"I still didn't ask you," Kate retorted.

She went to ready the bosun's chair, which hung from a block and tackle suspended from the yardarm. She tugged on the rope to make certain it was secure, remembering, as she did so, all the times the crew had lowered her to the site of a wreck, how she had crawled amid wreckage, searching for kegs of nails, barrel hoops, scraps of lumber—anything she could sell at auction.

Wrecking was a dirty and thankless job; the small amount of money Kate had earned had barely paid to keep the *Rose* afloat. She had often cursed that life, but now she blessed it. Her experience gave her a chance to save Olaf and her friends.

She was absorbed in her work with the chair, and the pistol shot startled her. The sound seemed unusually loud in the stillness, reverberating off the side of the mountain, echoing among the rocks.

"Do you see anyone?" Kate asked eagerly.

Thomas and Phillip stared over the rail, waiting.

Time passed, but no one answered.

Thomas looked back at Kate. "Now what do we do?"

"You and Phillip are going to lower me to the surface. The bosun's chair is over here."

Thomas glanced around the ship. "Where?"

"Right here," said Kate. She patted a wooden plank attached to two ropes.

Thomas stared in disbelief. "That's not a bosun's chair! That's a tree swing!"

Phillip grinned. "You're a child of luxury. You're thinking of the bosun's chairs carried by rich Estaran merchants: wooden seats with high backs, armrests, and comfortable cushions."

"This chair serves the same purpose," said Kate. "It's just not as fancy."

Thomas was still frowning.

"Trust me," said Kate. "I've used a chair like this hundreds of times. So has Pip."

"Then let Pip go. Or I will go," said Thomas.

"And how many times have you ridden in a bosun's chair that wasn't lined with velvet, Your Highness?" Kate asked.

Thomas flushed. "That's beside the point—"

"No, it isn't," Kate said. "I know what I am doing. Pip, you work the ropes. Thomas, come over here. I need your help."

Phillip inspected the block and tackle and gave the rope a couple of tugs. He appeared satisfied. "Ready when you are, Captain."

Kate grabbed the ropes.

"Hold the chair for me so that it doesn't start swinging," she ordered Thomas.

He held the chair steady. Kate took her seat on the plank, adjusting her weight so that she didn't tip and fall off.

"I wish you would reconsider, Kate," Thomas said earnestly. "Let me go search for your friends. I'm not talking about the danger. I'm thinking about what you might find . . ."

Kate knew what he meant but didn't want to say. He was thinking she might find them dead. He was truly concerned for her. She had to make him understand.

"They are my crew, Thomas," Kate said. "I am their captain. I am responsible for their welfare. My duty is to them. I cannot shirk it."

Thomas regarded her intently, his expression thoughtful. She expected him to continue to press his arguments.

He rested his hand over hers. His hand was cold and so was hers, but the touching of the two hands warmed them both.

"Good luck, Kate," he said.

Letting go, he stepped back.

"Ready?" Phillip called.

"Ready!" said Kate.

She was a little breathless, and not from fear. Phillip hoisted the chair with Kate in it off the deck and swung it out over the rail. He then began to slowly pay out the rope, lowering the chair down toward the island. Kate looked back up to see Thomas leaning over the rail, watching her descend. He gave her a reassuring smile and Kate looked away.

She didn't want him to smile at her like that. She didn't want him to make her feel fluttery and confused. She had told him not to kiss her, and yet, when he had been standing close to her with his hand touching hers, she found herself wishing he would kiss her.

"Look out, Kate!" Phillip called. "Riptide! Hold on!"

Kate had been thinking about Thomas and not watching what she was doing. The ripple in the mists flowed toward her and hit her chair, whipping her about, twisting the ropes, swinging her sideways. Kate clutched the ropes, her knuckles white. Once she almost slid off the plank and only a freak gust of wind saved her, pressing her back.

The riptide passed quickly.

She sighed in relief and hooked one arm around the ropes to give Phillip a reassuring wave, let him know he could start lowering the chair again.

"Let that be a lesson to you, Katherine Gascoyne-Fitzmaurice," Kate scolded herself as the chair resumed its descent. "Men are nothing but trouble, as your mother often told you!"

TEN

Kate kept careful watch on the mists from then on, searching for any sign of disturbance in the magic.

The Breath relented. For a moment the mists dissipated and the air grew calm. She heard the silence of the Deep Breath. Those who have never been there could not understand how one could hear silence, but Kate knew. What people termed "silence" in the world above was actually filled with the sounds of life if you listened closely enough. The silence in the Deep Breath was utter.

Wrapped in the silence, Kate drew near to the ship. As a wrecker, she had made her living off the carcasses of wrecked ships like this one. She had viewed with callous regard the lives that had been lost in the storm, the dreams destroyed. From now on, she would never look at a wrecked ship the same way.

She touched solid ground and slid out of the chair. She tugged on the ropes and waved to let Phillip and Thomas know she was safe. Thomas waved back and Phillip hauled the chair up.

As Kate looked around the site of the wreck, she was overwhelmed by hopelessness and despair. Nothing could have survived. Another riptide rippled past, almost blowing her over and causing the bosun's chair to swing wildly as it rose through the air.

"Olaf!" Kate shouted. "Akiel! Marco! Are you there?"

No one answered. Kate began to climb among the wreckage, shifting broken planks and shoving aside debris, searching for anyone who might be still alive.

Searching for bodies.

She was wearing the peacoat, but no gloves, and her hands were soon numb with the cold, which proved to be an advantage, or so she told herself. She couldn't feel the pain of the numerous cuts and bruises.

She found pools of blood and blood splatters. She found no survivors, but no bodies either and that puzzled her.

Then she understood.

"My brain must be going as numb as my feet," Kate muttered.

She started her search again, but now she left the wreck and concentrated on searching the area around it.

Akiel had explained to her that he required a spark from living things in order to fuel his spirit magic. That spark could come from something as small as a blade of grass, but he needed life. The ship had crashed onto the side of a mountain. The ground was barren and stony, no plants, no trees, not even lichen in the vicinity of the wreck. But Kate could see patches of green not far away.

She scrambled over the rocks, calling out for her friends.

"Olaf! Akiel! Marco!"

"Mum!" a voice called back. "Is that you?"

"Akiel!" Kate cried, overwhelmed with emotion.

The big man appeared, climbing over the top of a small rise, waving as he came. He had a wound on his head. The white, bloodstained bandage made a startling contrast to his black skin. But he was smiling.

Kate started toward him, but he waved her away.

"Wait there, mum!"

He looked back over his shoulder and motioned with his arm. "Come along!" he shouted.

"Olaf!" Kate yelled. "How is Olaf?"

In answer, she heard his voice. "Is that our Kate?"

"I'm here, Olaf!" Kate shouted.

"I knew you'd come for us!"

Olaf came in sight, hobbling over the uneven surface, propped up by a crude crutch made from a tree limb. Kate ran to him and flung her arms around his neck and clung to him as tears rolled down her cheeks. He dropped his crutch to put his arms around her, patting her on the back.

"Don't cry, Katydid," he said, chiding her. "Your tears will freeze."

He pulled back to observe her and his expression darkened. Akiel was staring at her, wide-eyed and frowning.

"Mum!" he exclaimed, shocked. "Where is your hair?"

"Your face is bruised. What happened to you, Kate? What did those Rosian fiends do to you?" Olaf demanded.

"It's a long story and it doesn't matter now," Kate said. She looked past Akiel, expecting to see the rest of the crew. No one else was there and Kate felt stifled. She looked from him to Olaf.

"Where are the others?" she faltered. Reaching out, she clutched Akiel. "There must be more!"

"We left them in the cave until we were certain who was here. Twenty-two survived. Eight dead," Olaf reported. He paused, then added, "Including Marco."

"Marco!" Kate gazed at him in dismay.

"He was standing at the helm. A cannonball . . ." Olaf didn't go on. "He died a quick death, Kate. He never saw it coming."

Kate remembered Marco, always cheerful and smiling. He had been saving money to buy his own ship.

"Oh, Olaf, this was all my fault," she said.

"Now, you know that is not true, Katydid," said Olaf stoutly. "Share the risks, share the rewards. Every man knows that when he makes his mark on the contract."

He rested his hand on her shoulder. "You did what you thought was best. It wasn't you that fired the cannonball that killed Marco."

"It was me who put him in the way of it," said Kate.

Olaf tightened his grip on her. Kate smiled and put her hand over his.

"Where are the rest of the crew?" she asked more briskly.

"In a cave we found," said Akiel. "When we heard the pistol shot, we couldn't see who was firing. Olaf was afraid it might be the Rosians come to finish us off. I told them to wait while I went to see what was going on. I told Olaf to wait, as well, but he is a stubborn old man."

"I knew it was you," said Olaf. "I knew you'd come for us."

His face was pinched with the cold. Akiel looked gray and haggard. They both must be starving, for they had gone days without food. They could say it wasn't her fault, but she knew better.

"I will go fetch the others," Akiel offered.

"Bring them to the site of the wreck," said Kate. "We can't sail down because of the riptides. We'll have to figure out how to transport everyone."

Akiel left, climbing back among the rocks.

"The *Rose* is up above, tied to a boulder," Kate told Olaf as they slowly made their way back to what remained of the *Victorie*. "They lowered me down in the bosun's chair. We can't haul everyone back up the same way, though. That would take hours and I'm not sure that the ropes would hold."

"How many times did I tell you to replace those old ropes?" Olaf scolded her, smiling.

Kate squeezed his hand. "I promise I will listen to you from now on."

Olaf snorted. "And pigs will fly like dragons. The riptides moderate around sunset. You could bring the *Rose* down then, though that will mean sailing through the Deep Breath after dark."

"We'll manage," said Kate. "No one wants to spend another night here. We don't have that far to travel to reach the cove. My crew are a couple of lubbers, but they'll do. You know one of them. Remember Pip?"

"Pip?" Olaf repeated, astonished. "You mean Captain Alan's Pip?"

"The same. I told you I met with him in Braffa when Dalgren and I were doing that job for Sir Henry. I ran into him again here in the Aligoes."

Olaf was dubious. "Pip, you say. That young man never drew a sober breath, leastwise not that I ever saw."

"He was putting on an act," Kate explained. "He was a spy for Alan. He did some very dangerous work during the war."

Olaf grunted, unconvinced. "Who else?"

"A friend of Pip's," Kate said. "His name is Tom. He . . . he's a soldier."

She felt herself blushing and that was infuriating because Olaf would think she cared about this man, and that wasn't true. Unfortunately, the more she tried to stop blushing, the more she blushed. She averted her face, rubbed her hands, and stamped her feet.

"I could use one of Akiel's warming spells about now!"

"We would be dead men if it weren't for Akiel," said Olaf. "I always mistrusted that spirit magic of his, as you well know. What with him talking to ghosts and trees and the like. But he kept us alive, Katydid. He tended to our wounds and found water. We managed to salvage a few bits of wood from the ship to burn, but once that was gone, he used his magic to heat rocks to keep us warm. He did all that even though he was hurt himself."

"Akiel will have a home with us for as long as he wants it," said Kate.

Olaf shook his head. "What sort of home, Katydid? Where will we go? We can't show our faces in the Aligoes. The Rosians brand us pirates. I suppose we could sail to Bheldem. No one knows us there. We could go back to wrecking . . ."

"Never!" said Kate firmly. "Being down here reminds me how much I hate that life."

"Then what?" Olaf asked.

"I have a plan," said Kate.

Olaf usually gave a disbelieving snort when he heard her say she had a plan, for he'd had some experience with her plans before, and none of it good. This time, he cleared his throat and wiped his red-rimmed eyes.

"You don't really, do you?"

"No, but I will," said Kate. She hugged him and they walked on in silence.

When they reached the site of the wreck, Olaf looked up at the *Rose* floating overhead.

"Good old girl," he said. "She never lets us down."

Kate could see both Phillip and Thomas leaning over the rail, worriedly gazing down at the wreck. When Kate waved to Phillip to let him know to send down the chair, he and Thomas both gave a cheer.

As Phillip began lowering the chair, Kate tried to estimate the amount of time remaining until sunset, but she was so cold she was finding it hard to think. She looked around the remains of her beloved ship. The helm she had salvaged and restored was gone, completely destroyed. Marco must have been standing there . . .

"Tell me what happened," she said.

"Akiel and I were on the quarterdeck," said Olaf. "The same shot that killed Marco took out the helm and the magic. The airscrews stopped, and the lift tanks failed. Then there was an explosion. Fire was everywhere, and we started sinking fast. That's all I remember until I woke up to find Akiel hauling me out of the burning wreckage. What happened to you?"

"The anchor was fouled. I finally managed to knock it loose, and I tried to go back on board," Kate said. "But then the powder magazine blew up. The Rosian marines took me prisoner. I heard the ship crash and I knew there would be survivors. I begged the Rosian captain to send a rescue boat, but he refused. They took me to prison . . ."

Kate faltered and fell silent.

"They were going to hang you, weren't they, Kate?" said Olaf.

"But they didn't," said Kate stoutly. "Pip and Tom helped me escape—"

"You shouldn't have come back for us. You put yourself in danger," Olaf said, glowering.

"If the Rosians hadn't been trying to capture me, we wouldn't have been attacked in the first place. They won't find me down here, at least," said Kate, smiling. "I'm safe enough for the time being."

She hurried over to catch the bosun's chair as it descended, telling Olaf, "Go up to the ship. Pip can take the helm, but he'll need your help. Bring the *Rose* down when you think it's safe. I'll wait here for Akiel and the others."

Olaf protested, insisting she should go back up in the chair, but Kate was adamant. She saw him settled on the plank, along with his crutch, then she waved to Thomas and Phillip to haul him up.

She watched nervously until Olaf reached the ship and Thomas signaled to her that he was safely on board. Kate sat down on a rock, huddled inside the peacoat, and clamped her jaw shut to keep her teeth from chattering.

The next hour she kept busy helping Akiel tend to the rest of the crew. Two men had broken legs and had to be carried. The others had various injuries ranging from burns and cuts to fractured arms and ribs. Akiel continued to keep them warm with his magic, but Kate could see that he was near exhaustion. She looked up at the *Rose,* hoping Olaf would come soon.

At last the gray mists began to darken. The *Rose* released the tether and sailed down to the site of the wreck. At the welcome sight of the old ship, the survivors raised a ragged cheer.

Once Olaf landed the *Rose* on a relatively level patch of ground not far from the wreck, Thomas lowered the gangplank and hurried down to help her with the wounded.

"Olaf says to work fast," Thomas told Kate. "He doesn't want to keep the ship here long."

Kate could see that for herself. The riptides might not be as severe, but magical currents were buffeting the balloons and whipping through the rigging.

"Don't say anything to Olaf about working with the Rosian navy," Kate said. "He's had a belly full of Rosians."

"I figured that out myself," said Thomas with a grin.

He worked tirelessly, assisting Kate with the walking wounded, helping to carry litters. He spoke cheerfully to the sailors, asking them about their families, trying to make them forget the pain and hunger and the bone-chilling cold, even though his own lips were blue. He kept an eye on Akiel, and he was at his side when the big man collapsed, his strength finally giving way now that rescue was at hand.

Sometimes, as they worked together and Thomas looked over at Kate and smiled, she couldn't help but smile back.

He must have been a good officer, Kate thought to herself. And then he had to ruin it by being a prince.

"That's everyone," Thomas reported when he had helped the last man come on board.

Kate cast a final look at *Victorie* in the deepening gloom. Akiel had told her that Marco's spirit had moved on, freed of the confines of flesh and bone. If *Victorie* had a spirit, perhaps the ship had moved on, as well. The two of them were together, sailing the Breath in some faraway place.

As for her dreams, she would find new ones.

"Hurry up, Kate!" Phillip called.

She said good-bye and hurried up the gangplank. Thomas pulled it up after her. Phillip sent magic flooding through the lift tanks. The *Rose* sailed into the night.

Kate did not look back.

ELEVEN

After a tense journey sailing blind in the darkness, the *Rose* at last broke through the mists and left the Deep Breath, emerging into a clear, warm night glittering with stars and a round, radiant moon. Kate guided the ship into the cove, where Thomas and Phillip tethered it to the trees. The survivors had been fed and were now sleeping on the deck, comforted by nourishment and warmth.

Kate insisted that Olaf sleep in her cabin. She fussed over him, covering him with blankets, making a pillow of her coat, and urging him to drink some cider. When he was settled, she sat down at his side.

"I was glad to see Pip again," said Olaf drowsily. "Even more glad to see him sober. I like his friend—that fellow, Tom. He thinks the world of you, Kate. He talked of nothing else."

"Tom is a glib talker," said Kate dryly. "Go to sleep."

Olaf sighed and closed his eyes.

"I knew you would come for us, Katydid," he murmured.

Kate clasped his hand and sat by his side until he drifted off, then she went back up on deck.

The ship was quiet save for the sounds of snoring. Akiel had wakened long enough to eat something and then he had stretched out on the deck and gone back to sleep. Kate moved among her crew, covering them with blankets, making certain all were as comfortable as possible.

Thomas and Phillip were both awake, deep in discussion on the quarter-deck. They spoke in low voices so as not to wake anyone, and stopped as Kate approached them.

"You two look guilty," said Kate. She was in a good humor with all the world at the moment. "What are you plotting?"

"Olaf wants to go back to running the Parrot, but he doesn't think he can," said Pip. "He's afraid he and the others will be arrested as pirates, and he's probably right. The Rosian navy will reduce its presence in the Aligoes, but they'll never leave altogether. Tom had an idea."

"I believe I can obtain pardons for them," said Thomas.

"Could you?" Kate gasped. "That would be wonderful!"

"Captain Favager is not well liked among the officers," Thomas explained. "No one believes his account of the battle. The dragons of the Dragon Brigade witnessed the entire incident. They reported to their captain that your ship had surrendered before he fired on it."

"Thorgrimson was also aware that you and your crew were privateers, men holding letters of marque from Freya," Phillip added. "Sir Henry will use this incident to embarrass King Renaud. The Freyan press will be howling for Rosian blood. It would be much better for everyone if the king can persuade the Admiralty to hush this up."

"The best way to do that would be for Renaud to issue pardons to your crew," Thomas said. "They would have to lie low for a time—"

"They can stay on board the *Rose*," said Kate eagerly. "The ship can shelter in the cove. We'll use the island hopper to ferry food and supplies from Freeport."

Thomas and Phillip both exchanged grave glances.

"I am afraid we cannot do the same for you, Kate," said Thomas. "Miss Amelia's newspaper stories about Captain Kate have made you notorious. Every week, Kate does battle against murderous Rosians who are depicted as bloodthirsty, cowardly swine. The Freyan public loves it, but, sadly, the entire Rosian nation truly hates you."

Kate brushed that aside. "Just as long as Olaf and Akiel and the others are safe and Olaf can go back home. I don't plan on staying in Freeport long anyway."

"Where will you go?" Thomas asked. "Back to Freya?"

Kate did not immediately answer. She had not planned on telling Olaf or anyone where she was going.

"You can trust us to keep your secret," said Phillip, mistaking her hesitation for doubt.

"I know I can," said Kate. "It's just . . . I need your help and I don't like to ask. You have done so much for me and my friends already."

"You can ask us for anything," Thomas assured her.

Kate plunged ahead. "I'm going to the Dragon Duchies to find Dalgren. I told you he went there to visit his family. That wasn't exactly true. He went back to stand trial for desertion from the Dragon Brigade."

"Desertion!" Thomas repeated, his expression grave and troubled. "That is a serious charge. In the Estaran army, he would stand before a firing squad."

"But he can't be guilty," Phillip protested. "Not Dalgren. This must be a mistake."

"He is guilty," said Kate. "But he had a good reason. There was a battle, he was wounded, and he saw his friends dying . . ."

Thomas shook his head. "Your friend Dalgren took an oath to serve his country and he broke it. He fled and left his comrades to face the danger."

He did not go so far as to accuse Dalgren of cowardice, but the words hung unspoken in the air.

Kate bristled. He had no right to judge. But when her gaze went to the scar on his cheek, a pale slash in the moonlight, she realized perhaps he did have a right to judge. Still, he didn't know the whole story.

"Dalgren was not a coward. He fought and was wounded at the Battle of the Royal Sail. Do you know what happened there?"

"I have read accounts," Thomas replied. "The battle is infamous in Estaran history."

"I've never heard of it," said Phillip. "What did happen?"

"During the Battle of the Royal Sail, a Rosian naval commander fired a broadside on his own dragons and their riders," Kate explained.

"Good God!" Phillip exclaimed. "Why would he do such a mad thing?"

"The Rosians were laying siege to a fortress claimed by the Estarans," said Thomas. "The captain of the Dragon Brigade had agreed to surrender terms for the fortress, saying the Estaran soldiers would be permitted to withdraw unmolested. A Rosian captain refused to honor the agreement, saying he was going to blow the fortress out of the sky and no one could stop him. The Dragon Brigade had given their word, and the dragons and their riders formed a line to protect the fortress. The captain fired on his own troops."

"That was how Dalgren suffered that wound to his leg," said Kate. "He was young, and he was grievously hurt. He had just seen his comrades die, killed by their own navy. He was upset and angry and confused. And so he left the Brigade and fled Rosia."

"I grant you that he and the other members of the Brigade acted bravely and with honor," said Thomas. "But that still doesn't excuse desertion."

"How did they catch him?" Phillip asked.

"He surrendered," Kate said. "When the Dragon Brigade came to the Aligoes, Dalgren turned himself over to them. He went back to the Dragon Duchies willingly to stand trial. And I need to be there to speak on his behalf. But I don't know where the trial is being held or when it will be."

She looked from Thomas to Phillip. "I was thinking one of you could find out."

"We can ask Captain Thorgrimson," said Thomas. "But, Kate, to reach the Dragon Duchies, you will have to travel through Rosia. You just heard what we told you."

"They will be keeping watch for you," Phillip agreed. "They have pictures of you from the newspapers."

"In those drawings I am jumping off the back of a dragon with a knife between my teeth," Kate said, laughing. "No one will recognize me, especially now that my hair is gone."

She grew serious. "Dalgren is my friend. He has been my friend for many years. I cannot let him down . . . again," she added, but softly, to herself.

"Say, here's an idea!" said Phillip. "Kate could fly to the Dragon Duchies on griffinback. That would be safer and faster than traveling overland."

"We could arrange with Little Dimitri for one of his griffins to carry her. Will that suit?" Thomas asked Kate.

Kate looked from one to the other. "I have said 'thank you' so many times, the words seem very stale and flat. I am truly, truly grateful for everything you have done."

"This means you owe me a second dance, Katherine Gascoyne-Fitzmaurice," said Thomas with a wink.

A night's rest, food, and warmth restored Akiel and many members of her crew. Kate informed them that her friends were working on a plan to obtain pardons for all of them. She couldn't promise them anything, but she was hopeful. They would have to remain hidden in the cove and some groused at that, but she reminded them of the danger they still faced from the Rosians. Eventually everyone agreed, and they set to work making camp.

Thomas and Phillip helped, hauling water from the stream, while Akiel went foraging in the jungle to find fruit and nuts. He also brought back some insects he claimed were edible, but Olaf said he would starve to skin and bones before he would eat a bug.

"I shudder now to think what you've been putting in my chicken stew all these years," Olaf growled.

Hearing that, Thomas and Phillip took their pistols and went out hunting for game. They returned with Dalgren's favorite treat: wild hogs.

The sailors took down the sails from the *Rose* and draped them over tree branches to form makeshift tents. Kate assisted Akiel in cooking up healing potions and salves to help the wounded.

When night came, they sat around the fire and told stories. Many of the crew remembered Captain Alan Northrop and the Rose Hawks, and Phillip kept them laughing with his tales of their adventures outwitting the Rosians, sinking their ships, and making off with their treasure.

Thomas sat apart. He often looked at Kate, as though he would like to talk to her, for this would be their last night together.

She avoided him. She did not want to hear anything he had to say. She stayed near Olaf. She had not yet told him she was planning to go to Dalgren's trial and she dreaded the argument that would ensue. Olaf felt the same as Thomas about Dalgren being a deserter. Olaf would not be happy to hear Kate was planning to go to the Dragon Duchies, putting herself in danger.

Kate considered just telling him she was going back to Freya, but her days of lying were over. Well, mostly.

She had a mission of her own to perform in Freeport, but she kept quiet about it, for she knew they would all be appalled, tell her the risk was too great. Kate didn't want to waste time arguing, though she knew they were right. The risks were great. She wrapped herself in a blanket and lay down on the deck. When Thomas came over to talk, she pretended to be asleep.

The next day, he and Phillip made preparations to leave.

"We can stay if you need us, Kate," Thomas said.

"No, we cannot," said Phillip sternly. "The griffins said they would return today and they will be furious if we're not there to meet them. Besides that, the Rosian navy must be deeply concerned over the fact that they have mislaid the future king of Freya. They will be sending out search parties, and that might endanger Kate and her crew. Time for the dream to end, Tom."

He gave his friend a meaningful look. Thomas looked grave and started gathering up his few belongings.

Kate was going to take them to Freeport in the island hopper. Once she did what she needed to do there, she would return to camp with the supplies. All was arranged, until Olaf announced he was going with her.

"I need to go back to the Parrot," he said. "Gert doesn't know anything about running a tavern. I probably don't have a customer left!"

"Olaf, it's not safe," Kate said

"You're going," Olaf said, glowering at her.

"Only as far as the lighthouse," said Kate, hoping she might be forgiven just one more lie. "You can't leave. You are second-in-command now that Marco is dead. You have to stay here."

Olaf grumbled, but he agreed.

Phillip and Thomas said their farewells, and Akiel gave them his blessing and bruising hugs. Olaf, in an emotion-choked voice, thanked them for rescuing Kate.

They boarded the island hopper, and Olaf threw off the lines and waved until they were out of sight.

Kate took the helm, and Phillip sat in the prow, ready to handle the sails and wield the boat hook. Thomas was supposed to be helping him, but he came instead to sit beside Kate, much to her ire.

"You're in my way," she said. "Go up with Phillip."

"I am leaving today, and I want to spend every moment I can with you," said Thomas.

His eyes were very blue in the early-morning sunlight, his gaze earnest, warm, and intense. The boat was small and he was forced to sit near to her. She was acutely conscious of his body close to hers, almost touching.

"What do you want from me?" Kate asked abruptly.

Thomas was startled by her question. "What do you mean?"

"You are obviously trying to make me fall in love with you. What do you expect in return?"

Thomas regarded her, troubled. He clearly didn't know how to respond.

"Suppose I do fall in love with you," Kate continued relentlessly. "You are engaged to be married. When you are the king of Freya, what will I be? The royal mistress?"

"No, of course not," Thomas said, flushing.

"Then what?" Kate asked.

He did not answer because at that moment, the boat entered the narrow, tree-lined channel that meandered through the jungle islands and Kate had to concentrate on negotiating a particularly narrow stretch of channel. Thomas, saying nothing, joined Phillip at the prow with the boat hooks, fending off rocks.

When the hopper had reached a clear place in the channel, Thomas returned to his seat.

"As for the Princess Sophia, I have reason to believe she is interested in someone else." He smiled as he said this, his gaze went to Phillip. Thomas regarded his friend somberly a moment, then he turned back to Kate. "As for me, if I were king, I would marry you."

"Marry a pirate?" Kate snorted in disbelief.

"Why not?" Thomas asked, adding with a teasing smile, "You are 'worthy.' Pip tells me you are the granddaughter of a viscount. Though I would marry you if you were the granddaughter of a—"

"Pirate?" Kate said archly. "Let me tell you about my grandfather the viscount. He gambled his way into debt then blew out his brains so as not to have to face the disgrace. He left my mother penniless and she died insane. My father was a gentleman rogue who swindled people out of their money and got his skull bashed in for his trouble. So, you see, Your Highness, my 'noble' blood is somewhat tainted."

"I am in earnest and you mock me," said Thomas. "I am falling in love with you, Kate!"

She shook her head. "You only think you are. I am the damsel of some romantic tale you've read about in the newspapers. Suppose I fall into your arms in the next installment? What happens to us in the chapter after that? You go back to your world of wealth and luxury and royal balls. I go back to my world of trying to survive. We were born to be what we are, Tom. Neither of us had a choice in the matter."

Her voice faltered. She tried to hide the tremor, but Thomas was quick to hear it.

"You are saying that if we *did* have a choice you could love me."

"I did not say that," Kate snapped. She jostled him with her elbow. "Go sit with Phillip."

Thomas smiled. "I believe you do love me. Maybe just a little, but that is enough for now."

He put his fingers on her lips, stopping her denial. "No, Kate, don't ruin my dream. You need to hear me out. I told you I hadn't been able to stop thinking about you since Braffa, and that is true. I was intrigued. You were so different from any other woman I have ever known. Since we have been together, my feelings for you have deepened. You made me think seriously about my life, Kate, about what it means to be a prince."

"Now *you* are mocking me," said Kate.

"Hear me out and I will explain," said Thomas. "My mother wants me to be king. She has plotted and schemed her entire life to put a crown on my head. I do have a claim to the throne of Freya, but the possibility that I would ever become king was remote. Queen Mary had an heir, the crown prince had a son. I never gave the matter serious thought. And then, Crown Prince Jonathan and his son both died and now, suddenly, I am the one with the best claim.

"Factions in Freya are against me. The queen terms me 'Pretender.' I have an army." Thomas frowned into the shifting mists. "Two thousand men and transport ships led by a Captain Smythe, who has trained them to accompany me to Freya to seize the throne by force. I would say they were men prepared to die for my cause, but the truth is they are mercenaries who will die for any cause so long as you pay them.

"I have never seen my army. I never planned on seeing it. I told my mother and my father and Captain Smythe that I will not be party to deposing the queen. Yet my mother keeps plotting and Smythe keeps drilling his blasted soldiers and my father keeps paying for all of it."

Thomas had been gazing into the mists. Now he looked back at Kate.

"Freya is teetering on the brink of disaster. The only other heirs are the queen's bastard half brother and her Rosian sister and they are both acquiring allies to vie for the throne. Freya could be torn apart by civil war. And what am I doing to help my people?" Thomas asked bitterly. "As you accused me, I am going to royal balls and dancing with princesses."

He was in earnest, sharing his fears and doubts and sorrows with her. Kate was silent, uncertain what to say. She felt ashamed of what she had said already.

"When you were sitting in the bosun's chair, Kate, you talked about what it means to be a captain. You were willing to risk your life because you are responsible for the welfare of your crew. That made me think. I need to be responsible for *my* people. I am the heir to a throne. I cannot abrogate those responsibilities just because I find them onerous or inconvenient.

"I love you, Kate. More than that, I admire you. When I leave here, I am going to obtain pardons for your crew and then I am going to go see this army of mine and talk to Captain Smythe, find out what is truly going on. I owe this to you, Kate."

Kate flushed. "Please don't say things like that. You don't know me . . ."

"I know you are strong and brave and smart. I know you are beautiful."

"Now I know you are making sport of me," said Kate, laughing self-consciously as she touched the red kerchief she wore tied around her shorn head. "I saw my reflection in the pool."

Thomas smiled. "Your hair will grow back. But for now, when the sunlight hits your eyes, the hazel shines and the gold dances." He raised his hand and gently touched her cheek. "I can see the fine bones of your face and the fullness of your lips." He added with a grin. "Although that may disappear when the swelling goes down."

He was teasing, but Kate could not laugh. Her breath came too fast. His touch seemed to thrill through every nerve. Thomas rested his hand on hers.

"I am not a romantic, Kate. I know that I will never see you again. You will go your way and I will go mine. My way will be easier if I know that you love me—just a little."

Kate watched the play of sunlight and shadow dapple his face as they sailed beneath the thick foliage. His eyes were bright blue in the sunlight, darkened to deep azure in the shadow.

"Maybe . . ." said Kate softly. "Just a little."

Thomas spoke gruffly, not looking at her. "Wherever I am, I will be loving you. And I will try to live up to the example you have set me."

He brought her hand to his lips and gently kissed it, then he stood up so quickly that he caused the small boat to rock alarmingly. He made his way forward to join Phillip.

Kate didn't know what to do or think. She was confused, upset, and angry. She was not angry at him for loving her. She was angry at him for making her love him when she would never see him again.

She didn't like the feeling, and she hoped when he and his blue eyes were gone, the pain of loving him would go with him.

Kate sailed the hopper to the lighthouse and tied up the boat. Phillip and Thomas hefted their gear and Kate led them through the jungle to the open field where they were going to meet the griffins.

They did not talk much. Shared danger and fear and sorrow, shared triumph and relief had brought the three very close. They had only one word left to say to each other and that was good-bye.

They arrived at the meeting site early; the griffins were not around. Thomas moodily walked around the field. Kate fidgeted, wishing they were gone, all the while knowing she would miss them. Phillip scanned the sky, searching for the griffins.

As generally happens, the three decided to break the awkward silence by all talking at once.

"I will send back a griffin—"

"You can tell the griffin to meet me here—"

"You must give me five days to negotiate the pardons—"

They each stopped talking, looked at one another, laughed, and felt better.

"You first, Pip," said Thomas.

"I was about to say that I will have Little Dimitri send a griffin here to take Kate to the Dragon Duchies," said Phillip. "I just hope Dalgren's trial doesn't start before you arrive."

"I am not worried about that," said Kate. "Noble dragons never do anything without formal ceremony and proper protocol. They will have to locate those dragons who served in the Brigade, as well as human officers who were present at the battle to give testimony. That will take time. I probably have a month or more before the trial could possibly take place."

"And as I was about to say, I will need time to negotiate for the pardons for your crew," said Thomas. "Can you give me five days? I will write you a letter and send it back with the griffin."

"Five days will suit me," said Kate. "I have my own business to attend to. Tell the griffin I will meet it here at noon five days from now."

"Speaking of griffins," said Phillip. "Time to be going."

They all looked up to see the beasts circling overhead. Thomas signaled to them and the griffins swooped down for a landing.

Phillip advanced to greet them, thank them for coming, and ask permission to stow their gear. Thomas took out one of the pistols and handed it to Kate.

"To remember me by," he said with a smile. He added, more seriously, "I think you might need it."

Kate was going to refuse, then she remembered her pistols were on the side of a mountain in the Deep Breath. She thanked him and thrust the pistol into her belt.

The griffins made certain the farewells were short. They did not like this place that smelled of dragon and they began snapping their beaks, indicating they were ready to leave—with their riders or without.

Kate held out her hands, one to Phillip and one to Thomas. "I owe you both a debt of gratitude that I can never hope to repay."

"I claim the privilege of an old family friend," Phillip said. He embraced Kate and kissed her on the cheek. "I hope all goes well with Dalgren."

Phillip went to mount his griffin, leaving his friends alone to say their farewell. The other griffin hooted and began to paw the ground in irritation.

"You better go," Kate said to Thomas.

Before she could stop him, he pulled her close and kissed her.

"Good-bye, Kate," he said, and walked away before she could utter a word.

Mounting his griffin, Thomas strapped himself into the saddle, then leaned forward to pat the griffin on the neck, letting the beast know he was ready. The beasts took off, loping across the field, spreading their wings as they ran, and taking to the air.

Kate stood watching them until they were out of sight and then she kept standing there, missing him already, feeling his absence like being lost and alone in the Deep Breath.

TWELVE

Leaving the field, Kate walked into Freeport. She had decided to go into town in the afternoon because it was the hottest part of the day and the road would be deserted. Most people chose this time to sleep. She entered the Parrot quietly, coming in through the back door.

She listened, didn't hear anyone around. The dinner crowd would have left. The supper crowd wouldn't come until the cool of the evening. She peeped into the kitchen and didn't see anyone. Probably Gert had gone home to nap.

Kate headed for Olaf's room. She sat down at the desk and was starting to write a note when she was confronted by a large and angry woman wielding a wooden spoon.

"Here, now, you rascal, what do you think you are doing?" the woman demanded, raising the spoon in a threatening manner. "You skedaddle this instant or you will get a thumping that will raise knots on your rascally head!"

"Gert, it's me!" Kate cried, jumping to her feet and backing up.

She had a healthy respect for that spoon. Gert had raised seven children, all of whom were now grown and all of whom had lived in terror of the wooden spoon, which their mother could wield with energy, skill, and surprising accuracy.

Gert frowned, eyeing her.

"It's really me," Kate said. "Just without my hair—"

Gert dropped the spoon and rushed forward to fold Kate in a bone-breaking hug that squeezed the breath from her body.

"I heard you were alive, but I didn't believe it! Goodness, child, what did those fiends do to you?" Gert held Kate at arm's length. "Half starved you, by the looks of it, and your poor hair! You sit down here and I will bring you a beefsteak pie—"

"Gert, no, please," said Kate. "I'm not hungry and I can't stay long. I came to pick up some supplies. First, tell me, are there any Rosian naval ships around?"

Gert looked worried. "The ships aren't here, Kate, but strangers turned up yesterday, asking questions about you. Bounty hunters, by the stink of them. Not one of us said a word, but you're not safe in Freeport."

Kate sighed. Bounty hunters. The Rosians must have put a hefty price on her head. This was just all she needed.

"I'm not planning to stay. I found the wreck of the *Victorie*. Olaf and Akiel and the others. They're safe— Well, some of them."

"Thank the good God!" Gert cried, and she hugged Kate again.

"I need information, Gert. Tell me what's been going on since I left."

"I will fetch us some ale, dearie, and we can have a good chat."

Gert bustled off and soon returned with two mugs and a bowl of rice and beans which she insisted that Kate eat.

"Where did the Rosian ships go?" Kate asked.

"They've moved on, so we hear. Chasing pirates out of the Imperial Channel."

"And Greenstreet?"

"He packed up and left. Good riddance to bad rubbish." Gert glowered.

Kate sighed. "I had unfinished business with him."

Gert grunted. "You and half the town!"

"Do you know if any of his men are still around?" Kate asked.

"They found Jules dead. Shot in the back. He must have crossed his master. No one's seen any of the rest. Everyone figures they left with Greenstreet."

Kate needed to find out if the dragon Coreg was still there or if he had gone, too. She couldn't ask, because no one in Freeport knew that Greenstreet had been working for a dragon.

"I'm thinking of one man in particular, a man called Trubgek," said Kate.

Trubgek had been Coreg's servant. If Trubgek was still around, then so was the dragon.

Gert frowned and shook her head. "I would have remembered such an outlandish name."

"Trubgek is a strange fellow," Kate said. "Maybe you saw him, but didn't pay much attention to him. He never has much to say. Dark hair, wears a leather vest."

"I haven't seen anyone like that around town, Kate," said Gert.

Kate sighed. "I'm also looking for someone else. A man who was here when the Rosians sank my ship. He's Freyan, tall, walks like a soldier, well spoken—"

"Mr. Sloan," said Gert at once. "He comes into the Parrot most nights."

"Did he ever say anything about me?"

Gert thought back. "He seemed pleased to hear you had escaped the Rosians, same as everyone else in town. But I don't think he ever mentioned you specific."

"Do you know why he is still here?" Kate asked. "Does he meet anyone?"

"He says he's here on business, though he doesn't say what. He met a man the first night he was here, but that man hasn't been back and Mr. Sloan always comes in alone. He did say he's planning on leaving tomorrow."

"Tomorrow!" Kate repeated, alarmed. "Gert, I need you to deliver a letter."

While Gert went to pack up food and other items for Kate to take back to the cove, Kate wrote a hasty note to Mr. Sloan. She did not sign her name, just said she needed to speak with him on a matter of the utmost urgency. She named a time and place: the Parrot, midnight tonight.

He would find that suspicious, but Kate dared not reveal that she was back in Freeport. She gave the letter to Gert and told her to assure him that no one meant him any harm, and that he could come armed if he wanted.

Gert knew where Mr. Sloan was lodging and promised to deliver the letter.

Kate ferried the supplies to the cove, saw to it that Olaf and Akiel and the others were safe and well, then made preparations to return.

"Where are you going?" Olaf asked.

"To the Parrot," said Kate. "I have business. I won't be back until tomorrow."

"This has something to do with Greenstreet, doesn't it?" said Olaf.

"He's left town, apparently," said Kate. "So I can't talk to him, but I can talk to Mr. Sloan. You've heard me speak of him. He works for Sir Henry. I believe Mr. Sloan is here to find out who killed the dragon."

"Or to find you," said Olaf, scowling.

"I have to chance it," said Kate. "The only way you and I can go back to Freya is for me to clear my name."

"Do you want to go back, Katydid?" Olaf asked.

She looked at him, amazed by the question. "Yes, of course. We'll sail back in the *Rose*. Our home is there, Olaf. You can live with me at Barwich

Manor. I still have a contract with Sir Henry, and while I don't have a ship, I can do other work for him."

Olaf shook his head. "I'm not going back."

"What are you talking about? Of course you are!" Kate said.

"I'm staying here with the Parrot. Winter is coming on in Freya and I never want to be cold again, Katydid. Not after what I've been through."

Kate was dismayed. "But you have to come with me! I can't do without you."

"You'll do fine, girl," said Olaf. "You have your life to live and I've already lived mine. I want to finish my days at the Parrot with my friends, taking my ease in the sunshine."

Kate suddenly saw how much Olaf had aged. She had not noticed before now. He moved slowly, leaning heavily on his crutch. His hair and beard were white, his face lined and seamed and haggard.

"I have to sail back to Freeport now," Kate told him, "but we'll talk about this later."

She climbed into the island hopper. Olaf stood onshore to release the ropes. He grinned and called out, "I'd tell you to be careful, Katydid, but I know I'd be wasting my breath!"

Kate left the hopper tied up at the lighthouse, hidden among the trees. Mindful of the bounty hunters, she once again slipped into the Parrot through the back entrance and locked herself in Olaf's room. She had a long time to wait until midnight and she whiled away the hours studying her father's maps of Rosia, planning the route she would take to reach the Dragon Duchies.

Gert reported that she had delivered the letter to Mr. Sloan at his lodgings. She said he had been surprised, but not overly concerned. He had questioned her about the person he was supposed to meet and the nature of the meeting. Gert had played dumb, told him she didn't know anything. When she said he could come armed, he had gravely nodded, thanked her, and promised he would be there.

Darkness fell and Kate lit a lantern and tried to read a book on seafaring crafting. She knew midnight was near when she heard Gert shooing the late-night stragglers out of the Parrot. She and her son began cleaning up, sweeping the floor and washing the dishes.

Rain showers rolled in, bringing a cool breeze blowing through the window, rustling the leaves in the trees.

Kate laid down the book. She checked the pistol Thomas had given her, made certain it was loaded, and placed it on the desk in plain sight. Mr. Sloan would know she was armed, but that she wasn't hiding anything.

As midnight drew nigh, Kate could not sit still. She walked the floor. Her future, her very life depended on the outcome of this meeting.

She heard Gert's son greet someone at the main entrance. Footfalls crossed the floor and Kate went cold all over. She forced herself to sit down in the chair, picked up a map, and tried to seem nonchalant.

Gert's son knocked on the door and called, "A gentleman to see you."

"Come in," said Kate.

Mr. Sloan opened the door and entered. He remained standing in the doorway. He was wearing a cloak against the rain and a tricorn. He had thrown back one side of the cloak and was keeping his hand near the pocket of his jacket.

He saw her and raised an eyebrow, evincing his surprise. He noticed the pistol on the desk, cast a swift glance around the room. Finding that they were alone, he lowered his hand from his pocket and removed his hat, shaking off the water.

"Should I close the door, Captain?" he asked.

"Please," said Kate.

Her mouth was dry, her hands were trembling.

"Thank you for coming, Mr. Sloan," she said.

Mr. Sloan sat down and placed his tricorn on his knee.

"I am glad to see you alive and well, Captain," he said. "I was sorry to hear of your capture. How did you escape?"

Kate brushed that aside. "I need to come to the point. I did not kill that dragon, Lady Odila. Miss Amelia said she told you about Coreg, how he's involved with Greenstreet and his criminal empire. Coreg knows who killed Odila and Greenstreet knows how to find Coreg. Do you know where Greenstreet has gone? I have to talk to him!"

"I am afraid you are out of luck, Captain," said Mr. Sloan. "Greenstreet is dead. And so is Coreg."

"Dead?" Kate gasped.

"They were both murdered. I saw the bodies."

Kate jumped to her feet. "I didn't kill them, Mr. Sloan! I swear I didn't! Oh, God!" She sank back down into the chair and lowered her head into her hands, overwhelmed by despair. "Now no one will believe me!"

"I believe you, Captain," said Mr. Sloan.

Kate raised her head to stare at him in astonishment. "You do? You believe me? Will you tell Sir Henry?"

"Sir Henry's friend Mr. Yates convinced him of your innocence. Sir Henry sent me here for the same reason you are here, to find out the name of the killer. Unfortunately, the killer reached the dragon first and silenced him."

"You said you saw the bodies of Greenstreet and Coreg, Mr. Sloan," said Kate. "Were they killed by magic?"

"I found Greenstreet's body lying in the tunnels. He had been felled by a pistol shot to the back of his head. The dragon was slain inside his lair. The murderer used the same magical spell to incapacitate Coreg that he had used on Lady Odila."

"I think I know who killed them, then," said Kate. "Coreg had a servant named Trubgek—"

"I met him," said Mr. Sloan. "A strange man, dark hair, empty eyes, dresses in leather, never smiles, almost never talks."

"That is Trubgek. And he is more than strange, Mr. Sloan," Kate said. "He is extremely dangerous. Coreg trained him in dragon magic."

Mr. Sloan frowned, clearly thinking Kate was exaggerating. "I am a crafter myself, Captain, and I have never heard of such a thing. How is that even possible?"

"Trubgek said that given enough pain, anything is possible. I have seen him cast powerful magic spells that no human crafter, not even a savant, could cast. He is more than capable of murder and he hated Coreg. The name Trubgek is not a name. In the language of dragons, it is an insult."

"He seems to wear it as a badge of honor," said Mr. Sloan.

"Be careful of this man, Mr. Sloan. Trubgek is deadly, and probably killed Coreg and Greenstreet."

"I appreciate the information," said Mr. Sloan, looking troubled. "I know for a fact, however, that Trubgek is not the murderer, although I do believe he was complicit."

"How do you know, Mr. Sloan? How did you find out?"

"Because I am currently friends with the man who did."

Kate stared at him.

Mr. Sloan rose to his feet. "I was wondering if you could do me a favor, Captain. Are you returning to Freya? I need someone to carry a confidential message to Sir Henry."

Kate shook her head. "I am not returning to Freya for at least a month. I am traveling to the Dragon Duchies. You remember my dragon friend, Dalgren. He is in serious trouble and needs my help."

"I am sorry to hear that," said Mr. Sloan. "I wish you both luck. And now, if there is nothing else, I must take my leave."

"The door is locked and the others have gone home. I will fetch the key," said Kate.

She picked up the lantern to light the way and stopped to retrieve the key that hung behind the bar. Outside, the rain continued to fall steadily and would likely do so throughout the night.

Kate unlocked the door.

"I bid you good night, Captain." Mr. Sloan paused, then added, "You say you are traveling to the Dragon Duchies. Perhaps you should inform the dragons about this Trubgek. You can tell them he sails tomorrow for Bheldem and might be found in the employ of the Marquis of Cavanaugh."

Mr. Sloan put on his tricorn, made a military bow, and stepped out into the rain.

After he was gone, Kate felt as though the weight of the Six Old Men had been lifted from her soul. Sir Henry knew she was innocent. Her future was once more bright with hope.

Kate had to find a way to extricate Dalgren from his predicament, but once that was accomplished, the two of them could return to Freya, continue working as privateers. She might even see Thomas. She had tried not to think about him, with the result that he was all she thought about. She imagined sailing a seventy-four gun, the HMS *Barwich Rose,* into the port of Haever, a Rosian treasure ship in tow, to be met by Thomas standing on the quay, hailing her as a hero.

"And pigs will fly like dragons," Kate said, laughing at herself. "The only way I will see him is when he rides past in his fine carriage, waving to the crowd."

She banished Thomas from her dreams after that and spent time working on repairing the real *Barwich Rose.* Once she and Dalgren were together again, she had planned to return to the Aligoes and sail the ship to Freya. But now that Olaf had decided to remain in the Aligoes, Kate was going to leave the *Rose* for him.

"My sailing days are over, Katydid," he said.

"Don't say that," said Kate. "You and Akiel will need the *Rose* to come to Freya to visit, see Barwich Manor again."

Olaf shook his head, but he did not argue. He and Akiel promised to keep the ship in good repair, should she ever need it.

"Which I have no doubt you will," Olaf said, grousing. "Knowing you, Katydid, it will be only a matter of time before you find yourself in trouble again."

Kate laughed. "From now on, I plan to be a staid and proper lady. Once my hair grows back, I might even start wearing dresses."

Olaf snorted, and Akiel regarded her gravely.

"I hope you mean that, mum. About staying out of trouble."

"I do," said Kate. "Trust me, dear friends, I have learned my lesson."

"She may not find trouble," Akiel remarked as Kate walked away. "But trouble has a way of finding her."

"Just like her father," said Olaf with a sigh.

Kate pretended she didn't hear.

After five days had passed, she returned to Freeport and went to the field to await the arrival of the griffin.

When the beast landed it indicated it was carrying something in its saddle-bags. Kate found a letter from Thomas.

> Dear Captain Kate,
> King Renaud has granted pardons to Olaf and the others, though not, I fear, to you. Captain Favager has resigned from the navy in disgrace, forced to do so when the king learned the truth—that he had fired upon your ship after you had surrendered.
>
> Dalgren's trial is scheduled to be held the last day of the month at a place in the Dragon Duchies known as Cieleterre. This griffin has been well paid to fly you to the border of the Dragon Duchies. (The beast refuses to carry you beyond that, I fear.)
>
> You will find a purse tucked into a secret compartment in the saddle. I know your first impulse will be to decline to accept the money . . .

"Damn right!" Kate muttered.

> But I hope you will reconsider. The journey will be costly. The griffin will need to rest at night and inns that provide accommodations for griffins are expensive. Dalgren saved my life in Braffa and I would like very much to contribute to his defense. Phillip says to tell you that you will need proper attire, for you cannot very well travel through Rosia or appear at a trial in a calico shirt and slops—no matter how much such clothes become you.

"Impertinence!" said Kate, yet she couldn't help but smile. Still, what he said was true. She was doing this for Dalgren. She must think of him first.

> Phillip has enclosed the name of a lady friend in Wellinsport who will provide you with suitable clothes.
>
> In closing, I know you will think it inappropriate to write to me to let me know how you are faring. Pip says you may write to him, for he is as good as a brother. I have included his address in Estara. I hope you will keep me informed through Pip about what you do and where you go. You are always in my thoughts, Kate. I hope that fond thoughts of me sometimes flit across your mind.
>
> Your obedient servant,
> Tom

Kate smiled. And then she sighed.

She folded his letter carefully, smoothed it with her hand, then tucked it into her belt. Examining the griffin's saddle, she found a purse containing a hundred silver rosuns.

She told the griffin to wait for her and sailed back to the cove to tell Olaf and Akiel and the others the good news. They were free men. They cheered her so loudly that she feared the Rosians might hear them all the way in Maribeau.

Now came the hard part: leaving Olaf and Akiel and her friends.

Kate kept the good-byes short, fearing she would break down if she did not. She shook hands with every member of the crew, hugged Akiel and told him in a whisper to look after Olaf. Akiel promised he would.

Kate clung to Olaf as to a father.

"Good-bye, dear friend," she said. "Dalgren and I will come to visit. So don't rent out my room."

"Take care of yourself, Katydid," said Olaf, embracing her. "That's all I ask."

He gave her a kiss on the forehead that was like a father's blessing. The last thing he said to her was "I knew you would come for us, Kate! I knew you would come."

THIRTEEN

Franklin Sloan, formerly of the Royal Freyan Marines, now retired, served as the private secretary to Sir Henry Wallace, known formally as the Earl of Staffordshire, known to the cognoscenti as Her Majesty's Spymaster and the most dangerous man in the world.

Sir Henry had dispatched Mr. Sloan to the Aligoes to question the dragon Coreg regarding the whereabouts of the murderer of another dragon, Lady Odila. The dragon's death had caused an uproar in Freya, shaking the stability of the country and creating an international incident. Henry's friend Simon Yates had provided a suspect: another former marine, who had served with Mr. Sloan. The man's name was Isaiah Crawford.

Sir Henry needed to know why Crawford had killed Lady Odila and what her death had to do with the Faithful, a secret cabal dedicated to advancing the claim of the Pretender, Prince Thomas Stanford, to the Freyan throne.

Mr. Sloan had sailed to the Aligoes and made his way to Freeport to find the dragon Coreg, only to run into the very man, Isaiah Crawford. The moment Mr. Sloan had set eyes on Crawford, he realized that he was too late. The dragon was the one being who could tie Crawford to the crime. He was not the type of man to leave this thread dangling.

Mr. Sloan had arrived at a fateful decision. He had attached himself to

Crawford, making use of their service together. He needed to communicate this decision, as well as the important information he had gathered, to Henry.

Mr. Sloan had considered writing a letter in code. But the mail in the Aligoes was untrustworthy, and codes can be broken. His mission was so extremely dangerous and so vital to the security of his nation that he did not want to put down anything in a letter that might imperil it.

He had hoped to send it by way of Captain Kate, but that had not worked out. The only other people he knew in Freeport were fellow customers he had met in the Perky Parrot. They were fine fellows in their way, but he did not consider any of them suitable for such a delicate mission.

Mr. Sloan woke early on the morning of the day he and Captain Smythe, as Crawford now called himself, were to leave for Bheldem. As Mr. Sloan packed his valise, he once more considered the problem. He had written a letter the night before, addressed to Simon Yates.

The letter was innocuous, letting Sir Henry know that he—Mr. Sloan— was going to be absent longer than he had anticipated, and apologizing for the inconvenience.

Sir Henry would realize that something untoward had occurred. He would connect Mr. Sloan's mission with the death of the dragon and perhaps even with Crawford/Smythe. Mr. Sloan was reluctant to send even this letter, however.

Mr. Sloan was a devout man, a member of the strict Fundamentalist sect, and as he closed and locked his valise, he decided he would place the matter in God's hands.

The ship sailing to Bheldem was due to arrive mid-afternoon. Captain Smythe had offered Mr. Sloan a job, and Mr. Sloan had arranged to meet Smythe at the Perky Parrot prior to their departure to go over the terms of the offer.

"Mr. Sloan, I know you are not happy in your current employment," Smythe had told him. "You have been of immense help to me in the business upon which I have been engaged this past fortnight. You are aware of the divine cause I serve and how important that cause is to bringing the word of God to the benighted. The marquis has recently promoted me to the rank of colonel—"

"Congratulations, sir," Mr. Sloan had said.

Smythe had modestly inclined his head in acknowledgment. "I need a new second-in-command. My former lieutenant turned out to be a drunkard. I need someone I can trust. I will soon set sail for Bheldem and I would like you to accompany me, Mr. Sloan—or should I say, Lieutenant Sloan."

Mr. Sloan had been expecting the offer. Indeed, he had been doing everything possible to ingratiate himself to Smythe for this express purpose.

Mr. Sloan had promised to give the matter prayerful thought and consideration. Smythe, also a Fundamentalist, had approved, saying he felt certain God would lead Mr. Sloan down the path of righteousness.

When Mr. Sloan entered the Parrot carrying his valise, Colonel Smythe rose to his feet to greet him.

"Have you made your decision, Mr. Sloan?" Smythe asked.

"I have, sir," said Mr. Sloan. "I accept your offer. I will be proud to serve with you."

The two men shook hands and then sat down to boiled ham and beans, which was seemingly the only meal Gert knew how to cook. Given her dexterity with the wooden spoon, none of her customers were inclined to complain.

Smythe was not one for idle chitchat. He ate rapidly and in silence, leaving Mr. Sloan to his own thoughts, which underwent a startling turn when the answer to his prayers walked in the front door of the Perky Parrot.

Mr. Sloan had never doubted for a moment that God would respond to his plea for help. Mr. Sloan was, however, considerably startled by God's choice of messenger, who turned out to be the outspoken and energetic journalist Amelia Nettleship.

Mr. Sloan knew Amelia and, unfortunately, Amelia knew him. She did not see him at once. The sun was bright and she had to pause in the doorway to allow her eyes to adjust to the gloom inside the Parrot. Mr. Sloan was in her direct line of sight.

He could envision the encounter. Miss Amelia would greet him joyfully, claim him as a friend, and ask about Sir Henry. All Mr. Sloan's careful work to gain the confidence of Smythe would be for nothing. Given the captain's bloodthirsty history, Mr. Sloan guessed his life would be worth less than nothing.

"Please excuse me, sir," said Mr. Sloan, hurriedly rising. "I find myself in some distress."

Gert's beans were known to have this effect upon people and Smythe merely nodded. The privies were located in the back of the tavern. Mr. Sloan bolted for the entrance.

His mind was apparently concentrating on his internal problems and he was not watching where he was going. He came level with Amelia just as she recognized him. When her eyes lit up and she opened her mouth, he barged into her, knocking the umbrella she always carried out of her hand and nearly bowling her over.

"I beg your pardon, Madame," Mr. Sloan said. Bending down, he recovered the umbrella and handed it to her. "Office. My signal," he said softly.

He then bowed and departed, hurrying out the door.

Amelia was a confirmed spinster in her forties, a journalist by trade. She was close friends with Kate and wrote the popular "Captain Kate" stories that had been running in serial form in the *Haever Gazette* during the past few months. Mr. Sloan guessed that Amelia had heard through her numerous sources her friend was in peril and had traveled to the Aligoes posthaste to try to save her.

Mr. Sloan respected Amelia, deeming her astute and intelligent, if a bit eccentric. He was confident that he would be able to rely upon her discretion, all the more so because she would be avid to know what was going on.

When he returned to the Parrot, he found Amelia in animated conversation with Gert, who was telling her about Kate's escape from prison. Amelia glanced at Mr. Sloan, dabbed her nose with a handkerchief, and looked away. Mr. Sloan resumed his seat at the table with Smythe.

"Forgive my absence, sir. I never thought I would say this, but I am actually looking forward to army rations," said Mr. Sloan, regarding his plate with disfavor. He shoved it away.

Smythe had finished his meal. "Food is merely nourishment for the body, Lieutenant. Nothing more." He drew out a pocket watch, checked the time, and rose to his feet. "I have some business to conclude with our friend before we depart."

Mr. Sloan remained in the Parrot, drinking ale. Smythe had been spending a great deal of time with "our friend," by which he meant Trubgek, the man Kate had claimed knew dragon magic. Smythe and Trubgek had been holed up in the lair of the dead dragon Coreg for days on end. Mr. Sloan had no idea what they were doing, for he was not in their confidence, but he guessed that the two were attempting to sort through the dragon's numerous nefarious business arrangements.

Once he was certain Smythe would not be likely to return to the tavern, Mr. Sloan rose to his feet, paid his bill, and took his leave. He saw Amelia rise and say something to Gert. The two of them departed, walking toward the back of the tavern.

Mr. Sloan took another trip to the privies, then entered the tavern through the back door. He passed Gert's son, who nodded in the direction of the office. Mr. Sloan opened the door to find Amelia pacing the floor, eagerly awaiting him.

Mr. Sloan shut the door. Amelia advanced to shake hands, then the two sat down at the desk.

"You know, first, that Captain Kate is safe," Mr. Sloan said.

"I just found out, Mr. Sloan," said Amelia. "When I read the news of her capture in a Rosian newspaper, I dropped everything and traveled to Maribeau.

I have been living in fear the entire trip that I would be too late to prevent her from being hanged. I was overjoyed to know that she has escaped."

Amelia took out her brown notebook and a pencil from her reticule and prepared to write. "Give me the details."

"I am sorry, I do not know them, Miss Amelia," said Mr. Sloan. "I spoke to Kate only briefly and we did not discuss that."

"Ah, well, I suppose I will just have to make them up," said Amelia. "I understand she is laying low due to the presence of bounty hunters. Do you know where she is?"

"She did not inform me of her plans, other than to say that her friend Dalgren was in trouble and that he required her help."

"Poor fellow," said Amelia. "I hope all goes well for him. You obviously did not summon me to talk about Kate. So what can I do for you, Mr. Sloan, other than pretend not to know you?"

"I am here to ask you an immense favor, Miss Amelia. When do you plan on returning to Freya?"

"My time is my own," said Amelia giving him a sharp glance. "I flew here by griffin. I can leave for Freya upon the hour."

Even in his urgent need, Mr. Sloan had to pause to regard Amelia in shock. He knew she was eccentric, but he had never imagined she would carry her eccentricity to such extremes. Traveling by griffin might be fast, but it was risky and uncomfortable and definitely not suitable for ladies.

Amelia guessed what he was thinking. "You are an old fuddy-duddy, Mr. Sloan. I learned to ride griffins when I attended Mrs. Ridgeway's Academy for Young Ladies. I can also drive a coach-and-pair. Mrs. Ridgeway believed we should be prepared for any contingency. What is it you need me to do, sir?"

Mr. Sloan ignored the use of the term "fuddy-duddy" in regard to himself and replied. "I need you to carry a message to Sir Henry, one that I dare not set down in writing."

Mr. Sloan cast a significant glance at the brown notebook. Amelia immediately packed it away, back into the reticule, folded her hands, and prepared to listen.

"I am all attention, Mr. Sloan."

Mr. Sloan lowered his voice so that he spoke hardly above a whisper. "Tell His Lordship that I have located Isaiah Crawford."

Amelia had to lean close to hear him. At the mention of the name, her eyes widened.

"The murderer!" she stated.

"How do you know that, Miss Amelia?" Mr. Sloan asked, astonished.

"Sir Henry told me," said Amelia. "He clearly did not want to, but he said he was afraid I would discover the name on my own and make my knowledge public, which would, of course, alert Mr. Crawford to the fact that we are 'on to him' as the police put it. I assume Sir Henry sent you here to find out what the dragon Coreg knew. Kate came here for the same purpose. I am sworn to secrecy, on condition that I will be able to tell the story when this is all finished."

"The story is a complex one," said Mr. Sloan. "Far more complex than we realized. Isaiah Crawford now goes by the name Jonathan Smythe, and he is the commander of the armies of His Highness, Prince Thomas Stanford."

"Merciful heavens!" Amelia exclaimed, startled. "How very extraordinary."

"I believe this has something to do with the Faithful. Do you know about them?" Mr. Sloan asked.

"Indeed I do, sir. To quote *The History of Freyan Monarchs* in regard to the Faithful. 'The Faithful began as a group of nobles loyal to the memory of King James I and are now alleged to be a secret society of noblemen devoted to restoring the male heir of the Stanford family to the throne,'" said Amelia. "Reads like the plot of a yellow-back novel."

"Sadly, this is not fiction, Miss Amelia," said Mr. Sloan gravely. "Mr. Yates has evidence that the Faithful are very much alive and are actively working to overthrow the monarchy. From certain things Colonel Smythe has said, I believe that he is in direct contact with these people. I further believe that some of them are highly placed in the government and may have managed to gain Her Majesty's trust."

"You fear Her Majesty is in danger, Mr. Sloan! These Faithful must be found and exposed." Amelia regarded him with narrowed eyes. "I believe such is your plan, isn't it, sir?"

Mr. Sloan hesitated. A cautious and reticent man by nature, he was averse to revealing his plan even to someone he trusted. He reflected that he had gone too far to stop now and that Henry would want to know.

"I have agreed to join Colonel Smythe's army in the capacity of lieutenant," said Mr. Sloan.

"I thought that might be the case," Amelia said, nodding. "Have you given careful consideration to this idea, Mr. Sloan? This Crawford or Smythe or whatever he calls himself is a trained assassin. He has killed six humans, as well as Lady Odila. And those are just the murders we know about."

"You may add to that list the dragon Coreg, the human Greenstreet, and several men in his employ," said Mr. Sloan.

Amelia sighed. "So he killed them before they could talk."

"Indeed, ma'am. They could have identified him as the murderer. Not only that, but I surmise the dragon was threatening to blackmail either Smythe or the prince."

"By all accounts, Prince Thomas Stanford is an estimable young man," said Amelia, troubled. "Do you believe he is involved in these murders?"

"His Lordship will want to believe it," said Mr. Sloan with a faint smile. "I must endeavor to find out the truth and this is a God-given opportunity to discover the inner workings of the Faithful. You understand why it is of vital necessity that I undertake this mission."

"I suppose I do," said Amelia grudgingly. "What is your plan?"

"Colonel Smythe and I are both devout Fundamentalists—"

"*You* are devout, Mr. Sloan!" Amelia interrupted indignantly. "I would not compare yourself to that loathsome creature, Smythe."

Mr. Sloan couldn't help but wonder if he wasn't closer to Smythe than he cared to admit. He had been giving the matter a great deal of thought lately. He couldn't take time to discuss that now.

"Colonel Smythe has been in need of a second-in-command for some time and he has found no one he trusts. We served together in the marines and he takes it as a sign from God that he and I happened to meet in this place at this moment in time."

"And I suppose you believe that God has brought you here to spy on Smythe and so you are putting yourself in danger." Amelia shook her head and added with a sniff, "Sometimes I think God would do well to mind His own business."

Mr. Sloan raised a shocked eyebrow, but refrained from comment. "Inform His Lordship that I am traveling to Bheldem with Colonel Smythe, ma'am, to take up my command. Once I am there, I will endeavor to find some way to communicate my discoveries."

"Put your mind at rest, Mr. Sloan," Amelia stated. "You may communicate through me."

"Ma'am?" Mr. Sloan raised both his eyebrows.

"As a journalist, I can go anywhere, even to Bheldem, without the least danger of arousing suspicion. I will discuss the matter with Sir Henry, of course, but I already have the inklings of an idea."

Mr. Sloan considered her suggestion and found it acceptable.

"One more thing, Miss Amelia," he said. "You need to warn His Lordship that a man called Trubgek has taken over Coreg's criminal enterprises. He and Colonel Smythe plan to use the money from weapons sales, smuggling, piracy, and so forth to fund the cause of Prince Tom."

"Trubgek!" Amelia repeated, her expression darkening. "Kate had a run-in with him. He is a dangerous man, Mr. Sloan."

"So Captain Kate has led me to believe, Miss Amelia. I will be on my guard." Mr. Sloan picked up his tricorn and rose to take his leave. "I am extremely grateful to you, Miss Amelia. You are the answer to a prayer. I say that quite literally."

"I have been called many things, Mr. Sloan, but never that," Amelia replied with a laugh. "Now that I know Kate is safe and well, I will immediately make arrangements for my return to Freya."

She extended her hand to him. He shook hands with her and she pressed his warmly. "Good luck, Mr. Sloan. You may rely upon me."

"I know that I can, Miss Amelia," said Mr. Sloan.

Amelia gathered up her reticule and umbrella, took a book from the shelf, and departed. He heard her calling out to Gert as she left that she had located the book she wanted to borrow.

Mr. Sloan waited a few moments, then left the tavern through the back entrance. He had committed himself. Up until now, he could have backed out. He was not concerned at all about physical danger. He was far more concerned about the danger to his spiritual beliefs, which had been profoundly shaken by the knowledge that he and Smythe were more alike than he cared to admit.

Mr. Sloan was revolted by the cold-blooded murders Smythe had committed and yet he had to confess that in this regard, his own hands were far from clean. Sir Henry had never had any compunction about removing people he believed represented a danger to his beloved nation, and Mr. Sloan had shared in that belief. This was war, and men died in war, whether they fell on the field of battle or were smothered in their sleep.

What troubled Mr. Sloan was the possibility that Smythe believed the same. He was a patriot who had committed these murders to advance the cause of his prince. Listening to Smythe recite the same passages from scripture that Mr. Sloan loved and knew by heart, he was plagued by doubt.

Is my own soul as black as Smythe's? Mr. Sloan wondered unhappily.

He reflected that part of the reason he was undertaking this dangerous mission was to find out.

FOURTEEN

Sir Henry Wallace put on his tricorn and was about to accept his greatcoat from the footman, only to turn around to find his wife, his beloved Lady Ann, holding it for him.

Henry slipped his arms into the coat and then gave his wife a kiss.

"I am going to the palace to meet with the queen," he said, as she buttoned his coat for him. "Do you have any message for her?"

"Only give her my love and tell her she has been in my thoughts. What with all this rioting in the streets, I worry about her safety," said Ann. "I worry about your safety, too, Henry. I wish you would hire a bodyguard. I know you cannot find anyone you trust as much as Mr. Sloan, but you should not be traveling about the city alone."

"Every man I have interviewed is a poltroon," said Henry. He placed his hand on his wife's hand and smiled at her. "I must say it pains me to hear my own wife lament that I cannot take care of myself."

"You have no care for your own safety and I fear your son is just like you," said Ann. "He wandered off yesterday and Nurse was frantic. The coachman, Baxter, found him in the stall with the carriage horses. Poor Baxter was white as a ghost when he told me. He tried to impress upon your son that he could have been kicked or trampled. Little Hal was not the least afraid, however, and couldn't understand what all the fuss was about."

"My brave boy!" said Henry. Seeing Ann frown, he added hurriedly, "Don't worry, my dear. I shall most certainly speak to him, impress upon him the danger."

"And your own danger?" Ann asked.

"I expect Mr. Sloan back any day now, so do not fret," said Henry in soothing tones. "And now, my dear, I must dash. You know how much your aunt is annoyed by those who keep her waiting."

He hurried out to the carriage, where he asked the coachman, Baxter, for a full account of the adventures of young Master Henry, now age three.

"You should have seen your lad, m'lord," said Baxter. "He was standin' in the stall, stroking Fred's nose and feeding him an apple. Gave me such a turn, m'lord, it's a wonder I have recovered. Fred is an ornery beast, as you know, m'lord. He laid up the stable boy for a week with a kick that busted his ribs and he'll nip me if he gets the chance. But with your lad, Fred stood there like a lamb. Master Henry looks at me, bold as brass, and says, 'Baxter, I should like to take Fred for a gallop.' A gallop!"

Baxter roared with laughter, then took his place on the box and shouted to the irascible Fred and his partner. The carriage rolled down the street.

Leaning back in the seat, Henry took a moment to bask in paternal pride. He would need to tell Hal, of course, that he should not go into the horse stalls, that horses could be dangerous. Yet he could not help but be proud of his son's fearlessness.

Henry's contentment did not last long, however. His wife, Ann, his son, and his baby daughter were among the few joys remaining in his life.

His beloved country, Freya, was in serious trouble and he had no way to save her. The near disastrous war with the Bottom Dwellers had left Freya on the brink of financial ruin. Henry's recommendation that Her Majesty invite Travian dragons to live in Freya and pay for the opportunity had filled the coffers, but had ended in disaster when their leader, Lady Odila, was murdered. Crown Prince Jonathan had died in an accident, his little son had died in an epidemic, leaving the succession in turmoil.

As the carriage left his quiet, upper-class residential neighborhood and entered the city proper, he had only to look out the window to see evidence of unrest among the populace: broken windows, stores looted and burned. He drew the curtain to shut out the dismal view.

He would never give up. He would fight for Freya with his last ounce of strength, give her the last drop of his blood. But he began to fear that the battle was hopeless. His country was headed for civil war and he could not stop it.

Queen Mary was yet another problem. Henry loved and honored her. She held him in esteem, as well she might, for Henry had placed her upon the throne. But the queen had always been a stubborn woman, often acting on impulse and then riding roughshod over the consequences. She would listen to his advice and occasionally accept it, but when once she had planted her flag and taken a stand, no amount of arguing or attempts to reason with her would cause her to retreat. The seven continents of Aeronne would shift position before she did.

The queen had unexpectedly summoned him to the palace for an urgent meeting this morning and Henry was deeply concerned. He feared she was going to tell him to announce that she had decided to make her sister, Elinor, her heir. Such a move would only plunge the country into more turmoil. Elinor had married a Rosian and moved to Rosia, which caused the Freyan people to view her as a traitor—and Henry agreed. If she named Elinor, Haever might well go up in flames. Henry had thus far kept the queen from making such a disastrous move, but he feared she was determined.

When the noise and tumult of the city began to recede, Henry drew back the curtain. The carriage had entered the park surrounding Covington Palace, a peaceful view he always enjoyed.

He took comfort in the sight of the palace with its arched windows and imposing battlements and crenulations. Unlike the ostentatious and ill-fated Sunset Palace of Rosia that for many years had magically floated among the clouds, Covington Palace was stolid and substantial; proud to stand on firm ground, proud to represent and defend the nation.

The park was open to the public. People were permitted to stand along the wrought-iron fence hoping to catch a glimpse of the queen strolling in her garden. Mary had sometimes been known to come to the fence to hand out sugar buns to the children.

The carriage had traveled about a half mile from the palace gates, rolling along a tree-lined avenue. Henry was absorbed in his thoughts and he did not notice anything was wrong until he heard shouts and curses and saw men rushing his carriage.

"That's him! Wallace!" one yelled.

The men grabbed the horses and dragged them to a halt. One man jumped onto the box and dragged Baxter from his seat and hurled him to the ground. He was attacked by several others, kicking and beating him.

Henry was not carrying his pistol. No one came armed into the presence of the queen. He kept a rifle and several loaded pistols in a secret compartment beneath the seat. If he opened that compartment, he would have access to the weapons, but so would the mob.

These thoughts passed in a split second. At the sight of Baxter lying bloodied on the cobblestones, Henry yanked open the carriage door and leaped out, bellowing for help. He seized hold of the horsewhip from its stand at the front of the carriage and began slashing at the men nearest him. His unexpected attack was so startling and so vicious that several of the mob took to their heels.

Others surged forward, fists clenched. Someone grabbed Henry from behind. He drove his elbow into the man's gut and he released his hold. A fist came out of nowhere, grazing his jaw. Henry jabbed the butt end of the horsewhip into the face and then two more leaped on him and started to wrestle him to the ground. Henry fought desperately to stay upright, knowing that once he was down he was finished.

He was saved by the sound of rifle fire and a stentorian command for the crowd to disperse. Members of the Royal Guard had opened the palace gates and were riding to the rescue. At the sight of armed resistance, the mob melted away, disappearing among the groves of trees and neatly trimmed hedge rows.

Henry hurried to check on Baxter. The coachman was battered and bloodied, but he had regained his feet and was roundly swearing and shaking his fist, which Henry took for a good sign.

The captain of the guard galloped up and reined his horse to a halt. He dismounted and hurried over to Henry.

"Are you all right, my lord?"

"I appear to be," said Henry. "My coachman has been injured, however. Please convey him to the palace."

Baxter didn't want to leave, but Henry persuaded him to have his wounds attended. Several guardsmen were trying to calm the excited horses, but Fred continued to lash out with his hooves, forcing the guardsmen to keep their distance. A few ruffians lay on the ground, groaning in pain. Fred had apparently managed to strike a few blows of his own.

"This lot picked the wrong carriage to attack," stated the captain. "Does Your Lordship require assistance?"

Henry regarded the distance he still had to cover. A good mile or more lay between the palace gates and the palace.

"A horse, if you please, Captain," said Henry. "I have an urgent meeting with Her Majesty."

"Take mine, my lord," said the captain.

Henry mounted the horse. He looked about and could see people standing in the shadows. Their faces were impassive, expressionless. They had not taken part in the attack, but neither had they come to his rescue.

He rode on toward the palace. He made a mental note to have the family coat of arms, now proudly emblazoned on the doors of the carriage, painted over.

Henry was well known in the palace, where he had his own small office. He waved away questions from the startled staff, who had yet to hear of the attack, and went to his office to survey the damage. He took off his great-coat, which was missing buttons and had a torn sleeve. His silk stockings were in tatters, there was a bruise on his jaw, and he was bleeding from a cut on the side of his face.

He kept a change of clothing in the office, and he considered washing up and changing before he went to his meeting with the queen. He was already late, however, and he decided that it might be good for the queen to see for herself the mood of the people.

He dabbed at his face with a handkerchief and then walked through the palace's famous Long Gallery, adorned with priceless paintings, porcelain, and statuary. He passed the Council Room where the queen met with her Privy Council, and headed to the queen's office, which was in the west tower. He encountered Farley, the Lord Chamberlain, coming from a meeting with the queen.

Farley regarded Henry in shocked dismay. "My lord! I just heard of the attack! Most distressful."

Henry agreed it was distressful. The Lord Chamberlain accompanied him into the Wait Room, which was across the hall from the office, and said he would inform Her Majesty.

The Wait Room was furnished with comfortable chairs. Henry longed to sit down, but he was starting to grow stiff and sore and he feared if he did, he might not get back up.

Fortunately, Her Majesty did not keep him waiting long. The Lord Chamberlain returned to say that he could go inside.

"Jo-Jo is with her, my lord," Farley added in an undertone.

Henry grimaced. "Thank you for the warning."

He entered the office. The room was spacious, light, and airy. Arched windows overlooked the park and the stables. Queen Mary had only to walk to the window to look out to see her horses taking their exercise.

This morning, the queen was at her desk, feeding grapes to her pet monkey, Jo-Jo, a gift from the former governor of Wellinsport in the Aligoes, who had been removed from office for corruption. Henry disliked Jo-Jo almost as much as he had disliked the governor.

Jo-Jo apparently felt the same about Henry, for at the sight of him, the monkey scrambled off the desk and ran back to its wooden stand, where it began to jump up and down and gibber at him.

Mary often insisted on conducting business with the monkey present, adding its shrill commentary and occasionally throwing grapes at him. Henry was never certain whether the queen kept the monkey by her side because she was fond of it or because she knew Henry wasn't.

He was therefore surprised and gratified when Mary rang the bell and ordered the servant to take Jo-Jo back to its cage in the conservatory. The office was blessedly quiet after its departure.

"Whatever have you been doing with yourself, Henry," Mary stated, eyeing him with disfavor. "You look as though you just stepped out of the boxing ring."

The queen was in her sixties. She had been athletic all her life, known for breeding griffins and fond of racing her horses in steeplechases and riding to the hunt. She was energetic, and restless, and had no use for reading or fancy work or gossip. She took pride in speaking her mind, leaving it to diplomats to be diplomatic. She was of medium height, solidly built, with shrewd eyes, and gray hair that she wore haphazardly pinned up in a bun.

"I heard your carriage was attacked," Mary continued. "I'm glad to see you are in one piece."

Henry bowed. "I would have changed clothes, Your Majesty, but I did not want to keep you waiting."

Mary wagged her finger at him. "Stuff and nonsense, Henry. We know your ways. You exhibit your bumps and bruises so that we will feel sorry for you and you can talk us around to your point of view. Help yourself to some brandy. We will have one ourselves."

As Henry went to pour the brandy, he wondered what was amiss. The queen never took strong drink in the morning. Henry carried the snifters, handed one to the queen, and then accepted her offer to sit down.

Mary fixed her forthright gaze on him.

"Tell us what happened. Old Farley was in such a dither we could make neither heads nor tails of what he was saying."

Henry recounted the attack, sticking to the facts without embellishment, as she liked.

The queen listened; she was a good listener. "We are sorry this happened, Henry. We will see to it that coachman of yours is well looked after."

"Thank you, ma'am," said Henry. "I would suggest you warn future visitors to the palace to come by way of the north gate. I will stop by the constabulary when I leave and ask them to increase their patrols in the park."

Mary nodded and sat in silence. She seemed abstracted, staring at the brandy that she did not drink.

"Your Majesty sent for me," Henry prodded. "How can I be of service?"

"You can't, Henry," said the queen. "No one can."

She reverted to the personal, dropping the royal "we." "I called you here to tell you that I am dying. I met with the Royal Physician yesterday. He says that there is nothing more to be done for me."

Henry watched his world grow dark. He had his own agents in the palace, for it was his business to know the queen's business, and he had received a report that the queen had met with her physician. She had not been feeling well of late, but he had not supposed the news would be this dire.

Mary took a healthy drink of brandy, made a face, and muttered, "Doctor's orders."

Henry knew the Royal Physician personally, for he had attended Lady Ann when she had given birth. Henry trusted the man implicitly, but he still said, "You should seek other opinions, ma'am—"

"Waste of time, Henry, and I have not much time to waste. The sawbones says six months, but the truth is he doesn't know. I could keel over tomorrow. Seems I am dying of the same thing that killed my father—tumor in my gut."

Henry had known Mary for years. They had been through a great deal together, starting with his fight to place her on the throne. He was deeply moved and for long moments could not speak.

"I am sorry, Your Majesty," he said at last, clearing his throat.

The queen regarded him with a fond smile.

"I know you are, Henry," she said. "That is why I wanted to tell you first. No one else knows."

"And no one must know, ma'am!" said Henry emphatically.

The nation of Freya was already teetering on the brink of disaster. Word that the queen was dying—and that she was dying without an heir—would push it over the edge.

Mary nodded. "I have impressed upon the Royal Physician that he is sworn to secrecy. He has assured me he will respect my wishes completely."

Henry made a mental note to speak to the Royal Physician himself, make it clear that if word were to leak out, the Royal Physician would find himself in need of medical treatment.

"And now, to business," said Mary. "I want you to make preparations for me to name Elinor as my successor."

Henry had known this command was coming, and he had been dreading it. Two people stood in line for the succession to the Freyan throne—three counting Prince Thomas Stanford (which Henry most certainly did not). One was King Godfrey's bastard son, Hugh, Earl of Montfort, and the queen's sister, Elinor.

Before he could say anything, Mary raised her hand in a peremptory gesture to stop him.

"I already know what you are going to say, Henry. I have given you a command and I expect you to obey."

"With all due respect, ma'am, I must strongly urge you to reconsider this course of action," said Henry.

The queen narrowed her eyes, tightened her lips, and thrust her jaw forward, reminding Henry strongly of one of her own griffins. Mary would have dug her talons into the carpet if such a thing were possible.

Henry attempted to mollify her. "All I ask is that Your Majesty take time to reflect upon such a drastic course of action. Your subjects will not accept your sister as their monarch. Elinor lives in Rosia and is married to a Rosian. She is a devout follower of the Church of the Breath and has stated publicly that she would like to see Freya return to the true religion."

"Meaning she would clean up the Freyan Church," Mary snapped. "Knock a few sanctimonious heads together. It would be all the better for it!"

Since Henry's father-in-law was Bishop of the Freyan Church of the Reformation and therefore one of those "sanctimonious heads," he had to bite his tongue.

"I suppose you would have us name that bastard half brother of ours, Hugh," Mary added, her lip curling in disdain. "He is a buffoon. You know that."

Her father, King Godfrey, had openly conducted a scandalous affair with a married woman, Lady Honoria. The union had produced two illegitimate sons. Godfrey had acknowledged both of them, given them money and titles and paid them far more attention than he had ever given his two legitimate daughters.

He had even wanted to name Hugh as his heir. Henry had feared this rash move could have sparked a civil war, for Mary had powerful nobles on her side. He had finally convinced Godfrey to permit Mary to inherit the throne. He had never thought he would have to fight such a battle all over again and, yet, here he was.

"Hugh is a member of the Church of the Reformation; his brother is the bishop," said Henry. "Hugh is known to the members of the House of Nobles, and while most of them do not like him, they do not actively dislike him— which would be the case with Elinor. May I speak freely, ma'am?"

"For God's sake, when do you ever do anything else!" the queen snapped, glowering.

"Your sister, Elinor, left Freya twenty years ago to pursue her religious beliefs. The two of you have not met since. You have written back and forth, since the war, but in truth you know very little about her."

"And you do, I suppose," Mary said.

"It is my business to know, Your Majesty," said Henry.

The queen glared at him, but said nothing, aware he was right. When she had begun dropping hints that she would like to name her sister as her heir,

Henry had planted a trusted agent in Elinor's household to intercept her letters, eavesdrop on her private conversations, and listen to the gossip of the
servants' hall.

The result was that Henry knew Elinor to be as stubborn as her sister,
while lacking Mary's keen intellect. He also knew she had the same streak of
cold, callous cruelty that had been her father, Godfrey's, worst fault.

"Would you like to hear what I have found out, ma'am?" Henry asked,
and steeled himself, knowing the ensuing conversation would be distinctly
unpleasant.

Mary fixed him with a glittering gaze. Henry met her gaze and held it.
Neither intended to give way.

At length the queen sighed and wearily passed her hand over her forehead.
She was looking pale and wan, despite the restorative effects of the brandy.

"Go home to your family, Henry. You have had a rotten morning. I will
take your objections under advisement."

Henry had won, but he took little joy in the victory. The queen he knew
would never have quit the field after only a few thrusts and parries. He was
seeing the effects of the illness upon her.

He rose to his feet, but he did not immediately leave. Walking over to the
desk, he gently took hold of the queen's hand and pressed it warmly.

Mary smiled at him and squeezed his hand in turn.

"Tell my niece and the children to come visit," she said.

Henry promised he would, and took his leave. Looking back, he saw the
queen had risen and gone to the window, where she stood gazing out, pressing one hand over her abdomen and grimacing in pain.

FIFTEEN

Henry needed a moment to himself before facing other people, and he entered the empty Council Chamber to spend a few moments in somber reflection. His country was facing a crisis, but he was not thinking about that. He was remembering the trials he and Mary had faced together, from the early days when he had fought for her to become queen to the more recent tragic death of her son and heir, and her little grandson.

The worst trial lay before them. Henry recalled Godfrey's suffering near the close of his life. No healing potions, magical or otherwise, had been able to relieve the terrible pain. He had begged them to kill him at the end. Henry remembered and shuddered.

Once he had composed himself, he went below stairs to the servants' quarters to check on Baxter. He found him in the kitchen, the center of attention. The physician's assistant was dressing his wounds with sticking plaster and bandages as Baxter related his adventure to the cook, two footmen, and four maidservants, all of whom were vociferous in their outrage, saying they really did not know what the world was coming to.

Baxter rose when he saw Henry, assured him he was fine, and asked anxiously about the horses. Henry told him to drive the carriage home, cautioning him to say nothing of the incident to Lady Ann or any member of the household staff. Should Lady Ann ask about the damage to the carriage, he was to say they had collided with a milk wagon.

Henry went to check on the horses, who had been taken to the palace stables. He was glad to find neither had been seriously injured and he asked the stable hands to be certain to give Fred extra oats as a reward for his valor. He then requested the loan of a horse, which was immediately granted, and left the palace by the north gate.

Henry did not return home. Love gave his wife the skills of the world's greatest detective, and she would know the moment she saw his face that he had not been in an accident with a milk wagon. She would be upset, and he was not equal to facing her questions, no matter how fond. He kept rooms at the Naval Club and he went there to dress in fresh clothes and to send a note home saying that he would be dining with Simon.

He then summoned a wyvern-drawn cab and directed the driver to the home of the Royal Physician. He spoke to the doctor, who confirmed the diagnosis.

"I have known about her affliction for some time, my lord," said the physician. "We tried various treatments, but none of them worked. She asked me to tell no one until the time came when we had exhausted all our options. She has months, perhaps weeks, to live. We will do our best to make her comfortable."

Henry impressed upon the doctor the need for secrecy, then returned to the carriage and ordered it to convey him to Welkinstead, the floating house that belonged to his friend Simon Yates.

The house had been built by an eccentric duchess and was considered one of the wonders of Freya. A scientist, gifted crafter, and collector, the wealthy duchess had caused the large mansion to be freed from its place on the ground, saying she was bored with looking at the same view out her windows. She had not wanted the inconvenience of moving to a different house and had decided therefore to move the house instead.

The duchess had equipped her mansion with lift tanks and airscrews and now Welkinstead floated above the capital of Haever, not sailing, but "drifting with panache" as the duchess termed it. She had willed the house to Simon at her death and he was now the resident, along with his manservant, Mr. Albright.

Simon had small interest in the view from his windows. Absorbed in his work, he allowed the house to float at will and thus Henry always had to track down Welkinstead whenever he wanted to visit.

He found the house near his own neighborhood and hoped little Hal would be able to see it. Henry had once taken his son for a visit and Hal had been enchanted, to the point that his father had spent several days trying to explain to Hal why they could not uproot their own house and cause it to fly.

The taciturn Mr. Albright greeted Henry at the door and silently ushered him inside. The manservant had no need to tell Henry where to find Simon, for he was always in one place and that was his office, where he and Mr. Albright lived in a perpetual state of disorder and confusion, which never appeared to bother either of them, although it could be disconcerting and sometimes dangerous for visitors.

The duchess had traveled the world over and had filled every room with rare and curious, strange and outlandish mementos of her trips. Welkinstead was therefore more like a museum than a home, although not nearly so organized.

Since the house was always on the move, drifting through the Breath, it would hit the occasional air pocket or a gust of wind would catch it or a storm shake it, causing the innumerable objects found in every room of the house to slide across the floor, tumble off side tables, or fall from the walls or ceiling. Henry often felt that reaching Simon's office, which was on the second floor, was akin to crossing a field of battle while under enemy fire.

This day nothing struck him, but he did see the remnants of a small crystal chandelier lying on the floor.

He found his friend seated in his wheeled chair at his desk, nearly lost behind stacks of documents, letters, and newspapers that came to him from Freya's agents all over the world. The only other furniture besides the desk and several chairs were the wooden and brass-trimmed filing cabinets that held even more letters, documents, and newspapers, all neatly categorized in a system only Simon and Mr. Albright knew.

Henry had called Simon Yates "Freya's secret weapon." As Welkinstead floated over Haever, Simon could be said to float over the world, gazing down on its people from the confines of his chair. He read their letters, journals, and newspapers, put together this fact and that, and was able to solve mysteries, unravel plots, and ferret out secrets.

As Henry entered, he found his friend perusing a document with a magnifying glass. Simon flicked a brief, preoccupied glance at Henry and went back to his work. He then turned his head to regard his friend more intently and dropped the document onto the table.

"What happened to you?" Simon asked.

"I was set upon by a mob outside the palace gates," said Henry. "I have only a few grazes."

"An unsettling experience, no doubt," said Simon. "But I wasn't referring to superficial injuries. Something far more upsetting has occurred that has shaken you to the depths of your being."

Henry gave a faint smile and sat down in a chair. He paused to master his voice, then said steadily, "Her Majesty is dying. She has a tumor."

"Are you certain?" Simon asked sharply. "Doctors have been known to make mistakes."

"I spoke to the Royal Physician," said Henry. "The diagnosis is not in doubt. There is a malignant growth in her abdomen."

"Poor woman," said Simon. "Who else knows?"

"The Royal Physician swears to me that he has told no one," said Henry. "We must keep this secret!"

Simon nodded his agreement.

Henry sighed. Rising to his feet, he began to pace about restlessly, at least as far as he could go without bumping into a file cabinet.

"Her Majesty asked me to start the process to name her sister, Elinor, as her heir. I cannot do it, Simon. I will resign first."

"What choice do you have, Henry? The queen will never agree to name Hugh. She hates him with a passion."

"And thus we are left in a stalemate," said Henry, brooding. "The House of Nobles, the Freyan Church, and most of the populace will never accept Elinor. Her Majesty will not accept Hugh."

"You do realize there is a third alternative—" Simon began.

"Out of the question," Henry snapped.

Simon continued as though he had not heard. "Prince Thomas Stanford has a far better claim to the throne than either Elinor or Hugh."

"Stanford would plunge us into a civil war that would destroy our country," said Henry. "To say nothing of the fact that you and I would be finished, along with Alan and Randolph. We would face ruin, exile, or worse. And we would not be alone. The Pretender and his Faithful have been waiting a hundred and fifty years to settle old scores, seize back the property they lost during the reign of James I. Meanwhile, the Rosians will happily watch us destroy ourselves then swoop in to feast upon the carcass."

"You make it sound as though Thomas was very, very old," said Simon. "One hundred and fifty. Whereas I believe the prince is nearer twenty-five."

"You know what I mean!" said Henry testily.

Simon smiled. "So what are you going to do?"

"I don't know," said Henry. "I came to consult with you. I was thinking I—"

He was interrupted by the appearance of Mr. Albright, who silently handed Simon a card.

"Your reporter friend, Miss Amelia Nettleship, is here," said Simon. He turned over the card, read on the back. "She requests an urgent audience with you."

"How the devil did she know I was here?" Henry asked.

"She probably called at your home. I assume you sent word to your wife," said Simon. "Send her up, Albright."

Albright disappeared and moments later they heard Amelia's quick, firm footsteps on the stairs.

Henry regarded her with amazement as she entered. Amelia was always neatly dressed in a severely tailored wool suit jacket—nipped in at the waist—and skirt of matching fabric, white blouse, and petticoat. She wore her hair pulled back in a neat bun, topped with a plain porkpie hat.

Today her clothes were wrinkled, her hat askew, her hair blown about her face.

"Forgive my rumpled appearance, my lord," she said, coming forward to shake hands. "I flew back from the Aligoes by griffin. Not a very ladylike mode of travel, as I am well aware, but I find griffin flight quite exhilarating. And in this instance, I deemed haste a necessity."

Amelia circled around the desk to shake hands with Simon. Mr. Albright brought up a chair and placed it next to Henry. Amelia sat down and took a moment to catch her breath, straighten her hat, and tuck in her hairpins.

"You left word you were traveling to the Aligoes to try to find out news about Captain Kate," Henry said. "Are the rumors we heard true? Have the Rosians hanged her?"

"Kate is safe, my lord, at least for the moment," said Amelia. "She managed to escape from prison. The Rosians are furious, as you might imagine, and are turning the Aligoes upside down in an effort to find her. Kate can take care of herself, however. That is not what brought me."

"Then what, Miss Amelia?" Henry asked curiously.

"I have an urgent message to you from Mr. Sloan."

"Mr. Sloan!" Henry repeated, concerned. "I have been expecting his return. Has something happened?"

"In a manner of speaking, my lord. I went to Freeport to find out about Kate, where I visited a tavern called the Perky Parrot. Imagine my astonishment when I ran into Mr. Sloan."

Simon and Henry exchanged grim glances.

"Mr. Sloan was there on a confidential assignment, Miss Amelia—" Henry began.

"Yes, yes, of course," said Amelia impatiently, chafing at the interruption. Her bobby pins were falling out and she paused a moment to try to tuck them back. "Mr. Sloan pretended not to know me and I knew something was wrong. We arranged a clandestine meeting and he gave me this message to give to you. He has found Isaiah Crawford—"

"Crawford! The man who murdered Lady Odila?" Simon said sharply.

"The very same. Crawford is now going by the name of Jonathan Smythe. While he was in Freeport he murdered the criminal Greenstreet, and his boss, the dragon Coreg—"

"Our witnesses!" Henry said to Simon. "We should have foreseen that Crawford would take care to eliminate them. I trust Mr. Sloan was able to gather proof—"

Amelia fixed Henry with a reproving gaze. "I know you have questions, my lord. If you will allow me to finish without interruption, I will be happy to answer them."

"Forgive me, Miss Amelia," said Henry. "Please proceed."

"Mr. Sloan said to tell you that this Smythe is now the commander of the army of His Highness, Prince Thomas Stanford—"

"Aha! I knew it!" Henry exclaimed with a triumphant glance at Simon.

Amelia glared at him and he added meekly, "I do beg your pardon, ma'am. I will henceforth sit in silence. You have my word."

Amelia pursed her lips, then continued. "Mr. Sloan infers from certain words that Crawford/Smythe let drop that he is in contact with members of the Faithful."

Henry opened his mouth and, catching Amelia's eye, immediately shut it.

"It seems that Mr. Sloan and Smythe/Crawford served together in the marines years ago. The colonel has been looking for someone to act as second-in-command and invited Mr. Sloan to take the post. Mr. Sloan has accepted. He is now traveling to Bheldem in company with Smythe to join the army of Prince Tom."

Henry stared in blank astonishment, unable to speak.

Amelia regarded him with concern. "I know this must come as a shock to you, my lord."

"Shock is not the word," Henry said, shaken.

"Albright, fetch the brandy," said Simon. "I think we could all use a drink."

Albright poured them each a brandy. Henry stared at his glass, but could not drink.

"The information he gathers will be invaluable, Henry," said Simon.

"Provided he lives to tell it," said Henry. He downed the brandy in a gulp.

"Mr. Sloan is extremely resourceful, my lord," said Amelia. "His most urgent need now is a safe way for him to communicate whatever he finds out. He said to tell you he was loath to put anything on paper, even in code."

"Understandable, considering the dangerous nature of the man with whom he is dealing," said Simon.

"I have an idea, my lord," said Amelia. "I can insinuate myself into the household of Prince Tom's mother, the marchioness, who currently resides in

Bheldem. I will propose to the marchioness that I write a series of newspaper articles on her as the mother of the young man who could be Freya's future king."

Henry thought this over. "That could work."

"I think the idea is excellent," said Simon. "The marchioness is extremely vain. She will delight in talking about herself and her son."

"Very well," said Amelia. "If we are all agreed, then I will put the plan into motion. It will take me some time to arrange matters with the marchioness, but that will provide Mr. Sloan with the time he needs to gather information."

"I understand, Miss Amelia," said Henry. "Let me know if you require any assistance."

"Thank you, my lord. Mr. Sloan also said to tell you that Coreg's servant, Trubgek, has taken over the dragon's criminal enterprises. This Trubgek is an extremely dangerous man."

"I would make no attempt to interfere in these enterprises, Henry," Simon cautioned. "You might draw unwanted attention to Mr. Sloan."

"I agree," said Henry.

"Do you have any questions for me, my lord?" Amelia asked.

"How did Mr. Sloan look?" Henry asked. "Was he well?"

"He is in very good health, my lord, and in good spirits. His primary concern was that his absence will be an inconvenience to you."

Henry was deeply moved, and could not readily respond.

Amelia rose to her feet. "And now, gentlemen, I will take my leave. Goodbye, Mr. Yates. Always a pleasure to see you. Good-bye, my lord."

"Good-bye, Miss Amelia, and thank you," said Henry. "Inform me when you hear from the marchioness. And do not worry about expenses for your journey. I will make all the arrangements."

"Thank you, my lord," said Amelia, and she went on her way, leaving a trail of bobby pins behind her.

"At least something is going right," said Henry after she had gone and Mr. Albright had gathered up the bobby pins. "Mr. Sloan will soon acquire the names of the members of the Faithful and we can expose them for the traitors they are. We also have proof that this Prince Tom is in league with assassins and raising armies to plot the overthrow of our government."

"You know nothing of the sort, Henry," said Simon. "Prince Tom is an officer in the Estaran army and he rarely visits Bheldem. He may have no knowledge whatsoever of Crawford's murderous actions."

Henry snorted in disbelief and was going to add something scathing when Mr. Albright entered, bearing a note. He handed it to Henry.

"This came to my club," said Henry. He tore open the note and grimaced. "A rotten end to a rotten day."

"What is it?" Simon asked.

"Hugh wants to speak to me on a matter of the utmost importance. I suppose I had better go see him."

Simon was grave. "You don't think Hugh knows about the queen's health, do you?"

"I hope he does not," said Henry. "He will be packing his trunk, prepared to move into the palace."

As he left, Simon called after him.

"Mr. Sloan could be gone for some time. You should employ a bodyguard, Henry!"

He pretended he did not hear.

SIXTEEN

Hugh Fitzroy, bastard son of King Godfrey and Lady Honoria Wesselman, lived on a grand estate near the hamlet of Chadwick, in Freya. The offices for his business were in Haever, however, and he had also a city house, which is where he had instructed Henry to meet him.

King Godfrey's affair had been widely known. He and his mistress had even appeared in public together. Hugh and his brother, Jeffrey, had grown up with the knowledge that people would smile to their faces and whisper about them behind their backs.

Hugh had reacted by adopting a brash and bullying attitude, going through life with his chin outthrust and his fists clenched, prepared to openly take on his detractors. Jeffrey had sought a quieter mode of life and had entered the church, where he had risen to become Bishop of Freya.

Hugh owned an iron mine and he had married the daughter of the owner of an iron works, thus gaining control of all aspects of the iron business. Aside from what his father had left him, he had become an extremely wealthy man in his own right. The union had also produced several children.

To Henry's mind Hugh's saving grace was that he was past his middle years and might not be expected to live all that long. His eldest son had the personality of a "bag of wool," as Henry had said to his wife, but he would make a safe, if not inspired, king.

Henry disliked Hugh, but he disliked him far less than he disliked the queen's sister, Elinor. Henry had never developed a close relationship with Hugh, knowing that Queen Mary would have been furious with him. Hugh detested Mary almost as much as she hated him. Henry had long ago given up trying to effect a reconciliation.

He had better luck with Jeffrey. As a man of God, Jeffrey was pleased to make peace with his half sister and was willing to overlook Mary's cutting, caustic remarks. The queen had rewarded him by bringing his eldest daughter, Ann, to court. Mary had given her in marriage to Henry, along with a title and a sizable estate.

Henry considered Hugh cunning and shrewd, but malleable. On those occasions when they had met, Henry had been able to talk Hugh around to his way of thinking. Henry saw no reason this should change. As he had told his wife, "I can manage Hugh. I cannot manage Elinor."

The house in town had been chosen by Hugh's wife, who spent the social season in the city. Hugh preferred to stay at his club, which was closer to his business, and thus Henry was surprised that Hugh had asked to meet at the house. It was a large and ostentatious edifice surrounded by a tall wrought-iron fence with elaborate iron gates that were an effective advertisement for the family business.

On his arrival, Henry was surprised to see that the house appeared deserted. The curtains were drawn, and no smoke rose from the chimneys. The social season was over, and Hugh's wife would have returned to the estate. Henry asked the driver to wait.

He knocked at the door and was met by Hugh's valet, who invited him to be seated while he went in search of the master.

The house was silent, the furniture covered by cloths. No fire had been laid in the marble fireplace, and no footman come to take his cloak.

The house was opened solely for my benefit, Henry thought to himself. Whatever is going on, Hugh does not want anyone to know about it.

When the valet returned, he took Henry's coat and tricorn and told him the earl was expecting him in the Trophy Room.

Hugh was an avid hunter. The room was filled with dead animals and birds that bleakly stared at Henry from the walls or regarded him without interest from their perches on tables. He regarded the trophies with disgust, but approved the exceptionally fine display of antique weapons.

No fire had been laid, but the covers had been removed from the furniture. Hugh stood, frowning, before a painting depicting a stag battling a pack of hunting dogs. He grunted at Henry and dismissed the valet, who shut the door behind him.

Hugh walked over to jiggle the door handle and give the door a shove. Apparently assured that it was closed to his satisfaction, he came back to where Henry was standing.

"Sit down, Henry, sit down," said Hugh, waving to a chair near the fireplace.

Henry stiffened at the familiar use of his first name. He barely knew Hugh. The two were not on intimate or even friendly terms. Hugh had been educated as a gentleman and on occasion he could even act like one. Other times, he behaved in a crude and boorish manner that would have made a street urchin blush.

Henry guessed Hugh was being deliberately offensive to gain some sort of advantage over him and he took care not to give him the satisfaction of seeing that he had annoyed him. He also knew better than to sit down. Hugh was a tall, heavyset, florid-faced man, an old hand at using his size to intimidate. Henry was not about to put himself at a disadvantage by allowing Hugh to loom over him while he cowered in a chair.

"Thank you, my lord. I prefer to remain standing."

Henry walked to the fireplace and turned his back to it, facing Hugh, who began to ramble on about the sad state of the country's finances and how this was affecting the sale of iron.

"If it were not for the nation of Guundar and their pressing need for steel, my business would be in a sad predicament," said Hugh. "I can do business with a man like King Ullr."

"I am glad to hear that, my lord," said Henry, wondering when Hugh was going to come to the real reason he had invited Henry to meet him in a cold and deserted house.

"And this is all Mary's fault," Hugh exclaimed angrily, slamming his fist on the mantelpiece. "She's been a rotten queen. She lets those imbeciles in the House of Nobles lead her around by the nose! The country is going to rack and to ruin. I'll wager you are sorry you backed her over me, eh, Henry?"

Hugh chuckled, as though his words were meant to be lighthearted and jesting. Henry saw no corresponding laughter in the man's cunning eyes.

Henry had to tread carefully. Hugh would be suspicious if he turned on the queen he had served for so many years. He could appear open to suggestion, however. He needed to find out what was going on. He wondered with growing unease if Hugh had found out the queen was dying.

"My loyalty is to Her Majesty, my lord," said Henry blandly.

"I know all about your loyalty," said Hugh with another chuckle.

He gave Henry a wink. Henry replied with a cool smile, all the while thinking how satisfying it would be to punch the man in his puffy jaw.

Hugh fidgeted. Going to the door, he thrust it open and glared out. He shut it again and crossed back over to the fireplace.

He's working himself up to it, Henry thought.

"The crux of the matter is this, Henry," said Hugh. "Something needs to be done about Elinor, and you are the man to do it."

Henry was startled.

"Elinor, my lord?" he asked, feigning confusion.

"Don't play coy with me, Henry," said Hugh. "You know damn well I mean Mary's bloody Rosian dog of a sister. Mary is going to name Elinor her heir unless something happens to stop her. From what I hear, you are the man to handle the job."

Henry knew perfectly well what Hugh was asking. The empty house, the lack of servants, all now made sense.

"I have spoken to Her Majesty about why her sister would be a poor choice, my lord. I fear I can do no more," Henry said coldly.

Hugh's face flushed an ugly red. He thrust out his jaw and loomed over Henry. "You can do a damn sight more! Elinor needs to take a tumble down the stairs and break her bloody neck. You've done this sort of thing before, or so I hear. Do it again."

Henry could not believe the effrontery of the man. Never mind that what Hugh said was true. Henry could have arranged for Elinor to break her neck. He had arranged such incidents in the past. As Admiral Baker sent men to their deaths in war, Henry was the general in a secret war waged by his counterparts around the world. His enemies were as ruthless as he was and for the same reason.

They were patriots, standing guard over their nations as he stood guard over his. They fought their desperate battles in the shadows, using garrotes and poison instead of bullets and cannonballs. Henry knew his counterparts and respected each one: the Countess de Marjolaine of Rosia, Monsieur Dubois of the Church of the Breath, Don Juan Amileo of Estara, Baron Rupert Grimm of Guundar, and Alderson Gouldsby, who worked for the Travian cartels.

But Hugh apparently considered Henry some sort of assassin-for-hire, obviously expecting him to make a servile bow and rush off to kill the queen's sister.

Henry Wallace was in his forties, tall and thin with a long face and a narrow, aristocratic nose. When he was angry, he possessed a soul-piercing look that could make a man feel as though a blade of cold steel had pierced his vitals.

He fixed Hugh with that look. "I fail to understand Your Lordship's meaning."

Henry thought for a moment Hugh was going to be stupid enough to repeat his demand.

Hugh thought so, too, for he opened his mouth. But then he must have realized he had placed himself in a dangerous and untenable position. He averted his gaze and made a clumsy try at repairing the damage with a blustering laugh.

"Come now, Henry, you know I was jesting," he said. "Don't be so damn sensitive!"

Henry made a stiff bow. "In that case, I believe we have said all we have to say to each other. I will take my leave."

He picked up his hat and coat, which the valet had draped over a chair, and walked to the door. Hugh remained standing by the fireplace, his puffy face creased in a scowl.

"You don't dare accuse me of anything, Henry," he snarled. "It's your word against mine."

"My lord," said Henry, pausing at the door. "I would never stoop so low."

He opened the door and walked out into the hall. He did not see the valet and he made his way through the house without escort. Once outside the gate, he gave the driver orders to take him to the Foreign Office. He then sank back into the seat and wearily closed his eyes.

"And to think," Henry remarked bitterly to the empty carriage, "this is the wretched oaf I am proposing to make a king."

BOOK 2

SEVENTEEN

Kate had taken to heart Phillip's advice that she should find suitable clothes for her trip to the Dragon Duchies. She was glad he had said something. Left to her own devices, she might not have given clothes a thought. She flew by griffin to Wellinsport to meet with his contact. She had to be on her guard in the city, for although Wellinsport was a Freyan stronghold, Rosian agents could be searching for her.

Phillip's contact turned out to be another of Henry's agents. Kate had met one of his agents before—a Mrs. Lavender, who ran a hat shop, and gleaned all manner of valuable information from the gossip of women as they tried on hats.

This agent was just as unlikely: a seamstress named Mrs. Brown, who traveled to the homes of the wealthy, oftentimes spending weeks as the guest of one of her clients while she worked on wedding trousseaus, gowns for young ladies who were "coming out," or new dresses for next year's social season. Mrs. Brown was a crafter, gifted in the art of sewing and removing magical seals from letters and replacing them so that no one ever noticed.

She was also something of a snob who was inclined to turn up her nose at the sight of Kate in her slops. Mrs. Brown studied Kate from head to toe, spent an hour taking measurements while Kate fidgeted, and finally nodded.

"I don't have time to sew anything. My clients have more clothes than they would wear in several lifetimes. They won't miss a few. Come back in two days."

Kate returned to find her wardrobe laid out on a bed. The seamstress had provided a warm, luxurious fur coat with a hood and a set of traveling clothes, consisting of a tailored wool jacket, vests and shirts, and two long split skirts made for riding horses, and which also were suitable for riding on griffin-back. Finally she brought forth a pair of elegant shoes and tall leather riding boots.

"Master Phillip ordered the shoes and boots from the finest cobbler in Wellinsport," said Mrs. Brown. "He had them specially made for you. See if they fit."

The shoes and boots fit perfectly. Mrs. Brown gave Kate an arch look. "It seems Master Phillip knows you well."

Kate flushed and mumbled something about her and Master Phillip being good friends, all the while remembering that it was Thomas who had pried the piece of broken glass from her foot and teased her about dancing with him.

The shoes were sensible, as Amelia would have said, extending above the ankle with a small heel and a buckle for decoration. The leather boots came to below the knee and were warm, and soft as butter. Kate held them in her hands, admiring them until she saw the seamstress slyly smiling. Hurriedly, Kate dropped the boots to the floor.

"Will you need dresses and petticoats for evening wear?" Mrs. Brown asked. "If so, you must give me another day."

Kate politely declined, saying with complete honesty that she did not have room to pack them.

"I do need gloves," she added, remembering the advice given to her by Mrs. Lavender, who had warned Kate that if she was planning to act the part of a pampered gentlewoman, she should wear gloves to conceal her "work-ing hands" with their calluses and sun-browned skin.

"I have two pair of gloves for you," said Mrs. Brown. "I also brought along a wig and silk scarves to replace that thing you are currently wearing around your head."

The "thing" happened to be Kate's red kerchief. She snatched it off and sat down in front of a mirror as the seamstress drew the wig over her head and primped and fussed with the curls and puffs.

"You can always say you lost your hair in the plague," said Mrs. Brown.

"It itches," Kate complained, regarding the wig with disfavor. "And I look ridiculous."

She declined the wig, then thanked Mrs. Brown and went back to her lodgings encumbered with boxes and bundles. She changed into the jacket

and riding skirt and pulled on the boots. She could not part with the red kerchief, and tucked it away in the valise. She regarded herself in her stolen
plumage and thought about the one fine dress she had owned, the green dress
Morgan had given to her on her birthday.

She had left the dress back in Barwich Manor, packed away in lavender.

Kate closed the valise and went to the stables to retrieve the griffin.

The trip from Wellinsport to the borders of the Dragon Duchies took seven
days and proved uneventful. Kate received some strange looks from innkeep-
ers when she and the griffin stopped for the night. Silver rosuns assured her
a warm welcome, though they did not buy her freedom from questions.

Women almost never traveled by griffin, and everyone was curious to hear
her story. Kate concocted a tale of rushing to the bedside of her dying father,
from whom she had long been estranged, and who wanted to see his dear child
before he passed.

Morgan would have approved.

Kate had never traveled beyond the coastline of Rosia and she enjoyed seeing new sights: flying over fields gold with wheat ready to be harvested, me-
andering rivers that glistened in the sunlight, shining lakes and thick woods.
Her enjoyment was always tempered by her fears for Dalgren. Flying on
griffinback reminded her of flying with the dragon.

Dalgren had talked to Akiel on his arrival in the Aligoes, telling him he
had decided to surrender.

"He was very unhappy, mum. He said he was tired of being a fugitive,"
Akiel had told her. "He brought disgrace and dishonor to his family and he
wants to try to make amends."

"He thinks I murdered that dragon, Lady Odila," Kate had said despondently.

"No, he doesn't, mum," Akiel had assured her. "He said to tell you he did
not ever believe that. He was upset and angry and he took out his anger on
you. He finally realized his anger was with himself."

Kate was grateful he no longer thought her a murderer, but she remained
worried about him. She worried about what would happen if he was
convicted.

Dragons never talked about dragons who broke the laws of dragonkind.
According to them, dragons never committed crimes. They made this assertion
not only out of pride, but out of necessity. Humans who lived among the
dragons had to be able to trust that these powerful and deadly creatures
could keep their terrible power in check and not go rampaging around the
countryside.

The weather was fair and Kate arrived at the border of the Dragon Duchies with four days to spare before the last day of the month, when Dalgren's trial was slated to begin. She was probably going to need that time, for once they arrived at the border, the griffin refused to continue. She pleaded with the beast to carry her to the city of Cieleterre, but it departed. The griffin was apparently convinced that dragons were lined up along the border of the Dragon Duchies waiting to devour any griffin foolish enough to trespass. Kate would have to make the rest of the journey by mail coach.

Phillip had recommended she stay at an inn known as the Half and Half, for half of the inn was on the dragon side of the border and the other half on the human side. As Kate retrieved her valise, she noticed she was not the only traveler choosing to stay here. An elegant wyvern-drawn coach-and-four stood in the yard. She could tell that the coach belonged to a Rosian of wealth and standing, for it was painted sky blue and decorated with gold gilt bees and a coat of arms featuring a bee.

A second, smaller coach accompanied the first. This one was piled high with luggage which several servants in livery were now removing.

The wyverns that pulled these carriages were by far the best-behaved wyverns Kate had ever seen. The stable hands were freeing the wyverns from their traces. Any other four wyverns would have been snapping and fighting among themselves or trying to bite their handlers. The coachman and servants had the beasts well under control, keeping them separated, stopping fights before they started.

Two women had apparently been the passengers in the first coach, for they were talking with the servants about which pieces of luggage to take to their rooms. Kate was eager to continue her journey and she barely spared a glance for the women, beyond noting that the younger of the two was holding a spaniel in her arms. Both regarded her with unabashed curiosity, for the sight of a woman riding a griffin was out of the ordinary.

Let them gawk, Kate thought, going to speak to the innkeeper.

"When will the mail coach to Cieleterre arrive?" she asked. "Will I have time to rest and order something to eat?"

"Madame will have a great deal of time," said the innkeeper. "The next mail coach is not due for ten days. Madame just missed the last one, which left this morning. We look forward to having you as our guest in the interim."

"Ten days!" Kate gasped. "But that is too late! I must be in Cieleterre four days from now!"

The innkeeper shrugged. "I am sorry, Madame. I do not know what to say. The mail coach travels to and from Cieleterre every ten days. And now if Madame will excuse me, I must attend to my other guests."

He hurried away. Kate stood in the yard, clutching her valise, gazing after the innkeeper in blank dismay as he bowed and fawned over his wealthy guests, the older of whom he addressed as "countess."

For their part, the countess and her young companion paid scant attention to him. They were far more interested in observing Kate. The countess asked the innkeeper a question, apparently regarding Kate, for she glanced at her as she spoke. After he responded to her, the countess and her companion began to whisper together.

Kate was tired, stiff, and sore. She had flown all this way and was now going to arrive too late to attend Dalgren's trial. She could have wept with disappointment and fatigue. She deeply resented the fact that these two pampered females apparently thought they had the right to gossip about her.

"Sir, could I hire a horse?" Kate called to the innkeeper, not caring that she was rudely interrupting his conversation.

Before he could reply, the countess came walking across the yard toward Kate, obviously intending to speak to her. Kate had no desire to satisfy this woman's curiosity and she started to turn away.

"Please forgive the intrusion, Madame," the woman called, her voice a rich contralto. "My companion and I could not help overhearing your predicament."

She lowered the cowl of her fur-lined cloak to reveal white hair arranged artfully about her face, whose beauty, even in middle years, was arresting. She regarded Kate with cool, intelligent eyes that observed everything about her from the scarf she had tied around her shaved head to the fine leather boots.

"My companion and I are traveling to Cieleterre ourselves," the countess continued. "Our coach is large and comfortable, and we hope you will allow us to convey you to your destination."

Kate was astonished and ashamed she had so badly misjudged the two.

"Thank you," she said in confusion. "Your Ladyship is too kind. I could not take the liberty . . ."

"You traveled alone and by griffin, Madame," said the countess with a smile. "You must be in need of haste."

"I confess that I am, my lady," Kate admitted. "But I would not want to intrude."

Her gaze went to the countess's companion. She was perhaps twenty, with brown hair and a frank and open face. She handed the spaniel to a servant and came over to join them.

"Please, do come with us, Madame," the young woman said, adding with a laugh, "The countess and I have talked about all our friends and spoken of every topic under the sun and now we are bored to death with each other's company. You would be doing us a favor."

"Traveling by horse will take you almost as many days as waiting for the

mail coach," the countess added. "The journey would be hard and uncomfortable. You will find no inns or way stops between here and Cieleterre. And
while the Dragon Duchies are safer than most places, lawless men have been
known to roam the outlands. A woman traveling alone by horseback would
not be safe."

Kate found herself liking these two. She was still reluctant to accept the
countess's offer, but she had to admit to the logic of her argument. Dalgren
needed her. She could not afford to stand upon her dignity.

"Your Ladyship has convinced me," said Kate. "If I am not intruding, I
would be very grateful for the chance to join you."

"Excellent," said the countess. "We are staying the night and will set out
early in the morning."

She held out her hand to Kate. "I am Cecile de Marjolaine and this is Her
Highness, Princess Sophia."

Kate gawked. Her traveling companions were the Princess Sophia—
the young woman to whom Thomas was engaged—and the Countess de
Marjolaine.

"If Henry Wallace is the most dangerous man in the world," Amelia had
once said, "Cecile de Marjolaine is the most dangerous woman."

Seeing Cecile frown slightly, Kate realized that she had been rudely gaping. She recovered herself enough to make an awkward curtsy. She would
now be expected to introduce herself.

Kate had been using her mother's maiden name, Rose Gascoyne, on her
travels and she was about to give them that name, when she realized lying
to them presented a problem. These two were traveling to Cieleterre, and
while Kate considered it highly unlikely they had anything to do with Dalgren or the court-martial, she couldn't take the chance. She was planning to
speak in her friend's defense and she had decided to do so under her own
name.

Rosian naval officers would be present. Kate might be placing herself in
danger, but she would deal with that when the time came. She could not tell
another lie in front of Dalgren. She had to prove to him she had changed.

"I am Katherine Gascoyne-Fitzmaurice, ma'am," Kate said. She gave an
awkward curtsy and watched closely to see if they recognized her as the notorious Captain Kate who had escaped the noose.

Neither appeared to do so. Sophia told her she was pleased to meet her.
Cecile said the same and Kate was breathing a sigh of relief when Cecile
spoke again.

"Gascoyne . . . I seem to know that name."

She paused, trying to remember.

Kate was caught. She didn't care what happened to her, so long as she

could save Dalgren. She needed to make the countess understand that she
had to reach Cieleterre.

"My lady—" she began.

"I seem to recall a Freyan viscount by the name of Gascoyne," Cecile said.
"Are you related?"

"He was my grandfather, my lady," said Kate.

The Viscount Gascoyne had been notorious for only one reason and that
was his suicide. Kate was spared from further comment by the spaniel, who
had managed to wriggle out of the arms of the maid and was now pawing and
sniffing at Kate's boots.

"Oh, you naughty Bandit," Sophia said, scolding him. "Don't jump on the
lady!"

"Don't scold him, Your Highness," Kate said with a laugh. "He must smell
the griffin."

She bent down to pet the dog, who sniffed her gloves and appeared to approve of her.

"I hope you don't mind sharing the carriage with him, Mistress Katherine," Sophia was saying. "Bandit goes everywhere with me."

"Not in the least, ma'am," said Kate, giving Bandit's silky head a pat. She
was so tired she wondered if she could stand up without falling. Cecile was
quick to notice.

"Come, Sophia," said the countess. "Mistress Katherine is fatigued from
her journey. We should let her rest."

"Of course," said Sophia. "I hope you will join us for supper, Mistress. We
dine at eight of the clock. I am so envious of you! I have always longed to fly
on a griffin! I want to hear all about it."

Kate knew enough about court etiquette from her mother to know that if
the princess invited you to dine, you did not decline the invitation, as much
as she longed to do so. Sophia was engaged to Thomas and she would be certain to talk about him. Kate had heard the young women of Freeport chatter
interminably about their young men. She would have to listen to Sophia
praise his dancing, his conversation, his blue eyes. Kate would have to smile
and pretend he was a stranger.

She made a feeble protest. "Please consider, ma'am, that I have spent seven
days in the saddle. My clothes are filthy and wrinkled and, as the little dog
can attest, I smell of griffin."

Sophia retrieved the spaniel and gave him a scolding. "Now see what you
have done, Bandit! You have left muddy paw prints all over the lady's skirt.
I am so sorry, Mistress. I insist that you dine with us, so that I can make
amends."

Cecile gave Kate a cool look.

"Of course Mistress Katherine will dine with us," said the countess. "I will send my servant for you at eight."

"Your Ladyship is too kind," said Kate.

She dropped another curtsy as the two women walked toward the inn, accompanied by their servants carrying enough luggage between them for a month's stay.

As she reached the door, Sophia looked back over her shoulder to smile at Kate and make Bandit wave his paw.

Kate sighed deeply.

EIGHTEEN

Alone in her room, Kate took one look at her clothes and despaired. She could not do much to clean them, but she could at least clean herself.

She had never ordered a bath at an inn, but she knew such things could be done. The procedure turned out to be extremely complicated, requiring the servants to haul in a brass tub. They heated copious amounts of water in the kitchen, then had to carry the jugs to her room.

The innkeeper might well have refused, but he had taken note of Sophia's friendliness to this guest, and went out of his way to accommodate her. The maids set up a folding screen to shield her modesty and even scattered rose petals in the water. They looked askance at Kate's shaved head, but carefully averted their eyes.

"I lost my hair in the plague," said Kate.

She had never felt anything so wonderful as sinking into the hot water. She stayed until the water grew too cool for comfort and emerged from the bath refreshed.

When she was going to dress, she found that her clothes were missing. Kate wrapped herself in a towel and confronted the maid and demanded to know what had happened.

"Her Highness says we were to take 'em to be cleaned, miss," the maid answered, seeming astonished that Kate would ask. "We will bring them to you in the morning, once they are dry."

"Her Highness!" Kate repeated, startled.

"The princess says her little dog jumped on you and got you all muddy, so we were to clean your clothes," said the maid.

"I am supposed to dine with Her Highness. What am I to wear?" Kate asked.

"Her Ladyship said that since you are traveling light, you might like to borrow something of hers. She sent this along for you. Beautiful, I call it!"

The maid produced a lovely gown, long and flowing, with lace at the elbows and neckline. The countess had also thoughtfully added a matching scarf trimmed with lace for Kate to cover her head.

Kate was at first resentful that the women had taken such a liberty, but she eventually calmed down and even smiled. They had probably done so out of their own self-interest. The three of them would be cooped up together in the carriage tomorrow and the countess undoubtedly did not care to travel with a companion who smelled of griffin!

Kate drew on the gown, which seemed to float over her body like a silky cloud. She tied the scarf around her head and held a serious talk with herself.

"Of all the strange things that have happened to you, this is one of the strangest. Keep your wits about you. Be careful of that princess. She can't possibly be as nice as she seems. And when she mentions Thomas, do *not* blush!"

The countess's servant came promptly at eight and escorted her to a private sitting room. Kate entered warily, not knowing what to expect, fearing some kind of social ambush.

What she found was Sophia sitting on the floor in a rumpled dress playing with Bandit. The countess was seated in a chair, reading a book by the light of the fire.

Sophia scrambled to her feet in a flurry of petticoats to welcome Kate.

"Bandit is here to act as guard dog," Sophia said, laughing.

Bandit licked Kate's hand, then proved his worth as guard dog by growling at the waiter when he entered.

The countess laid down her book. The servants served the meal, which consisted of salmon, trout, a meat pie, bread, and rice pudding, accompanied by both red and white wine. Sophia tied Bandit's leash to the leg of a chair and told him to be good—an order he obeyed by starting to bark.

Kate had not eaten since early morning and she was famished. The princess and the countess ate with hearty appetites, and although Sophia had said they had grown bored with each other's conversation, they did not give evidence of that at the table.

The countess acted the role of hostess and steered the conversation to politics. She and the princess discussed the political situation in Braffa and how the Braffans were attempting to manipulate the price of lift gas.

Kate knew nothing about politics. The mention of Braffa immediately brought Thomas to mind; she kept her head down, concentrating on the meal.

The princess and countess changed the topic of conversation to Estara. King Ullr of Guundar was trying to stir up trouble, laying claim to some islands Estara considered theirs. The princess's brother, King Renaud, was attempting to defuse the situation. Kate was thinking that the world was a far more complicated place than she had ever imagined, when the moment she had been dreading came.

"Speaking of Estara, have you heard from Prince Thomas, Your Highness?" Cecile asked.

Kate hurriedly took a gulp of wine.

"Yes, my lady," said Sophia. "I received a letter from His Highness before we left. This salmon is excellent, don't you think?"

Cecile was not to be deterred. "What does the prince write to you?"

"He writes that he is in the Aligoes with the Royal Navy chasing pirates," said Sophia.

Kate choked and was forced to hide her face in her napkin. She feared the shrewd eyes of the countess would notice her discomfiture, but Cecile was not paying attention to Kate. The countess focused on Sophia.

"Prince Thomas will soon be back in Everux, I have no doubt," said Cecile. "He must be counting the hours until he sees you again."

"If so, he will have a great many to count," said Sophia. "He does not intend to return to Rosia. He writes that he is next traveling to Bheldem to visit his mother and father."

"Bheldem!" Cecile exclaimed, displeased. "Prince Thomas should make the time to visit you, Sophia. He is, after all, your fiancé."

The princess made no comment, but asked the servant for another helping of salmon. Kate concentrated on her food, though she could not have said what she was eating. Cecile was in an ill temper and sharply ordered Bandit to stop barking.

The servants cleared the dinner table and brought in fragrant tea, sage cheese, fruit, and walnuts. The countess dismissed the servants, saying she would serve the tea herself. Sophia freed Bandit and rewarded him with cheese for having been good during the meal, though he had barked almost constantly.

The countess recovered her good humor. They discussed their journey tomorrow and she told them about the history of the city of Cieleterre, explaining that the name meant "land and sky" in the language of the dragons.

"What business do you have in Cieleterre, Mistress Katherine?" Cecile asked, handing Kate a cup of tea.

Kate had been expecting the question and trying to think of an answer that did not involve Dalgren. She wasn't ashamed of her friend, but she knew Dalgren was ashamed of himself.

She was going to say she was planning to visit an ailing relative, but before she could reply, Sophia spoke up.

"I hope you have a more pleasant reason to be there than I do. I must attend a court-martial."

Kate stared at her in confusion, wondering why she would be attending Dalgren's court-martial. Whatever the reason, Kate had to discard the ailing relative.

"I am here to attend the court-martial, as well," she said. "The accused is a friend of mine. I plan to ask permission to speak at the trial in his defense."

"You are Lord Dalgren's friend?" Sophia asked.

Kate nodded. She and the countess would soon find out the truth anyway. Might as well reveal it now and get it over with. "He and I have been friends for many years."

"I am so glad he has a friend to speak for him!" Sophia exclaimed. "I think what you are doing is splendid."

Kate looked up, startled. "You do, ma'am?"

Sophia was passionate. Her eyes flashed, her cheeks flushed rose. "The countess's own son was present at the battle. He was a lieutenant with the Dragon Brigade. He gave his word of honor that he would accept the enemy's surrender and he almost gave his life to keep his word. His dragon died when that horrible captain fired on his own forces. His Grace still grows angry when he talks about it. I think the dragons are very wrong to make Lord Dalgren stand trial!"

"Please consider, Sophia, that Lord Dalgren *is* a deserter," Cecile said in mild rebuke. "He swore an oath to defend Rosia. He broke his oath and fled the battle."

"I know you are right, my lady," Sophia said somberly. "But I remember the suffering we saw during the war and I cannot find it in my heart to fault anyone—man or dragon—who decides that he can no longer face the horror and brutality of war."

Sophia trembled in her earnestness.

"I know, my dear," said Cecile, her austere demeanor softening. "This is why I did not want you to come. I was afraid the memory of those dark days would return to upset you."

"I do not like to remember that terrible time," said Sophia in a low voice. "Yet I have always hoped that some good may come of it. I understand why

Lord Dalgren broke his oath and fled. That is why I wanted to be present at his trial."

Kate had no idea what they were talking about. She wondered very much how a princess could know the horrors of war. It was not her place to ask, of course. Sophia wiped away a tear. Cecile was gazing into the fire. Both seemed to have forgotten Kate. She was thinking she would quietly withdraw when Bandit, undoubtedly under the impression no one was watching him, chose that moment to jump on the table.

Kate made a deft grab and managed to catch hold of the dog. Bandit yelped in protest. Sophia looked up, startled.

"He was making a raid on the cheese," said Kate.

Sophia laughed, shook her head at the dog, and tweaked him on the nose by way of punishment. She then consoled him with a piece of cheese and returned to her chair, keeping Bandit in her lap.

The countess cast Kate a grateful look. Kate had the feeling she was thanking her not for saving the cheese, but for lifting the dark shadow that had fallen over Sophia.

"Will you sit in judgment on Dalgren, ma'am?" Kate asked.

Sophia shook her head. "I am attending the trial as an observer, representing the crown."

"I thought a court-martial proceeding was strictly a military matter," Kate said, confused.

"That would be true in the case of a human in the Rosian army or navy," Cecile answered. "The Dragon Brigade is far more than a branch of the military. Although the Dragon Duchies have their own laws, they are part of the Rosian kingdom and felt that they should share in the responsibility for the defense of their homeland. The King of Rosia and the Dragon Duchies drew up a treaty that created the Brigade and proudly proclaimed the bond between our two nations.

"The dragons will be represented at the trial by the Duke of Talwin, the Count of Whitcliff, the Countess of Rothvar, and Countess Anasi Deehaven. Her Highness represents the crown of Rosia. My son, His Grace, the Duke de Bourlet, will also be in attendance, both as a witness and a signatory to the treaty."

Kate regarded her in dismay. She had known Dalgren's offense was serious, but she had never imagined he would be facing the wrath of two nations.

"I am afraid I don't understand," said Kate.

"The dragons believe that service in the Dragon Brigade is a high honor," Cecile explained. "Those who serve bear the honor of all dragon clans. Lord Dalgren's crime brought disgrace not only upon himself, but on his family and the entire dragon nation. All dragons feel dishonored by his actions."

Kate was sick with fear. "Do you know what Dalgren's punishment will be? Will they put him to death?"

Cecile shook her head. "Dragons are far more civilized than humans. They do not kill their own kind. But I fear Lord Dalgren's punishment will be severe. The dragons are taking a very serious view of the matter. No other dragon has ever before deserted. They need to reclaim their honor."

Kate despaired. "Then they have already made up their minds. They mean to make an example of him. My testimony cannot help. Who am I? A nobody! Perhaps they won't even let me speak!"

Sophia dropped Bandit to the floor and came over to sit by Kate. She took hold of her hand and pressed it warmly.

"You are Lord Dalgren's friend. You have a better right to speak than any duke or count. I will make certain you are heard!"

"Thank you, ma'am," said Kate.

She looked down at her hand—brown and rough, her nails cracked and broken from grappling with the griffin's reins. Sophia's hand, by contrast, was white and soft. Rings sparkled on her fingers, and her nails were carefully trimmed and rounded.

Sophia gave Kate's hand a confident pat and smiled reassuringly. Kate realized suddenly that the princess did not notice the difference between the two of them. Kate was ashamed that she did.

Cecile gave a delicate cough. "You will be speaking before the Council of Dragons, as well as officers of the Royal Navy, Mistress Katherine. What are you planning to wear?"

"My riding skirt and jacket, my lady," said Kate, surprised. She had not given the matter thought until now. "They are the only clothes I brought with me."

She did not add that besides her slops, they were the only clothes she owned.

She had the feeling the countess guessed, however, for she said smoothly, "You were traveling by griffin and of course you lacked room to pack."

"But those clothes will not be suitable, will they," Kate said.

"I may not be able to help you win your case for your friend, but I can loan you a dress," said Sophia, adding with a laugh, "I always pack more clothes than I need, as the countess will tell you."

She regarded Kate with a thoughtful frown. "We must do something for a hat. I gather you don't like to wear wigs. I don't either. They itch. How did you lose your hair?"

"We must not pry, Sophia," Cecile said, mildly scolding.

"I am so sorry!" Sophia said, flushing. "I didn't mean to. It's just that I lost my hair once. I used to suffer from terrible headaches. One of the physicians gave me medicine that caused all my hair to fall out. My poor mama was in hysterics. She refused to look at me until my hair grew back!"

"I was thinking a draped turban," Cecile suggested.

"The very thing!" Sophia clapped her hands. "Draped turbans are extremely popular among the ladies at court. I learned how to drape them. Rodrigo taught me."

"Now that this is settled, we should retire, Sophia," said Cecile. "We must rise early in the morning."

Kate thanked both the princess and the countess for a lovely evening and then withdrew. She was grateful to return to the quiet and solitude of her own room to think.

She was tired, but when she lay down, she was wide awake. She blew out the candle and went to the window to look out at the Oscadia Mountains. Moonlight shone on peaks that were already white with an early autumn snowfall.

The city of Cieleterre was located in those mountains. Dalgren was there now, awaiting his trial. He had parted from her in anger and disappointment, and despite what he had told Akiel, he might still be upset with her. He might refuse to see her or the dragons might refuse to let her see him.

"I will make Dalgren listen to me," Kate said aloud. "I will make the dragons listen to me. Dalgren and I will stand together, never mind how many dukes and counts they line up against us. We might have to fight the whole bloody dragon nation, but we'll win, my friend. I know we will win."

NINETEEN

Kate woke up well before the hour appointed to meet Sophia and the countess. She tried to go back to sleep, but she was too worried about Dalgren.

When the maid brought in Kate's skirt, jacket, and shirt, cleaned and no longer smelling of griffin, she dressed and then went outdoors in the chill mountain air and roamed restlessly about the yard. She watched the countess's servants load the luggage and then enter their own wyvern-drawn coach. They made an early departure, presumably to have everything ready for the princess and their mistress when they arrived in Cieleterre.

Despite Cecile saying they needed to make an early start, Kate supposed that early meant noon. So she was pleasantly surprised when, not long after the servants had left, Sophia came downstairs, dressed and ready to travel.

The coachman drove the coach to the door, keeping the restive wyverns under control. Kate sat with her back to the wyverns, facing Sophia and the countess opposite, and Bandit resided in a basket on the floor.

The coach was warm and snug. They wrapped themselves in furs, and the servants had placed bricks heated by magical constructs on the floor at their feet. The coachman mounted the box and sent magic flowing to the lift tanks. He snapped the whip over the heads of the wyverns to get their attention, and gave the command to fly. The wyverns spread their wings, the coach rose effortlessly into the air, and within moments, Kate was in the Dragon Duchies.

"How long have you known Lord Dalgren?" Sophia asked.

"I met him when my father and I were visiting Westfirth," said Kate. "I saw the dragons of the Dragon Brigade performing their maneuvers in the sky above their fortress and I was entranced.

"The dragons were so magnificent and powerful that I longed to see them up close, and I sneaked onto the grounds where the young dragons were practicing. I ventured too close, and when Dalgren was coming down to land he nearly flattened me. A human officer saved my life. He was very kind, and he introduced me to Dalgren. That's when Dalgren and I became friends."

She fell silent, gazing out the window at the spectacular view of the mountains and not seeing it. She was vaguely aware of Sophia starting to ask another question and the countess stopping her with a silent pressure of her hand.

"Cieleterre is a fascinating city," Cecile remarked. "The oldest human colony in the Dragon Duchies."

"Being Freyan, my knowledge of Rosia is limited, my lady," said Kate, grateful that the countess had changed the subject for her benefit. "Have humans always lived in the Dragon Duchies?"

"Humans and dragons on Rosia began as enemies," said Cecile. "Dragons once killed humans for food. Humans killed dragons out of self-preservation. During the time of the Sunlit Empire, humans and dragons made peace, and the dragons formed the Dragon Duchies. During the Blackfire War dragons joined with Rosia to fight and defeat the Freyans. Afterward, the king invited them into the Rosian court and granted them titles. The Dragon Brigade was formed not long after.

"But humans did not then live in the Dragon Duchies, only dragons. As it happened, when the dragons visited Rosia, they were impressed by the beautiful palaces they saw. Their own caves seemed very dark and dismal by comparison. The dragons wanted to build palaces for themselves, but even dragon magic has its limitations. Dragons knew nothing about architectural design or even how to construct such massive buildings, and they hired humans to do the work.

"At first humans were reluctant to travel to the Dragon Duchies. The dragons paid them in gold, however, and soon architects and stonemasons, crafters and carpenters came here to work for them. The dragons developed a fondness for human culture and hired musicians to entertain them and artists to decorate their new dwellings. Human villages soon grew into cities as more and more humans moved here to work for the dragons.

"Cieleterre is the largest of these cities and the oldest. For many years, it was a thriving city with a large population. When King Alaric disbanded the Dragon Brigade, the dragons were outraged. They claimed the humans had broken the treaty and they cut all ties with the crown."

"My father didn't always make wise decisions," Sophia said. "But he loved me and that is what I like to remember."

"Your father loved you very much, my dear," said Cecile. "That is what you *should* remember."

Kate was struck by their remarks. Like Sophia's father, her own father had rarely, if ever, made wise decisions. But, again like the king, Morgan had loved her, at least as much as he knew how to love anyone. And she had loved him. She felt less in awe of Sophia, as if the princess had left her golden throne and come to sit with Kate on a shabby but comfortable sofa.

"When was the Dragon Brigade reestablished, ma'am?" Kate asked.

Dalgren had never told her anything about the history of the Dragon Brigade. He had rarely mentioned the brigade at all, except during those times when he was training Kate how to ride. Even then, he only talked about Captain de Guichen and Lady Cam and how they had trained him.

"The Treaty of D'eau Brisé reestablished the Dragon Duchies as a part of Rosia after the war with the Bottom Dwellers, and with that, King Renaud formally reinstated the Dragon Brigade."

Sophia asked the countess about the style of architecture used in Cieleterre. Kate, who knew nothing about such things, dropped out of the conversation, glad to be left alone with the view of the mountains and her thoughts.

At midday the coach descended at a wayside built by the dragons for the convenience of human travelers. The wayside was crude, consisting of a grove of fir trees, a table made of stone, and a clear, cold mountain stream for water.

The servants who had gone ahead were waiting for them, with dinner prepared. The women, wrapping themselves in their fur cloaks against the cool mountain air, ate beneath the fir trees. After they ate, Sophia said she needed to walk Bandit, for he would miss his exercise, and asked Kate if she would like to keep her company.

As it turned out, walking Bandit meant that Sophie walked while Bandit rode in comfort in her arms.

The two young women started talking about Haever, the capital of Freya, which was still at peace with Rosia since their wartime alliance, though the peace was now somewhat uneasy.

Sophia had been attending university in Haever, as a gesture to prove that the Rosians were serious about peace. She had come to love the city and its people, and asked about her favorite places.

Kate had lived in Haever with Amelia when she was working for Sir Henry, and she was able to tell Sophia that the pond in Whiteover Park was still home to black swans and that the famous floating house of the eccentric duchess continued to drift over the city.

Sophia put Bandit on the ground and watched the dog in silence.

"Are you tired?" Kate asked. "We could go back."

Sophia shook her head. Her cheeks were already rosy from the cold, but the rose color deepened.

"I know that Haever is a very large city with thousands of people, but I was wondering if you happen to know His Grace, Phillip Masterson, the Duke of Upper and Lower Milton?"

Phillip Masterson.

"You mean Pip?" Kate asked, astonished.

The moment she blurted out his name, she realized she'd made a mistake. She should have said she had never heard of Phillip Masterson, and Sophia would have dropped the subject. Why should she ask about him anyway? Kate wondered worriedly. Does she know who I am? Is this her way of telling me?

Kate stammered and tried to repair the damage. "I . . . have met His Grace . . . I don't truly know him . . ."

"Yet you call him by his pet name," said Sophia, smiling.

"The . . . uh . . . newspapers call him Pip. Just as they called Prince Tom . . . Prince Tom," Kate finished lamely.

Her excuse was very feeble and she was grateful to Bandit, who had caught sight of a squirrel and dashed off in pursuit. Sophia called after him, but the dog was oblivious, intent on the hunt.

"I will fetch him," Kate offered, glad for the reprieve.

The squirrel ran up a pine tree. Bandit jumped on the tree trunk as though he would climb it, and when that failed, he sat beneath it and barked. Kate caught hold of Bandit's jeweled collar and hauled him back to Sophia. The dog twisted about, trying to get away, still barking. Sophia took him in her arms and tried to calm him, burying her face in his fur. But not before Kate saw the flush staining Sophia's cheeks.

Kate was struck by a new and startling idea. She and Thomas had been talking of his engagement while they were on board the island hopper. Kate seemed to vaguely recall that when Thomas said that he believed Sophia liked someone else, his gaze had gone to Phillip. At the time, Kate had been trying to navigate the island hopper, as well as her own confused feelings for Thomas, and she had not given the matter much thought.

She was definitely thinking about it now. She knew she should let the dangerous subject go, shift the conversation to something else. But she was intensely curious to know how Phillip and Sophia knew each other.

"How do you know His Grace, ma'am?" Kate asked Sophia.

"He came to the palace with Prince Thomas when our formal engagement was announced," said Sophia, her flush deepening. "Phillip . . . I mean His Grace . . . saved my life."

"He did? What happened? Did someone attack you?" Kate asked.

"Oh, he didn't really save it, I suppose," Sophia said, laughing. "Though it seemed that way to me at the time. I was supposed to be attending the royal ball. I had locked Bandit in the closet, but somehow he got away. Imagine my horror when I found him in the ballroom standing on the dessert table eating a plate full of meringues!"

Sophia sighed. "My brother is the best brother in the world, but even he would have been furious. When I tried to catch Bandit, I ended up spilling chocolate all down the front of my ball gown. Phillip happened to be passing by and he rescued me. He helped me smuggle Bandit out of the ballroom before anyone saw us. Phillip was so quick-thinking and helpful. And Bandit loves him . . ."

Bandit isn't the only one who loves him, Kate realized.

"Don't you think he is the most handsome man you know?" Sophia asked impulsively.

Kate pictured Phillip with his perpetually rumpled hair, his too-wide mouth, and his odd eyes, one blue and one green. He was nice enough to look at, she supposed, but she certainly would not call him handsome.

She was saved from answering by one of the servants, who came with a message from the countess, telling them they should return to the coach, it was time to depart.

Sophia gathered up Bandit and the two women turned their steps toward the carriage.

"I fear you must despise me," Sophia said. "I am engaged to be married to Prince Thomas. I should not even be thinking about another man, much less talking about him."

"I do not despise you," Kate assured her. "My friend Miss Amelia says that there is a reason the poets use the term 'falling' in love. According to her, love is like you are walking along, happy and carefree, not looking where you are going, and suddenly you tumble into a ditch."

Sophia sighed. "That is exactly how I feel. Like I fell into a ditch! But I don't want to climb out. Yet the marriage is arranged. Our engagement has been made public."

"Why don't you tell the king? I am certain he would not force you to marry a man you do not love."

"He is the kindest brother in the world and he would end the engagement if I asked him, although the scandal would be very great. But I must do my duty to my country," Sophia said. "Freya and Rosia have been at war for centuries. So many lives have been lost. My marriage to the heir to the Freyan throne will ensure peace between our two nations.

"Prince Thomas is very nice," she added, unconsciously echoing what Thomas had said about her. "I will learn to love him. We have something in common, you see. He is also in love with someone else."

"Did he say he was?" Kate asked, alarmed.

"Oh, no. Prince Thomas would never breathe a word. He is far too polite," said Sophia. "My friend Sir Rodrigo told me. He said Phillip . . . His Grace . . . told him. Rodrigo told me because he was afraid I would find out and I would be hurt."

What a tangle! Kate thought. Phillip is in love with the woman who is engaged to be married to his best friend, Thomas, who is engaged to Sophia and he's in love with . . .

"Let me carry Bandit," Kate said hurriedly. "He must be getting heavy."

Sophia surrendered the dog. Bandit snuggled in Kate's arms and licked her cheek.

"He likes you," said Sophia. "He is an excellent judge of character. He once bit one of the servants on the leg. It turned out the man was a thief! They caught him trying to pawn some of my jewels. Bandit knew, you see."

Kate smiled. The two walked on in silence, then Sophia said impulsively, "I am glad to be able to talk to you, Mistress Kate. I have ladies-in-waiting, but I could never tell them my secrets. They are such gossips! They would spread it all over the palace."

"I will not tell a soul," Kate promised.

"I know I can trust you," said Sophia.

"But how can you know, ma'am? We have only just met," Kate argued. "You don't know anything about me." She remembered saying the same thing to Thomas, and her face grew warm.

"I know you are loyal," Sophia returned. "You are sacrificing a great deal to speak for your friend."

Kate had the uneasy feeling Sophia knew more about her than she was saying. She wondered how much the countess knew. Kate suddenly found it odd that the countess would so trustingly give a ride in her coach to a complete stranger.

The coach had come in view now. Cecile stood waiting for them at the door.

"I think you could confide in the countess," said Kate. "She loves you very much."

"The countess arranged the marriage. I would never do anything to disappoint her." Sophia added softly, "I owe her my life. When the Bottom

Dwellers kidnapped me and took me Below, she risked her life to rescue me. I would do anything for her."

Sophia waved to Cecile and called to her. "I am sorry if we have kept you waiting, my lady. Bandit chased a squirrel and then Mistress Katherine chased Bandit. I am afraid we lost track of time."

Cecile smiled. "You have not kept me waiting, ladies, but it is time we should be going. I want to reach Cieleterre before dark."

The women entered the coach, and Kate put Bandit in his basket. Fatigued from his strenuous exercise, the dog curled up and went to sleep. Sophia sat down beside the countess and leaned over to kiss her on the cheek. Cecile looked at her in surprise.

"What is that for, my love?" she asked.

"Just to say I am grateful to you for coming with me, my lady," said Sophia. "You are right. This journey has brought back sad memories."

"Remember, they are only memories, Sophia," said Cecile, regarding her with a fond smile. "They have no power over you."

Sophia and the countess settled themselves for an afternoon nap. Kate closed her eyes, pretending to do the same. Once she was certain the other two were asleep, she opened her eyes and gazed out the window at the pine forests below.

Kate let her thoughts wander.

Walking along, happy and carefree, and suddenly you fall into a ditch. You must promise me one dance. I think he is in love with someone else. I must do my duty to my country. You made me think seriously about what it means to be a prince. The most dangerous woman in the world.

Kate sighed. "Bloody hell . . ."

TWENTY

As the wyverns began to descend, Cieleterre came into view. The city was built on the floor of an expansive valley surrounded by mountains on all sides.

Cecile pointed out the sights as they drew near. Kate was particularly interested in the large amphitheater north of the city.

"This is where the trial will be held," said Cecile. "The amphitheater is a natural phenomenon formed by a dry lake bed. During the Dark Ages, storms raged over the world. The torrential rains created a lake. When the storms stopped, the lake dried up, leaving behind this circular, shallow bowl. The dragons decided this would be an excellent place to hold their Grand Gatherings. They paved it with flagstone and added benches for human visitors. They call it Grayhollow."

Kate pressed her face to the cold glass to see.

"I do not know how a court-martial is managed," Cecile continued. "In a Grand Gathering, each of the eight noble families is represented by the current head of the family, either male or female. The eight sit at compass points around Grayhollow. The highest-ranking dragons—the two dukes—sit at the head, which is north. The six dragon nobles range around them, each in his or her proper station."

Kate was daunted by the thought. Grayhollow was enormous. She tried to picture herself standing in the center of the amphitheater, surrounded by dragons, and her courage nearly failed her.

"Where do you suppose they are holding Dalgren?" Kate asked, shivering despite the warmth of the bricks in the carriage. "Is there such a thing as a dragon dungeon or prison?"

"I have never heard of one," said Cecile. "I will find out for you. My son and Sophia and I are the guests of a former member of the Dragon Brigade who has an estate not far from the city. He will know the answer. I will send you a message. Where are you staying?"

"I have no idea," said Kate, adding with a shrug, "I suppose there are inns . . ."

Cecile looked grave. "Not all the humans who work for the dragons are minstrels and portrait artists. Some of the inns in this city have a most unsavory reputation. A gentlewoman such as yourself cannot be too careful, especially as you are appearing before the Gathering. I recommend the Dragon Foot Inn. It is owned by a respectable widow, who will take good care of you. I will speak to the widow on your behalf."

Kate thanked her, grateful for the suggestion, though she couldn't help but inwardly smile to think of herself as a "gentlewoman."

The coach landed at the Cieleterre Docks. Large naval ships could not sail into the mountains. The Breath was far too thin here to support them. But smaller boats such as yachts were able to sail to the city, and required a place to dock.

The dragons had created berths made of wood that resembled cradles. The yachts rested in those, tethered to docking posts, their buoyancy neutral. The dragons had also built stables to house wyverns and horses, along with housing for grooms and drivers.

The coachman advised the ladies to remain in the carriage until the coach was safely docked and he and the stable hands released the wyverns and led them away.

While the ladies were waiting, two officers emerged from a yacht bearing the official emblem of the Brigade. They caught sight of Cecile's coach and came over to pay their respects to her and the princess. Cecile lowered the window to speak to them. Judging by their conversation, the officers were friends with the countess's son, for they asked about the Duke de Bourlet and where they might find him.

Cecile replied that the duke, as well as herself and the princess, were guests of Lord Haelgrund.

"Do you know where the dragons are holding the accused?" Cecile asked. "They have him secure, I trust."

"Your ladyship has no reason to worry," said one of the officers. "The accused has given his word he will not attempt to escape. Being a noble dragon, his word is his bond."

"I hear he is residing in a cave near Grayhollow," his friend added.

Cecile glanced at Kate, who thanked her with a smile.

"Look, my lady!" Sophia cried suddenly, pointing out the window to the dockyard. "Miri and Gythe are here! Did you know they were coming?"

"I did not, but I am very glad to see them," said Cecile with a warm smile.

The princess leaned out the window to call and wave her handkerchief. Kate was surprised to see she was waving to two women who were working on the deck of a Trundler houseboat tied up at the docks. With its gaily-colored balloons and bright sails, the houseboat looked very much out of place, like a wildflower blooming in the midst of a carefully manicured garden of the staid and elegant yachts.

A Trundler woman remarkable for her fiery red hair was busily sweeping the deck. The other woman, who was slight and blond, climbed like an acrobat among the rigging. A large orange cat roamed the deck with stately dignity, as though he were the true master.

Trundlers went everywhere, for the nomadic people claimed the entire world as home. Kate had never imagined they would roam as far as the Dragon Duchies, though, and she could not fathom how Trundlers could be on such intimate terms with a princess of Rosia.

"Come visit us, Sophia!" the red-haired woman shouted.

"We will! We promise! Miri is here," Sophia added, settling back in her seat. "I am so glad. That is excellent news for your friend Lord Dalgren. I hope we have time to visit with them."

"We will make the time," said Cecile. "I have not talked with them since the wedding. They have recently been Below with Father Jacob. I look forward to hearing news about him and how he progresses among the Bottom Dwellers."

Kate longed to ask what this "Miri" could have to do with Dalgren's case, but she didn't have the chance. The coachman told them that the wyverns were secure, the servants had unloaded the luggage, and they could transfer to the horse-drawn carriage sent by Lord Haelgrund to convey them to the dragon's castle.

Cecile asked the driver to take Kate to the Dragon Foot Inn. The carriage rolled through wide streets lined with picturesque buildings made of wood from the pine forests. Some of the buildings, especially the houses, appeared to be uninhabited. The city had been all but abandoned after the king had disbanded the Dragon Brigade, fearing the wrath of the dragons. Cecile had said that after the war, people were starting to return. The city was awakening from a long slumber.

They arrived at the inn, which was constructed of pine logs with lead-paned windows, a steep roof, and overhanging eaves. When they arrived, the countess descended to introduce Kate to the widow, while Sophia elected to remain in the carriage with Bandit to keep him from nipping at the horses.

"Good-bye, Your Highness," said Kate, holding out her hand. "Thank you for everything."

Sophia ignored Kate's hand to fling her arms around her in a warm embrace.

"I will come tomorrow to help you dress," Sophia promised. "I hope all goes well when you meet your friend."

Kate thanked Sophia, gave Bandit a pat on the head, and climbed out of the carriage. She found Cecile asking the inn's servants to remove a trunk from the top of the carriage.

"But that trunk is not mine, my lady," Kate said in a whisper, embarrassed.

"It is now, Mistress Katherine," said Cecile with a smile. "A gift from Sophia."

The inn's interior was rustic and cozy, warmed by a roaring fire in an enormous stone fireplace.

The proprietor was a woman in her middle years, dressed all in black. She was pleased to see the countess, and agreed at once to look after Kate, promising to give her the finest room in the house.

"I am only sorry I cannot stay here myself, ma'am," said Cecile. "We are guests of the dragon Lord Haelgrund and his mate. I hope your business is prospering."

"Better than it was before the war, my lady," the widow answered. "What with the signing of the treaty and dragons such as Lord Haelgrund building new palaces, people have started to move back to the city. And the court-martial has attracted quite a bit of interest. I have several officers staying here in order that they may attend."

She excused herself and bustled away to supervise the servants, who had entered with the luggage.

"I wish you and Lord Dalgren a fortunate outcome, Mistress," said Cecile, taking her leave.

"Thank you, Your Ladyship," said Kate. "Please, before you go, I came here with another purpose. I have information that could be of immense importance to the dragons, but I do not know who to tell. Perhaps Lord Haelgrund could help in that regard."

Cecile raised an eyebrow, then frowned. "Does this have something to do with Lord Dalgren?"

"No, my lady, it does not. I assure you," Kate replied. "I would confide in you, but I think the dragons should hear it first."

"I will speak to the Duke of Talwin," said Cecile. "Although I cannot promise he will receive you."

"Thank you, my lady," said Kate.

The countess gave her a final intense look, then departed. The widow showed Kate to her room.

"I hope you don't mind, Mistress, but I told the maids to unpack for you," said the widow. "Since you didn't bring a servant of your own."

Kate found the maids laying out a dress of lovely patterned silk in shades of muted rose and green, with elbow-length sleeves trimmed in lace, lace petticoats, delicate silk stockings, and silk undergarments.

Kate smiled, then sighed. She had come to like and admire Sophia so much that if Thomas were here, she would have told him he was a great fool not to marry her this instant.

The widow offered to bring Kate a late luncheon on a tray. Kate was too nervous to eat, however. She wrapped herself in her fur coat, tied a scarf around her head, and tucked a pistol into her boot. She then asked the widow for directions to Grayhollow, saying she planned to walk.

"The walk will be a long one, Mistress, and there is not much to see," said the widow.

"I am attending the court-martial tomorrow," said Kate. "I would like to acquaint myself with the setting."

The widow was immensely curious and plied Kate with questions, which Kate deftly avoided answering.

"If I could have a lantern, as well," said Kate. "I may not return until late."

"You should not be out alone after dark, ma'am," said the widow. "Let me summon a carriage and send one of the male servants to accompany you."

Kate was hoping to find Dalgren, and she did not want the encumbrance of a carriage or a servant. She assured the widow she would be fine, picked up the lantern, and hurried out the door before the widow could stop her.

The city of Cieleterre was charming. The streets were lined with maple trees and evergreens. The air was crisp with the scent of pine. The leaves of the maples were starting to change to blaze red. Many of the buildings were constructed of logs, similar to the inn, while others were made of native stone.

Cieleterre was now a busy, bustling city. Masons covered in stone dust talked to architects encumbered with sheaves of paper. A group of strolling musicians strummed their instruments. Taverns were doing a good business. A priest shepherded a flock of schoolchildren who were leaving school for the day. Wagons rumbled down the wide streets, hauling supplies that ranged from beer to barrel hoops to barley.

At any other time Kate would have enjoyed these sights, but now she scarcely cast them a glance. She hurried down the street until it came to an end, then followed the road that led to Grayhollow.

All she could think about was Dalgren.

TWENTY-ONE

Grayhollow was a place of stark beauty and awful majesty. Kate stood in the center of the amphitheater, surrounded by mountains, and felt isolated and alone, as though she was the only person left alive in the world.

The sun was already disappearing behind the western peaks, although the sky remained bright. Cold air flowed down from the mountains. Kate shivered beneath her coat and gazed around, wondering where to even start her search for Dalgren, and focused on two dragons relaxing in a field not far from Grayhollow.

The dragons were wearing the sashes bearing the insignia of the Dragon Brigade. Assuming that they must have something to do with the court-martial, Kate walked toward them.

The dragons had been watching her since her arrival and observed her approach with interest. They raised their heads to greet her, but did not rise. They sat with their wings folded, tails curled around their legs. She saw one say something to the other, probably wondering what she was doing out here by herself.

As Kate drew nearer, she became aware of the entrance to a cavern almost hidden by sheltering trees.

This must be the cave where they are keeping Dalgren, Kate realized. These dragons must be his guards.

She noticed a horse tied to a tree and she wondered if a human Brigade officer was also present, standing guard. She had not counted on having to explain herself to a human. Her nervousness and anxiety increased.

One of the dragons rose to greet her, uncurling his tail and politely extending his wings. He was an immense dragon, seventy-five feet from his head to the tip of his tail with the long, arching neck that indicated he was a dragon of noble blood. He was imposing, with vivid green scales and a dark green crest and mane.

"I am Lord Haelgrund of His Majesty's Dragon Brigade," said the dragon by way of introduction. "How may I be of assistance, Madame?"

Kate swallowed and drew in a deep breath.

"I would like to speak to Lord Dalgren."

Lord Haelgrund blinked at her in astonishment, his crest twitching. His fellow raised his head, equally astonished. The two dragons glanced at each other. Kate had the impression that such a circumstance was without precedent and neither knew what to do.

"What business do you have with the accused, Madame?" Lord Haelgrund asked.

"I am his friend," said Kate. "My name is Katherine Gascoyne-Fitzmaurice. I have known Lord Dalgren for many years and I have come to speak in support of him at his trial."

The two dragons conferred briefly in their own language, then Lord Haelgrund turned to her. "Lord Dalgren is currently with the Duke de Bourlet. You must ask permission of His Grace, of course, but I do not think he will mind if you join them."

Kate clenched her fists beneath her cloak in frustration. She wanted to talk to Dalgren alone, and now she had to contend with this duke who was, she recalled, the son of the Countess de Marjolaine.

"How is Lord Dalgren?" Kate asked abruptly. "Is he well?"

"He is at peace," said Lord Haelgrund.

Kate didn't like the sound of that. She gave a curt nod and turned her footsteps toward the cavern. As she went, she wondered why this duke would be talking to Dalgren.

"If he is saying anything to upset him, I will throw him out on his ear," Kate said to herself.

The cavern was dark. Kate had to pause to allow her eyes to adjust and even then she found it difficult to see where she was going. She could have lighted the lantern, but she was not yet ready to reveal her presence. She wanted to hear what this duke was saying. She quietly placed the lantern on the floor at the entrance and stole inside.

As her eyes grew accustomed to the darkness, she saw that the floor had been magically planed smooth, as were the walls and the ceiling. The atmosphere was oppressive, more like a mausoleum than a prison. She could hear a human talking in low tones, but she could not understand what he was saying. She crept closer, touching the wall with her hand to guide her.

A faint light shone in the very back of the cavern. As she drew nearer, she could dimly make out Dalgren. He was lying on his belly, his head resting on the cold stone floor. The man standing in front of him must be the Duke de Bourlet. He sounded angry, and Kate was incensed until she heard what he was saying and realized he was not angry at Dalgren.

"I confronted your father, Count Mirgrouff, last night. He has been spreading outrageous lies about you and I told him that if he did not stop, I would inform His Grace, the Duke of Talwin. Your father was at the Battle of the Royal Sail, but he has some deranged ideas regarding what happened there. I came to assure you that I do not believe his lies and neither do your comrades-in-arms."

"Thank you, Captain," Dalgren said in a low voice. "Your support means a great deal to me."

"I have been told you plan to refuse to speak in your own defense," the duke continued.

"I am guilty, Captain," said Dalgren. "I deserted my post. I will not make excuses."

"You would *not* be making excuses," the duke argued. "You need to tell the court what happened that terrible day. They need to hear how you and I saw our comrades blown apart by our own cannons! You were wounded. My dear friend Lady Cam gave her life trying to protect me."

"You did not desert, sir," said Dalgren.

"I considered it!" said the duke. "I was fortunate that King Alaric disbanded the Brigade soon after or I might be facing trial myself. The court needs to hear your story."

The man's voice sent a thrill through Kate. She knew him! She moved to where she could see his face reflected in the light. He was older, of course, but Kate would have known him anywhere. Every time she had looked at the little note she had written so long ago, she had heard his voice.

Fight for your dreams . . .

"Lieutenant de Guichen!" Kate gasped.

Stephano de Guichen was not a lieutenant any more, of course. He was now, apparently, His Grace, the Duke de Bourlet, wearing a frock coat and silk stockings, not the split leather coat of a dragon rider.

Stephano had been in his mid-twenties when she first met him. He must be in his forties now. His sandy blond hair was graying at the temples and his hairline was receding. He had not let wealth go to his belly, as the saying went. He was still fit, with the light-boned, slim build of a dragon rider. He turned to see her. His blue-gray eyes were shadowed, graver, more serious, and they were now narrowed in perplexity.

"You have the advantage of me, Madame," he said.

As Kate advanced, Dalgren opened his eyes wide. A flicker of light shone for an instant and then the light died. His eyes went dark.

Kate was chilled. She gave him an encouraging smile, then turned to respond to Stephano.

"I was a child when you last saw me, Your Grace. I had sneaked into the Brigade's fortress in Westfirth. Dalgren was coming down for a landing and I didn't see him. You knocked me down and threw yourself on top of me. You saved my life. I am Katherine Gascoyne-Fitzmaurice."

"Good God!" Stephano exclaimed, smiling. "The little girl with the big name!" He advanced to shake hands. "I have often wondered what became of that brash, adventurous little imp. Given your antics that day, I feared the worst. What are you doing here?"

"You introduced me to Dalgren that day, sir," Kate reminded him. "He and I have been friends ever since."

"Ah, of course," said Stephano. He was still smiling, but his eyes were thoughtful. "I should have known. Were you summoned to attend the court-martial?"

"I came on my own, sir," said Kate. "I hope to be able to speak in Dalgren's defense. I knew he would refuse to speak himself. He still bears the scars from that battle."

"We all do," said Stephano, looking grave.

"Could you arrange for me to speak, sir?" Kate asked.

"This is a Brigade matter and that decision will be up to those who sit in judgment," said Stephano. "I will put in a request, Mistress Katherine, but they may not permit it."

"Thank you, Your Grace," said Kate. She turned to Dalgren. "Even if I cannot speak for you, dear friend, at least you know I am here. You will not have to go through this alone."

Dalgren lowered his head so that his chin scraped her hand and made a soft rumbling sound deep in his chest.

Stephano looked from him to Kate.

"I must take my leave," he said abruptly. "My best wishes, Lord Dalgren. Whatever happens tomorrow, know that I am proud to have served with you."

Stephano gave Kate a reassuring smile and hurried off, leaving her and Dalgren alone.

"Duke or not, he is a true gentleman," Kate said, looking after him with admiration.

Dalgren seemed deeply affected by Stephano's words. He remained silent, however, gazing into the darkness, as though Kate was not there.

"Are you still angry with me, Dalgren?" she asked. "I need you to believe that I didn't kill that dragon! I was going to make Coreg tell me the name of the assassin, so that I would have proof, but Coreg—"

"I know you didn't, Kate," Dalgren said, interrupting her. "Thank you for coming, but there's no need to speak for me tomorrow. In fact, I wish you wouldn't. I have confessed my guilt. I will accept my punishment."

Kate was frightened. He had hardly glanced at her. He had not asked about Olaf or wondered how she had managed to escape the Rosian navy or ask what had become of her hair.

Dalgren closed his eyes. "I am tired. You had better go."

Kate regarded him in sorrow.

"I will see you tomorrow, my friend," she promised. "Try to get some rest. And eat something. You are nothing but scale and bone."

Dalgren didn't respond.

Kate sighed and left the cavern, remembering to pick up the lantern at the entrance. The sun had vanished, the afterglow was gone from the sky, and a few stars were visible above the mountain peaks. Lord Haelgrund was waiting for her, his bulk a deeper darkness in the night. Fire glimmered from his jaws.

"Captain de Guichen asked me to tell you that he is sending his carriage to take you back to the inn, Mistress," he informed her.

"That is very kind of him, but I could not possibly accept," Kate protested.

"The road back to Cieleterre is long and lonely," said Lord Haelgrund. "It would not be safe for you to travel."

Kate thought of the long walk back to the city in the cold and the darkness.

"The captain is very kind," she said.

Lord Haelgrund gave a fiery snort. "Kind! You obviously never trained under him. He was a stern taskmaster. I have seen him reduce dragon cadets to whimpering hatchlings with a single look."

Kate smiled faintly and sat down wearily on a boulder. "Dalgren said the same. Yet I think he would have flown to hell for the captain."

"We *did* fly to hell for him," said Lord Haelgrund grimly. "We flew with him to the bottom of the world. I will wait here with you until the carriage arrives, if that is agreeable."

"You are very kind, my lord, but that is not necessary," said Kate. "I know you have guests. You must want to join them."

"My mate will take care of our guests," said Lord Haelgrund. "She has hired minstrels and jongleurs and troubadours and a host of others to keep them entertained. I do not relish the prospect of sitting for hours on end with my wings politely folded, listening to a minstrel and trying not to disgrace myself by falling asleep."

Lord Haelgrund made himself comfortable nearby. He regarded Kate with concern.

"You are worried about Lord Dalgren."

"I have never seen him in such despair," said Kate. "He would barely look at me. He refuses to speak and he doesn't want me to do so. Captain de Guichen said something . . . I'm sorry. I mean His Grace—"

"Call him captain," Haelgrund said. "We all do. Personally I believe he prefers it."

"Very well," said Kate. "The captain said something about Dalgren's father, Count Mirgrouff, spreading lies."

Haelgrund scowled. His crest flipped in ire, his eyes narrowed to glowing slits.

"Count Mirgrouff is a wyvern's arse!" he said, snapping his teeth on the name as though he would snap Count Mirgrouff in half. "He hates Captain de Guichen, blames him for the fact that he was forced to retire from the Brigade. To my mind, Captain Thorgrimson should have thrown him out. Mirgrouff was a malcontent. He contested every order. He was constantly quarreling with his comrades. His own rider threatened to resign his commission unless he was given a different partner. No one likes him. Trust me, no one pays the least attention to what that pile of griffin shit says."

"Except Dalgren," Kate said somberly. "The count is his father. What is he saying?"

"I don't like to repeat it, but you should know," said Haelgrund. He added reluctantly, "The count claims his son fled the battle because he was a coward."

"That is not true!" Kate cried angrily.

"Everyone knows it isn't," said Haelgrund. "Unfortunately the count was present at the battle and will be given a chance to speak at the court-martial as a witness. Some of the officers who will be sitting in judgment do not know the count as we do. They may believe his lies."

"All the more reason I need to speak," Kate said. "Captain de Guichen said he would talk to the officers on my behalf."

"They will listen to him," said Lord Haelgrund. "No human is more respected among men and dragons."

Kate could tell by the dragon's guarded tone that he was merely being polite, not wanting to upset her. The truth was, he was convinced she would wasting her breath.

An elegant carriage arrived, driven by four magnificent horses—matching dapple grays—and marked with the coat of arms of the Duke de Bourlet: a rose entwined around the blade of a broadsword on a quartered field of silver and red.

As Kate entered the carriage, Lord Haelgrund added quietly, "Lord Dalgren is prepared to accept his fate, Mistress. As his friend, you should be prepared to accept it, as well."

TWENTY-TWO

At the appointed time the next day, the Countess de Marjolaine and Sophia came to the inn to help Kate dress, as the princess had promised. Sophia did not bring Bandit with her.

"He does not behave well on formal occasions," she said with a sigh. "He once disgraced himself at a knighting ceremony by nipping at the poor man's ankles as he knelt before me. Since then, he is not permitted to attend."

Sophia draped the turban around Kate's head. She and the servants helped Kate dress. Long trains were currently the fashion and Kate wondered how she would manage to walk without tripping over it.

"You have a loop here, attached to the hem at the end of the train," said Cecile. "Slip the loop over your wrist whenever you are in a crowd to pick up the train and keep it from dragging the floor."

"I failed to do that during a party and to my dismay a large Guundaran baron planted himself on my train and would not budge, no matter how many hints I gave him," said Sophia. "Rodrigo was forced to leave the room, he was laughing so hard."

Sophia held up a mirror. "You look splendid," she said.

Kate had to admit she did look good. Her hair was starting to grow back, and now covered her scalp with blond fluff. Sophia had arranged some of the fluff to show at her temples, pulling strands out from beneath the turban.

The dress was of heavy silk brocade, with an embroidered curling vine and rose pattern. She wore a chemise, silk stockings, and a lacy petticoat beneath. She had rebelled against stays. She had never worn them in her life and she was so nervous she already felt as though her chest was being squeezed.

"I hope I do not freeze," said Sophia. "I am wearing a flannel petticoat."

"I trust you are teasing, my dear," said Cecile.

"I am," said Sophia. "But I thought about it."

She was wearing an ermine-tipped fur cloak over a jacket and skirt of velvet the same color as the azure sky, and a crown of diamonds and sapphires. The countess wore a fur-lined cape of maroon silk that matched her dress. Jewels sparkled on her hat, which was trimmed with feathers. Kate tucked her red kerchief down her bodice for luck when neither was looking.

By the time their carriage arrived at Grayhollow, several dragons had already taken their places, ranged around the edge of the shallow bowl. A scattering of humans who had decided to brave the cold had gathered in a nearby field to observe the proceedings.

Kate searched for Dalgren, but could not locate him. She was impatient to leave the carriage, to see if she could find him. Cecile counseled her to wait.

"No need to leave the warmth of the carriage yet," she said. She indicated several humans and dragons who were waiting at the northern point of the compass. "Those are officers who will sit in judgment."

Kate recognized the two men who had spoken to the countess yesterday. Cecile had said these men had recently traveled from the Aligoes. Hopefully they would not connect the elegant Kate in silk brocade and furs with the convict who had escaped the hangman's noose.

The human officers were resplendent in their long leather coats, decorated with stylized dragons; plumed hats; shining brass buttons; wearing ceremonial swords and tall, polished riding boots. Each of the three noble dragons wore a silk sash in the Brigade colors of red, white, and gold around its neck.

The noble dragons crouched on the ground, their heads lowered to speak to the humans. Sunlight glittered on the scales of the dragons and flashed off the swords of the officers. As Kate watched, the human officers began to laugh uproariously. The dragons joined in, loudly chortling.

"They are enjoying themselves!" Kate said resentfully. "They don't give a damn about Dalgren!"

Cecile gave her a cool look. "You will hear much to anger and provoke you today, Mistress Katherine. You will do far better to remain calm. Let the judges see by your untroubled and relaxed demeanor that you have complete confidence in your defense of your friend."

"I will try, my lady," said Kate, who felt far from untroubled or relaxed.

"I see my son talking to the Duke of Talwin," said Cecile. "He must be arguing your cause. Stephano spoke quite highly of you to us last night, Mistress. He is most impressed by your loyalty to Dalgren."

The Duke of Talwin was an elder dragon of perhaps five hundred years or more. His scales had lost the brilliant sheen of youth and were a dull blue gray in color. His long neck was slightly stooped, his head hung down. His eyes were still bright, however.

The dragons swore fealty to the king of Rosia, but the Dragon Duchies were self-governing, each led by the head of a clan. Dalgren was a member of the Talwin clan and he always spoke of the duke with respect.

"Seeing him reminds me, I have arranged a meeting with the duke, as you asked, Mistress Katherine," said Cecile. "He will grant you an audience after the proceedings are concluded."

Kate had been so worried about Dalgren she had forgotten she had asked for the meeting. She murmured her thanks.

Stephano and the duke finished their conversation, and Stephano walked over to welcome them. He was joined by the Brigade officers, who left their dragon comrades and came to pay their respects to the princess.

The women left the carriage to greet them. Stephano performed introductions, and there was much bowing and doffing of hats, exchanging of compliments, regrets that the king could not attend, smiles and laughter.

Kate stood in the shadow of the carriage, seemingly forgotten. Only a few months ago, she and Dalgren had been flying together in the early-morning mists of the Breath as the Aligoes slept in the heat of the rising sun. She had worked hard to leave her life in the Aligoes behind. But now, more than a little overwhelmed, she wished with all her heart that she and Dalgren were back there.

She had no idea where to go or what to do. She did not even know if she would have a chance to speak. She fixed her gaze upon Stephano and waited. He was talking to a group of people and Kate did not dare interrupt. She was heartened when he glanced in her direction and gave her a nod, as though to say he had not forgotten about her.

He eventually was able to break free, and when he did so, he came straight to her.

"You will be glad to hear, Mistress Katherine, that I have obtained permission from the court for you to speak in Lord Dalgren's defense."

"Thank you, sir!" said Kate fervently.

"I hope you can help him," said Stephano somberly. He sighed when he spoke, as though his hope was a faint one.

Kate was now faced with a daunting prospect.

She could shout orders to her crew in the midst of a howling gale as her ship was sinking, and keep her nerve. But at the thought of standing by herself in front of men and dragons, her mouth went dry, her hands shook, and her stomach clenched. She pictured herself stammering and stuttering, making a fool of herself. She feared she might even throw up! She felt perilously close to sickness now, and she was tempted to run back into the carriage and hide.

And then she saw Dalgren being led forth from the cave by Lord Haelgrund. The rest of the assembly saw him at that moment. Conversation ceased, and they all turned to stare.

Dalgren walked with firm step, his head held high. He did not hesitate or falter. Lord Haelgrund escorted him to the top of a small hill away from the proceedings. Dalgren crouched on his haunches, head and neck erect, aware that all eyes were on him, and that most of the eyes were cold and disapproving.

He was putting on a brave front as befitted a soldier, but Kate could see that he was suffering. His mane quivered; he kept his jaws tightly clenched, so that not even a wisp of smoke escaped; his claws dug into the ground, his tail flicked nervously.

Kate was ashamed of her own fears.

I will not let you down, she promised silently.

The Duke of Talwin lumbered forth to escort Sophia to her place in Grayhollow. As she left, Sophia turned her head to give Kate a reassuring smile. Cecile and the others began going to take up their respective positions.

"Where do I go?" Kate frantically whispered.

"I will escort you," said Stephano.

He gave her his arm, regarding her with concern.

"Stage fright?" he asked.

Kate nodded and managed a faint smile. "I would rather be flattened by a dragon than talk before this assembly, sir. But I won't let Dalgren down."

"Good for you," said Stephano. "If it helps, don't look at anyone else. Pretend he is the only person in Grayhollow, and speak to him."

He led her to a bench located between the north and west compass points. A large dragon crouching nearby scowled at the sight of them.

"Your Grace." The dragon spoke with disdain.

Stephano answered with a smile and a polite inclination of his head.

"Count Mirgrouff," he said pleasantly. He added in a low voice for Kate's benefit, "Dalgren's father."

The count snorted a gout of flame in contempt. Stephano had not introduced Kate, for which was she glad, for then she would have had to say something to him, and she did not trust herself to be civil. As they walked past, the count stared fixedly at Kate. She knew enough about dragons to know he was trying to intimidate her. She boldly stared back at him. The count grunted and looked away.

"Why is he here?" Kate asked resentfully. "He doesn't care anything about Dalgren."

"The count is testifying against his own son," said Stephano.

Kate stared at him in shock. "*Against* Dalgren! Do you know what he will say?"

"No one knows," said Stephano. "But I fear it won't be good."

"Lord Haelgrund told me that no one in the Brigade likes him," said Kate. "Perhaps the judges won't believe him."

"Dragons are far more fair-minded than humans," said Stephano. "They do not allow personal feelings to cloud their judgment. I fear the count's testimony could be damning."

Sophia took her place upon the throne and the duke settled himself beside her, head erect, his wings folded, his tail wrapped around his feet. At this silent signal, the other dragons and humans seated themselves with a clattering of swords and a rustling of wings.

Kate sank down on the bench and clasped her cold hands together. She had looped the train over her wrist, but the loop was cutting off her circulation and she quickly released it. Her skirt with the long train fell in folds around her feet.

"I have to leave you," said Stephano. "My place is with my mother and the rest of the dignitaries."

He paused, then added, "You will hear testimony that will make you extremely angry, but you must keep silent. You may not speak until the court summons you."

Kate gave a bleak nod. She was shivering beneath her cloak.

Stephano rested his hand on her shoulder and gave her a reassuring pat. "Be brave and try not to worry."

He crossed the amphitheater, going to join his mother on a stone bench located at the east compass point to the right of the throne, directly opposite where Kate was sitting.

She kept her gaze fixed on him and was startled to notice that the Trundler women, Miri and Gythe, were sitting on the bench alongside the countess. Stephano appeared pleased to see them both. He shook hands with them and kissed each on the cheek. They moved aside to make room for him on the bench.

Kate couldn't imagine why the Trundler women would be here. The two certainly did not look like dignitaries. They were wearing typical Trundler garb: a skirt over pantaloons, peacoats, and knit stocking hats. Trundler women sailed their own boats and would often shed the skirt in order to climb the rigging. They looked warm and comfortable and very much at ease.

Stephano was talking to them and at one point he nodded toward Kate, causing the Trundlers to regard her with interest.

Four dragons wearing Brigade insignia took their places at the head of the amphitheater. They were flanked by three human officers. Since this was a dragon matter, the dragons would have the deciding vote.

Lord Haelgrund had explained the procedure of the trial to her, so that Kate knew what was going on.

A subaltern sat down on a camp stool behind the officers. He would be taking notes to be entered into the official files of the Dragon Brigade.

Dragons did not hold ranks in the Brigade as did humans. The dragon heading the proceeding would be the senior dragon in terms of years served. She introduced herself as Countess Anasi, a member of the Deehaven clan. Anasi was small for a dragon, being only about fifty feet in length, with the thick neck of a common dragon. Given that she was a countess, Kate guessed she must have married into a noble family. The scars on her body attested to her valor and courage. She had a booming voice that echoed off the nearby mountains and would have easily drowned out a cannonade.

She bowed to the princess, acknowledging the crown. Sophia rose to express her brother's regrets that he could not attend, and resumed her seat. Anasi wasted no time with further ceremony, but opened the trial.

"The accused, Lord Dalgren, son of Count Mirgrouff and Countess Faltihure, member of clan Talwin, will present himself."

Dalgren rose to his feet. Accompanied by his two escorts, he left the small rise on which he had been standing to take his place in Grayhollow. Dalgren had been wounded in the Battle of the Royal Sail and his left leg had not healed properly. He could use it, but the leg hung at an odd angle from his body and he often walked with a limp. Kate had teased him about it, claiming that his limp grew worse whenever he wanted to escape work.

Today he was making a conscious effort to put weight on his injured leg, and to walk as normally as possible.

If ever there was a time to hobble, Dalgren, this is it. Let them see you still carry the scars of battle, Kate silently urged him.

Dalgren was too proud to play for sympathy, however. He exerted every effort to disguise his injury. He took his place at the southern compass point and stood alone. His escorts settled themselves a short distance behind him.

Anasi resumed. "The account of the Battle of the Royal Sail as recorded in the official log of Commander Jeantrou, now deceased, will be read into the record by Captain Porcelli, senior Brigade officer in the absence of Captain

Dag Thorgrimson, who is currently serving in the Aligoes and is unable to attend."

Captain Porcelli came forward carrying a worn logbook in his hands. He opened it and began to read.

Kate glanced at Stephano. He sat braced, his back rigid, his expression grim; she imagined that steeling himself to listen to the account of the battle must he painful.

Following a request by General Dennis, the Dragon Brigade was dispatched to assist forces then engaged in besieging an Estaran flying fortress, the last remaining holdout of a larger enemy fleet that had sought to invade Rosia. The fortress had been strengthened by magical constructs that rendered it impervious to a week's prolonged bombardment by the Rosian navy.

The Dragon Brigade attacked the fortress. Dragon magic broke the magic of the Estarans and forced the fortress's commander to surrender. General Dennis specified the terms of surrender. I delivered them to Lieutenant Domingo Elizandro who had been left in charge of the fortress following the death of his commander. The lieutenant and Sergeant Dag Thorgrimson, commander of a unit of Guundaran mercenaries, agreed to the terms.

During the formal ceremony of surrender, a lone Estaran rifleman fired a shot at the Rosian fleet. The man was quickly subdued by Sergeant Thorgrimson and there was never a real threat. The commander of the fleet, Lord Captain William Hastind, now deceased, responded by ordering his ships' cannons to open fire on the unarmed Estarans.

The officers of the Dragon Brigade, led by Lieutenant Stephano de Guichen, had given their word of honor that the men who surrendered would not be harmed. They saw the ships running out their cannons and they flew their dragons between the fortress and the ships, hoping to ward off impending slaughter.

Lord Captain Hastind opened fire. The Estarans suffered eighty percent losses. The Dragon Brigade suffered two riders killed outright, five others were wounded.

I want to commend the dragons and riders that served at the Battle of the Royal Sail. They upheld the honor of the Brigade and the Kingdom, at a cost unseen since the Battle of Daenar. It is my wish to recognize the particular acts of heroism of Lieutenant Stephano De Guichen and Lady Cam, who was mortally wounded attempting to save her rider. In addition, I recognize

Lieutenant Fernel and his dragon, Lord Praigh; Lieutenant Moretti and his dragon, Lord Dalgren, for particular acts of bravery.

They have my admiration and my thanks. Unfortunately that is all I have to offer.

The captain finished reading and shut the logbook.

No one spoke. No one moved.

Captain Jeantrou had given a very spare account as required in a naval log until that last sentence, when he put his anger and emotion down on the page. Most of those present had served in the Brigade. They were veterans of military action and they could smell the gunpowder and the blood and hear the screams of the dying.

Stephano sat rigid and unmoving during the account. One of the Trundler women, Miri, gently rested her hand on his. Gythe whispered something to the countess, who clasped her hand. Sophia grew very pale and gave Dalgren a look of sympathy.

He had listened without any show of emotion until Captain Porcelli read the part at the end when Captain Jeantrou commended Lord Dalgren and his rider, Lieutenant Moretti. Dalgren blinked rapidly as though to clear a film from his eyes, and a thin wisp of smoke escaped from his mouth. He tightened his jaw and the smoke trailed away.

Kate glanced sidelong at Count Mirgrouff, who had been at the battle and had *not* been singled out for valor. He drew back his lip in a derisive sneer.

After a brief moment of respectful silence for those who had been lost, Anasi resumed.

"You may continue, Captain Porcelli. I believe you have something further to say to the court."

The captain reached into an inner pocket, drew out and unfolded a letter. "I received this from Sir Alonzo Moretti, formerly Lieutenant Moretti of the Dragon Brigade. Sir Alonzo was Lord Dalgren's partner. His Lordship is now living in Guundar, where he is undersecretary to our ambassador. He has asked me to read this into the record, if the court has no objection. The letter is . . . um . . . colorful, but to the point. I beg the court's pardon in advance for His Lordship's language."

Captain Porcelli cleared his throat and read.

"'I am told that Lord Dalgren is being put on trial for desertion following the unmitigated disaster I like to call the Battle of the Royal Numbskull. I want to state for the record that Lord Dalgren performed heroically during that debacle. He was the best damn partner I ever rode and in my opinion he showed remarkably good sense by quitting the Brigade, since it was obvious the goddamn navy had quit on us.

"'In fact, I would have followed his example, but I was laid up in hospital for weeks after our own bloody navy damn near blew off my head. I call it disgraceful that the Brigade has the nerve to try this heroic officer when that shit-eating horse's ass, Hastind, who gave the order to fire on his own troops, was awarded a medal. If you find Lord Dalgren guilty, you're a bunch of goddamn fools.'"

The human officers of the Brigade glanced at one another and appeared to have trouble maintaining their outward composure. Stephano put his hands to his lips as though to conceal a smile.

As Captain Porcelli folded the letter, he added dryly, "Sir Alonzo is notorious for speaking his mind."

"Indeed," said Anasi. "One can see why he is the undersecretary to the ambassador and *not* the ambassador. Thank you, Captain Porcelli."

The captain bowed and returned to his seat.

"Our next witness is Count Mirgrouff," said the countess.

Kate looked anxiously at Dalgren. He had dug his claws into the ground and braced himself as perhaps he had done that day when facing the cannon fire.

The count lumbered into the very center of Grayhollow. He did not stand erect, but crouched as though ready to spring. His head snaked around to look at the assembly.

"My name is Count Mirgrouff. I have the misfortune to be the father of the accused. I was present at the Battle of the Royal Sail. First, I want to state for the record that the account of the battle as reported by that imbecile Jeantrou is a damn lie! He and de Guichen were in collusion with the enemy commander of the fortress the entire time, as can be proven by the lamentable fact that Dag Thorgrimson is now commanding the Dragon Brigade. Captain Hastind was well within rights to fire on the traitors and all those who participated in their treachery, including my son. They got what they deserved."

Stephano sprang to his feet in anger, as Captain Porcelli and the two other officers began shouting in protest. Lord Haelgrund made a loud hissing sound, shooting flame from between his jaws. Count Mirgrouff regarded his former comrades with sneering contempt. Countess Anasi called several times for order, each time emphasizing her booming words with a thud of her massive tail.

"I am sorry you had to witness this disturbance, Your Highness," said Anasi, after the assembly had settled down. She cast a baleful glance at Lord Haelgrund. "One more outburst from you, my lord, and you will be asked to leave!"

Lord Haelgrund bowed his head, suitably chastened. Anasi shifted her gaze to Count Mirgrouff.

"These are extremely serious charges you make against His Grace, the Duke de Bourlet, my lord, and the memory of the late Captain Jeantrou. Can you prove them?"

"I know what I damn well saw," said the count sullenly.

"You are saying, then, for the record, Count Mirgrouff, that you have no proof."

Count Mirgrouff snorted and refused to answer.

Countess Anasi flicked her tail in displeasure and turned her head to the subaltern. "The count's testimony will be stricken from the record."

Count Mirgrouff lifted his wings, bared his fangs, and hissed. "Sniveling snakes, the lot of you! I would accuse you of licking the boots of this human king were it not for the fact that you are licking other portions of his anatomy!"

Sophia rose in anger. "How dare you, sir!"

The other dragons hooted in outrage. The Duke of Talwin rustled his wings and thumped the ground with his tail. Lord Haelgrund forgot himself and belched fiery disapproval.

Countess Anasi was furious. Her words came out wreathed in flame and smoke.

"You have insulted Her Highness, this court, and all those who are in attendance, Count Mirgrouff. I order you to leave Grayhollow and not return."

Count Mirgrouff shook his mane and stamped his forefeet. He was angry in turn and appeared prepared to defy the order. Mirgrouff was a large dragon. If Anasi had risen to her full height, mane and all, she would have come only up to his jaw.

She fixed him with a look, her eyes narrowed to glittering slits, and her head slightly lowered.

"I warn you, Count Mirgrouff, that if you do not leave voluntarily, I will have you removed by force."

Mirgrouff spat a gob of fiery goo onto the stones of Grayhollow, lashed his tail on the ground, lifted his wings, and flapped away. After he was gone, Lord Haelgrund walked into the center and cleaned away the defilement with a contemptive swipe of his tail.

Anasi gave dragons and humans a moment to recover from the shock. She shook herself all over, as though shaking off filth, and briskly returned to the business at hand.

"The accused will now be given a chance to speak in his own defense. Lord Dalgren, we have heard from the reading of the log and the testimony of your rider that you fought with valor and served with distinction. The court is interested in hearing your account of what happened during the Battle of the Royal Sail."

Anasi had softened her tone and was regarding him with compassion. The other dragons smiled and appeared to be trying to give him encouragement. Kate held her breath.

Dalgren lifted his head, faced the court, and spoke clearly, without a tremor.

"I am guilty of the charge of desertion. I have brought dishonor to my family and to all of dragonkind. I broke my oath. I deserve to be punished."

Anasi frowned. The human officers exchanged grim glances.

Kate forgot her fear and, with that, Stephano's warning that she should not speak until she was summoned. Jumping to her feet, she impatiently kicked aside the folds of her skirt that threatened to trip her and turned to face the court.

"I am here to speak in Lord Dalgren's defense."

TWENTY-THREE

The silence in Grayhollow was like the unending silence of the Deep Breath. The noise of life stopped and her words seemed to fall into a pit.

Dragons and humans faded into a blur so that all Kate could see were eyes and all the eyes were on her.

She looked at Dalgren and remembered Stephano's advice. Dalgren's eyes were the only eyes Kate saw, the only eyes she cared about.

"I beg the court's pardon for talking out of turn, my lady," Kate said. "Someone has to speak in Lord Dalgren's defense, especially after the lies his father told this court. I am Lord Dalgren's friend. I have known him for many years. I have asked to be allowed to say what he will not."

Countess Anasi was gracious.

"Your interruption is most irregular, Mistress Katherine. His Grace has granted you leave to appear as a witness, however, and we grant you permission. Next time, however," the countess added more severely, "you must wait until you are called upon."

"Yes, my lady," said Kate. "Thank you, my lady."

When she spoke, she spoke to her friend.

"Lord Dalgren was very young," Kate said. "He was fighting in his first battle. Those he trusted betrayed him when Captain Hastind ordered his forces to fire on their own comrades. Lord Dalgren bravely stood his ground, to defend his honor and that of the Dragon Brigade. Even when the muzzles of the cannons were aimed directly at him, he did not flee. He was wounded, struck by a cannonball. His rider was hit. He watched his best friend and mentor, Lady Cam, die a terrible death."

Dalgren was watching her in silence, his mane quivering. She continued to look at him. Her words were for him.

"Lord Dalgren was surrounded by death and fire and blood, and in that moment, he took an oath that was more important to him than the oath he had taken when he had joined the Brigade. Lord Dalgren vowed that he would never again take a life."

Kate drew in a shivering breath. Her voice trembled.

"Dalgren *is* a deserter. I admit that, as did he. But I want all of you to know that he did *not* leave because he was afraid he would be killed. He left because he was afraid that he might be ordered to kill others."

Kate stopped talking. The silence returned, flowing over her. She had no idea what the silence meant, if she had touched hearts, changed minds, or she had angered them all. She cared only for Dalgren. What did he think?

He looked at her, his eyes dimmed. His wings quivered. He lowered his head to hide his emotion.

"Thank you, Mistress Katherine," said Anasi.

Kate was shaking with relief. She was glad the bench was nearby, for she wasn't sure how far she could walk. She sank down on the cold stone and huddled beneath her fur coat to wait.

She did not have to wait long. Anasi brought the trial to a speedy conclusion. The judges withdrew to consider the evidence, the four dragons and three human officers walking into a nearby field to confer. Lord Haelgrund escorted Dalgren back to his cave.

Sophia was talking with the Countess de Marjolaine and the two Trundler women. Catching sight of Kate, the princess gestured to her, inviting her to come join them.

Kate was sick to her stomach. Her head ached. She didn't want to have to make polite conversation, talk about the trial or receive their sympathy. She pretended she didn't see Sophia and left Grayhollow, walking toward a grove of pine trees not far from the cave where Dalgren was being held.

She guessed there was no chance she would be able to talk to him, but she thought that she might be able to speak to Lord Haelgrund, get some sense of where he thought the trial might be headed. When she heard a dragon call her by name, she turned, hoping it might be Lord Haelgrund.

"Mistress Katherine, could I speak with you a moment?"

Kate looked around, but could not see him or any dragon, for that matter.

The pine trees shimmered in her vision and then slowly disappeared, revealing a stony patch of ground occupied by a female dragon.

"Forgive the illusion, Mistress Katherine," said the dragon. "I did not mean to frighten you. I had to use my magic to conceal myself. I am not supposed to be here."

"I wasn't frightened, my lady, only surprised," said Kate. "I am familiar with dragon magic."

Dragons had the ability to magically alter their physical surroundings; an old survival technique dating back to the days when dragons warred with each other and were fair game for human hunters.

Kate could tell the dragon was not a member of the Brigade, for she did not wear the insignia. She was, however, a noble dragon, judging by the sparkling blue-gray color of her scales and her long, graceful neck. When Kate saw the dragon had a twisted horn on her crest, she guessed her identity.

The first time she had met Dalgren, Kate had noticed him among the other dragons because of his twisted horn.

"You are Dalgren's mother," said Kate.

"Countess Faltihure," said the dragon, inclining her head. "I was glad to see you walk this way. I want to convey to you how much I appreciate your defense of my son."

"I was glad to defend him," said Kate, adding with a frown, "Dalgren needs the support of his friends and his family. Are you so ashamed of your own son that you choose to hide rather than be seen at his trial?"

Countess Faltihure winced. "I deserve your scorn. I hope that you will give me a chance to explain. Perhaps you will explain to my son."

"Very well," said Kate. "I am listening."

"You know that Dalgren visited Travia not long ago," said the countess.

"He went to visit his uncle," said Kate. "But I don't understand what that has to do with anything."

"Dalgren *does* have an uncle who lives in Travia," said the countess. "He did visit him, so he did not lie. But my son also came to Travia to visit me."

Kate shook her head. "Dalgren would have told me."

"He wanted to, but I begged him to keep my secret," said Countess Faltihure. "You see, no one in Rosia knows I am living in Travia."

"I don't understand," said Kate.

"You have met my mate, Count Mirgrouff," said the countess. "You heard his cruel accusations against our son. When the count threatened to disown Dalgren, I told him that if he did, I would leave him. The count had lost all reason by then and flew into a rage. When he denounced our son as a coward I was as good as my word. I left him. I flew to Travia to live with my clutch mate, Dalgren's uncle."

"I am sorry, my lady," said Kate. "I did not know. But why keep your departure a secret?"

"The count and I are forced to maintain the pretense that we are still together," said Countess Faltihure. "Dragons mate for life, as you know. Our population is small. We are meant to breed and continue our species. If our separation became general knowledge, the Duke of Talwin would be within his rights to bring the matter before the Gathering. Count Mirgrouff feared that the disgrace would ruin his military career and I feared it would harm Dalgren. I suppose that doesn't matter now," she added with a sigh. "Nothing matters now."

"Your testimony would matter a great deal to Dalgren, my lady," said Kate.

The dragon shook her head. "The count would hear I had testified and he would be furious. I have family who still reside in Rosia. The count has threatened to do harm to them if I interfere."

"Do you mean physical harm?" Kate asked, shocked.

"Nothing like that," said the countess. "But he could set fire to their forests, drive off their human workers, spread terrible rumors that would blacken their honor."

Countess Faltihure shrugged, saying grimly, "He is quite insane."

"But after the trial is over you can visit Dalgren," said Kate. "I will take you to him."

"I do not plan to stay for the end of the trial," said Countess Faltihure. "They will find Dalgren guilty and I cannot bear to see what follows. Farewell, Mistress Katherine. I am glad to know that my son has one friend in this world. Give Dalgren my love and tell him that his mother's thoughts are always with him."

The dragon made a low bow, touching her head to the ground in a show of respect before soaring into the clear sky. Kate watched the dragon until she was lost among the mountain peaks. Then she realized she had been standing still so long her feet were freezing.

She walked back and forth in the warm sunshine, afraid for Dalgren and the outcome of the trial. His mother had spoken of his punishment with horror, as a human might speak of the executioner and his bloody axe. She paced until she heard Countess Anasi raise her voice in a trumpeting call.

The sound chilled Kate's blood. The judges had reached a verdict.

TWENTY-FOUR

Kate searched the faces of Captain Porcelli and the other two human officers as they entered Grayhollow, hoping to see some indication of their decision. She wanted to believe that her testimony might have swayed them, that they had taken Dalgren's youth and inexperience into account. The officers were grim and stern as they stood at attention in front of the court.

The four dragons who wore the insignia of the Brigade returned to Grayhollow. They moved slowly, with studied formality, as they took their places around the circle. They, too, appeared grave and somber, their heads held high, wings swept back, as though they knew they had done their duty, no matter how distasteful.

None of them looked at Dalgren.

Amelia had told Kate once that a jury never looked at the defendant they have just convicted. She sank down onto the bench, sick and despairing.

"You should not be alone, Mistress Katherine," Countess Anasi said to her gently. "The court grants you leave to join your friends."

Kate looked across Grayhollow at Stephano and his mother, Miri and Gythe, and Sophia on her throne. The Trundlers and Stephano spoke together, not paying attention. Cecile was watching the proceedings with seeming fatigue. Sophia was fidgeting with her cloak, absently smoothing the fur. She seemed remote, abstracted.

None of them care anything for Dalgren, Kate thought resentfully. She wanted to sit here, alone, until she could be with him.

"Mistress Katherine," said Countess Anasi.

She was watching her expectantly. Kate realized that the suggestion had not been a suggestion. It was an order.

The human officers were seating themselves, shifting the ceremonial swords that hung at their sides, clanking and rattling. Kate remembered at the last moment to loop up her train. She rose to her feet with the feeling everyone was staring at her, and hurried across Grayhollow, hoping to escape notice, and not paying attention to where she was going. A shadow fell over her, and she looked up to see the Duke of Talwin looking down.

His eyes were opaque, yet his gaze followed her. Kate slid past the duke and came to stand several feet from Stephano and his friends, keeping the stone bench between them.

She hoped to make it clear she did not want their company, but apparently she failed, because Stephano walked over to speak to her.

"We have room if you would like to sit down, Mistress Katherine," he said.

Kate stared straight ahead, her arms folded across her chest. "Thank you, Your Grace, but I prefer to stand."

She was being deliberately rude, hoping he would walk off, offended. He looked grave, but he remained standing at her side.

The dragons crouched on their haunches, wings at their sides, tails curled around their feet. The humans stood with their hands on the hilts of their swords.

"Bring forth the accused," Anasi called.

Lord Haelgrund escorted Dalgren from his cave. He took his place in front of the court and waited, unmoving, to hear his fate.

"Have the officers selected to sit in judgment on the accused reached a verdict, Captain?" Anasi asked.

Captain Porcelli stood up. "We have, my lady."

"Is the verdict unanimous among men and dragons, Captain?"

"It is, my lady."

"What is the verdict, Captain?"

Dalgren stood rigid, staring straight ahead at the distant mountains. Perhaps in his mind he was flying free among the snow-capped peaks. Kate stopped breathing.

"We find Lord Dalgren guilty, my lady."

Kate clenched her fists and blinked back stinging tears. Stephano stirred, as though he would say something to comfort her. Kate turned away, not wanting to hear his empty platitudes.

The countess asked each judge in turn, first the humans and then the dragons. "Guilty," said one and "guilty" said another. When the final "guilty" echoed off the sides of the mountains and died away, Countess Anasi waited a moment in solemn, respectful silence, then addressed the assembly.

"You, the accused, Lord Dalgren of the clan of Talwin, have been found guilty of desertion. This is a most reprehensible crime, reflecting as it does upon the honor of all of dragonkind. Every dragon, noble and common, master and servant, civilized and wild, has been dishonored by your actions. The sentence for such a crime is severe. Lord Dalgren, step forward."

Dalgren had to walk only a few paces to reach the outer edge of Grayhollow. He maintained his courage, holding his head high, clenching his jaw.

"Lord Dalgren, you are sentenced to undergo the Banishing. Your name will never again be spoken by man or dragon. Henceforth, you will have no name. You are exiled from the Dragon Duchies. You are stripped of your lands and title. No dragon, on pain of suffering the same fate, will have any contact with you. You will go forth from here and never return."

Her words might well have been a barrage of cannon fire. Dalgren shuddered as each word slammed into him. His head sagged, his shoulders slumped, his body sank lower and lower to the ground.

"Stop it!" Kate shouted, choking on her rage and her tears. "Stop it! You are killing him!"

Countess Anasi fixed Kate with glittering eyes.

"Mistress, be silent—"

"Dalgren!" Kate cried, defiantly using his name. "Dalgren, *I* speak your name with pride! Come with me! You and I don't need these fools!"

Dalgren refused to even look at her.

Kate wanted to leave, to go talk to him, to be with him, to proudly stand at his side. Stephano placed a restraining hand on her arm and took firm hold of her.

"Sit down, Captain Kate," he said. "You are drawing unwanted attention to yourself."

Kate was about to angrily shake free of his grip when she realized that he was no longer calling her "Mistress Kate." He had called her "Captain." She stared at him, astonished.

"How did you know?" she asked in a low voice.

"I am not the only one with the ability to connect the name 'Katherine' with the sobriquet 'Kate.'"

He cast a significant glance at Captain Porcelli, who was staring at Kate with unusual intensity and frowning thoughtfulness.

"If he figures out that you are the Captain Kate who escaped from prison and cheated the hangman, you will be in serious trouble."

Kate sank down on the bench, biting her lip until she tasted blood mingling with her tears.

"Did Dalgren know about this . . . this Banishment?" she asked, choked.

"He knew of the possibility," Stephano replied, seating himself beside her. "He was clinging to the slim hope that the sentence would not be so harsh."

"He will always have a home with me!" Kate said vehemently. "He will always be Dalgren to me. He knows that!"

"But you do not know him if you think that would be enough," said Stephano. "He is a dragon without a name, without a nation, without a family. It is as if they had told him he is no longer a dragon."

Kate knew he was right. A name for a dragon meant far more than a word by which he was known. A name was an integral part of the dragon's being. The ceremony of acquiring a name was the most important event of the dragon's life. His name became the standard that he carried proudly before him.

Since dragon names were extremely long and unpronounceable, dragons generally had two names: the sacred name by which they were known to dragonkind and a name used by humans. Dalgren had once told Kate his true name and she had likened it to the sound of rocks cascading down the side of a mountain. But to Dalgren, using even his human name would be a disgrace. The wounds the dragons had inflicted upon him were mortal. He would slink off by himself to die of grief and shame and she would never see him again.

She turned to face Stephano. "Let me go to him, sir. I will make him listen to me! I don't care if they arrest me. I will give myself up after the trial."

"Hold your fire, Captain," said Stephano. "Now is the time for soft words, not bold deeds."

Kate frowned, not knowing what he meant.

"There *are* such times," Stephano added with a wry smile. "A hard lesson, I know. I had to learn it myself."

Kate decided to trust him. After all, she didn't have much choice. She resumed her seat.

"The convicted has the right to appeal this decision," said Countess Anasi.

Dalgren sank down on his belly and lay flat, crushed into the ground. He did not speak. He did not stir a claw or move a muscle.

Stephano glanced around at his mother, at Sophia, at the two Trundler women, and Kate realized with a sudden thrill that he was summoning them to battle. She could tell by the tension in his body, the faint smile on his lips, the expectant glitter in his blue eyes.

Soft words, he had said. *Not bold deeds.*

Sophia rose majestically from her throne.

"The crown appeals this decision on behalf of the accused," Sophia called out. "By the rights granted to Rosia under the Treaty of D'eau Brisé, the crown asks that the court hear one more witness—the Master of Dragon Lore."

Kate had heard of the Master of Dragon Lore. Dalgren had told her about this person—a human who spent a lifetime maintaining a written record of dragon history, traditions, heritage, and laws.

In the early days, dragon families had lived isolated lives in their caves in the mountains and relied on oral tradition to maintain family history, handing it down from one generation to the next. Over the centuries, the dragons forgot events, misremembered them, or even attempted to expunge them. Dragons grew concerned that much of their history, laws, and traditions were being lost.

When dragons first started to interact with humans back in the days of the Sunlit Empire, dragons were impressed with the human concept of keeping written records. The families employed human scribes to keep records for them and selected a single human, known and trusted by all, to gather and maintain the records. The human was known as the Master of Dragon Lore.

"The Master is welcome," said Countess Anasi. "We will hear the Master's judgment on this case."

Kate regarded Stephano in bewilderment. "What does the Master have to do with this?"

"When disputes arise between clans or family members, they can call upon the Master to resolve it, based on the reading of the dragon lore," Stephano said.

"There is hope?" Kate asked.

"There is always hope, Captain," Stephano replied.

Kate looked around Grayhollow and realized that the dragons had, of course, been aware of the presence of the Master of Dragon Lore. They had known all along that if the verdict went against Dalgren, the Master would have something to say about it.

Kate even had the impression they were looking forward to it, for they were making themselves comfortable, relaxing, settling down on their bellies, prepared to give the Master their full attention.

For their part, the human officers were alarmed. Dragons are passionately fond of legal arguments and can sit for days, happily debating some fine point of dragon law that went back a thousand years.

Only Dalgren paid no heed. The dragon crouched on his haunches, his head bowed so low that his twisted horn brushed the ground. Sunk in despair, he had no hope.

The red-haired Trundler woman, Miri, rose from the bench and, to Kate's astonishment, went to stand in front of the assembly. The dragons greeted her with respect, dipping their heads and gently thumping their tails. Kate recalled the countess saying that Miri's arrival was good news for Dalgren and now she understood why.

"Thank you, Countess Anasi," said Miri. She turned to the dragons and made a formal introduction, although by their looks of respect, they already knew her. "I am Miri McPike, the Master of Dragon Lore, and I am honored to be among you."

Miri was about Stephano's age, close to forty years, perhaps. She smiled at him as she took her place; Kate saw him return her smile.

Kate realized that they must have planned this all along. Stephano had known they would convict Dalgren. He had known that they would sentence him to the Banishment, and he had come prepared. Kate reproached herself. She should have trusted him.

Miri cut an odd-looking figure, bundled in her peacoat, her red curls flaring out from beneath the stocking hat, far different from the elegantly dressed princess and the Countess de Marjolaine. No one seemed to care how she was dressed. Miri certainly did not. She spoke with confidence and authority. The dragons listened with attentive interest.

"At the request of His Grace, the Duke de Bourlet, and His Grace, the Duke of Talwin, I have been asked to delve into the history of the sentence known as the Banishing.

"The sentence dates back to the time of the fall of the Sunlit Empire, being one of a series of laws created by the first Gathering. This is according to a human scribe who was given the task of recording these laws," Miri stated. "The Banishing was to be used for only the most heinous crimes, such as the willful killing of a human or another dragon. When the Dragon Brigade was formed, the dragons instituted the Banishment as the proper punishment for desertion, based on the fact that humans punish this crime by death.

"The Banishment strips a dragon of his name and exiles him from the land of his birth. The sentence is the most severe that can be handed down among dragonkind. Both the Duke de Bourlet and the Duke of Talwin have expressed concern, as have many of you, that the sentence is excessively harsh and cruel. Unlike other forms of punishment, the Banishing is singular in that it offers the guilty no hope of redemption."

The dragons appeared struck by this argument. Several exchanged glances and nodded their heads.

"I discovered in doing my research that when the Gathering first instituted the Banishment, they made provision that the dragon given this sentence could have the chance to earn back his name, restore his honor, and return to the land of his birth, if he so chooses."

"Oh, I am so glad!" Sophia cried, jumping to her feet and clapping her hands.

Countess Anasi and everyone else in Grayhollow looked at her. Abashed, Sophia blushed and sat back down.

Kate was watching Dalgren. He had at least raised his head; his eyes had lost their dull, uncomprehending stare.

The other dragons appeared to be reflecting on what they had heard, considering the possibilities.

"How can the Banished redeem himself, Master?" Countess Anasi asked.

"According to the old records, my lady, if the judges approve, the Banished can find redemption by—and here I quote from the old records—'undertaking a quest both perilous and selfless.'"

"Do you know why the chance for redemption was dropped from the records, Master?" the Duke of Talwin asked.

"I cannot be certain, Your Grace. We can only surmise that it was lost during the Dark Ages when records were destroyed in flood and fire."

"And what should be done?" Anasi asked.

"Provided the judges agree that the Banished should be given a chance to redeem himself, the court would devise a suitable quest for him. If the court pleases, I have a quest in mind which would, I believe, fulfill the requirements of the old law," Miri said. "I am friends with Father Jacob Northrop of the Arcanum—a human known to many of you for his interest in dragonkind, particularly dragon magic."

"Father Jacob is known to us," said Anasi, nodding her head.

"Father Jacob currently lives Below with those called the Bottom Dwellers. Many of you who served with the Dragon Brigade accompanied Captain de Guichen Below to put an end to the contramagic that was killing your children. After the war, the world Above forgot about the Bottom Dwellers, leaving them to survive in a land ravaged by terrible storms, bereft of sunlight and the contramagic that kept them alive. Father Jacob has been working among the people, helping them to rebuild their lives.

"I suggest to the court that if the dragon who has been Banished is willing to undergo a year of hard, physical labor assisting Father Jacob, he could petition the court for the opportunity to restore his name. While this is not exactly a 'quest perilous,'" Miri added with a grave smile, "many of you know I have traveled Below and can attest to the fact that the journey is dangerous."

"Thank you, Master of Dragon Lore," said Anasi. "The judges will retire to consider this new information."

The human officers rose with alacrity; hoping that the end of this trial was in the offing and they could return to their yachts or their inns. The dragons joined them and they retired once again to the field.

Kate turned to Stephano. "Will they agree to let Dalgren make this quest, sir?"

"I believe they will," said Stephano, smiling. "The Master is held in high regard."

Kate sighed in relief. "How long have you known who I was, sir?"

Stephano smiled. "The truth wasn't very hard to figure out, Captain. I knew that Dalgren had a human partner in the Aligoes. I had read the stories in the *Haever Gazette* about a 'dragon corsair' known as Captain Kate and her dragon partner. I would be a simpleton, indeed, if I did not make the connection when I heard your name."

"Does your mother know?" Kate asked anxiously. Before he could reply, she hurriedly added, "I should have told her the truth from the outset. She and the princess were both so kind to me—"

Stephano laughed. "My mother knew the truth the moment she heard you tell the innkeeper you were desperate to reach Cieleterre. Very little happens in the world that my mother does *not* know," he added dryly and somewhat grimly.

"And the Princess Sophia?" Kate ventured.

"She knows, as well, for the countess told her," said Stephano. "Indeed, you were the subject of much lively discussion at the dinner table between Lord Haelgrund, myself, my mother, and Her Highness last night. I am surprised your ears did not burn. We agreed you were most shamefully treated by the Rosian navy and that bastard Favager."

"I do not understand, sir," said Kate, bewildered. "How could you possibly know that?"

"My friend Captain Dag Thorgrimson wrote to tell me that your ship was fired upon *after* you had surrendered. Dag had heard that you and your crew were privateers, men holding letters of marque from Freya, and, as such, you were not subject to arrest or execution. The Lords of the Admiralty also received a letter from His Highness, Prince Thomas Stanford, accusing Captain Favager of submitting a false report and asking for pardons for your crew. You will be pleased to know that Favager will face court-martial himself. He has subsequently been relieved of his command."

Kate heard Thomas's name and a warm flush stole over her. Stephano had been so kind, she felt honor bound to tell him the truth now as she had done when she was a little girl and he had caught her sneaking onto the base.

"I did surrender my ship, sir, that much is true," said Kate. "But you should know that my surrender was a ruse. I planned to escape if I could, sail my ship down into the Deep Breath."

"I suspected as much," said Stephano. "I know that trick myself. I used it on occasion during my own smuggling days."

Seeing Kate's amazement, he added with a laugh, "I was not always a duke. I did not desert the Dragon Brigade, but I resigned my commission following the battle. My mother and I were estranged at the time. I would have starved to death before I asked her for a crust of bread. I had to earn a living somehow. But now we must worry about you."

"Do you think Captain Porcelli or any of the others suspect?" Kate asked.

"They have said nothing to me," said Stephano. "But I would not remain in Rosia long if I were you, Captain. Porcelli cannot arrest you while you are in the Dragon Duchies. Once you leave these borders, however, you will enter Rosia and you will be subject to Rosian law. I do not think they could execute you, since you were a privateer, not a pirate. But you did break the law by escaping from prison. I fear at the very least you would find yourself back in a Rosian jail."

Kate nodded absently. Her gaze was fixed on Dalgren. She didn't know whether to hope the judges granted him the right to redeem himself by undertaking a journey Below or to uphold the sentence of Banishment. Either way, it seemed to her Dalgren was doomed to die.

"You made the journey Below, Captain," she said. "What is it like? Is it as dreadful as they say?"

"I will never forget it," said Stephano. "To reach the land of the Bottom Dwellers, Dalgren will have to fly far below the Breath. He will have to endure bitter cold that freezes the blood and rimes his scales and his wings with ice. If he survives that journey, he will be forced to live among people who have no love for dragons. He will have to endure the fearsome wizard storms that still sweep the land and keep it in near constant night. He will rarely see the sunlight and never feel its warmth. And he will be constantly hungry, for the food supply is scarce for humans and far scarcer for dragons."

"Do you know this Father Jacob Northrop?" Kate asked.

All she knew about him was that he was a famous savant who had discovered the seventh sigil and revolutionized magic. But he was also a priest of the Arcanum, the most feared order in the Church of the Breath, tasked with upholding the laws of the Church and mercilessly tracking down malefactors. One glimpse of the priests in their black robes and people crossed to the other side of the street.

"Father Jacob is a good man," said Stephano. "Though a bit peculiar."

Kate sighed and chafed her cold hands. "I wish they would hurry! What is taking them so long?"

"You acted bravely and nobly, Captain, coming here to speak in defense of your friend when you risked discovery yourself. Keep up your courage," Stephano advised.

The judges did not confer long. They returned to Grayhollow and this time Kate could see that the humans, at least, appeared pleased, for they were smiling. The dragons were more difficult to read, but Kate saw some of them nod to Dalgren, when last time they had studiously avoided even looking at him.

"Have you reached a decision?" Countess Anasi asked.

"We have, my lady," said Captain Porcelli. "We have agreed that the Banished should be given the chance to redeem himself by performing the task suggested by the Master of Dragon Lore. The Banished is to spend one year Below, assisting Father Jacob with whatever he requires. At that time, he may return to the Dragon Duchies to petition the court to restore his name. We do stipulate that in so doing he will not regain his title nor his land holdings. He will, however, have the right to mate, start a family, and make his own way in the world."

Countess Anasi summoned Dalgren to come forward.

"Does the Banished choose to accept this challenge?" she asked.

Dalgren stood at attention, his head held high, his wings tight against his sides, his tail flat along the ground. The fire burning in his belly seemed to have illuminated his entire being. His eyes shone with newfound hope.

"I accept the challenge," said Dalgren. "I am grateful to the court for granting me this chance to redeem myself. I will travel Below and there I will work tirelessly to restore my name."

"Then this court is adjourned," said Countess Anasi.

TWENTY-FIVE

After court was adjourned, the dragons and humans were free to relax and mingle. Captain Porcelli and his fellows spoke of past times in the service with several dragon members of the Brigade. Humans and dragons alike were relieved the trial was over and that they could feel good about the outcome.

Sophia hurried over to hug Kate and congratulate her. Cecile expressed her pleasure to her son that all had ended well.

"The Battle of the Royal Sail has been a stain on the reputation of the Royal Navy for many years," Stephano said. "The recent treaty started to heal the festering wounds between the crown and the Dragon Duchies. This trial threatened to undo all that by forcing us all to relive it."

"I hope this puts an end to it," Cecile remarked. "I hope I never hear the words 'Royal Sail' again. We can put this tragedy behind us."

"So long as Dalgren pays for your sins," Kate muttered.

Stephano rounded on her, his expression grave. "What Lord Dalgren did was wrong, Captain. He deserted his post. He broke the oath he took when he joined the Brigade. Lady Cam gave her life for the honor of the Brigade. Lord Dalgren fled. He deserves to be punished and he, at least, appears to know that."

Kate was abashed.

"I am sorry, sir. I didn't mean that the way it sounded. Dalgren was will-ing to give his own life for the honor of the Brigade, but then he was wounded and nearly killed by his own comrades. Where is the honor in that?"

"I know that this seems very complicated," Stephano said. "I have done some things in my life that were not so honorable. The aforementioned smug-gling was my way of lashing out at the country that had wronged me. I am still trying to make up for my misdeeds, restore my own honor."

Kate looked at Dalgren, who was talking with Lord Haelgrund.

"When will he have to leave for Below, sir?"

"His Grace, the Duke of Talwin, will make that determination. He will likely assign a dragon such as Lord Haelgrund to escort Dalgren to Capione and the floating fortress. From there, he can fly down through the Breath to reach the city of Dunlow."

"He could die making that flight, couldn't he, sir?" Kate said.

"He could," said Stephano. He followed her gaze. "My guess would be that he and Lord Haelgrund are discussing that right now. You can go join them, if you would like."

"Thank you, sir," said Kate. "I especially appreciate what you did for Dal-gren. You and Mistress Miri saved his life. I also thank you for keeping my secret."

"I could not let Dalgren suffer for *my* sins, could I?" said Stephano with a wry smile. "A word of advice, Captain. Do not remain in Rosia long."

"I don't plan to, sir," said Kate.

Lord Haelgrund was offering advice about flying below the Breath. He spoke in serious tones and Dalgren was listening, but Kate wondered how much he was really comprehending. He seemed in a daze, as though he had been inhaling burley smoke, a dragon form of intoxicant. His head bobbed, his eyes glistened, his tail twitched.

Lord Haelgrund noticed Kate approaching and broke off the conversation.

"I will leave you two to celebrate in private. I need to talk to the Duke of Talwin."

"Thank you for everything, my lord," said Kate.

Lord Haelgrund looked grim. "Your friend has no idea of the danger he faces, not only traveling Below but once he arrives there. The Bottom Dwell-ers have no love for dragons. I tried to tell him, but he won't listen. Perhaps you can convince him. Being Banished trumps being dead."

Lord Haelgrund lumbered off, rumbling to himself.

Dalgren grinned at her, baring his fangs. "I am away to the Bottom of the world. Perhaps Akiel could cast one of his warming spells on me."

Kate rested her hand on his foreleg. "Oh, Dalgren—"

Dalgren closed his jaws, lowered his head.

"You must not call me by that name, Kate," he said. "I no longer have a name."

"The hell you don't! I'll call you whatever I damn well please!" Kate returned angrily.

Dalgren stubbornly shook his head. Kate sighed and rubbed his scaly skin.

"Are you sure about this decision you've made? Did you even listen to what Lord Haelgrund was trying to tell you?"

"I am as sure as I have ever been of anything in my life," said Dalgren. He spoke with dignity, and his eyes were clear. "Lord Haelgrund thinks I do not understand the danger. Perhaps I don't, for I have never been to the Bottom of the world and he has. But that doesn't matter. What if you had to go through the rest of your life never talking to another human being? Never again seeing your family or your friends?"

"You would have me," said Kate quietly.

Dalgren lowered his head to look at her in the eyes.

"I know I have you, Kate, and I am grateful. You are a true friend. But we must both face the truth. One day you will leave me and where you go, I cannot follow."

Kate knew what he meant. She might live to a ripe old age; she had heard of humans who had lived eighty or even ninety years. But those years were the blink of an eye to the long-lived dragons. When she was dead, Dalgren would be alone and without his kind, he would live alone, in unending silence. A living death.

"I do understand," said Kate. "And I am going with you."

Dalgren reared up with a bellow. "Like hell you are!"

Heads turned, conversations stopped. Humans and dragons were staring at them. Kate remembered a little late she should not be drawing attention to herself.

"Calm down! People are staring. How do you propose to stop me?" Kate asked.

"I won't have to," Dalgren muttered, glowering. "How do you propose to travel to the bottom of the world?"

Kate had to admit she had no idea. She had not given any thought to how she would travel or how this journey would disrupt her life. She would be leaving behind her dreams of working for Sir Henry, restoring Barwich Manor, perhaps of rounding a corner of the street one day and running into Thomas . . .

"I'll find a way," said Kate, smiling.

"You have no idea what dangers you will be facing!" Dalgren said angrily.

"Neither do you," said Kate. "So I guess we should face them together."

Dalgren snorted two gouts of flame from his nose, then he saw someone approaching and his demeanor abruptly changed. He lowered his head in respect.

Kate turned to see the Trundler woman, Miri.

"Master," Dalgren said, his voice trembling. "I cannot thank you enough. You have given me back my life."

"You may not thank me once you are Below," said Miri, smiling. She paused, then turned to Kate. "Forgive me, Mistress. I could not help overhearing your conversation. I admire your loyalty to your friend. If you are serious about accompanying Dalgren to Dunlow, you can sail with me and Gythe. We are leaving soon to carry supplies to Father Jacob."

"Thank you so much," said Kate. "But . . . well . . . a Trundler houseboat . . ."

Miri laughed. "Have no fear! We do not sail Below in our houseboat. We have a small ship that is specially equipped to make the journey."

"Then, yes, I accept," Kate said, casting Dalgren a look of defiance. "It will be an adventure."

Miri regarded Kate with earnest gravity. "Dalgren is right. You should understand the dangers *you* will face, Mistress. You will be in a strange and desolate land with people who have no love for you and will resent you for trying to help them. You will often be alone. A day in the world Below can seem a year. A year can seem forever."

"Whatever the danger, I will face it with my friend," said Kate.

Dalgren snorted again and rolled his eyes. But he shifted his forefoot closer to her, pressing against her. Kate rested her hand on his claw and gave him a pat.

"Good," said Miri. "Then that's settled. I came to tell Dalgren that His Grace has granted permission for you to go hunting, since you have already given your parole that you will return."

"Please thank His Grace," said Dalgren. "I haven't had much appetite lately and I am famished. But you should not use my name, Mistress—"

"Folderol!" said Miri. "You should use your own name for the sake of practicality, if nothing else. Believe me, Father Jacob will not want to constantly have to refer to you as 'Nameless Dragon.'"

She turned to Kate. "I am to remind you that you have an audience with the duke."

"Go find something to eat," Kate told Dalgren. "I have to say good-bye to Captain de Guichen and Her Highness and the others. I will come talk to you when you have returned. I have lots to tell you."

"I'll just bet you do," Dalgren growled.

Kate walked with Miri back down to Grayhollow. Miri introduced Kate to her sister, Gythe, who was talking with Stephano and Sophia and the

Countess de Marjolaine. Kate noticed that although Gythe sometimes spoke, her words were shy and halting, and that she was more comfortable using her hands to express her thoughts.

The group ceased their conversation when Miri and Kate arrived. Miri caused a sensation with her announcement.

"Mistress Katherine is sailing with Gythe and me when we go Below."

Sophia gasped and turned deathly pale. Cecile reached out to grasp her hand. Kate seemed to see the countess age, lines of sorrow and remembered fear rippling across the smooth complexion as though a pebble had been thrown into a still and placid pond.

Gythe gave her sister a reproachful look and punched her in the arm.

Miri flushed deeply. "I am so sorry, Your Highness. I should have realized that such news would upset you."

"I am fine, Miri," said Sophia. "Please don't worry. I think you are very brave, Mistress Katherine. The countess and I have been Below, you see. We know the dangers you and your friend will face. I am glad you will not let your friend go alone, though I will worry about you. You must come to visit me the moment you are back and tell me you are safe."

Hearing her voice tremble as she spoke, Kate recalled the princess saying how the countess had rescued her from the Bottom Dwellers. She had not realized they had carried her Below.

"I do understand the dangers," said Kate. "I have no love for the Bottom Dwellers. I saw some of the terrible atrocities they committed in the Aligoes. Friends of mine died during the war. But I want to be with Dalgren."

"The Bottom Dwellers are strong and resilient and they are working hard to survive and to make up for their misdeeds in their past," said Cecile. "You and Lord Dalgren could both learn from them."

Kate understood her meaning and flushed. While it was true she had misdeeds of her own to repair, she didn't need reminding.

Carriages had begun arriving to take the humans back to Cieleterre. Several of the dragons had already departed, taking to the sky, returning to their homes. Kate thought about the Countess Faltihure. She must remember to tell Dalgren to let his mother know the glad outcome. As for his father, Kate hoped he choked on his own flaming bile.

"Our carriage is here, Your Highness," Cecile said, placing her hand on Sophia's arm. "We should return to Lord Haelgrund's. I am half-frozen."

"And I am certain Bandit is causing all sorts of trouble for Lady Haelgrund," said Sophia. "Will you travel with us, Mistress Katherine? We can take you back to the inn."

"Thank you, Your Highness, but I would like to stay to talk with Dalgren for a while," said Kate.

"Mistress Katherine has a meeting with the Duke of Talwin," Cecile added.

"You can spend the night with us in the *Dragon Song*, Mistress Kate," Miri offered. "We are staying late. I want to speak to the duke myself, as well as Countess Anasi. You can return with us to Cieleterre. Our other boat is in Capione, which is where Dalgren needs to go. We can travel together."

Sophia smiled at Kate and impulsively kissed her on the cheek. "Promise you will visit me!"

"I promise, Your Highness," said Kate.

Cecile gave Kate her hand, which was long-fingered, cool, and smooth. "Please give Father Jacob my best regards."

"I will, my lady," said Kate.

Cecile cast Stephano a cool glance. "You and Lord Haelgrund are not to stay too long reminiscing with your friends, my son. We cannot sit down to dinner without you."

"We will be along shortly, Mother," said Stephano.

The countess and the princess entered the carriage. Sophia leaned out the window to wave. "Good-bye, Miri! Good-bye, Gythe! Give Doctor Ellington a kiss for me!"

As the carriage rolled away, Sophia called out to Miri, "And take care of Kate!"

"We will!" Miri called back.

Kate wondered about Doctor Ellington. "Do you travel with a physician?"

Gythe laughed and shook her head. She shaped her fingers into claws. Kate looked at her in perplexity.

"You must forgive my sister, Mistress Kate," said Miri. "Gythe is capable of speech, but she prefers to talk with her hands. Doctor Ellington is a cat."

"I hope you like cats," said Gythe, her words halting and soft.

Olaf had kept a cat around the Parrot to deal with rodents, but it had been a business-minded cat, not inclined to make friends. Kate did not know if she liked cats or not, although she did think that if a cat could travel safely Below, the journey couldn't be all that bad.

She assured Gythe that she would be fine traveling with a cat; then Miri and Gythe and Stephano excused themselves and left to go speak to Countess Anasi. Lord Haelgrund lumbered up to Kate.

"His Grace, the Duke of Talwin, will see you now, Mistress."

The duke was talking with Countess Anasi and several of the other dragons, discussing something in their own language. Seeing Kate approach, the dragons broke off their conversation and turned their heads in her direction.

"The Countess de Marjolaine said you had something of importance to tell us, Mistress," said the duke. "You may speak."

"Thank you, Your Grace," said Kate. "Have you heard of a dragon named Coreg?"

The dragons had been gently fanning the air with their wings, bobbing their heads. At the sound of Coreg's name, however, they stilled their wings, and their heads snapped around to fix Kate with unblinking eyes.

"We have heard of Coreg," said the duke. His tongue flicked over his fangs, as though he were ridding himself of a bad taste. "What about him?"

"I knew him, Your Grace," said Kate. "He was foul and corrupt. He was involved in all manner of criminal activities throughout the world. He murdered others, so perhaps it is just that he himself was murdered. But that is not what I came to tell you."

The dragons waited in silence. She had their undivided attention now.

Kate drew in a breath and forged on. "Coreg had many humans working for him. Most were flunkies who did his dirty work. They're dead, as well. But one was special and he is alive and extremely dangerous. Coreg called him Trubgek. Dalgren taught me some of your language and I know that is the most insulting word a dragon can use for a human."

"What makes this Trubgek special?" the duke asked.

"Coreg taught him dragon magic, Your Grace," said Kate.

The dragons gazed at her, still not moving. Then the Duke of Talwin smiled, lips parting, showing his yellowed fangs. Some of the other dragons stretched their necks and shook out their manes in what for dragons was a laugh. Countess Anasi politely endeavored to hide her amusement, but did not quite succeed, for little tendrils of smoke escaped from the corners of her mouth.

Kate was annoyed. "I am telling the truth, Your Grace. I have seen this Trubgek perform powerful magicks, far beyond those of which any human is capable. I am a crafter myself, and I know magic."

"He is likely nothing more than a talented savant, Mistress," said the duke. He glanced at the others and asked casually, "Out of curiosity, where is this human now? Do you know?"

"The last I heard, he was sailing to Bheldem and that he might be working for some marquis . . . the Marquis of Cavanaugh. I don't know more than that."

"Thank you for coming to us with this information, Mistress, but I don't believe there is any cause for alarm," said the duke. "We understand you are traveling Below with your friend. We wish you both luck."

The meeting was clearly at an end. Kate walked off, shrugging. She had warned them. If they chose not to believe her, that was their prerogative. She had done her duty.

The dragons strolled off in various directions. Miri and Gythe and Stephano began talking to Countess Anasi, laughing about something. Kate had no one and she felt isolated and alone. She went off in pursuit of Dalgren and found him hungrily devouring one deer with another carcass waiting.

Dalgren crunched bones, talking with his mouth full. "So tell me what happened to your hair and how you come to be in such exalted company, wearing fancy dresses and furs, hugging princesses and hobnobbing with dukes."

Kate sat down on a boulder. "They were all very kind to me—the dukes and the countesses and the princesses. They are good people. But they are not *our* people," she added, thinking of Thomas. "We don't fit into their world."

"True," Dalgren agreed somberly. "We belong at the Bottom."

That night, the Countess de Marjolaine was alone in her room in Lord Haelgrund's spacious palace. Like most dragon dwellings, the palace had been built with special rooms for humans, who prefer to sleep in warm beds with tapestries on the walls and cozy rugs on the floors as opposed to the cavelike rooms preferred by dragons.

Cecile sat before the mirror, brushing out her long hair, reflecting on the day's events. Someone tapped on the door. Her maid answered and came back with a letter.

"This was just delivered, my lady."

Cecile noted the paper, the type used by human scribes. The seal was that of the Duke of Talwin, a mountain peak wreathed with clouds.

Cecile broke the seal and opened the letter. It was brief.

> *The rumors regarding a human and dragon magic are true. The human is named Trubgek. He was last known to be sailing for Bheldem. Such information coincides with ours that he could be in the employ of the Marquis of Cavanaugh.*

As Cecile read the brief missive her brow wrinkled. She began to pace the floor, her weariness forgotten. Arriving at a decision, she crumpled the letter and threw it into the flames, then sat down at her desk to write. Her first letter was to an old and dear friend.

> *My dear Lord Ander,*
> *How pleased I am to write "Lord Ander" instead of "Sir Ander." I know you find the accolades heaped upon you embarrassing, but you richly deserve them.*

The last you wrote to me, you had retired from active duty to live upon the stipend given to you by His Majesty in return for your meritorious service. I would rejoice that you are at last able to rest after a long and glorious career, but, knowing you, I fear that you are already starting to find the life of a civilian frightfully dull.

If that is true, I was wondering if you could do me a great favor, the performance of which would certainly not be boring. I am returning to my son's palace shortly. I would be pleased if you would call upon me.

Yours always,
Cecile de Marjolaine

Her second was to Prince Thomas Stanford.

Your Royal Highness,
I hope I find you well and in good spirits. Sophia informs me that you are traveling to Bheldem to visit your dear mother, the marchioness. Please give her my warmest regards.

I am writing to invite you and your friend His Grace, Phillip Masterson, to attend an informal birthday celebration for Her Royal Highness, Princess Sophia. The party is being hosted by His Grace, the Duke de Bourlet, at Castle Dragonreach.

Her Highness is so much looking forward to sharing her special day with her affianced. I trust she will not be disappointed.

Yours sincerely,
Cecile de Marjolaine

She named a date and then added a postscript.

P.S. You may happen to meet a dear friend of mine while you are in Bheldem. He is Lord Ander Martel, Knight Protector. He is a soldier and I believe you two will have much in common.

Cecile's final letter was to Constanza, Marchioness of Cavanaugh.

Your Ladyship,
I trust this letter finds you well.
A dear friend of mine, Lord Ander Martel, Knight Protector of the Realm, is interested in visiting your estate. Lord Ander makes a study of architecture and he has heard that an old fort located

on your grounds is a fine example of the Twilight period. He is longing to see it.

You will be doing me a personal favor by extending an invitation to him. I look forward to hearing from you.

Yours sincerely,
Cecile de Marjolaine

Cecile closed and sealed the three letters, addressed them, then rang for the servant and instructed him to include them in the next day's post.

This done, she went to her bed. Before she slept, she made a mental note to send Lord Ander information on Twilight-period architecture and to inform Stephano that he was going to be hosting a birthday party for Sophia.

TWENTY-SIX

Mr. Sloan arrived at the Old Fort in Bheldem in company with Colonel Smythe and Trubgek. Mr. Sloan had seen almost nothing of Trubgek during the voyage, for the disturbingly strange man was often closeted with Colonel Smythe. Try as he might, Mr. Sloan could never discover what they discussed.

He found Bheldem to be a land of mountains and cliffs, ravines and crags, with grassy swards along the rivers and barren plateaus farther inland. The early inhabitants had built castles and fortresses along the banks of the rivers, which were the primary means of travel. No dragons resided in Bheldem and the native griffins and wyverns were wild, more likely to attack humans than allow them to ride on their backs.

The Old Fort, as it was known, had originally been built by some long-forgotten baron on a plateau overlooking the Artroughn River. Constructed of stone and concrete, the fort was so solid that the builders had not seen a need to reinforce the walls with magical constructs.

The fort consisted of a large square wall with four towers, one at each corner. The commander's quarters were located inside the wall near the front gate. The housing for officers and staff, horse and griffin stables, kitchens, a smithy and artillery depot were in the rear.

The Old Fort originally was designed to accommodate a small force of about one hundred and fifty men. The marquis had added additional barracks outside the wall on a strip of level ground between the plateau and the river, as well as a new and extremely modern shipyard.

The day they arrived, Colonel Smythe took Mr. Sloan on a tour of the fort and the shipyard. Mr. Sloan had been expecting to find an invasion force of ten thousand troops and a naval force. Instead he found about two thousand troops and eight three-masted troop carriers. Not a single frigate or warship. The older-model ships were crawling with carpenters and crafters.

"They are being refitted to use the crystalline form of the Breath instead of the liquid," Smythe explained. "A single crystal can provide lift for a ship for months."

Mr. Sloan feigned ignorance. "I have heard rumors of these crystals, but I was not aware that they truly existed. The expense must have been great."

"As it happened, the Braffans refused to sell them to us. His Highness, Prince Thomas, undertook a daring raid to obtain the crystals," Smythe said.

As Mr. Sloan walked the decks, he saw large lamps, similar to street lamps, hanging from the yardarms. When lighted, such lamps would illuminate a wide area, providing light enough to permit work after dark. That night, he heard the sounds of hammering and saw the lights shining in the shipyard.

The army was known as the Army of Royal Retribution, an appellation Mr. Sloan found deeply disturbing, for it denoted an army intent not only on conquering, but on punishing the sins of a hundred and fifty years ago, when the queen's ancestor had overthrown King James I.

"If and when the queen dies, the army will escort His Highness to Freya, where he will present his legitimate claim to the throne," Smythe told Mr. Sloan, adding with a shake of his head, "But I fear that unless God works in some unforeseen manner, we are a long way from that blessed day."

Listening to the workmen toiling day and night to ready the troop transports, Mr. Sloan wondered with a chill if Colonel Smythe intended to give God a nudge.

Mr. Sloan settled into his duties. His first care was to grow a long mustache. He did not think it likely he would run into anyone in Bheldem who knew him, but he did not take chances. He was fortunate in that the Guundaran officers all sported mustaches, and he fit right in.

He also had to obtain his uniform. Officers in the army were required to pay for their own uniforms, including the addition of magical constructs designed to protect against bullets, a lifesaving luxury the ordinary soldier generally could not afford. Mr. Sloan knew a great deal about this magic, for he had been responsible for hiring the crafters who worked on Sir Henry's clothing.

Mr. Sloan looked with disfavor on the Bheldem crafters Smythe had recommended to him. He considered their magic rudimentary, less than inspired. The constructs were designed to diminish the force of a bullet and deflect the point of a blade. When Mr. Sloan examined them he was not convinced they would do either. He would have liked to have strengthened the magic himself, but he was mindful of the fact that Smythe was a crafter and if he noticed anything out of the ordinary, he might grow suspicious.

The uniforms of both officers and footmen consisted of a russet-colored jacket that came to just about the knees, russet breeches, a white shirt with a wide collar, tall black boots, and a helm. The officers added braided trim to their jackets to distinguish their rank. The uniforms were comfortable and practical and, except for the mediocre crafting, Mr. Sloan approved.

He had to purchase another uniform, as well. This uniform filled him with foreboding, for it was an exact copy of the uniforms worn by officers in the Freyan army: blue jacket trimmed in gold, white trousers, tall black boots, white bandolier. The uniform had one small difference: the piping on the collar and jacket on Freyan uniforms was green; the piping on Mr. Sloan's was red.

Of course, thought Mr. Sloan. Those of us who serve in this army must be able to recognize each other.

"Pack that uniform away, Lieutenant," Smythe told him. "You will not need it until we sail to Freya."

The two thousand men—mostly Guundaran mercenaries—were divided into two regiments. Since many of the Guundarans spoke only limited Freyan, they had their own officers, who were fluent in both languages and thus able to translate Smythe's commands.

The Marquis of Cavanaugh, father of Prince Thomas Stanford, held the rank of general and was nominally in command, although thus far no one had ever set eyes on him. The true commander was Colonel Smythe. Mr. Sloan held the rank of lieutenant serving directly under Smythe, acting as liaison with the Guundaran officers.

Mr. Sloan had always prided himself on keeping in good physical condition. He ate only plain, wholesome food and eschewed strong spirits and wine. He drank ale, because it was considered nourishing, but not to excess.

He had faithfully exercised every morning using clubs weighted with lead, much like those clubs jongleurs are fond of tossing about. He would swing them above his head, cross them back and forth in front of his knees, whip them over his shoulders and perform other gyrations to keep up his strength.

He soon discovered, on arriving at the Old Fort in Bheldem, that he was not in such good shape as he had imagined. He had never considered his adventurous life with Sir Henry Wallace as "soft," but Mr. Sloan sadly discovered this was the case.

Colonel Smythe placed Mr. Sloan—now Lieutenant Sloan—in charge of drilling and instructing the soldiers in the use of new Freyan rifles, which had been obtained by the late Coreg on the black market and only recently had been delivered. Mr. Sloan subscribed to two theories: an officer should never ask his men to do anything he was not willing to do himself, and an officer led by example.

After the first day spent on the drill field, Mr. Sloan deeply regretted subscribing to both these theories. He went to his bed that night feeling every one of his forty-four years and woke the next morning feeling as if those forty-four years had been multiplied by two. He was scarcely able to move for the soreness and stiffness in his muscles, and he spent the first several days in such agony of mind and body that he had not been able to concentrate on the task at hand, which was to try to discover Smythe's plans.

By the end of the week Mr. Sloan had recovered, and he felt able to take stock of his situation and determine how to proceed.

Smythe maintained his living quarters and office in a building known as the Commander's House, a two-story blockhouse with two wings, one to be used as offices and living quarters, with the other wing intended for aides and servants. Mr. Sloan discovered, to his surprise, that the other wing was unoccupied.

"As the Scriptures teach us, Lieutenant, the godly life is the simple life," Colonel Smythe said.

He was true to his beliefs. He employed no secretary or servants. His aide-de-camp was little more than an errand boy. He did not keep his own cook, although there was a kitchen in the rear of the Commander's House. He ate the same food as his men, and, although he sometimes joined his officers for dinner, he generally ate alone in his quarters. He did not bother to post a sentry outside his office door.

The officers and men respected Smythe. He was a strict disciplinarian, but accounted fair. He drank no strong spirits himself, saying that was against his beliefs, but he saw to it that the soldiers had their daily ration of rum. If it were not for the fact that Mr. Sloan knew that this man had murdered several innocent people, brutally tortured and slain one dragon and killed another in cold blood, he would have esteemed him a good commander and a God-fearing man.

Mr. Sloan did know about the murders, however. He was here to discover what Smythe and his prince had planned for the future. After a fortnight, though, he was no closer to finding out what he needed to know than when he had arrived. He had been in Smythe's small office several times to receive orders and became convinced that what he needed to know was in there.

He knew better than to expect to stumble across detailed plans for the invasion of Freya. Smythe was an innately cautious man, secretive and reserved. He was unlikely to set anything down in writing that might compromise his mission.

But Smythe was also neat, regular in his habits, and a meticulous record-keeper. He kept account books and ledgers neatly stacked on shelves that had been built for the purpose. Mr. Sloan had learned from experience that seemingly dry columns of numbers had their own tales to tell if one knew how to read them. He hoped to find valuable information in these ledgers if only he could gain access to them.

Mr. Sloan was housed in the barracks inside the wall, along with other officers and staff. His room was small and sparsely furnished, but he was pleased with it, for the window looked out upon the compound and provided a clear view of the Commander's House.

He kept watch and noted that at night the sentries were posted at the gate and atop the walls. The compound was dark and deserted. Mr. Sloan should have no trouble slipping out of his quarters and sneaking into the Commander's House.

He chose a night when Smythe had said he was going to retire early and waited until long after midnight before venturing out of his quarters. He stayed close to the wall to avoid being spotted by the sentries, and arrived at the Commander's House without incident.

The main door to the colonel's quarters was unguarded and unlocked in case anyone needed to reach Smythe in an emergency. The absence of a sentry should have been cause for Mr. Sloan to rejoice. Instead, it troubled him. He had the feeling he knew the reason.

Smythe's office was located at the end of the hall. His quarters were on the floor above. A stairway at the end of the hall led upstairs.

The stone building had narrow windows and was pitch-dark inside. Mr. Sloan carried a bull's-eye lantern that he let shine only briefly in order to find his way. Reaching the door to the office, Mr. Sloan studied it by the light of the lantern and found nothing untoward. He drew a construct on his palm that radiated a small amount of diffused magical energy, allowing him to detect not only the presence of magical constructs, but to see them, as well.

As he passed his hand over the wooden door, the constructs on the door began to glimmer with a faint blue light. Here was the reason Colonel Smythe did not need to post a sentry.

Mr. Sloan gazed at the magic and he was both impressed and disheartened. An expert crafter himself, he could dismantle most ordinary wizard locks with relative ease. He might be able to dismantle these locks and warding spells and traps, but not without spending considerable time and effort. Every moment he spent here increased the likelihood of being caught.

As if to emphasize this point, he was committing the constructs to memory when he heard footfalls on the floor above his head. He recognized Smythe's heavy tread and beat a swift retreat out the front door. Mr. Sloan waited a few moments, hoping Smythe had just risen to relieve himself and would go back to bed. Seeing light flare in the window above him, Mr. Sloan gave up and returned to his quarters.

He copied what he remembered of the complex constructs onto paper. Reasoning that Smythe would not go to the trouble to place such complex magical constructs on a door if he had nothing to hide, Mr. Sloan was more determined than ever to break inside. He would need at least thirty minutes to dismantle the complex constructs, and once he had done that, he would require time to go through the books.

He watched for his opportunity, but, sadly, Smythe was apparently a man who required very little sleep for he was up all hours of the night. Mr. Sloan could never be certain that he would not be interrupted.

Trubgek was another problem for Mr. Sloan. The strange man was unobtrusive, kept to himself, and never spoke. But wherever Colonel Smythe went, Trubgek was sure to be lurking in the background, silently watching him.

Mr. Sloan had the impression that Smythe was not pleased to have this constant shadow, but he did nothing to stop him.

Everyone in the fort was by now familiar with Trubgek. Smythe had introduced him as a member of the marquis's household, here to go over the accounts.

"I do not like to lie," Smythe confided to Mr. Sloan. "But the fewer who know about the marquis's unfortunate business relationship with the man Greenstreet, the better. His Lordship is lucky that Greenstreet has fled the Aligoes and traveled to parts unknown. Their business dealings will be at an end."

Mr. Sloan knew, of course, that Greenstreet was dead, although he supposed that counted as being in "parts unknown."

The following morning, Mr. Sloan and Smythe were inspecting a shipment of long-barreled Estaran pistols set with the latest targeting constructs. Smythe had ordered the pistols for the use of the officers and he suggested that they take several of them to a field to test. Mr. Sloan, feeling a prickle on the back of his neck, looked over his shoulder to see Trubgek standing on a hill above the field, gazing down at them.

"That strange fellow is lurking about again, watching you, sir," Mr. Sloan said. "You are extremely patient with him. I would have thrown him off a cliff before now."

"The man is odd, but I believe him to be harmless," Smythe said, shrugging.

Mr. Sloan was intrigued. He would not term a human who knew dragon magic "harmless." Either Smythe was dissembling or he was ignorant of Trubgek's power. Mr. Sloan wondered, not for the first time, what Smythe knew about Trubgek.

"Where does he come from, sir?" Mr. Sloan asked.

Colonel Smythe loaded a pistol, aimed, and fired.

"I have no idea. All I know is that Greenstreet kept him around to run errands. I brought him along to assist in untangling Greenstreet's business dealings in Freya and to prevent him from exposing the marquis."

Plausible, since Trubgek was in truth involved in untangling Coreg's business dealings, and he was the only human who had been completely in the dragon's confidence. Coreg had lived comfortably in his cave. Trubgek had traveled the world, meeting with buyers, suppliers, removing enemies, rewarding friends. Trubgek knew where the dragon kept his wealth and how to access it. Coreg had not stashed his gold in a hoard in his mountain. He had kept it in banks and sent Trubgek to make the deposits.

Smythe had good reason to keep Trubgek around. But that did not explain why Trubgek was keeping such a constant and diligent watch on Smythe. And why Smythe appeared so unconcerned.

That afternoon, Mr. Sloan was on the drill field training the soldiers in the use of the new Freyan rifles. This involved a series of drills designed to walk the soldiers through each individual step of loading, priming, and firing the weapon, repeating this again and again until they could fire them in their sleep or, more important, while cannonballs were exploding around them and their comrades were lying dead at their feet.

Mr. Sloan allowed the men to rest after their exertions and allowed himself to rest, as well. He drank tepid water from his leather canteen as he casually observed his surroundings and again considered the problem of how to break into Smythe's office. He was interrupted in his musings by an aide-de-camp.

"The colonel's compliments, sir, and would you report to him in his office."

Mr. Sloan dutifully returned to the fort. The office door was open. Smythe was inside, holding a letter.

"You wanted to see me, sir," Mr. Sloan said.

"Yes, Lieutenant," said Smythe. "It seems we are to have a royal visitor. The marchioness writes to tell me that His Highness, Prince Thomas, will be here to review his troops. He arrives tomorrow morning."

"Does His Highness make such inspection tours often, sir?" Mr. Sloan asked.

"Quite the contrary, Lieutenant. His Highness has always before refused to take the least interest in his army," said Smythe.

"Why the sudden change, sir?"

"His mother writes that he is at last starting to take seriously his claim as heir to the throne. I hope she is correct. I regret to say Prince Thomas has not done so in the past. One can hardly blame him, however," Smythe added with a touch of asperity. "His mother talks of nothing else. Small wonder the young man is sick to death of hearing about it."

"I trust His Highness will take his responsibilities seriously when he is crowned king," said Mr. Sloan sententiously. "It is high time we had a God-fearing man on the throne."

"His Highness will be equal to the job," said Smythe. "He has proven himself to be a man of courage on more than one occasion."

"I am pleased to hear this, sir. I will make arrangements to receive him, although on such short notice, we will not be able to accommodate His Highness as befits royalty," said Mr. Sloan. "We have no wine to serve at dinner, for example, and since he arrives tomorrow, no time to obtain any. And where are we to house him and his retinue?"

Colonel Smythe considered. "They must stay in the empty wing of the Commander's House. I can think of nowhere else. Make the arrangements."

"Very good, Colonel," said Mr. Sloan. "How many are in the prince's party? Do you know their rank, titles? Will the marquis and marchioness be accompanying him?"

Colonel Smythe returned to the letter.

"The marchioness is hosting a female journalist from Freya and cannot possibly leave. His Highness will be bringing two gentlemen. One is a friend of the Countess de Marjolaine, who comes to study the architecture of the fort. The marchioness does not think it important to supply his name," he added dryly.

Whoever he is, he will be the countess's spy, Mr. Sloan reflected.

Colonel Smythe continued, "In addition, the prince is bringing along a Freyan nobleman, Phillip Masterson, Duke of Upper and Lower Milton. Do you know anything about this duke, Lieutenant?"

Mr. Sloan was alarmed. He knew Phillip very well and—more to the point—Phillip knew him. Masterson had been in the employ of Sir Henry and would recognize Mr. Sloan the moment he saw him.

Mr. Sloan had to swiftly think through the complicated situation. Phillip Masterson had switched sides, shifted his loyalty from Sir Henry to Prince

Thomas. Sir Henry would have given a great deal to see this young traitor drawn and quartered.

Smythe apparently didn't know any of this background, however. Mr. Sloan could lie, of course, and say he had not heard of the man. On consideration, he decided that in this instance, a slightly modified version of truth could be of more benefit.

"I have heard of him, sir," said Mr. Sloan grimly. "This young man, Masterson, is said to be in the employ of the Freyan spymaster Sir Henry Wallace."

"He is a Freyan spy?" Colonel Smythe was shocked.

"Yes, sir," said Mr. Sloan. "How close is he to His Highness?"

"According to the marchioness, this Masterson is the prince's best friend and confidant," Colonel Smythe answered, sounding troubled.

Mr. Sloan shook his head in dismay. "You mentioned that Prince Thomas has never before come to inspect his troops. I venture to suggest the idea came from Masterson, who is hoping to gather information in order to relay it to Sir Henry."

"If that is the case, we must expose this Masterson, imprison him," said Smythe. "We cannot have him near His Highness!"

Mr. Sloan took a moment to relish the suggestion. Nothing would make him happier than to see Phillip Masterson tossed into some bottomless pit. Mr. Sloan had to forgo the pleasure, however. As in the Aligoes, he could not very well expose Phillip without Phillip exposing him. He would have to again let the treacherous duke off the hook, at least for now.

"We must tread carefully, sir. If we make such a serious charge against Masterson, His Grace will simply deny it. We have no proof against him, and His Highness will believe his friend. Masterson is cunning and duplicitous. He would undoubtedly use this to turn the prince against you."

"I suppose you are right," said Smythe, his brow creasing. "Still, we cannot have this spy roaming the fort, observing our troop numbers and state of readiness and reporting what he discovers back to Wallace."

Mr. Sloan ventured to offer a suggestion. "You have been talking of sending the troops out on maneuvers, sir."

"His Highness is coming expressly to review the troops," said Smythe.

"But he has given you such short notice, sir," said Mr. Sloan. "I mean no disrespect to His Highness, but you need not be governed by a royal whim."

"Very true," said Smythe. "But what am I to do with the prince while he is here?"

"You could take His Highness and his guests to the shipyard, sir. Allow him to observe the crafters refitting the ships to make use of the Tears of God. Since His Highness risked his life to obtain these crystals, I am certain he will be highly gratified to see the significant progress we have made."

"A good idea, Lieutenant," said Smythe. He gave a grim smile. "And while we are touring the shipyard, you will search Masterson's belongings to discover evidence that he is a spy."

Phillip Masterson had been one of Sir Henry's most valued operatives. Mr. Sloan was well aware that rummaging through Phillip's valise would not turn up anything. The duke was far too clever to hide incriminating letters among his underclothes.

Mr. Sloan had another objective in mind, however, and this command to remain behind suited him very well. Indeed, if Smythe had not thought of it, Mr. Sloan had been prepared to suggest it himself.

He had one problem and it was a significant one. He wanted to be certain he was alone in the Commander's House.

"What do we do about Trubgek, sir?" Mr. Sloan asked.

He had no need to say more. Smythe knew what he meant, undoubtedly knew more than Mr. Sloan, who had no idea why Trubgek was here, or what he was after.

One possible reason was that Trubgek was blackmailing Smythe. Trubgek must have known Smythe had killed both Greenstreet and Coreg. Mr. Sloan decided to accept this as a working assumption.

Smythe was troubled, as Mr. Sloan had hoped. Even if Trubgek wasn't blackmailing Smythe, the strange man who had been Coreg's servant undoubtedly knew things about Smythe that the colonel would not want his prince to know.

"I will deal with Trubgek," said Smythe.

TWENTY-SEVEN

Curious as to how Smythe planned to "deal" with Trubgek, Mr. Sloan endeavored to find a way to eavesdrop on their conversation. He had not yet come up with any means of doing so, however, for he had myriad tasks to perform.

He had first to detail men to arrange accommodations for His Highness and his friends who would be quartered in the empty rooms in the Commander's House. In addition, Mr. Sloan was responsible for readying the troops to go out on maneuvers.

The Old Fort was soon the site of organized confusion. The soldiers welcomed any change in the boring routine of military life and went to work with a will, loading supplies onto wagons and packing their gear. Mr. Sloan also had to make arrangements for those soldiers remaining behind to serve as guards for the prince, since apparently he was not bringing any himself.

By nightfall, Mr. Sloan was relatively confident that barring the usual problems that would be certain to arise at the last minute, he and his staff and the Guundaran officers had everything in readiness for the morrow, when the troops would march out.

He ate a quick meal, then, as darkness was falling, picked up a lantern, and went to view the quarters for the royal party.

The Commander's House had two front doors, one for each wing. Smythe lived and worked in the north wing. Mr. Sloan entered the door to the south wing, which was to be given to the prince and his friends.

When Mr. Sloan inspected the rooms, he was pleased with the results. The men had managed to find real wood-framed beds with mattresses so that the prince and his friends would not be forced to sleep on cots. The mattresses were stuffed with straw, but that could not be helped. Each man had his own room, furnished with chairs, a desk, and lamps.

Mr. Sloan had asked how many rooms they would need for the servants, but Smythe had said he doubted servants would be accompanying His Highness.

"The marchioness doesn't trust them," Smythe had said.

The bed linens were clean, the floors and walls had been washed and swept, and the windows had been opened to air out rooms that had been kept shut for years. Each man had been supplied with a water jug and wash-bowl, and a chamber pot.

Mr. Sloan decided to take the opportunity to report to Smythe and find out if he had additional orders for him.

A door led directly from the south wing to the north where Smythe had his quarters, opening into the hallway that led to Smythe's office. Preoccu-pied with mentally going over his report in his mind, Mr. Sloan thrust open the door and proceeded down the dark hall.

He saw that Smythe's office door was closed and stopped, thinking the colonel had retired early. Mr. Sloan was about to leave for his own quarters when he saw a narrow strip of light shine beneath it and realized he could hear voices.

Mr. Sloan immediately doused the lantern and was interested to note that magical constructs on the door had been activated, shining with a faint blue light, ensuring that no unexpected visitor barged inside.

Smythe would not have gone to this trouble to meet with his aide.

Mr. Sloan padded soft-footed down the hall. Having studied the con-structs, he was aware that the slightest touch would activate the magic, so he stopped some distance from the door. Smythe had a deep voice that reso-nated, especially when he was annoyed.

"You must travel to Freya at once and that is an end to the matter, Trub-gek," said Smythe impatiently. "Gaskell refuses to deal with me and the fault is yours. You were the one who lied, telling Gaskell that Coreg was traveling to Freya! Now that fool Gaskell insists on meeting with the dragon before he will proceed with the plan."

Trubgek replied, but his monotone, lifeless voice was so low that Mr. Sloan could not hear what he said.

"I don't give a damn what excuse you use," Smythe returned. "Tell him

Coreg went to the devil, for all I care. You must deliver these orders and convince Gaskell that from now on he has to work with me. Either that or remove him and find someone who will."

Mr. Sloan heard a chair scrape. Realizing the conversation must be at an end, he retreated down the hall, opened the connecting door, and slipped into the south wing. He left the door ajar and peered out through the crack.

The door to Smythe's office opened, emitting a flood of light. Trubgek emerged, stuffing something inside his leather jerkin, probably the orders he had just been given.

Trubgek paused in the doorway. "I know the real reason you want to be rid of me. You fear I will tell your prince what I know."

"I want to be rid of you for your own good, Trubgek," said Smythe. "If His Highness sees you, he will take you for a lunatic and demand that you be placed in a straitjacket."

Smythe appeared to consider a moment, then added in a mollifying tone, "I will send Corporal Jennings with you. While you are in Freya, you may begin the work of carrying out our other plan."

"You said the time was not right," Trubgek returned. "That we were acting too soon."

"I want proof that you know what you are doing," said Smythe. "I am not entirely convinced that you are as gifted in magic as you claim to be."

"Then you must give me what I asked for. Now."

"Do you think I am fool enough to keep it lying about the office?" Smythe demanded. "I will give it to you in the morning, before you leave."

After Trubgek walked out the door and left the building, Mr. Sloan softly shut the connecting door and went out by the door in the south wing. He watched Trubgek—a dark figure in the lambent light of the stars—walk across the courtyard.

Mr. Sloan considered all he had heard. Trubgek traveling to Freya to talk to someone named Gaskell who had once done business with Coreg and was now going to be doing business with Colonel Smythe. What business? And what was the "other plan"?

Mr. Sloan rose before the dawn, hoping to observe the departure of Trubgek. The stars were fading in the east, though still bright overhead. The air was crisp and cool with a gentle wind, presaging a clear, fine day.

Mr. Sloan strolled over to the livery stable and found the men already at work feeding the horses. He exchanged greetings with the soldiers, noted that all the horses were present and accounted for, and walked on to the griffin stables, which were kept separate from the horse stalls. Griffins considered horse meat a delicacy.

Smythe employed six griffins, although only four were present at any one time. According to him, the griffins had once served in the Freyan army, and had agreed to come to work for him. They had been here for several years and mated with the Bheldem griffins, so that they had families who dwelt in comfort and security on high mountain peaks that their mates visited on a regular basis.

Only two griffins were present. Two of the griffins were missing.

"You're up early, Lieutenant," the griffin master remarked, seeing Mr. Sloan enter.

"I was thinking of riding Stone Claw today," said Mr. Sloan, referring to one of the griffins that was absent. "I was planning to observe the exercises from the air."

"I am sorry to disappoint you, Lieutenant, but Colonel Smythe and Corporal Jennings left just about a half hour ago, riding Stone Claw and Red Talon. The griffins are traveling to Freya, so they will be gone for some time. The other two are available for your use, sir."

Mr. Sloan said any of the others would suit and departed, disappointed. Corporal Jennings was a fellow Fundamentalist. Mr. Sloan knew little about him, for the corporal apparently had no interest in making friends, and his strict religious views made the abstemious Mr. Sloan look like a libertine. It was rumored that he had tried to persuade Smythe to force the soldiers to give up their daily ration of rum, which would have resulted in mutiny.

He guessed that Jennings and Smythe had flown to meet Trubgek outside the fort. Smythe had likely given one griffin to Trubgek, along with the mysterious payment, then handed him over to Corporal Jennings. The two were probably now winging their way to Freya.

Mr. Sloan had his theory confirmed when he saw Smythe cross the parade ground and go to his office. When Mr. Sloan asked if he could use Corporal Jennings to assist him with some project, Smythe told him that Jennings was carrying dispatches to Freya. No mention of Trubgek.

From that moment on, Mr. Sloan was thoroughly engaged in his duties and had little time to think of anything else. The soldiers of the battalions assembled on the parade field outside the barracks. The regiments were divided into platoons, with a vanguard and a rearguard, and officers assigned to each. Colonel Smythe inspected the troops and watched as they marched out of the fort, heading for the rugged countryside where they would skirmish with each other in lieu of an enemy.

Mr. Sloan should have accompanied them in Smythe's absence, but Smythe had asked Mr. Sloan to remain in the fort to assist with the prince and his retinue.

After Smythe returned to his office, Mr. Sloan waited to observe the arrival of His Highness. When he saw three griffins with riders flying in the direction of the fort, he assumed that these would be Prince Thomas, Phillip Masterson, and the unknown man sent by the Countess de Marjolaine.

Mr. Sloan alerted the griffin master to expect guests, and went to report to Colonel Smythe.

"His Highness and his friends are on their way, sir," said Mr. Sloan. "They are traveling by griffin. I have informed the griffin master."

"Thank you, Lieutenant," said Smythe, rising. "Come with me. I will introduce you."

Mr. Sloan had foreseen this possibility and, again, had recourse to the truth. "Begging your pardon, sir, but it might be best if I remained out of sight. Masterson might recognize me from his association with my former employer and that could put him on his guard. It would be best if we take him unawares."

"A good point, Lieutenant," said Smythe.

The griffin master and his men were there to meet the griffins when they landed and to assist the riders with their gear. While Colonel Smythe waited at the gate to greet his guests, Mr. Sloan stationed himself in the shadow of the wall to watch.

Mr. Sloan knew Phillip Masterson at once. He was hard to miss with his untidy hair and his customary cheerful demeanor. He found himself impressed with Prince Thomas. The young man had a clear, bright eye, a forthright and honest countenance, and an engaging smile. He carried himself with confidence, but not arrogance.

The two young men were talking with the third man, the unnamed friend of the Countess de Marjolaine, the man who had come to study architecture and spy for the countess.

He was older than the others, perhaps close to fifty. He still had the sallow complexion of one who has recently recovered from a severe illness, but he appeared to be strong and vigorous, and bore himself with the upright stance of a soldier.

"Which is only to be expected of the redoubtable Sir Ander Martel," Mr. Sloan said with an inward groan, recognizing him.

He should not have been surprised. Sir Ander had been a close friend to Cecile de Marjolaine for many years. He was devoted to her, and she valued him above most others. Sir Ander was no ordinary spy, however. The fact that the countess had sent her trusted friend on this assignment meant that it was one of the utmost importance.

Sir Ander Martel was a Rosian, a Knight Protector who had once worked for Father Jacob Northrop, a member of the feared Arcanum and a foe of Sir Henry Wallace. Despite the fact that Sir Henry and the cleric had been on opposing sides for years, dire circumstances had thrust them together in a desperate battle to save Freya from being broken apart by the evil magicks of the Bottom Dwellers.

The avowed enemies had been transformed into comrades-in-arms, fighting a terrible battle that had very nearly cost them their lives. Mr. Sloan had not been present at the battle, but he had been the one to locate the critically wounded men, and his timely arrival had saved them all, including Sir Ander and his charge, Father Northrop.

Mr. Sloan had not seen Sir Ander since that dreadful day. He had heard that he had been honored by the king for his service and that he had since retired from the military, due to an illness he had contracted when he had traveled Below. Having recovered, apparently he now had a new occupation: the countess's spy.

Colonel Smythe welcomed his guests and offered to escort them to their quarters, inviting them to take rest and refreshment after their journey.

Prince Thomas was looking about the fort in a puzzled manner.

"I came here to review the troops, Colonel, but I do not see any troops to review," said Thomas.

"The troops are away on maneuvers, Your Highness. If I had known in advance you were coming—"

"A last-minute decision," said Thomas. "When I was with the Rosian navy, the officers asked me so many questions about my army that I felt an utter fool not being able to answer them. I am sorry I cannot stay long this time. I have other obligations to fulfill. But next time, when I return, I intend to stay at least a month."

"We will be honored," said Colonel Smythe. "I was thinking that after you have rested, you would be interested to observe the progress we have made refitting the ships to use the crystals you and His Grace were responsible for obtaining."

"By God, *I* would be interested to see that!" said Phillip. "Especially given the ordeal we went through to obtain them. I will never forget being forced to listen to that lecture on the 'Magical Properties of Liquid Breath Before and After the Distillation Process.'"

"And I will never forget dodging bullets and our boat sinking beneath us," said Thomas with a laugh. "Still, I owe those crystals a debt of gratitude. They introduced me to a most remarkable woman. We will have something to eat, Colonel, for we are famished, and then we will go see your ships and our crystals. Is that plan amenable to you, Lord Ander?"

"I am game for anything, Your Highness," said Ander.

"I thought Your Lordship was here to study the architecture," Thomas said.

"I can do that later, Your Highness," said Ander. "I have heard a great deal about these Tears of God, but I have never seen them. I would be glad to accompany you to view the ships."

Colonel Smythe expressed his pleasure and took them to the mess hall, while aides carried their belongings to their quarters.

Mr. Sloan retreated to his room and posted himself at the window, eating a sandwich, reading the Scriptures, and keeping watch on the movements of his guests. The prince must have been eager to see the ships, for they soon emerged from the mess hall. Smythe had their horses waiting and they rode out, accompanied by one of Smythe's aides.

The journey would take at least half an hour each way. The colonel had promised to keep the prince and his party in the shipyard for at least an hour, perhaps longer.

The fort was quiet, and the sentries posted at the gate and those on the ramparts chatted together or stood yawning, looking bored.

Mr. Sloan laid down the book of Scriptures, picked up the drawings he had made of the magical constructs on Smythe's office door, and set out.

Mr. Sloan crossed the compound and walked to the Commander's House. He stopped to talk to the stable master in passing, recalling Sir Henry's advice: "When engaged in some nefarious activity, do not, for God's sake, look nefarious! A confident demeanor instills trust in the observer. Act as though you have a perfect right to be there."

Mr. Sloan had given orders that a sentry be posted outside the door of the south wing. Approaching the man, Mr. Sloan assumed a stern air and barked sharply, "Corporal, have you seen that fellow Trubgek around here this afternoon?"

"No, Lieutenant," the sentry replied, startled.

"He has not tried to obtain entry?"

"No, sir. Not while I have been on duty."

Mr. Sloan appeared relieved. "I have received some disturbing information regarding him. Keep watch. I will see if he has somehow managed to find a way inside."

Mr. Sloan entered the south wing, then closed and locked the door behind him. He walked down the corridor that led to the north wing, opened the connecting door, and arrived at Smythe's office.

The interior of the building was silent. The hall was dark, for it had only one window that admitted very little sunlight. In the darkness, the constructs gave off a faint blue glow.

Mr. Sloan consulted the diagram he had made of the constructs and began systematically to remove them. He first dismantled those that were the most difficult, the constructs that protected the lock and the handle. He had to be extremely careful, breaking them down sigil by sigil in the correct order. If he made a mistake, the blast would blow off his hands.

After the blue glow faded from the handle, he removed the constructs on the door itself. These were designed to alert Smythe if anyone tampered with the door. If triggered, the magic would cause the wood to expand and contract with sharp crackling pops that went off like gunshots.

This done, Mr. Sloan paused to draw in a breath. If he had miscalculated, he would find himself without hands, or at least be in for a very nasty shock. He placed his hand on the door handle and, with fast-beating heart, cautiously opened it a crack.

Nothing happened. Breathing easier, Mr. Sloan slipped inside the office and shut the door behind him. If for some reason Smythe returned early, he would notice at once that his constructs were gone. That could not be helped, however. Mr. Sloan was armed both with a plausible explanation and a pistol and felt himself ready for any eventuality.

He lighted the lamp, then removed his pocket watch, opened it and placed it on the desk. He had allotted himself one hour for his work.

Bookshelves on the wall were lined with volumes on military history and treatises on military discipline. If he were conducting a thorough search, he would have gone through all those looking for letters hidden among the pages. Given what he knew of Smythe, however, Mr. Sloan did not consider it likely that the colonel would keep letters.

He picked up the lamp and squatted down to look in the grate of the small fireplace. The grate was covered with a thin layer of ash and bits of charred wood. As he suspected, Smythe burned his correspondence. Mr. Sloan found three blackened fragments of what appeared to be letters. He carefully lifted these out. One disintegrated between his fingers, but he was able to salvage two remains, both of them the corners of burned letters.

He pictured Smythe holding the letter by the corner as it caught fire, then dropping the flaming paper into the grate.

Mr. Sloan placed the fragments carefully between the pages of his book of Scriptures, consigning them to God's protection, and then turned his attention to the accounts. He first picked up the account book and opened it to this week's date at the top of its ruled pages, along with the headings "Cash Paid" and "Cash Received."

He settled down to review Smythe's monetary transactions. By the time the little watch chimed the hour, Mr. Sloan had found enough information to confirm Sir Henry's worst fears and add new ones.

Mr. Sloan gazed at the watch. He was tempted to stay longer, try to discover more. He did not push his luck, however. The information he had already learned would be extremely valuable to Sir Henry. He dared not take the risk.

Mr. Sloan returned the ledger books to their proper place and looked about carefully to make certain nothing else had been disturbed. He extinguished the lamp, rose to his feet, and opened the door a cautious crack.

The hall was empty. He shut the door, locked it, and following the diagram, replaced the warding constructs.

He returned to the south wing, made a perfunctory search of Phillip's belongings, and, as expected, found nothing of interest with the exception of a folded handkerchief tucked beneath his pillow. The handkerchief was stained with what Mr. Sloan at first took to be blood. He sniffed at it and realized to his astonishment that the splotches were chocolate.

He could not fathom why Phillip would be carrying about a chocolate-stained handkerchief, nor why it alone should be carefully folded and placed beneath his pillow, when he had carelessly strewn the rest of his clothing about the room.

Mr. Sloan deemed the handkerchief an unimportant mystery he did not feel called upon to unravel. He left the south wing by the front door, making certain to say something to the sentry in passing. He reminded the man to keep an eye out for Trubgek.

If word got back to Smythe, Mr. Sloan could always claim he had heard a disturbing rumor about the strange man and had been concerned for the safety of the prince.

TWENTY-EIGHT

Mr. Sloan was safely back in his room when he heard a bustle at the gate indicating that Smythe and his guests had returned. He glanced out the window to see the four ride into the compound. Men came running to help them dismount and to care for the horses.

The visit must have gone well. Prince Thomas appeared to be in a good humor. He stood for several moments in the compound, talking and laughing with Phillip and Smythe.

Sir Ander was slow to dismount, and he grimaced when he walked, giving every evidence of being saddle-sore. He made his excuses and began to hobble toward the Commander's House.

Mr. Sloan observed Sir Ander stop to gaze in confusion at the two doors, as though trying to recall which door led to his quarters. He chose the door to the north wing and Smythe's private quarters. The colonel saw the knight's mistake, but the prince was talking with him and he could not very well run off.

Sir Ander blundered in through the wrong door and disappeared. When Smythe was at last able to free himself, he immediately headed for the Commander's House to retrieve the errant knight.

Sir Ander eventually reappeared, looking profoundly embarrassed.

Mr. Sloan saw with amusement that a good deal of the knight's stiffness had vanished. He accompanied the prince and Phillip, who had decided to climb the stairs leading to the ramparts to observe the view.

Sir Ander had managed to enter the north wing, but what could he possibly have hoped to accomplish in such a short span of time? He must have been aware that Smythe had seen him. Indeed, everyone in the compound had seen him.

What was he searching for? Why had the countess sent him here?

Such speculations were useless, and Mr. Sloan dismissed the matter from his mind. He was about to engage in delicate magic and he needed to concentrate on the task at hand. He made certain his own door was locked.

Sitting down at his desk, he picked up a blank sheet of paper, dipped his pen in the ink, and drew four sigils on the page: one at the top, one on each side, and one at the bottom. He then drew a line connecting each of the sigils, one to the other.

Carefully removing the first scrap of burned paper from the pages of the Scriptures, he laid it on the desk and held the sheet of paper with the sigils over it.

The partially destroyed letter had two separate components: the ink and the paper. If his spell worked as planned, the magical construct crafted on the sheet of paper should gently pull the ink from the burned paper and transfer it to the sheet on top so that he could read what had been written.

He had only one chance, for the spell would destroy the original letter. Mr. Sloan focused his thoughts on the magic. As he touched each of the sigils he had drawn on the paper, tracing them with his finger, the constructs began to glow. The black ink shone with a faint blue light.

He laid the glowing paper on top of the charred remains of the letter, and smiled as the two merged, proving the efficacy of his constructs. The glowing sigils appeared to absorb the burned letter, then the glow faded away.

When he read what was visible on the letter, he frowned down at the sheet of paper. His magic had recovered what appeared to be a valediction. The writer had not provided a signature (much to Mr. Sloan's disappointment), but had closed the letter with these words: *To the Day of Talionis*

Mr. Sloan quirked an eyebrow.

He was familiar with the legal term *lex talionis*, which meant "law of retaliation"—more specifically, the type of retaliation in which the punishment reflected the crime. Under this law, a blood mage who had drained his victims of blood in order to enhance his evil magicks would not be hanged for murder. He would instead be sentenced to be himself drained of blood, forced to endure the same slow and agonizing death as his victims.

Some strict Fundamentalists advocated a return to *lex talionis,* which system had its origins in the tumultuous time of the Dark Ages. They pointed to various writings of the saints that seemed to promote such punishment. Mr. Sloan could also find writings of the saints that denounced it. He knew of no day in the Fundamentalist religious calendar termed the Day of Talionis and he wondered if the ominous-sounding name had something to do with restoring Prince Thomas to the throne.

Mr. Sloan was deeply concerned. He needed to know more about this Day of Talionis; he turned to the second fragment hoping it would provide additional information. He repeated his crafting, drawing the sigils and placing the paper over the charred fragment to draw the words off the letter. He was left with a partial sentence.

—*hard to find those who know both magic and contra*—

This letter had a signature.

Gaskell.

In the conversation Mr. Sloan had overheard, Smythe had sent Trubgek to Freya in order to talk to a man named Gaskell, who was refusing to work with Smythe. Yet here was evidence that Smythe and Gaskell were already engaged in correspondence, which was at odds with what Smythe had told Trubgek. Presumably, Smythe had lied to Trubgek.

Mr. Sloan did not see how this letter provided much help. He could not fault Smythe for fabricating a story designed to remove Trubgek from the camp before the prince's arrival. As for this Gaskell, he would inform Sir Henry and he and Simon would undoubtedly try to find him, but the odds were against them. The name was a fairly common one in Freya and they would have no idea where to even start looking.

The partial sentence was intriguing. "Hard to find those who know both magic and contra—" The obvious answer was contramagic. "Hard to find those who know both magic and contramagic." That was not much help, however, since the description could be applied to a majority of crafters in Aeronne.

Contramagic had been outlawed by the Church for centuries, up to the time of the war of the Bottom Dwellers when Father Jacob had famously discovered the seventh sigil that bound the two together. Magic and contramagic were now being taught together, but people had been told for so long that contramagic was evil that crafters were loath to work with it, and parents refused to let their children study it.

Mr. Sloan rubbed his forehead, discouraged. Though he had gained a good deal of information from the ledger, he felt he had uncovered more questions than he had answered.

He could not sit here moping. The day was advancing and he had to impart to Sir Henry the information he had discovered. Mr. Sloan was accustomed to writing in code, but he deemed the information so vital that he dared not risk any misinterpretation. Besides, he was not going to mail the letter. Now that he knew Miss Nettleship had arrived in Bheldem, he would request a day's leave and deliver it to her directly.

He found it odd, for he generally did not like or trust journalists, but he had come to have a very high opinion of Miss Nettleship.

Mr. Sloan completed his letter and placed it in a packet. He did not seal the packet, however. Smythe was dining with the prince and his friends tonight. Mr. Sloan decided to take the opportunity to search Smythe's office one more time, hoping to find out more information regarding the Day of Talionis.

Colonel Smythe would be entertaining his guests in the mess hall. He had named a late hour, nine of the clock, in order to give everyone time to rest from their exertions of the day. Prince Thomas, Phillip, and Sir Ander were punctual, as became military men, emerging from the south wing of the Commander's House just as Mr. Sloan's pocket watch marked the hour. Colonel Smythe was waiting at the entrance to the mess hall to welcome them and usher them inside.

The colonel eschewed the elaborate dress uniforms worn by his counterparts in other armies, adorned with gold braid, frogs, and epaulets. He wore his customary uniform, which was plain, simple, and serviceable. The prince, Sir Ander, and Phillip were likewise informally dressed, wearing practical clothes in somber colors suitable for travel: shirt, cravat, breeches, long coats.

Mr. Sloan saw them enter the mess hall. He waited another half hour to give everyone a chance to settle in, then headed for the Commander's House.

He greeted the sentry on duty at the Commander's House, saying that Colonel Smythe had asked him to check the royal quarters to ensure that all was secure.

He did a cursory sweep of the south wing, in case the sentry was paying attention, which he probably wasn't.

The hour was about ten of the clock. Mr. Sloan did not expect them to return to their rooms until after midnight.

He opened the door that connected the two wings. The hall was dark and empty. The magical constructs on the door to Smythe's office gave off a faint glow.

Mr. Sloan hastened down the hall to the office. He removed the magical constructs and entered, closing the door behind him. He had brought with him a bull's-eye lantern and, by its light, he started to search the bookshelves. He had given the titles only a cursory glance and had taken them all to be military in nature. The title of one book seemed to suddenly leap into prominence.

Lex Talionis.

The volume was slender and easily missed for it had been tucked in between the *Handbook of the Freyan Army* and the *Official History of the Blackfire War*.

Mr. Sloan reached for the book and suddenly froze in place, his motion arrested by the sound of muffled footfalls and the creaking of the door on its hinges.

Mr. Sloan was caught. He could not retreat and he had nowhere to hide. He could only assume that Smythe had returned and, finding the warding constructs missing, had realized an intruder was inside his office.

Mr. Sloan was left with one recourse. He would shine the lantern's light full in Smythe's eyes, blinding him, then bowl him over and rush out into the night.

Mr. Sloan whipped about, aiming the beam of the lantern at the face that loomed out of the darkness. At that instant, the light from another lantern flashed on Mr. Sloan's face. Each man halted, staring, each extremely startled to recognize the other.

"Sir Ander!" exclaimed Mr. Sloan.

"God bless my soul! It's Mr. Sloan!" gasped Sir Ander.

Before they could recover from the shock, both men heard the door to the north wing open and the measured tread of heavy footfalls.

"That is Colonel Smythe!" Mr. Sloan whispered.

"I take it you're not supposed to be in here," said Sir Ander.

"No, my lord," Mr. Sloan returned.

"Then our only way out is each other," Sir Ander whispered. "I brought my own defense. You can play along."

He held up an egg-shaped silver container known as a spirit flask, commonly carried by Rosian soldiers as part of their gear.

Mr. Sloan nodded in understanding.

Sir Ander removed the stopper, took a healthy pull from the flask, splashed the rum down his shirtfront, and reeled backward. He fell against the door and caused it to shut with a bang.

The footfalls came to a sudden halt.

"Who is there?" Smythe called. "You should know I am armed!"

Sir Ander tumbled to the floor with a curse. Mr. Sloan hurriedly raised the lid to the strongbox, then bent over Sir Ander, who was loudly swearing at him.

"Devil take you, sir! What have you done with my bed?"

Colonel Smythe flung open the door and barged inside, pistol in hand. He stopped to stare in amazement. "Sir Ander! Lieutenant Sloan! What is going on?"

Smythe looked from Sir Ander floundering on the floor to Mr. Sloan bending over him, endeavoring to placate him, and lowered the pistol.

"Colonel Smithee!" Sir Ander bawled, catching sight of him. "To your very good health, sir!"

He raised the flask, took a drink, and belched.

Smythe grimaced in disgust. The room reeked of rum.

"I think you had better explain, Lieutenant," he said.

"I was on my way to report to you, sir, when I found this gentlemen in your office," Mr. Sloan explained. "Sir Ander appears to have imbibed more rum than is good for him. He is under the impression he is in his own quarters and that I have absconded with his bed."

"The door was wizard-locked, Lieutenant," said Smythe grimly. "How could he have managed to break inside?"

"Damn door wasn't locked," Sir Ander protested indignantly. "Wide open! You accusing me of being a thief?"

"No, Sir Ander, of course not," said Smythe hurriedly.

Mr. Sloan regarded the colonel with concern.

"His Lordship does have a point, sir," he said. "If he found the door ajar . . . Is anything missing?"

Colonel Smythe glanced around the room and immediately saw the open strongbox.

"Look to see if we were robbed, Lieutenant."

Mr. Sloan dutifully checked the strongbox and reported that the money was inside. "Of course, sir, we should count it—"

"I will attend to that," said Smythe. "Escort His Lordship to his proper quarters, then report back."

"Yes, sir," said Mr. Sloan.

He and Smythe between them managed to haul the drunken knight to his feet. Mr. Sloan put his arm around Sir Ander and steered him down the corridor that led to the south wing. Glancing back over his shoulder, Mr. Sloan saw Smythe investigating the door to his office.

Mr. Sloan opened the connecting door, and the two men stumbled through it into the south wing. Mr. Sloan closed the door behind them and they stopped to draw breath.

"I would ask you why are you here, Mr. Sloan," said Sir Ander, "but then you would ask me why I am here and our conversation would grind to a halt."

"Where are the prince and his friend, my lord?" Mr. Sloan asked, as they continued down the corridor.

"In the mess hall, undoubtedly shaking their heads over me," said Sir Ander. "Unless I am much mistaken, they take me for a drunken old sod."

He walked on, his head bowed, his brow creased. He suddenly stopped in the corridor and turned to face Mr. Sloan.

"Tell me one thing, Mr. Sloan. Did Wallace send you here to harm Prince Thomas?"

Mr. Sloan considered and decided he could answer the question truthfully. "No, my lord. I can assure you I had no idea the prince was planning to visit the Old Fort."

Sir Ander nodded, as though that accorded with his thinking. "I'm going to be honest, Mr. Sloan. I need your help."

Mr. Sloan was concerned. "You are a friend of the Countess de Marjolaine, my lord. Her Ladyship is an enemy of my country."

"This has nothing to do with politics. The countess sent me here to investigate a man with the ungodly name of Trubgek. She heard he was here in Bheldem, but he doesn't appear to be around and no one seems to know where he went."

"Trubgek," Mr. Sloan repeated, troubled. "What interest does the countess have in him?"

"So you know him?"

"Yes, my lord. He was here, but he has gone."

"Damn! The countess heard a rumor that this Trubgek knows dragon magic and she thought perhaps I would be able to discover the truth. I hoped I might find some reference to him among Smythe's papers, but you saw how *that* ended." Sir Ander grimaced. "Tell me one thing. Is this rumor true? Does this man know dragon magic?"

Mr. Sloan knew how the game was played. He was trying to make up his mind to a desperate course of action, and to receive, one first had to give.

"I do not have firsthand knowledge of that myself, my lord, for I have never seen Trubgek use magic of any sort," said Mr. Sloan. "A crafter who *has* seen him work magic warned me that he knew dragon magic. This crafter was astonished by his skill and power. Trubgek appeared to confirm it when questioned."

Sir Ander looked dubious. "How is such a feat possible?"

Mr. Sloan shook his head. "I have told you all I know about the matter, my lord."

"Did you believe this crafter?"

"I do, my lord," said Mr. Sloan. "Trubgek was in the employ of a dragon named Coreg, who was evil to the core of his foul being. If anyone could have conducted such a heinous experiment, it would have been Coreg."

They had arrived at Sir Ander's room. The hallway was quiet. The prince and his friend had not returned. Mr. Sloan switched off the bull's-eye lantern. Windows in the hall let in light enough to see, once their eyes adjusted, and Mr. Sloan did not want to call attention to themselves. Sir Ander drew out the key.

"If you would wait a moment, my lord," said Mr. Sloan. "I did you a favor. I have one to ask in return."

Sir Ander frowned. "What is that, Mr. Sloan?"

"Are you returning tomorrow to the marquis's estate?"

"Yes, sir," Sir Ander replied.

"I believe that a woman named Miss Amelia Nettleship is currently a guest of the marchioness."

"I have met Miss Nettleship," said Sir Ander, growing more and more puzzled. "She is a journalist who writes outlandish tales about some female pirate. What do you want with her?"

"I have important information to convey to her. I would be deeply obliged, Sir Ander, if you would deliver it for me."

Sir Ander glowered at him. "We fought together to defeat the Bottom Dwellers, but I am loyal to my country and would not put Rosia in peril for any consideration. I cannot oblige you, Mr. Sloan. I bid you good night."

He turned the key in the lock.

"You may first read the information and then decide, my lord," said Mr. Sloan. "I also give you leave to show it to the countess."

"I cannot think the countess would be interested in anything you have to say, Mr. Sloan!" Sir Ander said heatedly. "Good night."

"To the contrary, my lord," said Mr. Sloan. "The countess wants Prince Thomas to become king of Freya. Yet I cannot believe she would sanction the violent overthrow of a monarchy."

Sir Ander rounded on him angrily. "I can tell you for a fact, Mr. Sloan, that the countess would never sanction seizing the throne by violence, nor would Prince Thomas, for that matter!"

"If that is true, my lord, then he needs to know that the colonel of his army is making those plans for him."

Mr. Sloan's words fell into the silence of the dark, empty hall. Sir Ander was wary, eyeing Mr. Sloan, perhaps seeking some ulterior motive.

"Why don't you take this information to Miss Nettleship yourself, sir?" he asked, uncomfortable. "I assume you could make up some excuse."

"My lord, it is very possible that I could report back to Colonel Smythe tonight and find his guards waiting to arrest me," said Mr. Sloan.

"Damn it, you could escape now, Mr. Sloan," said Sir Ander. "Steal one of the griffins and fly back to that perfidious master of yours and leave me out of this!"

Mr. Sloan gave a faint smile. "Impossible, my lord. Colonel Smythe would immediately deduce that I had been spying on him. He would change his plans and my work would have been for naught."

Sir Ander still hesitated. He obviously suspected Mr. Sloan of trying to involve him in some sinister plot, yet he knew this information could be of immense value and he was loath to turn it down.

"Oh, very well, damn it," said Sir Ander. "I will relay this to Miss Nettleship."

Mr. Sloan reached into a secret pocket he had sewn into the jacket of his uniform, drew out the thick letter and handed it to Sir Ander.

Mr. Sloan did not like having to share his intelligence with the countess. Sir Henry would probably never forgive him for what he would consider an unforgiveable betrayal, but Mr. Sloan did not see that he had a choice.

"I must return to the colonel," said Mr. Sloan. "Thank you, my lord."

He left Sir Ander gazing after him in thoughtful perplexity.

He returned to Smythe's office in some trepidation, more than half expecting to find guards waiting for him. Instead he found Smythe alone.

"Come in, Lieutenant. Did you convey Sir Ander safely to his quarters?"

"I did, sir."

"Good. I have searched the office. Nothing was taken," he said. "Did you search Masterson's belongings?"

"Yes, Colonel," said Mr. Sloan. "As we surmised, I found nothing incriminating."

"A pity. I think it was Masterson who broke into my office."

"Indeed, sir," said Mr. Sloan.

"He left us during dinner, said he needed to use the latrine. He was gone quite some time."

"Do you think he found anything?"

"I have discovered no evidence of it. I blame myself. I should have posted a sentry outside my door. See to that before you retire, Lieutenant."

"And the wizard locks, sir?"

"I will restore those myself," said Smythe.

"Yes, sir," said Mr. Sloan.

He took his leave. Crossing the compound, he saw Prince Thomas and his friend leaving the mess hall. He kept to the shadows and they did not notice him in the darkness. The two were walking slowly, conferring in low voices. He could not understand what they were saying and, frankly, he was too weary to care.

He returned to his room, lay down on his bed, and gazed into the darkness. By passing on this information to the countess, he was setting the cat among the pigeons. He had no idea what would come of it.

Perhaps something good.

Perhaps a flurry of blood and feathers.

TWENTY-NINE

Thomas returned to his parents' home following his visit to the Old Fort to find the invitation to Sophia's birthday party waiting for him. His mother had opened it, of course, and she was thrilled. She could talk of little else.

Constanza even carried the elegant invitation about with her and showed it to their houseguests, Phillip, Lord Ander Martel, and the Freyan journalist, Miss Amelia Nettleship, an average of three times a day.

"The party will be splendid," she told her guests. "The Duke de Bourlet is hosting. It is to be held in Castle Dragonreach, which is in Argonne in the southern part of Rosia. The duke is fabulously wealthy, you know, Miss Nettleship. He owns a great many castles, but this is said to be his favorite. Did I mention, Sir Ander, that my son is engaged to marry the Princess Sophia of Rosia?"

"Only four times this morning, Mother," said Thomas with an apologetic glance for Sir Ander and Amelia.

"I am certain I have a right to be proud of my son," said Constanza, annoyed.

"Your Ladyship has every right in the world," Sir Ander stated gallantly.

"Indeed, my lady," added Amelia. "The newspapers in Freya speak of very little else."

"Little else except rioting in the streets, the dire financial crisis, and the turmoil over the succession," Thomas said to Phillip the moment they were able to escape his mother.

"You sound as though you do not want to go to the party," Phillip said. "There will be lawn tennis and pall-mall, flirting and dancing."

"I am depressed at the very thought," said Thomas.

He had traveled to Bheldem because of Kate. She had shamed him. Over and over he heard her words as she had prepared to descend into the Deep Breath in that flimsy excuse for a bosun's chair, risking her life to save her crew.

"These are my people," Kate had told him. "I am their captain and that makes me responsible for their welfare."

Thomas held the best claim to be heir to the throne of Freya and he had never given the Freyan people a thought. He had been selfishly thinking only of himself, lamenting the fact that he had been born to bear this burden. Phillip had made him realize that instead of railing against his fate, he could embrace it. Kate had made him see that he had a responsibility to his people.

He still found the thought unnerving. He hoped Queen Mary lived a long and happy life and that many years would pass before he was called upon to advance his claim. In the interim, however, he planned to take his duties more seriously. Thus he had visited his parents in order to visit his army—which he had never set eyes upon—and talk to his commander, Colonel Smythe. Thomas was embarrassed to discover that he knew so little. He was determined to rectify that.

The visit had proven unsatisfactory. Thomas had discovered on their arrival that the troops were out on maneuvers. Colonel Smythe had been extremely apologetic, offering Thomas's short notice as an excuse, saying he had planned the maneuvers for a long time.

"The colonel was lying," Phillip told Thomas over a game of billiards. "One of the stable boys told me that no one had breathed a word about field maneuvers until right before our arrival. He said the order came down suddenly and they marched out with little preparation."

"But why would the colonel not want me to see my own troops?" Thomas asked.

"I have no idea. I also wonder why he is working on those troop carriers day and night, when in all likelihood you will not need an escort to Freya for a good many years."

"Why didn't you say something?" Thomas asked, watching his ball go everywhere on the billiard table except where he had aimed it.

"Because Lord Ander was always about," said Phillip.

Thomas snorted. "The knight was far more interested in studying that flask of his than he was in us."

"He was no more drunk than those sentries on guard duty," Phillip said. "Probably less so. Lord Ander is a close friend of the Countess de Marjolaine. She is the one who wrote to your mother to invite him to visit."

Thomas stared at his friend. "Are you saying Lord Ander is a spy? But why would the countess send him to spy on me? She claims to support my cause. Next you will be telling me that Miss Nettleship is a spy!"

"She could be," Phillip said. "She is a friend of Sir Henry's. And say nothing to her about Kate. Miss Nettleship will land on you like a swooping hawk on a rabbit. She will guess your secret in a second."

"Good God!" Thomas exclaimed, shaken. "Why didn't you warn me before now?"

"Because I am not convinced either of them are here to spy upon you," Phillip replied. "Miss Nettleship made arrangements to visit before she knew you were coming. As you say, the countess is on your side. Be that as it may, Lord Ander is here to spy on someone. He could be here to spy on me. The countess still does not trust me."

At least while Lord Ander and Miss Nettleship were here his mother was forced to occasionally talk about something else besides the party. But the next day Sir Ander unexpectedly departed, saying that he felt unwell and feared he was suffering a recurrence of the fever he had contracted Below. The journalist, Miss Nettleship, also left, saying that Sir Ander had offered to escort her to Everux, where she had business.

Phillip gave his friend a significant glance. "Whatever they came for, they have found it," he whispered.

Now that Sir Ander and Miss Nettleship were both gone, Constanza spent all her time talking about the royal birthday party, advising Thomas on what to wear, what to say, how to dance, and urging him to set a date for the wedding. Thomas listened to her with a patient smile, nodded, and said only what was necessary to placate her.

"I am glad we are sailing this morning," Thomas told Phillip as they sat down at the breakfast table for the last time. "I look forward to the voyage to Castle Dragonreach. Perhaps we will run into a wizard storm and crash on some remote and deserted island."

"Keep your voice down," Phillip warned with a glance at Constanza, who was seated at the far end of the long table, sorting through the morning mail. "Come now," he continued. "You know visiting the duke's won't be so bad."

"That's very well for you to say," Thomas returned. "*You* are going to spend a fortnight in the company of the woman you love."

Phillip shook his head. "And I must watch you dance with Sophia and drape her shawl around her shoulders and hold her in your arms while you teach her how to swing a tennis racquet. All the while, the Countess de Marjolaine will be dogging my every step, trying to catch me slipping poison into the punch."

"Poor Pip," said Thomas, smiling. "And I do have at least one reason to look forward to visiting the duke."

"What is that?" Phillip asked, spreading butter on a slice of toasted bread.

"There may be a letter waiting there from Kate," said Thomas.

"At the duke's?" Phillip asked, surprised. "How did you manage that? I gave Kate our address in Maribeau."

"When I received the invitation from the countess, I sent instructions to our landlord in Maribeau to forward our mail to the Duke de Bourlet's castle. I could not very well have my correspondence sent to my mother's," Thomas added grimly.

Constanza gave standing orders to the servants that all correspondence was to be delivered to her the moment the mail arrived. She did not actually read letters that were addressed to her son in his presence, but she would study the paper, the handwriting, the ink, try to guess who had written them, and then spend the rest of the day endeavoring to persuade Thomas to tell her the name of his correspondent and the letter's contents.

"Whereas when we are visiting the duke, you merely have to worry about the countess reading your mail," Phillip remarked.

Thomas shrugged. "The countess does not know Kate. As far as she knows, you are receiving letters from a young lady of your acquaintance. Unless she thinks they are coded letters from Sir Henry."

"That is not funny," said Phillip in grave tones.

The luxurious yacht bearing the Stanford coat of arms, drawn by four wyverns, arrived in due course. The servants loaded the luggage on board. Constanza embraced her son and kissed him and gave him many loving messages from her to his future bride.

"I am sorry your visit to the Old Fort was a disappointment," she said, accompanying him to the yacht. "I cannot imagine what Colonel Smythe was thinking, sending away the troops."

"The fault was mine, Mother," said Thomas. "I should have given him more than a few day's notice I was coming. Besides, I will have many more chances to review them in the coming years. There is no hurry."

His mother cast him a sharp glance. "What do you mean by that remark, my son?"

Thomas was startled by her reaction.

"I meant nothing, except that I will likely have many more years to prepare—unless you know something that I do not know, Mother?" he added, half in jest.

"No, no, I know nothing," Constanza said. She patted his arm. "I am glad you are taking your responsibilities seriously at last. Please give dear Sophia my love and tell her that I wish her all the happiness in the world."

"Yes, Mother," said Thomas for the hundredth time.

THIRTY

The journey to Castle Dragonreach in Argonne in the wyvern-drawn yacht took about nine days. A larger ship could have sailed through the open Breath and traveled straight to Argonne, cutting the duration of the voyage in half. But the smaller yacht could not survive the wizard storms and strong currents of the open Breath and so they traveled first to the Aligoes, then east-north-east to Rosia, and finally along the Rosian coastline to Argonne.

When finally Castle Dragonreach came into view, Thomas and Phillip stared in awe.

Almost every landscape artist for the last century had done paintings of the castle, for the magnificent structure had been built atop cliffs overlooking the Breath and was said to be one of the most beautiful in the world. Thomas had seen the paintings, but no artist could capture the wild and rugged beauty of the shining white castle wreathed by the orangish-pink mists of the Breath, set against a backdrop of the famous black cliffs of Argonne.

"Sir Henry maintains that the late and unlamented King Alaric wanted this castle and these lands for himself. He made life so intolerable for the previous duke that he eventually rebelled against him. Stephano de Guichen was only a boy at the time, but he and his father, Julian de Guichen, were loyal friends of the duke's and they both fought in the ill-fated rebellion.

"Stephano's mother, the Countess de Marjolaine, had been Julian's lover and bore his son. She became the king's mistress in order to protect her son, and she persuaded King Alaric to spare Stephano from execution, although she could not save his father. From what Sir Henry says, Stephano was furious with her, blaming her for his father's death. They went years barely speaking to each other. They were reconciled after the war, but their relationship remains cool."

"What do you remember about your mother?" Thomas asked. "You never speak of her."

"Nothing to talk about," said Phillip with a wistful smile. "She and my father died in a carriage accident when I was young. They had loved each other from childhood and when I came along, they both loved me. She was pretty and happy. He was funny and loving. They led very simple and prosaic lives."

"We could all wish our lives to be like that," said Thomas.

"Indeed we could," Phillip agreed quietly.

Their Graces, the Duke and Duchess de Bourlet, were waiting at the grand entrance to greet Thomas and Phillip upon their arrival. Neither had ever met His Grace, Stephano de Guichen, although they had heard him highly praised by those who knew him, including Captain Thorgrimson of the Dragon Brigade and many other Rosian officers. The two young men reserved judgment, reminding themselves that the duke was the son of the formidable countess.

"How pleasant can he be?" Phillip had wondered.

As it happened, they discovered that Stephano was extremely pleasant. They liked his bluff, frank, and unaffected manner, his warm smile. He immediately made them feel at home, as did his wife, the duchess.

Juliette Corti was gracious and lovely. The daughter of a knight, she had met Stephano when she was a new recruit to the Dragon Brigade. Following the war, Stephano had retired as commander of the Brigade, but he had built a training ground on his estate. Juliette had been one of the first women to enter the ranks of the Dragon Brigade and had a distinguished military career before leaving when she discovered she was expecting their first child.

Juliette was as tall as Stephano, who was of medium height, and, like him, she had the lithe, slender-boned build of a dragon rider. She had dark eyes and long black hair, which she wore in a simple braid around her head. She seemed reserved and cool until she smiled and then her dark eyes warmed and the hint of a mischievous dimple creased her cheek.

"Welcome to Castle Dragonreach, Your Highness, Your Grace," Juliette said, extending her hands and giving them both a kiss.

"Thank you, Your Grace. Has Princess Sophia arrived?" Thomas inquired.

"She came yesterday with the Countess de Marjolaine," said Juliette. "And Sir Rodrigo de Villeneuve is a guest, as well."

Stephano and his wife escorted their guests inside the castle and personally showed them to their rooms, which were on the third floor.

"Rodrigo," Thomas whispered. "Isn't he the man who saved you when the countess caught you with Sophia at the ball some months ago?"

"Yes," said Phillip. "Wait until you meet him. He is one of the wonders of the world."

They met Rodrigo as they were ascending the stairs and he was coming down. Both young men stopped to stare, for Rodrigo was dressed in the fashion that might have been popular with a courtier of King James I. He wore puffy pants tucked into tall leather riding boots that came up his thighs, a slashed doublet of blue velvet trimmed with silver, a frilly white shirt, and a wide-brimmed hat with a curling white feather that slanted over one eye.

"Sir Rodrigo?" Thomas asked Phillip in a low voice.

"Sir Rodrigo," said Phillip. "Do not be deceived. He may look like a coxcomb and act like a popinjay, but beneath his fine feathers are the talons of a hawk who can rip you to shreds."

"Your Grace," said Rodrigo, pausing on the landing to extend a hand, first removing an ornate glove done in brown leather that matched his boots. "I am pleased to renew our acquaintance."

"Thank you, my lord," said Phillip. "Allow me to introduce His Highness, Prince Thomas Stanford."

"Charmed, Your Highness," said Rodrigo.

He swept off his hat with a flourish and bowed deeply, leg extended, and then straightened to give Thomas a languid hand. Thomas was about to dismiss him as a fop, despite his friend's warning, when Rodrigo's grip on his hand suddenly tightened. Thomas looked into eyes that were glittering and bright as those of the aforementioned bird of prey.

"What is that outlandish getup you are wearing, Rigo?" Stephano asked with a laugh. "You look as though you walked out of an old portrait titled *A Noble Musketeer of King Thibault.*"

"Laugh if you choose, my friend, but my *haute couture* will be all the fashion at the court this autumn," said Rodrigo, smiling and twirling the feather in his hat.

"Do you know the whereabouts of my mother?" Stephano asked. "I would like to introduce His Highness."

"The last I saw of her, the countess was in the solar writing letters," Rodrigo replied.

"Ah, then she will be steeped in some intrigue and we must not disturb her," said Stephano with a slight frown.

"Hush, my dear." Juliette reprimanded him gently. "Have you seen the Princess Sophia?"

"I saw the little dog this morning, but I have not seen Her Highness," Rodrigo replied. He turned to Phillip. "Feel free to call upon me if Your Grace finds himself lost. My room is down the hall from yours. I am going out now to give a piquet lesson to a certain lady of my acquaintance, but I will return after luncheon."

"Thank you, my lord," said Phillip.

Rodrigo bowed again, put his hat back upon his head, and proceeded down the stairs, the tops of his boots flapping around his knees.

"Piquet!" Stephano repeated, shaking his head. "He's playing at some game, but it's not piquet!"

Juliette raised her eyebrows. "My dear!" she exclaimed, shocked.

Stephano laughed and kissed her, then proceeded up the stairs with his wife, leaving Thomas and Phillip to follow more slowly.

"What did Sir Rodrigo mean by telling you to call upon him if you're lost?" Thomas asked.

"He reminds me of the night he helped me avoid the wrath of the countess when I first met Sophia. His way of telling me he needs to talk to me in private," said Phillip. He added thoughtfully, "I wonder why . . ."

Thomas grimaced. Phillip gave him a sympathetic smile.

"You had best become accustomed to intrigue, my friend, for it will swirl around you all the days of your life."

Thomas grimaced. "I have been steeped in intrigue from my birth. My mother lives to scheme and plot. I was hoping to escape it for a time."

"No such luck, I am afraid," said Phillip. "I will meet you later in the garden to impart what I find out."

The duke and duchess showed them their rooms, which were large and beautifully furnished and provided breathtaking views of the cliffs and the Breath. Phillip said he wanted to take a nap, and retired to his room. Thomas assumed he was going to wait until Rodrigo returned to speak to him.

Thomas asked his hostess if any letters had been delivered either for him or for Phillip. Juliette replied that she was sorry, she did not know of any. Thomas endeavored to conceal his disappointment, but he must have failed, for the duchess said she would ask the servants to make certain. She returned shortly afterward to say that neither he nor Phillip had received any letters.

Thomas, upset and restless, left the unpacking to the servants and went for a walk around the palace grounds. He began to wonder if he had misjudged Kate. Perhaps he had deceived himself into believing she was growing fond of him, when in reality, she was only grateful to him for saving her life. Perhaps he had mistaken gratitude for affection.

Hoping to shake off his dark mood, he went to view the training grounds utilized by the dragon and human members of the Dragon Brigade. He had asked the duke if he would be able to see some of the dragons and their riders in training, but was told the new recruits had flown to the Aligoes to serve in the war against the pirates.

Thomas walked the deserted training grounds and thought about Kate, remembering her story of how she had first met Dalgren. The dragon must have been court-martialed by now. Kate would be devastated if he was found guilty. Given that Dalgren had deserted and confessed to his crime, Thomas did not foresee a good ending.

Stephano would know the trial's outcome, but Thomas could not think of any way to ask without inviting questions that he could not very well answer. He had been hoping Kate would write to let him know. Apparently she had not cared enough about him to do so.

He strolled the grounds enveloped in gloom, oblivious of the magnificent scenery, until he deemed it time to meet Phillip in the garden, which overlooked the faintly swirling mists of the Breath. He paced the pebble-covered walkways and inhaled the fragrance of lavender and late-blooming roses and grew calm, allowing the tranquility and beauty to sink into his soul.

"Here you are!" Phillip cried, coming around a row of manicured boxwood hedges and spotting Thomas. "These blasted hedges! I have been searching for you everywhere!" He waved a letter. "It's from Kate!"

"Where did you get that?" Thomas asked, amazed. "I asked Her Grace. She said no letters had been delivered."

"Sir Rodrigo gave it to me," said Phillip, grinning.

"Why did he have it?" Thomas demanded.

"Rodrigo saw the letter on the entry table when the post was delivered. The countess still mistrusts me and he feared if she found it, she would read it. He carried off the letter before she saw it."

"So now Sir Rodrigo reads your mail?" Thomas asked scathingly.

"Perhaps he did," said Phillip, shrugging. "If so, he is very good at it. The wax seal is intact and I can detect no signs that anyone tampered with it."

Thomas shook his head, but he was too eager to hear from Kate to pursue the matter. "What does she say?"

"I have not yet opened it," said Phillip.

He broke the seal, unfolded the letter, and began to read. Thomas peered over his shoulder.

"Kate is fine," Phillip reported. "She writes that Dalgren was found guilty at his court-martial and that he was going to lose his name—whatever that means—but he was granted a reprieve. He is going to travel Below to work with the Bottom Dwellers. Good heavens! Kate is going Below with him—"

"Below! Let me see that!" Thomas was about to snatch the letter to study it more closely when they were interrupted by a young woman's excited voice.

"Did I hear someone mention Kate? How is she? How is Dalgren?"

Sophia came hurrying around the end of the hedge row, accompanied by Bandit. She stopped when she saw the two young men staring at her in astonishment.

"Oh, dear! I do beg your pardon, gentlemen!" Sophia blushed red. "I truly was *not* eavesdropping. I could not help overhearing your conversation and when I heard you mention Kate I could not contain myself. She has been in my thoughts. She told me she knew you, Your Grace."

"She did?" Phillip asked, his amazement growing. "How . . . where did you meet Kate?"

"At the court-martial," said Sophia, flustered. "I attended as a representative of the crown. Please do forgive me! Come here, Bandit! We must go and leave these gentlemen to their letter."

She tried to catch the little dog, but Bandit had trotted over to greet Phillip. The spaniel claimed him as a friend, pawing at his legs and barking.

"You naughty Bandit! Come here!" Sophia repeated. "I am so sorry, Your Grace."

Phillip bent down to pet the dog. "He remembers the night we met, Your Highness." He looked up at her with a smile. "As do I. Most fondly."

Sophia's flush deepened.

"You found me hiding under that table and now you find me hiding in the hedge row," she said, sighing. "You must take me for a most desperate character."

She shifted her gaze to Thomas. "I do hope you will forgive me, Your Highness."

"I find nothing to forgive, Your Highness," said Thomas, slipping the letter up the sleeve of his jacket. "Your reaction was quite natural. You heard the name of a friend and you were concerned about her welfare."

He knew he should let the matter drop, change the subject, talk about the weather or pet the dog or ask her about her travels. He could not help himself, however. His curiosity was too great.

"You said you attended the court-martial, ma'am, and that you met Kate . . . I mean Mistress Katherine . . ."

He stammered over her name, but Sophia was recovering from her own embarrassment and did not appear to notice his.

"The countess and I were traveling to the Dragon Duchies," Sophia explained. "Kate had come to speak in Dalgren's defense, but the griffin wouldn't take her to the dragon lands. The countess was happy to offer Kate a ride with us in our carriage."

"Good God!" Phillip murmured.

Thomas was too stunned for words. He could only stand and stare.

Fortunately Sophia was trying to catch Bandit and did not notice. "That bench at the end of the walk offers a beautiful view of the harbor," she added after she had captured the dog. "We could make ourselves comfortable and you can both tell me how you came to know Kate."

"I am certain Tom would like nothing better, but he has a pressing engagement—" Phillip began.

Thomas elbowed him in the ribs. "I would very much like to see the view."

"What the hell are you doing?" Phillip whispered to his friend, as Sophia and Bandit led the way to the bench. "You shouldn't be talking about Kate at all, much less with the young woman to whom you are engaged! Escape now, while you have the chance."

"Sophia attended the court-martial!" Thomas whispered back. "She knows what happened to Kate. If that is true about her going Below, I need to find out!"

"And how are you going to tell her you know Kate? Will you say, 'I met Kate, Your Highness, when she threatened to shoot me,'" Phillip mimicked.

"I will think of something," Thomas muttered.

The three sat down on the bench, Thomas on one side of Sophia, and Phillip on the other. The scent of pines mingled with the fragrance of the flowers, and a faint breeze shook some of the yellowing leaves from the walnut trees and stirred the mists of the Breath. Bandit lay on the ground at Sophia's feet, growling at the butterflies he was too lazy to chase.

"And so, sir, tell me how you know Kate," Sophia said, turning to Thomas.

Before he could reply, she was struck by a sudden horrifying thought. "Your Highness was recently with the Rosian navy! Was it your ship that attacked her ship and sank it?"

Thomas didn't know how to answer.

Phillip came to his rescue. "You heard about that? You know Kate is a pirate?"

"Privateer," Sophia corrected, smiling. "I know all about Kate. Stephano told us. And I have read the stories about her."

Thomas had been going to claim he had met Kate at the home of a friend, but that would not suit. He had been ranting and raving about hating lies and intrigue. He could not tell a lie now. Looking at Sophia, pretty and happy, Thomas made up his mind at that moment that he would not lie to her. Ever.

"First, let me assure you that I did not sink Kate's ship, ma'am," said Thomas. "The story of how she and I met is long and complicated and could potentially turn into an international incident involving four governments, so I dare not tell it, not even to you. Suffice it to say, Kate and I were each trying to liberate some cargo from a ship. It ended up sinking and her dragon, Dalgren, came to our rescue."

"How exciting!" Sophia turned to Phillip. "What about you, sir? How did you meet Kate?"

Phillip hesitated, then said, "Well, since we are being completely honest—"

"Always a bad policy, Your Grace," said a grave voice. "I do not recommend it."

Bandit sat up with a growl. The three young people jumped and turned to see Rodrigo saunter out of the shadows of the boxwood hedge. He fended off Bandit, who was fascinated by the high leather boots, and smiled at Sophia.

Phillip and Thomas exchanged alarmed glances.

Thomas rose to his feet to confront him. "You should have made yourself known, sir. You do not act the part of a gentleman."

"I never do," said Rodrigo complacently. "And please do not challenge me to a duel, Your Highness. I survived one affair of honor, but that was only because a man in a tree shot my opponent. Allow me to I assure you, sir, that I did not hear anything except that ill-advised statement made by His Grace that he intended to be honest."

Thomas did not believe him. He disliked the man, disliked his sly, foxlike face and his clever eyes. Phillip stood up hurriedly.

"I believe I will go back to my room to take a nap before dinner," he said. "Thomas, don't you have letters to write?"

"I do, Pip. Thank you for reminding me," Thomas said.

"I am sorry you have to go," said Sophia. "We will finish our talk another time."

They made their excuses and departed. Thomas, glancing back, saw Rodrigo settle himself on the bench at Sophia's side.

"Sir Rodrigo is our host's best friend," Phillip admonished him as they walked off. "It would never do to start a quarrel with the duke."

"I do not understand how His Grace can stomach that gentleman. Stephano has the reputation for being an honest, courageous, honorable man," said Thomas. "From what you tell me, this Rodrigo is a philanderer, a fop, a gossip—"

"And a war hero," said Phillip. "His selfless, courageous actions during the war with the Bottom Dwellers contributed to their defeat."

"Makes one believe in doppelgängers," Thomas muttered.

"Go hide in your room so that you may read and reread Kate's letter," Phillip suggested. "And from now on, I would suggest rather less honesty. You never know who might be listening."

Rodrigo and Sophia sat together on the bench overlooking the harbor.
Rodrigo observed that Sophia was not enjoying the breathtaking view of
the white-sailed ships far below them, nor was she paying attention to Bandit, who was currently engaged in rolling on his back in the grass, undoubtedly in something disgusting.

Her gaze and, Rodrigo guessed, her thoughts were following Thomas and
Phillip as they walked along the path among the fading flowers and the falling leaves. Sophia was focused on one of the gentlemen in particular and he
was *not* the gentleman to whom she was engaged.

When Thomas and Phillip were lost to sight, Sophia gave a faint smile, a
small sigh, and absently smoothed the folds of her skirt. Rodrigo regarded
her with concern. She might be a magical savant, with talents far beyond
those of ordinary crafters, but she was still only eighteen and she had no one
in whom she could confide.

Her mother had declared her an ungrateful child and departed in high
dudgeon after Sophia had defied her wishes and chosen to attend university
rather than marry some aged, gout-ridden count. Sophia was attended by
ladies-in-waiting when at home in the palace, but both the countess and Rodrigo had warned her never to tell them her secrets, for at least one and
probably more were undoubtedly in the pay of foreign governments. Sophia
generally confided in Cecile, for she loved the countess, who had been more
than a mother to her. But while Cecile loved Sophia dearly, she disliked and
distrusted Phillip, knowing that he had once been an agent for Sir Henry
Wallace. Cecile was also the one who had arranged the marriage with Prince
Thomas. No, Sophia could not very well confide in her.

"That leaves me," said Rodrigo.

The time had come for him to take action—a bold move, for he was far
better suited to a life of indolence and comfort.

"My dear girl, I am your uncle Rigo," he said. "You know you can be honest with me."

Sophia smiled and shook her head at him. "I just now heard you advise
His Grace that he should never be honest with anyone."

"I am not his uncle," said Rodrigo. "Admittedly, I am not your uncle either,
but I have undertaken to act in that capacity. I have seen you color prettily
when His Grace smiles at you—"

"I do not!" Sophia protested, her cheeks flushing.

"And I have seen that a single look from you reduces the Duke of Upper
and Lower Milton to bread pudding," Rodrigo continued. "The two of you

are falling in love faster than any two people I have ever encountered, with the possible exception of myself."

Sophia ducked her head so that her face was shadowed by the brim of her hat, and began plucking at the lace on her shawl.

"I cannot let myself fall in love with him, Rigo," she said. "I am to marry Prince Thomas."

"True," said Rodrigo. "Are you aware that he is in love with someone else?"

"You mean Kate," Sophia said. "I didn't know for certain, but I saw him 'color prettily' when her name was mentioned."

Rodrigo gave her an approving look. "You have been taking my lessons in *affaires de coeur* to heart. Far more useful, in my opinion, than studying Advanced Theorems on the Application of Magic in the Modern World."

"The advanced theorems are so much easier to grasp!" Sophia said with another sigh. "I believe that Kate is in love with him."

"You two traveled together in the Dragon Duchies," said Rodrigo. "Traveling is a dull business and one tends to pour out one's heart just to alleviate the boredom. Did Kate pour out her heart to you, my dear?"

"Oh, no. Kate is much like the countess. She wraps her heart in lavender and packs it away in a brass-bound chest."

"So how did you find out?" Rodrigo asked.

"The countess and I were discussing Prince Thomas at dinner one night. Kate had been very talkative up to that point. When the countess spoke his name, Kate suddenly was very quiet. She pushed her food around on her plate and couldn't eat, and when I said something about Prince Thomas being in the Aligoes chasing pirates, she choked on her wine."

"Tongue-tied, loss of appetite, choking: all symptoms of love," Rodrigo agreed. "So, what are we to do to fix this?"

Sophia rested her hand on his. "There is nothing to fix, Uncle Rigo. I am engaged to Prince Thomas and I am certain I could do far worse. He is handsome, kind, and honorable. Phillip would not be such close friends with him if he were otherwise."

She tried to speak with matter-of-fact calm, but Rodrigo heard a tremor in her voice and observed her closely. "The countess arranged this marriage. You know your doting brother would never force you to marry anyone against your will."

"But I am not marrying the prince against my will," Sophia protested quickly. "I agreed to this marriage for the sake of our two nations, as did His Highness. In time, we will learn to love each other."

"Or you will both continue to love others and be miserable," Rodrigo said.

"I cannot be miserable if I am doing what I know to be right, Uncle Rigo," said Sophia. "When I was being held captive by the Bottom Dwellers, I was frightened, lost, and alone. The countess went willingly into that hell to find me. She was prepared to give her life for me. I owe her everything."

"You do not owe her a lifetime of unhappiness, Sophia," said Rodrigo, unusually serious.

"You talk as though the countess was an ogre who has me locked in a tower!" Sophia said. "She explained to me the benefits of this marriage to both Rosia and Freya. She left the decision entirely up to me. I agreed to the engagement with all my heart."

"But that was before you met Phillip," Rodrigo said.

"My feelings for him will not affect my decision, Uncle. I trust the countess. I know that she loves me and she would not do anything to hurt me. All she is asking of me is to marry a very handsome prince. Not a terrible sacrifice," Sophia added with a light laugh.

Rodrigo would have continued to argue, but he was interrupted by Bandit, who had managed to become entangled in the thorns of a holly bush and was emitting frightful howls. Sophia hurried off to rescue her dog.

Rodrigo gazed after her, deep in thought. He was a romantic. He believed in love. He loved being in love. He felt he owed love a debt of gratitude and he decided to hurl himself into the fray in love's name.

Sophia returned carrying Bandit, who sank down, panting, at her feet and growled at the holly bush.

"May I ask you a question regarding proper decorum, Uncle?"

"Decorum! Good heavens! How fatiguing!" Rodrigo said, alarmed.

"I would like to continue to be friends with His Grace while we are together this fortnight," Sophia said. "There would be nothing improper in talking to him, would there, Rodrigo?"

"You must be careful not to rouse suspicion, of course," said Rodrigo. "Laugh coquettishly at every word the prince utters and yawn and roll your eyes when you are with the duke."

"I am in earnest, Uncle," Sophia scolded.

Rodrigo reflected. In his experience, if two people were walled up together for an extended period of time, enduring days of enforced fun and frolic, they either fell more deeply in love or they grew heartily sick of one another. He generally belonged to the latter category, though he had a feeling that Sophia and Phillip would belong to the former.

"If I were your duenna, I would advise you to keep well clear of His Grace," said Rodrigo. "Since I am only an uncle, I see nothing improper in being friendly."

"Thank you, dear uncle!" Sophia gave him a kiss. "I must go. I promised Juliette I would help her tat lace for a baby cap."

She gathered up Bandit and departed.

"I must do something to help," Rodrigo said to himself. "Though I must admit that pairing a prince with a pirate will be a challenge for even my advanced skills at matchmaking."

THIRTY-ONE

Thomas shut the door to his room, told the servants he did not want to be disturbed, and sat down in the window seat to read Kate's letter by the waning light of the sun.

> *My dear Pip,*
> *I promised I would let you know the outcome of Dalgren's court-martial. He was found guilty and sentenced to be stripped of his name. I will not go into what that entails, but the punishment is terrible among dragons. I feared he would not survive.*
>
> *He was granted a reprieve, however. A dragon-lore master found an ancient law which says that a dragon can redeem himself and earn back his name if he performs a sacrifice that benefits others.*
>
> *The upshot is that he has agreed to travel Below to work for a priest named Father Jacob Northrop. I plan to go with him. He is my friend and he should not go alone.*
>
> *Please do not worry about me. I am traveling with two Trundler women named Miri and Gythe. They are dear friends of the Duke de Bourlet and these two sisters make the journey on a*

*regular basis and they take their cat with them! How perilous can
it be?*

*I trust you are well, Pip. Give my best wishes to our mutual
friend.*

Yours sincerely,
Kate

P.S. Dalgren sends his warm regards.
*P.P.S. I will be forever grateful to you and our mutual friend
for your help.*

He read the letter again and again until he was interrupted by the sound
of a gong ringing through the hall of the castle, announcing dinner. Thomas
hurriedly struggled into his evening finery, thrust Kate's letter into the inner
pocket of his blue brocade jacket, and ran down the stairs, wondering how
he was going to steer the conversation to two Trundler women.

The fortnight passed quickly. Thomas enjoyed himself far more than he had
anticipated. He and Phillip and Sophia were inseparable. The days being crisp
and sunny, they spent much of their time outdoors. They hiked up the cliff to
view a waterfall that tumbled with a cascade of white foam into the Breath,
and visited the dragon training ground with Stephano.

They played croquet and lawn tennis, walked in the garden, and helped
Juliette gather the last flowers for the bouquets that filled the rooms with
fragrance. They celebrated Sophia's nineteenth birthday with a quiet family
party, for Sophia did not want to make a fuss.

Thomas grew to like Sophia, finding her cheerful, funny, and intelligent.
She had an excellent grasp of world affairs and was able to give Thomas in-
sights into the politics of many major world powers. She readily credited the
countess as her teacher and he could see how much she loved and admired
Cecile. Thomas's own trust and estimation for the countess rose as a result.

They did not see much of Cecile. She spent her days in the solar, receiving
visitors who came and went at all hours and who appeared to be from various walks of life. The family and servants studiously took no notice of the
strangers, beyond Stephano's occasional grim mutterings and dark looks.

"Something is amiss," said Rodrigo one evening as he joined the young
people at the card table, playing quadrille. "I fancy it has to do with Lord
Ander Martel. He came to visit the countess here not long ago."

Thomas and Phillip exchanged startled glances.

"Your bid, Your Grace," said Rodrigo.

"Oh, uh, yes, sorry," Phillip said.

"I did not know Lord Ander was here," Sophia said. "I did not see him."

"He did not make himself known. He slipped into the palace without ceremony, spent an hour closeted in the solar with the countess, and departed in haste."

"How do you know all this, Rigo?" Sophia asked with a laugh as she played a card.

"Can you truly ask me such a question, dear girl?" Rodrigo returned with a smile. "Your turn, sir. Are you certain you want to play that card?"

Thomas had not been paying attention. He picked up the card and laid down the right one.

"Lord Ander is the countess's dearest friend," Sophia continued. "I am surprised she said nothing to me about his visit."

"Judging by his grim expression, Lord Ander was not here to pay a social call," said Rodrigo. "Not long afterward, the countess's secretary, D'argent, left on some sort of urgent mission and we have seen little of the countess since. I believe it is your turn, Your Grace."

Phillip laid down a card and cast a glance at Thomas. He was thinking again how much he disliked Sir Rodrigo. He did not have a chance to talk to Phillip until they retired for the night.

"Lord Ander was here! He must have come to see the countess after he left Bheldem," Phillip said to Thomas as they climbed the stairs to their rooms. "What do you make of that?"

"More intrigue," Thomas said bitterly. "That man Rodrigo introduced the subject deliberately, to see how we would react. He knows more than he is telling."

"If he didn't then, he does now," said Phillip. "One look at our guilty faces and he had his answer."

As the days passed, Thomas saw Sophia and Phillip falling deeper and deeper in love. He watched the two walk together, drawing close, hands sometimes touching, though never for long. At such times, they were completely wrapped up in each other, leaving him forgotten. He envied his friends at these times and felt very much alone.

The autumn rains began and their walks were spoiled by gray clouds, and sheets of water pouring from the sky. Thomas and Phillip and Sophia stayed indoors, playing round games, cards, chess, and checkers. They read books in the library and took their exercise as afternoon strolls up and down the long gallery.

One afternoon, near the end of their stay, Thomas was by himself in the library. He had been chagrined to discover his ignorance of world affairs, especially compared to Sophia, who knew far more than he did. He was resolved to learn more. He chose a book on Braffa, but instead of reading, he listened to the rain fall and gazed into the fire, thinking of Kate.

He was relieved when a knock on the door interrupted his melancholy mood. Expecting Phillip, he was surprised to see Sophia enter, accompanied by the ever-present Bandit.

"I am sorry to interrupt you—" Sophia began.

"No, no, please do!" said Thomas, rising to his feet. "This book is rather heavy going, I'm afraid."

Sophia glanced at the title and laughed. "*The History of the Braffan Oligarchy.* I am surprised you are still conscious."

"I fear I would have succumbed if you had not rescued me," said Thomas.

He stirred the fire, for the library was an immense room and a chill wind whispered through the lead-paned windows and disturbed the curtains.

"May we talk, Your Highness?" Sophia asked, sitting down in a chair. Bandit curled up in front of the fire. "I leave tomorrow for Freya and I did not want to go without letting you know that I am aware of your regard for Kate."

Thomas jumped up once more to stir the fire and hide his confusion.

"I am sorry," he said politely. "I do not take your meaning."

"I know you like her very much, and so do I," Sophia explained. "I think she is splendid. If it is any comfort, I believe she feels the same for you."

Thomas remained standing by the fire, although he had stopped stirring it. "Did she mention me?"

"Oh, no. Kate would never talk about anything that personal. She was not aware that I saw how she feels. But I think I am right," Sophia said calmly.

Thomas did not know what to say. He thought he should apologize for loving someone else, but then he looked at Sophia. She was regarding him with understanding and sympathy, and he felt as though he was confiding in a beloved sister. He returned to his chair and brought it closer to her.

"So what do we do now?"

"Our duty," said Sophia.

Thomas shook his head.

"Our marriage will unite the people of Rosia and Freya and bring two warring nations together," Sophia said.

"I am not king of Freya and there is every likelihood I will never be," said Thomas with a rueful smile. "You could be buying a prince in a poke."

Sophia laughed. "You are a member of the Estaran royal family. Your father is Marquis of Cavanaugh. The countess says that if you choose, you can exert your influence over Freyan politics even if you do not wear a crown."

If I choose . . . Thomas thought again of a plan he had been half forming in his mind. He said nothing, however. He had not told anyone. Not even Phillip.

"Do you know why the countess arranged for you to be my husband?" Sophia asked. "I had many suitors," she added in matter-of-fact tones. "All of them wanted to marry me for my influence or power or to gain some advantage in their home countries. The countess chose you for two reasons. The first is that she hopes to bring about lasting peace between Rosia and Freya. She says she does not want to see another war in her lifetime."

"The second reason?" Thomas asked.

"Because you are close to my age and she believed you were someone I could love," said Sophia. "I think I could have . . ."

"If you had not met Pip," said Thomas. "I will not ask if you are in love with him, Sophia, for, of course, a lady would refuse to answer such a delicate question. But if it is any comfort to you, I know he loves you with all his heart."

Thomas took her hand in his, to make a vow. "When we are wed, I promise that I will be a good and faithful husband to you, Sophia."

She clasped his hand in hers. "And I promise I will be a good and faithful wife. I am so glad to know that I will be marrying a dear friend."

They shook hands to solemnize their oath, only to be interrupted by Phillip, who opened the door and thrust his head inside.

"Thomas? The countess is asking for us—" Phillip saw Sophia and stopped. "I beg your pardon, Your Highness. I thought Thomas was alone."

"I was just going," said Sophia, rising. "I am glad we spent this time together, Thomas."

She gathered up Bandit and left Thomas with a smile, giving an even warmer smile to Phillip as she passed him. Phillip stood gazing after her.

"She is to leave tomorrow," he said softly.

"I know," said Thomas. "What did you come to tell me?"

"Oh, yes, sorry," said Phillip. "The countess sent me to find you. She wants to see both of us now in the solar."

"Both of us? Did she tell you what this meeting was about?" Thomas asked.

"She did not," Phillip answered. "But I saw her private secretary, D'argent, enter the palace about an hour ago; the dust of travel was on his cloak. I think the party has ended."

THIRTY-TWO

A servant guided Thomas and Phillip to the solar, a room in one of the upper stories of the palace, used by the family, particularly the women, as a private sitting room. Small and intimate, the solar was the ideal place to retire in solitude and peace, escape the bustle of servants and guests.

The solar was charming, with old-fashioned, ornately carved woodwork covering the walls, a large stone fireplace, and comfortable high-backed chairs. A deeply recessed window faced west to take advantage of the bright afternoon sunlight. Thomas and Phillip found the countess standing at this window, gazing out of it, her arms folded across her chest.

When the servant announced them, Cecile turned to greet them with a cool and gracious smile.

She was elegantly though simply dressed in a gown of gray silk with a lacy shawl around her shoulders. Her only ornament was a gold ring on her left hand. She did not invite them to be seated. She was clearly deeply troubled.

Cecile did not waste time in niceties. Confronting Phillip, she said abruptly, "Your Grace was in the service of Sir Henry Wallace."

"I *was* in his service, my lady," said Phillip, laying emphasis on the past tense. "I have assured Your Ladyship before that I no longer work for Sir Henry. My loyalties are to His Highness."

Cecile impatiently brushed his words aside. "Be that as it may, are you acquainted with a man named Franklin Sloan?"

Phillip was startled and wary. "Sir Henry has a private secretary who goes
by that name."

"Would you say this Mr. Sloan is a man to be trusted? That is . . ." Cecile
rephrased her question. "Would Sir Henry be likely to trust him?"

"Mr. Sloan is more than a secretary to Sir Henry," said Phillip. "He is a
valued friend and confidant. Sir Henry would trust him implicitly."

Cecile gave a grave nod. "That was my assessment, as well."

She fell silent, lost in thought, twisting the ring on her finger.

"Let us sit down," she said abruptly. "We could be here some time."

She indicated a sofa by the fire. Thomas sat down near the fire, Cecile took
her place at his side, and Phillip drew up a chair to sit near Thomas.

Cecile turned to face him. "You visited an army encampment while in
Bheldem, Your Highness."

"I did, my lady," Thomas said.

"You accompanied Prince Thomas, Your Grace. The two of you spent a
day and a night there."

"Yes, my lady," Phillip answered, exchanging puzzled glances with
Thomas.

"Were you aware that Mr. Sloan was present in the fort at the same time?"
Cecile asked.

Phillip was taken aback. "That is not possible, my lady! I would have recognized him immediately."

"Mr. Sloan feared you would recognize him and took pains to keep out of
your sight," said Cecile. "He was there, I assure you, to gather intelligence
about Your Highness's plans to invade Freya and overthrow the queen."

Thomas gaped at her. "But . . . that is ludicrous! I have no such plans!"

Cecile studied him searchingly. Thomas realized she was trying to find out
if he was lying and he flushed beneath her scrutiny and said angrily, "I assure
Your Ladyship I have no plans to invade Freya!"

"You may not, sir. But your colonel has," Cecile said.

She reached over to an end table on which stood a large inlaid chest made
of ebony and rosewood. She opened the chest, drew out a sheaf of papers,
and placed them on the table in front of Thomas. He made no move to touch
them.

"Mr. Sloan discovered that Colonel Smythe and your parents are making
these plans in your name. He relates all this in his report. I did not truly think
you had knowledge of these plans, but I had to make certain," said Cecile.

"I don't believe it. This man, Sloan, is a creature of Sir Henry's!" said
Thomas, giving the papers a glance of contempt. "We cannot trust him."

"We can, because he wrote this report for Sir Henry," said Cecile.

"I don't understand," said Thomas.

"Mr. Sloan is unshakably loyal to Sir Henry," Phillip explained. "He would not give him false information."

"Very well, I grant you that. But if this was intended for Sir Henry, how did you come by it, my lady?" Thomas asked.

"Lord Ander," said Phillip promptly.

"Your Grace is very perceptive," said Cecile dryly. "Lord Ander was there on another mission, one that has nothing to do with Your Highness. He was as astonished to see Mr. Sloan as Mr. Sloan was to see him. The two knew each from the war against the Bottom Dwellers. Lord Ander owes Mr. Sloan his life and despite the fact that the two are avowed foes, they have developed a certain amount of trust.

"Mr. Sloan was in desperate straits. He needed to find a way to send this information to Sir Henry. He found out Lord Ander was staying at your home with a female journalist who, it seems, was there for the sole purpose of receiving information from Mr. Sloan."

Phillip cast Thomas a glance that said, "I told you so."

"Miss Nettleship has presumably delivered the information to Sir Henry. Lord Ander was so troubled by what he read that he made a copy and immediately brought it to me.

"I dispatched D'argent to Freya to try to confirm Mr. Sloan's information. Colonel Smythe is very clever, however, and D'argent could not discover much. What he did find is disturbing."

"And that is?" Thomas asked.

"Colonel Smythe is involved in a plot with your mother, Thomas, and a group of people in Freya who call themselves the Faithful. They plan to overthrow the queen, foment revolution, and take advantage of the unrest to place you upon the throne.

"As proof, Mr. Sloan found that vast sums of money are being sent to Freya to hire and train armies and provide them with weapons and ammunition. These armies are being raised in secret locations in northern Freya. When the time comes, they will be positioned near strategic cities."

"This answers our questions about the troop carriers," said Thomas. "My mother has done nothing all her life but scheme and plot to make me a king. I should not be surprised."

"You did not choose your fate, Thomas," said Cecile. "But you can choose how to deal with what fate has given you."

Thomas gazed into the flames, silent. He had no choice. He had to act. But once he told them about his idea, spoke the words, they could change his life forever.

"What will happen when the queen dies?" he asked abruptly.

"Civil war will break out," Cecile replied. "Hugh and Elinor are already planning for that eventuality. They are garnering support from various factions, raising money for their own armies. Neither will accept the other on the throne."

Thomas was silent, considering. He had seen armies marching in the streets during the war, people living in fear and dying in terror. He recalled Sophia talking about their duty, bringing peace to warring nations.

Phillip was regarding him with a troubled expression. Thomas had not mentioned this plan to his friend, but Phillip knew him well and could probably guess what Thomas was going to propose. Thomas could also guess that his friend would not be happy.

Thomas made his decision. "My lady, could you arrange for me to meet with the queen of Freya?"

"I could, Your Highness," Cecile replied, with a slight frown. "Such a journey would be fraught with peril, however. You would need to have a very good reason to undertake such a dangerous mission."

"I believe I do," said Thomas. "I have been thinking about this for some time. I would like the chance to introduce myself to Her Majesty. Persuade her that I am not a power-seeking, vainglorious youth interested only in my own aggrandizement. I want to convince her that I would work hard to be a good ruler. She could name me as heir and trust that I would elevate myself to the country."

"An interesting idea, sir," said Cecile in thoughtful tones.

"I think it's madness!" Phillip exclaimed. "I beg your pardon, my lady, but if Sir Henry discovered Tom was in Freya, he would most certainly have him arrested or killed!"

Thomas made an impatient gesture, but Phillip was not to be deterred.

"And let us say, for the sake of argument, that the queen does name you her heir. How would that stop your mother and Smythe?"

"The Faithful would stop them," said Cecile. "If Her Majesty proclaimed that Thomas, the heir to King James I, would be her heir, she would validate the Faithful, reward a century of loyalty and dedication. They would be glad to wait years, if need be. They do not want war. They would withdraw their support for a revolution."

"Such was my thinking," said Thomas. "I am glad to have Your Ladyship's confirmation."

"What about Hugh and Elinor? They will never accept Thomas as king," said Phillip, pursuing the argument.

"The prince is already immensely popular with the people due to the stories about him in the newspapers," said Cecile. "Those backing Hugh and Elinor do so reluctantly, for neither is well liked. Given a better choice, the nobility would be quick to switch their allegiance, especially if Thomas were to actively seek their support. The Faithful could assist you with that endeavor."

Cecile rested her hand on his. "Your proposal is a good one, Your Highness. I know what it cost you to make it."

"And what it could cost him to go through with it," Phillip said grimly.

Cecile ignored him. "I will reach out to a high-ranking member of the Faithful to assist with the arrangements. His name is Sir Richard Wallace. He is a member of the House of Nobles and has direct access to the queen."

"I believe I may have met this man," said Thomas. "My mother introduced me to a member of the Faithful she called 'Sir Richard.' She made him seem very mysterious, of course. She would not tell me his surname."

"Was he tall, balding, beaked nose, slight stoop, and a bit of a paunch?" Phillip asked.

"That description fits him," said Thomas. "Do you know him?"

"Richard Wallace is Sir Henry Wallace's elder brother," said Phillip gravely.

Thomas was startled. "Did you know that, my lady?"

Cecile raised an eyebrow. Thomas flushed.

"I beg your pardon, Countess. Of course you knew. But how can Sir Henry's own brother be a member of the Faithful? Did you know that about him, Pip?"

"I did not. And neither, I'll wager, does Sir Henry," said Phillip. He shook his head in wonderment. "He has long feared the group had members at the highest level of government and he is apparently right. Sir Richard is a leading member of the House of Nobles and, as my lady has said, he has direct access to the queen."

"Richard Wallace has been a member of the Faithful since his father's death," said Cecile. "The secret is passed on to the eldest child or closest kinsman. The Wallace family backed King James I. When he was forced from the throne, the family lost everything. King Alfred, fearing that James's adherents would try to oust him, stripped them of their lands, their money, their power. Like most of the Faithful, Sir Richard hopes to recover the family's glory. The Faithful believe that the time is at hand."

She paused, thoughtful, then said, "I wonder if that has something to do with this reference to *lex talionis*."

"What does that mean?" Thomas asked.

"The Law of Retribution," said Cecile. "Mr. Sloan refers to it."

Thomas brushed that aside. He wanted to discuss Sir Richard.

"If Richard is Henry Wallace's brother, how can we trust him?" Thomas asked.

"Sir Henry and his brother have never been close," Phillip said. "Richard is considerably older. He did not approve of Henry's choice of friends, particularly Captain Northrop, or his involvement in royal intrigues. The brothers did not speak for years, until Henry married the queen's niece. Then Richard took care to renew their acquaintance. Now they dine once a month. Henry refers to Richard disparagingly as the 'Old Chap' and talks of how he uses him to influence votes in the House of Nobles. All this time, it seems Richard has been the one using Henry."

Phillip added reluctantly, "I must admit that if someone told Henry that Richard was plotting against him, Henry would burst into laughter. He would never believe it. If you insist on this mad course of action, Tom, Her Ladyship is right. I would choose Sir Richard to act as an intermediary."

"I will write to the queen and to Sir Richard this day and dispatch D'argent with the letters tomorrow," said Cecile. She fixed them with a look, particularly Phillip. "You understand, gentlemen, that this secret must not leave this room."

"You have my assurance that I will tell no one, my lady," said Phillip.

"*My* only worry is that Sir Richard will tell my mother," Thomas added. "If she found out that I was meeting with the queen, she would immediately rush to Haever to prepare for my coronation."

"D'argent will emphasize to Sir Richard that he must keep your secret, particularly from the marchioness. Sir Richard is devoted to you, sir. He would not risk placing you in jeopardy."

"When do you think you will receive Her Majesty's answer, my lady?" Thomas asked.

"In a month's time, perhaps longer," Cecile replied coolly.

"A month!" Thomas repeated, dismayed. Now that he had made a decision, he was ready to act.

"They say that diplomacy is the art of taking a long time to do very little," said Cecile. "In this instance, we are trying to do a great deal. The journey from here to Haever takes five days by griffin and that depends on a fair wind and good weather. Once D'argent is in Haever, he must meet with Sir Richard and they must meet with Her Majesty, and convince Queen Mary to meet with you. She will want time to consider. If she agrees, we have arrangements to make, how you will travel, where you will stay. If she refuses, Sir Richard will need time to try to change her mind."

"I understand, my lady," said Thomas. "I will endeavor to be patient. In the interim, Phillip and I will return to Estara—"

Cecile shook her head. "I strongly suggest that you remain at Castle Dragonreach, Your Highness. When we receive the queen's answer, we need to be prepared to act, although I fear you will find this place very dull. Sophia and Sir Rodrigo will soon be leaving for Freya and my son and his wife will be traveling to Everux to be near Juliette's parents for the birth of their child."

Thomas could think of nothing more boring than wandering about an empty castle for a month. He understood Cecile's reasoning, however, and he assured her that he and Phillip would remain if the duke would grant his permission. Thomas tucked the papers from Mr. Sloan into an inner pocket and they left the countess alone to write her letters.

Phillip suggested that they walk in the garden.

"Perhaps we will run into Sophia," said Thomas, knowing why his friend chose the garden.

"I cannot believe she is to leave tomorrow," said Phillip, sighing. "I meant to ask. What were you two talking about in the library."

"Our duty," said Thomas somberly.

The garden paths were deserted, much to Phillip's disappointment. He and Thomas strolled along the path that ran near the wall overlooking the harbor. They watched the ships and the drifting mists of the Breath.

"You know Queen Mary, Pip. What do you think of my chance for success?" Thomas asked.

"To be honest, about the same as the ground on which we are standing suddenly giving way and plunging us into the Breath," Phillip replied. "Mary is very fond of her sister, Elinor. Sir Henry has been trying to dissuade her from naming Elinor as her heir, but without success. Their half brother, Hugh Fitzray, is a bumbling fool, but he is preferable to Elinor, who would bring back the priests and burn heretics at the stake."

"Do you still disapprove of my going?" Thomas asked.

"On consideration, no," said Phillip. "For I will be going with you."

"You will not!" Thomas stopped walking to remonstrate with his friend. "I will not permit it! Sir Henry Wallace deems you a traitor to your country. He would have your head on the block! I am only surprised you have not been assassinated before now. I shudder when I think that man Sloan was lurking about within feet of you."

"I imagine I presented a very tempting target to poor Mr. Sloan," Phillip agreed, laughing. "I cannot believe I did not see him. Such a lapse would have been the death of me in the Rose Hawks days. But to return to our argument, you might as well save your breath, for I will not let you travel to Freya alone."

"Out of the question, Pip. The risk you would run is too great."

"And your risk is not?" Phillip countered. "Sir Henry knows that if you ascend to the throne, he will be ruined. You could revoke his title, seize his lands; even send him into exile."

"He has a right to be worried," said Thomas grimly. "The man is a scourge."

"Henry is not so bad," Phillip said. "He is a patriot, as am I. We are both loyal to our country. He and I happen to differ on what is best for our country, that is all. Consider this argument, Tom. You know no one in Freya. You will be a stranger in a strange land at the mercy of strangers. If you find yourself in trouble, you will need someone you know you can trust."

"Sir Rodrigo will be in Freya," Thomas said dryly. "So will Sophia for that matter. Confess the truth. She is the real reason you want to come with me."

He grinned, meaning the suggestion in jest. He was taken aback when Phillip rounded on him, his face dark with anger.

"Do you seriously believe I would involve Sophia in this mad venture? Do you think I would put her in danger? If so, Tom, our friendship is at an end!"

"I am sorry, Pip," said Thomas. "I know you would not. I was teasing."

"Well, don't do that again. You gave me a fright," said Phillip. "You must take this seriously, Tom. Do not worry about me. I have contacts in Haever, safe places to stay. I will keep out of Sir Henry's sight."

"I should not let you put *yourself* in danger on my account," said Thomas. "But I suppose I cannot stop you, short of chaining you to the dungeon wall."

"The countess would do that herself if she suspected I was coming with you," said Phillip. "So what do we do now?"

"We wait," said Thomas grimly.

THIRTY-THREE

Henry Wallace examined his reflection in the dressing room mirror. He was wearing evening attire: a long blue velvet coat trimmed in gold brocade; matching blue weskit, also trimmed in gold; blue breeches and silk stockings. He was wearing a stock, then the fashion, which had replaced the wider cravat.

He deliberately twitched the stock out of place, knowing his wife took pleasure in fussing over him and setting it right with her own hands.

Sir Henry and Lady Ann were hosting a formal dinner party, a rare occurrence since Henry abhorred entertaining. He viewed his home as a sanctuary, a calm haven in the center of the chaotic storm that was his life, and he did not like having it invaded. Ann insisted that they host at least three dinner parties during the year, to fulfill their own social obligations, and Henry acceded to her wishes, as always.

Henry was actually looking forward to this party, for hosting it had been his idea. His friends Captain Alan Northrop and Admiral Randolph Baker, of Her Majesty's Expeditionary Fleet, had returned to Haever for refitting. Their ships were going to switch from using the liquid form of the Breath to the far more efficient crystalline form.

The ships were now in the Naval Yard, attended by a swarm of crafters and carpenters. Alan and Randolph were on leave and they were coming to dine this night, along with their other friend, Simon Yates, another rare occurrence. Simon did not like to take time from his work and his friends had spent considerable time and effort convincing him to leave his house for a few hours.

Henry, satisfied that he would pass inspection, left his dressing room in search of his wife. He found Ann in the dining room studying the arrangements with a critical eye. They had invited twenty people for dinner. The table was resplendent with gilt-edged porcelain plates, gleaming silver tableware, and glittering crystal glasses. Three large cut-glass vases held flowers that filled the room with fragrance.

Henry watched his wife, unobserved, as she frowned over place cards and, at one point, switched two of them. He marveled now, as he marveled every day, that he had been so fortunate as to gain her love. She felt his gaze upon her and turned to smile at him.

"I hope you have not put Lord Percy next to Randolph, my dear," Henry said, advancing into the room. "They will get into a blazing row over some long-forgotten naval battle that will end with Randolph chucking the fish at Percy's head."

Ann came over to greet Henry and tilt her head to receive his kiss. She then frowned at him and twitched his stock back into place, much to his delight.

"I have put Lord Percy at one end and Randolph on the other. I was switching cards to seat Alan next to Lord Alfred's charming niece, Lady Annabelle. Her brother is currently serving in the navy and that will give the two of them something to talk about."

"They can also discuss the fact that she is unmarried and, by remarkable coincidence, so is Alan," said Henry wryly. "My wife the matchmaker."

"They would suit each other perfectly," said Ann. "I have put Simon at your right hand. Do not allow him to discuss the intestinal diseases in cattle as he did the last time he was here. Poor Lady Penelope complained that she could not eat beef for a month."

"I will make the attempt, but you know Simon," said Henry. "Seat Miss Amelia next to him. She will talk about cow intestines. She has undoubtedly written an article on the subject at some point in her career."

"Miss Amelia is to sit next to me and Lady Susan. We want to hear about Captain Kate's latest thrilling adventure. She was almost hanged!" said Ann.

She was interrupted by a flurried maid who came to say that Cook urgently needed to speak to her mistress regarding some potential culinary disaster, and then by another servant, who came to say the first guests were arriving.

They could both hear Randolph's booming voice resounding throughout the house. "Damn your eyes, you lubber, you've nearly upset Master Yates! Do that again and I will have you flogged round the fleet!"

"Stop swearing at the servants, Randolph!" Simon returned, peeved. "You are the one who was blocking the door!"

Ann flashed her husband an alarmed glance. "I will deal with Cook. You must do something, Henry. The last time Randolph was here, the butler gave notice. I do not want to lose Jacobs."

Henry went to the entry hall to welcome his friends and save their newly hired butler.

Jonathon Jacobs was in his fifties. He had been born to household service, his father having been a butler before him. He had served in the Royal Navy and entered his father's profession following his retirement.

He came highly recommended by Alan Northrop, who had said, "Jacobs is calm under fire, Henry. Just what you need, given that people have a tendency to shoot at you."

Jacobs was not Mr. Sloan, but he was adept at running the household and he did not appear the least unnerved by Randolph's withering attacks.

"This blasted lubber almost dumped Simon out of his chair, Henry!" Randolph boomed, divesting himself of his cloak and hat and throwing them in the general direction of a maid.

"Randolph was the one who nearly upset me," Simon stated as he floated into the hall. "Henry, I need a word with you in private. I will meet you in the library."

"Simon, I can't talk now," Henry protested. "I have guests—"

"This is important," said Simon. He whipped his chair around and headed down the hall.

Ann appeared at Henry's shoulder. "Go talk with Simon, my dear. I will take care of Admiral Baker. Captain Northrop has just arrived. He will assist me."

Henry cast his wife a grateful glance and followed Simon. He looked over his shoulder to see Alan latching onto Randolph.

"What news from the dockyard about our ships? I heard you were there today," said Alan, steering him toward the parlor. "How is the work on the *Valor* progressing?"

"The refit is complete," Randolph stated, adding with a snort, "No thanks to those blasted crafters."

Alan winked at Henry and led their friend, grumbling about the ineptitude of ships' crafters, to the parlor.

The library was the most secure room in the house. It had no windows and only one door. The walls were lined with shelves filled with books that were there not just to be read and enjoyed, but also served to dampen sound. Mr. Sloan had inscribed the magical constructs that strengthened the walls, and the warding constructs that guarded the door. Henry never entered this room without thinking of his secretary and friend.

Henry ushered Simon inside, then shut the door.

"Well, Simon, what is so important that you take me away from my guests?" Henry asked.

"I have finished studying the reports we received from Mr. Sloan," said Simon. "What he has uncovered is shocking, Henry. This Colonel Smythe— and we must never forget that he is really Isaiah Crawford, the man who murdered six humans and two dragons—commands an army of mostly Guundaran mercenaries in Bheldem and, in addition, has secret armies hidden in various parts of Freya. He has apparently been plotting this for months without my knowledge. I am sorry to let you down, Henry," Simon added despondently. "I had no idea."

"You could never let me down, Simon," said Henry. "Do not blame yourself. We will send in our own army to deal with them."

Simon made an impatient gesture. "You do not understand, Henry! I know these secret armies exist, but I can't locate them!"

Henry was concerned. "How can you hide an army, Simon?"

"That is the point. You can't. And yet it seems they have. I have searched through my files, looking for clues: a farmer chasing after soldiers roaming about his hay field or a griffin rider spotting men marching along a road. Nothing. Absolutely nothing!"

Henry could not recall seeing his friend so unsettled by anything. He sat down to face him. "Mr. Sloan could be wrong—"

"We both know better, Henry," Simon interrupted impatiently. "I was thinking that your privateer, Captain Kate, might have better luck. With her dragon, she could search from the air. If I were going to hide an army, I'd do so in parts of northern and western Freya. Perhaps along the coastline. That area is uninhabited, but Kate and her dragon— Why not? What's the matter?"

Henry was shaking his head. "I have no Captain Kate. According to Miss Amelia, Kate's dragon got himself into some sort of trouble and she is fleeing bounty hunters. They have gone to ground."

"That's a damn shame," said Simon. "Then perhaps you should ask the Countess de Marjolaine. She has the same information. No doubt *her* Freyan agents have already located these armies."

"If you cannot find them, Simon, no one can," said Henry. "As for the countess, Mr. Sloan did what he had to do by permitting her to read the information. I do not fault him."

"Nor do I, Henry," said Simon. "Pay no heed to my rants. In truth, I believe the countess is acting on the reports. Her secretary, D'argent, is in Haever."

"Not surprising," said Henry. "Sir Rodrigo de Villeneuve and Princess Sophia have only just arrived. The countess will be keeping a watchful eye on them, even as she and the Pretender plot to overthrow our queen."

"I have told you before, Henry, and these reports confirm my opinion, that Prince Thomas knows nothing about these secret armies—"

Henry snorted. "Bah! Of course he does! He is behind this! He intends to march into the palace at the head of his army and seize his throne by force!"

"I do not think so, Henry," said Simon. "More importantly, neither does Mr. Sloan. He believes Smythe and the marchioness are keeping the prince in the dark. Mr. Sloan adds that Lord Ander shares his belief."

"So I have lost you, as well, Simon. It seems I must fight this battle for my country alone," Henry said bitterly, rising to his feet. "And now, my other guests are waiting. If you will excuse me—"

Simon steered his chair around so that he was blocking the door. "Henry, do you want me to tell you what you want to hear, or the truth? I can do one or the other. I can't do both. The choice is yours."

Henry gave his friend a grim look and was silent.

"I'm sorry. We can discuss this at a later date," said Simon.

He began to maneuver his chair toward the door. Henry stopped him, placing his hand on his shoulder.

"I am the one who should apologize," said Henry. "My queen is dying, Simon, and I am alone in this hellish darkness. I cannot see where I am going. I could be strolling down a smooth highway toward success or I could be teetering on the edge of a precipice, one false step from disaster. And yet, whatever I do, I have to keep walking! I dare not stop!"

"You are not alone, Henry," said Simon, reproving. "You have friends who walk with you. Granted, we are not good for much: I am a cripple, Alan is a hothead, and, by the sounds emanating from the parlor, Randolph has just now broken a very expensive vase. But in addition to us, you have your estimable lady wife and the courageous Mr. Sloan, who is risking his life to provide us with this information."

"Thank you, Simon," said Henry, moved. "Thank you for reminding me."

He resumed his seat, took a moment to collect himself, then said briskly, "Let us suppose you are right. The marchioness and the members of the Faithful are in league with Smythe to seize the throne for Prince Thomas, all the while keeping the prince in the dark. For what reason?"

"According to Mr. Sloan's reports, as well as those from your own former agent and friend, Phillip Masterson, Prince Thomas is an honorable young man who would be opposed to seizing the throne by force."

"You believe he is a gentleman and thus all is well, then," Henry said, his lip curling.

"I do not," said Simon, ignoring the sarcasm. "I think the fact that he does not know puts us in even graver danger, which is what I need you to understand. If Smythe and the marchioness fear the prince will put a stop to their plot, they could find it necessary to take immediate action. I think the countess feels as I do, which could be why she has sent D'argent to Haever."

"Or the countess could be in league with the marchioness and Smythe," Henry said. "God! This is a tangle! I assume you have agents following D'argent."

Simon gave a faint smile. "The man has served the countess for many years, Henry. He knows what he is about. He let it be known he was in Haever by openly meeting with the princess. That was a ruse to put us off the trail, for shortly after, he gave my best man the slip and vanished. I have no idea where D'argent may be, how long he has been here, or even if he is still in Freya."

Henry sighed. "One last question. Have you found out anything about this mysterious mention of this Day of Talionis?"

"The answer is obvious. *Lex talionis.* Law of Retribution. Day of Talionis. Day of Retribution," Simon replied. "On that day, these people will act to take retribution for whatever crime they believe has been committed against them."

"But who are *these people?*" Henry demanded. "What day? What time?"

"Shouting at me won't help, Henry," said Simon. "The date could be a specific time in the future or any day they choose to act. As for the crime, the Faithful blame the queen and her family for every outrage committed in the past one hundred and fifty years. We have no way of knowing."

"Teetering on the precipice," Henry muttered. "I am sorry I shouted."

Simon gave him a sympathetic look. "I'm the one who should be sorry. I am spoiling your evening."

"No, no," said Henry. "As you said, I need to know."

They heard the sound of another crash coming from the vicinity of the parlor.

Simon smiled and waved his hand. "Go to your guests, Henry. You need to save your furniture from Randolph."

Henry had played many roles in his life. He was not only a spymaster, he was himself a very good spy. He was fluent in many languages and he had a variety of aliases and disguises secreted in locations about the world. He could transform himself into a dull-witted Guundaran thug, a cunning Travian cartel owner, a dissolute Braffan oligarch. This night, he had to set aside his troubles and transform himself into a gracious host.

The transformation did him good, made the night in which he wandered seem less dark. Lady Ann was a superb hostess. She and Cook had done an excellent job planning the menu. The meal consisted of many courses and was excellent. Lord Percy and Randolph were at opposite ends of the table. Alan apparently found the charming niece charming, for he devoted all his time to her. Amelia told stories of Captain Kate to an enthralled audience. Simon did not once mention intestinal diseases in cattle, although he did enlighten the assembly on the subject of truffle pigs.

Henry was pleased to see his guests enjoying themselves. When his wife and the other ladies rose at the end of the meal to leave the gentlemen to their port, he caught his wife's eye and smiled to let her know he was proud of her.

As the gentlemen handed the port around, the subject started to turn to Freyan politics, complaints about the queen, the economy, and so on. Henry could say nothing to defend the queen without starting an argument. He was grateful to Alan, who began to discuss the prospects of this autumn's grouse shooting. Lord Percy said that grouse shooting reminded him of the battle between HMS *Falcon* and the Rosian *Belle Fleur,* which upon hearing the remark made Randolph flush purple. And with that, Henry rose to say they should join the ladies for tea.

Randolph sat down at the card table, and Alan settled himself on the love seat with the charming Lady Annabelle. Simon and Amelia began discussing King Ullr, and Henry was about to join the card players when Jacobs intercepted him.

"I apologize for disturbing you, my lord, but there is a person to see you."

"A messenger from the palace?" Henry asked immediately.

"Far from it, my lord," Jacobs replied. "To judge by the fact that he attempted to persuade me to bet on a horse, I believe him to be a racecourse tout. He first asked for Mr. Sloan. I said he wasn't available and asked to know his business. The man refused to tell me. I would have sent him upon his way, but you gave orders that if anyone came asking for Mr. Sloan, no matter what time of day or night, I should apprise you at once—"

"Quite right, Jacobs," said Henry. "Where is he?"

"Given his unsavory appearance, I deemed it best if we kept him out of sight in the butler's pantry. George, the footman, is with him now."

"I will come at once," said Henry.

When Lady Ann saw Jacobs speaking to her husband, she raised an inquisitive eyebrow in his direction. Henry smiled to let her know all was well, and accompanied Jacobs down the stairs.

Henry judged that this man must be one of Mr. Sloan's many informants and he again lamented the absence of his secretary, who would have dealt with the situation effectively and discreetly, and left Henry to his party.

The butler's pantry was a small service and storage room located off the kitchen. Henry found George, the footman, listening to the blandishments of a short, slight man, probably a former jockey, who was attempting to lure George into parting with his money.

"I tell you straight up, George, my lad, that Candy Apple is a sure bet for a win in the derby tomorrow. The only reason I'm giving you this tip is because I like you, George—"

"That will be all, George," said Henry, entering the pantry.

George departed in haste, looking relieved. The man turned to Henry with a beaming smile and rakish air.

"How 'bout you, my lord? Candy Apple is guaranteed to run away—"

"Thank you, no," said Henry, shutting the door. "You asked for Mr. Sloan. I am sorry he is unavailable. What is your name?"

"Jenkins, my lord," said the tout, doffing a jaunty hat.

"Do you have a tip for me on something other than a horse, Jenkins?" Henry asked.

"Might be nothin', my lord, but Mr. Sloan is always very happy to hear from me."

"Very well, Jenkins, what information do you have?"

"I've been hangin' about the grog shops by the docks, my lord. The dockworkers aren't happy. They've not been paid in a month—"

"Get to the point," said Henry sharply.

"There's talk of a strike, my lord. The workers plan to march on the Naval Yard—"

"When?"

"Tonight, my lord."

"Tonight!" Henry repeated, startled. He had heard no rumors of trouble among the dockworkers. "How many men are involved?"

"A handful are doing the talkin' right now, my lord. They're buyin' the grog and workin' the crowd into a lather."

"Thank you for the information, Jenkins. Wait here," said Henry.

"One other thing I should mention, sir—"

"Well, Jenkins?" Henry said, thinking this better not be about Candy Apple.

"The men who are buyin' the grog and talkin' trouble are not from around here, my lord. Leastwise, I don't recognize them and I know most everyone who works the docks," he added with pride.

"I'll bet you do," Henry muttered.

He left, shutting the door behind him, and sought out Jacobs.

"Give Mr. Jenkins a silver talon and show him the door. See to it that he does not talk to any of the other servants," Henry instructed.

He mulled over what Jenkins had said and pondered what to do. The ships of the fleet were currently docked in the Naval Yard where they were being refitted.

Henry knew the dockworkers were unhappy. The government was teetering on the brink of financial ruin. The navy had to allocate what funds they had and the Admiralty had decided that refitting the ships to use the crystallized form of the Breath as opposed to the liquid was a high priority. The crystals provided more lift; ships could fly longer and at higher altitudes. They had taken pains to explain this to the dockworkers and appeal to their patriotism to keep working.

Still, the workers could not eat patriotism nor feed it to their children. Yet Henry considered it likely that Jenkins was exaggerating the seriousness of the situation, just as he was undoubtedly exaggerating the merits of Candy Apple.

But even a few men marching on the Naval Yard was bound to draw a crowd and could end in another riot. Henry was also troubled by Jenkins's information that the men who were stirring up the trouble were apparently strangers. Henry sighed and rubbed his forehead, and gave orders to send for his coach.

When he returned to the parlor, his wife was pouring tea. He bent down to say softly, "I am summoned to the palace, my love. I am sorry, but I must go."

"Oh, dear," said Ann, dismayed. "Must you leave now?"

"I am afraid so," said Henry. He kissed her and added, "With luck, I will be gone only a short while."

Henry cast a glance around the room. The charming Lady Annabelle was playing the spinet with Alan sitting beside her, turning the pages for her; Randolph was glaring at his cards as though they had personally offended him; and Simon and Amelia were deep in discussion regarding the current refusal of shortsighted parents to allow their children to study contramagic.

Seeing that no one was paying attention to him, Henry slipped out a side door and went to the front hall. He sent the footman to fetch his hat and greatcoat and stood looking out the window for the coach.

"There he stands, Randolph," said Alan. "The wretch. Thinking he could give us the slip."

"As if we wouldn't notice him sneaking off like a goddamn thief," Randolph grumbled.

"Were you really intending to leave us behind while you have all the fun, Henry?" Simon asked in a hurt tone.

Henry turned to see his friends assembled in the hall, eyeing him with mock severity.

"I am going to the palace—" he began.

"No, you are not," said Simon. "I saw you go below stairs with Jacobs. You came up looking worried, whispered to your wife, and then tried to sneak away before we noticed."

"The truth, Henry," Alan added. "We will have it out of you sooner or later."

Henry regarded them with exasperation. "If you must know, I received a report that some of the dockworkers are threatening to shut down the Naval Yard—"

"Goddamn dockworkers!" Randolph burst out angrily. "Treason! That's what it is! I say we hang the lot of them!"

"They haven't been paid in a month, Randolph," Simon remonstrated. "They have families to feed."

"Still . . ." Randolph growled. "Unpatriotic."

"And is it patriotic to starve children?" Simon demanded.

"Stop it, both of you," said Alan with a meaningful glance at Henry, who was looking grim.

"Sorry, Henry," said Randolph. "I know this goddamn mess isn't your fault."

"We are definitely coming with you," Alan stated. "Don't worry. We won't delay you. Simon already asked Jacobs to fetch our coats."

"My chair won't fit in your coach," Simon added. "I've sent Albright to bring my conveyance around. We'll follow you."

"Now see here!" said Henry, losing patience. "I can slip out of the party unnoticed, but if all of four of us leave, people will talk. Lady Ann will be extremely upset—"

"Lady Ann was the one who sent us, Henry," said Alan. "Your wife said on no account were we to allow you to go alone."

Henry stared, amazed.

"Oh, come now, Henry," said Simon. "Your wife is an intelligent and perceptive woman who was raised in a palace fraught with intrigue. Did you really think she believes your tales of urgent late-night summonings to attend Her Majesty?"

"I did, rather . . ." said Henry, dazed. "But . . . our guests . . ."

"Lady Ann has made our excuses," Alan said.

"She is even keeping that goddamn female journalist occupied so she doesn't rush after us," Randolph said.

"You have a wonderful wife, Henry," Alan said. "I hope you know you do not deserve her."

"Trust me, I know," said Henry.

The coach rolled up, and shortly after, Mr. Albright arrived with Simon's wyvern-drawn carriage that had been specially designed to hold his chair.

"Albright, we will fly my carriage over the Naval Yard," Simon ordered. "Take a look around."

"You will not!" Alan protested, alarmed.

"Have you forgotten what happened when that goddamn house of yours accidentally floated over the Naval Yard?" Randolph demanded.

"You were lucky the patrol boats didn't open fire on you!" Henry said.

"All that ruckus over a simple miscalculation in wind speed," stated Simon, nettled.

"You are making far too much out of a few disgruntled dockworkers," Henry said, putting on his hat. "Once the men sober up, they will think better of it and go home to their beds. Still, if you insist—"

"We do," said Alan.

He and the others walked outside, heading for the coach, while Mr. Albright came to assist Simon.

Henry paused before leaving to look back into the parlor. His wife was standing beside the spinet, singing a duet with Lady Annabelle. Ann felt his gaze and half turned her head to smile at him.

"I do not walk alone in the darkness. Your heavenly light will guide me into eternity," Henry reflected. "Alan is right, my love. I do not deserve you."

"Henry, stop goddamn lollygagging!" Randolph roared.

THIRTY-FOUR

The Royal Naval Dockyards, known more simply as the Naval Yard, was located on Zak Street near the harbor, where the ships of the Freyan navy floated at anchor in the Breath. The dockyards were massive, for all the materials needed to refit, repair, and build ships were manufactured here under the watchful eye of the Admiralty.

The Naval Yard could be likened to a small, self-contained city within a city. The vast complex included warehouses, forges, metalworking and woodworking shops, roperies, crafting facilities, victualing yard, ballooning equipment, and repair shops, and the armory with its vital stores of gunpowder, ammunition, swivel guns, cannons, and cannonballs. The Admiralty had administrative offices here, as well as barracks for resident officers, ships' crafters, and guards.

A number of ships were in the dockyard, currently being refitted to use the crystalline form of the Breath. Among these was Randolph's flagship, the *Valor*; frigates and warships belonging to the Expeditionary fleet; and Alan's ship, the *Terrapin*, so called because the hull was protected by a "shell" of Pietro Alcazar's famous magical steel plates.

Alcazar had relocated his own shop to the Naval Yard, because Henry planned to build another ship similar to the *Terrapin*, using the same steel—now much improved—and with an advanced design. Unfortunately, a lack of funds had put a stop to the project, at least for now.

As Randolph had informed Alan, the work on his flagship, the *Valor*, had been completed. The ship was now ready for a test sail. The workers were just finishing the *Terrapin*, which had needed extensive work. The weight added by the steel plates meant the ship required more lift and thus would have to use more of the precious crystals unless the crafters could devise some means to reduce the amount. They had done so and were close to completing the task.

The grog shops located near the dockyards catered to both sailors and dockworkers. The shops were doing a brisk business tonight. Looking out the coach window, Henry could see people milling about in the streets outside the shops, singing and laughing. He saw no signs of trouble.

"I think Jenkins just needed betting money," Henry said.

Alan laughed. "If that's the case, we should return to the party. I promised Lady Annabelle that we should go out riding in the park tomorrow. She is a most charming young woman."

The Naval Yard was surrounded by a brick wall eight feet in height with only two entry points. One was the harbor itself and the other a gate consisting of magically reinforced, solid iron bars with spikes on top set between two large stone watch towers. Street lamps illuminated the highway that ran in front of the Naval Yard. Lamps shone on the gate and inside the watchtower, where soldiers stood guard.

Patrol boats guarded the harbor, where each ship had its own cubbyhole-like berth. Those needing extensive repair could be hauled ashore and laid on their sides if necessary. The harbor was guarded day and night by the boats that sailed along the shoreline.

Another patrol boat guarded the air above the Naval Yard, as Simon had lamentably discovered. Ships, wyvern-drawn carriages, yachts, and griffin-riders were forbidden to fly over the dockyards. The marines aboard the boat would order the offender to land or face being blown out of the sky. They would then escort the interlopers off the property and hand them over to the police.

The coach drove up to the front gate, which was closed and locked for the night. Henry and Alan and Randolph climbed out and approached the gate. Mr. Albright assisted Simon with his chair and he joined them.

A wicket gate opened in the side of the wall and a guard came out to meet them. The corporal was young and clearly disconcerted by the arrival of four gentlemen in evening attire, one of them in a floating chair.

Alan stepped into the light of the lantern that hung over the gate.

"I believe you know me, Corporal. Captain Northrop," Alan said.

The corporal saluted. "Captain Northrop, sir."

He was relieved, but also puzzled. Then he caught sight of Randolph and his eyes widened. He stiffened and saluted. "Admiral Baker!"

Alan continued the introductions. "Sir Henry Wallace and Mr. Simon Yates. We would like to speak to the officer of the watch on a matter of some urgency."

"Yes, sir. Right away, sir," said the corporal.

He ushered them through the wicket gate, looking startled as Simon's chair whisked past him. The corporal sent a fellow marine to fetch the officer of the watch.

"How has the watch gone tonight, Corporal?" Alan asked. "Anything out of the ordinary?"

"Quiet as a churchyard, Captain," the marine reported.

The watch commander arrived to confirm the marine's report. "Why do you ask, Captain Northrop? Are you expecting trouble?"

"We had a report that some disgruntled dockworkers might march on the yard," said Alan. "Apparently our informant was wrong."

"I hope you didn't pay that goddamn tout too much, Henry," said Randolph.

"The grog shops close in a hour or so," said Henry. "We will wait around just to be certain."

"Then let's go someplace warm," said Randolph, rubbing his hands.

The lieutenant invited them into the office, where he had lit a fire in an iron stove. The five were a tight fit in the small room, especially with Simon's chair, but Alan had brought some brandy in a flask and they spent a pleasant time sharing the brandy, listening to Randolph complain about his rotten luck at whist and Alan extol the virtues of the charming niece, Lady Annabelle.

The party was interrupted by the sound of running feet and a loud knock on the door. A marine burst inside almost before the lieutenant granted permission.

"Sir, men are marching in the street and they're headed this way," he reported.

"How many, Corporal?" asked the lieutenant.

"At least a hundred, sir," said the marine. "Maybe more. They're carrying torches."

The lieutenant made his excuses and left in haste. "Torches!" Henry repeated, casting an alarmed glance at his friends.

"They're planning to set fire to the Naval Yard!" said Alan, jumping to his feet. "Think of it! The lumberyard is filled with conifer logs, planks, masts, spars. The wood is seasoned, dry . . . The entire dockyard could go up in flames!"

"Then there's the armory . . . If that caught fire . . ."

Henry looked at his friends, all sharing the same terrifying thought. Freya was dependent on her navy to protect the nation and her interests around the world. The loss of a fleet of ships, not to mention the dockyard, the equipment, and stores would be a devastating blow to the navy and Freya's overall defenses, and a financial disaster for the country.

"This could well drive Freya to her knees," said Henry, shaken.

"I'll be goddamned if a goddamn mob is going to destroy my country!" Randolph stated.

The alarm bell sounded, rousing the soldiers, calling them to man the walls. Flares burst in the night sky, alerting the patrol boats that the yard was under attack.

"Our drivers, Baxter and Albright!" Henry exclaimed, suddenly remembering. "They are waiting for us outside the gate. We need to warn them."

"We could send them for help," said Alan. "The yard has its own fire brigade, but we'll need more than that—"

"Good idea," said Henry. "Perhaps I can talk to these men. Reason with them—"

"You can't reason with a mob, Henry!" Randolph said.

"I have to try. The alternative is marines firing on our own people! The rest of you go with Baxter for help, then return to the party. I'll handle this."

"Once again, gentlemen, he's keeping all the fun to himself," said Alan, grinning. "You know we won't let you do this alone, Henry. But we should be armed."

"I have rifles and pistols, shot and powder in the coach," said Henry. "We shoot only in self-defense. I don't want to start killing civilians."

"Wait a minute!" said Simon as they started to leave. "Alan, how far can you hurl a lighted torch?"

"What the hell—" Alan began.

"Answer the question."

Alan stopped to consider. "Over an eight-foot wall? Maybe forty yards at the most."

"The lumberyard is at least a quarter of a mile from the wall," said Simon. He motioned out the door. "Look at our surroundings. What do you see? Brick walls. Stone pavement. Torches landing around here would fizzle and go out. I suppose they *might* set a roof ablaze, but that would be the extent of the damage."

"Unless the mob breaches the gate," said Henry, frowning.

"Is that likely? How many marines are stationed here?"

"In peacetime and with the budget cuts? Sixty-five total," Alan replied.

"Sixty-five . . ." Simon repeated. "How are they deployed?"

"Sixteen on duty at any one time," Alan said. "Two at the gate. Two guarding the armory. Six on the patrol boat that sails the coastline and the docks and six on the patrol boat that keeps watch from the air. The rest would be asleep in the barracks. They will be wide awake now."

"All of them armed with rifles. The two patrol boats with swivel guns and rifles firing at them from above. Breach the gate!" Simon scoffed. "Henry, what did Jenkins tell you? Be precise."

"Simon, I don't have time—" Henry began.

"This is important," Simon snapped.

Henry hurriedly recounted the conversation.

"'Men buying grog, urging the dockworkers to attack,'" Simon muttered. "Who are these dockworkers who have money enough to buy grog for their fellows when they haven't been paid in a month?"

Henry was troubled. "Jenkins did say he didn't recognize them. They were strangers."

Simon fell silent, ruminating. He appeared to have forgotten they were there.

"Let's go—" Henry began.

He and Alan and Randolph started for the door. Simon suddenly propelled his chair forward and stopped in front of them, blocking the way.

"Henry, you cannot try to reason with this mob."

"You talk very glibly about marines with rifles, but they will be killing Freyans, Simon," said Henry, losing patience.

"You can't reason with this mob because it isn't a mob," said Simon. "It's a diversion."

The three stared at him.

"Go to the coaches," Simon said. "Bring weapons and meet me back here. And send Albright with the carriage."

"Simon—"

"No time! Go!"

Henry glanced at the others, then they hurried out the door, heading for the gate. Alan ran alongside with Randolph huffing and snorting behind them.

"Diversion? For what reason?" Alan asked.

"I have no idea," said Henry. "But what Simon said does make sense."

"If you're Simon," Alan grumbled.

Arriving at the wicket gate, they had a brief argument with the lieutenant, who did not want to let them outside the wall. They insisted and since the lieutenant could not very well oppose the wishes of both a captain and an admiral, he reluctantly agreed to open the gate and ordered one of his men to accompany them.

Henry found his coachman, Baxter, in conversation with Mr. Albright. Both of them were watching the approach of the mob with interest.

"You know where I keep the weapons?" Henry said to his friends.

"Beneath the seat," said Alan.

He and Randolph hurried to the coach. Henry explained the situation to the two drivers and issued orders.

"Baxter, once we have removed the weapons, take the coach and go for help. Alert the fire brigade and the constables. Then you can return home. Not a word of this to Lady Ann!"

Baxter nodded and hurried off to assist Alan and Randolph, who had pulled up the seat and were hauling out the weapons.

"Albright, fly the carriage over the wall. You need to take Simon home."

"Master Yates won't want to leave, my lord," Albright stated, one of the few times Henry had ever heard him speak.

"I'll handle Simon," said Henry, with more confidence than he felt.

Albright gave a silent nod and mounted the box. The wyverns were nervous, disturbed by the smell of smoke, and were snapping at each other. He cracked the whip over their heads, and sent power flowing to the small lift tanks. The carriage rose into the air.

Henry glanced down the street at the mob. The number of people was hard to determine, for they packed the street. The torchlight cast a lurid glow on the surrounding buildings. He thought about what Simon had said.

"Henry!" Alan shouted. "We could use some help!"

Henry ran for the carriage. Randolph was pulling out rifles and pistols and handing them to Alan, who was thrusting pistols into his belt and dumping powder horns and bags of bullets into his pockets. Henry grabbed two pistols and two rifles, stuffed the pistols into his belt, and emulated Alan's example by filling his pockets with ammunition.

The mob was getting closer. They could hear the roar of angry voices.

Randolph jumped out of the carriage, carrying two rifles, and more pistols.

"Go!" Henry yelled to Baxter, and he slapped one of the horses on the rump.

Baxter cracked the whip over the heads of the horses. Already skittish from the sound of the mob, they surged forward. The coach rattled off down the street.

Henry, Alan, and Randolph made a dash for the gate. Someone in the mob saw them and they began shouting and hurling rocks. The marine fired a warning shot in the air. Henry and his friends rushed through the wicket gate, followed by the marine. Two waiting marines slammed shut the gate behind them and bolted it.

Alan paused to speak to the lieutenant. "Order your men to fire into the air. We don't want Freyans killing Freyans if we can help it."

"Yes, sir," said the lieutenant.

More marines were already coming to reinforce those at the gate. The three ran back to the office where they had left their friend. Albright had already landed the carriage and dismounted.

Henry entered the office. "Albright's here to take you home, Simon. I won't stand for any argument! One bullet in the spine is quite enough—"

He stopped talking and looked around.

"Simon?"

The office was empty.

"Hellfire and damnation!" Henry swore.

He dashed back outside.

Armed marines were running past him, their uniforms askew, half buttoned. The two patrol boats had seen the flares and heard the alarm. They were sailing toward the gate.

Each of the patrol boats was armed with a single nine-pound cannon mounted at the bow and several swivel guns. Henry could hear the officers giving orders to load the cannons. A large lamp mounted on the bow cast a wide beam of light, sweeping the ground below.

"Did you see Simon?" Henry asked.

Alan and Randolph were loading the weapons. They looked up, shook their heads.

"Isn't he in the office?"

"No, he's gone," said Henry. "Give me a pistol."

He could hear the dull roar of the mob, the thud of stamping feet, shouts and jeers. He could smell the acrid smoke of the blazing torches.

"There he is!" Alan said suddenly.

Henry turned to see Simon propelling his chair at a rapid rate over the ground, rushing toward them.

"I know what they're plotting!" he cried excitedly, bringing his chair to a halt. "They're going to try to steal a ship! Henry, I think we may have found a portion of Colonel Smythe's army!"

Simon touched his hand to the brass helm, but before he could sail off again, Henry grabbed hold of the chair's armrest.

"Explain, Simon," he said. "Or we're not going anywhere."

Simon glared at him. Henry was firm and Simon condescended to explain.

"After you left, I went to take a look around. I saw the patrol boats sailing this way, leaving the harbor unguarded. It occurred to me that if my objective was to steal a ship, a mob attacking the front gate would be an excellent diversion."

"He has a point," said Henry, looking at his friends.

"Who is Colonel Smythe?" Randolph asked.

Alan was doubtful. "Simon, did you actually *see* any activity around the ships?"

"Be sensible, Alan," Simon returned irritably. "The night is dark and the harbor is over a mile away. How could I see any activity?"

"Then you don't know for certain someone is trying to steal a ship," Alan argued.

"Who the hell is Colonel Smythe?" Randolph demanded.

The mob had reached the gate. People were shouting and jeering, hurling rocks and bricks and vegetables. Someone tossed a single torch over the wall. The torch landed on the pavement not far from Henry. A marine ran over with a bucket and doused it with water.

"I will meet you at the docks," Simon said, and whipped his chair around, deftly avoiding running down Mr. Albright, who made a lunge to stop him and missed.

"Simon! Wait!" Henry shouted. "It's too danger—"

Simon ignored him and sped toward the harbor.

Mr. Albright looked helplessly at Henry. "Should I go after him, my lord?"

"You'll never catch him on foot," said Henry. "Alan, signal that patrol boat."

"You realize Simon ran off on purpose!" said Alan in exasperation. "He knows we'll chase after him."

Another torch sailed over the wall. This one fizzled out on impact.

"We either trust him or we don't," said Henry. "What ships are in the harbor?"

"The *Valor*. She was the first to be refitted," Randolph answered. "Do you think they're trying to steal my goddamn ship?"

The *Valor* was one of the largest ships in the Freyan navy, one hundred seventy-five feet long, with three gun decks. The ship carried one hundred cannons along with forty swivel guns.

"We can't take a chance," Henry said. "And we have to retrieve Simon."

Alan and Randolph both waved their arms and shouted, hailing the patrol boat that was about level with the rooftops. The sailor operating the lamp shone the light down on them.

"Captain Alan Northrop of the *Terrapin*!" Alan yelled, blinking in the bright beam. "I need to speak to your commander!"

"Reynolds, sir," said a lieutenant, leaning over the rail. "Perhaps you remember me, Captain. I was midshipman under you on the *Terrapin* two years ago."

"By God, so you were!" said Alan, staring up. "Is there any open area around here large enough for you to land?"

"No, sir, not nearby," said Reynolds.

"Then send down a ladder! My friends and I are coming aboard."

Reynolds ordered his men to toss down a rope ladder. They had to leave the rifles behind; they couldn't very well carry those and climb a rope ladder. Alan stuffed pistols into his belt, then ascended nimbly and turned to help Henry, whose ladder-climbing days were well behind him. Randolph came last, fumbling to find a foothold, swearing as the ladder lurched, refusing all offers of help and damning the eyes of everyone in sight.

Henry shouted to Mr. Albright to follow them in the carriage. Alan explained the situation to the lieutenant, who looked dubious, but ordered his helmsmen to return to the docks. The patrol boat was light and fast and they sailed swiftly over the Naval Yard. Randolph seized hold of a spyglass and focused on the harbor where the *Valor* rode at anchor.

"Do you see Simon?" Henry asked Alan, whose eyesight was the best of any of them.

Alan stared into the night. "No. But he had a good head start and that chair of his is fast. Who is this Colonel Smythe anyway?"

"Keep your voice down," said Henry quietly, glancing at the deck that was crowded with sailors and marines. "I cannot talk now, but I will tell you this. If these people are trying to steal a ship, I need them alive. Tell the lieutenant."

Alan raised an eyebrow, then went to pass along Henry's instructions. Henry checked to make certain his pistols were loaded. The patrol boat sped through the night, sailing above the rooftops of the warehouses and office buildings, and the ships in various stages of repair, lying in specially designed cradles. The harbor came into view, a gaping expanse of black.

Pinpricks of light marked the location of the *Valor*. Randolph lowered the spyglass, rubbed his aching eyes, and raised it again. The rushing wind ruffled Henry's coattails and almost took off his hat. He jammed it down on his head.

For so many weeks, he'd been forced to sit in his dark, dreary office, doing nothing except fret and fume, plot, and manipulate all to no good end. His queen was dying. The fate of his country hung in the balance and he had been powerless to help her. Until now.

Henry smiled. He had to admit it. He was enjoying himself.

Alan must have shared his thoughts, for he clapped him on the back. "You throw one hell of a dinner party, Henry."

THIRTY-FIVE

Simon Yates had grown accustomed to his friends trying to protect him. Years ago, he would have been angry at them. But then, he reflected, years ago, after the shooting that had left him paralyzed, he had been angry at everything.

Henry had undertaken to find out who had attempted to assassinate Crown Prince Godfrey. The four young men had spent an enjoyable time attempting to solve the mystery until the rousing adventure had turned serious. A bullet had felled Simon.

Feeling guilty, his friends had tiptoed around him, treating him as though he was some fragile piece of porcelain to be handled with great care, tenderly wrapped in cotton wool. Simon had resented their pity. He had answered their kindness with cruel and cutting remarks. He saw the hurt in their eyes and he reveled in the knowledge that he was inflicting pain.

"At least I am not the only one suffering," he would say to himself.

He had been especially rude to the eccentric old duchess who had taken him into her crazy floating house and nursed him. She had endured his abuse until the day she saved his sanity.

Simon began the day by refusing to eat. He knocked the tray of food to the floor and turned his face to the pillow.

"What's the use?" he muttered.

The duchess picked up the spilled food and left him without a word. He was lying in bed, bitterly enjoying his misery, when the duchess suddenly barged into his room.

"Heads up," she shouted in her stentorian voice and threw a book at him. Simon acted out of instinct, catching it before it struck him in the face.

"What the hell—" he demanded peevishly.

"I thought you might like something to read," said the duchess.

Simon looked at the book. It was of the type commonly known as a chapbook, a small paper-covered book that could be published cheaply. Such books generally contained bad poetry, sentimental ballads, or dire warnings that the Evil One was coming to lay waste to the world.

The chapbook was old; the pages were yellowed and gave off a musty smell. He glared at the duchess resentfully, but he was bored and he read the title.

A Defense of Contramagic.

Simon felt the hair on the back of his neck prickle. He looked at the duchess in shock.

"Where did you get this?"

"I wrote it," said the duchess. She made herself comfortable, plopping down on his bed. "I was quite young at the time. I thought you might find it entertaining."

"Good God, Duchess! The Church has issued a ban against even speaking of contramagic, let alone writing about it!"

"So you are one of those who subscribe to the belief that contramagic is evil," the duchess said.

"Magic is neither good nor evil," Simon said impatiently. "Magic *is*!"

The duchess winked at him. "Let me know what you think of the book."

"If the Church finds out you wrote this, they will lock us both in prison, Your Grace. Or worse!"

"I don't think they burn heretics these days," the duchess said, laughing.

Simon waved the book at her. "For you, they might make an exception!"

He smiled at the memory. He had, of course, read the book. He devoured it. He discreetly sent the duchess to find other books on the subject of the so-called evil magic, only to discover that they had all been confiscated by the Church.

In the process of studying the forbidden contramagic, Simon had come to realize that while he might not be able to use his legs to walk, he could use his mind to leap and soar and fly.

And now Simon was propelling his chair at a rapid rate of speed along the street that led to the harbor. His friends would follow, of course.

Simon grinned. He had left them little choice.

He was traveling several feet off the ground, but he could not yet see the harbor. Tall brick buildings blocked his view. He knew where he was, however, for he had visited the Naval Yard a month ago to instruct the *Valor*'s crafters, crew, and officers on how to best utilize the crystals known as the Tears of God.

The *Valor* was the first of the ships of the Expeditionary Fleet to be refitted. Randolph had wanted time to be able to test the crystals, see how the ship handled, make necessary adjustments. Randolph and his flag captain had planned to take the *Valor* out into the Breath only a few days from now.

Simon propelled his chair along the empty street, rounded a corner, and the lights of the harbor came into view. He could clearly see the *Valor*. The ship had been moved out of its berth and was now riding at anchor in the harbor, held in place by ropes attached fore and aft to two iron bollards. Those on board had lowered the gangplank and it was still in place for they were loading the ship with supplies. The *Valor* displayed her running lights, as well as masthead lights.

Her flag captain was ashore, but he would have detailed a small crew to keep watch under the command of a lieutenant. The crew would not be expecting trouble.

Simon dropped his chair to the ground and shut down the lift tanks to roll along the street, using the airscrews to propel the chair. The street ended at the pier. Simon kept to the shadows cast by the buildings and halted some distance from the ship.

The night air was crisp and cold. Beyond the lights of the *Valor*, the Breath was black. The very world seemed to come to an end. Simon removed a spyglass from one of the compartmented cabinets Mr. Albright had built into his chair and put it to his eye.

He assumed the enemy would come by boat, but he could see nothing. He lowered the glass and settled himself to wait.

"They will have to act soon," he said, talking to himself as he generally did since he was usually the only person around. "They have planted instigators in the mob, they must worry that the people at the gate will eventually grow bored with yelling and throwing rocks and will head back to the grog shops. Either that or the marines will open fire, in which case the mob will flee."

Simon heard the boats before he saw them. The faint hum of airscrews broke the silence of the night. He raised the spyglass and turned it toward the direction of the sound.

He saw three shore boats that had been painted black creeping toward the *Valor*. The boats did not have balloons and they had not raised their sails. They were relying on the airscrews alone. Their progress was slow, but steady.

"Now would be an extremely good time to arrive, Henry," Simon remarked, twisting his head to look over his shoulder. He saw no sign of the patrol boat, and turned back to observe the enemy.

The three boats headed straight for the pier, taking care to stay in the shadows, avoiding the light that shone from the ship. The sailors keeping watch on board the *Valor* had not noticed their peril. They would probably not notice until they were under attack, and by then it would be too late. These men were armed and they had come to fight.

Simon considered his options.

"I need to alert the crew to the danger. I can accomplish that by means of magic, but I will have to reveal my position, which is precarious, for there is little cover close to the pier. Therefore the best way to achieve my goal is to take to the air."

Simon waited until the three boats drew near the pier and men began jumping from the boat onto the dock. They were dressed all in black to blend in with the night, but he could tell by their bearing and their disciplined movements that they were soldiers. He counted six in the first landing party and guessed there would be equal numbers in the other two boats.

Someone gave a single command in a foreign language, which Simon recognized.

"Guundaran mercenaries," he murmured.

The soldiers from the first boat crept soft-footed across the dock toward the *Valor*. As they drew closer, Simon could dimly see them in the reflected glow of the masthead lights on the wooden dock. The soldiers were armed with clubs and pistols.

Arriving at the gangplank, the first group came to a halt, waiting for their fellows in order to storm the ship in a rush that would overwhelm the small crew.

The first boat left, returning to the Breath, and the second boat sailed up to the dock. The soldiers jumped out and moved toward the gangplank. All was carried out in orderly, military fashion and almost total silence.

"That, at least, is going to end," Simon said.

He glanced over his shoulder and was heartened to see the patrol boat, flying low, just managing to clear the steep roof of the Admiralty building. Simon could picture Alan standing on deck, eager for action, with Randolph beside him, fretting about his ship. Henry would be the cool head, advising them to proceed with caution.

The third boat was drawing near the dock. Simon adjusted the direction of his chair's airscrews and propelled his chair into the air, relying on the sounds of the boat's airscrews to mask his own.

The mercenaries jumped out of the third boat and ran to join their comrades. Their attention was focused on the ship. No one had seen or heard him.

Simon was pleased. He had been hoping for a chance to test his newest invention, one he called a "cracker" for it resembled the bonbons known as crackers—paper cylinders tied at each end with ribbon that emitted a sharp crack when pulled apart.

The cracker he had invented consisted of a glass rod, six inches long and an inch thick with a twist in the center. One side of the cracker was etched with magical constructs. The other was etched with contramagic. When the tube broke, the two energies would collide with force that Simon trusted would do more than crackle.

He ran his finger over the constructs he had etched into the glass, the magic and the contramagic. The cracker began to glow a faint blue at one end and green at the other.

He kept the glowing tube concealed so that no crafter would notice the light, and flew his chair until he was within range.

The last group of soldiers joined their comrades and stood waiting at the end of the gangplank for the order to attack.

Simon hurled the cracker.

Designed to explode on impact, the cracker hit the dock and blew up in a dazzling ball of blinding blue-green light. A concussive boom bowled over those unfortunate enough to be standing nearby.

Lights flared on board the *Valor*. Sailors shouted and ran to look over the rail. The mercenaries were thrown into confusion. Three lay unconscious on the ground. Most of the others were bleeding from cuts where they had been struck by shards of glass.

"Prepare for boarders!" an officer shouted, and the crew of the *Valor* ran to grab cutlasses and pistols.

Simon took out another cracker and began preparing the magic. Henry and his friends on board the patrol boat could now see what was happening and would hopefully increase their speed.

The mercenaries assumed that they had come under attack from the sailors on board the ship. They dashed up the gangplank, ready to fight the sailors who were running to meet them.

Simon flew overhead and dropped another cracker. It landed on the gang-plank in the midst of the warring groups. The blast and blinding light momentarily incapacitated both friend and foe.

The mercenaries now realized that they were being attacked from the air. They looked up and spotted Simon. The Guundarans appeared considerably amazed by the sight of a man floating in a wheeled chair about fifteen feet off the ground, but they were professionals. Nothing rattled them for long. They raised their pistols.

Simon tossed a final cracker in their general direction, then turned the airscrews on full and made a rapid retreat. He heard shots, but he wasn't particularly concerned. He was a moving target, barely visible in the darkness, and the soldiers were firing into the air.

He even performed some nice calculations as he fled regarding the trajectory of the deteriorating arc of a lead ball that is fired upward as compared to one fired in a straight line.

The patrol boat had arrived, and the Guundarans were now facing armed marines, swivel guns, and the cannon. The mercenaries were not being paid enough to sacrifice their lives in a hopeless cause, and they decided to retreat.

Their comrades in the waiting boats saw the danger and returned to the rescue. The mercenaries picked up their wounded and ran for their boats. The sailors from the *Valor* streamed down the gangplank and chased after them. The mercenaries made an orderly retreat, holding off the sailors with pistol fire as they boarded the boats.

The patrol boat had reached Simon. He looked up to see Henry anxiously gazing down at him and he gave an exuberant wave. He then looked back at the battle on the dock, where the *Valor*'s enraged crew was trying to seize the enemy boats.

Sailors and mercenaries were locked in close combat. The marines on the patrol boat had to hold their fire, for if they shot into the confused mass of men, they were likely to kill as many of their own as they would the enemy.

The mercenary boats eventually managed to take to the air. A few die-hard sailors intent on fighting to the last were forced to jump from the boats as they sailed off.

"After them!" Henry shouted and the patrol boat sailed off in pursuit.

Simon doubted it would catch them. The black-painted boats would undoubtedly sail off in different directions and would be nearly impossible to see in the darkness of the Breath.

Simon lowered his chair to the ground. A few moments later, Albright arrived in the carriage and landed near Simon. He jumped off the box before the carriage had stopped moving.

"Are you hurt, sir?" he gasped, rushing over.

"I am fine, Albright. Stop hovering," Simon said. "You know how that irritates me. Go wait with the carriage. I will join you in a moment."

Mr. Albright reluctantly returned to the carriage. The patrol boat had lost the mercenaries, as Simon had foreseen, and returned. Once the boat had docked, Henry and Alan and Randolph hurriedly disembarked.

Alan and Henry ran to Simon. Randolph ascertained that his friend was all right and then told them he was going aboard the *Valor* to check on his ship, adding that he would spend the night on board.

"I'm afraid I may have inadvertently injured some of your crew," Simon told him. "Give them my apologies. I had not anticipated that the concussive blast created by the mixture of the two magicks would be quite so powerful."

Randolph gaped at him, too astonished to even swear. He then stomped off, shaking his head and muttering.

Henry turned to Simon. "What the devil did you think you were doing running off on your own like that? You could have been killed."

"You should have waited for us," Alan added.

"By that time, the *Valor* would have been in the hands of the enemy," Simon replied. "I calculated the risks and I was in very little danger. As a matter of fact, I rather enjoyed myself. I have been wanting a chance to test the crackers and I was pleased to find out they worked as planned."

"Too bad the attackers escaped," said Henry. "I was hoping to question them, find out if they are part of this plot to put the Pretender on the throne."

"Which was, of course, why they had to escape. Once they saw that their venture had failed, they fled, even making certain to carry their wounded away with them so that they would not fall into your hands.

"These men were well-trained Guundaran mercenaries," Simon added. "I think you may safely say they were part of Smythe's secret army. We know from Mr. Sloan that Smythe employs such mercenaries. Smythe has troop carriers, undoubtedly converted merchant vessels. But he could use a warship and he would not find one such as *Valor* lying about unattended."

Henry cast him a grim glance.

"Sorry, Henry," said Simon. "I did not mean that remark the way it sounded. You had no way of knowing the *Valor* would be in danger."

"Still, I should have foreseen it, posted guards," Henry said.

"Are you two talking about this Smythe again?!" Alan said impatiently. "I trust one of you will tell me what is going on."

Henry drew out his pocket watch. "It is too late to return home. Let us go back to Simon's for a brandy and I will explain."

Henry and Alan walked Simon to his carriage. Alan was in a jovial mood, exhilarated by the chase, teasing Simon about his inability to make an accurate throw. Henry was more somber. He thrust his chilled hands into his pockets.

"It's all so outlandish," he stated. "Secret societies, secret armies, days of retribution. Like one of Miss Amelia's novels. Yet I should have realized the danger."

"You've had a great deal to occupy you of late, Henry," said Simon. "Will you tell Her Majesty?"

Henry shook his head. "She has not been well. I do not want to burden her."

"I am on the job," said Simon. "And so are you, Henry. If it hadn't been for your informant, Smythe's plan would have succeeded."

"We will drink a toast to the tout," said Alan, hoping to cheer his friend. "Given our good luck tonight, I suggest that tomorrow we each place a considerable sum on Candy Apple for the win."

"We can use the money to pay the dockworkers," Henry muttered.

THIRTY-SIX

Kate and Dalgren flew to Capione, a city in the southern part of Rosia. They were going to meet Miri and Gythe here, to make the cold and perilous journey Below. Once they arrived, they had to wait for Miri and Gythe to catch up.

Trundler houseboats were not known for their speed. They tended to "trundle" along at a leisurely pace, stopping in various floating Trundler villages along the way.

"They fly so slowly I'm afraid I'd fall asleep in midair," Dalgren said to Kate.

Lord Haelgrund had provided Kate with a dragon saddle and helm. Stephano had loaned Kate a heavy leather coat specially designed for members of the Brigade.

"I suggest you and Dalgren keep to yourselves. Camp in the wilderness, avoid cities and towns," Stephano had advised Kate. "You are still a fugitive."

"At least none of the officers recognized me," said Kate.

"Oh, yes they did." Stephano had smiled.

Kate had stared at him, astonished. "But if so, sir, why didn't they arrest me?"

"You were safe from arrest while you were in the Dragon Duchies. The dragons do not recognize Rosian law."

"But when I am in Rosia they could arrest me—"

"Princess Sophia informed the officers that you were under her protection."

"Her Highness never told me . . ." Kate had said.

"You had worries enough," Stephano had said dryly. "I would not tempt fate, if I were you. The Rosian navy might not be looking for you, but bounty hunters are. The protection of a princess means nothing to them."

Kate took Stephano's advice. She and Dalgren packed supplies enough to last the journey and took care to land in remote fields, far from civilization. The two had time to talk and hear about each other's adventures. That is, Dalgren heard about Kate's adventures. He did not want to talk about what had happened to him.

"I have a lot to think about," he said.

He was pleased and touched to hear his mother had attended the trial.

"I wrote to her," said Kate. "I told her the verdict and how you are going to work to restore your name. We'll fly to Travia to visit her when we return."

"I am the cause of her estrangement from my father," said Dalgren unhappily. "I brought shame and dishonor to both of them."

"Your father brought shame and dishonor on himself," said Kate.

But Dalgren only shook his head.

Kate, too, had a lot to think about. Miri had been intrigued to find out Kate was a ship's crafter.

"Gythe and I are still working on our ship. You can help us with the magic. Read this," said Miri, and she had handed Kate a slim volume.

Kate read the title, *The Seventh Sigil: A Crafter's Musings on the Marriage of Magic and Contramagic. Unholy Union or Sacred Alliance?* The author was Rodrigo de Villeneuve. Kate recalled Amelia mentioning this book to Olaf.

Already daunted by the title, Kate opened the book and viewed its diagrams and sample constructs with considerable dismay.

"I am certain I will find this interesting," she had said politely, being extremely certain she wouldn't. "But why do I need to know how to use the seventh sigil?"

"Because it is what keeps us flying," Miri had responded with a smile.

Kate had not understood, but she was deeply indebted to Miri for saving Dalgren, and so she had dutifully read the book. She had been surprised to find that she was interested in the subject and that she understood it.

To put it in the simplest terms, dear reader, crafters have known since the beginning of time that magical constructs are built using six basic sigils: earth, air, fire, water, life, death.

Saint Xavier discovered the existence of contramagic, which makes use of the same six constructs, only reversed. The constructs are mirror images, and since every action requires an equal and opposite reaction, they destroy each other. Thus the early Church deemed contramagic evil and forbade its use in the world Above.

Father Jacob Northrop did not accept the idea that magic is good and contramagic evil. He believed they were two halves of the same whole. He theorized the existence of a seventh sigil, one that represents God. When the seventh sigil is used in a construct containing both magic and contramagic, it blends the two together as God intended, making the combined magicks far more powerful.

Kate was dubious. She had seen contramagic do a great deal of evil.

Arriving in Capione, she and Dalgren made camp far from the city to wait for Miri and Gythe at a prearranged location: a lake not far from the coastline. They did not have long to wait. Miri and Gythe appeared only a few days after their own arrival. They took Kate to the secluded cove where they kept their ship.

"Why do you hide it?" Kate asked.

"You will see," said Miri.

The ship rode at anchor among the trees. Kate took one look at it and she understood why they had to keep it hidden. Also why she needed to know the seventh sigil.

The name of the ship was *Anáil Naofa,* which meant Holy Breath in the language of the Trundlers. And as far as Kate was concerned, the name was ill-conceived. For the ship was a black ship, one of those heinous vessels used by the Bottom Dwellers to wage war on those Above.

The black ships had been infamous for their use of blood magic and their green beam weapons—cannonlike guns that fired a beam of contramagic that had the effect of wiping out magical constructs.

The contramagic weapon had the potential to destroy every object that relied on magic on the face of Aeronne, and since magic was used in the construction of everything from privies to cathedrals, the green beam was capable of vast devastation. The weapons had sunk the naval warship *Royal Lion;* shattered the beautiful Crystal Market in Everux, killing hundreds; and blown up the massive gun emplacement that had once guarded the harbor of Westfirth.

Adding to the horror of the attacks, the Bottom Dwellers made use of human sacrifices to fire the weapon, killing them in blood magic rituals that enhanced the power of the contramagic. They would bind their victims to the guns, then cut their throats and bathe the green beam weapons in blood.

Designed to make the perilous journey from Below to the world Above, the black ship had a wide beam, short wings, reinforced hull, four airscrews, four lift tanks, and a large cargo hold designed to transport troops and prisoners. The helm was enclosed, providing shelter for the helmsman as the ship traveled through the frigid Deep Breath. The green beam weapons had been mounted on platforms on the bow.

The black ships took their name from the color of the dried blood of the victims that had been used to reinforce the contramagic on the hull. The hull of this ship was gray, not black, and there was no green beam weapon mounted on the foredeck. But Kate felt the same horror that she had known when she had seen her first black ship in the Aligoes. She turned to regard Miri and Gythe with revulsion.

"I want no part of this evil thing," Kate told them. "And neither does Dalgren. We will find our own way Below."

She started to walk away.

"You are very quick to judge us, Kate," said Miri. "You were a wrecker. You told us how you salvaged a Rosian warship that had once killed Freyans."

"That was different," said Kate, rounding on her. "My ship wasn't 'anointed' in blood!"

Gythe had been holding the cat, Doctor Ellington, but she dropped the indignant cat to the deck and began to talk. Her eyes flashed and so did her hands. She made rapid gestures, jabbing her finger at the ship, slashing her hand across her throat, shaking her head.

"Gythe says to tell you that our ship was never used in battle," said Miri. "We found it on Glasearrach at the end of the war. The ship was built with contramagic, that much is true. But it was never 'anointed' as you put it. The war ended before they had a chance to put it into action.

"We needed a ship that could make the journey Below to help Father Jacob in his work among the people. We sailed this back Above and made it our own."

Kate looked back at the ship glowing with the green light of the contramagic; the sight made her skin crawl. She tried to tell herself that magic was not good or evil, but she had heard all her life that contramagic was the tool of the Evil One and she found it hard to divest herself of the notion, no matter what the book claimed.

She could see places, particularly on the deck and the masts, the sails and balloons, where the green magic and the blue blended together. Gythe had been using the seventh sigil to combine the two magicks, make them stronger, as well as making it easier for her to manage the ship. And she'd said she had been hoping Kate would be able to assist her.

"It brings back memories . . ." said Kate.

"For us, as well," said Miri. "The Bottom Dwellers attacked our old boat, the *Cloud Hopper*. That's when we were with the Cadre of the Lost. Stephano was sailing with us then. They boarded the ship to try to steal Gythe. We fought them off, but Gythe was so terrified she retreated into her mind, went to some dark place. We almost lost her."

Miri smiled fondly at Gythe. "Not long after that, she and I were prisoners in one of these ships. The Bottom Dwellers locked us in the hold. I was worried when Father Jacob gave us this ship that it would stir up those same dark memories in Gythe. She is fine. She says the souls of men are dark, not wood and sailcloth."

"And now you carry food and supplies to those who mistreated you," Kate said, shaking her hand. "How can you help them?"

Gythe pointed to herself and Miri and Kate, then flung her arms wide as though she would embrace the world.

"What is she saying?" Kate asked.

"They are not *them*," Miri explained. "They are us. True, the Bottom Dwellers committed terrible atrocities, but we did the same to them. We sank their island and left them to perish in the darkness at the bottom of the world."

"No ghosts on our boat," said Gythe, bending down to pet the Doctor. "Only a cat."

Miri sniffed. "Give me a nice, quiet ghost over that dratted beast any day. Come on board, Kate. We will show you around."

Kate boarded the *Naofa,* feeling somewhat reassured. She was impressed with the idea of the "wheelhouse"—a term Miri borrowed from ships that sailed on water—that protected the helmsman from the elements. Kate had been forced on more than one occasion to stand at the helm while being pelted by hail or soaked in the driving rain. She considered the shelter an excellent idea.

"We had to replace the helm," said Miri. "The original was etched with contramagic. Gythe managed to use it on our first journey here, but she was almost dead from exhaustion by the time we arrived."

Officer and crew quarters were on the berth deck, along with the galley, the head, and a large storage closet. The cat, Doctor Ellington, took a special interest in the galley, but turned tail and fled when Miri opened the storage closet.

"We lock him up in here when we go Below," Miri explained, laughing. "He's afraid that every time we open the door we're going to chuck him inside."

Miri and Gythe slept in the captain's cabin, which was the largest. They gave Kate a smaller cabin directly across the corridor.

"How do the two of you sail a ship this big?" Kate asked.

"We couldn't if we were traveling any great distance," said Miri.

"We don't sail," said Gythe. "We just go down and up."

"The city of Dunlow, the capital of Glasearrach, lies almost directly below us," Miri explained. "We sail a short distance from land, then reduce the lift in the tanks and sink."

"I've done that myself," said Kate thinking back to when she had gone down to save her crew. "I never traveled very far. It was too dangerous."

"The journey will not be a pleasant one," said Miri. "But as bad as it is for us, it will be worse for Dalgren."

Two days later, the *Naofa* made its descent to the bottom of the world. Kate stood shivering in front of the small porthole on the middle deck of the black ship. She was wearing a heavy sweater Miri had given her, her slops with thick woolen stockings beneath, her peacoat, mittens, and her woolen hat—and she was still half frozen.

At least she was safely inside a ship. Dalgren was out there, exposed to the cold. He would have to endure worse, for he would have to fly through the Aurora—a phenomenon created when the severe cold of the Deep Breath caused the Breath to liquefy and form a layer of congealed mist that hung suspended between Above and Below.

Lord Haelgrund had made the historic journey Below in company with Stephano and the Dragon Brigade. He had warned Dalgren that the journey would be difficult and dangerous.

"My body temperature dropped," Haelgrund told him. "My reaction time slowed. I grew sluggish and found it hard to think clearly. Ice rimed my scales and coated my wings, slowing my flight. At one point I was so exhausted I remember thinking it would be easier if I just quit struggling and gave up, let myself plummet into oblivion."

Kate craned her neck to try to see her friend through the porthole. Dragons could use their fiery breath to burn through the Aurora, but Miri had suggested that the *Naofa* enter the Aurora first and punch a hole in the liquid. Dalgren could fly through the opening; far safer than having to fly through the congealed mists, which Miri likened to sailing through jelly.

Kate could not see the dragon for the thick fog and eventually she gave up trying to find him. She tried jumping up and down to warm herself, then felt a tap on her shoulder.

She turned to see Gythe offering her a steaming mug of hot cider. Kate could tell by the smell it was laced with Calvados; she drank it gratefully.

"You should be back in the galley where it's warm," Kate said. Her facial muscles were so stiff the words came out a mumble.

At the sound of her voice, the Doctor gave an indignant yowl, reminding them that he was still locked inside the storage closet, just in case they had forgotten him.

Gythe went over to give the door a reassuring tap and the howling subsided. Coming back to the porthole, she pointed to the deck above and placed her hand over her heart.

"You're worried about Miri," said Kate.

Gythe nodded and sighed. "I always worry."

Her sister was at the helm, inside the shelter of the wheelhouse. Gythe had placed magically heated stones around her feet to keep her warm. The wheelhouse was little more than a shanty, however, with windows on all four sides so that the helmsman could see to navigate. No amount of heat from magical stones could hold the warmth for long.

Gythe latched onto Kate and drew her closer to the porthole. She pointed out the glass. The fog was starting to dissipate. Pale light from a sickly looking sun filtered through the porthole.

"The Aurora," said Gythe.

Kate looked down on what appeared to be a river of gray ice flowing beneath the ship.

"How did it come by its name?" Kate wondered.

"Watch," said Gythe.

The pale sunlight hit the Aurora and suddenly myriad rainbows flowed across the shimmering, icy surface in an ever-changing dance of incredible beauty.

Kate gazed in awe mingled with growing uneasiness. The Aurora appeared to be rushing up to meet them at a high rate of speed. As she continued to watch, the rainbows faded, and the liquid Breath changed to a viscous, undulating mass of gray.

The boat plunged down toward the gray mass. Kate braced herself, although Miri had assured her that they would feel no impact.

"The ship will slide through the Aurora like a spoon through jelly," Miri had said.

The ship struck the gray mass, shuddered slightly, and slipped through with ease. The sunlight disappeared as they descended further. Thick, gray-white slime slid down the glass of the porthole and then the *Naofa* was through.

Kate peered up through the slime and saw Dalgren. He was flying slowly, his movements labored. Icy fog coated his scales and rimed his wings. A white beard of frozen saliva hung from his jaws.

He sucked in a breath and then let it out in a blast of fire that struck the congealed liquid, melting it and widening the hole through which he would have to fly.

The gray slime sliding down the window started to diminish. Sunlight returned, dim at first, then growing brighter as the ship emerged from the Aurora.

Kate looked out on a rugged, barren landscape. The jagged peaks of Mount Glabhar Cloch rose in the distance, shrouded by gray clouds. Smaller peaks trailed along behind it—the mountain ridge known as the Spine. The capital city of Dunlow lay directly below, a hodgepodge of buildings sprawling across the foothills, dimly visible through the clouds.

The bright sunlight vanished as the ship passed through the clouds. The sky grew dreary, dismal. A light rain began to fall.

"Welcome to the doomed isle of Glasearrach,"* said Gythe.

She tapped Kate on the shoulder and indicated with signs of her hands that it was now safe for them to go up on deck. Kate had been cooped up long enough, and she eagerly opened the hatch and climbed the stairs that led to the main deck.

With rain pattering on her face, she drew in a deep breath of moist air and waved to Dalgren, who caught sight of her and breathed a triumphant blast of flame in response. The worst, most dangerous part of the journey was over. They had only to endure life at the bottom of the world for a year and then they could return to sunlight and blue sky and Dalgren would have his name back.

Kate helped Gythe and Miri prepare the ship for landing.

"Where are the docks?" she asked Miri, who was still in the wheelhouse, her hands on the helm.

"They were destroyed during the war and have yet to be rebuilt," Miri said. "They're not really needed. Few ships brave the journey from Above. We land in a shallow ravine on the outskirts of the city."

"A ravine?" Kate repeated, startled.

"We have to remain afloat to accommodate the airscrews," said Miri.

"Of course," said Kate, feeling silly. "I should have thought of that."

The weight of the hull would crush the airscrews if the ship set down on land. In a proper dockyard, the ship's hull could rest in a large cradle.

Miri must have guessed her thoughts. "Lumber is scarce. People need homes, not dockyards."

She lowered the *Naofa* into the ravine, which had the extra advantage of providing them with water, for a stream ran at the bottom. When the ship was hovering safely a few feet off the ground, Gythe and Kate jumped off and attached the mooring lines to boulders.

---

* We tell the complete story of Stephano de Guichen and the Cadre of the Lost in the three-volume series titled *Dragon Brigade*.

Dalgren had flown away to hunt and rest in the caves of Mount Glabhar Cloch. The caves had been used by the dragons of the Brigade during the war and Lord Haelgrund had recommended that he make his home there.

Once the ship was safely tethered, Miri emerged from the wheelhouse. She looked cold and exhausted. Kate asked if she could be of help.

"I'm half frozen," said Miri. "I think we could all use some rest and a cup of the brew to warm our bones."

The brew consisted of boiling hot water, Calvados, honey, cinnamon, and nutmeg. Gythe filled mugs and handed them around. The three sat down at the small table in the galley to eat a long-delayed supper.

They were interrupted by angry yowlings and thumpings coming from the storage closet.

"We forgot the Doctor!" Miri exclaimed.

Gythe jumped to her feet and hurried to free the cat from the closet. He bolted out, looking irate, and stalked past the table with his tail in the air, refusing to acknowledge them until Gythe offered him a bit of sardine by way of apology. He showed them he forgave them by jumping onto the table and trying to eat the butter.

Miri hauled him off and dumped him on the deck. Nonplussed, the Doctor curled up in front of the stove to rest after the rigors of his journey. Gythe made signs with her hands, a hugging motion with her arms.

"You want to go see Father Jacob," said Miri. "You know there are chores to be done."

Gythe spread her arms as though they were wings, then clapped her hands over her mouth and danced about in a mock frenzy of terror that made Kate laugh.

"She says she's afraid people will be terrified of Dalgren. Very well," Miri agreed crossly. "You can go. Kate and I will do the chores. I will write a letter of explanation for Father Jacob, warning him we've brought a dragon and that he's peaceful, so people don't panic."

"This priest won't panic, will he?" Kate asked. "I know you said this Father Jacob would help Dalgren, but I also know that most priests hate dragons. They claim they are in league with the Evil One."

"Father Jacob Northrop is not one of those priests," Miri said. "He lived among dragons for a long time. He is a close friend of the Duke and Duchess of Talwin. He might have even met Dalgren."

Kate remained doubtful, but she kept her doubts to herself. She had never heard of a priest who was friendly to dragons, particularly a priest who was Freyan and a member of the Arcanum.

Kate had another reason for distrusting Father Jacob. She had learned that he was Captain Alan Northrop's older brother. Alan had never even told her he had a brother. When Miri found out Kate knew him, she told her the story of the old scandal, how Jacob had disgraced the family by refusing to renounce his faith and fled to Rosia following the Reformation in Freya.

"Alan was so angry he tried to kill him," Miri said. "The two are reconciled now, but they were estranged for many years."

Miri descended to her cabin to write her letter, Gythe cleared the table, and Kate went to fetch water for washing up. By the time she returned, Miri had finished her task. Gythe tucked the letter into the pocket of her skirt, gave the Doctor a kiss on his head, then departed, running lightly down the gangplank.

"Be back before nightfall," Miri called. "I don't want you tumbling into a gorge in the dark. And ask Father Jacob if he has news about the young folk."

Gythe promised she would with a wave of her hand and walked across the field toward the town.

"Funny how that girl always finds something else to do whenever there is work to be done," Miri said, sniffing. "You put on the kettle and I'll haul out the washtub."

"What's happening with the young folk?" Kate asked.

"They've been leaving home." Miri placed the small washtub on the table.

Kate, remembering the dilapidated-looking buildings and war-ravaged city over which they had flown, couldn't very well fault the young people.

She poured the hot water into the tub. The Doctor viewed the preparations with alarm and bolted up the stairs to the deck above. Miri laughed at him. "I occasionally decide the Doctor smells a little too strongly of sardine and I insist on a bath."

Miri plunged the wooden trenchers into the water and began to scrub while she talked.

"We Trundlers have always been proud that our clans maintain law and order among our people, not counting the occasional blood feud, of course, and in that instance a few cracked skulls and a knife wound or two generally settles the matter. All that's changed down here, however.

"Dunlow is divided into clans, like Trundler floating cities above. After the war, the clan leaders decided that they would take over running the government. The clans had worked together to fight the blood mages and they wanted to try to remain united."

Miri handed Kate a plate to dry.

"Lacking an enemy to fight, however, the clans began fighting among themselves," Miri continued. "Old rivalries and feuds surfaced. If you ask a McPike and a McDougal if water is wet, a McPike would say no just because a McDougal said yes. And so now nothing gets done. The young people have no work and no prospects. They gather in the local taverns and drink fermented goat's milk and talk revolution. We've been hearing reports of parents waking to find their sons and daughters have packed up and left."

"Where are they going?" Kate asked.

"The center of the rebellion is said to be in Kilean, a town in the western part of Glasearrach near the marshland. The problem is that once the young folk leave, they don't come back. Their parents never hear from them again. Father Jacob is doing what he can to help rebuild the city and try to settle the feuds, but that takes time and the young don't want to wait. They want change to happen immediately."

Kate stacked the trenchers in a cupboard. She and Miri carried the dish tub outside and dumped the water into the ravine. Now that the washtub was put away, the Doctor returned and began rubbing around Miri's ankles.

Miri sat at her ease, glad to rest. Kate walked the deck, feeling restless and watching the clouds mass overhead. Lightning flickered in the distance. Miri had said the storms that swept the land were not nearly as bad as they had been prior to the war, but this was the second rainstorm since they had landed.

Kate gazed out at the dismal prospect and tried to picture a year in this place. The time had seemed very short when she had first heard Dalgren's sentence. Now it seemed interminable.

"Do you have any more chores for me to do?" Kate asked.

"I didn't like the way the helm answered after we came through the Breath," said Miri. "Sometimes the magic of the Aurora damages the constructs. Perhaps you could take a look."

Glad to have something to occupy her mind, Kate started to go inspect the helm. Before she could look at it, Dalgren appeared. The dragon circled overhead, searching for a place to land on the rugged, uneven ground. He spiraled down and made a safe, if inelegant, landing, thumping forward onto his chest when his hind leg slipped into a crevasse.

He lumbered toward the boat, moving stiffly. His crest drooped and his injured left leg slightly dragged on the ground. He looked tired and hungry.

"Did you find food?" Kate asked.

"If you could call a couple of tough stringy mountain goats food," Dalgren grumbled. He looked discomfited to see Miri coming to greet him. "Sorry, Mistress, I didn't mean to complain."

"Good evening, Dalgren," she said, smiling. "I am afraid food is not plentiful for anyone on Glasearrach. We have to learn to live on short rations down here."

"Yes, ma'am," said Dalgren, chagrined. "I am most grateful—"

"I know," said Miri. "You won't find life easy here, either of you." Her earnest glance included Kate. "You *will* find it rewarding, I believe."

"Yes, ma'am," said Kate.

"I am certain I will, ma'am," said Dalgren.

"And that ends my lecture," said Miri, laughing. "Ah, good, here comes Gythe."

Miri caught sight of her sister hurrying toward the ship and walked down the gangplank to meet her.

"I truly am grateful for this opportunity to regain my name," said Dalgren to Kate. "I hope Miri knows that."

"She knows," said Kate. She affectionately rubbed his snout with her hand.

Dalgren gave a huge yawn, causing Kate to wave her hand and back away.

"Sulfur fumes," she said, grimacing.

"I could sleep for days," Dalgren said. "I came to make certain you were all right after the journey."

"I thought I'd been cold before, back when I was wrecking in the Deep Breath," said Kate. "I never knew what cold was!"

A shudder rippled across Dalgren's body, making his skin twitch. "I was covered in icicles. I don't want to make that trip again any time soon."

"We won't," said Kate somberly. "We're stuck here for a year."

"I'm not complaining," Dalgren reiterated.

"Neither am I," said Kate. "They say the Pirate King used to live around here. Maybe I'll spend my time searching for buried treasure."

Dalgren rolled his eyes and snorted fire from his nostrils.

"Father Jacob is coming tomorrow at midmorning," said Miri, returning with Gythe. "He is bringing men to help unload the cargo and he wants to meet with you then, Dalgren."

"I can help with the cargo, ma'am," said Dalgren.

"I am certain Father Jacob will find all sorts of tasks for you," said Miri. "And now you should go get some sleep. Hopefully you'll find something more to eat."

"Yes, ma'am, thank you, ma'am." Dalgren said.

He ducked his head and backed away so as not to accidentally take down a mast with a swipe of his tail. Once he was clear of the ship, he spread his wings and made a running leap into the air.

"He really is grateful," said Kate. "We both are."

"Tell me that in six months," said Miri.

THIRTY-SEVEN

Dalgren arrived well in advance of the time set for his meeting with the priest. He looked better rested and better fed than the day before. Kate greeted him, but she didn't have time to talk. She, Gythe, and Miri were working down in the hold to ready the cargo for transportation.

Dalgren asked if he could help. Miri, eyeing his massive size, said he could keep watch and let them know when the priest and his helpers were coming.

Dalgren settled down on the ground to wait. Miri opened the hatch and she and Kate started to descend into the hold. Miri stopped to look around.

"Where is the Doctor?" she asked sharply. "I don't want that cat down there. Last time he ripped open a sack of flour and made such a mess that I almost never got it cleaned up."

Gythe pointed to Dalgren.

Kate was mystified. "What does Dalgren have to do with it?"

"The Doctor doesn't like dragons," Miri explained. "That means he'll be hiding under one of the lift tanks, which is where he can stay until we're finished."

Dim light filtered into the hold, for the sun was visible in the sky this morning, shimmering faintly and giving no heat.

Kate was going to bring a lantern with her to light the hold, for it had no portholes. Miri shook her head.

"Gythe uses her magic."

Gythe cupped her hands together, as though she were holding a bird. She sang a few words then opened her hands to reveal a globe of bluish-white light. She flung the globe into the air and smiled to see it float upward to hover near the wooden beams, filling the hold with light.

The three of them lowered the netting that held the cargo in place and began to tug loose the ropes that kept it from shifting during the voyage. Shifting cargo could prove deadly to a ship, causing it to list dangerously and potentially sending it plunging into the Breath.

The cargo consisted of sacks of rice and wheat to grind for flour, barrels of salted pork and beef, and sacks of seeds for crops that grew well in low sunlight, such as lettuce, carrots, and spinach. They carried more than food. They had filled wooden chests with books for the school run by Brother Barnaby, Father Jacob's assistant. The books ranged from the history of Aeronne to primers on magical constructs. Other boxes contained bottles of tinctures and potions and unguents used for healing, as well as herbs and oils and spices for medicine and cooking.

"Who pays for this?" Kate asked.

"The people of Dunlow," said Miri. "When we make our return voyage, we haul blankets and clothing made from the merino wool for which the Trundlers of Glasearrach were once famous. The woolen goods fetch high prices in the world Above and we are able to provide these people with the means to earn a living, maintain their pride."

Dalgren gave a trumpeting hoot that was so loud and unexpected even Kate jumped. The Doctor shot down into the hold, his eyes wild, every hair standing on end.

"I hope that means Father Jacob is coming and not that the world is ending!" Miri gasped. "Look now! See what that dratted cat has done! Gythe, clean up those seeds he's spilled, then come greet our guests."

"You go," Kate told Gythe. "I'll clean this up."

Gythe thanked her with a flashing smile and started to run up on deck.

"Don't leave that cat down there!" Miri called irritably.

Gythe grabbed the Doctor and carried him to the deck above. Kate scooped up the seeds from the deck and stored them in another sack. When she was finished, she came on the deck in time to see a group of men dressed in shabby clothes gathered around the gangplank. Several other men remained seated on wagons drawn by sturdy little shaggy horses. She presumed the man in the cassock, talking to Miri and Gythe, was Father Jacob.

He was certainly not what Kate had expected.

His cassock had seen better days. It was rumpled and worn; the hem was frayed and covered in cream-colored dirt while the same dirt stained the area of the knees and his sleeves. The top button near the clerical collar was missing. The collar itself was no longer white, but a dingy gray.

Kate searched for a resemblance to Alan, but saw little. Father Jacob was perhaps in his early fifties, and thin, but then so was everyone on Glasearrach. He was well-built with broad shoulders. He wore his iron-gray hair in the traditional tonsure, but it was ragged and unkempt. He gave Gythe a fatherly hug and smiled at Miri, who was scolding him on the state of his clothes.

"You look as though you have been crawling around in the mud, Father!"

"That's because I have," Father Jacob answered with a chuckle. "I've come from the construction site. I've been helping to lay bricks for the new houses."

"You lay bricks?" Kate asked, startled.

She had never known a priest to get his hands dirty.

Father Jacob turned to her with a smile that crinkled the lines around his eyes and deepened the lines around his mouth, almost as if he knew what she was thinking.

"Father, this is Mistress Katherine Gascoyne-Fitzmaurice," said Miri.

He started to hold out his hand, then noticed it was covered in dirt. He wiped it on his cassock, causing Miri to mutter and shake her head. Father Jacob offered Kate his hand again.

"I am Father Jacob Northrop."

Kate was entranced by his eyes, finding it hard to look away. They were gray-green in color, piercing and intense, surrounded by a web of lines. He seemed to see through her body to her soul. She supposed that must be a job requirement for a priest, but the feeling of intrusion made her uncomfortable.

"Mistress Katherine," said Father Jacob, shaking hands. He had a firm grip.

"Please call me Kate, Father. I know your brother, Alan," Kate added, flustered, trying to avoid his gaze. "I knew him from the Aligoes. When he was a Rose Hawk."

"Indeed!" Father Jacob said, his eyes warming. "How is Alan? I hope he is well. Is he still a privateer?"

"He is now a captain in the Royal Navy, Father," said Kate.

"Good for Alan," said Father Jacob. He released her from his scrutiny with a smile. "I must write to congratulate him. And now, Mistress Kate, please introduce me to your friend."

Dalgren held himself at rigid attention, sitting back on his haunches, his neck stiff, eyes staring straight ahead, his wings at his sides. The Bottom

Dwellers who had accompanied the priest kept their distance, arms folded, eyeing the dragon askance.

"This is Dalgren, Father," said Kate.

"No, I am not," Dalgren stated, his voice grating. "I do not have a name."

Father Jacob regarded the dragon with interest. "Miri wrote to me about the trial and your sentence. I know the history of the Battle of the Royal Sail. I am friends with Father Antonius, whose magic kept the fortress from crashing to the ground after the navy fired on it. Do you think you deserve the sentence that was handed down by the council?"

Dalgren had not expected the question. He shifted his head to look down his snout at the priest. His claws dug into the ground.

"I deserted the Brigade, Father," he said, his voice grating. "I admitted my guilt. I broke my oath."

"One could say that the navy broke its oath to you," Father Jacob remarked. "You were doing your duty, guarding those who had placed their lives in your care when they surrendered. Why did you desert? Was it cowardice?"

Kate stirred in anger, but she kept silent. Dalgren would not appreciate her interference. The Trundler men were watching and listening. A few scowled, but more appeared to be curious to hear what Dalgren had to say.

He was clearly startled by the question. He thought it over in silence, then breathed out pale smoke. His rigid defensive posture relaxed. His claws uncurled, his jaws parted slightly.

"If I had stayed in the Brigade, they would have ordered me to kill again and I could not do that. I had seen too much death already. My choice was to either desert or disobey my commanding officer. I deserted."

He lifted his head, his crest flared. "I realize now I should have stayed to fight for my beliefs, as did Captain de Guichen and the others. I will work hard to earn the right to bear my name again."

"Good," said Father Jacob, smiling. "Since the name you lost is your dragon name and none of us could pronounce that anyway, I believe we could call you by the name you go by among humans. Would that be correct, Master of Dragon Lore?"

He glanced at Miri.

"Indeed it would, Father," she replied.

Dalgren gave a faint smile, his lip drawing back slightly, barely showing the tips of his fangs.

"If the Master approves, then so do I, Father."

"Welcome, Dalgren," said Father Jacob. He rubbed his hands. "And now, let us get to work unloading this ship."

The Bottom Dwellers greeted Miri and Gythe as old friends, but their smiles vanished when they turned to Kate. They rebuffed her attempts to be friendly and shouldered her out of their way when she offered to help.

"You are an outsider," Miri explained. "The Bottom Dwellers don't trust strangers, especially those from Above. Give them time to come to know you. You're going to be here a year."

Kate thought that over and sighed.

They loaded the cargo into the wagons. Miri and Gythe were going to go back to the city with them to help store and distribute the supplies. Father Jacob asked if Dalgren would like to pay his respects at Droal's Cairn, a memorial dedicated to a dragon who had died during the war.

"Come with us, Kate," said Miri, as they were leaving the *Noafa*. "I know these people don't seem very friendly, but they will warm up to you."

Kate shook her head. "I'll stay here. I need to make those repairs to the constructs."

"But you don't have to do that right now," Miri protested. "We're not going anywhere in the ship. Besides, Gythe is the one who should be making the repairs."

Gythe made a face and pointed at Kate, who laughed. "Gythe is right. I don't mind the work. Gives me a chance to practice using the seventh sigil. Tell Father Jacob that I'd like to talk to him about it, when he has time."

"I'm sure he will make time," said Miri. "He likes nothing better than to talk about magic."

Gythe thanked Kate with a wave and ran off to climb onto one of the wagons where she laughingly settled herself among the sacks and barrels. The driver looked back to see what had become of Miri.

"We will be home before nightfall," said Miri, hurrying down the gangplank. "Don't let that cat trick you into feeding him!"

Kate promised she wouldn't and stood at the rail to watch the procession. The wagons led. Father Jacob and Miri and the others followed on foot, while Dalgren soared overhead. He dipped his wings to Kate, then flew lazy circles to keep pace with the wagons.

"He looks happier than I've seen him in a long time," Kate remarked to the Doctor.

The cat was not interested. He yawned and licked his paws, then followed Kate as she went over to inspect the brass helm. The cat insinuated himself between her and the helm and began to purr loudly.

"Absolutely no sardines," Kate told him. "You heard Miri."

She rubbed the Doctor's head to ease the disappointment, but the cat would have nothing more to do with her. He stalked off in ire, heading down to the galley in the faint hope that Gythe had mistakenly left the butter on the table.

The helm wasn't badly damaged, and after Kate made the repairs, she was satisfied it would answer. She turned her attention to the lift tanks.

Unlike any other ship Kate had ever seen, the lift tanks on the black ship were located underneath the base of each wing, built into the structure of the hull. The helmsman could therefore adjust the amount of lift in each tank to control the pitch and yaw of the ship; critical when sailing the Deep Breath.

In order to access each tank, Kate had to open a hatch on the main deck, then lower herself down to the platform on which the tank rested. The space was tight and she had to crawl around on her hands and knees to view the constructs on each tank. She went over all the rows of sigils, searching for breaks and making repairs.

Miri was right. The constructs had been damaged, though not severely. Kate was intrigued. She had been making repairs to magic since she was ten and she had never seen breaks quite like this. It was as if the magic of the Aurora had run down the lift tank in rivulets, washing away the sigils wherever it touched them. Kate was surprised that the lift tanks hadn't failed completely.

The constructs were a combination of magic and contramagic. Making the repairs was draining, both physically and mentally, for she had to adjust her thinking to understand the contramagic and to make it work with the seventh sigil.

By midday, she decided to take a break. Her knees were sore, her back ached, and the constructs were starting to blur before her eyes. She realized she was hungry and remembered Miri saying something about a dish of salt pork and cold beans she'd left in the pantry.

As Kate climbed back through the hatch and onto the main deck, she was startled to hear a rustling sound and catch a glimpse of movement out of the corner of her eyes. She turned swiftly and could have sworn she saw someone peering at her from over the rim of the gully.

The moment she turned, the person vanished, ducking down out of sight.

Kate didn't want to stare. If someone was out there, she didn't want to let the person know she had seen him. She put her hands on her hips and bent forward, easing the kinks from her back and casually scanning the area.

The landscape was rock-bound and desolate, reminding her of the islands in the Deep Breath. Scraggly weeds seemed to be reaching desperate hands to catch every ray of the pallid, fickle sunlight.

The ground was uneven, broken by gorges, ravines, gullies, and ditches, littered with boulders and trees bent double by the winds of fierce wizard storms. If someone was out there, she might never find him.

Kate wasn't particularly frightened. Miri kept a loaded pistol beneath the helm and an axe within easy reach. She could deal with any threat, but she found the idea that someone was lurking among the rocks, spying on them, disquieting.

The most logical explanation was that the Bottom Dwellers didn't like her, didn't trust her, and had posted someone to keep an eye on her. But she couldn't help thinking of the stories about blood mages pouring fresh blood over the decks of the black ships. Her skin crawled.

Kate didn't want to leave the deck, but she had worked hard and she was hungry. She hurried to the galley, grabbed the plate of cold beans, salt pork, and brown bread and carried it up onto the foredeck to eat where she could keep an eye on things.

The Doctor accompanied her, disdainful of beans, hoping for pork. She offered him some bread. He sniffed at it, then looked up at her, seeming to ask if butter went with that. Finding it did not, he ate it anyway and then curled up on a pile of rope and went to sleep.

Kate cast surreptitious glances every so often at the ditch, but saw no signs that anyone was out there. Eventually she grew tired of wondering and decided to go see for herself. Taking Miri's pistol from under the helm, Kate walked down the gangplank and out into the field.

Miri had said that other Bottom Dweller boats used this area for landing, for it was close to the city. The *Naofa* was the only ship here now, but Kate could see indications that other boats had landed here: depressions in the soil, remnants of campfires. There was no refuse, though. The Bottom Dwellers had so little they never discarded anything.

The afternoon was gray and gloomy. No sun this day. The ground was muddy and difficult to walk, and brush and scrub trees impeded her way.

"And, of course, the only thing that grows in this godforsaken country would be brambles," Kate muttered, sucking on her bleeding thumb.

As she approached the gully, she drew the pistol.

"I know you're here!" Kate called, speaking Rosian. "Show yourself. Why are you spying on me?"

The only sound was the wind whispering among the rocks. She peered into the gully. It was empty, but fresh footprints covered the ground. Some were deep, as though the person had been standing there a long time. Others were shallow. She could see them coming and going.

Kate followed the footprints for about a mile until the gully ended at a jutting rock formation. The person had climbed out of the gully onto stony ground. The footprints ended. But they had gone off in the direction of Dunlow.

Kate looked back at the footprints. They appeared to belong to a man wearing boots. Every man she had seen from Dunlow had been wearing boots.

Night came early and fell quickly on Glasearrach. The shadows were closing in and Kate had not thought to bring a lantern. She hurried back to the ship before she was caught out in the bramble-laced, rock-strewn field in the dark. She reached the gangplank at the same time as a wagon delivered Miri and Gythe.

"What were you doing? Exploring?" Miri asked as they walked up the gangplank. "I'm afraid there's not much to explore around here. Unless you are making a study of the many varieties of brambles," she added, seeing the scratches on Kate's hands and arms.

Kate told them about the glimpse of movement and the footprints in the gully.

"Someone was out there spying," Kate said.

Darkness had fallen, deep and thick, by the time they were on deck. As she did nightly, Gythe clapped her hands and started to cast balls of brightly glowing magic up into the rigging to fill the deck with light.

Miri stopped her. "Better not tonight, Gythe. Let's not tell all of Glasearrach where we are until we figure this out."

"Do you have any idea who it would be watching us or why?" Kate asked.

Miri was clearly upset. "I can't think of any. We don't have anything of value on board now that we've unloaded the cargo. Still, we shouldn't take any chances. We'll raise the gangplank for the night. Gythe, you and Kate check to make certain there are no holes in our defenses."

Kate and Gythe checked the warding constructs on the hull and the deck, the masts and the rigging. The constructs were contramagic that gave off a faint green glow.

"The contramagic provides protection, so Gythe and I decided not to change it," Miri had explained.

They ate their evening meal and over mugs of hot tea as they sat on the deck talking and keeping watch. Miri described how Dalgren was already working to assist in the construction of new houses to replace those destroyed in the war.

"He's proving invaluable," said Miri. "We use timber from ironwood and hemlock trees to build houses. These trees only grow on the small islands in the marshland, which is about a hundred and fifty miles from Dunlow. The only way to haul the logs is by boat and by oxen. The journey could take weeks. Dalgren can easily lift and carry the whole trees and make the journey in a day."

"I'm glad," said Kate. "Now I need to find some way to make myself useful. That is going to be hard when your people don't trust me."

Gythe gave Kate a sympathetic pat on her shoulder.

"I was thinking of something you could do to help earn their trust," Miri said. "Ours is one of the few ships in Glasearrach capable of sailing through the

Aurora. The black ships that survived the war were refitted to use lift gas, not blood sacrifices, but they encounter the same problem we did—the magic damages the constructs.

"The Bottom Dwellers knew nothing of our kind of magic until after the war. They are slowly learning, but few can do the kind of intricate, complex work you do. You could help them learn."

"That's a good idea," said Kate, and she tried to sound cheerful.

Her attempt must have been a dismal failure, for both Miri and Gythe were regarding her with concern.

"Are you all right?" Miri asked.

Kate couldn't very well tell them that the thought of spending a year in this desolate place among people who hated her filled her with dismay. She was isolated, alone, cut off from her friends. Thomas and Sophia might be married in a year. Sir Henry would forget about her. He would never offer them employment now.

She had imagined herself and Dalgren working together to earn back his name. Instead the dragon would be spending his days hauling wood and she would be crawling about on the decks of ships, eating cold beans and salt pork and knowing she should be grateful for that. Most of the Bottom Dwellers had far less.

Kate rubbed her eyes.

"Just a headache," she said. "Probably from staring at sigils all day. I'll be fine in the morning."

"A headache. I can help that," said Miri. "Gythe, go to the herb box. Bring feverfew and passionflower."

"Truly, I'm fine . . ." Kate protested.

"This won't take long," said Miri.

Gythe returned with the herbs. Miri placed them in the teapot, added hot water, and sang softly beneath her breath. When she deemed the brew had steeped sufficiently, she poured it into a mug.

"Feverfew for pain and passionflower to calm the restless spirit," Miri said.

"I hope you have a plentiful supply," said Kate with a smile.

She took the steaming mug to her cabin, closed the door, and drank her tea in the dark. Miri and Gythe were in their cabin, which was directly across from hers. She could hear Miri talking, her voice faint and indistinct. Gythe's responses were silent, unspoken. The Doctor remained on deck.

"He likes to make us think he's earning his keep, catching mice," Miri had said with a sniff.

Kate pulled off her slops and dragged the calico shirt over her head. She flung her clothes on the floor, too tired to bother folding them. Sitting on the edge of the bunk, she finished her tea and then lay down. Her headache had eased and she did feel calmer.

When Kate closed her eyes, she could still see the afterimages of the sigils burned on the backs of her eyelids.

THIRTY-EIGHT

Kate woke with a start, listening for the noise that had wakened her. After a moment, she heard the noise again—a thunk and then creaking sounds on the deck above her cabin.

"Dratted cat," Kate muttered.

She dragged the blanket over her head and closed her eyes, then sat straight up when an angry, pain-filled screech split the silence. Kate froze, listening.

"What the hell was that?" a voice demanded.

"A cat, sir! Sorry. I didn't see it in the dark."

"Hoist those sails and be quick about it. No need for quiet now. You've wakened the city. Lock that hatch to the berth deck and stand guard. Don't let those women up here."

Kate jumped out of bed and groped blindly for her clothes in the dark. She hurriedly pulled on her slops, drew her shirt over her head, and grabbed the pistol she kept under her pillow. She found her stockings lying on the deck, but had to search for her shoes. Moving quietly, her heart pounding, she opened the door a crack.

"Miri! Gythe!" Kate whispered, peering into the darkness. "Are you all right?"

Their door opened. Kate could see the two sisters outlined against a faint glow of candlelight.

"Kate! I thought you'd been murdered!" Miri gasped in relief. "What was that terrible scream?"

"The Doctor. I think someone stepped on him."

Kate slipped out of her room and into the corridor. She looked up at the hatch that stood at the top of the stairs. Miri came to join her. She was wearing a long white nightdress and her hair was unbound, cascading down around her shoulders. Gythe remained in the cabin, peering out the door, her eyes wide with fear.

Kate could hear people moving about on the deck above. Miri stared at the hatch as though she could see through it.

"Who are these people? I'm going up there," Miri stated angrily.

"You can't," said Kate. "They bolted the hatch."

"But why? What do they want?"

"Your ship. I think these people are here to steal it."

Miri paled in anger. "We'll see about that!"

Kate smiled. "You might want to get dressed first."

Miri grunted and went back to her cabin. She emerged moments later carrying a lantern, wearing her skirt and pantaloons with a shawl wrapped around her shoulders. Gythe was dressed, but she stayed in the cabin, refused to come out.

"She's acting strangely," said Miri. "Best if she stays in there, away from the trouble."

They could hear the sounds of the sails being released from the yardarms, people running across the deck, the creaking of the wooden supports as magic flowed into the lift tanks.

"Fetch the women!" the commander ordered.

They heard the bolt being thrown. Footsteps clattered as two men hurried down the stairs. One carried a lantern, making him an excellent target.

Kate raised her pistol and took aim. "I am armed. Stop right there or I'll shoot!"

The young man in the lead came to a halt at the foot of the stairs. His fellow stopped at the top. The first held up the lantern and by its light Kate could see that the two men were young, perhaps sixteen. They were not armed and they were staring at her pistol in shock, not knowing what to do.

"Keep quiet," said Kate. "Raise your hands—"

Miri's angry voice exploded behind her.

"Garrick Duffy and Ian McDougal! What the devil do you think you are doing, waking decent folk in the middle of the night and treading on our cat? Kate, lower that pistol! There'll be no killing!"

Kate reluctantly lowered the pistol, but she kept hold of it.

Miri shouldered past her. Her red hair blazed in the lantern light and she advanced on the two young men like some vengeful angel threatening them with the wrath of God.

"What is the meaning of this, Garrick?" Miri struck him in the chest, knocking him backward. "Are you and your good-for-nothing friends here to steal my ship?"

She struck him again.

"We're going to bring it back," Garrick mumbled, trying to avoid the on-slaught.

"We're sailing to Kilean," Ian added. "To join the rebellion."

"Rebellion!" Miri snorted and hit Garrick a third time, then kicked him in the shins for good measure. "You louts aren't going to Kilean or anywhere else. So get off my ship this minute! Wait until I tell your parents!"

Garrick backed up the stairs, bumping into his friend. The two turned, and Kate thought they were actually going to leave when a man shouted down at them.

"What is that caterwauling? Bring those women here!"

His voice was deep and accustomed to being obeyed. He was speaking Rosian, but with a strong accent.

"He's Freyan!" Kate whispered. "Do any Freyans live on Glasearrach?"

"Not that I know of," Miri returned. "You can go to hell!" she shouted, glaring up the stairs. "Get off my ship!"

"Madame," said the commander. "You can either walk off or my men will carry you."

Miri bristled. "I'd like to see you try!"

"Mistress Miri!" Garrick pleaded. "Commander Franklin means what he says. Please, you and Mistress Gythe should just leave. They won't hurt you. They promised."

Miri folded her arms over her chest and planted her feet firmly on the deck. "Where my ship goes, I go!"

"I'll talk to her," said Kate. "Give me a moment."

Garrick and Ian remained standing uncertainly by the stairs.

Kate plucked at Miri's sleeve and leaned close to whisper, "These young folk look scared to death of this commander. They're only doing this because he is making them. If we shut him up, they'll back down!"

"How?" Miri asked, frowning. "No killing."

Kate released the hammer on the pistol and thrust it into her belt. "Gythe could use her magic. She's a savant. She can cast a spell on a whim. She could blind him with dazzling light or cause the yardarm to hit him in the head or something."

Kate looked back through the door. "Where is Gythe? She was right here."

She heard a strange sound and looked into the cabin. Gythe was huddled in a corner, curled up in a ball, her hands covering her head.

"Miri," Kate said, frightened. "Come quickly! It's Gythe! Something's wrong."

Miri came hurrying back to the cabin and crouched down beside her sister.

"Gythe, what is wrong? Are you hurt?"

Gythe sat up. Her hair was disheveled, her eyes wild and staring. She shivered with fear.

"Bottom Dwellers! They've come for me! Where is Stephano? He will stop them!"

"Oh, God!" Miri gasped. She looked up at Kate. "Years ago, during the war, the Bottom Dwellers attacked our boat, the *Cloud Hopper*. They tried to kidnap Gythe."

"What does she mean about Stephano?" Kate asked.

"Sometimes Gythe . . . goes away from me," Miri faltered. "She's gone back to that time. She thinks she's on the *Cloud Hopper* and that Stephano is here with us."

"Stephano?" Gythe clutched at her sister. "Where is he? What about Dag?"

Miri gathered her sister into her arms and said soothingly, "Stephano and Dag are both here, Gythe. They won't let anything happen to you."

"What can I do?" Kate asked, feeling helpless.

"We have to take her to Father Jacob!" Miri said. "Help me lift her."

Kate put her arm around Gythe and assisted Miri to raise her sister to her feet. Gythe cowered in their grasp.

"Don't let them take me!" she begged, hanging back. "I can hear their voices! I know they're up there waiting for me!"

"You are safe. We won't let them touch you. We are going to find Father Jacob," said Miri. "He will protect us."

Gythe whimpered, but she gulped and nodded. Miri and Kate helped her from the cabin into the corridor and started toward the stairs. Gythe looked up, caught sight of Ian and Garrick and screamed. She covered her face with her hands and sank to the deck.

The two young men stood staring at her, wide-eyed. Miri gave them a furious glance.

"I hope you two are proud of this night's work!"

Neither answered. Both lowered their eyes.

Kate and Miri managed to help Gythe climb the stairs and out through the hatch onto the deck. The sails were set and starting to catch the air. A lantern shone in the wheelhouse where a man was running his hands over the brass helm, sending air to start to inflate the balloons.

People hauled at the lines, making the ship ready to sail. Kate noticed that they were all young, about the same age as Garrick and Ian.

The commander was waiting for them.

"About damn time." He eyed Gythe. "What's wrong with her?"

"You've scared her out of her wits!" Miri said, glowering at him. She added grudgingly, "Will you still let us leave the ship?"

"Of course, Mistress," he said. "I am sorry we upset her."

Miri snorted and muttered something in her own language. Gythe shrank away, moaning, and tried to go back down the stairs. Kate caught hold of her. She and Miri managed to half drag, half carry Gythe down the gangplank.

"Miri, do you recognize that man?" Kate spoke quietly. "The one they call 'Commander'?"

Miri shook her head. "I've never seen him before. He's not a Bottom Dweller, I can say that much."

"How do you know?" Kate asked.

Miri sniffed. "He's too well fed."

They had just reached the end of the gangplank, when Gythe suddenly stopped, opened her eyes, and looked around.

"The Doctor. Where is the Doctor?"

Kate and Miri exchanged startled glances. Neither of them had seen or even thought about the cat.

"He will be fine, Gythe," said Miri. "Now come away . . ."

Gythe shook her head. "I won't leave him!"

"I'll find him," Kate offered. "Where does he go when he's frightened?"

"Look under the stairs by the wheelhouse," Miri answered. "If he's not there, try the storage room. We'll wait for you here."

She put her arm protectively around Gythe.

"I need to come back on board!" Kate called. "I have to find our cat. Gythe won't leave without him."

The commander looked exasperated. "Very well, but be quick about it. I think I saw the beast run under the stairs."

The stairs led to the platform near the wheelhouse where the Bottom Dwellers had mounted their green beam weapons. Glancing around, Kate counted fourteen young people on board, a mix of girls and boys. They were wearing the clothes typical of Bottom Dwellers: skirts and shawls worn criss-crossed over their chests for the women, baggy trousers and shirts for the men.

The commander and the man at the wheelhouse wore similar clothes, but they were obviously not Bottom Dwellers. They both had tanned, leathery skin common to men who were used to being outdoors in the strong sunshine. And, as Miri had said, they looked as though they had always eaten three meals a day.

Kate crouched down on her hands and knees to peer underneath the stairs. Two yellow eyes stared back at her. The Doctor flattened himself against the hull and hissed at her. When Kate tried crawling toward him, her hand outstretched, he lashed out with his claws. She sat back on her heels, wondering how she was going to pry him loose.

Being near the wheelhouse, she could hear the commander talking to the helmsman, both of them speaking in Freyan. At first she was too preoccupied with the Doctor to pay much attention until she realized the men were talking about her.

"I watched that woman with the cropped hair work on the helm and the lift tanks today, sir," said the corporal, adding in grudging tones, "Looks like she did a good job. The helm is responding. Still, I'm not certain I trust sailing a strange ship through the Aurora."

"Since our other ship is now lying at the bottom of a swamp, we have little choice, Corporal," the commander returned dryly. "Did you stow the pistols?"

"Under the helm, sir. Are you expecting trouble?"

"Not from the recruits. But one can never be too careful."

"What about those women, sir?" said the corporal. "I don't like leaving them behind. They're friends with that dragon, the Evil One's minion. What if they summon it, send it after us?"

"The dragon will be in his lair, asleep," said the commander.

"What if the women talk, sir?"

"Let them. God be praised, now that we have this black ship, we won't have to return to this hellish place. Carry on with your work. Where the devil is that wagon with the parts and the swivel guns? Those cost me two months' pay. They should have been here by now."

"Sorry, Doctor," Kate muttered.

She reached beneath the stairs, grabbed hold of the cat by the scruff of his neck, and dragged him, scratching and clawing, out from under.

The commander was just leaving the wheelhouse as Kate hurried past him, carrying the hissing cat at arm's length and sucking blood from a scratch on the back of her hand. As she passed, she shot a quick glance at him.

He was of medium height with the stern, intense expression of a soldier devoted to duty to the exclusion of all else. It was clear to her that he was military through and through, from his upright stance to his squared shoulders.

She lugged the Doctor down the gangplank and thankfully handed him to Gythe. The cat immediately stopped hissing and gave a pitiful yowl, wanting her to know he'd been mistreated. Gythe held him tight and buried her face in his fur.

"How is she?" Kate asked.

"She's calmer now that we're off the ship," said Miri.

"Good," said Kate. "I need to talk to you. Come over here where they can't see us."

Gythe seemed quite content to leave the ship now that she had the cat. Miri and Kate led her into the field, some distance from the *Naofa* in the shadow of some brush. When Kate deemed they were far enough that the commander had lost sight of them, she stopped.

"Those men are Freyan military," she said to Miri. "They were the ones who were spying on us. They wanted to make certain I'd made the repairs to the magic and they knew how to take down our defenses."

"Those fool youngsters did this," said Miri, her voice burning with anger. "Garrick and Ian are both crafters and would know how to use contramagic to burn holes through Gythe's magic." She shook her fist. "Wait until I get hold of them. I'll smack them silly!"

"You won't have the chance," said Kate. "They are *not* taking these young people to Kilean, Miri. The commander is sailing the *Naofa* to Above."

Miri stared at her, aghast. "Above? Are you certain?"

"I heard him talk about traveling through the Aurora. He is tricking these youngsters, Miri. And this isn't the first time. You said other young folk had disappeared. I'm thinking now we know why. Once they are Above, they would have no way to come back."

"But why would the Freyan military be kidnapping our children?" Miri asked, bewildered.

"I've been wondering that myself," said Kate. "The commander said he stole your ship because his sank in a swamp. And he said this was his last voyage. He's done this before."

As they were talking, a wagon rolled into view, bumping and jolting across the uneven ground in the darkness. They heard the commander order several of the young people to unload the supplies.

"The fool children think they're going to Kilean to start a revolution," said Miri bitterly. "They'll find themselves in a strange land, friendless and alone." Her lips pursed in anger. "I'm going to put a stop to this!"

She rolled up her sleeves and started to storm off, heading back for the ship.

"Miri, you can't!" Kate protested, grabbing hold of her. "The two soldiers are both armed. You need to think about Gythe."

Miri cast a worried glance at her sister. Gythe was swaying back and forth, cradling the Doctor and softly singing to him. The song was in Trundler, strange and eerie-sounding.

"It's a long walk back to town in the dark," said Kate. "You stay here with Gythe. I'll go fetch Father Jacob. Tell me where to find him."

Miri didn't answer. She was gazing at the ship.

"I can't stop them," she said abruptly. "I can't leave Gythe. But you can, Kate."

Kate gaped at her. "Me? How?"

"Go back on board the ship and warn them!" Miri said. "Tell the young folk the truth, that these men are lying to them."

"Miri, you're not thinking clearly," said Kate. "If the commander even gave me a chance to speak, he would only deny it. Or he might just shoot me!"

Miri sighed. "You're right. Well, at least we can tell Father Jacob. He can send a message to the Arcanum. The priests will find out what is going on and bring our young folk home."

They stood watching the wagon that was now surrounded by young people, hauling sacks off the wagon bed and carrying them on board ship. Kate saw two of them lift out a long wooden crate. Two more followed with another similar crate. Gythe was still singing to the cat, a song about some- one named Annie and goblins snatching children from their beds.

Kate stood pondering.

"I have an idea. There might be a way to rescue the young people *and* steal back your ship. It means I'll need to sail with them."

Miri shook her head. "No, Kate! That is far too dangerous. Forget I said anything. I had no right to ask you to risk your life."

"You saved Dalgren's life," said Kate, smiling. "You have every right. Be- sides, I will only be gone a short while."

"I can't let you," said Miri. "If anything happened to you, I would never forgive myself."

"Nothing is going to happen," said Kate. "Once the young folk find out they've been duped, they'll be only too happy to help me take over the ship."

Miri was still shaking her head. Gythe dropped the cat to the ground and took off her skirt, sliding it down over her pantaloons. She handed the skirt to Kate, pointing at her slops.

Kate immediately understood.

"Good idea," she said, and hurriedly dragged the skirt over her head. The skirt would help to hide the bulge made by the pistol in her belt, and if she stayed in the shadows, the slops could pass for pantaloons.

"You'll need this, too," said Miri.

She took off her shawl and tied it around Kate's shoulders.

"God go with you, Kate!" Miri gave her a fierce embrace.

"Not a word to Dalgren!" Kate said. "I'll be back before he knows I'm gone."

She ran to the wagon, picked up a sack of rice, and slung it over her shoulder. She arranged the sack so that it partially concealed her face, and walked toward the gangplank, keeping to the shadow. She was nervous, thinking every moment one of the young people would recognize her and call her out. She trudged up the gangplank, weighed down by the sack over her shoulder, and carried it into the hold.

A young man took her sack from her. The hold was dark, lit by only a single lantern. He was working fast, and never bothered to glance at her.

Kate sneaked back up on deck. The corporal was still in the wheelhouse, along with the commander. Once the supplies were stored, they would be ready to sail. The young people were emptying the wagon. Kate watched for her chance, and when no one was in view, she ran down the stairs that led to the crew quarters.

The storage closet was located at the end of the corridor. Kate slipped inside and shut the door behind her. The closet was pitch-dark, but she didn't dare light a lantern. She groped her way about in the darkness, moving slowly and cautiously to keep from knocking anything over.

They would find her eventually, preferably after the ship had set sail. The corporal would be occupied in operating the helm and Kate didn't think it likely the commander would go rummaging about the storage closet. If he needed something, he would send some of the young people. She would be able to talk to them, tell them they had been duped.

The commander and his corporal were outnumbered. Kate would urge the young people to turn on them, overwhelm them, seize control of the ship, and return to Dunlow.

She hoped they would believe her. She was an outsider, after all, but they had seen her with Miri and Gythe. If nothing else, she would plant doubt in their minds and perhaps they would confront the commander, demand to know the truth.

A good plan. Kate didn't see any reason why it wouldn't work. But she decided to conceal the pistol, just in case. Gythe had made a bed using some old gunnysacks for the Doctor during those times he was locked in the closet. Kate found the sacks, hid the pistol inside one, and then stuffed the sack in a corner behind a barrel.

She heard the commander give the order to raise the gangplank. The airscrews began to whir, and Kate felt the jolt when the ship rose off the ground. She took off the skirt, sat down on a barrel, and waited for someone to come find her.

Miri stood with her arm around Gythe and watched their ship rise into the air and vanish into the darkness, taking Kate with it.

"Mistress Miri," said a muffled voice. "I can give you a lift."

She turned to see the driver of the wagon walking toward them. He wore a handkerchief tied around his nose and mouth and his hat was pulled low so that he wouldn't be recognized.

"I don't want to leave you both stranded."

"You should have thought of that before you stole my ship!" Miri snapped. "How much did you get paid for this night's work?"

The man gazed out into the night. "Do you want a ride or not?"

"What I want to do is kick you where you would feel it," Miri retorted. She glanced at Gythe, then said grudgingly, "But we'll take the ride."

The man assisted Gythe to climb into the wagon. He wrapped an old blanket around her and offered to hold the Doctor, but Gythe would not let him go. She lay down in the back of the wagon and curled up, cradling the cat.

Miri climbed up on the seat next to the driver. He slapped the reins of the horse and the beast walked off. The wagon was old, and shook and rattled as it lurched over the rocky ground. The man again slapped the reins on the horse's back to try to hurry it, but the horse didn't pay much attention. He kept going at the same plodding speed.

"You know I will tell Father Jacob about this," Miri stated.

The man shrugged. "Doesn't matter. The Top Dwellers have all the youngsters they need. They won't be back."

"Meaning our children won't be back," Miri said, her voice quivering.

"Mayhap that's not such a bad thing," the man said. "This life is no good life for children."

As they neared the outskirts of the city, the horse appeared to perk up a bit, probably because he was close to home. Suddenly the beast shied and neighed in terror.

Miri heard the sound of wings flapping overhead. She looked up to see Dalgren looking down. Flames flickered from between his teeth.

"Mistress Miri, what is going on?" he demanded. "I was out hunting when I saw your ship sail away. I find you and Mistress Gythe here, but no sign of Kate. Where is she? She's in some kind of trouble, isn't she?"

The horse bucked and reared, almost falling in the traces. The driver yanked on the reins.

"I can't hold him!" he shouted to Miri.

Miri jumped off the wagon. "Take Gythe to Father Jacob!"

The driver barely had time to nod. He slapped the reins and the horse lunged ahead, eager to leave. The wagon lurched off.

Dalgren circled overhead, waiting for her answer.

"She's doing me a favor. She asked me not to tell you," Miri said. "She was afraid you'd come after her and she knows you need to rest."

Dalgren grunted, shooting flame from his nose. "What's Kate done now?

I'm going after her in any case, so you might as well tell me what I'm likely to find."

Miri relented. "Two Freyan soldiers stole our ship and kidnapped some of our young people. Kate stowed away on board the ship. She has a plan to bring the children back. She won't be gone long."

Dalgren circled overhead in silence. Miri waited on the ground, worrying about Gythe. She shivered in the cold night air.

Dalgren shook his head. His lips parted in a wry smile, fire flicked out from between his fangs.

"Kate has a plan . . ." He sighed deeply and shook his head again. "Thank you for what you tried to do for me, Mistress Miri."

"Dalgren! No! Wait!" Miri called after him.

The dragon made a sweeping, banking turn and then flew off.

"Tell Father Jacob I am sorry," he called, and then disappeared into the darkness.

THIRTY-NINE

The young people discovered Kate around dawn, when everyone on board was preparing to sail through the Aurora. A young woman opened the door to the storage closet and saw Kate, sitting on the barrel. The young woman gasped in fright and nearly dropped her lantern.

"I won't hurt you," Kate hastily assured her, raising her hands to show they were empty. "I need to talk—"

The young woman slammed the door and ran off, leaving Kate locked in the closet. After a short interval, the door opened again. One of the young men Kate had met earlier walked inside.

"Keep your hands up," he ordered. "Where is your pistol?"

"I gave it to Miri," said Kate. "Your name is Ian, isn't it? You need to listen to me. These men are not taking you to Kilean. They lied to you. They are taking you to the world Above and once you're there, you won't be able to ever come home! You need to warn the others—"

"Hands behind your back," said Ian.

He was holding a length of rope and he bound her wrists.

"Didn't you hear what I said?" Kate asked him. "This ship is sailing Above!"

"I heard you," said Ian.

He took hold of her arm and led her to Miri's cabin. He shoved her inside.

"The commander says you are to wait here. He will deal with you after we have navigated the Aurora," Ian told her. "They are taking us to Freya."

"Freya?" Kate repeated, stunned. "But you and that other boy told Miri you were going to Kilean. To join the revolution."

"We lied," said Ian.

He left, shutting the door behind him.

He forgot to lock it. Kate slipped out of her bonds, crept soft-footed to the door, and put her hand on the handle. Green light flared. The resultant shock numbed her arm to the elbow.

Kate swore and rubbed her tingling hand. Now that she bothered to look, she could see the constructs glowing with a faint green light. She wasn't an expert in contramagic, but she knew enough to realize that if she tried to tamper with them, she'd only get shocked again.

She had to resign herself to the fact that she wasn't going anywhere. Not until someone came to let her out. She flung herself on the bed, stared at the beams above her head, and wondered what the hell she was supposed to do now.

"I stowed away, risked my life to rescue some kids who don't want to be rescued," Kate muttered. "And now, seemingly, I'm on my way to Freya! Unless the commander decides to shove me overboard!"

The temperature began to drop. They were nearing the Aurora. She rummaged through a chest and found Miri's peacoat and knit hat. Wrapping herself in a blanket, she went to peer out the small porthole.

She could see the Aurora above the ship, shimmering with a yellow-whitish light, and the sun shining through it, looking like a copper coin. Kate looked down to see the city of Dunlow and the field where they had been docked. She caught sight of movement almost directly underneath the ship.

Dalgren was down below, flying after the ship.

Dismayed, Kate pressed her face to the porthole to try to get a better view. She knew well enough what she was seeing, however.

"No! Oh, no!" she said softly. "Damn it, Dalgren! Turn back!"

She had no idea how he had found her. Perhaps he'd been out hunting, perhaps Miri had told him. Or perhaps he'd just seen the ship leave and wondered what was going on. Kate hammered on the porthole with her fists, thinking she could break the glass and shout to him.

All she accomplished was bruised hands.

"You can't fly through the Aurora again," Kate told him. "You're exhausted and half starved. You'll never survive!"

Kate ran to the door and called through the keyhole, careful not to touch it.

"Let me out! I need to talk to the commander!"

The sunlight vanished. Gray mists closed around the ship, streaming down the porthole. They were entering the Aurora. No one came to the door, and after another few moments of shouting into silence, Kate realized that no one was coming. The young people were probably holed up in the crew quarters. The commander would be keeping watch, the corporal in the wheelhouse. Kate ran back to the porthole.

She peered down, trying to find Dalgren, but she could not see through the fog. She kept her face pressed against the glass, ignoring the cold that bit into her flesh.

The fog grew thicker. The ship shivered and shook as though it, too, was freezing. She could hear the airscrews turning, propelling the ship through the congealed layer of the Breath.

In her mind, she was flying with Dalgren. She pictured the ice forming on his wings, the cold creeping into his lungs. His flight would slow, his breathing grow labored, as he tried to gain altitude, claw his way up through the Aurora.

"He is sensible," Kate said to herself. "He will realize this is hopeless and he will go back. Miri will explain what happened. He'll be furious with me, but at least he will be safe."

But she didn't leave the porthole. The ship broke through the Aurora and the bright sunlight of the world Above flooded through the porthole, half blinding her.

She rubbed her eyes and stared down into the Breath, not knowing whether she was hoping to see Dalgren still pursuing the ship or hoping that he had given up the chase.

Those were the only two options she allowed herself. She chose not to consider the third.

She was still watching when she heard someone open the door. Another young man walked into the cabin. He was Garrick, Kate recalled. She glanced at him and looked back out the porthole.

"The commander says I'm to bring you to the helm," Garrick said.

"In a minute," Kate snapped.

"He said now," said Garrick.

Kate suddenly wondered if the commander had seen Dalgren. Freyans hated and feared dragons. She remembered the commander had brought swivel guns on board. Bullets would not penetrate a dragon's scaly hide, but they could tear the thin membrane of his wings. She turned away from the porthole, half frozen. Her face was numb from where she had pressed her cheek to the glass.

Once they reached the main deck, Garrick pointed to the wheelhouse.

"Commander Franklin is waiting for you there."

Kate cast a glance out into the Breath. She longed to run to the rail and look over to see if she could find Dalgren. She didn't dare, however, for fear she would draw the commander's attention.

She continued on to the wheelhouse. The air was still cold, although not as cold as in the Aurora.

Commander Franklin and Corporal Roberts had discarded their Bottom Dweller clothes. Both were wearing the same uniforms as those worn by members of the Freyan army: blue jacket, white trousers. She longed to ask what members of the Freyan army were doing kidnapping young people, but she was in enough trouble and she kept quiet.

Franklin fixed her with a grim look.

"You left the ship and now I find you hiding in the storage closet. Why? What are you doing on board?"

Before Kate could answer with the lie she had concocted, the corporal interrupted her.

"Rate of ascent is slowing, sir."

Franklin's lips tightened. "The magic on the lift tanks is starting to fail. Our last crafter perished in a shipwreck. Corporal Roberts is also a crafter, but I need him at the helm. He says you can handle the repairs. Is he right?"

"How would he know?" Kate demanded, casting the corporal a baleful glance. "Unless he was the one who was spying on me yesterday."

"Answer the question," said Franklin curtly. "Can you repair the magic or not?"

"You know I can," said Kate. "Promise me safe passage to wherever it is you're going and I will."

"You are hardly in a position to make demands," said Franklin dryly. "If this ship sinks, you go down with us."

"The *Naofa* is not sinking," Kate returned with a snort of disgust. "The ship's just slowing a bit and that's the fault of your inept helmsman, not the lift tanks."

Franklin regarded her in cold, narrow-eyed silence.

"I'll take a look at the magic," Kate said grudgingly. Franklin accompanied her to the port side, walking with his hands behind his back.

Kate leaned far over the rail and peered down into the Breath, looking for Dalgren. Seeing no sign of him, she breathed easier. He must have flown back to Dunlow. Now she just had to get back to him.

"The lift tank is not down there," Franklin said.

"No, but the airscrew is," Kate said, straightening. "Do you hear that rattling sound?"

Franklin listened and frowned. "No."

"Well, I do," said Kate. "I think one of the blades is bent. Could have been damaged when we set sail. I have no way to fix it, not while we're aloft. How long before we reach our destination?"

"How long will it continue to function?"

Kate shrugged. "A few days, a year. Just depends."

Franklin nodded. "Work on the lift tanks."

Disappointed that she had not found out where they were going, Kate pulled open the access hatch and climbed down the ladder to the platform on which the lift tank rested.

Franklin remained on deck, watching her from above.

"You know how to use the seventh sigil," he said.

"You better hope I do," said Kate. "We won't get far without it. The original magic on these tanks was contramagic. It worked, but it needed blood magic to enhance it."

She glanced up at him. "I take it you're not going to be slashing throats this voyage?"

Franklin was grim. "Such evil doings are not the subject for jest."

Kate was relieved. Miri had said Garrick and Ian were both crafters. The thought had occurred to Kate that perhaps Commander Franklin was recruiting young blood mages.

"You were in the war?"

"I was," said Franklin flatly. "I asked you about the magic."

"Gythe and I used the seventh sigil to blend the magic and the contramagic. The problem is that the magic of the Aurora damages the constructs. I fixed these once. All my work wasted."

"What is your name?" Franklin asked.

"Kate McPike," she answered, borrowing her surname from Miri and Gythe.

"You are a Trundler," Franklin observed. "What were you doing on Glasearrach?"

Kate recalled Morgan saying, *If you want people to swallow a lie, feed them a morsel of truth.*

"I lived in Wellingsport," she replied. "Owned my own boat. I traded in goods that were . . . hard to come by."

"You were a smuggler," said Franklin.

He would find that easy to believe. Trundlers traveled the world over, owed allegiance to no country, and lived by their own laws. Most of them were smugglers. It was a way of life.

"When the Rosian navy came to clean up the islands, they put out a bounty on me," Kate continued. "Dalgren was my partner. The Dragon Brigade was after him. He and I had to leave in a hurry. Miri and Gythe offered to take us with them to Glasearrach. I wasn't particular about where I was going and Dalgren had to make himself scarce, so we left."

"Then why didn't you stay on Glasearrach?" Franklin asked. "You stowed away on this ship, leaving your friends behind, including your dragon friend. Why?"

"I had no idea you were sailing Above," said Kate, aggrieved. "The boy told us the ship was bound for Kilean. I have business there. Business of my own that doesn't involve anyone else. Where are you bound?"

"Freya, of course," Franklin replied.

Kate looked up at him. "I was born and raised there, at least as much as any Trundler is raised anywhere. What city?"

Franklin didn't answer. He was inspecting her work. Kate noted his intense stare as he studied the constructs on the lift tank. A person who had not been born to magic could not have seen them, yet he had said he was not a crafter.

"You're a channeler, aren't you," said Kate. "Does my work pass muster?"

"You have done well," Franklin conceded.

"I have a proposal. You need a crafter and I have friends in Freya," said Kate. "I'll keep the ship afloat, earn my passage."

Franklin sat back on his heels. He seemed to be considering. Kate impatiently wondered what he had to think over. He surprised her with his response.

"Our army is sorely in need of crafters. The pay is ten talons a day and we provide food and lodging."

Kate gave him a puzzled look. "Since when is the Freyan army short of crafters?"

"We are not members of the Freyan army," said Franklin with a slight curl of his lip.

"You're wearing their uniform," Kate pointed out.

"You would be joining the Army of Royal Retribution."

"I've never heard of it," Kate scoffed.

"Not now," said Franklin gravely. "But soon the whole world will hear of us. Would you be interested in enlisting?"

"First, tell me this," Kate countered. "What are you doing with these youngsters? You call them recruits. Did they enlist? And if so, what for?"

"You ask a great many questions that are none of your business," Franklin returned coldly. "Ten talons a day."

Kate considered. She had not yet given up hope of convincing the young Bottom Dwellers to seize control of the ship. She decided to play along, allay his suspicions.

"Ten talons a day. I'll take it."

"Commander Franklin," called Ian, joining him on deck. "Corporal Roberts has a question about the route. Could you please come, sir."

Franklin stood up and walked off. Ian remained, gazing down through the hatch at Kate. He was not accustomed to the bright sunlight. His eyes were slits, red-rimmed and swollen and streaming with tears.

"Come down here," said Kate. "The light isn't as bright."

Ian hesitated, glancing back over his shoulder.

"It's all right," Kate added. "I've just joined your army. Commander Franklin hired me as a crafter."

Ian climbed down the ladder. He looked relieved to be in the dim light of the platform. At least he was able to partially open his eyes. He wiped away the tears and looked with interest at her work.

"What is the purpose of that construct?" he asked, pointing.

"Miri told me you were a crafter," Kate asked. "Do you know magic?"

"I know how to craft contramagic," Ian replied. "I've been doing that all my life. But I want to learn magic."

The construct she had selected was a basic one. She had been creating such magic on lift tanks since she was eight years old and no longer gave it much thought. She wondered how to explain it, then remembered how Olaf had explained it to her.

"If you think of the Breath in the lift tank as water in a kettle, then this construct acts like the flame beneath the kettle. It heats up the water so that it boils. The helmsman sends magical energy to the constructs on the lift tank through these cables. The constructs on the tank stimulate the magical energy of the Breath inside the tank, increasing the amount of lift."

"I know what the sigils are," said Ian. "Father Jacob taught us those in class. I have trouble putting them together. Can you teach me? I want to be able to use magic when I'm living in the world Above."

"I can teach you," said Kate. "Why did you join the army? What are you and the others going to be doing in the world Above?"

"I don't know. The commander brought those of us who are skilled in contramagic. He promised us food and money in exchange for our work."

"Contramagic? Why would the army need contramagic?" Kate asked, puzzled.

Ian shook his head. "I don't know."

"Do you trust this commander to keep his promise?"

"It doesn't matter. All we care about is that he is taking us to a new world, a new life."

"Was your old life so bad?" Kate asked.

Ian gave a bitter smile. "You were only in Dunlow a day. You saw how wretched it was. Imagine living there all your days. Never enough to eat. I've seen little children starve to death. Any life Above is better than the life Below."

"People struggle in the world Above," Kate said somberly. "Children die there, too."

"But not in darkness," said Ian. "My eyes hurt. I'm going below deck with the others. Do you mind if I ask you more questions about magic sometime?"

"I'm glad to help," Kate said.

He climbed back up the ladder and she could hear him walking across the deck.

Kate sighed. So much for convincing these young folk to seize the ship. If she proposed taking them back to Glasearrach, they would be the ones to throw her overboard.

She finished work on the port-side tank and then glumly walked over to start on the repairs to the magic on the starboard.

She had no idea how she was going to get back to Dalgren.

Once she repaired the magic on the lift tanks, the *Naofa* rose rapidly through the Deep Breath, so rapidly that the helmsman, Roberts, was forced to slow their ascent for fear the lines might give way.

She checked the rest of the magic on board the ship. She was alone on deck. Franklin had gone down below. The Bottom Dwellers were holed up in the crew cabin, keeping out of the sunlight. Kate thought she might visit with Roberts, see if he was more inclined to talk.

When she got to the wheelhouse, the door was open, letting in the fresh air and sunshine. Roberts was standing at the helm, his hands on the brass plate. He was younger than Franklin, but he had the same stern and humorless air about him.

"Having any trouble with the helm's magic, Corporal?" Kate asked in friendly tones.

Roberts gave her a look of disgust, as though she was something he'd found soiling the bottom of his boot.

"A wanton woman is the devil's handmaiden," he said, and slammed the door in her face.

Kate turned to see Franklin crossing the deck, coming toward her.

"Let him be," he said.

"I didn't do anything," Kate protested. "I was just asking him if he needed me to look at the magic on the helm. He called me the devil's handmaiden or something like that."

"You should dress more seemly," Franklin advised. "I noticed your cousin left behind some female clothing that would fit you."

"You try crawling around under the lift tank in a skirt," Kate told him.

"Is this army of yours fighting a religious war? Some sort of avenging army of God?"

Franklin ignored her question as he ignored most of her questions.

"Come with me to my cabin. You need to sign the contract of enlistment."

Kate followed him to the berth deck below. Franklin walked with long strides; she hurried to keep up. She wondered if these two were Fundamentalists. She had met people who belonged to that sect before, including Sir Henry's secretary, Mr. Sloan. But if that was true, why were Fundamentalists recruiting contramagic-wielding young Bottom Dwellers?

Ian and Garrick and the other young people were sitting around the small table in the galley, out of the bright light of the sun. They were talking in low voices; when they saw Kate watching them, their conversation ceased. She smiled; they did not smile back.

Franklin entered the cabin that had once belonged to Miri and Gythe. He had bundled their clothes and belongings into a chest in a corner and appropriated Miri's small desk. On top was a document one page in length, handwritten, bearing an official-looking wax seal and ribbon.

The ship's logbook was also lying on the desk. The book was open; Franklin had apparently been making recent entries.

He sat down at the desk, picked up a pen, dipped it in the inkwell, and began to write on the document. He did not ask Kate to sit down, but kept her standing.

Kate took the opportunity to study the logbook, hoping to find out their location. The book was facing Franklin, which meant she had to read it upside down. That was not difficult. Franklin's handwriting was large, clear, and bold, and she had no trouble seeing what he had written.

The *Naofa* was to the south of the continent of Freya, heading west toward the western coast. Kate found that odd. The major port cities, such as Haever, were located on the eastern side of Freya. The only large city in the south was Port Crighton. The western coast of Freya was mostly forested woodland and mountains, generally considered to be uninhabitable.

Kate tilted her head to get a better view. Franklin looked up, saw her, and closed the logbook.

"Sorry, sir," said Kate. "I've sailed the Breath around southern Freya before. Don't you think we're too far west, Commander? You'll miss taking advantage of the Easterlies. Those winds could cut a half day at the very least off our journey to Haever."

"We are not bound for Haever," he said.

"Of course. You don't want to be caught by the Royal Navy," Kate said. "They'd certainly be curious about a black ship sailing into Freyan territory, even if you are wearing Freyan uniforms. So where are we bound? I can tell you how to avoid them."

Franklin slid the document toward her and handed her the pen.

"Sign your name there," he said, indicating a space at the bottom.

Kate accepted the pen, but did not put it to the paper. "What am I signing?"

"A contract with the Army of Royal Retribution stating that you are enlisting to serve as a ship's crafter for a period of four years from this date," said Franklin. "You will hold the rank of Crafter Private and be paid ten talons a day, as I told you."

"Mind if I read it before I sign?" Kate asked.

"Suit yourself," said Franklin.

Kate scanned the document, hoping to learn more about the army she was now joining. The contract specified the ten talons, mentioned food and drink and lodging. She would be charged for her uniform. Nothing different from contracts she'd made with her own sailors.

Then she came to the last paragraph.

I, the undersigned, do solemnly swear that I will support and defend the true and rightful heir, His Highness, Prince Thomas Stanford, against all enemies . . .

"Bloody hell!" said Kate.

FORTY

"Bloody hell!" Kate repeated, staring at the document. The words were a jumble, blending together. None of it made sense except two: Thomas Stanford.

Franklin regarded her with a stern eye. "I will not tolerate such language."

Kate looked up. "I'm sorry . . . What did you say?"

"I will not tolerate swearing!" Franklin returned, glowering.

"Sorry," Kate mumbled.

"Are you going to sign or not?" Franklin asked. "If not, I have work to do—"

"I have some questions."

"You are trying my patience, Mistress McPike." Franklin was grim. "Ask your questions."

"Who is this prince, Commander? And why does he have an army?"

"I forget you have been living in the Aligoes," said Franklin dryly. "Prince Thomas Stanford is the true and rightful heir to the throne of Freya. His army, the Army of Royal Retribution, is tasked with removing the whore of the Evil One, Queen Mary Chessington, from the throne to prepare the way for our prince to become the true and rightful king."

"Bloody hell," Kate said again, but this time she said it to herself.

"If you are not going to sign—" Franklin reached out to take the document.

"I'll sign," said Kate.

Her hand shook and she remembered only at the last moment to use the name "Kate McPike." Her signature was practically illegible.

Franklin added his signature, then placed her contract in a stack with others, probably those of the young Bottom Dwellers.

"Are you taken ill?" he demanded. "You do not look well."

"I'm fine, sir," said Kate. "I haven't eaten anything since yesterday."

"You will berth in your own cabin. You can wear some of your cousin's clothes. Get something to eat and then check the magic on the lines that run from the helm to the lift tanks and the airscrews."

Kate nodded. "All right."

"Yes, sir," said Franklin sternly.

Kate looked back at him, puzzled.

"When I give you an order, Private, the correct response is 'Yes, sir,'" said Franklin. "And you do not leave until you are dismissed."

"Yes, sir," said Kate.

"You are dismissed," said Franklin. "Don't forget to change your clothes."

Kate rummaged through Miri's things and found a blouse and a skirt that would fit her. She rejected the frilly pantaloons, knowing she would feel silly. Roberts couldn't complain if she wore her skirt over her slops. She carried the clothes to her cabin, shut the door and slumped down on the bed.

"I am now a soldier in the Army of Royal Retribution," Kate said to herself. "I just vowed allegiance to Thomas."

He would have laughed uproariously. But the situation was not funny. Whatever Franklin and Roberts were doing, they were doing it in the name of Thomas Stanford. And Kate had the feeling he knew nothing about it.

She tried to remember what Thomas had said about his army. He had described the commander of his army as a Fundamentalist, a man named Smythe who had once served in the Freyan army.

"A Fundamentalist," Kate murmured. "Like Franklin and Roberts."

Franklin had referred to Queen Mary as the "whore of the Evil One." And he was trying to put Thomas on the throne. By kinapping children?

Kate pulled on the skirt and decided to take Franklin's advice and eat something. She didn't care what; she was too preoccupied with her thoughts to taste. She went back up on deck and headed for the lines that carried the magic to inflate the balloons.

Kate cast a quick glance at the braided leather lines and found, as she had expected, that the magic needed repair. The work was relatively easy. She didn't have to think about it. She could concentrate on Thomas.

She could see him so clearly: his generous smile; his striking blue eyes. He was very real in that moment. She could almost feel the warm touch of his lips. He reached out to her.

She pushed him away, kept him at arm's length.

"Did you lie to me when you claimed you had never seen this army of yours, knew nothing about it? Or were you the one who commanded your soldiers to seduce discontented young people, persuade them to leave their families and fight and die to make *you* king? Because if you lied to me about that, you lied to me about everything. You don't love me. I amused you, that's all. I was a way to pass the time until you could marry your princess."

Thomas laughed out loud. "Amuse myself! I haven't known a moment's peace since I met you, Kate! Look at the grief you have caused me. I had to save you from being hanged! Would I go to all that trouble, risk my life for you, if I didn't truly love you?"

"I suppose not," Kate said grudgingly. "Say I concede that point to you. Do you know what your army is doing in your name?"

"What can I say, Kate?" Thomas asked. "If I don't know, then I'm a fool. If I do know, then I'm a liar and a knave. Which would you have?"

Kate sighed. She didn't know, but she was going to find out. She didn't have much choice. Wherever the black ship was bound, she was going with it.

"I am not paying you to daydream, Private," Franklin said tersely.

Kate jumped, startled. She had been so lost in her musings, she had not heard him come up behind her.

"I wasn't, sir," Kate protested. "I was trying to figure out what was wrong with this construct."

Franklin looked at the leather braid. "Nothing that I can see, Private. Now get to work."

"Yes, sir," said Kate.

She recalled, belatedly, a piece of advice from Amelia.

"Stay out of court intrigue, Kate. Put a foot wrong in that foul morass and you will sink to the bottom and never be found."

"I'm not putting a foot wrong," Kate muttered as she worked. "I'm diving in headfirst."

The *Naofa* sailed the Breath for two days, stopping at night to rest and to avoid crashing into the small islands created when chunks of the larger land-masses broke off and floated out into the Breath. Kate had only the vaguest idea where they were. She guessed they were near Freya, for the floating islands grew more numerous as they drew closer to the continent.

Franklin kept his cabin locked, denying her access to the logbook. She loitered on deck whenever he took the navigational readings, hoping he might say something to her, but the only person he told was Roberts, who marked the ship's location on a map in the wheelhouse. Whenever Kate tried to pay him a friendly visit, he slammed the door shut.

Roberts clearly detested her. He had been displeased to hear the commander had recruited her and he had made his displeasure known. He scowled whenever Kate came near. Oddly, though, Kate would sometimes feel his gaze on her. She remembered that he had been the one spying on her in Dunlow. She took to avoiding him.

The Bottom Dwellers stayed below unless Franklin needed their help around the ship. But even at that they were practically useless, for they were still having trouble adjusting to the sunlight. Kate felt sorry for them with their swollen, teary eyes, and often offered to do their chores herself.

She was glad to have work. The voyage seemed endless, especially as she had no idea where they were headed or how long it would take them to get there. Franklin generally ignored her, unless he had orders for her.

Olaf told a story about a ghost ship that sailed the Breath, manned by a spectral crew that tried to lure other ships to their doom. Kate decided that the dead men aboard that ship would be considered jolly companions compared to those on board the *Naofa*.

She tried to relieve her loneliness and boredom by teaching the Bottom Dwellers lessons in basic crafting, and answering their questions about the world Above. She soon discovered that the young Bottom Dwellers faced life with grim resolve and burning resentment for those who dwelt Above. They were willing to learn from Kate. Indeed, they appeared to believe they were entitled to the knowledge and begrudged the fact that it had been kept from them. But they did not like her. Whenever she laughed or tried to tease them or make a little jest, they would stare at her in frozen silence and talk among themselves in their own language.

They were eager to learn, and they soon grasped the theory behind magic and how it differed from contramagic. But they could not make the constructs work.

"You are wasting your efforts," Franklin said after finding Kate and her students in the galley tracing constructs on a kettle. "We have tried to teach their kind before and failed. That is why we are recruiting crafters, such as yourself."

"Given time, I think they could learn, sir," Kate said. "What is it you are trying to teach them to do?"

"What they are told to do," Franklin responded curtly. "The same goes for you. No one asked you to teach them anything. Take another look at the lift tanks. We will be docking soon and the corporal says that the magic is weakening again."

Kate could have told him the magic did not need repairing. The problem was Roberts. He was a rotten helmsman, and no magic in the world could fix that. She had found out from something Franklin said that he had not sailed with Roberts before. Judging by his tone, he had no intention of ever sailing with him again.

On the third day, Franklin spent the morning on the foredeck, a spyglass to his eye, scanning the mists to the east.

"What are you looking for, sir?" Kate asked. "Perhaps I could help."

She expected a rebuff, but the commander must have been in a good mood.

"We should be within sight of the coast," he said. He lowered the glass and pointed. "There!"

The mists of the Breath parted and Kate saw towering cliffs and hulking, snow-topped mountains. Waterfalls cascaded over the edge of the continent, plunging into the Breath.

"Do you know where we are, sir?" Kate asked.

"If I have judged our position correctly, that should be the largest of the North Milton islands."

Gray mountains, lightly brushed with snow, floated on gray mist. The island clusters were designated North Milton and South Milton on maps, but most people, including their duke, Phillip Masterson, knew them as "Upper" and "Lower" Milton. Kate looked at the lonely, desolate coastline and no longer wondered why Phillip rarely visited his home.

"Two days' sailing with no sight of land to aid you, and you've reached Freya, sir," said Kate. "That is a fine job of navigating. Where do we go from here?"

Franklin must have been pleased by her praise, for he answered her question. "We continue up the western coast of Freya to our destination."

"What destination, sir?" Kate asked. "There's nothing in that part of Freya except mountains."

Franklin lowered the spyglass. "Make certain the magic on the swivel guns is working, Private. We need to be prepared in case we encounter naval patrol boats."

"You won't find any patrol boats here, sir," said Kate, laughing. "There's nothing to patrol."

"Check the guns, Private," said Franklin. "That's an order."

He walked over to the wheelhouse to confer with Roberts. Kate heard him tell the corporal to search for a suitable place to dock for the night. The *Naofa* sailed inland, creeping along the coast.

Kate climbed the stairs to the foredeck to look at the two swivel guns that had been mounted on the rails, one on the port side and one on the starboard. She could tell at a glance that the magic on the guns needed only minor repairs. She made those easily, then spent her time gazing at the rugged coastline at the edge of the continent. Calling up a chart of Freya in her mind, she tried to figure out where the *Naofa* could possibly be headed. The western part of Freya was mountainous and magnificent, empty and desolate. The only inhabitants were goats and the birds that nested among the rocks.

The sunlight waned with the coming of evening and the Bottom Dwellers left the lower deck where they lived like bats in the darkness during the day and ventured on deck. They gathered along the rail to stare at the land that would soon be their new home. They gazed in awe at the mountains, exclaiming over the waterfalls, admiring the beauty.

A flicker of movement out in the Breath caught Kate's eye. She turned her head and saw Dalgren.

The dragon was flying toward the coastline and he appeared to be on the verge of collapse. He flew with his head down, his tail drooping, legs dangling. Every beat of his wings was an effort. Rivulets of smoke trailed from his gaping mouth. He was fighting to draw breath.

If he had been paying attention to his surroundings, he must have seen the ship, for he was not far from it. But he was focused on the rock-bound coast, willing himself to keep flying despite pain and exhaustion. If he failed to reach land, he would sink into the Breath and die.

The dragon's green scales glistened in the last rays of the setting sun, clearly visible against the backdrop of dismal gray stone. Apparently no one else had seen him for no one had raised the alarm. But it would take just one glance in that direction.

Franklin knew Kate was friends with a dragon. He had asked her about Dalgren. The Bottom Dwellers must have seen him when he was assisting Father Jacob in Dunlow. Seventy feet from snout to tail, Dalgren was hard to miss.

Kate had no idea what Franklin would do if he was alerted to Dalgren's presence. Given that the commander had gone to a lot of trouble to keep this voyage secret, he wouldn't be pleased to find out that Dalgren had followed them and might decide to attack. And while bullets from the swivel guns would bounce off Dalgren's scales, they could strike him in the head or tear the fragile membrane of a wing.

Kate needed to do something to draw their attention. The canisters containing the bullets for the survived gun lay beneath the weapon, ready for use. She grabbed a canister, fit it into the gun, and fired.

The sound of the rounds going off shattered the peaceful silence. The Bottom Dwellers gasped and cried out and turned to stare. Franklin came running out of the wheelhouse, shouting at her, demanding to know what was going on.

Kate was watching Dalgren. At the sound of the gunfire, he raised his dull eyes and shifted his gaze to the ship. Flame flickered from his jaws. He was still a short distance from land. With a final, valiant effort, he soared over the cliffs. The last Kate saw of him, he was plummeting out of the sky. He vanished among the jagged rocks.

Kate kept watching, her heart in her throat, but he did not reappear.

Franklin had been yelling at her the entire time. He came running up the stairs to the foredeck, his face flushed with anger.

"The magic on the swivel gun works, sir," Kate reported.

Alone in her cabin that night, Kate sat down on her bed and put her head in her hands. She had convinced herself that Dalgren had been forced to turn back. She should have known better. He was her friend. She had gone to Glasearrach for him. Fearing she was in danger, he had come after her.

He had left Father Jacob and Miri and undoubtedly lost his chance to redeem himself, regain his name. He would be forced to live the rest of his life as an outcast, an exile. And now he was somewhere in Freya, lost and alone.

"But he knows how to find me," said Kate, lifting her head. "He saw the *Naofa*. He knows I'm on board and he knows the ship is headed north. Once he's rested and recovered, he will come looking for me.

"We'll find another way for him to earn back his name!"

BOOK 3

FORTY-ONE

The countess's private secretary, D'argent, had been gone over a fortnight now, making arrangements for Thomas's clandestine meeting with the queen. They had heard no word from him and Thomas was growing worried.

"My dear fellow, D'argent is traveling by griffin," Phillip reminded him. "Flying from the southern coast of Rosia to Haever and back will take five or six days and that is pushing it. He might have run into bad weather, especially this time of year—"

"He could have been arrested by Sir Henry," Thomas said.

"In which case, D'argent would raise hell, for he is a citizen of Rosia traveling to Haever on business of the countess," Phillip replied soothingly. "If D'argent is gone past a month, then I give you permission to be concerned."

"If he is gone past a month, I will not be concerned," Thomas said. "I will be a raving lunatic."

He found the wait increasingly difficult. Now that he had decided to take such drastic action, he wanted to have the matter settled, one way or the other, and he chafed at the delay.

He and Phillip had only each other for company these days, if one didn't count a household staff of about a hundred. Stephano and his wife were in Everux, awaiting the birth of their child. The countess remained in the castle, but she was occupied with matters of state and stayed in the solar most of the day. They saw her only at dinner, and those encounters were awkward and uncomfortable.

The countess had expected Phillip to leave when his host left and she had not been pleased to hear he was remaining with his friend. Cecile still did not trust Phillip and she made it clear that she considered he had overstayed his welcome. She spoke almost exclusively to Thomas. If Phillip ventured to voice an opinion on a subject, Cecile would fix with him a crystalline look, say coolly, "Indeed, Your Grace," and resume her conversation with Thomas.

"I should go back to Estara," Phillip told Thomas.

"And leave me here alone with the countess?" Thomas added. "You will do no such thing. I am terrified of that woman."

The two were walking in the garden after breakfast. The morning was bright, but the air was cool, and both men were bundled up in scarves and greatcoats. They would have been more comfortable if they had been reading their newspapers by the fire in the library, but the garden was the only place where they could be assured that they could speak in private.

The garden was lovely with the coming of autumn's colors: the reds and golds of the changing leaves; the scarlet roses, blooming their last. Thomas found no joy in the beauty. D'argent had been gone eighteen days now and Thomas was convinced that something had gone wrong.

"The countess is so remote, beyond my reach," Thomas continued. "I have no idea what she is thinking. Does she value and respect me or does she despise me? Is she advancing my cause or using me to advance her own?"

"The countess is much like Sir Henry," said Phillip. "They are both duplicitous, ruthless, merciless. Both patriots, fiercely loyal to king and country."

Phillip smiled sadly, his tone softened. "That said, Thomas, the countess is trusting you with Sophia, who is dearer to her than a daughter. She would not permit Sophia to marry a man she despises. Which is why I have no hope," he added with a sigh. "She still more than half suspects me of being Sir Henry's agent."

"If the countess truly wanted you somewhere else, you would be somewhere else—most likely the penal colony on the Chain of Pearls," said Thomas. "She permits you to stay because she values your opinion."

"Or because I know too much and she wants to keep an eye on me," Phillip said. "I wonder if the countess is aware that you confide in me?"

"She knows everything about everyone," said Thomas. "If King Ullr sneezes, she knows the color of his handkerchief."

"Be grateful she is on your side," said Phillip, laughing. "You may have noticed that I feel safe drinking my port only after you have tasted yours."

Thomas grinned. "Speaking of Sophia, she has written to me."

He drew a letter out of his pocket and waved it tantalizingly in front of his friend, keeping it just out of reach.

"You cad!" Phillip exclaimed. "Why didn't you tell me? Let me see it? What does she say?"

"She writes to me, her fiancé, but I have a feeling the letter is intended for your eyes. She asks several questions regarding Freyan customs that could be answered only by a native such as yourself."

"Give that to me, you fiend!" Phillip said, snatching the letter from his hand.

He sat down on a bench to read it. Thomas took a seat beside him.

"She writes that she enjoys being in Freya, although she finds the political situation distressing," Phillip said. "Her fellow students know that she is engaged to be married to the handsome 'Prince Tom,' made famous by the stories in the *Haever Gazette*."

Thomas shook his head.

"The young women are all in love with you. They ask her countless questions about you. Sophia says she refers all questions to Sir Rodrigo," said Phillip, laughing.

"God help me!" Thomas intoned.

When Phillip read on, his laughter died. "She says all of Freya is eager for the wedding."

He folded up the letter and handed it back to his friend.

"At least you hear news of Sophia," said Thomas. "You know she is happy and well. I know nothing of Kate. I do not know where she is or what has become of her. She might be dead for all I know."

"I thought you were never going to think of her again," said Phillip with a faint smile.

"Unfortunately the more I try *not* to think about Kate, the more she is in my thoughts," said Thomas.

Phillip looked grave. "My friend . . ."

"I know that is wrong," said Thomas. "Don't lecture me, Pip!"

"I was not going to lecture you," Phillip said. "I was going to warn you that you might want to lower your voice. A servant is coming this way."

"Her Ladyship sends her regards, Your Highness," said the servant. "She wonders if you could spare a moment to meet with her in the solar."

"Has Monsieur D'argent returned?" Thomas asked.

"Monsieur D'argent was with the countess when I left her, Your Highness," the servant replied.

Thomas and Phillip exchanged glances.

"Please inform Her Ladyship that I will come now," said Thomas.

Phillip rested his hand on Thomas's shoulder.

"I will meet you in your room."

"Have brandy waiting," said Thomas.

The servant opened the door to the solar. Thomas found the countess and D'argent standing by the window, deep in conversation. D'argent was still wearing his traveling clothes: heavy cloak and riding boots. He had apparently come immediately to the countess, not even going to his room first to change clothes. He and Cecile both looked exceedingly grave.

The servant announced him. The countess and D'argent stopped talking and turned to greet him. D'argent bowed. The countess made a graceful curtsy.

"Thank you for coming, Your Highness," said Cecile, rising. "That will be all, D'argent. You have earned your rest. I will send for you if I have need."

"Yes, my lady, thank you," said D'argent.

"I hope you had a safe journey, Monsieur D'argent?" Thomas asked, as the man walked past him.

"I did, sir. Thank you for your concern."

D'argent left, taking care to close the door behind him. Cecile followed him and turned the key in the lock. She then took the precaution of adding a magical warding spell, murmuring words beneath her breath and passing her hand over the door frame.

"Please take care not to touch it, sir," she said.

"Something has gone wrong," Thomas said.

"Not wrong, exactly. Unexpected," Cecile replied.

She indicated a chair. Thomas sat down and she took her usual place on the sofa. Thomas was too restless to remain still, and he almost immediately stood up.

"Her Majesty has changed her mind, refused to meet with me."

"On the contrary, sir, the meeting is confirmed. D'argent has made all the arrangements," said Cecile. "Her Majesty is most eager to meet with you."

"Then what is wrong?" Thomas asked, sitting down again.

Cecile was dressed in shimmering gray silk with little decoration, only a touch of delicate white lace at her throat, like a froth of sea foam. She wore a shawl of soft white lambs' wool about her shoulders. She smoothed the folds of her gown, then clasped her hands and regarded Thomas with earnest gravity.

"Queen Mary is dying."

Thomas stared at her. He did not know the queen, and his first thought was the pity one feels at the news that any fellow mortal is dying. Then, suddenly, he comprehended the enormity of her words. He refused to believe it.

"I have been reading the Freyan newspapers, my lady, and I have seen nothing . . ."

"Her illness is a closely guarded secret," said Cecile. "I can count on one hand the number of people who know."

"But then how did you hear about it?"

Cecile smiled, but her smile chilled him. "Do not ask me. Never ask me, for you would not want to know. Suffice it to say, I know this news to be true."

She regarded him with concern. "I know this comes as a shock."

"I am reminded of the time when I went walking on a frozen pond," Thomas said. "The ice broke beneath my feet, plunging me into the freezing water. The cold stopped my breath and nearly stopped my heart. I feel something like that now."

He shook his head. Still in denial. "The queen is only in her middle years."

"Mary is dying of the same affliction that killed her father. A malignant growth in her stomach."

"How long . . ." Thomas asked.

"Months, perhaps," said Cecile. "Weeks. No one can say."

Thomas sat staring down at the carpet. He noticed it was beige, decorated with a vine and dragon motif done in soft, muted colors of green and blue. He thought it odd that he should be so aware of the carpet.

"Poor woman," he murmured.

"God give her ease," said Cecile.

Thomas stirred and looked up. "Is this why D'argent was gone so long?"

"He had to make plans," said Cecile. "We believe the queen will name you her heir. Sir Richard is honored to have you as his guest. This development means you must remain in Haever until . . ."

Cecile hesitated.

"Until the queen dies. I am to remain on death watch," Thomas said grimly. "I will do nothing so ghoulish!"

"You must and you will, Your Highness," said Cecile. Her voice was cold, stinging. "Put aside your pity. Put aside your compassion. Such feelings do you credit, but they are luxuries you cannot afford."

Thomas was so angry he did not trust himself to speak. He rose from the chair and walked to the window. Cecile came over to stand beside him.

"When the queen dies, you must be present in Haever to assert your right to the throne. Her Majesty will have documents drawn up making the succession legal and official, but I doubt she will announce it publicly, knowing she would put you in danger. Most likely she will publicly name you from her deathbed, as her father named her."

Thomas shuddered and bowed his head.

Cecile clasped his hand, her nails piercing his flesh. Her fingers were as cold as the frozen water of that long-ago pond. "The waiting will be dangerous and tedious, for you must remain in hiding. We will have to find a plausible excuse for you to extend your stay, for Sir Richard cannot know the truth. I was thinking you could fall ill with an ague. The symptoms are easy to fake and the illness would leave you weak and unable to travel."

"An ague . . ." Thomas repeated.

He sank down in a chair and stared at a vase of chrysanthemums, the last blooms of the fall before the onset of winter. When spring came and the flowers bloomed again, he could well be king of Freya.

"I need time to think," he said.

"I am sorry, Thomas, but there is no time," said Cecile. "You must leave tomorrow at first light. D'argent has made the arrangements for your journey."

"So soon . . ." Thomas murmured.

"D'argent spoke to several of my contacts in Haever, remaining discreet, of course," Cecile continued. "He heard nothing that caused him alarm. No one knows the queen is ill. Freya remains in turmoil; riots occur almost daily. A mob actually attacked the Naval Yard. The unrest works to our advantage. Sir Henry is completely occupied with the worsening political crisis to the exclusion of all else. We must take advantage of the situation.

"As for Sir Richard, he is overjoyed to hear that you will be meeting with the queen." Cecile added with a sigh, "He presents something of a problem, however."

"What is that, my lady?" Thomas asked.

"He is deeply concerned for your safety while you are in Freya. Sir Richard tends to be an alarmist. He sees assassins behind every bush, and he was at first insistent that you travel with a military escort.

"D'argent attempted to explain that you would be far safer traveling alone, incognito. He reminded Sir Richard that you are a soldier with training in arms so you can take care of yourself. He was able to convince him, but Sir Richard remains dubious."

"Did D'argent impress upon Sir Richard that he must not tell my mother of my journey?" said Thomas.

"No need to worry on that account. Sir Richard knows your mother, and while he admires her, he views her as a rival. His great fear is that once you are king, your mother will rush to Freya, supplant him, and take charge herself. Sir Richard is loyal to you, Thomas, but he is also ambitious; something we can use to our advantage."

Thomas scarcely heard her. He had not been in that icy water long. His mother had never let him go anywhere on his own and when he had fallen through the ice, an army of servants had rushed to his rescue. They had carried him inside, blue with the cold, dripping wet and shivering so that his teeth chattered. His mother had fainted at the sight of him, sodden and shaking, and he had not been allowed to go near the pond ever again, even in the hottest days of summer.

The chill he now felt was the same, creeping over him. His hand shook and he clenched his fist to hide it.

"What would happen if I were to reconsider, my lady?" Thomas asked.

"Has this been a game to you, Your Highness?" Cecile was angry. She spoke with a calm fury that was like the prelude to a deadly wizard storm.

"Not a game, my lady!" Thomas returned. "I thought I had years ahead of me to make the adjustment. Years during which I could study to be king. I am not ready. I am not prepared! I am . . ."

He faltered. He could not say what was in his heart—he was afraid.

Cecile heard the unspoken words, and her tone grew gentle. She said softly, "No one is ever ready, Your Highness."

She understood, and proved she did by answering his question. "Let me tell you what will happen if you do not take the throne. Queen Mary will name her sister, Elinor. Hugh will not stand for that. He is already plotting with his wealthy friends to seize control, even as Elinor is conspiring with the Council of Bishops of the Church of the Breath to help her stay on the throne."

"What will keep both of them from turning on me?" Thomas asked.

"You have your own armies, both in Bheldem and the secret army your colonel is raising in Freya. In addition, Sophia brings as her dowry the might of Rosia," Cecile replied. "You must, of course, be married immediately following your ascent to the throne, thus cementing the Rosian alliance. Neither Hugh nor Elinor will dare contend against the might of Rosia."

"You have thought of everything, my lady," said Thomas.

"That is my job, Your Highness," said Cecile.

"I will go to Freya," said Thomas. "I will meet with Her Majesty. Beyond that, I can make no promises. The future is in God's hands. We have no idea what will happen."

"I, too, have misgivings," said Cecile. "You are right, we do not know what may happen. I considered traveling to Haever myself, to be on hand if you need advice."

She smiled and shook her head. "Stephano would never forgive me if I missed the birth of my grandchild. And, to be honest, I would never forgive myself."

Cecile opened the rosewood box, withdrew a piece of paper and handed it to him.

"Here are the names of my most trusted agents in Haever. Contact them if you are in desperate need. That said, your best resource if you are in trouble is Sir Rodrigo."

Thomas started to smile, then saw she was serious.

"Rodrigo? Truly, my lady?" he asked, astonished.

"Do not underestimate him, Your Highness," said Cecile. "Rodrigo has hidden talents. Although I admit at times they can be *well* hidden. And now I must be going. I am leaving for Everux this afternoon."

Thomas accompanied her to the door of the solar. She turned to leave him, then paused.

"You must say nothing about any of this to His Grace," said Cecile.

"I hope you will have a safe journey, my lady," said Thomas politely. "Please give my best wishes to your son and his lady wife."

Cecile gazed at him. "I know you trust Phillip, despite the fact that he betrayed you. Ask yourself this: Do you trust him with your life?"

Thomas did not answer. He met her gaze and held it. Cecile sighed and lowered her eyes.

"God go with Your Highness," she said. "Wait here. I will send D'argent to you. He will provide you with what you will need for the journey."

Pressing his hand, she left him.

Thomas stood alone in the doorway. He remembered that his fingers had turned white after the plunge into the frozen pond. He had lost all feeling in them.

When the feeling returned, the pain had been excruciating.

FORTY-TWO

Thomas met with D'argent and received his instructions for his journey to Freya: where to stay, how to act, who to trust (essentially, no one). Left on his own at last, Thomas went to find Phillip. He discovered his friend in his room, lounging in a chair, reading a book of poetry.

Phillip looked up with a smile, until he saw Thomas's face. His smile vanished. He jumped up from his chair.

"Tom! My God, you're as white as the bed linen. What has happened? What is wrong?"

Thomas looked up and down the hallway, saw it was empty. He shut the door. "Keep your voice down. Did anyone see you come in here?"

"I don't think so," said Phillip. "The servants are preparing for the countess's departure and no one paid attention to me. Sit down. Let me pour you a brandy."

"I would choke on it," said Thomas. "We need to talk."

He grasped Phillip by the arm and dragged him to a remote corner of the bedchamber, far from the door. The servants had laid a fire in the old stone fireplace, but they had not lighted it. The room faced east to receive the morning sun and was dark and shadowy in the afternoon.

Thomas pulled up a chair for himself and one for Phillip and placed them in front of the unlit fire. That done, he stood looking at the chairs. He did not sit down; neither did Phillip.

"What I am about to say goes no further. I am trusting you with my life," said Thomas.

"You can, Tom," said Phillip, troubled. "You know that."

Thomas smiled and felt his tension start to ease.

"I do know that, Pip." He drew in a deep breath, then let it out. "Queen Mary is dying. Her Majesty has months, maybe weeks, to live."

Phillip stared at him, wordless, then he abruptly sank down in the chair.

"Oh, my God, Pip!" Thomas rested his hand on his shoulder. "I am sorry! I was thinking only of myself. This dreadful news touches you close to home."

"I have known the queen all my life," Phillip said. "She and my father were friends. She carried me in her arms when I was a child. She taught me to ride . . ."

He could not go on. Shaking his head, he put his hand to his eyes.

"I will pour us both a brandy," said Thomas.

He left his friend to himself, giving him a chance to recover. Going to the sidebar, he poured brandy from the crystal decanter into the first glasses that came to hand and carried them back to the cold fireplace. He handed one to Phillip and kept one for himself.

Thomas raised his glass. "To Her Majesty, Queen Mary."

"To the queen," said Phillip.

They both took a drink. Thomas sat down opposite his friend. They looked at each for long moments.

"That was the countess's news. Her Majesty is going to name you the heir to the throne," Phillip said.

"So the countess believes," said Thomas. "What do you think? You know the queen."

Phillip was thoughtful. "Mary is cross-grained and stubborn, impatient with fools, loyal to her friends, and implacable toward her enemies. But she is eminently sensible. I think now that she is faced with the knowledge that she must soon quit the world, she realizes that choosing either Elinor or Hugh would plunge the country into war."

"Why would she choose me? She has never met me. She knows nothing about me, beyond those fool newspaper stories," said Thomas.

"She does know you," said Phillip. "Better than you think." He added with a faint smile, "I never told you this, but after I had made up my mind to confess to you that I had been Sir Henry's spy, I wrote to Her Majesty. You will recall that night, when I made my confession to you, I expected to be arrested and executed.

"I knew Sir Henry would blacken my reputation, brand me a traitor to the queen. Queen Mary loved me and I did not want to die leaving her to believe that I had betrayed her. I wrote to her in secret. I told her about you. I said that by supporting your cause, I was supporting my country. I said that in my opinion, you would be a good and wise ruler."

"You are my friend, Pip," said Thomas, uncomfortable. "Your judgment is skewed."

"I do not think so," said Phillip. "Apparently the queen does not think so, either."

Thomas did not know what to say. Never comfortable hearing himself praised, he left the fireplace to walk over to the window. He looked out to see the countess's yacht had landed on the castle grounds.

The countess owned several yachts; elegant wyvern-drawn yachts and yachts like this one that was large enough to sail the Breath. Designed for a woman who might need to sail anywhere in the world at a moment's notice, the yacht had been built for speed and endurance, with luxury an afterthought. The yacht had two full decks and a forecastle, two masts and two balloons. Wings ran the length of the hull, supporting three airscrews on each side.

Footmen hauled heavy trunks up the gangplank, followed by maids carrying hatboxes and jewel cases. The countess's lady's maid was already on board, directing the servants where to stow the luggage.

As Thomas watched, Cecile emerged, wrapped in a fur cloak. She paused, as though she felt his thoughts touch her, and looked up at his window. Her expression was enigmatic, her face impassive. She turned and boarded her yacht, disappeared below deck.

Thomas remained at the window, watching the crew prepare for departure.

Phillip joined his friend at the window. "Trust me, my friend. The queen would not just take my word on your worth. She has done her own investigating. You may depend upon that."

The helmsmen sent magic to the lift tanks and the airscrews. The yacht rose into the sky. Sails billowed and caught the breeze. They watched the yacht circumnavigate the mountain peaks and vanish into the mists of the Breath.

Both young men gave an involuntary sigh of relief.

"The countess is a formidable woman," Thomas remarked.

"She chills me to the marrow of my bones," said Phillip.

He offered Thomas another brandy, then said briskly, "I assume D'argent has made all the arrangements for your journey: safe places for you to stop for the night, fresh griffins awaiting you each morning, a false identity, that sort of thing."

"I have spoken to him," said Thomas. He turned away from the window. "He has thought of everything. He will have a griffin saddled and ready for my departure tomorrow morning with money and weapons, maps and other necessities in the saddlebags. I know where I am to stop along the way. I am to keep my face hidden and speak to no one. When I arrive in Haever, Sir Richard's servant, Henshaw, will meet me at a secret location in the dead of night and convey me to his master's house where I will be wrapped in cotton wool and locked up in the wine cellar."

Phillip regarded him with concern. "Thomas, this is no time to act the fool. You must take this seriously."

"I will. I do," said Thomas. "It is just . . . You know that Sophia and I must wed the instant the crown touches my head."

"Of course you must," said Phillip, his voice steady, matter-of-fact. "You will need the Rosian alliance to serve as a bulwark against your foes as you work to secure the kingdom."

"You are like the countess. She talked of alliances, of securing the kingdom, of my enemies plotting against me," said Thomas. "All I could think about was the time when I was a little boy and I plunged through the ice into freezing water."

"An apt analogy," said Phillip, smiling in sympathy. "I spoke out of habit. You must remember that I studied statecraft at the knee of Sir Henry Wallace. Do not worry, Thomas. You will learn and, in the meantime, you will rely on trusted advisers."

Thomas snorted. "Trusted advisers! I have been told to trust no one—except Sir Rodrigo."

"And your humble servant," Phillip reminded him. "I will be there."

Thomas shook his head. "You should not go, Pip. Especially not now. The risk of discovery is far too great."

"We have been through this before, Tom. I will not let you go alone. You will need someone who knows Sir Henry, who knows Haever. *Especially* now."

Thomas gave a deep sigh. "I am being selfish, but I admit I will be glad to know you are in Haever."

"We should not travel together," said Phillip. "Since you are planning to leave tomorrow morning, I will depart this evening before dark."

"Where will we meet in Haever? I have no idea when I will arrive."

"Find some excuse to visit Oak Hill Park," Phillip said.

"I doubt Sir Richard will let me out of the wine cellar," said Thomas. "The countess says he is deeply concerned for my welfare."

"Good for him," said Phillip. "But he cannot deny you exercise. At the north end of Oak Hill Park there is a famous round knob of a hill topped by a ring of oak trees. Every morning at nine of the clock, I will sit on a bench near the pond reading a copy of the *Haever Gazette*. I will remain there an hour. If you do not appear, I will leave and return the next morning and the morning after that and so on."

"Oak Hill Park, knob, pond, bench," Thomas repeated. "I believe I have it. Do you know where you will be staying?"

"I have a couple of places in mind. I must study the situation before I decide. See who's watching who's watching who's watching who, as Sir Rodrigo would say."

Phillip glanced at the clock. "If I am to leave before dark, I must pack and tell the stable hands to have my griffin ready."

He and Thomas shook hands.

"Have a safe journey," said Phillip.

"You, as well," said Thomas. He paused, then said, "I must give up all hope of Kate."

"My dear fellow, face facts," said Phillip gently. "There never was any hope."

FORTY-THREE

The next two days, the *Naofa* sailed north, traveling up the western Freyan coastline toward some unknown destination. Kate tried more than once to find out where they were bound. She asked the Bottom Dwellers, but they had no idea nor did they care. In this strange and unfamiliar world, one place was much the same as another. She thought Franklin might stop at Trellingham, but the ship gave the small logging and mining town a wide berth, avoiding the barges that carried logs and coal and iron ore around the southern tip of Freya to Haever or other manufacturing towns.

Kate kept watch for Dalgren during the journey, and once or twice, she thought she caught a glimpse of him. She could not be sure. The Brigade had trained him to conceal himself in the mists or soar high among the clouds. He knew now that the ship was armed with swivel guns and he would take care to keep out of sight.

Kate had little work to do aboard ship; the magic did not need repair, leaving her with time to try to figure out what was going on. She supposed there could be some reasonable and innocent explanation for secretly smuggling contramagic-wielding young people to the deserted western coast of Freya, but she was damned if she could think of one.

"I trust Thomas," Kate would say to herself in the long, silent watches of the night. "I do. But is it really possible he knows nothing about this?"

She would lie awake, staring into the darkness and doubting.

Early on the morning of the third day of the voyage, Franklin announced that they would soon be docking. He told the young people to gather their things and then stand ready to assist. Excited, they hurried below. Kate was also excited, for at last she would find some answers. She was about to go pack up her belongings when Franklin summoned her.

She expected him to ask her to keep an eye on the magic of the lift tanks or some such thing. His question took her by surprise.

"Do you know how to use signal flags, Private?"

"Yes, sir," said Kate. "As I told you, I operated my own boat when I was in the Aligoes. Why?"

"Our former crafter handled the signaling. I can do it, but I will have to assist Corporal Roberts with the docking, so that leaves you."

"What signal do you want me to send?"

"You will have to use the flags to spell it out," said Franklin. "I will write it down for you."

He handed her a piece of paper with the word: "Talionis."

"What does it mean, sir?" Kate asked.

"It means you will have to use the flags to spell it out," said Franklin.

Every ship was equipped with signal flags that were used to alert other ships of dangerous conditions, transmit orders to other ships during battle, or invite another captain to dine. Each letter of the alphabet had its own flag, as well as flags that could be hoisted to warn that the ship was under quarantine and to keep away. Kate went to the locker where the flags were kept and selected those she needed to spell out the mysterious word. She attached the flags to the line, and stood by, ready to hoist them when ordered.

Franklin conferred with the corporal at the helm. Roberts altered the ship's course and the *Naofa* headed toward shore. As the ship drew closer, Kate could see they were sailing toward a harbor formed by two heavily forested peninsulas that extended out into the Breath and curved inward like arms reaching out to embrace the ship. The *Naofa* was bearing down on the gap between the two.

Franklin came over to inspect the flags. Satisfied, he gave her the order to show the signal.

Kate hoisted the flags and watched the wind catch them. She searched for some indication of a town or even a military camp, but all she could see were gray cliffs, heavily forested with fir trees. Watching the flags flap in the wind, Kate had an idea.

"Begging your pardon, Commander, but how would you like to salute the prince?"

Franklin was watching the ship creep toward the shore and he turned to regard her in puzzlement. "What prince?"

"Prince Thomas," Kate explained. "We don't have any cannons, but we could raise a flag in his honor. Or maybe a royal ensign?"

"The flags you have raised will be sufficient, Private."

"Begging your pardon again, sir," said Kate, carefully deferential, "but won't His Highness be offended if we sail into the harbor without saluting him?"

"Ah, now I understand," said Franklin, amused. "I forget you are a Trundler. Do you truly imagine His Highness would visit us in this godforsaken part of the world? Princes leave military business to their commanders. They do not involve themselves with such matters."

Kate looked at the Bottom Dwellers, lined up on deck, shivering in their thin coats and squinting against the light of a pallid sun as they looked on this land that was going to be their new home.

"Perhaps they should," she muttered.

The ship entered the gap, moving slowly. The entrance to the harbor was narrow, and shrouded in mist. When the ship was close, Kate saw two gun emplacements, one on either side of the entrance to the harbor. The guns were concealed by trees and brush and magic. A fleet of naval patrol boats could have sailed past that harbor twice a day and never noticed them.

The signal, *Talionis*, would let the gunners know that the ship was friendly and could safely pass.

The narrow entrance opened into a large natural harbor with a wharf that would have been able to accommodate at least five ships much larger than the *Naofa*. Several troop carriers and two Travian merchant ships were docked here.

Kate wondered at first why Travian merchants would be here; then she saw that the ships were being overhauled. Workmen had taken down the Travian colors and were painting over the Travian names. The ships were relatively new and had probably been captured. The merchant vessels were now being transformed, probably into more troop carriers.

Kate searched for some sign of a town to house all these people. The only buildings were a couple of large warehouses near the wharf. Beyond that was forest.

Yet people must live somewhere. Soldiers had been manning those guns. Sailors and crafters were working on the merchant ships. More sailors waited on the wharf, ready to assist the ship in docking.

Kate stood at the rail, trying not to laugh as she watched Roberts com-

pletely bungle the docking. Each ship had its own berth, iron bollards driven
into the rock to hold the anchor and poles to which the ship could be tethered. Roberts sent too much magic to the starboard airscrew; the ship veered,
and those standing on the wharf ran for their lives as the ship almost plowed
into them and nearly knocked down one of the tethering poles.

Kate dared not look at Franklin, who was standing with his jaw clenched,
his expression grim.

Once the ship had finally made a safe landfall, soldiers came on board to
round up the Bottom Dwellers. Half blinded by the sun, the young people
trooped off the ship clutching their few possessions tied up in sacks. The soldiers escorted the Bottom Dwellers to the end of the pier and they disappeared into the forest.

The sacks reminded Kate that she had not yet retrieved the pistol she had
wrapped in a gunnysack and hidden in the storage closet. Roberts had also
disappeared, probably to avoid the wrath of his commander over the inept
docking procedure. Soldiers began descending into the cargo hold to unload
the supplies.

Kate kept an eye on Franklin, hoping he would disembark and give her an
opportunity to sneak below. He did not leave the ship, however. He paced
the deck as though waiting for someone, and smiled to see a man coming up
the gangplank. He went forward to shake hands. The man was wearing the
uniform of a Freyan army officer, similar to the one Franklin wore, only
trimmed in the gold braid that denoted a captain.

Kate realized now, seeing the two together, that the uniforms were different, although the difference was minor, scarcely noticeable. The decorative
piping on the jacket was in red, not green. Anyone observing these soldiers
marching down Freyan streets, setting up camp in Freyan fields, would not
give them a second glance.

Seeing the two engrossed in conversation, Kate decided she could slip
away and not be missed.

She headed for the storage closet, only to find her way blocked by more
soldiers hauling up the two heavy, wooden crates. Kate had seen the young
people carry the crates on board. She had wondered then, as she wondered
now, what was inside. The soldiers carried the crates off the ship and loaded
them into a waiting horse-drawn wagon.

Kate could not waste time speculating. The door to the closet was open.
The Bottom Dwellers had taken all the remaining foodstuffs with them, force
of habit for those who had never been certain when they would eat again.
Kate slipped inside and groped her way to the back. She found the pistol,
wrapped in the gunnysack, where she had left it.

She tucked the pistol into the waistband of her slops, pulled the skirt over it, and buttoned her peacoat over that. She was heading for her cabin, when she heard Franklin and his friend coming down the stairs.

Kate darted into her cabin, hoping to avoid detection, but she was too late.

"Private, what are you doing down here?" Franklin demanded.

"Packing my belongings, sir," said Kate.

"You can do that later," said Franklin.

"Yes, sir." Kate tried to sidle off.

Franklin stopped her. "Come with me. You are not in trouble, Private. Captain Martin and I need to speak to you."

Mystified, Kate accompanied the two men to Franklin's cabin, which was directly across the corridor from hers. Kate allowed them to go first, acutely conscious of the pistol hidden beneath her clothes as she followed them.

Franklin unlocked the door and he and the captain walked inside. He brought a chair for his friend and then sat down in the chair behind the desk. He did not invite Kate to sit down, which was fine with her. She remained standing near the door, ready for a quick escape should that prove necessary.

The captain cast her a disapproving glance.

"Who is this woman, Franklin?"

"Kate McPike. The crafter I was telling you about,"

The captain frowned. "You did not mention she was a Trundler."

"Beggars cannot be choosers, Martin," said Franklin dryly. "She knows how to use the seventh sigil."

"Are you certain? She is a Trundler, after all," Martin grunted. "And a stowaway. She could have lied so you wouldn't throw her off the ship."

"I am certain, Martin," said Franklin, sounding irritated at being doubted. "She has repaired the magic on the lift tanks using the seventh sigil. You can see for yourself."

Kate shifted restlessly. The two were discussing her as if she were a prize hog they were planning to purchase.

"How did you come to find her on Glasearrach?" Martin asked.

"She is related to the two Trundler women who own this ship. She ran afoul of the law in Wellinsport and traveled with them to Glasearrach to escape bounty hunters."

Martin cast her a disparaging glance, then shook his hand. "A Trundler! God works in mysterious ways, Franklin."

"God be thanked for His miracles, both great and small," said Franklin. "You are dismissed, Private. Go finish your packing, then wait on deck. Someone will show you to your quarters."

"Yes, sir," said Kate. "Thank you, sir."

"Leave the door open," said Martin. "Stinks of Bottom Dweller in here. Makes me want to retch. I don't know how you stand it, Franklin."

"You get used to it," said Franklin. "I don't smell it at all anymore."

Kate hurried into her cabin, closed the door, then sat down on the bed to listen to the conversation from across the hall, hoping to hear something of interest. She was disappointed. The two were apparently just exchanging the latest camp gossip.

"I heard from one of the men that Gaskell is gone," Franklin was saying. "Somewhat mysteriously, as I understand. I cannot say I am sorry, Martin. Between his drunkenness and debauchery, he was a constant threat to discipline."

"Gaskell's dissolute behavior was not surprising, given he was in league with that spawn of the Evil One—the dragon Coreg."

Kate sucked in a startled breath, wondering if she had heard right. She crept over to her door, opened it a crack, and waited to hear more.

"God be thanked, we do not have to deal with either of them anymore," Martin was saying. "From now on, we deal directly with Colonel Smythe. He has taken over acquiring the weapons from the black market himself."

"Good news," said Franklin. "Smythe is a God-fearing man by all accounts. What happened to Gaskell?"

"He did something to displease the colonel," Martin replied. "Smythe sent a man to deal with him."

"Why the grimace?" Franklin asked.

"Wait until you meet Weasel," Martin growled.

"Weasel?" Franklin repeated. "Is that his name?"

"He goes by some heathen name no one can remember. He never speaks, except once to me to ask me where the Travian dragons lived. As if I would know or care! He is always sneaking about. One of the men said he reminded him of a weasel, and the name stuck. Colonel Smythe wrote that this fellow could prove useful to us in refurbishing and refitting the guns. I can't fathom why Smythe would say that, for the fellow claims to know nothing about crafting."

"Strange," said Franklin.

Martin grunted. "Between you and me, I think our colonel wanted to be rid of him and foisted him off on us. It is a pity. I could use another crafter since Huston died."

"Huston is dead?" Franklin sounded shocked. "What happened?"

"The fool got the lunatic idea into his head that the Bottom Dwellers were going to turn on us. He began carrying a loaded pistol with him everywhere. He was at work in the armory when there was some sort of accident; no one is really certain how, but the contramagic reacted with the magic in his pistol and blew a hole in him the size of a cannonball. I hope this Trundler is all you claim," Martin added grumpily. "What with losing Huston and the man you lost in the shipwreck, we are running low on crafters."

"I will have the private start work tomorrow. Speaking of guns, here is the inventory of the replacement parts. Do you want to go over it now?"

"No, I need to return to camp, make certain these new recruits are settled. Bring the list along when you come."

Chairs scraped as the two men stood up. Kate softly shut her door and stood with her back against it. Franklin and Martin walked past her cabin, heading for the stairs.

"How did you find a black ship in such good condition?" Martin was asking.

"The Bottom Dwellers told us about this one. The two Trundler women who owned it are friends with some Rosian priest. They risked their lives carrying food and medicine for these people, who then turned around and betrayed them." Franklin added in a tone of disgust, "The Scriptures tell us to love our fellow man, but I confess I find it difficult to love Bottom Dwellers."

"Too bad we didn't kill them all off during the war," said Martin. "I can't stand the sight of them with their fish-belly skin and squinty eyes. I'll be glad when this job is finished and we can be rid of them."

They proceeded up the stairs. "Leave the balloons partially inflated. Make certain the ship is securely tied down. I'll have the lift tanks refilled."

Their voices trailed off.

Someone pounded on her door. "It's me, Corporal Roberts."

"What do you want?" she asked.

"The captain sent me to find you. I have orders to take you to the barracks."

"I haven't finished packing," said Kate.

"Make haste then," Roberts said. "Leave your chest in your cabin. One of the soldiers will bring it over."

"I can carry it," Kate said, not wanting some stranger pawing through her things.

"I said leave it, Private," Roberts ordered. "You have ten minutes."

He walked off. Kate dragged the chest out from under the bed, wondering if there was some way for her to steal the ship and fly it back to Glasearrach. Dalgren could go with her, make his apologies to Father Jacob.

Kate let herself dream for a moment, then came back down to reality. The black ship required at least a crew of three to sail and those three needed to be experienced sailors. Even if she came up with the crew, she didn't know how to find Glasearrach without navigational charts.

She went back to her packing, which didn't take long. She hadn't brought that much with her, considering she had been planning to remain on Glasearrach for a year. Two calico shirts, an extra pair of slops, undergarments, stockings, red kerchiefs and—always mindful of Miss Amelia's dictum regarding sensible shoes—sturdy boots as well as the slippers she wore on deck.

She had also brought with her the two most cherished things she owned: the pistol Thomas had given her and the letter he had written to her when she was in the Aligoes.

Kate had hidden the letter in the false bottom she had fashioned for her chest—an easy task for the daughter of a smuggler. She had been amused at herself for keeping it, telling herself she was being silly and sentimental, and she had made up her to mind to burn it, but found she couldn't destroy it.

Reducing his letter to ashes would be like reducing their relationship to ashes. And although Kate could tell herself that they had no relationship, and that Thomas was engaged to another woman, she couldn't bring herself to consign his letter to the flames.

She read it over, although she had the words memorized. She was relieved to think Thomas had no idea what was going on with his army in Freya, even as she was aggravated with him for not making it his business to find out.

She slid the letter back into its hiding place and toyed with the idea of hiding the pistol with it. She decided to keep the pistol where it was, hidden beneath her skirt and the peacoat. She tied one of the red kerchiefs around her neck. When Dalgren found her, she could use it to signal to him, as they had in former times, when they had gone wrecking together.

Those days seemed very far away. She closed the chest with a sigh and went back up on deck.

Roberts greeted her with a sullen look and ordered her curtly to follow him.

The sun was in the west; only a few more hours of daylight left. Kate wondered where everyone had gone. The *Naofa* swung at anchor, balloons partially deflated, sails furled. The crews working on the other two ships had all departed. The dock was almost deserted. The forest stretched as far as she could see, deep and empty, filled with shadows.

Kate glanced back at the ship. It might be hidden from other ships in the Breath, but not from a dragon. Dalgren would be able to see the *Naofa* from the air and know how to find her, although she had no idea what good that would do either of them, for they would not be able to talk.

"I'll think of something," Kate muttered.

"What did you say?" Roberts demanded. "You are always muttering to yourself. You are not a witch, are you?" He scowled at her. "Witches constantly mutter spells, or so I have heard."

Kate thought to herself that it was lucky for Roberts she wasn't a witch. Otherwise he would be a hop toad by now.

"I was wondering where we were going," she said. "I don't see any sign of a barracks or encampment."

"That's because it's underground," said Roberts with a smirk.

"A cave!" Kate said, impressed. "I'll be damned."

A road paved with crushed rock led to two wrought-iron gates that guarded the entrance to the cavern. The entrance was large enough for two wagons to roll through the gate side by side. The gates had been built directly into the stone and stood open with two soldiers guarding it.

The soldiers eyed Kate suspiciously and would have stopped her, but Roberts vouched for her, saying she was a new crafter. The soldiers allowed her to pass.

Kate entered the cave and stopped to stare, awed. The Army of Retribution was not bivouacking in some dank hole, as she had supposed. They had built an underground city.

The cavern's interior was vast. Crafters must have spent months shaping and expanding the natural limestone. Huge square pillars located at regular intervals supported the ceiling.

The vast interior was lighted by constructs glowing softly on glass plates set into the ceiling, all connected by a complicated system of leather cords. The lighting was dim and Kate wondered why, at first, then remembered the Bottom Dwellers. Like moles, they must enjoy living underground in the dark.

"Those are the barracks." Roberts pointed to buildings carved out of stone. "The Bottom Dwellers live in the north barracks and we live in the south. Officers quarter there. The crafters have their own barracks toward the rear. That's where you'll be. Men and women are housed separately. Over there is the mess hall and beyond that the latrines . . ."

He kept talking, but Kate wasn't listening. She had the strange feeling someone was staring at her, a prickling sensation on the back of her neck, as though a tick was crawling into her hair. She glanced around and saw that someone *was* staring at her. He was leaning against a pillar, his arms folded across his chest, watching her with such intensity she had felt his eyes.

Dark, empty eyes. A dark, empty face.

Trubgek.

FORTY-FOUR

"What are you standing there gawking at?" Roberts demanded. "I told you to follow me."

He had apparently walked off, only to realize she was not behind him. He had come back to retrieve her and now stood glaring at her angrily.

"Sorry, sir," Kate said faintly.

But she could not take her gaze from Trubgek. She was bewildered, confounded. He was in the Aligoes. He couldn't possibly be here. And yet here he was.

"Who is that man, sir?" Kate asked. "He's not wearing a uniform."

Roberts glanced at Trubgek. "Him? He's called Weasel. And stop making eyes at the men, temptress! You may have fooled the commander, but you do not fool me. We flog any woman caught whoring herself. I will be watching you. Modest women keep their eyes lowered."

Kate barely heard him. She recalled Franklin and Martin talking about someone they called "Weasel," who did not know anything about magic and had asked where the Travian dragons lived. She had never connected that man with Trubgek, who was the most powerful crafter she had ever met, for he knew dragon magic.

Although in a way, Kate thought, he had told the truth. Trubgek knew nothing about ordinary, everyday crafting. He could work dragon magic and he could use it to bring down the mountain.

He might be a weasel, but he was a dangerous weasel, and apparently no one here knew the truth about him.

She followed Roberts, but all she could think about was Trubgek. When Roberts wasn't watching, she cast a swift glance over her shoulder.

Trubgek was gone.

Startled, Kate looked around the cavern. The central floor area was vast and unbroken except for the enormous pillars and they were spaced far apart. Soldiers were going about their duties. Some of the Bottom Dwellers had emerged from the living quarters to welcome the new arrivals. No sign of Trubgek. He had vanished so completely Kate began to wonder if she had imagined him.

Kate felt she should tell someone the truth about Trubgek. Unfortunately, he knew the truth about her.

Trubgek knew her true name. He knew that she worked for Sir Henry Wallace. If Trubgek told Franklin what he knew, Franklin might well leap to the conclusion that Kate was here to spy on the army at Wallace's behest.

A long leap, admittedly, but Kate couldn't chance it. The fact that she had lied was enough to land her in serious trouble.

She had to talk to him. Fleeting as her glimpse of him had been, she had the impression from the crease between his black brows and the flicker in the usually empty eyes indicated that Trubgek had been as unpleasantly shocked to see her as she had been to see him.

She tried to rid herself of Roberts, saying she could find her quarters on her own, in order to look for Trubgek. Roberts insisted on remaining with her until he had marched her to the door of her quarters.

"The Scriptures say that the 'mouth of strange women is as a deep pit; he that is abhorred by the Lord shall fall into it,'" Roberts admonished her. "Report to Commander Franklin at the armory tomorrow morning at eight of the clock."

He walked off and left her. Kate wondered what she was going to be doing at an armory. She was a ship's crafter, not a weapons smith. She shrugged, figuring she'd find out tomorrow, and entered her quarters.

The army valued crafters, apparently, for each had his own room, unlike the barracks where the soldiers slept on rows of cots. The crafters also had a certain amount of privacy for each room had a door, although the door did not lock.

The room was small and square, with smooth-planed stone walls, a stone floor, and stone ceiling. It contained a cot and a nightstand, a blanket, a chamber pot, a chair, and a lantern powered by magic. The soldiers had delivered her chest, for it was standing beside the cot.

Kate cast a warding spell on the door before unpacking. The spell was simple, mainly designed to keep out unwanted visitors, such as Roberts. As for Trubgek, no lock, magical or otherwise, could keep him out if he wanted to get in.

She opened the chest and immediately saw that someone had gone through her things. The magical construct she had placed on the false bottom remained intact, however, so no one had discovered it. She was going to hide the pistol in the chest, then decided to put it beneath her pillow. Roberts had talked about the sins of the flesh with far too much relish.

This done, Kate went in search of the mess hall, keeping a lookout for Trubgek. She was eager to talk to other crafters, find out all the information she could.

The underground cavern was surprisingly comfortable. The temperature would remain constant, winter and summer. The lighting system made it seem almost as bright as a dreary day. Roberts had told her an underground stream provided fresh water for drinking, washing clothes, and bathing.

The mess hall was noisy and crowded. The Bottom Dwellers sat apart from the soldiers and talked in low voices. The lighting in the mess hall was dim, presumably for their benefit. Even so, many were wearing spectacles with smoke-colored lenses.

The officers had their own table at the head of the hall. Franklin was sitting with his friend Martin, the camp commander. She searched for Trubgek, but he wasn't around.

As she stood in line to pick up her ration of beans, ham, and bread, she asked the soldier in front of her where the crafters were sitting.

"I'm a ship's crafter," she said. "I'd like to talk to the others, find out what's expected of me."

The soldier shrugged. "Sit anywhere you like. There aren't any others."

"No other crafters?" Kate asked, startled.

"They're hard to come by. The last one, Huston, blew himself up," said the soldier. "I don't know what they are paying you, but it's not enough."

The cook slapped a ladleful of beans onto the tin plate and told her that the bread was at the end of the line. Kate ate by herself.

After supper, she roamed around the cavern, still looking for Trubgek and familiarizing herself with the layout. The caverns had only one way in, which was also the only way out. The doors were shut and locked after dark with soldiers standing guard.

Kate wondered why Martin bothered. The cliffs and the mountains and the wilderness were the only guards he needed. None of the Bottom Dwellers knew where they were and probably very few of the troops. She could not find Trubgek anywhere.

She went back to her room, lit the lantern, and sat down on the cot to assess her situation. She was in one hell of a predicament. She was a crafter and that was a benefit, although seemingly a dubious one. Crafters were in high demand, but only due to the fact that they kept dying.

Her only hope of escape lay with Dalgren. She had no idea how long he would have to search the coast before he found the *Naofa*. And when he did, how would he find her underground?

She sighed and had started to unbutton her shirt when she saw two eyes reflecting the glow of the lantern light, staring at her from a dark corner of the room.

Kate thrust her hand beneath the pillow to grab the pistol. It wasn't there.

Trubgek raised her pistol to the light and remained standing, staring at her from the shadows beyond the lantern's light.

"Why are you here? Did they send you?" he demanded, his voice grating.

Kate had to calm her breathing before she could answer. "No one sent me. Who are you talking about?"

"The dragons," said Trubgek.

"What dragons?" Kate asked, puzzled.

"The Rosian dragons. I know you warned them about me."

Kate was going to deny it, but she couldn't speak. Her tongue seemed swollen. Her heartbeat clogged her throat.

Trubgek sat down in the chair, folded his arms. He was still holding the pistol.

"I don't blame you," he continued. "I don't blame the dragons. I blame Coreg. He is dead. I watched him die."

Kate shuddered. His voice was cold and as empty as his eyes. She licked her lips and moistened her dry mouth.

"The dragons did not send me," she managed to say, but the words were scarcely audible. She coughed and tried again. "They didn't even believe me . . ."

Her voice trailed off.

"They believed you," said Trubgek. "Coreg had spies among the dragons and now his spies are my spies. The dragons are hunting me: Rosian dragons, Travian dragons, wild dragons. They all fear me, and if they find me, they will kill me."

Kate was terror-stricken. Trubgek had done nothing more than place the palm of his hand on a wall in Barwich Manor, and without speaking a word or moving a finger, he had sent quakes through the walls, nearly destroying her house.

"I never intended . . . Please, you have to believe me . . ."

"I am not going to harm you," said Trubgek. "You knew my name and what it meant. I had another name once. I was Petar. I tried to go back, but I couldn't. I am what he made me."

Kate said not a word. She wished desperately he would leave.

"Where is your dragon? The one who lost *his* name?" Trubgek asked abruptly.

"Dalgren?" Kate shook her head. "I have no idea. Somewhere Below, I guess."

Trubgek regarded her in silence. He stared at her so long that she knew he knew she was lying. He rose to his feet, placed the pistol in the seat of the chair, and walked out the door.

Kate sprang from the bed, grabbed the pistol, shut the door, and cast the most powerful warding spell she knew. She then shoved the wooden chest against it. After a moment, she dragged over her chair and put it on top of the chest. This done, she picked up the pistol, wrapped herself in her blanket and sat on the bed, facing the door.

She stayed there all night, until she heard the people walking about in the corridors. The pistol lay on the bed beside her. She didn't want to leave the room, but need drove her.

Roberts had said something about an area where women could bathe and perform their ablutions. Kate moved the chair, dragged aside the chest, and took down the warding spell. She opened the door with trepidation, saw people around and felt better.

She set out to find the latrines. The soldiers had dammed an underground stream, collected the water in a pool, and curtained it off so the women could have some privacy. Kate plunged into the cold water. The shock to her system helped drive away the lingering terrors of the night.

She even took a moment to look at herself in a crude mirror one of the women had propped up against the stone.

Her hair was growing back; her head was covered with blond ripples that curled at the tips. She had lost weight during the journey to and from Glasearrach. Or perhaps she had lost weight last night. Her face was thinner and paler, and that made her eyes seem bigger. She ran her fingers through her hair, ruffling her curls, thinking that might help her looks. It wasn't much of an improvement.

At breakfast she did not bother to look for Trubgek, knowing now she wouldn't see him unless he wanted to be seen. After she had eaten, she walked to the cavern entrance. The double doors stood open to allow those working on refitting the ships to attend to their duties.

The day was clear with only a trace of mist. The sun was shining. Dalgren would have a good view of this place from the air. Kate smiled at the two soldiers standing guard and started to walk outside.

"Where are you going?" one of the soldiers asked, stopping her.

"I am a crafter. I have work to do on the black ship," said Kate.

"No crafter is allowed to leave without an escort," said the soldier.

"I have permission—" Kate began, then she saw Roberts approaching, scowling at her.

"The commander is looking for you," said Roberts accusingly. "You were supposed to report to him at the armory this morning."

Kate suddenly remembered Roberts giving her the order. The encounter with Trubgek had driven it out of her head.

"I'm sorry, Corporal," said Kate. "I forgot."

Kate trailed along after him to a building on the western side of the cavern, set apart from the living quarters. A sentry stood at the door.

Franklin was waiting for her. He did not look pleased.

"Here she is, sir," said Roberts. "I caught her trying to leave the cave."

"I just needed some fresh air, sir," said Kate. "I'm not used to living underground. I was starting to feel suffocated."

"You get accustomed to it," said Franklin. "Follow me."

He led her into the armory, where Kate was expecting to see the usual: barrels of gunpowder, stacks of cannonballs, stands of weapons, cases holding rifles, sacks of canisters for swivel guns. But if any of those supplies had ever been in the armory, the soldiers had moved all of it out, and Kate understood why. The room was lit by the soft green glow of contramagic. Bottom Dweller crafters were busily at work on what Kate, in the dim light, at first took to be some sort of overlarge guns similar to swivel guns, only bigger.

Looking more closely, she realized what she was seeing.

"Green beam guns!" Kate exclaimed, scowling. "What are you doing with those?"

"Nothing, at the moment. That's the problem," said Franklin. "We need you to use the seventh sigil to make them operational."

Kate shook her head. "No, sir." Turning on her heel, she started to walk off.

"Private!" Franklin grabbed hold of her arm and yanked her around to face him. "Listen to me. We are trying to make them operational without the use of blood magic."

"You can do it without me!" Kate said angrily. "I won't touch them. Have Roberts or the Bottom Dwellers or someone else work on them."

"The other crafters do not have the needed skills," said Franklin. "The Bottom Dwellers can make them work without blood magic, but not very well. One of our crafters, Sergeant Huston, discovered that by combining the magic with the contramagic through the use of the seventh sigil, the weapon will work."

Kate cast the weapons a look of revulsion. "They are steeped in blood! Not to mention blood magic! I doubt if even the seventh sigil could remove that!"

"These guns have never been fired. No blood magic was ever used on them. Our supplier discovered this cache of weapons hidden in the Aligoes and offered them to the captain. Colonel Smythe is a God-fearing man. He inspected them and was convinced they were never used. Otherwise he would never have purchased them."

Franklin didn't name the supplier, but Kate could guess: Coreg. The dragon must have had dealings with the Bottom Dwellers who had terrorized the people of the Aligoes years ago during the war.

Kate conceded that it was possible Franklin was telling the truth. He was a Fundamentalist, a veteran soldier, and, as far as she could tell, earnest and sincere in his beliefs. Still, she wanted no part of this. Thomas would never sanction the use of such weapons, blood magic or no blood magic.

"I've seen what these guns can do!" Kate said. "They fire beams of contramagic that can sink a warship!"

"So can a broadside," said Franklin with grim exasperation. "What is the difference?"

Kate was confounded by that argument and chose to ignore it. "I heard how Huston died—"

"The sergeant's death was his own fault," Franklin said. "The fool was a crafter. He knew better than to be carrying a magic-enhanced pistol near a contramagic gun."

"Which makes such weapons ideal for a battlefield," Kate said scathingly.

"We are not planning to use them in battle. We only need one to work at the moment and we need it soon." Franklin was grim. "I have been patient with you thus far, but let me put this another way, Private. We are planning to set sail in a few days. If you want to sail with us, you will find a way to fix this weapon. Otherwise you can stay here and rot."

Kate saw that he was in earnest and she realized she had made a mistake. She should have been cooperative with him from the start. Now he was suspicious of her and might restrict her movements, refuse to allow her to leave the cave.

"I am sorry, sir," she said. "Those guns brought up some bad memories for me. What do you need me to do?"

Franklin eyed her grimly, clearly doubting her sudden change of heart.

"Come with me. I will show you what Huston was doing before he died."

He led her to a small chamber off the main cavern where a single green beam weapon had been mounted on a truck, like a cannon.

"Huston worked on this and, according to his theory, the magic and the contramagic combined with the seventh sigil should allow us to fire the weapon. Thus far, we have been unable to do so. He died before he had a chance to determine what was wrong."

Kate was loath to touch the gun, but Franklin was watching her and she had to convince him she was reliable.

"How is it supposed to work, sir?" Kate asked. "I don't understand the mechanics."

"The contramagic was the basic power source," Franklin explained. He indicated a brass disc set with a green crystal. "These crystal and brass discs were set with contramagic constructs charged with energy. The gunner would load the disc into the chamber of the weapon. They used blood magic to enhance and amplify the energy of the crystal disc. Huston theorized that the blood magic could be replaced by magic and the seventh sigil. The magic and contramagic would then combine to make both stronger. The power of God is stronger than the power of the Evil One."

Kate wondered if God appreciated his power being used on a weapon designed to kill. She kept that thought to herself. She studied Huston's magic and, despite herself, began to grow interested in his work, which was impressive.

"How are you planning to use this gun? You said it wasn't going to be needed in battle." Kate suddenly understood. "This is why you needed a black ship, isn't it! This operates like a pivot gun. The mountings for it are already in place on the foredeck. You are going to mount this on the black ship."

"I don't see what that has to do with getting it to work," said Franklin.

"There's nothing wrong with the magic on the green beam gun that I can see, sir," said Kate. "It's the magic around it."

She made an expansive gesture with her hands. "Look at this chamber, sir. The crafters who built it used magic to shape the walls and the ceiling, smooth the floor. They strengthened the pillars with magic. You could read a newspaper from the glow given off by the constructs. The strong magic inside the cavern is interfering with the more delicate magic of the seventh sigil."

Franklin was a channeler. He might not know anything about the seventh sigil, but he could see the myriad magical constructs that overlapped, intertwined, forming a complex web of magic that glowed above them, around them, and underneath their feet.

"We need to move the gun out of the cave," Kate added.

"I see," said Franklin, impressed. "Once it is away from the magic, you are saying it will work."

Kate had no idea if it would or it wouldn't. She had made up the theory on the spot.

"I'm not saying it will, sir. I don't know what Huston wanted this weapon to do. If I knew what he intended to use it for—"

"He intended for it to work," said Franklin dryly. "I will have the gun transported to the black ship."

He hurried off to give the orders. Kate was growing more and more troubled about this army. Franklin might claim the green beam gun was comparable to a cannon, but she knew better. A single beam of contramagic could be far more destructive than a broadside fired by the thirty-nine cannons of a ship of the line.

She would continue to try to find out. But at least now she had an excuse to leave the cave, and once outside, she could keep watch for Dalgren.

"As for this infernal gun," Kate said under her breath as she eyed the weapon with repugnance, "what I make, I can bloody well break."

FORTY-FIVE

Phillip arrived in Freya after a bitterly cold but otherwise unremarkable journey by griffinback. He bade farewell to the griffin on the outskirts of Haever, changed from his traveling clothes into clothing more suited to the persona he planned to adopt, and, gripping his valise, walked to the inn he had chosen for his stay.

The streets were crowded with people returning from work. He was jostled and knocked about on the sidewalk, almost run over by a wherry, and had to fend off the advances of an aggressive female who was determined he should spend the night with her and pay for the privilege. He left her screaming curses at him and reached for his pocket watch to check the time, only to encounter the small hand of a young pickpocket trying to steal it. The lad dashed off the moment he realized he had been caught. Phillip shouted after him, then found himself grinning.

He was home.

His joy was short-lived, tempered by the sobering thought that he would find no safe haven in his homeland. He was in far more danger here than he had been abroad.

He had selected his lodgings with care. He had a town house in Haever, but he avoided that, knowing that Sir Henry would be having it watched. He chose the Two Swans Inn because it was on the mail coach line, which meant there would be a steady stream of strangers coming and going. And no one was likely to recognize the wealthy Duke of Upper and Lower Milton among the corset salesmen, hostlers, and bootblacks.

The inn had another advantage of being located near Oak Hill Park, one of two royal parks in Haever, where he had arranged to meet Thomas. Unfortunately he had not taken into consideration the fact that Oak Hill Park was only a few blocks from the university and that he might run into Sophia. He had no way to contact Thomas, however, to change the location. At least they would be meeting in a secluded part of the park, away from the lanes and bridle paths.

Phillip walked to Oak Hill Park the next day, arriving an hour ahead of the time he had appointed to meet Thomas. Phillip sat down on the bench near the pond, opened the latest issue of the *Haever Gazette,* and waited. The newspaper served as excellent cover, for he could pretend to be absorbed in his reading, all the while keeping watch for Thomas.

Phillip had adopted the clothes and attitude of an idle young gentleman of no particular occupation, living above his means and hiding from his creditors. His suit coat was of good quality, but worn. The cuffs were frayed, his trousers shiny at the knees. His leather shoes had been mended. He knew his disguise had succeeded when the innkeeper eyed him distrustfully and demanded payment for a month's lodgings up front.

The news in the paper was grim: increasing unrest among the populace of Haever; people injured in rioting near the parliament building; members of the House of Nobles coming under attack; speeches denouncing the opposition, who gave their own speeches in return; bills being proposed; votes being taken. And so on and so forth, unending. No wonder young boys were reduced to stealing watches.

Phillip turned with relief to the back pages. He was pleased to see that the energetic Miss Amelia Nettleship was still writing stories about Captain Kate and her Dragon Corsairs. In this installment, Captain Kate was being held captive by an evil Guundaran count, who bore a remarkable resemblance to King Ullr.

The hour came and went with no sign of Thomas. After waiting another hour, Phillip folded his paper and departed. He returned the next day and the day after that. Thomas did not come and Phillip was starting to grow worried.

The fourth day, he took his place on the park bench and opened the paper. He was applauding Captain Kate, who had just kicked the evil count in the teeth, when he became aware of a man bundled in a greatcoat coming toward him. Phillip recognized Thomas despite the fact that a muffler covered the lower part of his face and a large hat concealed the upper. He walked slowly, giving the impression of a patient convalescing after a long illness, out for a restorative stroll.

Thomas took his seat on the bench a short distance from Phillip, who nodded as one does to a stranger, and continued reading the paper.

"You are late," Phillip observed. "Is everything all right?"

"Ran into foul weather," said Thomas. "I arrived the night before last, much to Sir Richard's relief. He was so thankful to see me he practically wept over me. I would have come here yesterday, but he was so alarmed at the thought of my venturing out of the house that I deemed it better to remain with him."

"How did you escape today?" Phillip asked, turning a page.

"He had to go to the House of Nobles. Once he was gone, I then had to dodge his manservant, Henshaw, who had been instructed to watch over me. A doting grandmama would not be more solicitous of my welfare," Thomas said, shaking his head.

"When is your meeting with the queen?"

"That is another problem," said Thomas.

"What? Is something wrong?" Phillip asked, looking up in alarm.

"Nothing is wrong. Her Majesty has left Haever. She has gone to her estate in Kerry," said Thomas. "The trip was unexpected. According to Sir Richard, the queen received news that her favorite male griffin had fallen ill. She breeds her griffins in Kerry, and she did not trust his care to anyone except herself. She is not expected to be gone long, but no one seems to know when she will return."

Thomas frowned. "Does Her Majesty do this sort of thing often? Run off to nursemaid a griffin?"

"She has been known to," said Phillip, smiling and lowering the paper. "Queen Mary is very fond of her griffins. To be fair, Thomas, Her Majesty did not know when you were coming. Sir Richard could not very well arrange the meeting with her until you were safely upon Freyan soil."

"I suppose you are right," said Thomas, sighing. "But the delay means I am left to the ministrations of Sir Richard. He is a fine fellow, but he acts as though I had flown down from heaven on angel's wings. I am not permitted to do anything for myself. He would have had his manservant cut my meat had I not rebelled. His conversation is dull in the extreme. He spent one hour expounding on the legal distinction between points of law as opposed to questions of fact."

"He can't be as bad as that," said Phillip.

"You have no idea," said Thomas darkly. "Sir Richard claims his wife is away on a visit, but I am convinced she died of wasting boredom and Henshaw buried her body in the garden."

Phillip started to laugh, stopped to stare at something up the hill, then suddenly dove behind his paper.

"What is wrong?" Thomas asked.

"Sophia and Sir Rodrigo!" Phillip whispered, agitated. "Have they seen me?"

"They have not, but Bandit has sniffed you out," said Thomas. "He is running toward us. Stay hidden. Sophia is calling him to come back. And, of course, he is not listening. She is running after him. I am afraid you are soon to be discovered."

Phillip groaned. "Leave before they see *you*! Go back to Sir Richard's."

"Let me know what happens," said Thomas. "I will take a stroll in the garden after dinner."

"Yes, yes! Now go!" Phillip ordered.

Thomas pulled his hat low and departed in haste, heading for the grove of oak trees on a hillock that had given the park its name.

Bandit jumped on Phillip, claiming him as a friend.

"Bandit!" Sophia scolded. "Come off that gentleman. You do not know him!"

Phillip leaned down to the pet the dog as an excuse to keep his face concealed. All the while, he was watching Rodrigo, who was gazing after Thomas with a frown.

"I believe I know that gentleman—" Rodrigo began.

"Sophia, Sir Rodrigo!" Phillip exclaimed, springing to his feet. "What a nice surprise."

Sophia gasped in astonishment. "Phillip! Is that you?"

"He might be. Or he might not be," said Rodrigo with a quirk of his eyebrow. He cast another glance at Thomas, who was disappearing beyond the hill, then gave Phillip a knowing smile.

Turning to Sophia, Rodrigo added gravely, "We should leave, my dear. The duke is undoubtedly here on a secret mission and we do not want to reveal him to his enemies."

"Nothing so dramatic as that, I am afraid, sir," said Phillip, laughing.

He doffed his hat. Sophia gave him her hand to kiss. She was wearing a fur-lined cape over her dress, while Rodrigo had adopted the long flowing black gown with the blue silk hood that denoted a professor of crafting. They were accompanied by two servants: a lady's maid carrying a sketchbook, pencil box, and a blanket; and a male servant encumbered with a picnic basket.

"Who was that gentleman in the muffler?" Rodrigo asked. "Something about him seems familiar."

Phillip shrugged. "I have no idea. He asked if he could share the bench, sat for a few moments as though recovering his breath, and then departed."

Rodrigo gave Phillip a shrewd, perceptive, glittering look, accompanied by an airy smile. The look said, "I know you are lying." The smile added, "But I have lied in my day and I understand."

Phillip turned to Sophia. "What brings you to the park, Your Highness?"

"My magic tutor has told me to take up drawing, and I am here to sketch the oaks," said Sophia, making a face. "She maintains that transferring what I observe from my brain to the paper helps to concentrate the mind and makes me attentive to detail, thus improving my crafting ability."

"I know that I find transferring a glass of wine from the bottle to my mouth improves my powers of concentration immeasurably," said Rodrigo. "Speaking of wine," he added, turning to the servants, "go spread the blanket over there in the sunshine and open the bottle. The red needs to breathe.

"Now that they are gone, we may speak freely," Rodrigo added. "Why are you furtively lurking about the park in that dreadful suit, Your Grace?"

"Rigo, you must not interrogate His Grace!" said Sophia.

"I don't mind answering your question, my lord," said Phillip. "I received a letter from my banker saying I had to come to resolve matters regarding my estate. I am doing nothing more sinister than signing a few papers and yawning over account books."

"Still, you are in peril," said Sophia, regarding him with concern. "You have made a great many enemies by supporting Thomas."

"I am taking precautions," said Phillip. "Thus this dreadful suit. Please do not worry about me."

They walked up to the top of the hill. The servant had opened the wine and was taking crystal glasses from the basket.

"Will you join us, Your Grace?" Rodrigo asked.

Phillip would have liked nothing better than to spend the morning lounging beside Sophia, drinking wine and admiring her sketches. The hour was nearing noon, however, and more people would be coming to the park. Phillip did not dare risk being recognized by anyone else.

"Thank you, my lord, but I have an appointment with my banker."

"Will I see you again?" Sophia asked softly.

Phillip reluctantly shook his head. "I do not think that would be a good idea."

"Of course, you are right," said Sophia. "Please take care of yourself."

She gave him her hand. Her fingers tightened over his. He remembered the Trundler good-luck charm she had once magically inscribed on his palm. He gently released her hand, bade farewell to Rodrigo, and walked away.

The oaks' dead leaves rustled beneath his feet.

The next time I see her, Phillip said to himself, she will be Thomas's wife.

———

Thomas returned to Sir Richard's house—a staid and stately old building the walls of which were so thickly covered by moss and ivy it was almost impossible to see the brick beneath. The house had been built during the reign of King Oswald II, when the Wallace family's fortunes were on the mend.

Trees surrounded the mansion and a wall surrounded the trees, hiding the house from the street and muffling the noise of the world outside. Thick intertwined branches cast deep shadows that plunged the house in gloom during even the brightest day. Shade-loving plants grew thick beneath the trees, almost covering the stone walkway that led to the front door.

A cab dropped off Thomas at the gate. He paid the fare, then opened the gate that creaked from disuse and walked through with a sigh. The house was always dark and always silent. The servants trod softly and rarely spoke. Sometimes, the only sound Thomas heard for hours was the ticking of the clock on the mantelpiece.

Henshaw opened the door before Thomas could lift his hand to knock.

"We are glad to see you safe, Your Highness," said Henshaw. "His Lordship has been extremely worried."

"I am sorry to have been the cause of any concern," said Thomas, unwinding the muffler and divesting himself of his hat and cloak. "Where is Sir Richard?"

"His Lordship is in the study," Henshaw replied.

Thomas walked the darkened halls, following Henshaw. After a barely heard knock, Henshaw quietly opened the door to the study to announce Thomas's safe return.

Sir Richard Wallace was in his fifties, tall and thin. He was going bald, but scorned to wear a wig. His most prominent feature was the Wallace family beaked, aquiline nose. He had been accustomed to employing the same tailor for thirty years and he was proud to claim that his choice of cut and style and fabric had not changed in all that time.

He gave every appearance of dull, staid respectability and only a very few knew that this dull, gray man was leading a double life, belonging to a secret society known as the Faithful, dedicated to restoring the heir of James I to the throne.

Richard rose to his feet, grave and relieved. "Your Highness, I am glad to see you safe. You gave us a fright, disappearing like that without a word. We have all been extremely worried."

"I felt the need for fresh air and exercise and I took a walk, sir," said Thomas, trying to keep the impatience from his voice. He resented being scolded like a truant schoolboy. "I was not gone above an hour."

"Leaving the house for even a moment is unwise, sir, as I have endeavored to impress upon you. The streets are not safe."

Richard removed his spectacles to regard Thomas with a faint smile. "You are young, with the energy and restlessness of youth. I know you must find me a stodgy old fussbudget, but you must realize that you can no longer think only of yourself. You have a duty to your people, to your nation."

"Have you heard any news of the queen?" Thomas asked, changing the subject.

"She remains in Kerry," said Richard, adding dryly, "We must hope the griffin is recovering. I know you find the wait tedious."

He replaced his spectacles and picked up a large, heavy tome. "I found an excellent account of the Cousins War, starting with the reign of your esteemed ancestor, Frederick I, and concluding with the fall of King James. I borrowed it from the library at my club. I sought it out following our conversation at dinner last night when you expressed a wish to know more about the family history."

"Thank you, sir," said Thomas, regarding the massive book with dismay. "I look forward to reading it."

"And I have the morning edition of the *Haever Gazette*. I asked the maid to light a fire in the library for your convenience. I will be attending a debate in the House that will go on for hours. I have left orders with Henshaw to obtain anything you should desire."

Thomas accepted the book and the newspaper, which was the same one Phillip had been reading. Henshaw marched him to the library and left him there. Thomas was surprised he didn't lock him inside.

The library was as dark and gloomy as the rest of the house and was filled with law books. The fire struggled to combat the chill.

He placed the book on a table, sat down in a chair, and opened the newspaper to the back. The first article he saw was the lurid account of Captain Kate escaping from the clutches of the evil count by crawling out her prison window and nimbly climbing down a knotted bedsheet.

Thomas could so clearly see Kate in another prison, lifting her eyes to his in fear and despair, then hope and wonder. He remembered her shaved head, the guard's boots that were too big for her, the cut on her foot . . . He remembered holding her in his arms . . .

He stood up and flung the paper into the fire, causing it to instantly flare up so that he feared for a moment he had started a conflagration. The flames consumed the paper quickly, however, and went back to licking the wood.

Thomas picked up the book that told the story of his ancestors: Frederick, who had been deposed by a younger brother and gone meekly to his tower; numerous Oswalds who had at least shown some spirit by fighting for their crowns, and ending with poor, weak James, whose one accomplishment in life appeared to have been dying a hero, though he had certainly not lived as one.

Thomas settled down resolutely to read.

Henshaw waited a moment with his ear to the door, to make certain that Thomas was not going to try to bolt. Hearing the rustle of the newspaper, Henshaw was satisfied and returned to Richard, who was waiting for him in the study.

"What is your report?" he asked

"I followed His Highness to Oak Hill Park, where he went to meet someone, my lord," Henshaw said.

Richard frowned. "Do you know who?"

"The person made an attempt to disguise himself, but I recognized your brother's agent—His Grace, Phillip Masterson."

"He has duped Thomas into trusting him," said Richard. "His arrival in Haever proves that the duke is still doing my brother's dirty work. He would not dare to return otherwise. Undoubtedly he and Henry are plotting to lure the prince into some sort of trap. Were you able to overhear their conversation?"

"I regret to say I could not, my lord," Henshaw replied. "Masterson chose the place for their meeting in a secluded area of the park. They did not speak long, and their conversation was interrupted by the arrival of the Princess Sophia and a friend of the Countess de Marjolaine, Sir Rodrigo de Villeneuve."

"Good God!" Richard was alarmed. "Did they recognize the prince? Speak to him? Her Highness would be discreet, but de Villeneuve is a rattlebrained gossip!"

"Prince Thomas had the presence of mind to hurry away before they saw him, my lord," said Henshaw. "I saw him get into a cab and heard him give the driver this address. Knowing he was safe, I followed Masterson to his inn. We now know where he is staying."

"Excellent. We must keep him under surveillance."

"I took the liberty of doing so, my lord. I contacted the usual agency you hire in such circumstances. Their people are on the job. Will you tell His Highness?"

"It would do no good," said Richard bitterly. "I attempted to convince the marchioness that Thomas should have nothing to do with the duke, but she is blinded by his wealth and prestige, just as Thomas is blinded by his professions of loyalty and friendship."

"His Grace is very clever, my lord."

Richard sat down at his desk, drew forth a sheet of paper, picked up a pen and dipped it in the inkwell.

"Prepare yourself for a journey to Bheldem, Henshaw. I promised His Highness I would say nothing to his mother, but his safety is of paramount importance. I must take matters into my own hands."

FORTY-SIX

Queen Mary had grown up in Kerry Court, the royal family's country estate located in Kerrington among the rolling foothills of the Glenharris Mountains. She and her younger sister, Elinor, had spent idyllic summers here in the care of their governess, happy to escape the heat of Haever and the hotter quarrels that resounded throughout the palace.

King Godfrey had been involved in a very public affair with a married woman, fathering two sons by her. His wife, Queen Jane, had not suffered in silence. She had loudly vented her fury on her husband, trying to shame and humiliate him in the vain hope that he would end the affair.

Godfrey had made it plain that he wanted nothing to do with his wife or his daughters. The girls felt abandoned by their father and found no comfort in their mother, for she attempted to turn them against him. Queen Mary had once confided in Henry that she had preferred Godfrey's cold dislike to her mother's querulous complaints and screaming rages.

Mary loved Kerry and had chosen to live here following her marriage, prior to becoming queen. Her only son, Jonathan, had been born here. She had built eyries for her racing griffins here, and lavished care and attention upon them. Her griffins were admired by racing enthusiasts the world over; their young fetched high prices.

The queen's illness was still a closely held secret, and when she had collapsed three nights ago, her confidential secretary had transported her in the dead of night to Kerry for treatment. Henry had approved the decision. The servants at Kerry had been with Mary since childhood and were incredibly loyal. When Henry told the press that the queen was in Kerry to minister to one of her beloved griffins, no one questioned the veracity of the story.

Mary was attended by the Royal Physician, Dr. Broughton, and the Royal Healer, Sister Hope. The two put aside professional jealousies to work together, using all their powers—science, faith, and magic—to try to save their patient.

Henry had been roused in the night by the news. He had rushed to the estate and had remained here in case he was needed. This morning, a week after the queen had fallen ill, he ate a solitary breakfast with little appetite, then lingered over his tea as he read the paper.

His first concern was to make certain that the reporters had no idea of the truth. This done, he had little care for any other news and he threw the paper aside. He sat gazing out at the green hills and denuded trees, black lace against a cloudless steely blue autumnal sky, and waited in dread for news.

The day before the queen had fallen ill, Mary had sent Henry a message saying she had made her decision about the succession and asked him to come to the palace the following day to discuss it. That night, she had lapsed into unconsciousness and she had been too ill to speak to him ever since. He fully expected her to name Elinor as his future queen. He had already written his letter of resignation.

Henry was genuinely grieved to think of his world without Mary. He had known her for many years and he would miss having her berate him, cajole him, exasperate and confound him. She was far more than his queen. She was a dearly loved friend and he had no idea what he would do with himself when she was gone.

Henry picked up his teacup, absently took a drink, only to discover he had let it grow cold. He grimaced and was about to ring for hot water when Dr. Broughton entered the room. The physician was gray with fatigue, for he had slept very little.

"Good morning, my lord." Dr. Broughton looked about vaguely. "If it is morning. I am not certain. I have lost track of time."

"I will ring for more tea," said Henry. "How is Her Majesty?"

Dr. Broughton gave a weary smile. "The crisis is past. The problem is with her heart, not the tumor. Her Majesty is weak, but she is conscious and resting comfortably."

"Thank God! When will you allow me to speak to her?" Henry asked.

"You may do so now, although against my better judgment," said the doctor. "I advised rest and quiet, but, of course, Her Majesty refuses to listen to me. Do not stay long, my lord, and try not to antagonize her."

"I will do my best," said Henry with a faint smile.

"I must warn you to prepare yourself, my lord. Her Majesty survived this attack. She will not survive the next. The malignancy is spreading."

Henry did not trust himself to speak. He gave a brief nod and departed.

An old servant ushered Henry into the queen's bedchamber. The curtains had been drawn and the windows closed, leaving the room dark and hushed and stuffy, smelling of sickness and some herbal remedy Sister Hope had concocted.

Queen Mary lay at ease in the enormous four-poster bed, propped up among a mountain of pillows. Sister Hope stood beside the queen, taking her pulse.

Mary was exceedingly pale. She seemed to Henry to have aged years. Her plump cheeks sagged, and her eyes were bruised and sunken. She still retained her indomitable spirit, however. Always a proud woman, she had taken time to prepare herself to receive visitors. She wore a lacy cap over her braided gray hair and a brightly colored silk dressing gown, with a woolen shawl around her shoulders.

She was fondly watching the monkey Jo-Jo gambol about the bed, performing his one trick, which was a little bobbing bow, in return for grapes. Sister Hope had ordered the servants to bring the monkey to the queen's bedside, saying that animal energies had healing benefits. Henry doubted this was true, but, seeing the queen smile at the monkey's antics, he could almost admit to liking the annoying little creature.

His moment of tender feeling did not last long.

Jo-Jo caught sight of Henry, gave a shrill shriek, and scrambled up the bed curtains. The monkey crouched on top of one of the bedposts, chittering at Henry and refusing Sister Hope's attempts to persuade him to come down.

The queen laughed, but her laughter ended in a gasping cough. Sister Hope gave her a drink of a posset and Mary breathed easier. She lay back among the pillows.

Henry advanced quietly, walking with slow and measured tread so as not to disturb her.

"For mercy's sake, Henry, step a bit livelier," Mary ordered peevishly. "You are not following our casket to the graveyard. Not yet, at any rate."

She coughed again and motioned for Sister Hope to give her a drink of the posset and to help her sit up.

"You may leave now, Sister," said Mary. "We need to speak to Sir Henry in private."

Sister Hope flashed a cautionary look at Henry as she passed him. "No more than ten minutes, my lord."

"Shut the door, Henry," said Mary.

Henry did so and returned to her side, trying to ignore Jo-Jo, who was jumping up and down on top of the bedpost and screeching.

"Now open that window," said Mary. "We need sunlight and fresh air."

"Your Majesty, I don't think that would be wise—"

"Do as you are told, Henry," Mary said, wagging her finger at him. "And while you are at it, dump out that green mess that is stinking up the room."

Henry drew aside the curtains and opened the window a crack, letting in the crisp, cool air. He did not empty the pot of steaming herbs, not choosing to brave the wrath of Sister Hope, but he did remove it to a far corner of the bedchamber.

Mary called to Jo-Jo and bribed him with grapes to come down from the bedpost. The monkey regarded Henry with intense dislike and Henry returned the favor.

"We trust you would like us to have him removed," said Mary with a smile.

"If Your Majesty would be so kind," said Henry.

The queen rang for the old servant, who took Jo-Jo away, still screeching imprecations at Henry. Mary propped herself up among the pillows, waving away offers of assistance. She pointed to a chair by her bedside.

"Sit down, Henry. We have much to discuss."

As Henry drew up the chair, he saw Mary grimace, suck in a sharp breath, and clench her fists.

"Should I summon the doctor?" Henry asked anxiously.

Mary shook her head. He stood at her bedside, feeling helpless, his heart wrung with grief to see her suffering. The spasm eased. The queen gave a shivering sigh.

Henry took his seat by her bedside. "The sister can give you something for the pain, ma'am."

"Laudanum," said Mary, grimacing. "Muddles the wits and we need a clear head. We need to discuss the matter of our heir."

"This can wait until you are stronger, ma'am," said Henry. "The doctor assures me that you are going to make a full recovery—"

"Pish-tosh, Henry! For a spymaster, you are a dreadful liar!" Mary snorted. "Be quiet and listen. We have made our decision regarding our heir. Our attorneys have drawn up the paperwork so that all is legal. Hand me that dispatch pouch."

Henry did as she ordered, handing over the leather pouch. Mary opened it, drew out a letter, and gave it to Henry. The letter was sealed shut with the royal seal. The outside bore his name and the words "To Be Opened After My Death," along with the queen's signature. Henry turned the letter over in his hands.

"Are you going to tell me your decision, ma'am?" he asked quietly.

"No, we are not," said Mary, fixing him with a stern eye. "We have a few matters left to resolve. We can always change our minds. We just wanted you to know in case this damn malignancy carries us off before we are ready."

"I accept your desire to keep the matter confidential, ma'am," said Henry, choosing his words carefully, "although I venture to suggest that my knowing in advance would be extremely helpful in making the requisite arrangements—"

"Why would you need to do that, Henry?" Mary asked with a glint of mischief in her eyes. "According to you, we will be making a full recovery."

Henry was silent, pressed his lips together.

"Now don't sulk, Henry," said Mary, giving his hand a playful slap. She then clasped her hand over his. "You have served us well and faithfully for many years, dear friend. We could not have asked for a more loyal and devoted servant."

Henry swallowed, unable to speak, and muttered something about the damn herbs clogging his windpipe.

"We ask you . . ." Mary paused, then amended her words. "*I* ask you as a friend, Henry. Be the same devoted servant to your new monarch."

Henry recalled his own letter lying in his desk drawer. "In truth, I was thinking of retiring from public service, Your Majesty. I am no longer a young man. Lady Ann complains that I am never home. I must oversee young Henry's schooling . . ."

"Do this for me, Henry," Mary said softly. Her voice was ragged with fatigue, pinched with pain, yet her grip on him was firm. She sat up straight, drew near him. "Or, if not for me, then do this for your country. You have devoted your life to Freya, Henry. Do not abandon her when she will need you most."

Henry thought of Elinor. He clasped the letter and gave a bleak sigh. "Very well, ma'am."

"Give me your word, Henry," Mary urged, pressing him. "I know you and I know that once you give your word, you will not break it."

"I give you my word, ma'am," said Henry.

He brought her hand to his lips, then gently rested her hand down upon the silken coverlet.

"Thank you, Henry," said Mary, sinking back among the pillows. "The doctor assures us we will be fit to travel within a week's time. Make the arrangements for our journey and then go home to Lady Ann and the children. We will send for you if we have need."

Mary closed her eyes, her strength exhausted. "Close the window. There is a decided draught. And send for Sister Hope."

Henry did as she asked, closing the window and drawing the curtains to darken the room. The queen appeared to sleep. Henry paused by the door to take out his handkerchief, wipe his nose and try to compose himself.

"You have my word, Your Majesty," he repeated.

FORTY-SEVEN

Franklin spoke to his superior, Captain Martin, about Kate's idea to move the green beam weapon outside the cavern so that the magical constructs on the walls did not interfere with the contramagic on the gun.

"We might as well go ahead and haul the weapon to the ship," Franklin added. "We have to do that anyway."

Martin agreed. Soldiers loaded the weapon into a wagon and drove it to the black ship, which was tethered to the dock. Kate at last found out what was contained in those two large crates: the crystal discs that were apparently the ammunition and spare parts for the green beam weapons. The gun was to be mounted on a carriage affixed to a rotating platform on the forecastle. The rotating platform allowed for a wide field of fire.

Franklin oversaw the work. The gun was heavy and awkward to lift, and mounting it on the carriage proved difficult, for neither he nor any of the sailors knew how the gun had been fitted into the carriage. The Bottom Dwellers had little knowledge of the weapon; most had been too young during the war to have served on board the black ships.

The Freyan sailors had been forced to guess how it was to be mounted. Judging by their dark looks and mutterings, they were not much happier than Kate about working with the heinous weapon. They did as they were ordered, however, not wanting to risk a flogging or the threat of being left behind.

While Kate worked, she kept a hopeful watch on the sky for Dalgren, and a nervous watch around camp for Trubgek. She did not see either one, but she had the uneasy impression Trubgek was lurking somewhere, watching her. She eventually grew weary of searching the shadows, and tried to forget about him. She had other worries.

The crew had reached an impasse trying to attach the weapon to the rotating platform. Franklin talked about returning the gun to the cave. Kate couldn't allow that to happen. But the gun seemed to crouch on the platform like some evil beast, mocking her by stubbornly refusing to lock into place.

"Swearing at it won't help," Franklin told Kate impatiently. "Neither does standing around staring at it."

"'When all else fails, hit it with a hammer,'" said Kate, quoting one of Olaf's favorite sayings.

She did not have a hammer, but the blunt edge of an axe proved a convenient substitute. Before Franklin could stop her, she grabbed the axe and gave the gun truck a whack. The weapon dropped into place.

Franklin shook his head over her methods, but he was pleased to report to the captain that the gun had been successfully mounted on the foredeck. Martin ordered him to test it, see if it worked.

"The captain wants us to test it," Franklin told Kate the next day.

"Are you sure that is wise, sir?" Kate asked nervously. "We don't want to set the woods ablaze."

"The firing mechanism should work without using ammunition," he replied, referring to the brass and crystal discs.

"What is the firing mechanism?" asked Kate.

Franklin indicated a complicated construct, an elaborate knotwork of magic enscribed on the barrel near the breech.

"According to Huston, this construct should glow when the weapon is charged and ready to fire," he said. "As you can see, it remains dark."

Kate studied the magic on the gun and shook her head. "The constructs covering the weapon are all breaking down. You can see the fading constructs on the crystal rods and here on the brass muzzle. Huston used the seventh sigil, but it's not working. I can't figure out why."

"You had better," said Franklin grimly. "Captain Martin does not tolerate failure."

Franklin had to return to his other duties, but he assigned a corporal named Jennings to assist her.

"The corporal is a channeler. He says he might be able to help," Franklin told her.

"Do you know anything about the seventh sigil, sir?" Kate asked Jennings. He shook his head.

"Then you won't be of much use," Kate said, but she said it beneath her breath, guessing that Jennings was not here to help her, but to keep a watchful eye on her.

The corporal perched himself on a camp stool beside the gun. He was a nondescript young man of medium height, going prematurely bald. He wore spectacles and looked more like a clerk than a soldier.

"Jennings . . ." Kate tried to think where she had heard his name and suddenly remembered. "You traveled with that fellow they call Weasel. He's a strange one. Where did you dig him up? Out of a molehill?"

Jennings blinked at her from behind his spectacles. "I am here to observe, not to engage in idle gossip."

"I haven't seen Weasel around lately," Kate said, trying again. "Do you know where he went? Did he leave?"

"He might have," said Jennings. "We traveled here by griffin and the beasts were ordered to remain in case of need."

Kate was elated. Trubgek must have departed. She went back to her work in better spirits, able to concentrate on studying the magic.

The crafting involved connecting the seventh sigil to the contramagic constructs already in place on the weapon, then adding magic constructs that mirrored the contramagic. The seventh sigil was necessary, for without it the contramagic would destroy the magic. The use of the seventh sigil caused the two halves to work together, with the result that the energy of the whole far exceeded the energy of the two halves. Or at least that was how it was supposed to work.

"What does this construct do?" Jennings asked, pointing.

"That's the seventh sigil," Kate said. She looked at it more closely. "Mirror image . . ."

She left the forecastle and ran down the stairs that led below deck.

"Where are you going?" Jennings demanded.

"To find the answer," said Kate.

She went into her cabin and eventually located de Villenuve's book on the seventh sigil under her cot. She carried it back up on deck with her. Jennings had summoned Franklin, who was waiting for her with a displeased expression on his face.

"I know what's wrong, sir," Kate said, before he could open his mouth. "Was Huston self-taught in magic? Never mind. It doesn't matter." She pointed to an illustration in the book. "He was using the mirror image of the seventh sigil, not the actual sigil. The mirror image worked to combine the magic and the contramagic, but not very well. The contramagic weakened the magic, which began to break down."

"I hope you are right, Private," said Franklin.

Kate began her repairs on the weapon. She kept an eye out for Dalgren, but eventually gave up watching when clouds rolled down from the mountains. Mists twined around the trees and dripped off the pine needles. If he was searching for her from the air, he wouldn't be able to find her, and she wouldn't be able to see him.

The next day the wind shifted. The clouds vanished and the sun shone brightly. Kate kept an eye on the sky as she repaired the magic. The work was incredibly delicate and often frustrating, for if she made a mistake with the seventh sigil—as Huston had done—the contramagic would seep through it and devour the construct before she could stop it. She would have to start over. And she had to repair innumerable constructs.

Despite the clear sky, she saw no sign of Dalgren again that day and she began to worry that he had been injured or had completely lost track of her. The next day dawned clear and bright. Kate and the ever-present Jennings began work early.

Franklin came out daily to inspect her work. He could see for himself that the constructs were starting to glow again and he was pleased. Kate's only worry now was that she would be finished in a day or two and she had still seen no sign of Dalgren.

That afternoon, she was down on her knees, stringing together a row of magical constructs, not paying attention to the sky, when Jennings said suddenly, "There's a dragon."

Kate stood up so fast she made herself dizzy.

Soldiers and sailors working to load supplies onto the troop ships stopped their tasks to stare. The dragon was Dalgren. Kate knew him by the dangling foreleg, the twisted horn on his head, the way he flew.

"No need to stand there gaping at the beast, Private," Jennings told Kate irritably. "Dragons live around here. We see them occasionally when they go out hunting. We were alarmed at first, but they are Travian, not Rosian. They leave us in peace and we do not bother them."

Dalgren flew nearer. The troops continued to watch him, glad for a break in their routine. Dalgren was careful to pay no attention to the humans gathered below. He swooped above the treetops in large, lazy circles as though hunting for deer. From his vantage point, he would be able to clearly see the black ship tethered to the dock. He would be watching for a signal.

Kate untied the red kerchief from around her neck. She flapped it several times in the air as though to shake out the creases, then let it flutter in the breeze.

"What are you doing?" Jennings demanded.

"Sorry, sir, but the beast makes me nervous," Kate offered in apology, using the kerchief to wipe her face. "Do you know what they use this gun for?"

"Only the captain and commander know the target," Jennings grunted. "Stop wasting time and get back to your duties."

Kate tied the kerchief around her neck again and went back to work, all the while watching Dalgren. He ducked his head and dipped his wings, letting her know he had seen her. He made another sweeping circle, then flew back out into the Breath.

"Good news, sir," Kate told Franklin that afternoon when he came to make his inspection. "The gun is ready to test. We could do so tomorrow, if you'd like."

Franklin was pleasantly surprised. "Captain Martin will be pleased. We will schedule the test for early morning. He will want to witness it."

"We shouldn't fire the gun around here, sir," Kate warned. "I have no idea how the magic will work. It might not work at all or we might burn down the forest. We should take the ship out into the Breath."

"A sensible precaution," Franklin agreed. "And that will allow us to train the ship's crew in the use of the weapon."

The *Naofa* set sail the next morning with Captain Martin on board along with the crew and some of the Bottom Dwellers. Wearing their smoke-colored spectacles, they still kept to the shadows and squinted in the bright sunlight.

The ship neared the entrance to the harbor and then slowed its speed. Kate did not see Dalgren, but she was confident he was out there somewhere. Now that he had discovered her location, he would take up residence nearby and keep watch.

"Signal the soldiers at the gun emplacements," Franklin ordered Kate. "Ask if there are any other ships in the vicinity."

Kate laid out the signal flags and then sent them up.

The soldiers raised flags in turn.

"They say they don't understand, sir," Kate reported.

Franklin glanced up at the flags Kate had sent up.

"That's the wrong flag," he told Kate.

"Sorry, sir," Kate said.

The first flags had been a private signal to Dalgren, telling him to meet her tonight. Kate replaced them with the correct flags.

The ship cautiously emerged from the hidden harbor into the Breath and set sail up the deserted coastline. Martin and Franklin observed the landscape through spyglasses, searching for a suitable site to test-fire the weapon.

At last they found what they wanted, seemingly, for Franklin ordered the helmsman to reverse the airscrews, slow the ship's flight, and then steer the vessel so that the weapon, which was mounted on the forecastle, was aimed at the side of a cliff.

Kate did not see how firing at such an enormous target was going to prove anything. When training her own gun crews, she would launch barrels tethered to small balloons and then order the gun crews to try to blast them out of the sky. They had to make allowances for the wind, the movement of the ship, and a host of other factors in order to hit a target that was bobbing up and down in the sky.

The cliff was miles long and standing still.

Franklin climbed the forecastle to fire the gun. He took his time, loading one of the green crystal discs into the breech, sighting in on his target, adjusting the weapon, taking careful aim.

Kate knew in theory how the weapon should work. Provided her magic worked, firing it was relatively simple. The constructs set in the disc stored a large amount of contramagic energy. When activated, the constructs set into the barrel of the weapon enhanced, channeled, and magnified that energy. She fidgeted nervously, wanting him to get on with it, not liking the thought of what could happen to her if the gun failed.

Franklin fired the weapon. The green beam struck the rock, sending chunks of stone flying, blowing a sizable hole in the cliff face.

Franklin straightened, looked at Martin, who nodded his approval, then ordered the ship to sail over to inspect the hole they had blown in the cliff. Both were impressed at the extent of the damage.

Franklin fired the weapon several more times after that, adjusting the range. Every time he fired, the ship would sail back to the wall and he and Martin would study the results.

Eventually Martin ordered the ship to return to camp. He and Franklin were in an extremely good mood. As they drew near the gun emplacements, Franklin ordered Kate to send up the flags to spell out the same mysterious signal: *Talionis*.

"That has special significance this day," Martin said, grinning.

"Indeed it does, sir," Franklin replied.

The ship sailed into the harbor and the crew tethered it to the dock. Kate lingered on deck, choosing her moment to approach Franklin when everyone else had left the ship.

"Could I speak to you, sir?" Kate asked.

"Of course, Private," said Franklin. "You have done good work. Captain Martin is thinking of promoting you."

"Thank you, sir," said Kate. "I would like your permission to remain on board, continue working. I need to make some refinements to the magic on the green beam gun."

Franklin frowned. "I see no reason why. The weapon worked well."

"Yes, but for how long, sir?" Kate argued. "The connection between the magic and the contramagic is tenuous. You've seen for yourself how contramagic starts to degrade the magic. If the seventh sigil fails, the contramagic will eat through the magic, and at that point, I don't know if I could fix it. I would like to find a way to strengthen the bond between the two."

He regarded her narrowly. "I think you should leave well enough alone."

Kate shrugged. "Suit yourself, sir. You know best how critical this weapon is to your plans. If the magic fails . . ."

Franklin was silent, eyeing her, thinking.

"Very well," he said finally. "I have to meet with Captain Martin now. You can work on it tomorrow."

"Begging your pardon, sir, but the contramagic could be destroying the magic on every single construct on that gun this very moment," said Kate. "If we do nothing until morning, I might have to start all over again and that would take days of repair work. If it could be repaired at all by that time."

Franklin hesitated.

"I can show you what I'm talking about, sir," Kate offered.

"I have no time. Carry on by yourself, then," Franklin said grudgingly. "Remember that the gates close at dusk. No one will be around to let you back inside."

"Yes, sir," said Kate. "Where is Corporal Jennings?"

"He has other duties. I will check your work first thing in the morning."

Franklin left the ship and Kate sighed in relief, glad to be rid of Jennings. She climbed the stairs to the forecastle to inspect the green beam gun. The constructs had degraded after use; a natural occurrence, nothing alarming. Quite the opposite. The seventh sigil appeared to strengthen the magic, reduce the possibility of wear and tear. But if Franklin had accepted her offer to inspect the gun, Kate could have pointed out the deterioration to him.

She was working on the magic when she saw Franklin emerge from the cave in company with Jennings. Kate wondered if Franklin had changed his mind and was coming to inflict Jennings on her.

Franklin paid no attention to her, however. Jennings gave an earsplitting whistle. Within a few moments, a griffin appeared, flying down from the mountains.

The beast landed on the dock, not far from the *Naofa*. Jennings entered a warehouse and emerged with a saddle and bridle, which he proceeded to strap onto the griffin.

"Here is my report to Colonel Smythe. God grant you a safe journey,

Corporal," Franklin said, handing over a leather pouch. "We leave in a few days for Haever. We will meet you there."

"Yes, sir. Thank you, sir." Jennings took the leather pouch and placed it in one of his saddlebags, then put on his helm and mounted the griffin. Franklin watched until he was gone, then returned to the cavern.

"Haever!" Kate said exultantly.

She had been wondering about their destination and now she knew. Once the black ship arrived in Haever, she would have an easy time escaping, lose herself in the crowded city. She did wonder how they would hide a black ship in Haever, but that wasn't her problem.

The sun began to set, and shadows lengthened. She heard the clang as the sentries closed the gates for the night and grinned.

She went below, sat down on her bed and tried not to think about how hungry she was, for she was missing dinner.

When the darkness deepened, she went back up on deck. The stars were out. A sliver of moon began to rise, but then the clouds rolled in again. Moon and stars vanished.

Kate was not concerned about being missed. No one ever bothered to check on her once lights were out.

She put on her peacoat, for the night was growing cold, then lit a dark lantern and paced the deck, waiting for Dalgren. Every so often, Kate opened the dark lantern, aimed it at the sky, and flashed it three times short and three times long.

The lookouts stationed with the gun emplacements across the harbor might see her signal, but she didn't think that risk was too great. If the lookouts were even still awake, they would be keeping watch on the Breath, not back in the harbor.

The troop ships rode at anchor at the end of the wharf. Each had a skeleton crew on board, but they had orders not to show a light, for fear a passing ship would see it. They would have set a watch, but not one of great vigilance; no one here thought they had anything to fear.

She heard Dalgren before she saw him. She heard his rasping breath and the creak of his wings and she smelled the faint smell of sulfur that always clung to him. He seemed disembodied, for all she could make out in the gloom were his eyes and his snout. He was aware of the sailors standing watch and he had dived down below the surface of the Breath and was flying up from beneath the ship.

His head was now about even with the keel. Kate leaned over the rail to talk to him.

"I'm glad to see you," she said. "But you shouldn't have come after me.

You could have died in the Aurora. You should have stayed in Dunlow, earned back your name."

"You said it yourself, we stand together," Dalgren returned, lifting himself until he was level with her. "I knew you'd land yourself in some sort of trouble."

Kate cast a worried glance at the troop ships. They were dark, silent.

"I was going to save the young people, but they didn't want saving," she said. "What will you do about your name?"

"While I was Below, Father Jacob took me to Droal's Cairn. Droal was a dragon who was killed during the war, fighting to save people who didn't want saving," said Dalgren. "I didn't want saving because I was angry and I didn't think—deep down—that I did anything wrong. I understand now that I fled because I *was* a coward. I didn't have guts enough to stay to fight for my beliefs. I can earn my name back anywhere, Kate. The only one who can save me is myself."

"With maybe a little help from a friend," said Kate, smiling.

"It appears my friend is the one who needs the help," said Dalgren. "What are you doing here? Are these people holding you prisoner? Do you need me to help you escape?"

"I was going to ask you, but now I've decided to stay."

Dalgren grunted and cast a glowering glance at the green beam weapon. "What are they planning to do with this piece of *augverdef*?"

"I don't know," said Kate. "I'm trying to find out. Coreg discovered a stash of the weapons in the Aligoes. Speaking of Coreg, that horrible servant of his is here. Trubgek."

"The human who knows dragon magic," Dalgren said. "What's he doing here?"

"I guess he's working for this army now," said Kate. "Some colonel sent him. You need to watch out for him."

"Me? Why?" Dalgren grunted.

"He asked me about you. He knows I warned the Rosian dragons about him and he believes they are hunting for him."

"He's probably right. Our magic is born within us. We have learned over centuries the discipline required to wield such vast power. Why do you think I have sworn to never take a human life? Because it would be too easy for me. This human has the power, but not the discipline. Are you in danger from him?" Dalgren demanded.

"I don't think so," Kate said hesitantly. "I knew what his name meant, that Trubgek was an insult in the dragon language. He seemed pleased. He seems to think I understand him. I don't. And I don't want to."

Kate reached out her hand to rub Dalgren on his snout. "Just watch out for him."

"That's going to be hard when I've never set eyes on him," said Dalgren.

"You'll know him," said Kate with a shiver. "You look into his eyes and nothing looks back."

The clouds were starting to drift away. Kate could already see a few stars and the sliver of a moon. She looked again at the troop ships.

"You better go. Someone might see you. We're sailing to Haever. Once I'm in a big city, I can easily escape. I will meet you in that cave where you stayed when we first went to work for Sir Henry, the one overlooking the harbor. We'll ask him for our old job back."

Dalgren hovered in the air, his wings stirring a gentle breeze. Puffs of smoke trailed out from between his fangs.

"What's really going on, Kate? Why are you staying?"

Kate gave a faint smile. "Because I need to find out what is really going on. A friend of mine is somehow involved with this army and I don't think he knows that they are stealing children and salvaging green beam weapons. Once I figure out what they're plotting, I'm going to tell him."

"Do I know this friend?" Dalgren asked.

Kate felt herself blushing and was grateful for the darkness. "I doubt you would remember him. Now please go. You're going to get me into trouble!"

"You can do that without any help from me!" Dalgren grumbled. "I will meet you in Haever. Take care of yourself—if that's possible."

"I will," Kate promised. "And, Dalgren—"

"What?" He snaked his head around.

"We both need saving," said Kate. "Thank you for coming back for me."

Dalgren grinned. Flames flashed from between his teeth, reflecting in his eyes. He sank down below the ship, and the mists of the Breath swallowed him up.

FORTY-EIGHT

Mr. Sloan was overseeing rifle drill on a particularly fine morning. The air was crisp and cool. The troops were in high spirits. Rumors had been floating about for a week that they would soon be going into action. The troop transport ships had been refitted and were ready to sail.

When an aide summoned Mr. Sloan to report to Colonel Smythe, he was not surprised to receive orders to start preparing the ships to receive men and supplies.

"I do not yet have a firm date for departure," Smythe stated. "I am awaiting news from Freya in regard to obtaining a warship but that could come at any time. We must be ready to sail at a moment's notice. I have sent an urgent message to the marchioness to inform Prince Thomas that the day of his ascension to the throne is almost at hand. He needs to join us here. His Highness will travel with his forces, so we must arrange for his accommodations aboard one of the ships."

He and Mr. Sloan discussed what needed to be done. Smythe was thorough and efficient in his planning, detailing what work was to be done in advance, such as loading weapons and supplies, and what had to wait until they had a firm departure date.

"I trust His Highness will arrive in the next day or two," Smythe added.

"We have preparations to make before we sail. I pray God that the queen listens to reason and agrees to our demands and that she will abdicate in favor of Prince Thomas. But we must be prepared for her to resist, in which case she will be arrested and the prince must be ready to lead his people to war."

"Yes, sir," said Mr. Sloan, maintaining his calm with difficulty.

"I already have troops in place to prevent the queen's sister, Elinor, from leaving Rosia. I have given orders to arrest the queen's half brother, Hugh, who will most certainly attempt to make trouble, as well as the queen's friends and allies among the Freyan nobility. They will also need to be rendered harmless."

Smythe did not name Sir Henry, but Mr. Sloan knew with certainty that he would be among those "rendered harmless"—arrested or perhaps even killed.

"I must say that I am disappointed that His Highness is not already here," Smythe remarked. "He was spending time with his fiancée at the palace of the Duke de Bourlet, but that was weeks ago. The marchioness expected him back before now and she has not heard from him. I hope nothing is wrong."

Mr. Sloan hoped Prince Thomas had tumbled down the side of a mountain and broken his neck. He went off to carry out his orders.

As he worked, he tried to think of some means of sending a warning to Sir Henry. He contemplated carrying the warning himself and was again deterred by the fact that if he did so, Smythe would realize he was a spy and would alter his plans, rendering worthless the information Mr. Sloan had gleaned.

He had another reason to remain. He was missing pieces of vital information. Sir Henry would want to know where the troops were going to land, for instance, and when Smythe planned to launch the attack. Henry would ask about the Faithful. Mr. Sloan knew they had forces stationed in Freya, ready to assist in the uprising, but he had no idea of their numbers, where they were located, or who was leading them. He could warn Henry that members of the Faithful were in the queen's inner circle, prepared to do her harm, but such a warning was useless since he did not know who they were.

Mr. Sloan kept hoping for an opportunity to once again slip into Smythe's office, search through his dispatches and letters, and read the account books. He did not find a chance. Mr. Sloan had his own duties, which kept him busy during the day. He tried his luck a couple of times at odd hours of the night, only to find Smythe awake and at work.

A week passed without hearing any word from Prince Thomas. He still had not arrived in camp, nor was anything known of him. Smythe was growing increasingly restless and he sent yet another urgent message to the marchioness.

Mr. Sloan was in the colonel's office, delivering his daily progress report, when Smythe's aide entered with word that a messenger had arrived by griffin.

"Corporal Jennings has returned, sir," said the aide. "He says he is carrying an urgent letter."

"Send him in at once," said Smythe.

Mr. Sloan recalled that Jennings was the corporal who had escorted Trubgek to Freya, thus relieving the camp of his odious presence. Smythe must have been thinking the same, for he asked, as the aide was about to depart, "Is Corporal Jennings alone?"

The aide replied that as far as he knew, he was. Jennings entered the office, saluted, and handed the colonel a leather dispatch pouch. Smythe removed a letter from the pouch, broke the seal, and swiftly scanned it. He actually smiled.

"Good news, I hope, Colonel," Mr. Sloan said.

"The best," said Smythe. "Very good, Corporal. Go get some food and rest. I will have dispatches for you to take back."

The corporal departed. Smythe glanced through the letter again, then laid it to one side. Mr. Sloan continued with his report until they were once more interrupted.

"A wyvern-drawn carriage seeking permission to land, sir," said the aide. "It bears the Stanford family coat of arms."

"That will be His Highness!" said Smythe, his smile expanding. "We must go welcome him. You will accompany me, Lieutenant."

He rose to his feet and put on his uniform coat. Mr. Sloan rose as well, his eyes on the letter. He lingered a moment after the colonel had left, pretending to be engaged in buttoning his jacket. When the colonel was out of sight, Mr. Sloan snatched up the letter, read the few words that were written on the paper, frowned in perplexity, then returned it to its place on the desk.

The carriage descended rapidly and landed in the courtyard with a jolt that must have been very uncomfortable for the passengers. The coachman had obviously plied the whip on the way, driving the wyverns to their limits, for the beasts stood panting in their traces, too exhausted to misbehave.

The coachman hurriedly descended and opened the door. The marchioness burst out of the carriage in a torrent of silk, her hat askew, her clothes in disarray. Her dark eyes flashed. She refused the coachman's assistance and stormed over to confront Smythe.

"Marchioness, where is His Highness?" the colonel demanded.

"Thomas is in Freya!" Constanza hissed. "He is meeting with the queen!"

Smythe went livid, his eyes widened, and his face contorted. He could only stare at her, unable to speak.

Constanza waited for him to say something, and when he did not, she exclaimed angrily, "Pah! Idiot! Have you gone deaf? Did you hear what I said?"

Smythe recovered himself. Constanza's shrill voice had attracted attention. Soldiers had stopped to stare.

"Lieutenant Sloan, send these men about their duties, then join me in my office," Smythe ordered.

Looking grim, he took hold of Constanza's arm and forcibly escorted her into the headquarters building. Her shrill recriminations were cut off by the slam of his office door.

Mr. Sloan obeyed orders, bellowing that he would take the name of any man who was still in his sight after two seconds. Then he hastened to the office. He could hear the marchioness raging behind the closed door, and he could not help but hesitate before opening the door and slipping inside. Constanza was on her feet, pacing back and forth, the tapping of her heels emphasizing her words. Smythe cast Mr. Sloan a grim look. Mr. Sloan shut the door and then took his place in a corner of the room.

The marchioness vented her fury at her son, saying he did not appreciate her years of sacrifice and accusing him of betraying a mother's love, all in a torrent of mostly incoherent rantings, switching from Estaran to Freyan and back again so rapidly that Mr. Sloan had difficulty understanding much of what she was saying.

As near as he could gather, the marchioness had received a letter from the servant of a man she referred to as "Sir Richard" telling her that Prince Thomas had traveled in secret to Freya for a clandestine meeting with the queen. Sir Richard was deeply concerned about the prince's safety while he was in Freya.

When Constanza had to pause for breath, Smythe was able to ask a question. "Has His Highness met with the queen?"

"I do not know! What difference does it make?" Constanza demanded.

"It makes a great deal of difference, my lady," said Smythe. He was rigid, grim. "What did Sir Richard tell you?"

"He said something about that stupid woman leaving the palace to tend to a sick griffin . . ."

Smythe rose to his feet. His lips were pressed tight, his jaw clenched. He flung open the door and walked out, calling for his aide.

Constanza glared at his retreating figure, then stormed after him, knocking over a chair and gesturing wildly with her fan.

"What do you think you are doing, Colonel?" she cried. "Where are you going? I have not finished speaking to you! How dare you turn your back on me!"

Smythe paid no attention to her, but continued to shout for his aide. He met him at the entrance and the two walked outside together.

"Peasant! Poltroon!" Constanza shook her fan at him, but he kept walking.

Constanza found herself alone with no one paying any attention to her. She decided to remedy that, apparently, for she sank to the floor in a swoon.

Mr. Sloan was not one to leave a lady in distress, despite being fairly certain her distress was self-inflicted. He hurried to her aid and reached the fainting woman about the same time Smythe returned. He stood gazing down at her with dispassion.

Mr. Sloan chafed her hand and fanned her face. "Perhaps we should send for her maid, sir—"

"I doubt she brought one," said Smythe. "She distrusts servants. Take her to the infirmary. Have the sawbones tend to her."

Upon the utterance of this dire threat, Constanza gave signs of life. She moaned. Her eyelids fluttered. Mr. Sloan raised her to a sitting position and she reached out her hand to Smythe.

"You must not worry about me, Colonel. You must go to my son. Foolish boy! He has ruined everything. He will get himself killed! After all that I have done for him!"

She burst into hysterical sobs.

"Take her to my office," said Smythe.

Mr. Sloan carried Constanza to the office. Smythe righted the overturned chair and they settled her in it.

"I will fetch some brandy, sir," Mr. Sloan offered.

"First, I need a word with you, Lieutenant," said Smythe. He drew Mr. Sloan back into the hall. "I am traveling to Haever, Lieutenant."

"You believe her story about His Highness, then, sir?" said Mr. Sloan, sounding dubious. "That the prince is in Freya?"

Smythe nodded. "I know Sir Richard. He is a man of solid sensibilities. He would not have raised the alarm if he did not truly fear for the prince's safety."

"I understand, sir," said Mr. Sloan.

He was thinking that once Smythe was gone, he would have the chance to go through his papers, discover all the information he could, then travel to Haever himself, report to Sir Henry. He could always make up some excuse to give the Guundarans.

Smythe's next words took Mr. Sloan completely by surprise and unraveled his plans.

"I have given orders to have two griffins saddled. Be packed and ready to leave within the hour."

Mr. Sloan was dismayed. He wondered uneasily if Smythe distrusted him and did not want to leave him on his own.

"Begging your pardon, sir, but what about my duties here?"

"You will soon have no duties here, Lieutenant," said Smythe. "I have given orders to complete the supplying of the troop ships. The troops are to set sail as soon as possible. We must ensure the prince's safety. In two days' time the fortress will be empty."

"Yes, sir," said Mr. Sloan, relieved and grateful.

The troop ships would take a week to reach Haever, assuming they did not run into bad weather. Traveling by griffin, Mr. Sloan could be in Haever, warning Sir Henry that the queen was in peril, in two days.

"I will be ready to leave within the hour, sir."

"Very good, Lieutenant," said Smythe. "I am putting the Guundaran officers in charge. Give them their orders. Oh, and be certain to change into your Freyan army uniform."

He returned to his office and shut the door. Constanza had calmed down, and Mr. Sloan could hear the two speaking in lowered voices. Mr. Sloan would have given a great deal to eavesdrop, but he needed to speak to the Guundaran officers, then pack his few belongings.

In addition, he had to change into the uniform worn so honorably by so many brave soldiers. He had to admit the idea was genius, even as he regarded the uniform with revulsion. Freyan soldiers would be tricked into thinking they were seeing friendly forces advancing on them and not bother to defend themselves. They would not realize they had been duped until the bullets smashed into their bodies.

As he sought out the Guundarans, Mr. Sloan reflected on everything that had happened, and especially on the words he had read in the letter.

God's Glory awaits. Lex Talionis. Franklin.

FORTY-NINE

The coachman of the horse-drawn carriage of the Countess de Marjolaine brought the elegantly appointed vehicle to a stop in front of a modest house in an upper-middle-class neighborhood of Everux. He wondered uneasily if he had misunderstood the address.

The three-story house looked pleasant enough as houses go, but was not, in the coachman's mind, a suitable residence for His Grace, the Duke de Bourlet. Fearing that he had made a mistake, the coachman descended from the box and opened the door in some trepidation, expecting a reprimand.

"I am afraid I misunderstood the address you gave me, my lady," he said. "I will endeavor to correct my error—"

"No, no, Jarvis," said Cecile, smiling. "The address is correct."

"If you are certain, my lady," said Jarvis, eyeing askance the neighborhood children who had clustered around the coach.

He lowered the step and gave Cecile his hand to assist her to descend.

"Do you require me to wait?" he asked, valiantly attempting to ignore one young lad of about six who was tugging on his coat and loudly demanding to know the names of the horses.

"You may leave. I am to stay to dinner," said Cecile. "My son will escort me back to the palace."

"Very good, my lady," said the coachman.

He cast a baleful glance at the six-year-old, removed the child's grubby hand from his coattail, climbed back onto his box, and drove off down the street. The children ran after him, hooting and shouting.

Benoit, the aged steward, was waiting for her at the front door. Cecile paused to look at the house before entering. Stephano and Rodrigo had lived here many years ago, after King Alaric had disbanded the Dragon Brigade and Stephano had resigned his commission in anger.

Joining forces with their friends Miri and Gythe McPike and Dag Thorgrimson, they had formed the Cadre of the Lost, earning a living by undertaking various jobs for people, some less respectable than others.

Cecile had never been to this house before. She and her son had not been on speaking terms. They had reconciled in the days after the war, although their relationship was still tenuous. He could not understand her and she understood him far too well.

Benoit made a stiff and rickety bow as she entered. He took her cloak, then said in doleful tones, "I am sorry you find us living in such reduced circumstances, my lady."

"On the contrary, Benoit, I approve of this house," said Cecile. "My son knew love and friendship and laughter here. I can think of no better place for his child to be born."

"Far be it from me to disagree with Your Ladyship," said Benoit, and then proceeded to disagree with her. "I might point out that Your Ladyship doesn't have to climb those stairs a hundred times a day."

Cecile knew for a fact that Benoit had likely never set foot on those stairs. He spent all his time comfortably seated in front of the fire ordering the maid up and down the stairs.

"How is Lady Juliette?" Cecile asked.

"Extremely well, my lady," Benoit said. "Far too well, if you ask me. 'Tisn't right. A proper lady should not leave her bed for a week and Her Ladyship actually came down to tea last night."

He lowered his voice to a ghastly whisper. "She is nursing her baby herself!" Benoit sniffed. "Respectable women hire wet nurses. So I told Her Ladyship, but she only laughed and said she never had any pretense of being respectable. Perhaps you could speak to her, my lady. Her Ladyship is currently napping. The young master had a fractious night. But I could wake her—"

"Please let her sleep," said Cecile. "Where is my son?"

Benoit was pained. "If Your Ladyship will wait in the drawing room, I will send him to you."

"Nonsense, Benoit," Cecile said crisply. "I want to see my grandchild."

"He is with the young master in the kitchen, my lady!" said Benoit, aggrieved. "It's not right! The son of the Duke de Bourlet should not even know where to find a kitchen, much less be cavorting with the scullery maids."

"The baby is a week old, Benoit," said Cecile soothingly. "I am certain he will not be cavorting with anyone."

"I hope you are right, Your Ladyship," said Benoit, but he sighed heavily, fearing the worst, and with tottering steps led the way to the kitchen.

He was going to announce her, but Cecile stopped him. She wanted to watch the scene in front of her.

Stephano was walking up and down before the fireplace, holding his son in his arms, gently rocking him back and forth and talking to him.

"And so you see, my son, in order to mount a dragon, you step on the foreleg and then hoist yourself up into the saddle. This requires some practice, but you will soon become accustomed to it. I remember the first time my father put me on a dragon—"

Stephano paused and looked up. "Mother! I thought I smelled perfume." He added, teasing, "I assumed it was Benoit."

The old man snorted and tottered over to the most comfortable chair in the room, located in the warmest corner. He settled himself with a contented sigh and closed his eyes.

Cecile held out her hands. "Let me hold my grandson."

Stephano carefully laid the baby in her arms. "Mother, meet Julian Rodrigo Dag de Guichen."

"You named him after your father," said Cecile softly, tears coming to her eyes.

She gazed down at the baby, searching for some resemblance to the face she had loved and still held in her heart. The baby regarded her with intense, grave eyes, as if he knew the secrets of the universe, but chose not to reveal them.

"The child is well?" she asked.

"Thriving," said Stephano proudly.

Cecile touched his hand with her finger and, as if in answer, the baby curled his tiny fingers around hers.

"And Juliette?" Cecile asked.

"She is radiant," said Stephano. "I know she will want to see you."

"Benoit said she was sleeping."

"We have hired a nursemaid, but she insists on taking care of the baby herself. I will go wake her."

"Please don't," said Cecile. "Let her sleep. She must be exhausted."

Cecile marveled at the small human in her arms. She had not been allowed to hold her own baby. She had been sixteen, and unwed, at Stephano's birth.

When her father discovered her pregnancy, he had banished her to a convent and threatened to kill her lover. She had deemed it best for the sake of her son and for the sake of the man she loved to give up both of them. The sisters had taken the baby away from her after his birth. Julian had raised Stephano, who was taught to believe his mother had abandoned him for the sake of her ambition.

"I will be in your life, little Julian," Cecile promised the baby. "I will be there to see you take your first steps and hear your first words. I will teach you to dance, and proper court etiquette, for God knows your father will not."

The baby fell asleep in Cecile's arms. She rocked him gently back and forth.

"Let me put him in his cradle, Mother," Stephano offered.

"You will do no such thing," Cecile said softly.

She walked before the fire, holding the baby in her arms. The house was quiet save for the ticking of a clock, and Cecile wished she could silence that. She wanted time to stand still and leave her suspended forever in this moment of simple, sublime happiness; she had almost forgotten what such a feeling was like. She wanted to hold the moment close, revel in it, not let it go.

The moment was just that: a moment. The ticking of the clock was drowned out by the cawing of wyverns, the shouts of the driver, the jingling of harness, and the clatter of wheels landing on the pavement.

The baby woke and began to whimper.

"That's a carriage," said Stephano. He cast her an accusing glance. "You told D'argent where to find you."

"The carriage could be someone visiting a neighbor, Stephano," said Cecile.

"Not likely," Stephano muttered.

Cecile ignored him and began singing to the baby. The song was an old one; she dimly remembered her own mother singing it.

"'Lullaby, child, lullaby. Sleepy time, the young one sleeps. The child will sleep, oh so soon.'"

The coachman was swearing at the wyverns. Someone knocked loudly at the door. Stephano glared at his mother, then went to shake Benoit by the shoulder.

"Benoit! Someone at the door."

The old man hunched down in the chair, tightly closed his eyes, and began to snore.

Stephano shook him harder. "Benoit! The door!"

Benoit blinked, opened his eyes, groaned, and cupped his hand to ear.

"Eh?" he said.

Stephano gave him a grim look. "You can hear a whisper of gossip three blocks away and you can't hear someone banging on the door?"

"The floor, did you say, Master?" Benoit asked.

"Oh, for mercy's sake!" Stephano exclaimed, and he stalked off, running up the stairs to the entry hall.

Benoit winked at Cecile, closed his eyes, and resettled himself comfortably.

Cecile kept singing, "'A white hen is there in the barn. It will lay an egg for the child who is sleeping. Lullaby, child, lullaby.'"

Stephano came down the stairs. "D'argent is here, Mother," he said dourly. "He begs pardon for the intrusion, but says the matter is urgent. I put him in the drawing room."

"Little Julian is very beautiful, my son," Cecile said. She kissed the baby on his forehead, then carefully transferred the slumbering child to Stephano's arms. "Your father would be so proud."

Stephano smiled, his grim expression softened. "I wish he could be here to see his grandson."

"He is watching," Cecile said. "Be certain of that."

She smoothed her skirt and said briskly, "Where do I find the drawing room?"

"Benoit, show my mother to the drawing room," Stephano ordered.

"Yes, Master," said Benoit. He tried to stand up, groaned, and fell back into the chair. "My poor joints . . ."

"The drawing room is up the stairs, Mother," said Stephano. "First door to your left."

Cecile gave her grandson a long, last, lingering look, then turned away, the moment gone.

She entered the drawing room to find D'argent waiting for her. He handed her a letter. "I am sorry to intrude on this joyful occasion, my lady, but I thought you would want to see this at once. The letter is from Lady Rosalinda."

A Rosian noblewoman, Rosalinda had married a Freyan earl and was now living in Haever. She was well liked in the Freyan court and was a confidential friend of the queen's. She was also one of Cecile's most trusted agents.

Cecile broke the seal and opened the letter. As usual, it was filled with the latest court gossip.

> *An old friend is in town, Lord Phillip, someone I have not seen in Haever in quite some time. He travels incognito to avoid his creditors, and it cost me considerable effort but I managed to locate him. You say he claims to have spurned the advances of our dear Henrietta. Since few can resist that lady's fatal charms, I find that hard to believe. Thus far, however, all seems well. Henrietta is away from home and I am certain she would rush back to the city if she knew Lord PM was here.*

You will be interested to hear that Lord Phillip has talked with another lady, our beloved Mademoiselle S! The two met in the park quite by accident. Not a happy accident, you will say. He has also met with Count T. That was some days ago, but he and the count have not met since. I trust nothing has gone amiss.

Cecile read the letter again to make certain she understood, then handed it back to D'argent. He thrust it into an inner pocket of his coat.

"Phillip Masterson accompanied Thomas to Haever and has met with him there," Cecile told D'argent. "The young fools! I warned Thomas the duke was dangerous, but he would not listen."

"Has His Grace informed Sir Henry the prince is in Haever, my lady?" D'argent asked in concern.

"Sir Henry has left Haever, which is a good sign. Lady Rosalinda believes he would return if he knew the duke was in the city."

"We have no evidence that His Grace is still working for Sir Henry," D'argent said.

"I am inclined to believe he is sincere in his high regard for the prince," said Cecile. "But even if Phillip is not working for Wallace, he might inadvertently lead Wallace to Thomas. There is another matter that concerns me. Phillip and Sophia have met."

"That is indeed troubling news, my lady," said D'argent.

"If Phillip has not told her Thomas is in Haever, she may have guessed. Or if she has not, then Rodrigo will most certainly figure it out. I should have gone with them."

Cecile stood in silence, twisting the ring on her left hand. She knew what she had to do. D'argent knew, as well, for he was regarding her with sympathy. The baby's christening was in a week. His Majesty the king was hosting a celebration at the palace. This would be a proud moment in Stephano's life and, once again, she would not be there.

"I will leave for Haever this afternoon, D'argent. Have the yacht ready. My maid will know what to pack."

"Very good, my lady," said D'argent. "Will you share my carriage or should I summon another?"

"I will go with you," Cecile continued. "I must inform His Majesty and cancel my meeting with the envoy from Travia. I have to first tell my son."

"I will wait for you in the carriage," said D'argent. He paused, then said, "I am sorry, my lady. His Grace will be disappointed."

Cecile gave a faint smile. "His Grace will be furious. But there is nothing new in that."

D'argent left the house and she returned to the kitchen. Stephano had placed the baby in his cradle and was making tea, while Benoit watched him from his chair.

"I heard D'argent leave," said Stephano. "Sit down, Mother. The tea will be ready in a moment."

"Thank you, my son, but I have only come to tell you that I must leave as well," said Cecile. "I travel to Haever this afternoon."

Stephano regarded her, frowning. "The christening is in a week, Mother."

"I know, my son. I am afraid I must miss it."

Stephano flushed and drew in an angry breath.

"Don't shout, Stephano," Cecile added. "You will wake the baby."

Stephano glanced at his sleeping child. His lips compressed. He stood glowering at her. The rift between them was wide, had existed since his childhood. They had built a bridge across it in these last few years, but it was shaky, at best.

"Give Juliette my love," said Cecile and started to walk away.

The teakettle began to whistle. Benoit nimbly leaped out of his chair and hurried to snatch it from the flame.

"You could refuse to go, Mother!" Stephano said, coming up behind her. He laid his hand on her shoulder. "You could tell the king you quit. Tell him to find someone else to steam open letters and hide in closets!"

Cecile regarded him with dignity.

"Guard your child, Stephano," she said. "Keep him safe. And know that somewhere I will be doing the same."

She retrieved her cloak, left the house, and climbed into the carriage.

She had plans to make. The journey would take her five days with good weather. She would send D'argent ahead by griffin to make arrangements.

The driver brought the wyverns under control. The carriage took to the air.

She could still feel the baby's warmth in her arms and she closed her eyes and murmured the words to the last verse of the lullaby.

Everyone is calm. All around, it is the time for all to sleep. Sleep will come soon.

For some, perhaps. But not for her.

FIFTY

Mr. Sloan arrived in Haever two days after leaving Bheldem. He and Captain Smythe, along with two Guundaran mercenaries as escorts, traveled day and night, with only brief stops in Wellinsport and Dunham to change griffins and grab a bite to eat.

The flight was brutally cold. Mr. Sloan was muffled to the eyebrows in his uniform jacket, two shirts, a thick coat, two pairs of stockings, leather gloves, greatcoat, and a knit hat beneath his helmet. Icy wind and sleet clawed its way through his clothes to gnaw at his very bones.

They flew into Haever at night. Mr. Sloan had seen the lights of the city from far off. As they drew nearer, he could see the glowing walls of the palace. The walls were constructed of a colorful mixture of blocks of yellow limestone, red granite, and orange sandstone infused with magical constructs that glowed softly at night. Thus, it was said, the light of Freya's monarchy shone as a beacon in the bleakest night.

Mr. Sloan was overcome with pride and love for his country and he grieved to think this light could be extinguished. When the griffin landed and he was once more able to set foot upon his native soil, he was glad for the helmet that concealed his emotions.

Mr. Sloan was stiff from the cold and from being in the saddle and he stifled a groan as he climbed down from the griffin's back. The journey had been wearing on all of them; even the tough Guundaran mercenaries staggered as they dismounted. Colonel Smythe grimaced in pain and was forced to hobble around the stable yard in an attempt to ease a cramp in his leg.

Mr. Sloan told the mercenaries to unpack the saddlebags and help the stable hands to unharness the griffins, then went to see if he could assist his colonel.

"I have done business with this stable before," said Smythe. "The owner is sympathetic to our cause. Tell him we require a carriage and we need housing for the griffins for several nights. I also need someone to carry an urgent message."

Mr. Sloan went to talk to the owner, who was pleased to accommodate them. He sent stable hands running to harness horses to a carriage, and offered his son to serve as messenger.

Smythe removed a letter from an inside pocket and handed it to the boy. "The address is on the front. You will deliver the letter and say, 'Ten of the clock tomorrow morning.' The person who receives the letter will understand. Do you have that?"

"Yes, sir," said the boy. "Deliver the letter and say, 'Tomorrow, ten of the clock.'"

"Good lad," said Smythe.

The boy took the letter, climbed on a horse, and rode off. The stable hands rolled out a closed carriage drawn by two horses. The Guundarans stowed the saddlebags in the carriage, along with weapons, including rifles, powder, and ammunition, their bedrolls and other gear.

"Do you require a driver, Colonel?" the owner asked.

"My lieutenant will drive," said Smythe, indicating Mr. Sloan.

"Very good, sir," said the owner.

"The owner is a good man, but the fewer who know our plans the better," Smythe remarked to Mr. Sloan as they waited for the Guundarans to finish loading.

"Where are we going, sir?" Mr. Sloan asked.

"A member of the Faithful who owns a real estate agency purchased and renovated several abandoned warehouses and office buildings for our use as headquarters when the troops arrive," Smythe replied. "We will spend the night there. I am meeting with him tomorrow. The address is Meek Street. I have not been to Haever in many years and I confess I am unfamiliar with it. Do you know it, Lieutenant?"

"I do, sir," said Mr. Sloan, shaken.

Meek Street was named for Augustus Meek, the owner of an import-export business which was, prior to the war, the largest in the world. He had built warehouses and offices and even his own private dockyard to accommodate a fleet of ships. The end had come when the Bottom Dwellers began to attack and seize merchant vessels. Trade throughout the world dwindled to a trickle during the war. Meek had been forced to declare bankruptcy.

With its warehouses and office buildings empty, Meek Street fell into squalor. Vagrants moved into the abandoned buildings, living in filth and dying of cold and starvation. The area became a blight on the city.

Eventually a real estate agency purchased the buildings and began renovations. No one paid much attention except the vagrants, who were forced to find other accommodations. According to Smythe, the agency had transformed office buildings into military headquarters, converted abandoned warehouses into barracks, and repaired the dockyards.

Mr. Sloan tried to recall the name of the real estate agency that had purchased Meek's property, but he had paid scant attention at the time, and if he ever knew, he had forgotten it.

The Faithful have been laying the foundation for our destruction for years and we were none the wiser, Mr. Sloan reflected in despair. Indeed, Her Majesty had applauded their community spirit! We have been blind. Blind as dormice!

Mr. Sloan did not like to have to include Sir Henry among the dormice. He found it almost impossible to believe his employer could have made such a blunder.

Still, Mr. Sloan reflected sadly, we are all human—even Sir Henry.

He mounted the box and took the reins. Colonel Smythe and the Guundarans entered the carriage and Mr. Sloan drove off.

The church clocks struck midnight. Windows were dark and shuttered. Behind some of those windows, people slept. Behind others, people were awake, plotting the downfall of the country. Mr. Sloan had not slept much in the last two nights. Looking at the dark windows, he felt a kind of horror creeping over him. He had to force his weary brain to concentrate, determine his next move.

He had at least a week before the troop carriers arrived and that was with good weather, which was unlikely this time of year. That gave him time to warn Sir Henry and gave him time to warn the queen, alert the military, and end this rebellion in its infancy.

Mr. Sloan could go to Sir Henry tonight. He still lacked information, however. He knew the first question His Lordship would ask him. "Who are the members of the Faithful involved in the rebellion?"

Mr. Sloan would have to confess he did not know, and that could prove disastrous. Even if Smythe was in prison, the Faithful would merely find another commander for their armies. They would still be able to use their money and influence to carry on with their attempt to put Prince Tom on the throne.

Tomorrow Smythe was meeting with a member of the Faithful.

I will remain one more day to discover this man's identity, Mr. Sloan decided. Once that is known, Sir Henry can denounce him to the queen and we can start to dismantle this treacherous fellowship.

When Mr. Sloan turned the carriage onto Meek Street, it was deserted. The workmen had long since gone home for the day, and the buildings were dark, unoccupied. Mr. Sloan could see signs of extensive renovation, however, the most notable being that the street lamps were lighted. Glaziers had been at work replacing broken windows, and crafters had erected scaffolding and would be working to strengthen the magic on the walls. They had cleared the streets of garbage and piles of refuse.

Mr. Sloan brought the carriage to a halt in front of a three-story brick building.

"This is the address, sir," Mr. Sloan reported.

Smythe climbed out and stood looking at the building. He gave a nod of satisfaction. He ordered the Guundarans to unpack the gear, then drive the carriage around to the stables in the rear.

"When you return, carry in the bedrolls and the rest of the equipment," Smythe concluded. "We will spend the night in this building."

The Guundarans obeyed orders. Once they had unpacked the gear and piled it on the sidewalk, they drove the carriage down a side street to the rear of the building. Smythe and Mr. Sloan mounted the two steps to the front door, which was padlocked. Smythe opened a leather pocketbook and took out a large brass key. He paused a moment to gaze at it.

"I have been in possession of this key for a year," he said. "God gave me to know then that the Day of Retribution would come, and now it is almost at hand. We will save Freya from her foes, and restore her to her days of glory."

"Great are God's miracles, sir," said Mr. Sloan, saying what was expected of him.

He wondered—not for the first time—how Smythe reconciled his vile crimes with his faith. Mr. Sloan had thought at first that perhaps Smythe was shamming, pretending to be a religious man, although Mr. Sloan could not conceive of a motive. He eventually decided that Smythe was a devout man, sincere in his belief in a God, although his God was not Mr. Sloan's God. Smythe's God was one who could apparently overlook the murders of innocent crafters and the brutal killings of Lady Odila and Coreg; pass them off as the means to a desired end.

Smythe unlocked the padlock and opened the door. He entered the building and Mr. Sloan followed.

The street lamp outside shone through the windows, providing some light. Smythe had brought a dark lantern with him and he and Mr. Sloan inspected the premises. They came first to a large reception room where Meek's secretary would have greeted visitors and invited them to wait.

A door to their left still bore the name MEEK stenciled in black letters on frosted glass.

Other offices ranged along a hallway off the reception room. A staircase at the rear of the reception area led to the upper stories. The building smelled strongly of fresh paint and wet plaster.

Mr. Sloan opened the door marked MEEK and looked inside.

The office was spacious, occupying an entire corner of the building, and was lined with windows. Mr. Meek had been able to look out his front window to see the street that bore his name, and from the side windows observe the warehouses and other buildings that all bore his name.

Mr. Sloan wondered what had become of Meek. He seemed to dimly remember he had gone mad and been confined to a lunatic asylum. A large desk covered in ink blots and a single chair were all that remained of the once great man.

"Bring the bedrolls, Lieutenant," said Smythe. "We will make arrangements for more comfortable accommodations tomorrow, but tonight we will sleep on the floor."

Mr. Sloan and the Guundarans hauled in the bedrolls and other equipment. Smythe spread out his bedroll into Meek's office. The Guundarans made camp in the reception area. Mr. Sloan chose an office down the hall, close to the rear entrance.

The room was cold. It was furnished with a small stove, but he was too exhausted to search for wood. He unrolled the blanket, took off his coat and his boots and lay down on the floor. He fell almost immediately into a deep and dreamless slumber.

FIFTY-ONE

Mr. Sloan had trained himself to wake at five of the clock every morning and this day was no exception. He woke to the faint light of dawn in the window and pain in every bone and muscle.

He lay on the floor, reluctant to move, knowing that it would hurt. He needed to prepare for his escape, however, and now was the time, before Smythe and the Guundarans were up and about.

Gritting his teeth, Mr. Sloan sat up, pulled on his boots, and managed to stagger to his feet. He had draped his uniform coat over a chair. Before putting it on, he checked the magical constructs that covered the fabric to make certain that none were broken or starting to fail.

Such a check was routine, a task every marine officer carried out daily until it became an unthinking habit, just as checking to make certain his sidearm was loaded. The task took on special significance this day. Mr. Sloan trusted he would be able to escape tonight without being seen, but he was not one to take chances.

He put on his coat and hat and quietly opened the door. He could hear the Guundarans snoring. No sound came from the office where Smythe was sleeping. Mr. Sloan softly stole past the slumbering soldiers and crept up the stairs, heading for the room directly above Smythe's office.

He studied the floorboards and found several that were loose. He experimented and discovered he could pry up one without much effort, allowing him to listen in on the meeting Smythe would be having with the member of the Faithful.

He went back down the stairs and out the rear exit to the privies, which were located in a separate building. The privies had been constructed during Meek's time, but they bore evidence of having been cleaned and refurbished. Mr. Sloan completed his ablutions, then went to the stables, which were a new addition, since Smythe would require mounts for himself and his officers. The stables contained a tack room and stalls for about twenty horses. Griffin stables would be located somewhere else, since they could not be near the horses, lest the griffins indulge their taste for horseflesh.

Mr. Sloan saw signs that the Faithful had prepared for the army's imminent arrival. Someone had brought in straw, hay and oats, and fresh water; rakes and brooms for mucking out; and sponges, towels, and brushes for currying. Unfortunately, he could not find saddles, bridles, or harnesses. Unless those were delivered today, he would either have to ride bareback or walk to Sir Henry's, which was several miles distant.

Mr. Sloan then recollected that Meek Street was not far from Market Street, a busy thoroughfare. He might be able to find a cab on Market Street, even late at night.

This settled to his satisfaction, he set to work in the stables, acting on the off chance that Smythe might have seen him enter and wonder what he was doing. Mr. Sloan fed and watered the carriage horses and he was brushing them when he saw Smythe head for the privies. The colonel stopped by the stables on his return.

Smythe regarded Mr. Sloan curiously. "I thought I heard someone. I did not expect to find you, Lieutenant. You are not a stable hand."

"I needed the exercise, sir," said Mr. Sloan. "My muscles were so stiff, I could barely climb out of bed this morning. This is not work for me. I have liked horses since I was a boy."

Smythe raised an eyebrow. "I require you with me, Lieutenant. You are an officer. Leave the mucking out for the Guundarans."

The day was one of those rare days in autumn when one could imagine it was springtime. The air was warm, the sun bright. They could have entered the building through the back door, but Smythe chose to inspect the building's exterior and they walked around the building, taking the side street that led from the back of the building to the front.

"As you know, I am expecting a visitor shortly," Smythe said. "We will meet in the office. You will need to find two more chairs, one for our guest and one for yourself, and a small desk where you will sit to take notes."

"Yes, sir," said Mr. Sloan, pleased that he would not have to eavesdrop.

"I have found it advantageous when dealing with the Faithful to have the conversation recorded in writing," Smythe continued, adding dryly, "Noble lords and ladies often suffer from convenient lapses of memory. Sir Richard and I will be discussing matters of importance, and I want a record of what is said so that there is no misunderstanding."

So I am to meet the mysterious Sir Richard, Mr. Sloan thought. The man who is sheltering Prince Tom! If all goes as planned, Sir Richard and Smythe and Prince Tom will be in custody by tomorrow morning and this conspiracy at an end.

He located a second desk, which he placed near the front window, so that he might take advantage of the sunlight, and found additional chairs. He busied himself with other tasks and waited impatiently for the clock to strike ten.

The hour appointed for the meeting came at last. Smythe paced in front of the building to await the arrival of his guest. Mr. Sloan laid out the writing materials he would need and watched out the window.

A private carriage arrived. The carriage was well appointed and obviously belonged to someone of means, though it bore no armorial markings. Smythe descended the steps to greet his visitor. The driver opened the carriage door.

Sir Richard Wallace, brother of Sir Henry, stepped out.

Mr. Sloan stared, riveted. The shock was paralyzing and for a horrible gut-twisting moment he could not move, could not even breathe. Mr. Sloan had known Sir Richard for years.

And Sir Richard knew him.

Smythe and Sir Richard shook hands and started up the steps toward the door. They moved slowly, for Sir Richard was always mindful of his dignity and could never be hurried. He was the quintessential "Old Chap," an eminently respectable attorney-at-law, member of the House of Nobles, and part owner of a real estate agency (Mr. Sloan remembered that with an inward groan).

Richard Wallace was dull and staid, gray and boring, and for God knew how long, he had apparently been a member of the Faithful, plotting rebellion, raising armies, and turning warehouses into barracks.

Mr. Sloan drew back from the window. He had to overcome his shock, decide what to do and he had only moments. He considered flight, but immediately discarded the idea. The office opened into the reception area and he could hear their voices at the door. He would rush out of the office only to end up in their arms.

Mr. Sloan decided to stand his ground. He had been granted a God-given opportunity to discover the secrets of the Faithful and he would not shirk his duty out of cowardly regard for his own safety. He had to pray that Sir Richard did not recognize him.

The odds were in his favor. Mr. Sloan had not seen Sir Richard Wallace in at least two years. Sir Richard was a little nearsighted and Mr. Sloan was greatly altered in appearance. His skin was tanned and weathered. He had shaved his head, grown a mustache. He was wearing a uniform, which tended to make him just another faceless soldier.

Yet, Mr. Sloan did not discount Sir Richard. He was very like his brother in some respects: cunning, clever, astute. Mr. Sloan now had proof of that. Sir Richard had for years kept his dangerous secret from a brother whose job it was to ferret out dangerous secrets.

The two men entered the reception area. Mr. Sloan could not move the desk, but he hastily shifted his chair away from the bright sunlight streaming in through the window and placed it at an end of the desk that was in shadow.

Smythe stood back to allow Sir Richard to precede him. He then made introductions.

"Sir Richard, this is Lieutenant Sloan, my second-in-command. He will be taking notes."

Mr. Sloan knew a bad moment, fearing Sir Richard would connect "Lieutenant Sloan" with his brother's secretary of the same name.

Sir Richard had no care for a mere lieutenant. He acknowledged the introduction with a vague, preoccupied glance and started to look away. He frowned, however. His gaze sharpened and he turned his head to regard Mr. Sloan more closely.

Mr. Sloan was sweating beneath his leather coat.

"Shut the door, Lieutenant," Smythe said, moving to stand behind his desk. "We do not want to be disturbed. Please, my lord, be seated."

Mr. Sloan moved with alacrity. He closed the door and then crossed to his desk. He sat down and began to busily arrange the ink bottle and select his pens, keeping his head lowered.

He heard a chair scrape behind him. Sir Richard sat down. Mr. Sloan cast a surreptitious glance at him. He was sitting with his back to him and appeared completely absorbed with his own affairs. Given that he was plotting rebellion, these affairs would hopefully be serious enough to claim his undivided attention.

"How is His Royal Highness?" Smythe was asking.

"He is well, sir," Sir Richard replied. "Bored and restless, as one would expect of a young man forced to remain in confinement. He roams about the house like a caged lion."

"He is a high-spirited lad, my lord," said Smythe with a smile. "I take it, then, that you were able to convince him of the wisdom of remaining indoors. He has not met again with Masterson?"

"No, sir, thank God!" said Sir Richard. "His Highness has not met with anyone nor has he corresponded with anyone. He may be young, but he is sensible and intelligent."

"So I have found His Highness," Smythe agreed. "What about Masterson? Is he still in Haever? I trust you are still having him watched. Has he been in contact with your brother?"

"Not that I am aware," Sir Richard said, his voice grating. "Henry has been out of town, or so I was informed by the Foreign Office."

"I should like to speak myself with the agent regarding Masterson. Could you send him to me?"

"By all means," said Sir Richard, though he sounded faintly surprised. "I will have the man report to you this afternoon. As for His Highness, he is impatient for his meeting with the queen, which was put off due to Her Majesty's sudden need to rush off to treat a sick griffin. Folly, if you ask me."

"Has a date and time been set for the meeting, my lord?"

"The queen returned to the palace yesterday and summoned me to see her."

Sir Richard sat up straight, cleared his throat, and spoke slowly and solemnly, as though he were addressing the assembly in the House of Nobles.

"Her Majesty asked to meet His Highness on the twenty-eighth day in the evening, at the hour of eleven of the clock. I am to bring him to the palace."

"That is the day after tomorrow," said Smythe, displeased. "That does not give us much time to prepare. I have only just arrived. Why didn't you delay?"

"Reflect, sir, upon the danger to His Highness!" said Sir Richard, shocked at the question. "Masterson knows he is here. With every day that passes, the prince may be discovered!"

"True," said Smythe. "Well, we must make the best of it. What are the arrangements?"

"The meeting is secret, known only to myself and His Highness. She promised to tell no one, not even my brother. I am to escort His Highness into the palace through the back entrance, along a secret passage that leads to the Rose Room. We are to wait in the Rose Room until Her Majesty sends for us."

"Where is this Rose Room, my lord?" Smythe asked. "I am not familiar with the palace. That reminds me, could you provide me with maps of the palace grounds and the interior?"

"Certainly, Colonel," said Sir Richard. He drew out a small book and made a note. "I will send the information with the agent. The Rose Room is located on one of the upper levels. You need not worry, sir. Not even the servants will be aware we are there. Will you have troops in place by then?"

"I will have soldiers stationed nearby, ready to move onto the palace grounds the moment you give me the signal. I will place Her Majesty under arrest and my men will escort her to Offdom Tower."

Mr. Sloan gripped the pen tightly to keep his hand from trembling, and dropped a blot of ink upon the paper.

"The other members of the Faithful and I are opposed to having the queen arrested, Colonel," Sir Richard said stiffly. "If she names Thomas her heir, as we pray she will, we have accomplished our goal. He will be crown prince now and king upon her death. The transfer of power will be quite peaceful."

Smythe was grim. "I have not worked all these years, built up this army, planned for a revolution only to wait years for this woman to die or our plot to be discovered. Queen Mary is known to be capricious. Only a few days ago she wanted to name her sister, Elinor, as her heir. Today she wants Prince Thomas. Next week, she could change her mind and disown him in favor of her bastard half brother Hugh!

"God is handing you and the Faithful the opportunity to achieve the goal you have been waiting to obtain for one hundred and fifty years! God is giving you the chance to restore the true and rightful king to the throne! Will you take this opportunity now or risk losing it, perhaps forever?"

Sir Richard was impressed by the argument, but not entirely convinced. "When we first made our plans to take the throne by force, I was convinced Her Majesty would insist on naming her sister. But now she is going to name Thomas . . . I don't like the thought of having Her Majesty arrested! The populace would be in turmoil. And I fear His Highness will not be at all pleased."

"You have not told him our plans, have you, my lord?" Smythe demanded in alarm.

"*I* have not, sir," said Sir Richard. "The same cannot be said for the marchioness. She may be a woman of spirit, but she lacks common sense. I warned her not to reveal our plans to His Highness, but she paid me no heed. She told him several months ago that we intended to have the queen arrested and imprisoned. His Highness was furious. He informed me himself only last night that he would not be a party to such action."

"His Highness is young and idealistic. When the time comes, he will see reason," said Smythe. "As for the populace, they will be pleased to have Prince Tom upon the throne. The only people you will see marching in the streets will be throngs of his cheering supporters."

Sir Richard remained troubled. Smythe eyed him grimly.

"I need to know that you and the Faithful are committed to this cause, that His Highness, Prince Thomas, has your undying loyalty and support."

"You may be assured of that, sir," said Sir Richard.

"Good," said Smythe. "I will take your views and those of His Highness into consideration. Perhaps he could persuade the queen to abdicate the throne. No need for having her arrested in that instance. Our troops will be in place to assure a peaceful transistion, prevent the other heirs from causing trouble."

Sir Richard brightened. "She might well consider abdicating. Her Majesty has not looked well for months. She could be glad to retire to tend her griffins."

Mr. Sloan noticed Smythe's lip curl in a faint sneer and marveled that Sir Richard could be so obtuse as to believe the colonel would ever permit the queen to remain at liberty. His brother, Sir Henry, would have seen through Smythe in an instant. He wondered if Sir Richard had considered the fact that the queen would not be the only person going to prison. Smythe could not allow Sir Henry to remain at liberty, nor members of the queen's family such as her niece, Lady Ann, and her children.

"When are the troops from Bheldem due to arrive?" Sir Richard asked.

"Not for at least a week," said Smythe. "I have five hundred troops within a day's march of Haever. They are only waiting on my order."

Sir Richard consulted his watch, then rose to his feet. "I must be going. I have scheduled a meeting with other members of the Faithful to give them the news. We will draw up a petition to the queen, urging her to abdicate."

"You will not forget to send the agent to me about Masterson," said Smythe.

"I will notify him prior to my meeting," said Sir Richard.

Smythe accompanied Sir Richard to his carriage. Mr. Sloan remained at his desk, finishing his note-taking so long as the two men were within earshot. They proceeded out the front door and down the steps, then paused for a moment by the carriage door to continue the discussion.

Mr. Sloan felt stifled and he set down the pen to tug at the collar of his shirt and unbuttoned his coat.

Mr. Sloan no longer had a week to warn Sir Henry. He had until the day after tomorrow; the day when the Faithful would avenge themselves on the queen whose ancestors had deposed King James by restoring his heir to the throne. *Lex Talionis*. The Day of Retribution.

Every moment was now of the essence. He could not wait for even an hour. Yet he could not simply rush off. He needed an excuse to leave so that Smythe would not be suspicious.

Mr. Sloan kept watch out the window and saw Sir Richard enter the carriage. The driver mounted the box and drove off. Smythe gazed after the carriage for a moment, deep in thought, then turned and headed back inside. Mr. Sloan completed his work on the notes. Hearing Smythe enter, he rose to face him.

"What are your orders, sir?" Mr. Sloan asked.

"I need you to deliver a message, Lieutenant," said Smythe.

"I can leave at once," said Mr. Sloan, trying not to sound too eager. "Who is the message for, sir?"

Smythe came to within a couple of paces of Mr. Sloan, drew a pistol, and aimed it at his breast.

"Sir Henry Wallace," said Colonel Smythe.

He drew back the hammer. The muzzle was inches from Mr. Sloan's breast. He had a split second before the bullet tore through his chest and pierced his heart.

Mr. Sloan struck out with his left hand, shoved the pistol to one side, away from his chest, and lunged sideways.

Smythe fired. The bullet crashed into Mr. Sloan's rib cage as he smashed his fist into Smythe's jaw. He fell to the floor and lay still. Mr. Sloan grabbed a chair and flung it at the window. Glass shattered. He leaped on top of the desk and jumped through the window, falling heavily onto the street below. He did not wait to see what had become of Smythe, but ran down the street toward the stables.

Adrenaline started to ebb and Mr. Sloan could now feel the pain. Every breath was agony. His shirt was wet with blood and he could both feel and hear his shattered bones grinding. But he had to keep running or die.

He expected any moment to feel another shot slam into him, but no shot came. He had put all his fear and hatred into the blow that had felled Smythe and he hoped he had put him out of the fight, at least temporarily.

He staggered into the stables, his hand pressed over his wound, trying in vain to stanch the bleeding. He approached one of the carriage horses. The animal reared back his head at the smell of blood, but he knew Mr. Sloan from this morning and calmed down at the sound of his voice.

Carriage horses were accustomed to having postilions ride them, although not bareback. Mr. Sloan prayed that the horse would not fling him off or bolt, for that would be the end of him. Groaning, he pulled himself up onto the broad back. The horse turned its head to eye him curiously, but permitted him to mount.

Mr. Sloan managed to fling his leg over the horse and sit more or less upright. He kicked his heels into the horse's flank and the animal trotted out of the stable. The fastest route to Sir Henry's home would be to take Meek Street to Market. Mr. Sloan guided the horse to the front of the building.

The two Guundaran mercenaries came dashing out the door, armed with rifles, with Smythe behind them, his face a mask of blood. He pointed at Mr. Sloan. The Guundarans raised their rifles and fired. Mr. Sloan flung his arms around the horse's neck and ducked down as best he could.

Warhorses are trained to endure fire. Carriage horses are not. One of the shots clipped the horse's ear, the other struck him in the rump. The bullets did little damage but the pain and the cracks of the rifles terrified the animal.

The horse bolted, breaking into a gallop and rushing headlong down the street. Mr. Sloan had no harness, no way to try to restrain the maddened animal. He could only hang on as best he could, which meant pressing his chest against the horse's neck. The pain was excruciating and he had to fight to remain conscious.

The Guundarans fired again, but by now the horse's frantic pace had carried him out of rifle range, though there was some question as to whether Mr. Sloan should count himself fortunate.

He was going into shock from pain and loss of blood and finding breathing increasingly difficult. The horse's hooves clattered on cobblestone. Mr. Sloan had a dim impression of nearly being run down by a dustman's cart and of men running into the street, shouting and waving their hands in an effort to stop the crazed beast.

The next thing Mr. Sloan knew, he was lying on his back on the pavement looking into a crowd of faces gathered around him, peering down at him and loudly discussing him. Several pronounced him dead and a group of boys jostled with each other to view the corpse. Someone noted that he was wearing a uniform, which meant he was a soldier. Another man stated that he had been in the war and knew a gunshot wound when he saw one.

Mr. Sloan stirred and attempted to sit up, and cries rose that he was alive, at which someone thought to summon a constable.

The constable arrived and took charge. He ordered men to take a door off its hinges to use as a litter and they jumped to the task. The boys squatted down to peer at Mr. Sloan, probably hoping he would die again. The makeshift litter arrived. Several men picked up Mr. Sloan and placed him on it.

"There, my man, just lie still. We'll take good care of you."

"Henry . . ." Mr. Sloan whispered.

"We're going to take you to the Sisters of Mercy Hospital, sir, just lie still."

The men lifted the litter. Mr. Sloan had to try one final time to make them understand. He managed to gasp out the name.

"Henry!"

"Just you rest now, Henry," said the constable, giving him a pat. "We'll soon have you set to rights."

Mr. Sloan closed his eyes and gave up.

FIFTY-TWO

Phillip waited for Thomas in the park for several days after their first meeting, but to no avail. Thomas did not come, nor did he try to contact his friend. Given what he had heard of Sir Richard, Phillip guessed that Thomas had been locked in the nursery and forbidden to go out.

"Undoubtedly for the best," Phillip reflected.

He had been uneasy of late. He had the feeling he was being watched. He had no real basis for the fear. He had not seen anyone following him or loitering outside the inn or taking too great an interest in his movements. The feeling persisted, however, and he did not discount it. He had learned through the years to trust his instincts.

He was reasonably certain Sir Henry had not discovered him, mainly because he was still alive. Henry was not one to shilly-shally around. He would simply order one of his agents to "shoot the bastard" and that would be that.

But Haever was a city crawling with spies. Every foreign government had spies who lived in the shadows as well as diplomats, ambassadors, and envoys who were also spies, but walked about in the open.

Phillip was acquainted with most of them, for they all knew each other, because they all needed one another. They fed each other false information, used each other, spied on each other, and each pretended not to know the other. Everyone knew the rules of the game, and so long as no one crossed anyone, few ever came to real harm.

But they would all have heard that Phillip had given his support to Thomas and several might be concerned enough to keep him under surveillance.

Phillip considered leaving Haever, but he was reluctant to depart without knowing what was to become of Thomas. He did not know if the queen had returned to the palace. He thought about sending Thomas a note warning him not to come to the park, it was too dangerous. He knew Thomas, however, and knew his friend would not rest until he had questioned Phillip to find out what was going on, which would rather defeat the purpose.

Phillip decided his best course of action was to keep to his routine, which consisted of leaving his inn every morning, buying a paper, reading it in the park, and returning to his inn. If anyone was following him, they must be heartily bored by now.

He came to the park today, as usual, and waited for Thomas, who did not appear. Phillip was folding up his paper and preparing to go back to his cheerless inn when a boy ran up to him.

"Message for you, guv'nah," said the urchin, touching his hat.

He held out a piece of paper in a grubby hand.

"For me?" Phillip asked, startled. "Are you sure?"

"Yes, guv," said the boy.

"Who gave it to you?" Phillip asked.

"The bloke up yonder." The boy pointed.

Phillip looked to see Rodrigo, resplendent in sky blue, strolling along the path, talking to a woman who was hanging on his arm and regarding him with adoring eyes. Rodrigo glanced his way, put his hand to his hat, then continued on.

"Thank you, lad," said Phillip. "I'll take that now."

The boy held the note out of reach. "The bloke said you'd give me a talon."

"He did not. In fact, the 'bloke' already paid you, didn't he?" said Phillip.

The boy grinned and shrugged. "No harm in trying, guv." He handed over the note and dashed off.

Puzzled as to why Rodrigo would be sending him a note, Phillip quickly opened it.

> I have vital information. Meet me at my dwelling. The address is 1100 Clattermore Street. Tonight, the twenty-sixth day of the eleventh month, seven of the clock.

The note was signed *Rodrigo*.

Phillip frowned. He should decline the appointment, of course. He could be putting both himself and Rodrigo at risk. Phillip searched for him, planning to signal to him he could not attend. Rodrigo and his companion had walked on, however. They were still within sight, but Phillip did not want to draw attention to himself or to them by dashing after them.

He returned to his inn, wondering what to do. He was going to send Rodrigo a note, saying he couldn't come, but he was troubled by Rodrigo's message. What was his information? Did it have something to do with Thomas?

He recalled something Rodrigo had told him when they had first met in the palace in Everux.

"I delight in the follies and foibles of mankind," Rodrigo had said. "I make it my business to seek out every rumor, savor every bit of gossip, revel in every hint of scandal. I hear every whisper, I see every furtive glance. I know the meaning behind every coy smile."

"If there is even a chance he has heard something in regard to Thomas, I have to visit him," Phillip said to himself. "I have to find out."

He had brought no evening attire, but he trusted Rodrigo would understand. He spent the afternoon watching out the window, trying to see if someone was keeping an eye on him. He had chosen this inn because it was on a busy street and he could blend in among the crowd. The problem was that the inn was on a busy street and his tail could blend in with the crowd.

Phillip saw no one behaving in a suspicious manner, yet the feeling of unease did not abate. He prepared for his meeting, taking the usual precautions. He wore unremarkable clothing, such as might be worn by any gentleman-about-town: fawn-colored breeches, tall black boots, weskit, and knee-length suit coat. He pulled a tricorn low over his face, wrapped himself in a cloak, tucked a pistol inside his jacket, and left the inn by the back door.

He hailed a cab and gave the driver an address several blocks from Clattermore Street. Alighting from the cab, he walked the rest of the way. Night came early in the city as the sun sank behind the tall buildings, and the lamplighter was making his rounds. The streets were quiet; few people were walking abroad after dark in Haever in these troubled times. If someone was following him, Phillip would certainly have seen him.

He watched Rodrigo's house, saw no one about. He waited until a carriage drove past, then crossed the street, ran up the steps, and rang the bell.

Rodrigo himself answered the door. He was dressed all in black. His coat was black and trimmed in black. He wore black stockings and a black cravat. His hair was tied back with a black ribbon.

Phillip could only suppose some close relation must had died and offered his condolences.

"Ah, dear boy," said Rodrigo with a heavy sigh. "You have no idea."

He ushered Phillip inside with the air of an undertaker leading the family to view the body.

"I gave the staff the night off," said Rodrigo in sepulchral tones. "Allow me to take your cloak."

He took Phillip's cloak and hat and then looked about vaguely, uncertain what to do with them.

"The servants always deal with cloaks and hats and whatnot," said Rodrigo. "I am positive there is a cloakroom but I'm damned if I know where."

Phillip could offer no help, and in the end, Rodrigo draped his cloak over the top of a large, freestanding clock in the hallway and rested the hat atop a marble bust of a gentleman in a full-bottomed wig.

"I have grown quite fond of the portly chap," Rodrigo said, admiring the effect of the hat on the bust.

"Who is he, my lord?" Phillip asked.

"No idea," said Rodrigo. "I am renting this house during my time in Freya and the portly chap came with it. The owner was going to have him carted off, but I could not bear to part with him. I mean—look at that wig! I am having one made for myself. This way, please, Your Grace."

"My lord, if you could tell me—"

"Hush, not here," Rodrigo warned.

He picked up a lamp and showed Phillip into a darkened parlor. Phillip thought perhaps they would hold their clandestine meeting here, but Rodrigo passed through the parlor into a darkened sitting room. He kept up a steady stream of conversation, talking of the Freyan weather, which he considered perfectly foul, and lamenting the rented furniture, which he also considered foul.

"I invested heavily in antimacassars," he confided. "That way, I can't see what's underneath."

Rodrigo crossed the sitting room and was about to open yet another door. Phillip stopped him.

"My lord, you said you had urgent information for me. I took a great risk coming here. What do you have to tell me?"

"Have you dined, Your Grace?" Rodrigo asked imperturbably. "I asked the servants to prepare a light supper."

Phillip was losing patience. "Thank you, my lord, but I must insist—"

Rodrigo threw open the door to the dining room ablaze with candlelight. Sophia stood smiling at him.

"Please forgive me for the subterfuge, Your Grace," she said, flushing. She was holding Bandit and had her hand clamped over his muzzle to prevent him from barking. "I wanted a chance to talk to you in private and Rigo told me he would arrange a meeting. Ouch! You naughty Bandit!"

The spaniel had been trying to free himself from his mistress's grasp to greet Phillip. Failing at his previous attempts, the dog resorted to nipping at her fingers. Sophia dropped him to the floor and Bandit ran to Phillip and began to paw at his boots, begging for treats.

Phillip could only gaze at Sophia. He was accustomed to seeing her wearing her court finery: silk and ribbons, tulle and lace, hoops and petticoats. Tonight she was dressed in a plain woolen skirt and white blouse decorated with tiny pearl buttons. Her hair was done simply, gathered in curls that framed her face. She had never looked more beautiful.

"I do not mind a secret that ends in a delightful surprise," he said.

He stooped to pet Bandit, then walked forward to kiss her outstretched hand. Her fingers were cold and her hand trembled. She regarded him with sorrow mingled with regret.

"Phillip, I have been thinking. I am engaged to Thomas. It is not fair to him . . . And it certainly is not fair to you . . ." Sophia drew in a deep breath, gathering her courage. "I believe we should end—"

"This discussion until after we have dined," Rodrigo interjected. "Where are your manners, Sophia? The poor man has traveled all this way. You might at least offer him a glass of wine and a cold chicken wing before you break his heart. Especially since I went to all the trouble of ordering the servants to prepare this meal."

"Oh, dear! I am so sorry!" Sophia said. "Of course, you must be famished. Bandit, leave His Grace alone! He does *not* have a treat for you. Please, do sit down."

She picked up Bandit and led the way to the table. Phillip wasn't the least hungry, but he was grateful for the reprieve, if only for a short time. The table was small with seating for six. Rodrigo took his place at the head.

"We will be cozy, like a family," he said, with an emphasis on the word that made Sophia blush. "Your Grace will sit at my left, Sophia to my right." He fixed Bandit with a cold stare. "The dog on the floor."

Light gleamed on the elegant silver and delicate porcelain plates. Rodrigo was a charming host. Neither Phillip nor Sophia knew what to say and he kept the conversation flowing.

Phillip was not relegated to dining on a cold chicken wing. The dinner consisted of filet of beef and sauté of veal, shrimp and mussels, and plover's eggs. Rodrigo poured the wine and was in the midst of telling a scandalous tale when Bandit suddenly jumped to his feet with a growl. He glared at the door that led to the sitting room, continuing to growl. His hackles rose, his ears flattened.

"He interrupted my best story," Rodrigo said.

"I am so sorry, Rigo," said Sophia. "Bandit, what is the matter? Stop growling! There is no one there—"

"Yes there is," said Phillip softly, reaching for his pistol. "I hear voices . . ."

Bandit fled, diving under the table. A man threw open the door and entered the room, closely followed by two companions. They wore dark coats, tricorns with black silk masks. The first man aimed his pistol at Phillip. The other aimed his weapon at Rodrigo and the third trained his pistol on Sophia.

"Drop your weapon, Your Grace," said the first. "Come with us quietly and your friends will not be harmed."

Phillip could tell at a glance that these men were professional assassins. They knew their business and were going about it calmly. He rose with alacrity, his only thought to lead them away from Sophia. He raised one hand in the air and dropped his pistol to the floor.

"I will come with you," he said.

"No, you will not!" Sophia cried. She rose imperiously to her feet. She was pale, but she was angry. Two crimson spots burned in her cheeks. "His Grace is not going anywhere with you!"

"That's true, he isn't," said Rodrigo. "You rudely interrupted our meal. We haven't had dessert."

He exchanged glances with Sophia. She gave a little nod. Rodrigo began idly playing with the silver salt cellar.

The three men cocked their pistols. The first man gestured. "Make haste, Your Grace."

"I am coming with you," said Phillip, casting an agonized glance at Sophia.

He started to walk toward the men. Before he could reach them, Rodrigo flung the contents of the salt cellar at the assassins and spoke a single word. Each grain of salt burst into dazzling blue light.

As the men squinted, trying to see, Sophia lifted her hands. One hand burned with blazing green fire. The other hand flamed blue. She waved her hands and sent the magical fire roiling across the room. The threads of flame, blue and green, mingled and engulfed the three men.

Their pistols began to glow green.

"You should drop those weapons," Rodrigo advised in grave tones. "The green glow is contramagic. When the green mixes with the blue of the magic on your weapons, they will explode and blow off your hands. You have mere seconds."

The men hesitated. The green glow intensified and, cursing, they flung their weapons to the floor.

"And now, I give you permission to leave with your lives," said Rodrigo magnanimously.

The first grunted, thrust his hand in his coat and drew a knife.

Sophia spoke a word and clapped her hands.

Sparks of blue flame snapped and crackled around the three like fireworks, burning their faces, their hands, their clothes. One tore at his smoldering silk mask, ripping it off his face in panic. Another slapped at the sparks on his cheek and the third was frantically wringing burned hands.

"The witch is going to roast us alive!" one cried and dashed off, crashing through the door. A second followed. The leader remained, angrily slapping at the flames as though he was in a swarm of biting mosquitoes. He cast a grim glance at Phillip, then left. They heard the front door slam.

Now that they were gone. Bandit growled menacingly from beneath the table.

The green and blue light vanished, leaving the room dark by contrast. Afterimages of green and blue danced in Phillip's eyes, half blinding him. He realized he had stopped breathing and drew in a gasping breath.

"Good God!" he muttered, shaken.

He ran to make certain the assassins had truly departed and were not hiding somewhere. He opened the front door and saw the three of them piling into a carriage and driving off.

"That's odd," Phillip reflected, puzzled. "I would have expected them to have reinforcements."

He waited and watched as long as he dared, but no one appeared. He returned to the dining room, worried about Sophia, only to find her and Rodrigo in an animated discussion regarding the magic.

Sophia was breathing fast and trembling with excitement. Her face was flushed, her eyes shining. "Did you see that, Rigo? You were right! Our spell worked wonderfully!"

"You have proven my theory, my dear," said Rodrigo, regarding her with pride. "When used by a savant, magic can be combined with contramagic. You held the image of the seventh sigil in your head?"

"I did," said Sophia. "It wavered at first, probably because I was so afraid that they would hurt Phillip. But I gained courage and the image grew stronger."

"Please remember to make notes tonight before you sleep, while the spell is still fresh in your mind," said Rodrigo. "I shall write a treatise—"

"I am sorry to interrupt, my lord," said Phillip urgently, "but there is no time! Those men were professional killers, not the type to take defeat well. Is there a back way out?"

"The servants' entrance," said Rodrigo. "Through the kitchen. You two stay here. I will fetch your cloaks—"

"No time!" said Phillip.

He picked up his pistol, thrust it into his belt. He glanced at the pistols the men had dropped and saw that the green glow had died away. He could still feel the contramagic sparkling in the air, however, and he did not touch them.

Rodrigo lifted a lamp and led the way to the back of the house. Phillip and Sophia followed, with Bandit trotting along behind. They hurried through a maze of hallways.

"You saved my life, Sophia," Phillip said softly, reaching out to find her hand.

She clasped him tightly and pressed close to him. "Sir Henry sent those men, didn't he? Phillip, you must leave Freya! It's not safe."

"I know," he said quietly. "I will."

"Promise me?" she whispered.

"I promise." Phillip paused, then said, "What was it you wanted to tell me?"

Sophia hesitated. The next moment, she was in his arms.

"That I love you!" she whispered.

Phillip held her close and kissed her. She kissed him, and they clung to each other, arms entwined. Bandit dashed about them in circles and started to bark.

"Bandit, hush!" Sophia whispered, alarmed.

"I'll carry him," Phillip offered.

"Where are you two?" Rodrigo asked, coming back to find them. "I am love's champion, but there *is* a time and a place."

Sophia lifted Bandit and gave him to Phillip and they hurried after Rodrigo. They passed through the kitchen, down a flight of stairs, and arrived at a door.

Rodrigo doused the light.

"Let me go first," said Phillip.

He handed Bandit to Sophia, then drew a pistol and stealthily opened the door. Once his eyes had adjusted to the darkness, he could see a yard, small, but with several well-kept flower beds, and a walkway that led to an alley.

Phillip swept his gaze around the backyard and saw no one. The alleyway was dark and deserted.

He came back to see Rodrigo had found a cloak for Sophia hanging on a hook near the servants' quarters.

"I don't see anyone," Phillip reported. Again he found that puzzling. "The alley will take you to one of the main streets. You can catch a cab from there."

"Trust me, Your Grace, I am an expert on running down alleys," said Rodrigo airily. "Although generally I am being pursued by enraged husbands, not assassins. What will you do?"

"I will wait here to make certain no one is following you, then I will make my way back to my inn," said Phillip.

"Promise me you will leave Freya tonight," said Sophia.

"I promise," he said. "Word of honor."

Sophia kissed him again, still holding Bandit, who took the opportunity to lick his face.

"Come, my dear," said Rodrigo.

"Write to me!" Sophia said softly. "Let me know you are safe."

"I will," Phillip said. "Please go!"

Rodrigo guided her to the alley, keeping close to her, his arm around her. Phillip soon lost sight of them, but he could follow their progress by the dwindling sounds of Bandit's barks. He kept watch until they, too, faded away.

He was still in danger and he needed to think, to decide what to do. That was difficult when he could still feel Sophia in his arms, still smell her lingering perfume, still see her smile.

He shook himself out of his blissful reverie and returned to the house. He closed the back door, picked up the lamp, and searched the lower level until he found what he sought in the housekeeper's small sitting room: a desk and writing paper.

He sat down at the desk. He remained alert for sounds that the assassins had returned, although they must know that by now their prey would have fled.

Phillip wrote four words on a sheet of paper.

Discovered. Leaving tonight. Godspeed.

He folded the note and tucked it into his pocket, then doused the lamp and groped his way through the darkened house until he reached the front door. He retrieved his hat from the bust of the portly gentleman, took his cloak down from the clock, and let himself out.

The street was empty. Phillip left the house and walked down the sidewalk, avoiding the light of the street lamps. He kept watch, but no one followed him and no carriage with blackened windows came racing around the corner. He was still surprised the assassins had given up so easily. Sir Henry Wallace did not take kindly to those who failed him.

I might not be the only one leaving Haever in haste tonight, Phillip reflected with a grim chuckle.

He had a long walk ahead of him, but that gave him time to think. He left the quiet residential streets behind, entered the noisy streets of the tavern district. Coming across several enterprising young lads pitching coins against a wall, he asked if one would be willing to deliver a message.

One lad immediately presented himself.

"I'm your man, mister," he said, and held out his hand.

"Here is the note," said Phillip. "When you arrive at the house, ask for Thomas. Give it to him and no one else. Here is money to deliver it. You will receive more money from Thomas. This message is urgent."

"Yes, sir," said the boy.

"So urgent, I am going to send you in a cab."

The boy grinned in delight and stuck his tongue out at his friends, who were jeering and called him a "toff," saying next he'd be going to visit the queen.

Phillip put the young man inside a cab, gave the driver the address, and paid the fare to Sir Richard's and back. As the cab rolled away, the young man waved out the window at his friends, who hooted derisively.

Phillip pondered what to do next. He was loath to return to his inn, in case the assassins were watching it. But he had to hire a griffin and they did not come cheap. Phillip had some money with him, but not nearly enough. He had hidden the rest of his funds in his room.

By the time he reached his inn, the church clocks were chiming two in the morning, and the inn was dark. Phillip concealed himself in the doorway of the building opposite and kept watch.

He waited for half an hour, shivering. The street remained empty. He could see no one lurking in the shadows.

Phillip made his way across the street, and entered the inn. The night manager slumbered at the desk. He woke, grumbling, and handed Phillip the key to his room.

Phillip drew his pistol and climbed the stair. He inserted the key in the lock and cautiously opened the door. He waited a moment, but heard nothing. No quick, indrawn breath, no cough.

He lowered the pistol, turned to shut the door.

The three men burst out of the room across the hall and were on him in a rush. One punched him an expert and savage blow to the gut, driving the breath from his body and doubling him over. He fell to the floor, gasping for air, helpless. One took the pistol from his limp hand. Another hauled him into his room and the third shut the door.

The men worked with swift efficiency. Two of them tied his hands behind his back, while the third prized open his jaws and poured liquid into his mouth.

Phillip recognized the bitter taste of opium and he choked and tried to spit it out. His assailant clamped his jaws shut, tipped back his head. The liquid trickled down his throat.

The men had only to wait for the drug to take effect. Phillip had a dim and awful awareness of being carried from the room and thrown into a waiting carriage.

After that, he knew nothing but horror.

FIFTY-THREE

The black ship and the troop carriers sailed north up the western coast in calm weather with a fair wind and headed east. When they neared the port city of Glenham, the troop carriers, under the command of Captain Martin, remained behind, anchoring on the coast within a day's journey of the city. The soldiers were wearing Freyan uniforms, the ships flying Freyan flags.

Martin had left most of the Bottom Dwellers behind in the cavern to work on the green beam weapons, assembling and repairing them. The young people still required a crafter familiar with the seventh sigil to make the guns operational, but they were clever and skilled in crafting and Kate had no doubt that some would soon grasp the concept of the seventh sigil and be able to bring the green beam guns to life.

She determined the location of the cavern on the Freyan coast as best she could before she left, planning to warn Sir Henry to send a force to seize it and shut down the work. Perhaps he could help the young Bottom Dwellers to find new and better lives Above, employed in a more productive occupation.

As for Trubgek, he had disappeared. No one had seen him depart, but the griffin he had ridden was no longer around and everyone assumed he had left with it. No one missed him, least of all Kate.

The day before the *Naofa* parted company from the troop carriers,

Martin visited Franklin on board the black ship. The two talked in Frank-lin's cabin with the door shut. Kate loitered about the corridor to hear.

"When is Jennings supposed to arrive with your orders from the colonel?" Martin asked.

"We are to start keeping watch for him on the twenty-seventh," said Franklin. "We might have to wait several days, depending on the weather. I assume you will receive your orders to march into Fort Glenham at the same time. I trust you will meet no resistance from the troops there."

"We will probably be welcomed with open arms," Martin said with a chuckle. "We come to reinforce them, after all. The fort will be in the hands of the Army of Retribution and none the wiser."

"Godspeed your mission," Franklin said.

"Godspeed yours, my friend." Martin added in somber tones, "*Lex Talionis.*"

After parting with the troop carriers, the *Naofa* continued eastward, sail-ing only at night, for this part of the Breath was well traveled. Ships carrying lumber and iron ore plied the Breath from Glenham to Haever. Merchant ships arriving from Guundar and Travia also sailed this part of the Breath. The Freyan navy patrolled the coastline. Any ship, no matter what nation, would be highly alarmed by the sight of a black ship armed with a green beam gun prowling the Freyan coast. The *Naofa* hugged the coast by night, and went into hiding during the day.

Their progress was far too slow for Kate, who was growing increasingly worried about the mission of this Army of Retribution. She needed to reach Haever, to warn Sir Henry and then find a way to get word to Thomas.

Kate also was growing more and more uneasy about the green beam weapon and its intended use. She felt responsible, for she was the one who had brought the monster to life.

She could cripple the gun by reversing the seventh sigil, but her plans were thwarted by Franklin, who hovered over the weapon like a new mother over her firstborn child.

As the sun rose on the morning of the twenty-seventh day of the eleventh month, the black ship once again scuttled into hiding, anchoring on an is-land off the eastern coast of Freya.

This day was different, however. In the past, the black ship had taken ref-uge in secluded coves or tree-covered inlets. Today, Franklin anchored on an island known as Falcon's Rock, about twenty miles from the coast, within a few hours of Haever.

Falcon's Rock was well known, marked on all the charts, for it was the site of a famous shipwreck. HMS *Falcon* had crashed on the island in calm weather, for no reason that anyone could fathom, killing all hands on board. Kate recalled that Jennings was supposed to meet up with them on the twenty-seventh and she guessed Franklin had chosen this island so that Jennings could spot the ship from the air.

The day passed peacefully. Kate, as one of the crew, tried to rest during the day, for they would be awake all night making the perilous voyage along the coastline in the dark. But Kate couldn't sleep. She tossed and turned, wondering how to sabotage the gun.

She had not been able to discover the weapon's target or Franklin's secret mission, but she could not banish the sight of the green beam blowing up the side of a cliff. Kate's worries were interrupted by the lookout shouting, "Deck there! Griffin rider!"

"Jennings is back," she muttered and hurried up on deck.

A griffin carrying a rider was circling above the ship, searching for a place on the shoreline to land. Franklin noted Kate loitering about the deck and turned to frown at her.

"Have you no duties, Private?"

"I would like permission to work on the magic on the helm while we're anchored, sir," Kate replied. "The helmsman was complaining he was having trouble with the rudder."

Franklin gave Kate permission, then turned back to watching the griffin settle down on a large outcropping of rock near the shoreline.

Kate entered the wheelhouse and began to work on the constructs that operated the rudder. The helmsman had complained that the rudder was sluggish and slow to respond, so he would confirm Kate's story. She was convinced that the fault was not with the magic, but with the rudder, which had been poorly designed. She wanted an excuse to hear and see what Franklin and Jennings had to say to each other, and working on the helm gave her reason to be on deck.

The rider dismounted, unpacked his gear, and dismissed the griffin, who flew off. As he approached the ship, Franklin stood waiting for him at the top of the gangplank.

"Corporal Grunnel, sir," said the rider formally, removing his helmet. "Permission to come aboard."

Franklin was startled. "Grunnel?"

"I served under you when we were in Bheldem."

"Yes, I remember. It is good to see you again, Corporal, but where is Corporal Jennings? I am in need of a crafter."

"I am a crafter, sir, as you'll recall," said Grunnel. "That is the reason the colonel sent me. He expected you would need assistance."

Grunnel handed Franklin a leather pouch tied with string and affixed with a seal. "Your orders, sir. As for Corporal Jennings, he remained in Haever to assist Colonel Smythe—"

"Wait a moment, Corporal," said Franklin, startled. "Are you telling me that Colonel Smythe is in Haever? I assumed he was still in Bheldem with the army. Why has he traveled to Haever? Has something gone wrong?"

"His Highness, Prince Thomas, secretly traveled to Haever," said Grunnel. "He's there now."

Kate gave an audible gasp, then smothered it by putting her hand over her mouth. She was not the only one shocked by the news.

"His Highness in Haever!" Franklin was astonished. "He was supposed to remain in Bheldem until we secured the city. Did the colonel sanction this trip?"

"He did not, sir," Grunnel replied. "The colonel was forced to leave Bheldem and travel to Haever posthaste. Our orders were changed. My brigade was stationed outside Haever, near Illwick. We had to break camp and set sail. We moved into the new barracks on Meek Street last night."

"What reason did the colonel give for the prince's actions?"

"Colonel Smythe passed it off as high spirits. Rumor has it that our colonel is none too pleased with the prince."

"I can imagine," said Franklin. "I know Colonel Smythe from our days in the marines. He is a man who does meticulous planning and would not like to have his plans overset. The prince has placed himself in peril and our plans in jeopardy."

"We must act more quickly than we had anticipated," said Grunnel. "And the colonel has added another mission. You will find the details in your orders."

"When do we strike?" Franklin asked.

"Tomorrow night, sir," said Grunnel. "The twenty-eighth day of the eleventh month. *Lex Talionis!*"

The corporal was enthusiastic. Franklin was not.

"Tomorrow!" he repeated angrily. "I do not know if we can be ready! My crew is new to handling a black ship. Even a seasoned crew would find our mission difficult, and not one of my men has ever sailed this type of vessel. I had hoped to have at least another week to train them!"

"No one is happy, sir," said Grunnel, hastily tempering his enthusiasm. "Least of all the colonel. 'God wills it,' he told my commander. What happens if we don't reach Haever in time, sir?"

"As I said, I know Colonel Smythe. He will have made contingency plans. I know he is counting on us, however. We will not fail him." Franklin sounded resigned. "When you have stowed your gear, inspect the green beam weapon.

If we are going into action tomorrow, I want to be damn sure it is in working order. I hope you have studied the seventh sigil."

"Yes, sir. As it happens, I am something of an expert on it," said Grunnel with pride.

He carried his gear below. Franklin remained on deck. He unsealed the pouch and took out a letter. The orders were brief, apparently, for he read them in the space of a few moments. He went over them again, to make certain he understood, then replaced the letter in the leather pouch.

Kate hoped he would take it to his office, thinking she could find a chance to sneak in and read it. Unfortunately he tossed the pouch into the Breath. The pouch must have been lined with lead, for it dropped into the mists and sank immediately.

He walked over to the wheelhouse to check the logbook and seemed astonished to find Kate. She was down on her hands and knees beneath the helm, checking on the braided leather ropes that transmitted the magic.

"What are you doing here?" Franklin demanded, ill-pleased.

Kate hurriedly scrambled to her feet.

"I was checking on the rudder, sir. The helmsman was complaining about it."

"Yes, right," said Franklin. "I had forgotten. We will be setting sail soon. Were you able to do anything about the rudder?"

"Not much, sir," said Kate. "The problem isn't the magic. It's the design of the rudder. The Bottom Dwellers weren't very capable shipbuilders. Did Corporal Jennings return, sir? I saw a griffin landing and I figured that must be him. I want to show him the work I've done on the green beam weapon."

"Jennings is not coming back," said Franklin. "You will report to Corporal Grunnel. He is below, stowing his gear. When he is finished, he and I will meet you on the forecastle."

He walked off, shouting orders for all hands to weigh anchor and hoist the sails. The crew streamed up on deck, as Kate climbed the stairs to the forecastle. Standing in the shadow cast by the green beam weapon, she tried to make sense of what she had heard.

Thomas was in Haever! The news was both astonishing and deeply troubling. For someone who had declared he knew nothing about his army, Thomas certainly seemed to be involved with it up to his neck.

She wanted to trust him, to believe he truly did not know that these men were plotting to overthrow the government and place him on the throne. He was making trust increasingly difficult for her.

Kate began to pace back and forth. She could alter the magic on the lift tanks, prevent the ship from sailing. Unfortunately, Grunnel could fix that, too, and she would put herself in danger.

"Besides, I need to reach Haever myself and this ship is the fastest means of travel," Kate reasoned. "Once I'm there, I'll jump ship and find Sir Henry . . ."

Kate stopped pacing, brought up short by a terrible realization. She couldn't follow through with her plan to tell Sir Henry. He hated Thomas, calling him the Pretender. If she told Sir Henry that Thomas was in Haever, planning to overthrow the queen, Sir Henry would find him and arrest him. Or perhaps not even go to all the bother. Perhaps he would just kill him.

Kate stood in front of the green beam weapon and regarded it with loathing. The crew had covered the gun with a tarpaulin, on the chance some passing ship might see it. The gun crouched beneath the tarp like a hideous, shapeless monster.

"I can't tell Sir Henry. I've lost the opportunity to disable the magic on the gun. I should have told Dalgren to melt the damn thing!"

Kate heard Franklin and Grunnel talking as they climbed the stairs to the deck, discussing the magic on the green beam weapon. Kate stood by, not wanted. She was disheartened to discover that Grunnel really was something of an expert on the seventh sigil.

"Tomorrow will be a glorious day, sir," said Grunnel in a tone that was almost reverent.

"Prince Thomas crowned king at last," Franklin agreed.

FIFTY-FOUR

Thomas was wakened in the middle of the night by a thunderous knocking on his door. He sprang out of bed in alarm, thinking the house was on fire, and hurriedly flung on his dressing gown, then threw open the door.

Sir Richard stood before him in his bedclothes, holding a candle and glaring at him.

"A street urchin has come to the door asking for you, Your Highness. *By name!*" Richard emphasized, incensed. "He claims to have a message for you and he insists upon giving it to you in person."

Thomas knew at once the message must be from Phillip and that it must be important or Phillip would not have risked sending it. Thomas lit a candle that was on the nightstand and hurried down the stairs. He expected Richard to return to his bed and was annoyed to find him at his shoulder.

"Thank you, my lord, but I can deal with this matter," said Thomas. "I am sorry you were disturbed."

"Imprudent, Your Highness, highly imprudent!" Richard seethed, doggedly pursuing him. "No one is supposed to know you are in Haever and this guttersnipe asks for you by name!"

Thomas knew Phillip better than that. "What were his exact words, my lord?"

"He said he must give the message to Thomas," Richard returned angrily.

"Please note that was all he said, my lord. There must be a hundred men named Thomas in Haever."

"An assassin needs to kill only one, Your Highness," said Richard. "The right one."

Thomas pressed his lips together to keep from saying something he would undoubtedly regret. He arrived at the first floor to find Henshaw standing in the entry hall in his dressing gown and nightcap, holding a pistol.

"For God's sake, Henshaw, put that away before you hurt someone!" Thomas exclaimed angrily. He fixed his grim gaze upon Richard. "I said I would deal with this matter, my lord."

Richard was not pleased, but his prince had spoken. He and Henshaw retreated a few paces, waiting for him at the bottom of the staircase.

Thomas approached the closed door with caution, not quite as unmindful of his own safety as his host made him out to be. He opened the door a crack and looked out into the night.

A boy with a dirty face and shrewd eyes fidgeted on the door stoop, holding his cap in his hand.

Seeing no one about to toss a bomb at him, Thomas opened the door. "You have a message for me?"

"That depends," said the boy, eyeing him warily. "You Thomas?"

"I am," Thomas replied with a smile. He indicated Richard and Henshaw. "These gentlemen will attest to that fact."

The boy sized him up and decided he must be telling the truth, for he took a piece of folded paper from his cap and handed it over.

Thomas opened it, glanced at the four words. He crumpled the note and thrust it into the pocket of his dressing gown.

"Thank you," he said, then raised his voice. "Henshaw, we must pay this lad for his trouble."

Henshaw left, heading for the kitchen. He returned with several coins, which he gave to the boy. The lad studied them carefully, then, satisfied they were real, he stuffed the coins into his shoe.

"Thanks, guv," he said, and started to dash off.

"Do you have some way to get back home?" Thomas asked.

"Yes, guv!" said the boy. "The t'other guv'ner sent me in a cab."

The boy grinned, tipped his hat, and ran off.

Thomas shut the door and walked back toward the stairs.

"Is everything all right, Your Highness?" Richard asked.

"It is, thank you, my lord," said Thomas.

"If I might ask Your Highness—"

"You may not, my lord," said Thomas.

He continued up the stairs. Pausing on the landing, he looked down to see Richard and Henshaw with their heads together, deep in conversation. Thomas went to his bedroom and slammed the door. He drew the note from his pocket, smoothed it, and read it again.

Discovered. Leaving tonight. Godspeed.

Thomas sighed, afraid for his friend. Henry Wallace must have discovered Phillip was in Haever. He was safe enough for the time being, apparently, for he had been at liberty to send Thomas a note. Hopefully by now he was riding a griffin, winging his way back to Estara.

Thomas envied him. He could not stand to be cooped up in this house another moment. The countess wanted him to remain in Haever to be present when the queen died, but from what Thomas had heard, the queen appeared to be in good health and spirits, for she had gone off to tend to a sick griffin. His meeting was scheduled for tomorrow night.

Tonight, he amended, hearing the clock chime one.

He set fire to the note and dropped it in the grate. He watched it burn to ashes, then stirred the ashes and went to bed.

The next morning as he came down to breakfast, he passed Henshaw on the stairs.

"If you are going to my room to look for the note, you can save yourself the trouble," said Thomas. "I burned it."

He did not stay to hear Henshaw's response.

Sir Richard was not at breakfast, for which Thomas was grateful. He picked up the *Haever Gazette* and noted the date at the top of the page. The twenty-eighth day of the eleventh month.

The date he could well be named heir to the Freyan throne. The paper shook in his hands and he folded it and laid it down, unread. He went outdoors for a cheerless walk in the walled-in garden. The day was cold and raw. Dead leaves crackled beneath his feet. He walked until he had released some of his pent-up energy, then went back to the house and retired to the library.

He did not see Sir Richard until dinner, which was good, for by that time Thomas's anger had cooled. The two men could not discuss in front of the servants the only subject that was on both their minds, which was the meeting with the queen in a few hours. Thomas ate little and drank only a single glass of wine. He wanted to make certain he had a clear head.

At the best of times Richard had nothing much of interest to say, and he was extremely solemn and formal tonight. His eyes grew moist with emotion whenever he looked at Thomas, and he spent most of the dinner gruffly clearing his throat.

The clock chimed seven times. They were not due to leave for the palace until nine. The hour was still early, but Thomas went to his room to dress.

He had not packed any court clothes, having traveled by griffin and in haste. He had with him only the evening attire he had worn while visiting the Duke de Bourlet.

Henshaw had offered to serve as valet. Thomas had politely refused, saying he would dress himself, and he was not pleased to see Henshaw enter his dressing room carrying a large trunk.

"A gift from your lady mother, Your Highness," said Henshaw.

Thomas stared at the man. "My mother? She does not know I am here!" He paused, then added grimly, "Or does she?"

"No, no, of course not, Your Highness," Henshaw said smoothly. "Her Ladyship sent Sir Richard a message over a year ago, requesting that he have this suit of clothes made for you in preparation for the day you entered court. Sir Richard thought you would want to wear it this evening."

Henshaw unpacked the trunk and laid out the clothes. Thomas had to admit that they were far more elegant than the clothes he had brought with him. His mother had many faults, but she had exemplary taste in fashion.

The jacket was of robin's-egg-blue silk velvet. The front was trimmed in glistening bands of silver embroidery with double bands of embroidery around the cuffs of the sleeve. The weskit was of matching velvet, also embroidered, though more ornately than the embroidery on the jacket, which was intended to be worn open. The breeches were of blue velvet, embroidered at the knees.

The weskit and the breeches were adorned with silver buttons bearing the Stanford coat of arms. The same buttons trimmed the jacket. A shirt with lace cuffs and a lace-trimmed cravat completed the ensemble.

Henshaw held up a powdered wig, but Thomas refused. Wigs were hot and the powder made him sneeze. He combed his hair, and tied it back with a blue velvet ribbon.

He regarded himself in the mirror. He seemed older, with grave blue eyes, pensive brow, and an unusually serious expression.

He credited Phillip with making him understand that his people needed him. He credited Kate with showing him by example that he had a duty to them. He wished both of his friends could be here with him. He would hold them close within his heart and someday he would tell them all about this.

Henshaw knocked again at the door.

"The hour is nine of the clock, Your Highness. Time to leave for the palace."

FIFTY-FIVE

The *Naofa* sailed during daylight hours now, heading south for Haever. They traveled over land, sailing southwest from Illwick, avoiding the coast and navy patrol boats. They had fair weather and made good time, arriving just north of Haever after dark.

As the lights of the city came into view, Franklin ordered the helmsman to slow the ship. He sent the crew to extinguish all lights except for a small lantern hanging above the helm.

"We will maintain strict silence," he told the crew. "If I hear so much as a cough, I will throw that person overboard."

Franklin stood outside the wheelhouse, his spyglass to his eye, directing the helmsman. He took out his pocket watch and set it on the brass helm where he could see it, keeping track of the time.

The *Naofa* crept into Haever, sailing about forty feet above the church steeples.

"Ten of the clock," Franklin said softly to the helmsman, and he was corroborated by the church bells sounding the hour; the chiming and gonging seemed to stretch on endlessly until the last bell fell silent.

Kate had nothing to do except grow increasingly nervous. Grunnel had taken over her duties as crafter for the green beam weapon. He was on the forecastle, standing by the weapon, prepared to activate the magic when ordered. Kate had offered to help, but Franklin had curtly rebuffed her. He told her to remain near the wheelhouse in case the helmsman encountered problems with the helm's magic.

The crew had been speculating as to their target, some even placing wagers. The favorite was blowing up the parliament building, although destroying the ships in the Naval Yard had emerged as a strong contender.

The black ship sailed steadily onward. The crew had mounted the two swivel guns on the rail, one on the portside and one starboard, prepared to fight if necessary. Discovery seemed unlikely, however. The black ship was one with the night, silent and nearly invisible. Franklin continued to provide the helmsman with directions. He glanced at his watch again.

"Half past the hour," Franklin told the helmsman. "Start your descent."

Kate stood fidgeting by the rail near the wheelhouse. From her vantage point, she could look down on the rooftops and chimney pots as the ship drifted slowly closer. The lamplighters had made their rounds and street lamps shone at regular intervals, forming a sparkling grid.

Kate thought the streets seemed unusually deserted, buildings unusually dark. This time of the night, the streets were generally crowded with cabs taking people home from the theater or to their clubs, gambling houses, restaurants and taverns. Those establishments should be busy now, bright lights shining. They were dark and shuttered.

As in times of plague or war, Kate thought uneasily.

Franklin had been keeping watch ahead of them. He shifted the spyglass to look off to the west. Kate followed his gaze. The only object of interest in that direction was Haever's famous floating house drifting among the stars.

Kate stared out into the night, searching for other landmarks. She didn't see anything that looked familiar until she caught sight of the distinctive conical towers of the university. The *Naofa* sailed over a park, and now Kate had some idea of their location. She still could not guess where they were bound.

The ship flew on, descending lower and lower. The helmsman slowed his speed almost to a crawl, for they were so close to the buildings he had to avoid knocking down chimneys and navigate around steeples.

A broad swath of darkness opened up ahead. Covington Palace came into sight, a radiant star in the night. The glowing palace was easy to see from the sky and from the ground.

Franklin picked up his watch and left the helm, going up to the forecastle to join Grunnel.

"Prepare the weapon for firing," Franklin said.

Grunnel loaded the brass disc into the breech and activated a series of constructs that completed the power circuit between the barrel and charging disc. Franklin raised his spyglass, looked to the west, toward the palace's front gate. He watched intently for several moments, then lowered the spyglass.

"There is the signal. Our troops are in position. We may proceed." He glanced at his watch. "The time is nearing eleven. We are right on schedule."

Kate now knew the target. Those who had bet on parliament or the Navy Yard were out their money.

The target was the palace.

She could see again the green beam blow an enormous chunk of stone out of the cliff, see the rock shatter, split apart, and she was overwhelmed with horror. Fear tightened her throat, her mouth went dry, her hands gripped the rail.

The ship crept closer and closer, gliding silently through the night. The magic on the green beam weapon started to come to life, the constructs glowed. Her constructs. Her magic.

"The gun is ready to fire, sir," Grunnel reported.

"Go take command of the swivel guns," said Franklin. "Do not fire unless I give the order! Thus far no one has seen us or heard us. I want to keep it that way."

Grunnel left the forecastle and ran down to the main deck. Franklin took his place behind the green beam weapon, spyglass trained on the palace. The magical constructs on the green beam gun glowed blue and green, connected by the seventh sigil.

The palace grounds were surrounded by a tall stone wall pierced by the main gate. The gate would be well guarded and Kate was not surprised when the helmsman altered course to avoid it, veering off to the west.

The ship was close. The wall was only about a mile away. But the grounds were extensive, and the palace was still far beyond the wall. Kate looked down to see rooftops directly beneath her.

She flashed a glance at the green beam gun. The only way she could disable the magic was to remove the seventh sigils and to do that, she would have to be able to touch them. Franklin was wearing his sidearm. He would kill her before she could come close.

Frustrated, Kate looked desperately about the ship, searching for an idea. Her eye fell on the rack holding the boarding axes.

The crew members were staring at the glowing palace. Franklin was intent upon his target. The helmsman was concentrating on his task. The only person she had to worry about was Corporal Grunnel, who was standing on the main deck, manning the port-side swivel gun. To reach her objective, she would have to get past him.

Kate glided over to the rack, grabbed one of the axes, and pressed it close to her thigh so no one would notice. She then walked back toward the stern, swearing under her breath.

"The damn airscrew would choose this time to fail."

A few of the crew glanced at her, but they were used to her going about the ship repairing the magic, and no one stopped her.

Kate continued toward the stern. The distance across the deck from the front of the ship to the rear seemed interminable, and she longed to break into a run. Someone would take notice at that and alert Franklin. Kate gritted her teeth and kept walking. Her palms were sweating, and the axe handle was slippery. She gripped it so tightly her hand started to ache.

She drew level with Grunnel and the swivel gun. He was supervising one of the crew members who was busy loading it. Neither looked at Kate. She reached the stern in safety.

She could hear the airscrews, one on the port side, one on starboard, whirring beneath her. She glanced over the rail. The last of the rooftops was coming into view. Beyond that was the broad thoroughfare that ran in front of the palace, then the outer wall and the palace grounds.

Kate came to the place on the deck known as the "crafter's cut." The braided leather that carried the magic to the airscrews ran mostly below deck. At this juncture, a hatch allowed access to the line as it traveled down to the airscrew.

Kate threw open the hatch, positioned herself above the line, and raised the axe. She heard a smothered shout, the sound of feet pounding across the deck, and looked up to see Grunnel bearing down on her. He had drawn his pistol, but he didn't dare fire for fear someone would hear the shot.

Kate brought the axe down on the braided leather with a strength born of fear, and sliced through it with a single stroke, just as Grunnel slammed into her with his shoulder. He knocked her off balance and she dropped the axe. He tried to grab hold of her, but she kneed him in the groin and he doubled over with a groan. Kate started to pick up the axe, to disable the other aircrew, but more crew members were now aware of the danger and were rushing to stop her.

She climbed onto the rail and looked down. The ship was above a building with what looked like a flat roof about six feet below.

A hand grabbed her foot. Kate stomped on the fingers and the hand let go with a curse. She sucked in a deep breath and jumped.

She landed on the roof with a jarring thud that seemed to jam her spine into her skull, and had to take a moment to recover from the paralyzing shock.

She looked up at the black ship. She had managed to cripple it; she could hear the sound of only one airscrew. A ship could continue to sail with one airscrew, especially a small ship such as the *Naofa*. She had not stopped it, as she had hoped, but she had managed to slow it down, giving her time to warn someone.

She could see Franklin in the darkness, glaring down at her, helpless to do anything. The ship sailed on, crossed the boulevard, and headed toward the palace wall.

The roof sloped at a slight angle to allow runoff, and she slipped and skittered precariously on the slate tiles as she made her way to the edge and tried to figure out how to get down.

An iron gutter ran around the roof. A street lamp stood on the corner and she could see by its light that her options were an old and rickety-looking drain spout or a two-story drop.

Kate was still jarred from the last jump, so she opted for the drain spout. She gingerly lowered herself onto it and clasped her knees around it, intending to shinny down the drain spout the way she shinnied down a mast.

The drain spout was not like a mast, however. It was anchored to the building and she couldn't get a proper hold on it. She clung to it as best she could, scrabbling with her feet for a toehold and slicing her hands on rusted iron. The drain spout solved her problem by breaking beneath her weight. She plunged to the ground and landed amidst the wreckage of the drain spout, shaken, bruised, and bleeding.

Kate staggered to her feet and looked for the black ship, but it had sailed over the wall onto the palace grounds and was almost lost to sight.

All she could see was the faint green glow of the gun that had blown up a cliff.

FIFTY-SIX

Henry Wallace was sitting in his favorite leather chair in his study before the fire. He had come here to read the newspaper, but the *Haever Gazette,* dated 11/28, lay unopened in his lap. He held in his hands the queen's letter announcing the name of her heir. He had not removed the seal. He would not read it until the time she had dictated. He had given her his word and, as she knew, his word was inviolate.

His wife had gone out for the evening to dine with friends. They had invited Henry, but he had declined to go, pleading fatigue from his recent travels. Alan and Randolph had urged him to join them for dinner at the Naval Club. Simon had wanted him to come to Welkinstead, saying he wanted to discuss a theory he had regarding liquid Breath in the Aligoes. Henry had refused both invitations.

He was not fit company for anyone tonight, including his friends. He was tired, as he had said, although the weariness was more of spirit than of the flesh.

He had accompanied the queen back to the palace two days ago. She had been smiling, in a good humor, and had ordered Henry to stop fussing over her and go back to work. He had spent the next two days at the Foreign Office attempting to repair the damage done in his absence by bureaucratic

fools who had blundered into delicate situations with all the grace of prize
hogs and had then come begging him to pull them out of the muck.

In addition, he had to deal yet again with the Travian dragons. One of
their number had been killed in a rock slide; a tragic event, but one which
was an act of God, over which he had no control. Yet they were now in
an uproar, claiming the rock slide had been triggered by magic; that this
was murder. He was extremely sorry he had ever involved himself with
dragons.

Henry tapped the queen's letter on his knee and frowned at the fire, mus-
ing over a report that the Countess de Marjolaine had arrived unexpectedly
in Haever. She had let it be known that she had come to visit the Princess
Sophia and to give a lavish ball in the princess's honor.

The countess was perfectly free to visit Freya. The two nations were not
at war. She was known to take an interest in the princess's education, and,
although the countess was viewed with suspicion and hostility by the Freyan
nobility, the fools would be tumbling all over themselves to secure an invitation to attend her ball.

Henry thrust the queen's letter into the inner pocket of his coat. He carried
it with him at all times, placed it beneath his pillow when he slept. Rising
from the chair, he to went to pour himself a brandy, still thinking about the
countess.

The reason Cecile had given for being in Haever seemed perfectly logical,
except that Henry had just read an announcement in a Rosian newspaper
that the Duke de Bourlet and his wife were the proud parents of a baby boy.
Cecile de Marjolaine would never absent herself from home at such a joyous
time. Henry knew her as he knew himself. She had some urgent reason to
travel to Haever and it was not to give lavish balls.

"That blasted woman is up to something," Henry said, drinking his
brandy.

The great clock in the hall chimed eight times. Henry drew out his pocket
watch to check its accuracy and discovered he was a minute behind. He corrected his watch and smiled to think his wife would soon be home. He always
waited up for Ann when she was away for the evening. Given the unrest in
the streets, he was never easy until she was safely in the house.

The clock chimed a quarter past and he went to the window. He drew
aside the curtain and looked out just in time to see her carriage arrive. The
coachman, Baxter, assisted Ann to alight. She looked up, saw the light in the
study, and knew he was watching. She smiled and touched her hand to her
lips.

Henry smiled back. He lowered the curtain, returned to his chair, and realized suddenly that he had let the fire go out, and the room was cold. Ann

would come to the study to share with him the gossip of the evening. He reached for the bellpull to order the servants to relight the fire.

He halted, frozen, his hand in midair.

A woman screamed and kept screaming, not once but over and over, the high-pitched shrill shriek of hysteria. Her screams were accompanied by a commotion—the sounds of shouts and people running. Alarmed, Henry was about to yank open the door to find out what was going on when the door burst open of its own accord.

A maid stood gasping and wringing her hands. "Oh, sir, the mistress says to come quick! It's Mr. Sloan!"

Henry bolted out the door, almost knocking down the maid, and ran down the stairs. He stopped about halfway down, arrested by the astonishing scene.

The front door stood open. One of the maids was screaming hysterically in a corner. His wife and Amelia Nettleship were propping up Mr. Sloan, assisting him to enter the house. He was partially clothed in a torn and bloody uniform jacket, trousers, and shoes, but no shirt or stockings. His torso was swathed in bandages that were stained with fresh blood. He collapsed as he crossed the threshold and fell to the floor.

Henry dashed down the stairs as Amelia quickly shut the door behind her. She caught sight of him and gave a shake of her head, as though to say "a bad business." She then proceeded to deal with the hysterical maid.

"Stop shrieking, my girl! The neighbors will hear you!" Amelia said sharply. "One of you, take her to the kitchen and be quick about it."

Ann was on her knees beside Mr. Sloan. She had removed her own cloak and was wrapping it around him, as she issued orders to the staff.

"Jacobs, send someone to fetch Dr. Vollmer. We will convey Mr. Sloan to the downstairs bedroom, so see to it that there is a fire. Tell Cook I will need boiling water and bandages. The wound has broken open and we must stop the bleeding."

Henry hurried down the stairs. Finding Mr. Sloan was unconscious, Henry looked to Amelia for answers.

"I received word that a man had fainted on Market Street and was found to be suffering from a gunshot wound. I went to the hospital, of course, to see if I could obtain the story and was astonished to find the victim was Mr. Sloan. He said he needed to speak to you on a matter of the utmost urgency. He was in no condition to be moving about, so I told him I would fetch you or I would carry the message. He said he could not stay in the hospital. He feared those who had shot him would come searching for him, to silence him. He asked me to help smuggle him out and bring him to your house. I did so and that is all I know," Amelia concluded.

"Thank you, Miss Amelia," said Henry, opening the front door. "You have my eternal gratitude. We will deal with this matter now."

"Hear me out, my lord. If I had not come across Mr. Sloan, I would have come to you anyway," said Amelia. "Something is amiss in the city tonight."

"I will read your article about it in the morning," said Henry.

He did not exactly shove her bodily through the door, but he came close, maneuvering her across the threshold and out onto the door stoop. He quickly clapped the door shut behind her. Looking out, he saw her hesitate on the stoop and then she turned and walked down the sidewalk.

Henry hurried back to his wife.

Ann looked up at him. She was pale, but quite composed. "Mr. Sloan was conscious and tried to say something just now, but he passed out before he could. I fear he has lost a vast quantity of blood."

"Mr. Sloan!" Henry knelt beside his friend and pressed his hand.

Mr. Sloan roused at the sound of Henry's voice and opened his eyes. "Sir, I have to tell you—"

"Not now, Mr. Sloan!" Henry interrupted. He glanced around at the servants. "Some of you men, help me convey him to the bedroom."

"Sir," Mr. Sloan said weakly. "Please! . . . *Lex Talionis*! I must—"

"No more talking, Mr. Sloan. Time enough when you have rested."

Ann had been watching Mr. Sloan. He was gray and haggard, his eyes sunken, his face bathed in sweat. He gazed at Henry with a fixed intensity.

"Henry," Ann said. "I think you should hear what he has to tell you."

"I will, my dear," said Henry. "When he is settled—"

"Henry, listen to what Mr. Sloan has to say now!" Ann spoke sharply. "He has risked his life to bring you information he considers urgent."

Henry stared at her in shock. His "Mouse" had never raised her voice to him or to anyone that he had ever known.

"His Lordship is listening, Mr. Sloan," Ann said.

"Yes, Franklin, you have my complete attention," said Henry. "Tell me."

Mr. Sloan had to summon strength. His words came out in gasps. "Prince Tom . . . here. Meeting Her Majesty . . . tonight, eleven of the clock . . . Plot to overthrow . . . Troops . . . our uniforms, queen arrested . . ."

"Good God!" Henry exclaimed in horror. "When?"

"This night . . . Your brother . . ."

"Richard?" Henry was puzzled. "What has he to do with this?"

Mr. Sloan moistened his lips. "The Faithful . . . Sir Richard . . . part of the plot . . ."

Anne cast her husband a stricken look.

"You must be mistaken, Mr. Sloan," said Henry.

Mr. Sloan clasped Henry's hand tightly. "I am sorry, my lord. So very sorry . . ."

His head lolled. His eyes closed.

Henry gently laid down his hand and rose to his feet. He glanced at the clock.

"Half past eight. I must leave at once."

"Take the carriage!" Ann told him, rising to her feet. "Baxter will not yet have unhitched the horses!" She added softly, "Mr. Sloan may be wrong about your brother, my dear."

"He is not wrong," Henry said. He kissed his wife's hand. "Stay with him, my love."

"I will not leave his side," Ann promised. "Be careful! Pray God you are in time!"

Jacobs stood ready with Henry's cloak and hat. Henry put them on, hardly knowing what he was doing, and ran outside, shouting at the coachman, who had started to drive the carriage around back to the stables.

"To the palace with all possible speed. Kill the horses if you must!" Henry added grimly, "It is a matter of life and death!"

He jumped into the carriage and shut the door, only to see the door open on the other side. Amelia nimbly climbed in and took a seat across from him.

"Miss Amelia, this is an outrage!" Henry cried, glaring at her.

He would have pushed her out, but the coachman used the whip and urged the horses forward at a gallop. The coach lurched, flinging Henry backward and almost sending Amelia forward into his arms.

She regained her seat, hanging on as the coach shook and rattled.

"You need to listen to me, my lord! I told you something was amiss! It is said that animals sense when a storm is in the offing and seek shelter. The citizens of Haever have gone to ground. Doors throughout the city are locked and bolted. Shops have closed. I have heard reports of secret gatherings of armed men. I have no idea what it means . . ."

"I do," said Henry. "There is a plot to overthrow the queen."

"Ah," said Amelia. "I thought it might be something like that. The Faithful."

"The Faithful," Henry murmured.

Amelia opened her mouth. "My lord—"

Henry raised his hand. "Please, Miss Amelia. Your questions will have to wait. I need to think."

Amelia nodded. "I understand, my lord."

She clutched her reticule in her hand and gazed out the window.

Henry tried to concentrate on the danger to his country, but his thoughts kept twisting back to his brother.

The Old Chap, gray and staid, dull as dirt, boring as cold mutton, plotting to bring down the monarchy.

And yet it all made sense, now that Henry thought about it. Their father had always deplored the fact that their misguided ancestors had lost the family fortune and title by backing the wrong side in the Cousins War.

Henry had laughed at what he termed "ancient history," said their ancestors were fools for supporting a weak-willed King James and they got what they deserved. Richard, however, had always taken their father's side, speaking of James as a martyr and Alfred as a monster who had robbed the family of their due.

Henry stared out into the night.

My own brother could be hanged for treason.

The coach bounded over the cobblestones and took a corner at high speed, throwing Henry and his fellow passenger hard against the door.

"Are you all right, Miss Amelia?" Henry asked.

"Please do not concern yourself with me, my lord," said Amelia, recovering her hat and picking up the reticule. "I am the least of your worries."

Henry had work to do. He would deal with Richard when the time came.

"I need your assistance, Miss Amelia," he said. "I must ask you to move. I need to lift up your seat."

The swaying of the carriage tossed them both about, but between them they managed to open the secret compartment. Henry drew out several pistols, powder, and shot.

Amelia assisted him in loading the weapons. This proved difficult not only because of the erratic motion of the carriage, but they had to wait until it passed beneath a street lamp so they could see what they were doing.

"I don't suppose it would do me any good to recommend that once we arrive at the palace, you take a cab for home, Miss Amelia," said Henry. "There will likely be trouble."

"None in the slightest, my lord," said Amelia. She patted her reticule. "I always go armed, as you know." She added in hardened tones, "I hope we arrive in time to put a stop to this nonsense!"

Henry did not answer. He shut the compartment, sat back in his seat, and took out his watch.

A street lamp illuminated the dial.

The time was thirty minutes past the hour of nine.

FIFTY-SEVEN

The elegant little clock on the mantelpiece in the Rose Room chimed the half hour.

Thomas noted the time, thirty minutes past nine. At the hour eleven of the clock, he would be bowing before the queen and his life would change forever. He could not sit still, but paced the room, watching the clock, thinking that time had never moved so slowly. Or so fast.

The Rose Room was located on the fourth floor in the family's private wing of the palace. The room was named for the rose-colored walls, the roses on the carpet, and the roses on the curtains that were drawn across the room's sole window. The chairs and sofas and love seats were adorned with cushions embroidered with petit point roses.

Sir Richard had brought him to the Rose Room by way of a secret passage that wound up a great many stairs and led to a panel concealed behind a painting.

Sir Richard had shut the panel behind them and it had disappeared into the wall.

A vase filled with roses stood on a table in the center of the room. The mantelpiece clock told the time in roses. Thomas thought that he would never again see a rose without recalling this night.

The servants had lighted the lamps, filling the room with warm magical light. The queen had provided food and drink: hot tea and a plate of assorted sandwiches, tea cakes, and sweetmeats, a decanter of brandy, a bottle of wine, and a pitcher of water.

"Will Your Highness take some refreshment?" Sir Richard asked, pouring himself a brandy.

"Thank you, sir, no," said Thomas.

He was too nervous to eat. He sat down in a chair near the fire, stretched out his legs and stared at his shoes. Sir Richard drank the brandy at a gulp, then walked over to the window. He drew aside the curtains and Thomas saw glass-paned doors that opened onto a balcony. Richard stared intently outside.

Thomas was glad to have something to do besides admire the roses. He walked over to join Sir Richard.

"What do you find so interesting out here, my lord?" Thomas asked.

Sir Richard had not heard his approach, apparently, for he gave a nervous start and jerked his head around.

"What? Oh, er. Nothing, Your Highness. I was . . . um . . . wondering if we were going to have rain."

He let the curtain fall and left the window.

Thomas thought it extremely odd that Richard should be worrying about the weather at a time like this. He said nothing, however. Parting the curtains, he glanced curiously outside.

The balcony overlooked the paved courtyard that ran in the front of the palace. The magical light shining from the walls illuminated the courtyard. Thomas could see sentries at their posts, but nothing more interesting.

"You should not let yourself be seen, Your Highness!" Sir Richard scolded. "Please close the curtains!"

Thomas let the curtain fall and returned to his chair. He gazed at the painting, which was a full-length portrait of a woman from a bygone era holding a bouquet of roses. He was idly wondering who she was and was about to ask Sir Richard when the painting began to move, swinging like a door. The panel in the wall behind it opened suddenly, without warning. A woman entered the room.

She was short and stout, perhaps in her early sixties. She wore a gown of green brocade trimmed in gold, a ruby and diamond necklace, and several sparkling rings on her fingers. A jeweled band of gold perched somewhat askew on her gray hair. She leaned on a walking stick.

Thomas could only stare, startled by the intrusion. Richard was momentarily shocked, but then he sprang to his feet in confusion.

"Your Majesty!" he exclaimed.

The queen acknowledged him with a nod. She shot a sharp glance at Thomas, then turned to speak to a lady standing behind her in the passageway.

"Wait here for me. I won't be long."

The queen shut the panel.

Sir Richard bowed low, his hand on his heart.

Thomas rose to his feet and bowed. He was too amazed to do more than murmur incoherently.

Queen Mary was pale beneath her rouge, but her step was firm, not faltering. Her intelligent eyes took in every part of him, from the buckles of his shoes to the blue ribbon that tied back his hair. Her scrutiny was intense. She took her time.

"So you are Thomas Stanford," she said at last. "Otherwise known as Prince Tom."

"His Highness is—" Sir Richard began.

"Please be quiet, my lord," said Mary, giving him an annoyed glance. "We need to speak to this young man and our time is short."

She returned her gaze to Thomas and waited for his answer.

"I am Thomas Stanford, Your Majesty," he said, adding with a faint smile, "Prince Tom is a character in the serials, ma'am. He and I bear little resemblance."

"Hah!" Mary exclaimed, but she seemed pleased with his answer.

She rested both hands on the walking stick, thrust her head forward to fix him with a shrewd gaze.

"Why do you want to be king, Thomas Stanford?"

Thomas was astounded by her question and did not know how to answer. He knew what he ought to say, knew what Sir Richard had been coaching him to say, knew what his mother would want him to say.

Sir Richard had written out a speech. *If I am so honored as to earn Your Majesty's trust, I vow before God that the Freyan people will be my first and only care. I view their welfare as a sacred responsibility given to me by God, and one that with His help and guidance, I will do my best to faithfully discharge.*

The speech went on to talk in moving terms of his love for his country (which he had never visited), of his fondness for the people (whom he had never met). Thomas knew at once that such twaddle would diminish him in the eyes of this woman who knew she was dying and needed to leave her country and her people in the hands of someone she could trust.

Mary was patient, giving him time. Her eyes were small, set in a face that had once been pudgy, but which had now dwindled to folds of sagging skin.

Her time was short.

"The truth is, I do not want to be king, ma'am," Thomas said.

Sir Richard stared at him in horror. Mary struck her walking stick on the floor.

"Then why the devil are you here, Thomas Stanford?"

"By accident, ma'am."

Richard appeared to be on the verge of apoplexy.

"The will of God, Your Majesty!" Richard cried, dismayed. "You are God's chosen!"

Mary ignored him, kept her gaze on Thomas.

She did not seem displeased.

"Explain yourself, sir."

Thomas hoped he would not offend her. He had no idea of her religious views. He was bound to tell her the truth, however. She had the right to know.

"A tragic accident aboard ship felled your son, the Crown Prince. His little son died of a contagious disease, which he had the misfortune to contract. I do *not* believe God struck them down to bring me here to stand before you, Your Majesty.

"I am here because the accident of my birth makes me heir to King James and I have been led to believe that if you name either your sister or your half brother as your heir, the one you rejected would wage war to seize it. Whereas if you name me, the supporters of the other two would shift their support to me. Am I wrong in that belief?"

"You are not wrong," said Mary quietly.

"I am here out of duty, to try to bring peace and stability to Freya." Thomas paused, drew in a breath. "I cannot promise Your Majesty that I will be a wise and powerful ruler. I do promise that I will strive to be a good man who hopes someday to be a good king."

"You remind me of my son," said Mary. "He never wanted to be king, either."

She propped the walking stick against the wall and took hold of a ring that sparkled on her finger. Drawing it off, she handed the ring to Thomas.

"This ring belonged to poor James, your unhappy ancestor," Mary said. "The man made a pig's breakfast of being king, damn near ruined the country. Still, he was the anointed king and my own ancestors were wrong to plunge Freya into a bitter and bloody civil war to overthrow him."

Mary placed the ring in his palm. The ring was gold with black diamonds and blue sapphires set in intricate patterns, like a mosaic. The ring was still warm from her touch. She closed Thomas's hand over it, then rested both her hands on his and looked into his eyes.

"You and I, between us, must do everything within our power to keep Freya strong and united, Thomas Stanford. I do my part by naming you heir to the throne. You do yours by doing your duty."

Thomas bowed his head as one receiving a benediction.

Mary gave his hand a maternal pat, then released him and retrieved her walking stick.

"We will speak more in my office when you come to formalize matters later this night. I must have you sign documents and all that rot." The queen gave him a mischievous grin. "Forgive me for springing a kingship on you, young Stanford, but I wanted to catch you off guard. I needed to hear what was in your heart, not the platitudes Sir Richard undoubtedly urged you to memorize."

Thomas smiled. "I look forward to having the chance to talk with you many more times after tonight, ma'am. You have much to teach me and I have much to learn."

"More than you know, dear boy," said Mary with a sigh.

The queen touched her hand to a magical construct concealed in the ornate carved frame around the portrait. The painting moved and the secret panel slid open. The queen paused before she entered the passageway and turned to Thomas. "Tell that rapscallion friend of yours Pip that he was right about you. And let him know he should come visit me. He's not to worry. I won't let Henry chop off his head."

Mary gave a barking laugh and walked out of the room, joining an older woman who hovered solicitously in the passageway, wanting to assist the queen. Many gave her an irritated scolding for her pains, then closed the panel.

Thomas stood facing the portrait. He was not ready to receive Richard's effusive congratulations. The moment was too solemn, too reverent. He slipped the ring on the little finger of his left hand—the only finger it would fit, and closed his hand over it.

The ring had belonged to James, but it would always remind Thomas of the queen and of this moment.

"Your Royal Highness!" Sir Richard cried jubilantly, coming up behind him. "I am so pleased. You must allow me to congratulate you!"

Thomas drew in a breath and turned to face his destiny with a smile. Sir Richard seized hold of his hand and heartily shook it. He then asked to see the ring.

"Immensely valuable," he said, admiring it. "A painting of King James in the Royal Academy shows him wearing this very ring. It is thought to have been a gift from his wife."

Richard gazed thoughtfully at the ring. "I never liked Queen Mary. She has led our country to the brink of ruin, but I freely admit that in naming you her heir, she has done the right thing. I would not have expected it of her."

"I esteem Her Majesty highly," said Thomas. "I believe she and I will be good friends. I look forward to spending time learning from her."

Richard cast him a frowning glance, then looked away. He seemed about to say something, then checked himself.

"What is it, my lord?" Thomas asked.

Richard cleared his throat. "Nothing, sir. I am a little overwhelmed, that is all."

He walked to the sideboard and poured a glass of brandy. He drank it off quickly.

The clock chimed ten. Thomas sighed. Another hour of waiting, cooped up in this room.

"If you will excuse me, my lord, I feel in need of some fresh air."

He walked over to the balcony and started to open the door.

Richard came up behind him, put his hand on the door and pushed it shut. "You cannot go out there, sir."

Thomas rounded on him angrily. "I have a great deal to think about, my lord. I would like some privacy."

"I must insist you remain concealed, sir."

Richard waited and finally Thomas went back to the chair in front of the portrait and sat down. He had nothing else to do except wait and he could either watch the hands crawl over the face of the clock or he could study the face in the portrait.

He chose the portrait.

The lady was dressed in the fashion of the court of King Frederick with a ruff about her neck, her hair bound with strands of pearls. She was about Thomas's age. She was not wearing a wedding band, but she wore a miniature of a gentleman on a velvet cord around her neck. Perhaps her portrait had been painted on the occasion of her wedding.

His thoughts went to his own wedding. He thought about Sophia and their pledges to each other. He thought about Kate and wished he could talk to her, tell her why he had made this decision. He hoped she would understand. She was the one who had taught him about duty.

The lady in the portrait seemed to regard him with sympathy and understanding. He wondered if her marriage had been arranged. If she had been happy.

The clock chimed three quarters of the hour.

Sir Richard rose to his feet. "We should go, sir. We will be a trifle early, but Her Majesty is punctual to a fault. I suggest we put on our hats and cloaks. If anyone stops us, we can say we are visiting friends."

Thomas picked up his hat and draped his cloak around his shoulders. Sir

Richard did the same. They were advancing toward the front door when someone knocked on it.

Thomas looked at Richard, startled. "No one is supposed to know we are here!"

Richard frowned and shook his head, enjoining silence.

"A mistake!" he whispered. "The person will go away."

The person did not go away, but knocked again, adding in deferential tones, "Sir Richard, please open the door. I have an urgent message for His Highness."

Sir Richard glowered and opened the door a crack.

"Yes, what is— I beg your pardon, sir!" Richard exclaimed, stumbling backward as a member of the palace guard, armed with a rifle, thrust open the door and shouldered him to one side.

The guardsman saluted Thomas. "Your Highness, I require you to come with me at once. You, as well, Sir Richard. I have orders to remove you both to a place of safety."

Thomas saw more guardsmen waiting in the hall, all of them armed, rifles over their shoulders.

Richard saw them, as well. He cast them a disparaging glance. "I am not going anywhere, sir, until I receive an explanation!"

"You and Prince Thomas are in danger, my lord," said the guardsman. "This room is compromised. There could be a bomb."

"A bomb!" Richard repeated, snorting. "I don't believe it. We've been sitting here for over an hour. If some damn anarchist was going to blow us up, he would have done so by now!"

The guardsman eyed him grimly. He was beginning to lose patience.

"I think we should do as they say, my lord," said Thomas quietly. "Nothing to be gained by arguing."

The guardsman cast Thomas a grateful glance. He walked out of the room into the hall. Richard stalked after him.

"I will get to the bottom of this!" he muttered.

The officer turned to one of his men with orders.

"Go out on the balcony and give the signal that His Highness is safe," he ordered. "Leave the lamps lighted and the door open."

One of the guardsmen entered the room, picked up a lamp, and headed for the balcony. Thomas noted that the officer had not given orders to search for a bomb.

"This way, gentlemen," said the officer. "Down the hall. The Yellow Drawing Room. The next room, to your right."

"Next door! Hardly far enough to escape a bomb blast," Richard said caustically.

"Down the hall, to your right," said the officer and they proceeded down the hall to their right.

"This is Henry's doing!" Richard muttered, seething. "Do not worry, Your Highness. You have the ring. Her Majesty has made the succession official. My brother can do nothing!"

Thomas thought of a great many things Henry Wallace could do and none of them pleasant. He was careful to take note of his surroundings as he left, thinking he might need a means of escape. He wondered how many people knew about that secret panel.

"What part of the palace are we in, my lord?" he asked Richard in an undertone.

"This hall is known as the Principal Corridor, sir," said Richard. "The main hall of the east wing of the palace."

The corridor was wide with polished marble floors, ornately carved woodwork, and a high, vaulted ceiling. The walls were papered with flocked velvet done in red against a gold background. The hall was dimly lit by lamps with porcelain bases decorated with peacocks holding up glowing globes of light. Crystal chandeliers hung from the ceiling, but they had not been lighted.

"Where does this lead?" asked Thomas.

"The north gallery at the end of this hall," Richard replied. "That is the Skylight gallery and it leads to the western wing, the queen's offices, and the Grand Entrance."

"Behind us?"

"The south gallery," said Richard. "Overlooking the palace gardens."

Thomas fixed the map in his mind.

The officer came to a halt in front of the door to the Yellow Drawing Room. He knocked first, then opened the door and indicated they were to enter.

Thomas walked inside and looked around. He wondered how the room had come by its name as the Yellow Drawing Room, for the walls were green, the furniture and carpet blue. The room was considerably smaller than the Rose Room, more intimate.

Guards were already in the room. Two were posted in front of glass-paned doors at the far end. The curtains were open and Thomas could see another balcony outside, similar to the balcony in the Rose Room. He heard raised voices and turned to find Richard standing in the hall, arguing with the officer.

"I will not stir a step!" Richard stated. "Not until you tell me what is going on!"

"You can either walk inside, my lord, or I have orders to force you," said the officer, polite, but firm.

Sir Richard breathed hard, but he required only a moment to realize he had no recourse. He gave the officer an enraged glower and stalked into the room.

"I apologize for the inconvenience, gentlemen," the officer said. "I will be outside if you require anything."

He bowed and walked out, shutting the door behind him. Thomas heard a key turn in the lock and feet stamping, rifle butts thudding on the floor. The guardsmen were taking up positions outside the door. The two guards-men in front of the balcony door stood facing them, rifles on their shoulders, their faces expressionless.

Sir Richard tightened his lips. Anger flushed his cheekbones and two white dents appeared, one on either side of his nose.

"Henry!" He choked on the name.

FIFTY-EIGHT

Henry placed one loaded pistol on the seat beside him, thrust another beneath his coat, and held one in his hand. Amelia had opened the reticule and brought out the curious little two-barreled corset gun. They both kept watch out the windows.

He made plans. He would first see to it that the queen was taken to a place of safety. He decided on the ancient castle where the dragon Lady Odila had been murdered.

Castle Lindameer was old and ugly, not a very pleasant place in the best of times, never mind that the blood of the dead dragon still stained the flagstones of the lower level.

The castle had the advantage of being located in an isolated part of the country and was deserted the better part of the year, so no one would be in residence. It had been built centuries ago, during a time when castles were designed to withstand armies, not host a hundred guests for dinner and dancing. No enemy would think of looking for Her Majesty there, giving time for Henry to summon the forces he needed to defend the queen and his country.

The carriage rumbled through streets that should have been clogged with cabs and wagons and carts, coaches and carriages. Henry saw a few vehicles, but those scurried off like rats diving back into their holes. The city had gone to ground, as Amelia had said.

"Mr. Sloan is a hero, my lord," Amelia commented.

"He is," said Henry, gruffly. "I will see to it he receives a knighthood for this. Did he say who shot him or why?"

"He did not, my lord," said Amelia. "He was barely conscious. I believe he was reserving his strength to talk to you."

The lights blurred in Henry's eyes. He rubbed them and rode the rest of the way in silence. The carriage arrived at the palace at a little after thirty minutes past the hour of ten. Henry had feared they would arrive in the midst of a pitched battle and he was vastly relieved to find all appeared peaceful and quiet.

The gate was closed, but that was customary. The palace guard were in position. Nothing was amiss except a drunken sailor engaged in an altercation with a guardsman.

Henry opened the carriage door before the carriage had come to a stop and jumped out. Amelia remained inside, undoubtedly realizing that if she climbed out, Henry would not allow her back in.

The guards recognized him and began to open the gate. The commander advanced to greet him with a smile that vanished when he saw Henry's grim expression.

"Is Her Majesty in the palace?" he demanded.

"Yes, my lord," the captain replied, startled.

"Has the queen received any visitors this night? Anyone not known to you? Did any stranger try to gain entry?"

"Her Majesty dined with the Princess Sophia," said the captain.

Henry brushed that aside. "Anyone else? A young man, black curly hair and striking blue eyes?"

"No, my lord," said the captain, mystified.

Henry swallowed, then asked as calmly as he could manage, "Has my brother, Sir Richard Wallace, been here?"

"No, my lord. The only visitor was the Countess de Marjolaine—"

"The countess!" Henry repeated sharply. "Is she here? When? Was she expected?"

"Yes, she is here and no, my lord, she was not on the list of visitors," said the captain. "She arrived about twenty minutes ago in a wyvern-conveyed coach. The countess requested admittance, saying the matter was urgent. I had no orders to keep her out, and I permitted her to enter."

"Damn!" Henry swore.

He jumped back into the carriage, then heard the guardsmen shouting at someone to halt. Henry looked around to see the drunken sailor running toward the cab. The sailor ducked beneath the arm of the captain who tried to stop him and seized hold of the door as Henry was shutting it.

The sailor yanked open the door and tumbled into the carriage.

Henry raised his pistol.

"Get out or I will shoot you dead." He cocked the hammer.

"Stop, my lord!" Amelia cried frantically, reaching out her hand. "Don't shoot! It is Kate!"

"Kate!" Henry exclaimed, astonished.

He would not have recognized her, for she had cut off her hair. Her face was flushed, smeared with grime and blood. She was wearing slops and a man's calico shirt, her clothes torn and dirty.

"Kate, what are you doing—" Amelia began.

"No time, Miss Amelia!" Kate gasped. She turned to Henry. "You have to listen to me, my lord! They're going to attack the palace! And they are wearing Freyan uniforms! So no one will know!"

Henry recalled Mr. Sloan saying the same. He released the hammer, lowered the pistol, and leaned out the window.

"Baxter, drive on! Close the gate after me, Captain!" Henry shouted as the carriage rattled off. "Do not let anyone in or out. Sound the alarm. The palace could come under attack at any moment! The assailants could be disguised as our own troops!"

The captain stared at him, openmouthed. Henry fell back against the seat as the carriage plunged forward. Kate held on to the seat, swaying in the rattling carriage and trying to catch her breath.

"Then you were warned about the black ship, my lord!" she said, relieved. "I am so glad!"

"Black ship?" Henry repeated. "What black ship?"

"The black ship with the green beam gun! It sailed over the palace walls only a few moments ago. I thought you saw it!"

"Dear God in Heaven!" Amelia gasped.

"Tell me what you know and be quick about it," said Henry, feeling a tightness in his chest.

"I was on board a black ship until a few moments ago when I managed to jump off," Kate replied. "They have a green beam gun mounted on the forecastle and they intend to use it to knock down the palace. I did manage to disable one of the airscrews and that will slow the ship down and make it more difficult to steer. But it won't stop them."

"Them! Who is 'them'?" Henry demanded.

"They call themselves the Army of Retribution, my lord," said Kate. "I know it sounds as though I am mad, but there really is a black ship. It belonged to Miri and Gythe. I don't suppose you know them, but they used it to go Below to help Father Jacob. This army stole it from them—!"

Miri and Gythe and Father Jacob. Names floating out of the mists of the past. Henry stared intently out the window searching for a ship. Trees lined the lane leading to the palace. Their leaves almost all gone, they were skeletal, their bony limbs shaking in the wind. He saw no sign of a ship, but he saw moving shadows and pictured an army out there, trampling the dead roses and hollyhocks, taking up position behind marble cherubs and empty fountains. The carriage rocked back and forth. The horses' hooves pounded.

Henry stood up, swaying perilously, and rapped on the roof of the carriage. "Baxter, stop!"

The carriage slowed.

"Miss Amelia, I need someone to carry a message to Captain Northrop, warning them of the peril," said Henry. "They are dining at the Naval Club. If you could find someone—"

"I will go myself, my lord," Amelia offered. "Godspeed, both of you."

She climbed out of the carriage, slammed shut the door. Baxter slapped the reins on the backs of the horses and the carriage rattled on.

Henry turned to Kate.

"You said you were on board this black ship. Are you in league with them? Are you working for the Pretender?"

A cannon boomed, followed by another and then a third. Kate flinched and looked out the window.

"What is that?" she asked. "Are we under attack?"

"Not yet. The guardsmen are sounding the alarm," said Henry. "Turning out the palace guard. I asked if you were working for Thomas Stanford."

"No, why would I be?" Kate asked, but Henry saw her flush.

"Because he is even now inside the palace plotting to arrest the queen," said Henry.

Kate stared at him in horror.

"Inside the palace!" she gasped. "That's impossible! Thomas would never—"

"Thomas . . ." said Henry, grinding the name in his teeth. "You call him by his first name. You are on very familiar terms, it seems."

"I am *not* working for him, my lord!" Kate insisted. "He is a friend. I know him through Phillip—"

"Another traitor!" Henry said angrily.

"Please tell me, my lord. Is Thomas inside the palace?" Kate asked desperately. "He could be in danger!"

"Danger!" Henry gave a bitter laugh. "That young man is in danger, all right! When I catch him, I will lock him in the darkest cell in the deepest dungeon in the strongest tower until he dies of rot or old age, whichever comes first!"

"You are wrong, my lord!" Kate cried. "Thomas knows nothing about tonight's attack. I heard the soldiers talking—"

Henry sneered. "And yet, this night, he is inside the palace waiting for his chance to seize the throne."

Kate sank back against the seat. Her face was drawn and haggard. She grimaced, and rubbed her shoulder.

"He doesn't know anything," she said.

Henry snorted.

The carriage was drawing near the palace and Henry opened the window to get a better view. The cold wind struck him in the face and cooled his temper. He again searched the sky for some sign of Kate's black ship. He still could not see anything, however.

What he could see was the countess's elegant coach, emblazoned with the de Marjolaine coat of arms, brazenly parked in front of the palace.

"As though she owns the place," Henry muttered.

The countess was wealthy enough to keep her own coach in Haever. She did not have to hire one. The six wyverns that pulled the large coach crouched quietly on the ground, patiently waiting. Cecile would not tolerate wyverns that shrieked and brawled.

Henry smiled in grim satisfaction. The fact that the countess was here in the palace on the night the Pretender tried to usurp the throne was all the evidence he needed that Rosia was conspiring against Freya.

"I will arrest that woman *and* Prince Tom! The Rosians will be humiliated! King Renaud will crawl to us on his knees!" Henry stated in triumph.

Baxter shouted at the excited horses, dragged on the reins, and brought them to a clattering halt. Henry thrust two pistols into his belt, threw open the door and climbed out.

"You are coming with me," he said to Kate.

"Damn right I am!" she told him. "You're wrong about Thomas!"

Henry ordered Baxter to wait for him. "Drive round back to the stables. If I have need of you, I'll meet you there."

Baxter nodded and urged the weary horses to continue. Henry started toward the palace on the run, planning to order the guards to shut the doors and bar the entrance. He had taken only a few steps when he came to a startled halt.

The orders he had not yet given had already been obeyed. The great doors stood closed. Armed guardsmen, rifles at the ready, lined the steps, barring entry, while additional guardsmen were setting up barricades.

Someone caught sight of Henry and Kate; within seconds, they found ten rifles aimed at them.

"Stand and be recognized!" one of the guardsmen shouted.

Henry halted, his hands in the air.

"Sir Henry Wallace," he replied. "I am on urgent business to the queen! Where is your captain?"

"Here, my lord," said the captain, coming forward. "My apologies. We were ordered to take no chances."

"Who gave the orders?" Henry demanded.

"The Countess de Marjolaine, my lord," the commander replied, looking confused. "She said the queen was in danger. She showed us a writ with your name and your seal."

"Damnation!" Henry swore. "Open those doors!"

The guardsman frowned at Kate. "Who is that with you, sir?"

"An informant," said Henry. "She comes with me."

He seized hold of Kate and ran up the palace stairs. Two guardsmen dragged open the heavy doors that were two stories tall, made of brass banded with iron and bearing the seal of House Chessington, with its two lions guardant on either side of a sun in splendor.

The doors opened onto an enormous rotunda. The domed ceiling soared six stories above the floor. A grand staircase led to a mezzanine, where two more staircases branched off the first, one leading to the palace's western wing and the other to the east.

Huge glass globes in golden baskets floated above, lighting a scene of confusion. Palace guardsmen were setting up more barricades in front of the stairs and at the door. Harried-looking servants were dashing up the stairs and banging on doors, calling for the queen.

The clocks in the palace began to chime eleven times.

The Countess de Marjolaine paced back and forth in the center of the rotunda. Hearing the great doors open, she looked up and caught sight of Henry.

"Thank God, you are here!" she breathed, and came hurrying toward him.

"What the devil is going on?" Henry roared. "You forged documents—"

"My lord," Cecile said, cutting him off. "I had to get inside the palace. I have reason to fear the queen is going to be assassinated!"

"Assassinated!" Henry repeated, stunned.

"One of my most trusted agents sent word that the assassination will take place tonight. I came to the palace the moment I received the information to warn Her Majesty, but no one can find her! The servants are searching the palace. An assassin could have slipped past the guards—"

"Not an assassin! The black ship!" Kate cried.

Henry had forgotten all about her. Cecile was staring at Kate in amazement.

"Captain Kate? What are you doing here?" She looked at Henry. "My agent feared a black ship might be involved."

Henry didn't immediately respond. He didn't know how these two women knew each other. They could be his enemies, his friends, friends of his enemies. He had a split second to make up his mind. He decided to err on the side of caution and turned to Kate.

"Which direction was the ship headed?"

"The west side of the palace, my lord," Kate replied, pointing.

"Her Majesty's office is located in the west wing," Henry said. He looked for the largest guardsman he could find. "You, sir! Run as fast as you can to Her Majesty's office! If the queen is there, warn her to leave! If Her Majesty refuses, carry her out bodily!"

The guardsman nodded and broke into a run. He was young and strong and he dashed up the stairs, taking them three at a time, without seeming to even breathe hard.

Henry motioned to two more guards. "Keep this young woman in custody."

The guardsmen took hold of Kate and dragged her off. Henry ignored Kate's frantic protests and turned back to the countess.

"Tell me, my lady, is Thomas Stanford inside the walls of this palace?"

"I know only that he was supposed to be here, my lord. He was scheduled to meet in secret with the queen. She was considering naming Thomas her heir. I questioned the servants, but no one has seen him."

Cecile was adept at keeping her true thoughts hidden, and Henry was equally adept at reading the thoughts people tried to keep hidden. He noticed a furrow in the countess's brow deepen in concern, her eyes grow shadowed.

Henry decided that she was telling the truth, or at least as much of the truth as she ever told anyone.

"I was told the Princess Sophia is here," said Henry.

"Her Highness was here," said Cecile. "She dined with the queen at seven. The servants assured me that she has safely departed. I have sent my own people to escort her to my yacht, where she will be safe until I can take her away from Haever."

Henry regarded her grimly. "I must go to the queen. We both know that I cannot detain you, my lady, but I ask that you remain within the palace. I have a great many questions for you."

"Of course, my lord. I trust you will not mind if I speak to Captain Kate in the interval," Cecile said. "She is a friend of Sophia's."

Henry doubted they would be talking about Sophia, but he couldn't take time to sort out whatever schemes the two were hatching. He ran up the stairs, taking them one at a time and having difficulty with even that. He was no match for the guardsman, who was already lost to sight.

Henry had almost reached the top when he was aware that the countess had gathered up her skirts and was running up two stairs behind him.

"Go back, Your Ladyship," Henry told her when she caught up to him. "It is not safe."

Cecile gave a faint smile. "We are neither of us likely to die in our beds, are we, my lord?"

Henry glared at her. He didn't trust her, but short of pulling out his pistol and shooting her, he couldn't stop her.

They entered a gallery lined with windows that overlooked the palace grounds. The glow emanating from the magical stone walls lit the grounds, but only for a short distance, then the light made everything beyond darker by contrast.

The interior wall opposite the windows was lined with famous paintings, most of them depicting griffins, either hunting or racing. Henry had often walked here with the queen, listening to her criticize the paintings, remarking that the artists didn't know one end of a griffin from the other.

"Her Majesty's office is at the end of the gallery," said Henry.

The guardsman had ranged far ahead of them. Henry could see his blue uniform. He pressed on. The countess kept pace with him, despite being hampered by having to clutch large folds of silk and petticoats.

Henry kept watch outside the windows, but could see nothing; no sign of a black ship. He decided Kate had made this up, though he could not fathom her motive. The long row of windows was coming to an end. The queen's office was not far, down a hall and to the left.

Henry glanced back to see Cecile start to slow. She pressed her hand to her side. Corsets were not made for strenuous athletics.

"Go on!" she said to him. "I will catch up!"

Henry started to turn his head. He saw a flash of blue-green light outside the window. A bright green beam lanced through the night.

Henry reached out his hand, grabbed hold of Cecile, and pulled her into the hallway, as far from the windows as he could manage. He shoved her to the floor and dove on top of her.

The blast seemed to blow apart his world.

Glass shattered. Walls shook. He heard wood rending and a horrendous crash. Debris rained down around him, pelting him, hitting him on the head and the back and his legs. He had closed his eyes, but he could still see the bright green light, even through his eyelids. He remembered that terrible light. The last time he had seen it, the beam had destroyed his house.

He scrambled to his feet the moment the shaking stopped. Plaster was still falling all around him. Dust was rising, smoke began to drift down the hall. He looked behind and saw the gallery floor covered with splinters of broken glass that would have torn them to shreds if they had been standing there.

The countess lay on the floor, covered in plaster and dust, but apparently unharmed. She coughed and pushed herself up on her hands and knees.

"I am all right, Henry!" She choked on the smoke and coughed, motioning with her hand. "Go to the queen! Run!"

Henry ran through the dust and broken paintings and smashed furniture. He coughed in the smoke, rubbed grit from his eyes, spit dirt from his mouth, and still he kept running. Trying to outpace despair.

He was brought to a halt by a gigantic wooden beam that had split apart and crashed through the ceiling. The guardsman lay beneath it in a pool of blood. The beam had fallen on top of him, crushing him. He was still outside the office, or what was left of it.

Henry tried to call, but his mouth was dry and gritty. He moistened his mouth, spitting out the dirt.

"Your Majesty!" He broke off, coughing.

The floor gave a shudder like a living thing in pain. The danger had not ended with the blast. The contramagic was still at work, eating away every magical construct in the vicinity of the blast and spreading beyond. It would devour every construct in the stone walls, gnaw at the mortar between the stones. The magic would grow weaker and eventually stop, but this part of the palace might well collapse before that happened.

Henry shouted again for the queen. No response.

The hall that he knew so well was now unrecognizable; reduced to mounds of rubble, twisted iron, and smoke. He came to a door clogged with wreckage. He kicked aside debris and entered.

He could feel cold air on his face and realized it was blowing through a gigantic hole in the wall. The room was dark, lit only by an eerie white light. Henry couldn't place the strange light for a moment, then he realized the magical glow came from the broken chunks of stone that had once formed the palace wall. Their magic was already starting to dim, as the contramagic ate it away.

He looked on a scene of utter destruction. The heavy timbers in the ceiling had cracked and fallen. The bookshelves that lined the walls had been knocked down; the floor was knee-deep in leather and vellum.

The furniture had been pulverized. Chairs were reduced to sticks of wood with bits of stuffing poking out. The chimney had toppled, filling the grate with bricks that smothered the fire. A few flames still flickered. Smoke drifted out, blown away by the wind.

"Your Majesty!" Henry called desperately, his voice ravaged by grit and smoke and fear.

He had only to look at the destruction to know she would not answer.

The queen kept her desk in front of the window, for she liked to be able to look out at the garden, at the trees and the flowers. She enjoyed watching the snow fall and her dogs playing in the yard. She ordered the grooms to walk her horses beneath the window so she could admire them.

He could not see the desk for the rubble that covered it.

Henry crawled and pushed and kicked and shoved his way through the debris. He hoped, prayed, that the queen had not been in her office. He told himself she was asleep in her bed. He made himself believe and he more than half expected to hear Mary come storming down the hall, bellowing in outrage and demanding to know who the devil had blown up her palace.

Henry at last reached the avalanche of debris. He smelled the stench of blood and looked down at his feet. The carpet was covered with blood, black in the eerie white light. His throat clogged, his tongue felt thick, and there was a horrid taste in his mouth. He dropped to his hands and knees, desperately hurling aside broken chunks of stone. He uncovered a small, crumpled body.

The monkey, little Jo-Jo, lay dead, covered in blood that was not all his own. He had his tiny paw wrapped around a hand; all that was visible of another body buried beneath the twisted beams, shattered glass, and broken stone.

Henry touched the upturned palm and felt the wrist. The flesh was cold, the pulse stilled. He knew Mary's hand as well as he knew his own, but he continued to hope—until he saw the signet ring on her thumb. He could not count the number of times he had watched Her Majesty press that ring into the hot wax, stamping her decrees with the royal seal.

Henry gripped the queen's hand and doubled over in wrenching grief.

"My lord . . ." Cecile called to him from the hall.

"Don't come in here!" Henry warned, his voice rasping. "It's not safe!"

"Her Majesty . . ."

"Dead," said Henry.

"God give her ease," said Cecile. Her voice tightened. "Was she . . . is there anyone else . . . ?"

"Meaning is Thomas Stanford here?" Henry asked harshly. He swallowed, then said, "I do not think so. The queen died alone."

He shuddered and the palace shuddered with him, as though sharing his grief.

"My lord, the ceiling might give way!" Cecile told him. "We must go."

"I will not leave Her Majesty," said Henry.

"You can do nothing—" Cecile began.

She stopped speaking and stared out past the shattered stones into the night, listening. Henry heard and raised his head. The crackling sounds carried clearly on the night air.

"That was gunfire!" Cecile said.

A cannon boomed and then another.

"The palace is under attack! My lord, you must come away!"

Henry shook his head and held fast to the queen. Cecile ventured into the room, following the path Henry had cleared through the ruin. Her hair straggled down over her shoulders. Her face was covered in dust and plaster. Blood trickled down her arms.

"Henry, listen to me!" she said, her words sharp and cold. "You know as well as I do that anyone associated with the royal family is now in danger and your wife is the queen's niece! The Faithful could be in your house this very moment!"

Henry looked up at her.

"The dead have no more need of you, my lord," Cecile said. "Your duty is to the living."

Henry bowed his head and bade good-bye to the woman he had served and loved for so many years. He drew the signet ring from the queen's thumb and closed his fist over it, pressed the queen's cold hand to his lips, as he had done so many times before, and then stood up. He and Cecile made their way back through the wreckage.

"We will take my coach," Cecile said.

"I have my own carriage," said Henry harshly.

"And how far do you think you will get through the palace grounds before the soldiers stop you?" Cecile asked.

They reached the hall and heard cries and shouts and the rattle of gunfire, sounding closer.

"My coach is parked in front of the palace," said Cecile, frowning. "We must avoid the front entrance. The Faithful could have troops there already."

"How do you know you won't be arrested?" Henry asked.

"I am known to them," said Cecile simply. "They will allow me to pass."

Henry rounded on her. "You are known to them! They have killed my queen! Damn it, how the devil can I trust you?"

"Rebellion is contagious, like the plague," Cecile said. "I swear to you I knew nothing about this plot. I serve a king. I would never sanction the murder of a king and neither would Prince Thomas. He wanted peace for Freya and so did Queen Mary. She knew she was dying and she feared the chaos that would follow. That was why she agreed to grant him an audience."

Henry remembered the queen's words: her last words, their final meeting.

We have made our decision regarding our heir. Our attorneys have drawn up the relevant paperwork so that all is legal . . .

You have served us well and faithfully for many years. We could not have asked for a more loyal and devoted servant . . . I ask you as a friend, Henry. Be the same devoted servant to your new monarch.

He carried the letter naming the heir with him, forgotten, in an inner pocket. He was aware of it now. It seemed to burn his flesh. He had no doubt what he would read when he opened it.

"This way, my lady," said Henry. "I know a secret passage that will take us to the coach."

FIFTY-NINE

Two guards had taken Kate into custody on Sir Henry's orders.

"I need a word with the prisoner," Cecile said in her cool, imperious tone. "Sir Henry sent me."

"Of course, my lady," said one of the guards.

They did not move, but remained near Kate, one on either side.

Cecile bent near and spoke in Kate's ear. Kate was acutely conscious of Cecile's elegant clothes and faint fragrance of spring, contrasting with her own torn shirt, filthy slops, and rumpled curls.

"Thomas is somewhere in this palace and he is danger. I dare not search for him, for I am being watched. Find him and warn him. Look first in the Rose Room."

Kate had to know something first. "My lady, is Thomas involved in this plot?"

"He is not," said Cecile. "But Sir Henry will never believe that. I must go now. Godspeed!"

Cecile squeezed her hand and departed, leaving Kate to stare after her in astonishment. The countess seemed to take it for granted that Kate knew Thomas, when she had been so careful never to mention his name to either the countess or Sophia.

Cecile also appeared to take it for granted that Kate could escape her guards and then find Thomas, who was in the Rose Room, wherever that was.

And all the while the black ship was sailing nearer and nearer, coming to blow up the palace.

"Bloody hell," Kate muttered.

The guards marched over to a wall and made her stand facing it, toes up against the decorative wainscott, like a naughty child told to stand in a corner. Out of the corner of her eye, she could see Cecile gathering up her skirts and running after Sir Henry.

The rotunda was the scene of confusion, as guards shoved heavy furniture across the ornate doors to barricade the main entrance and rifleman smashed glass out of the windows and took up positions, ready to defend the palace. Courtiers had heard the commotion and came running to the rotunda to find out what was going on.

The clock had chimed eleven times ages ago—or so it seemed to Kate— and nothing had happened. Perhaps she had done more damage than she had thought and the ship had crashed. Perhaps she had been wrong about the target. Perhaps the green beam weapon hadn't worked.

She felt the blast at the same time she heard it, a dull, rumbling roar that rolled down the halls and sent tremors through the building. Paintings fell from the walls and statues toppled over; people gasped, cried out, or froze in shock. Frightened and confused, they looked at one another for answers.

Someone shouted that it was a bomb, and that set off a panic. Some ran toward the doors, but the soldiers had barricaded those and were instantly caught up in a swirling knot of screaming confusion. Some ran up the stairs, colliding with people running down from upper levels.

Kate jammed her elbow into the ribs of one of her guards, dodged around the other, and made a dash for the stairs. Her guards cried for someone to stop her, but their shouts were lost in the tumult. She climbed the stairs as fast as she could, bumping into people, stumbling, and falling. She pushed herself back to her feet and finally made it to the mezzanine. Kate looked down to see her guards angrily thrusting people aside, trying to reach her.

The countess had told her to look for Thomas in the Rose Room, but there must be hundreds of rooms in this palace and she had no idea where to even start searching.

She would have to ask someone, but now her main task was to avoid being caught. The guards were pursuing her gamely, though they were now bogged down by a torrent of bodies. She ran down the first hall she found, avoiding people when she could, shoving them aside when she couldn't. People stared at her and called out to her, but no one tried to stop her.

She paused to catch her breath and look behind her and there were the damned guards, still doggedly chasing her. She reached the end of the hall, where she saw a tower with a narrow staircase that spiraled up and down.

Kate did not know where the stairs led, but anywhere was better than where she was. She started to go down, then realized that the guards might assume she would go down because that was easier, so she ran up instead. She climbed two flights, her breath coming in ragged gasps, and her legs burning with the effort. She quit climbing, pulled open a door and ran through it.

Clapping the door shut behind her, she fell back against it and gulped in air.

She heard the guards running up the stairs and she stopped breathing, afraid they might hear her. The guards paused at her door, but then continued on, going up the next flight. Kate sucked in a few gasping breaths, then looked around.

She was standing in a long, wide gallery with a vaulted ceiling made of panes of glass. Looking up, she could see the stars. The gallery was dark except for the starlight and appeared to be deserted.

Kate held her breath, listening, but she could not hear any voices, or footsteps. No lights shone. At a time when the entire palace had been roused by the explosion, the silence here was odd, foreboding.

Kate was frustrated. She had no idea where she was, much less how to find the Rose Room. She had hoped to ask a servant, but this hall appeared to be unoccupied. Any moment the guards would realize they had lost her, retrace their steps, and come looking for her. She hurried down the hall, trying door handles, hoping to find someone, anyone, to ask.

Most of the doors were locked, but she finally came across one that wasn't and opened it. The room was dark. The chandeliers were wrapped in white cloth, and white cloths covered the furniture. The carpets had been taken up and stashed in a corner, and the floor was covered in dust.

Kate shut the door and continued down the hall and tried another. This room was shrouded in the same cloths and the same dust. The entire floor must be closed up, sealed off.

She stopped to ponder what to do. She no longer worried about the guards. They must have given up the search by now. Her only concern was to save Thomas before Sir Henry found him. Sir Henry had said he would place Thomas under arrest, but if the assassination attempt had succeeded and the queen was dead, Thomas would face a far more terrible fate.

Just as she was thinking that, she heard the crackle of gunfire. The sound was distant, coming from outside the palace, but she still shuddered.

Kate looked up through the skylight, into the night, and was startled to see the *Naofa,* her sails black against the frosty stars. The ship was sailing away from the palace, bound on its second mission, whatever that was. She had never been able to find out.

Kate shivered. The ship was a long way off. They could not possibly see her, yet she had to resist a temptation to run into a room and hide.

She looked around, desperate and frustrated. The palace was four stories tall with three wings, hundreds of rooms, dozens of hallways, passageways, and stairs. She could search for days and not find the Rose Room. At this point, she was beginning to wonder if there was anyone left to ask.

She continued down the long, empty gallery. She might have been in the Deep Breath: the same cold, the same emptiness, the same drowning silence.

Just as she began to feel a little panicked that she might never find her way out, she saw a glimmer of light far ahead. She increased her pace, and saw the light grow brighter. The ghostly hall was coming to an end at last, intersecting with another hall that ran at right angles, forming the shape of a *T*.

Kate could now hear men's voices, and she slowed to listen. They were talking in even, measured tones, not yammering in panic. She could not make out what they were saying, for their voices were low, but she could distinguish one voice speaking with authority, as though giving orders.

She had come all this way only to run into the palace guard.

They could have been sent by Sir Henry to search for Thomas or they might even be looking for her. She flattened herself against a door in the darkened hall, near the intersection, and watched and listened, trying to understand what the guardsmen were saying.

She could hear brisk footfalls coming down the well-lighted hall and a voice call out "Colonel Smythe!" and the sound of a man running down the hall to catch up.

Kate recognized the name. Franklin had spoken of a Colonel Smythe and so had Thomas. He was the commander of this Army of Royal Retribution and if he and his soldiers were in the palace, then Thomas must be safe.

Kate sighed in relief, then felt guilty for being relieved. These men were responsible for the queen's death. She had Cecile's assurance that Thomas was not involved and Kate hoped that was true. Still, his own army would see to it that he was protected.

"I questioned the staff as you ordered, Colonel Smythe," the soldier was saying breathlessly. "The woman I saw in the hall could have been the Princess Sophia. She was dining with the queen and no one actually saw her leave the palace."

"Two of you go see if you can find her," Smythe ordered, sounding annoyed. "Where were you when you saw her?"

"In this hallway, sir."

"Search every room. I will be with His Highness," said Smythe.

He and his escort continued walking down the hall, coming closer to where Kate was hiding.

She was concerned to hear that Sophia was still in the palace, but she was safe, apparently. She had not been caught in the explosion. Thomas was safe, as well, it seemed. Kate thought for a moment of trying to find Thomas, but immediately abandoned the idea.

"He might well be king now," Kate said softly.

The soldiers trooped down the hall. They were wearing the same uniforms as the palace guard. The man in the lead wore a red sash around his waist and carried a sword and sidearm, which generally denoted an officer.

Kate assumed that this must be Colonel Smythe. He was almost past her when he turned to speak to one of the men behind him.

Kate saw his face. His nose was broken and his jaw was bruised and swollen, as though he had been in a fight, but she had no trouble recognizing him.

She began to shake; her gut wrenched; her mouth went dry; and her hands shook. She could never forget that face. She was looking straight up into that when he struck her to the floor, grabbed hold of her hair, dragged back her head, and held a drug-laced handkerchief over her nose and mouth.

Colonel Smythe, the commander of Thomas's army, was also a cold-blooded killer, the man who had murdered Lady Odila and Coreg.

Kate gave a little gasp and then pressed her hand over her mouth. She was too late. He had heard her.

"Who is there?" Smythe called out sharply, staring intently into the shadows.

Kate shrank back against the wall and closed her eyes, as though blotting him from sight would make him vanish.

"You two, go search," Smythe ordered.

The soldiers entered the hall. They were carrying dark lanterns and their lights flashed around the hall and into the alcove. Both lights shone right in her eyes.

Kate raised her hands.

"It's a sailor, Colonel," reported the soldier.

"A sailor?" Smythe repeated in disbelief. "What the devil is a sailor doing here? Bring him."

Kate had recognized Smythe, but perhaps he might not recognize her. He had seen her only in the darkness and only for a few seconds.

The soldier grabbed hold of her arm and dragged her into the hall, bringing her to stand before Smythe.

Kate kept her head lowered, touched her hand to her forehead, and broke into a mumbled explanation.

"I was in the servant's hall, sir, visitin' my girl, Jenny, when we heard a blast. Terrible loud it was, sir. We didn't know what had happened and we started runnin'. I lost hold of Jenny and I come here lookin' for her."

Smythe frowned at her. "Why do I know you?"

"I'm sure I couldn't say, sir," said Kate gruffly, shuffling her feet.

She shot a quick glance around. The soldiers were regarding her with amusement. Smythe was still frowning and then his eyes fixed on her, narrowed and glittering.

Kate shoved past him, darted through a gap between the two guards, and ran down the hall.

"Catch her!" Smythe ordered. "She's not a sailor. She's an agent for Sir Henry Wallace! And don't kill her. I need to question her."

Kate ran as fast as she could, but she was already exhausted, and she could feel her strength flagging. The soldiers pounded after her. She ducked around a corner and dove into another hall, hoping to lose them. Too late, she saw more guardsmen posted near the end of the corridor.

Kate stumbled to a halt and looked frantically for a place to hide. She saw only long stretches of wall with niches and alcoves, few doors and no windows. The guardsmen who were in pursuit dashed around the corner. They caught sight of Kate and shouted to their comrades at the far end of the hall to stop her.

Kate was cornered. She couldn't go forward. She couldn't go back.

The soldiers closed in on her.

Kate raised her hands and opened her mouth to tell them she surrendered.

The corridor was suddenly plunged into darkness as black as the Deep Breath. Kate couldn't see a thing and neither could the soldiers. She heard them clatter to a confused halt.

Before she could think what to do, a ghostly figure seemed to materialize at her side. The apparition reached out, took hold of her wrist with a very real hand, and pulled her through a red-and-golden-papered wall.

SIXTY

Kate stood, shaken, on the other side of the wall, wondering what had just happened. She heard the muffled sound of a door being softly, stealthily closed, and the ghostly figure put her fingers on Kate's lips.

"Hush, Kate! It's me, Sophia! Keep quiet!"

Kate had no trouble obeying the command. Her breath came in ragged gasps, and her heart seemed to be beating in her throat.

In the hall outside, soldiers were blundering around in the darkness, shouting for light.

"Wait here," Sophia whispered. "I'll fetch the lamp."

"Won't they see the light?" Kate asked, alarmed.

"We are inside a room behind a closed door," Sophia explained. "The soldiers won't see anything if they look, not even a door. I cast an illusion spell. If they ever do manage to light the lamps in the corridor, all they will see is a wall. Are you all right?"

"I will be when I can breathe again," said Kate. "You scared me half to death. I've never seen magic like that!"

"I'm a savant," said Sophia, shrugging. "It's my one useful skill. Keep your voice down. They can't see us, but they might be able to hear us. Come onto the balcony with me. We can talk out there."

Kate followed her across the room that smelled of roses. She passed a sideboard and the sight of a pitcher made her realize her throat was parched.

"Is there water?" Kate asked.

"Yes, and brandy, too," said Sophia. "Here, let me."

Kate tried to pour the water into a glass and ended up sloshing most of it all over the table. Sophia poured the water for her, and Kate gulped it thankfully.

"You're shivering! Here, take my cloak." Sophia draped a fur-lined silk cloak over Kate's shoulders.

Kate clutched it around her.

"I saw him, Sophia," she said, shuddering. "And he saw me. He knew me."

"Who did you see?"

"That man, Colonel Smythe."

"The commander of Thomas's army?" Sophia said, amazed.

Kate shook her head. "Smythe is a murderer, a cold-blooded killer. Thomas doesn't know the truth about him. Smythe is behind a plot to kill the queen. You heard the explosion? They might have succeeded!"

Sophia paled. Kate started to tell her more, but then she heard men talking right outside the door.

"We will be safer outdoors," Sophia whispered.

She extinguished the light of the lamp and drew Kate through the darkened room and out onto the balcony. Drawing the curtains closed, she shut the door.

"How long will the illusion last?" Kate asked, still a prey to fear.

"Until someone who is familiar with this part of the palace realizes that there should be a door there instead of a wall," said Sophia. "We don't have to worry about these soldiers. They are not the palace guard. They are disguised to look like the palace guard. A real guardsman would see through the illusion."

Kate sank down on a stone bench and almost stepped on Bandit, who was eating his way through a plate of sandwiches and tea cakes.

She looked around and saw another balcony close to theirs, not more than twenty feet away. The curtains covering the doors leading to the balcony were shut, but she could see light shining from behind them.

"Is someone in that room over there?" Kate asked.

"I don't know," said Sophia. "That is the Yellow Drawing Room. I can see the light, but no one has come out on the balcony."

She sat beside Kate and leaned down to pet Bandit.

"I had to feed him to keep him quiet. I was afraid they would hear him bark." Sophia spoke softly and added, with a glance at the balcony next to theirs. "I'm sorry we have to sit in the dark, but if someone did come out, they might see us."

"What are you doing here in the palace, Sophia?" Kate asked. "The countess told me—"

"The countess!" Sophia interrupted with a breathless gasp. "Is she in the palace? Where is she?"

"The countess *was* in the palace," Kate answered. "She and Sir Henry ran to warn the queen. They left me in the rotunda, under guard, and then there was the explosion . . ."

"Is the queen safe?"

"I don't know," Kate said. "I hope they reached her in time. But what are you doing here? The countess was worried when she heard you had been dining with the queen. The servants told her you had left."

"I was going to leave," said Sophia. "Oh, Kate, it is all so confusing, like a strange, horrible dream."

She picked up Bandit, who had finished off the sandwiches, and held him in her lap. The dog closed his eyes, his stomach full, and went to sleep.

"I dined with the queen," Sophia said. "Her Majesty was in good spirits. Bandit barked at Jo-Jo and the monkey threw something quite nasty at poor Bandit. I thought Her Majesty would be angry at Bandit, but she laughed and laughed. She said she knew a few members of the House of Nobles who deserved the same treatment."

Sophia patted the dog on his head and then put him down on the floor at her feet. Bandit yawned, rolled over on his side, and began to snore gently.

"The queen looked pale and seemed very tired and so I left early, at about nine of the clock. One of the servants and I were walking down a hall when Bandit suddenly jumped out of my arms. He ran over to a closed door and began barking at it. I tried to make him come back to me, but he was frantic, and began pawing at the door. The servant bent down to grab him and I am afraid Bandit bit her.

"The poor woman's hand was covered in blood. I felt terrible. I told her to go to the servants' quarters and have someone tend to it. She didn't want to leave me, but she was dripping blood on the carpet and I ordered her to go. I knelt down on the floor to try to convince Bandit to leave and a voice called my name through the door."

Sophia took hold of Kate's hand. "It was Phillip!"

"Phillip?" Kate repeated, stunned. "What is Pip doing here in Freya?" She answered her own question. "He came with Thomas."

"I didn't even know Thomas was here," said Sophia. "Not until Phillip told me. He warned me that I was in danger and so was Thomas. He said Thomas was in the palace, in the Rose Room."

"The countess told me the same thing," said Kate. "I was searching for it. What else did Phillip say?"

"That I must find Thomas and tell him and we were to leave. Oh, Kate, Phillip sounded so strange. His words were slurred and he had trouble talking. I peeked under the door and I could see him lying on the floor, as though he had collapsed."

"Was he drunk?" Kate asked doubtfully, thinking of the Pip she had known in Wellinsport.

Sophia gave an emphatic shake of her head. "He was drugged. I know what being drugged is like. When I was young, I had terrible headaches. They used to give me laudanum to ease the pain and Phillip sounded like I used to feel. I tried to open the door, but it was locked. I asked him if he was all right, but he only kept repeating over and over that Thomas and I were in danger. And then . . . he didn't say anything more.

"I didn't want to leave him. I kept hoping someone would come. Then I saw the green light and heard the explosion. The blast shook the floors and the walls. Something inside the room fell down with a crash. I was frightened for Phillip and I decided to go to the Rose Room to see if I could find Thomas.

"I was hurrying down this hall, to the Rose Room, when I saw three members of the palace guard at the far end of the hall. I was so relieved! I started to call to them, but they acted very strangely. They stared at me and began whispering. I heard one say, 'That's her, the princess.'"

"They looked so grim, not at all like the palace guard, who are always very gallant and polite to me. I didn't trust them. The door to the Rose Room was standing open—"

"*This* is the Rose Room?" Kate asked, interrupting. "But if that's true, where is Thomas?"

"If he was here, he left before I came," said Sophia. "The room was empty. I picked up Bandit and ran inside, then cast the illusion spell. I could hear the men outside in the hall. They had seen me enter a room, but they couldn't find the door. I knew, then, that they weren't really palace guards.

"They said something about telling the colonel, and left. I didn't know what was happening and then I heard voices and men shouting.

"I peeped out the door and saw you running down the hall. I caused all the lights to go out, opened the door, and pulled you inside. And here we are. I don't know what has become of Phillip. I am so afraid for him and now I'm afraid for Thomas, as well. What is going on, Kate? Who are those soldiers?"

"They belong to Thomas's army," Kate said.

"Thomas's army? No, that's not possible!" Sophia protested, shocked. "Phillip told me to warn him—"

"The countess says he doesn't know the truth; he's not involved."

Light suddenly shone on the balcony of the room adjacent to theirs. Someone had parted the curtains and was opening the glass-paned doors.

A man stepped out onto the balcony. He was speaking to someone over his shoulder, answering impatiently, "I will be perfectly fine, Sir Richard. The room is stuffy. I need a breath of air."

Kate and Sophia stared at each other.

"Thomas!" Kate whispered.

"At least he is safe," said Sophia. "Do you think we should call to him? Ask him about Phillip?"

"Who is Sir Richard?" Kate asked. "Do you know?"

Sophia shook her head.

Kate longed to talk to Thomas. She hesitated, then remembered that the guards were searching for Sophia as well as for herself. "As you say, he is safe. We need to find out more."

Thomas walked onto the balcony, glancing over his shoulder, perhaps to see if he was being watched. He hurried to the railing and leaned over it, as though trying to gauge how long a drop it would be to the ground below him.

The drop was a long one, too long for a leap in the darkness if that is what he contemplated. He slammed his fist into the stone in disappointment, then turned his gaze to the ivy, as though that might be of some use to him.

A man called to him from inside the room. Thomas made an annoyed gesture.

"I told you, my lord, I am fine!"

A guardsman walked out onto the balcony.

"Colonel Smythe is here, Your Highness. He respectfully asks to speak with you."

"Smythe?" Thomas repeated, amazed. "That's not possible. The colonel is in Bheldem!"

"He is here, sir, as commander of your forces."

Thomas appeared relieved. He started to return to the room. "Smythe! It is you. What the devil is going on?"

Sophia whispered frantically, "We have to warn him!"

"Thomas!" Kate cried, jumping to her feet. "Don't trust him!"

Her call woke Bandit, who flipped over and jumped to his feet with a growl and a snarl. Sophia grabbed the dog and clapped her hand over his muzzle.

Thomas stopped and turned to stare into the night. "Who is there? Is someone there?"

Kate started to reply. A soldier walked out onto the balcony of the Yellow Drawing Room and she shrank back down on the bench, out of sight.

"Is everything all right, sir?" the guardsman asked.

"How do you know Colonel Smythe?" Thomas asked abruptly. "You are a member of the queen's guard. You serve Her Majesty."

"I serve you, sir," said the guardsman. "I am with the Army of Royal Retribution. Forgive the deception. It was for your own good. We feared for your safety. But victory is ours this day, sir!"

Thomas stiffened. His jaw tightened. His hands clenched to fists. "I don't understand. What is going on?"

"You will be king, sir," the guardsman said, excited and enthusiastic. "Colonel Smythe has arrived. He will tell you the glad news."

The guardsman stood waiting. Thomas cast a glance toward the other balcony, perhaps hoping to hear again the voice that had called to him.

Kate didn't dare speak, but she willed her thoughts to touch him, willed him to know she believed in him and she was sorry for ever having doubted him.

"Sir," said the guardsman. "Colonel Smythe is waiting."

Thomas straightened his shoulders, braced himself as though for battle, and walked back into the room. He did not close the doors behind him, but left them open. Perhaps he had felt her touch.

SIXTY-ONE

Thomas entered the drawing room to find Colonel Smythe, accompanied by several officers, all wearing the uniforms of the palace guard. Smythe bowed low, as did the other officers.

Sir Richard rose in outraged dignity. "Colonel Smythe. I demand to know what is going on! We have been most shamefully treated!"

Smythe ignored him.

"God save Your Royal Highness," he said. He seemed to be in earnest, his tone respectful, even reverent. "The blessed Day of Retribution is at hand."

"I do not understand, Colonel," said Thomas, carefully maintaining his composure, modulating his voice. "You are going to have to explain."

"The queen is dead, sir," said Smythe. "Long live the king."

"The queen is dead . . ." Thomas repeated with a catch in his voice.

"That explosion . . ." Sir Richard sank into his chair, pale and unsteady, supporting himself with his hands. "Oh, God, Smythe! What have you done? Queen Mary was an anointed monarch! You assured us she would not be harmed!"

Smythe regarded him with cool pity. "Claim ignorance if it eases your conscience, my lord, but you and the other members of the Faithful knew we could not achieve victory unless we took swift and decisive action. *Lex*

Talionis. Day of Retribution. The Faithful devised the name. What did you gentlemen think it meant?"

"Not murder!" Richard cried. He turned to Thomas with outstretched hands, begging for understanding. "The queen was to be arrested, sir, removed to Offdom Tower. I swear before God I did not know—"

"You knew, my lord," Smythe remarked caustically. "You were the one who alerted me that the prince was about to upset our plans by coming here in secret. You were the one who shared the time of the meeting, so that we would know where to find the queen and when."

Richard swallowed and moistened his lips. "I feared for your safety, Your Highness. I tried to warn you that Masterson was working for my brother. You would not listen to reason . . ."

"Phillip Masterson was not the one who betrayed me," said Thomas. "He did not betray his queen!"

Richard lowered his eyes and sank, trembling, into the chair. He put his hand over his eyes. "I did not know . . ." he repeated.

Thomas stared at the wretched man and started to turn away. Then he realized, sick with horror, that this is what he always did. He turned away.

He had not comitted the crime, but he was still responsible. His was the sin of omission, if not commission. He had been in that army camp, seen the troop carriers. He had heard his mother talk of the violent overthrow of the queen. He had turned away, averted his face, looked somewhere else; anywhere else except at the truth.

The accident of his birth. Thomas wished to God he had never been born.

"I must apologize for detaining Your Highness," Smythe continued gravely. "I needed you to be inside the palace in order to establish your claim to the throne, but I had to ensure your safety."

"What you mean is that you had to keep me from dying alongside the queen," said Thomas harshly.

"I did what was necessary to secure your crown, sir," said Smythe. "The queen's half brothers, Hugh and Jeffrey, and her sister, Elinor, have been taken into custody. The other members of the royal family of House Chessington are being apprehended as we speak."

He glanced at Richard. "Including your brother, Henry Wallace, and his lady wife."

Richard shuddered as though he had been struck a blow.

Smythe continued. "Armies loyal to Your Highness are now marching on the port cities of Whithaven, East Aulkin, and Fort Upton."

"They are not my armies!" Thomas cried. He drew the ring the queen had given him off his finger and threw it to the floor. "You might as well arrest me, too, Colonel, for I want no part of this bloody insurrection. I renounce the throne."

Smythe gave a grave nod. He bent down, picked up the ring. "I anticipated Your Highness would be reluctant." He gestured to one of the guardsmen. "Bring the duke."

The man opened the door and called, "Bring Masterson."

Two soldiers entered. They carried Phillip between them, dragging him by his arms. The soldiers flung him facefirst to the floor. One of them shoved him with his boot, rolled him over so that he lay on his back. His face was battered and bloody.

He groaned. His eyelids fluttered. He tried to talk, choked and retched. Thomas knelt beside him.

"I am here, Pip," he said. He looked up at Smythe. "He needs a physician!"

"Masterson will be fine. The laudanum will soon wear off," said Smythe. "Probably sooner than he would like."

"Why are you doing this, Smythe?" Thomas demanded. He rose to his feet and turned to face him. "What do you want from me?"

"Ah, now we get to the nub of the matter. When I undertook this command at the behest of your mother and the Faithful, I believed I was doing God's work. We would remove a profligate, corrupt family from the throne and restore Freya to her rightful position as a power in the world. I believed in you, Your Highness, and in your cause," said Smythe. "And then I came to know you.

"You are a man of honor and strong principles. I have been told these are excellent qualities in a king." Smythe shrugged. "Sadly, you are also a fool who doesn't have the wit to know what to do with the power God has given you.

"I *do* know what to do with power, Your Highness. I have plans for Freya and her people," Smythe went on. "For years, I watched a feeble queen and her lackwit councilors such as Sir Richard beggar my country and grovel before godless infidels such as King Renaud. I could no longer stand idly by and watch my country sink into the stew of corruption.

"But then, I thought, who will pay heed to me and my ideas?" Smythe asked. "Who am I? A man of low birth. A common soldier, as your lady mother delights in reminding me. The meanest beggar on the street would pay no heed to me. Your Highness speaks and kings jump to do your bidding."

"I see what you are planning and I would sooner dance with the devil," Thomas said with contempt. "You might as well put a bullet in my head now, Smythe, for I will not be a party to this deranged scheme of yours."

"I will not harm you, sir," Smythe replied. "You are the true and rightful king. I need you and I hope you will eventually realize that you need me. We will make a good team. But in case you don't come to your senses, I am holding the duke as surety for your good behavior, as well as your mother and father, who are now prisoners in Bheldem. They will remain safe, so long as you do what you are bidden. Your first test will come with the dawn."

"You are mad!" said Thomas.

Smythe nodded in understanding. "I can see why you would think that. But consider this, sir. My armies control one of the most powerful nations in the world. That is not the work of a madman. That is the work of a man whom God has chosen to rule."

The sound of gunfire coming from outside laid emphasis to Smythe's words. The palace guard would resist, but Thomas doubted they could hold out long against an army of Guundaran mercenaries; the same army that had been "out on manuevers" when he had gone to the fort to review the troops.

I was a fool, Thomas thought in bitter self-recrimination. And now men are paying for my folly with their lives.

Smythe drew close to Thomas. "You have no choice, sir. If you try to publicly denounce me, I will say truthfully that the death of the queen was done in your name. You ordered the armies to march, to arrest those who oppose you. And who will say differently? Not one of my men. They are loyal to me."

"*I* will denounce you," cried Richard, livid with anger. "The Faithful will denounce you!"

Smythe drew his pistol, cocked it, aimed, and fired.

Richard fell back into his chair with a cry, and gazed in disbelief at a hole in the brocade. Blood began to flow. He clasped his hand over his arm and the blood welled out from between his fingers.

Thomas heard the faint sound of barking through the open door. The barking was quickly stifled.

"There was no need for that!" Thomas cried angrily raising his voice hoping Smythe had not heard the dog.

"I have no patience for fools," said Smythe as he thrust the pistol back into his belt.

Thomas went to Sir Richard's side and drew aside the bloody fabric. The bullet was lodged in the man's upper arm. Richard groaned in pain.

"Forgive me, sir," he said, clasping Thomas's hand. "He is right. I was a fool."

"And so was I, my lord," said Thomas quietly. "I trusted this man." He cast Smythe a grim look. "I want no more bloodshed. What would you have me do?"

"A wise decision, sir," said Smythe. "In the morning, when Haever is firmly under my control, you will appear before the people. You will express your grief at the queen's death at the hands of the Rosians—"

"The Rosians?" Thomas repeated, aghast. "You will start a war!"

"Such is my intent," said Smythe. "That reminds me. Corporal Jennings, have the men found Princess Sophia?"

"No, sir," said Jennings. "She was last seen on this floor. She could not have gone far. I could conduct a search, go room by room."

"Do so," said Smythe. "Take the sergeant with you."

"What do you want with Her Highness?" Thomas demanded, as the two men departed. He could guess, now, the identity of the barking dog and knew Sophia must be close by.

"The princess is a witch, sir, and must not be allowed anywhere near Your Highness," Smythe replied. "I have proof, for she used her foul magicks to attack several of my men."

"You cannot be serious. Sophia is not a witch," Thomas protested, incredulous. "She is a savant, unusually gifted in the art of crafting."

"So the corrupt priests have led the populace to believe, sir," Smythe said gravely. "The truth is that these so-called savants have obtained their skills by pledging their souls to the Evil One. We will find Your Highness a more suitable wife."

Smythe continued talking, saying something about the ring of King James and laying claim to the throne, assuring the people that their nation was blessed by God.

Thomas was no longer listening. He remembered looking over the balcony to the pavement so far below. He could not go through with this. Death would be preferable. All he had to do was turn and run . . .

"One of you, shut those doors," Smythe ordered. "His Highness finds the sound of gunfire distressing."

He walked over to Thomas and rested his hand almost gently on his shoulder. "Make up your mind and this trial will be easier for you. You will be king, Your Highness, for as long as I say you will be king."

Kate and Sophia sat on the balcony in the darkness, their hands clasped as they listened to the conversation coming from the Yellow Drawing Room. They could not hear everything, but they had heard enough.

Kate grieved for Thomas and feared for him. She remembered Dalgren, and how, crushed by shame and dishonor, he had sunk to the ground when the dragons had pronounced his sentence,.

"Corporal Jennings, have the men found Princess Sophia?"

The reply was muffled, but Kate and Sophia both heard clearly the words "search room by room."

"Jennings mustn't find us here!" Kate said urgently, jumping to her feet. "He knows me. Smythe will know we were eavesdropping!. We have to leave. Quickly, before the search gets organized!"

She flung open the balcony doors. Sophia picked up Bandit and hurried after her. The room was dark, but their eyes had already adjusted to the darkness and they hastened toward the door doing their best to avoid bumping into the furniture.

"But Corporal Jennings, there's nothing's here," said a voice right outside the door. "This is a wall."

"We are meant to think this is a wall, Sergeant. But it isn't. It's an illusion spell. Remember, the princess is a witch."

"A witch?" Sophia gasped, shocked.

"No time! Hide!" Kate whispered frantically.

Sophia crouched down behind a sofa, holding Bandit in her arms, her hand clamped on his jaws. Kate ducked behind a curtain. The room was dark. She hoped Jennings would just open the door, give a cursory glance around, and, seeing nothing, he would shut the door and move on.

Kate parted the curtain a fraction and peeked out to see the door open.

Jennings and the soldier entered, both carrying bull's-eye lanterns. They walked a short distance into the room and sent their lights flashing about.

"Close the door, Sergeant," Jennings ordered. "And light one of those lamps."

Kate bit her lip. She was near the fireplace. There would be a fireplace poker, if only she could lay her hands on it.

As the sergeant turned and started to light a lamp, Jennings drew his pistol and savagely struck the man on the back of his skull. The sergeant dropped to the floor. Jennings stepped over the body, shut the door, and then turned around.

"I know you are in here, Your Highness," he said. "Only a savant could cast such a spell."

Sophia slowly straightened up from behind the couch. Bandit wriggled in her arms and started to growl. Kate walked out from behind the curtain and went over to stand protectively near Sophia. She cast a longing glance at the fireplace, but had to give up the idea of grabbing the poker. Jennings was still holding the pistol.

Jennings gave a start of surprise on seeing Kate, but he had no time for questions. He turned to Sophia.

"I am glad I found you, ma'am. We must hurry. We don't have much time."

Sophia faced him with defiance. "I don't know what you mean. What are you going to do with us?"

"I am going to take you to a place of safety, ma'am," Jennings said. He thrust the pistol into his belt and held out his hand to her. "I am an agent for the Countess de Marjolaine."

SIXTY-TWO

The countess's wyverns were well trained and exceptionally fast, but they were not fast enough for Henry. He was seated on the box, beside the coachman, to provide the man with directions to his house. He watched the city flow beneath them, a swirling river of fear. Mobs filled the streets, firing off pistols, breaking into stores, looting and burning, spreading chaos and terror.

Soldiers of the Army of Retribution were in the streets, as well, seizing control of government buildings, rounding up opponents. Henry looked down on the Foreign Office as the coach flew over it to see soldiers entering the building.

When he and the countess were leaving the palace, the guard had come to their aid, holding off the foes until Henry and Cecile could safely enter the coach. Henry had seen the enemy massing outside the gates. The palace guard were outnumbered. The palace would not stand long.

He thought of his wife and children, alone in the house, with only the servants and the wounded Mr. Sloan standing between them and the soldiers who had orders to seize those related to the queen and her supporters. Lady Ann was the queen's niece. He was . . . had been . . . the queen's trusted spymaster. The soldiers were being led by a man who had committed murder before now and would not hesitate to kill again. Henry was a prey to such agony he could scarcely refrain from leaping from the coach and running to his home on foot.

"Are we close, my lord?" the coachman asked. "I need to know when to start my descent."

Henry tried to determine their location. He stared down at the streets below him, but they were only streets. He had no sense of where he was; only that he was not where he desperately needed to be.

Then he saw beacon lights shining from a church steeple, serving as a warning to flying vehicles and griffin riders that they should not approach.

Henry gripped the coachman by the arm. "The church is only a few miles from my house. Follow this street. You can start your descent now."

The coachman ran his hand over the small brass helm that controlled the lift tanks and shouted an order to the wyverns. The coach began to descend.

"My lord, look there!" The coachman pointed with his whip.

A troop wagon drawn by four horses was turning onto the street where Henry lived. The wagon was filled with soldiers and he knew with sickening certainty they were bound for his house.

"Do not fear, my lord," said the coachman, a big, burly man named Cousailles. "You will find two rifles located beneath the seat. A brace of pistols, as well."

"Are they loaded?" Henry asked, reaching down.

"Yes, my lord," said Cousailles. "I always go armed when I drive Her Ladyship."

"Knowing Her Ladyship, I will wager you've had occasion to use them," said Henry with a faint smile.

"That I have, my lord," said the coachman. "I'm a crack shot, if I do say so myself. I was a soldier in the Royal Fusiliers. This coach is armored in magic, as well. Her Ladyship and I will see to it that no harm comes to you and yours."

Henry found the man's cheerful confidence comforting. The coach left the troop wagon some distance behind and he lost sight of them in the darkness. He was close now. He could see his house in the light of the street lamps. The windows were dark and for a moment his heart constricted in fear.

Then he reminded himself that Mr. Sloan was with his family, and with his unfailing good sense, he would have foreseen the danger and ordered the servants to douse the lights, draw the curtains, bolt the doors, and shutter the windows.

The coach made a smooth descent. The wyverns landed on the lawn, nearly touching the door stoop, coming as close to the house as the coachman dared. The beasts sensed the tension and started to act up, biting at each other's heads. The coachman sent a flicker of magic through the harnesses, giving them a mild jolt, and the wyverns settled down.

"Drive around back," Henry instructed, jumping from the box. "I will meet you there."

Cecile opened the door and climbed from the coach.

"You should remain inside, my lady," Henry said curtly.

"Nonsense," she replied coolly. "You may need my help. We must be quick. The soldiers have seen us."

Henry glanced down the street. The wagon carrying the soldiers was yet some distance away, but it had increased its speed. Cousailles drove the coach around the house to the rear, plying the whip. The wyverns lumbered over the grass, trampling shrubs and flower beds. Henry ran to the front door and was about to hammer on it when it swung open.

The butler, Jacobs, stood in the entrance, armed with a pistol.

"Thank God you are safe, my lord!" he exclaimed.

Henry bounded inside, shoving past Jacobs, who was staring in amazement at Cecile. Her face was smeared with grime and blood. And though she had taken time while in the carriage to braid her hair to be out of the way, it was covered in dust and dirt, a mockery of wig powder. Yet she entered the house as coolly and serenely as she would if she were arriving for dinner and an evening of cards.

"The Countess de Marjolaine," Henry said hurriedly by way of introduction.

Jacobs was eyeing the countess uncertainly, perhaps unsure of the proper etiquette for receiving her. The *House Servant's Directory* did not cover such situations as the household fleeing arrest and imprisonment.

"Where is my family?" Henry demanded.

"Lady Ann and the children are with Mr. Sloan in the library, my lord. He deemed it the safest place in the house, due to the magical protection."

"The rest of the servants?" Henry asked.

"Her Ladyship sent them away," said the butler. "I took it upon myself to wait for your arrival, my lord. Baxter has returned with the carriage. He said to tell you he would wait in the alley around back."

"You have done well, Jacobs," said Henry, as he hurried toward the library. "Shut this door and lock it. The warding magic won't stop the soldiers, but it will slow them down. Do you have some safe refuge?"

"I do, my lord. I am friends with Sir Reginald's butler. His Lordship is out of town. I will be safe there."

"Then off you go, Jacobs," said Henry. "Thank you!"

"I will take your pistol, Jacobs," Cecile said.

Jacobs handed over the pistol, then departed, heading for the servants' entrance in the back.

Cecile tucked the pistol into the waist of her skirt, then pulled her cloak over it.

"One can generally judge people by the loyalty of their staff. You must be a good master, Henry," she remarked.

"I cannot take the credit. It is all Lady Ann's doing," said Henry.

They arrived at the library and found the door closed.

"Don't touch the handle!" Henry warned Cecile.

Mr. Sloan would have activated the magical warding constructs that would give anyone trying to force the door an extremely nasty shock. Henry raised his voice.

"Mr. Sloan!" he called. "The soldiers are down the block. We do not have a moment to lose!"

The handle glowed blue; the magic was bright as Mr. Sloan disarmed it.

"Safe now, my lord," Mr. Sloan called.

Henry flung open the door. Ann was inside the room, holding their baby daughter in her arms. Young Hal was standing protectively at his mother's side, trying very hard to look brave.

"Oh, Henry!" Ann gasped when she saw his disheveled state. "Are you all right? What has happened?"

Before speaking, Henry gathered his family in his arms and held them close.

"No time for explanations, my love," he said, brisk and businesslike. "The Countess de Marjolaine has kindly offered to convey you and the children to Everux. You will be safe there. Her Ladyship's coach is waiting around back."

"The Countess de Marjolaine?" Ann repeated, staring wide-eyed at her husband's most implacable foe, now standing in her library.

"Lady Ann, I am only too glad to be able to offer my help," said Cecile. "Are you ready? Is there anything I can do to assist you?"

"Mr. Sloan warned us we should be prepared to travel," Ann replied. "The children are warmly dressed. I have my jewels and the family documents."

Ann gave Henry a conscious look as she said this and he realized that the "family documents" must be important papers Mr. Sloan considered too valuable to be discovered.

"I will take you and the children to my coach, Lady Ann," Cecile offered. She reached out to Hal. "Master Henry, would you be so kind as to serve as my escort?"

Hal glanced at his father, who nodded. "Go with your mother and the countess, son."

Hal's lower lip trembled, but he made a little bow and took the countess's hand.

"I will show you the way, my lady," he said gallantly.

Cecile gave Henry a reassuring smile. Ann paused long enough to give him a kiss. "My aunt? Is she safe?"

"You must go, my love," said Henry.

Ann paled. She tightened her lips, gave him a trembling smile, and hurried past him and out the library door. Henry could hear his son saying to Cecile in a confidential tone, "Mummy doesn't know it, but I sneak out the servants' door when I don't want Nurse to find me."

Henry smiled, touched by his son's confession, and had to take a moment to swallow the choking sensation in his throat. He had no idea if or when he would ever see them again.

Mr. Sloan was on his feet. He appeared extremely weak and his bandage was stained with fresh blood. He did have some color in his face, however, although Henry guessed the flush had come from the brandy decanter.

"My lord, I am gratified to see you safe," said Mr. Sloan.

"Not safe as yet, Mr. Sloan. Soldiers are in the street," said Henry. "They could be here any moment."

"I anticipated as much, my lord," said Mr. Sloan. "Everything is in order. We have only to shut the door and the magic will activate."

"Very good, Mr. Sloan," said Henry. "If you will wait a moment, I have one task I must attend to first."

He reached into his pocket and drew out the queen's letter. She had written on the front in her firm, untidy hand: *To Be Opened on the Event of My Death*.

He broke the seal. The document was brief.

I, Queen Mary Elizabeth Ann Chessington, hereby appoint His Royal Highness Crown Prince Thomas James Stanford my heir to the throne in accordance with the Palace Law on Succession.

The letter was dated, signed, and sealed with the royal signet ring; the same ring Henry had removed from her cold, still hand. He folded the document and thrust it inside his coat.

"We can go now, Mr. Sloan."

They left the study. Henry closed the door behind them. Mr. Sloan passed his hand over the door handle, activating the magic. He was about to do the same for the door itself when he grimaced and stifled a groan. Sweat covered his forehead.

"You should accompany your family, my lord."

"I have done without your services for far too long, Mr. Sloan," said Henry. "I'll be damned if I'm going to lose you again. Finish the crafting, then give me your arm."

Mr. Sloan demurred, but Henry was adamant. He put his arm around Mr. Sloan and the two men hurried down the hallway. Behind them, they could hear sizzling and crackling sounds and screams coming from the front of the house. Some poor devil must have tried to open the front door.

"Queen Mary is dead, Mr. Sloan," said Henry.

"I am truly sorry, my lord," said Mr. Sloan. "Her Majesty was a good queen and a great lady."

"She was, Mr. Sloan. She was," said Henry.

Mr. Sloan hesitated, then asked, "Is there news of your brother, Sir Richard . . . ?"

"I cannot think about him now, Mr. Sloan," said Henry.

"I understand, my lord."

They exited the house. The coach was parked in the kitchen garden. The wyverns were kneading their claws into the herb beds and the smell of crushed rosemary scented the air. He saw Baxter sitting atop the box of his own carriage in the alleyway and waved to let him know he had seen him.

The countess was standing by the door to her coach, holding the pistol.

"Your wife and children are safely inside, my lord. Mr. Sloan, there is room for you, as well."

"Guard my family, Franklin," Henry said, assisting him to climb into the coach.

"With my life, my lord," said Mr. Sloan.

The coachman, Cousaille, indicated he was ready to depart. He had one hand on the brass helm and was holding a rifle in the other.

Ann leaned out the coach window to grip Henry by the hand. "I know you must stay behind, my love. For my sake, take care of yourself."

Henry kissed her hand, too emotional to speak. She withdrew back into the coach and shut the window. Henry rested his hand on the side of the coach, loath to let her and his children go, knowing he had no choice.

"I will take care of your family," Cecile promised. She handed him the pistol.

"I have not words enough to thank you, my lady," said Henry.

Cecile gripped his arm tightly. "You can do something for me in return. Thomas Stanford is a good and brave young man. If what I fear has come to pass, he will need your help, Henry. Do not abandon him."

He did not answer, but thought of the letter he carried. Cecile climbed inside the coach and shut the door. Henry gave the signal. Cousaille roared a command to the wyverns and sent the magic flooding through the lift tanks. The coach rose from the ground and flew off, using the treetops as cover.

Most of the soldiers were inside the house, ransacking it, but some must have seen the coach depart, for Henry heard shouts, and someone fired at it. The coach was armored with magical constructs, and bullets would have no effect, but he did not stir until he was certain it was safely away.

He then had to consider his own danger. The soldiers would probably think he had escaped inside the coach, but he took no chances. He ducked down, making himself as small as possible, in case anyone came around to the back to search for him, and ran to his carriage.

Baxter was sitting on the box, armed with a rifle.

"I have fresh horses, my lord," he said.

"Good work, Baxter," said Henry. "I'll take the rifle and sit up top with you."

He climbed onto the box and settled himself, then looked back at his house in time to see and hear the explosion. A portion of the wall in the vicinity of the library glowed bright blue and began to crumble. Baxter slapped the reins and the horses broke into a gallop.

"Where are we bound, my lord?" Baxter asked.

Henry had been thinking about where to go, what to do next. He had sent Amelia to warn Alan and Randolph that their country was in peril and he trusted his two friends were now on their way to the Naval Yard to defend their ships.

He thought of Simon and he glanced skyward. He could see Welkinstead peacefully drifting among the stars. Simon would be absorbed in his work, as usual, with no idea of the death and destruction taking place on the ground. Henry touched the letter secreted in his pocket. If ever he needed Simon's advice, he needed it now.

"I need a griffin. I must reach Welkinstead," said Henry.

"The Naval Club, my lord?" Baxter asked. The Naval Club kept griffins for the use of their members, and Henry had on occasion used their beasts. But he could not do that now.

"The Naval Club is one of the first places the soldiers would attack. The officers are probably fighting for their lives."

"Then we will make for the Regent's Arms, sir," said Baxter. "It's not far and they have a griffin hostelry there."

As the carriage reached the end of the alley, Henry looked back over his shoulder. The blue glow still lit the night. The soldiers would be attempting to salvage papers from his library, but they would have little luck. Mr. Sloan's magic would have obliterated his papers and books, reducing them to cinders and ashes. The library itself would now be a pile of rubble.

Henry turned back with a sigh.

"I saw the de Marjolaine coat of arms on the coach. Her Ladyship and the little ones will be safe, my lord," said Baxter, trying to reassure him. "Where does Her Ladyship does her yacht?"

"Hampton Yard," Henry replied. "The countess docks there when she is in Haever."

Hampton Yard was an exclusive, private docking facility that catered to a noble and wealthy clientele. King Ullr kept his yacht there when he traveled, as did King Renaud of Rosia. The yard was well guarded, as Henry had reason to know, for he had once sent his agents to try to break into Ullr's yacht and the guards had driven them off.

"The soldiers will be far more interested in warships than a few elegant yachts," Henry added. "They are probably now fighting to seize the Naval Yard."

"A bad business, my lord," Baxter said. "Mr. Sloan explained some of it to me while we were waiting."

Henry did not reply. He was mentally with his family inside the coach. Cecile and Ann would already be friends, and Cecile would gently break the news about the queen. Ann would be deeply grieved, for she loved her aunt. She would be worried about him, but she had royal blood in her veins and would put her country first. He was proud that she had not wept over him and pleaded with him to stay.

"My Mouse," he said to himself, and he remembered that it was Queen Mary who had given Ann her nickname.

"She's a mousey little thing," Mary had said to him. "But she will make you a good wife, Henry."

Henry put his hand to his eyes and let the tears trickle through his fingers.

The Regent's Arms was ablaze with lights and awash in rumor. All the guests were awake, either running around in their nightclothes, demanding to know what was going on, or shouting for their carriages.

Baxter pulled into the yard.

"There, my lord!" he said, indicating a hired griffin saddled and ready to fly. "Made to order."

A gentleman was standing beside the beast, berating the stable hand, claiming the man had not properly secured his luggage. Henry climbed down, giving final instructions.

"Drive to the house in Staffordshire, Baxter. If the soldiers are there, let it be known that I have fled the country. You should be safe. Keep the carriage hidden. If possible, my friends and I will meet you there."

"Yes, my lord," said Baxter. "Godspeed!"

He drove out of the yard and Henry hurried to the gentleman who had settled the issue of his luggage and was preparing to mount the griffin.

"Excuse me, sir, but I am in haste and I require this beast far more urgently that you do." Henry drew out his pocketbook. "I will pay you any amount you require as recompense for the inconvenience."

The man eyed Henry with contempt, for which Henry couldn't really blame him. He was filthy and disheveled and must look like a vagrant.

"Go to the devil," the man said, and put his foot in the stirrup.

Henry was in no mood to argue. He seized hold of the man by the collar, flung him to the ground, and aimed a pistol at his head.

"I will take the griffin and your helmet, as well, sir," Henry told him.

When the man swore at him, Henry cocked the pistol.

"I really do not want to put a bullet in you or the helmet, sir, but I will if I must."

The man yanked off the helmet and threw it at Henry with a snarl. Henry picked up the helm, put it on, then removed the man's luggage and tossed it in the muck. He mounted the griffin, who was glaring at him.

"I'm extremely sorry for the row," Henry said to the beast by way of apology. "I don't have time to explain, but you might want to depart these stables and not return. Otherwise you could find yourself conscripted into a rebel army."

The griffin must have been listening to the rumors, for after some consideration, it appeared to agree with Henry's assessment. Henry strapped himself into the saddle, just as the innkeeper came running outside in response to the commotion.

"I will be keeping the griffin," Henry called to him, and he tossed his pocketbook to the man.

As the griffin flew off, Henry saw the innkeeper pick up the pocketbook, open it and smile in satisfaction. He then tried to placate the other guest, who was sitting in the muck, shaking his fist at Henry and shouting imprecations.

The griffin shifted its head to seek instructions.

"The floating house," said Henry. "Welkinstead. Are you familiar with it?"

The griffin nodded and they took to the air. Henry located the house; the odd-looking combination of turrets and steeples, chimneys and towers, made a strange-looking blot against the stars.

The griffin suddenly opened its beak and gave a screeching caw, startling

Henry, who wondered what was wrong. The beast was staring off to the east. Henry raised the visor on the helm to follow the griffin's gaze, and saw another blot on the starlight: a black ship.

The griffin gnashed its beak. Griffins had served in the war against the Bottom Dwellers and had no love for them.

Henry gripped the reins and watched the progress of the ship, wondering where it was bound. Following the ship's trajectory with his eyes, he stiffened.

The black ship was sailing straight for Welkinstead.

Henry could not believe it. Why would this Colonel Smythe target Simon Yates? As far as most people knew, Simon was nothing more than the eccentric owner of a flying house. Only a few knew that Simon was, as Henry termed him, Freya's "secret weapon." Simon's unique ability to read, remember, gather, and sift through mounds of seemingly irrelevant and insignificant details was invaluable to the nation.

And, as such, he was a threat.

But how had Smythe found out? Simon's role in Freya's intelligence network was a closely held state secret. Only the queen and a handful of others knew his value to the country.

A handful of others . . . including Richard Wallace.

A leading member of the House of Nobles, Richard was one of the few who knew that Simon worked for the crown. And as a member of the Faithful, he must have shared that information with Smythe.

"You have a great deal to answer for, Brother," said Henry grimly to the dark night. "By God, if you are responsible for killing Simon, I will dance at your hanging!"

The black ship was sailing straight toward the floating house, but it was moving slowly, seeming to crawl through the mists. Kate had disabled one of the airscrews and that had reduced the ship's speed, plus it was flying a little off kilter. Its green beam weapon had long range, however. The ship would not need to be close to the house to open fire on it.

Welkinstead was made of magic, as the saying went. The duchess had been a renowned crafter, as well as architect, artist, musician, scientist, and God knew what else. Magic imbued the walls and kept the towers standing and the house floating. The green beam with its contramagic could utterly obliterate it.

Henry leaned forward over the griffin's neck and shouted so that the beast could hear him.

"That black ship is bound for Welkinstead! We need to get there ahead of it!"

Griffins generally flew at a moderate pace, so as not to create discomfort for their riders, but the beasts were powerful fliers, capable of bursts of speed. Henry could feel the griffin gathering itself, feel the strong muscles bunching together. The griffin dropped its wings, then raised them, spread them, and began to soar.

Henry slammed shut the visor, crouched low in the saddle and hung on.

ACKNOWLEDGMENTS

The lullaby Cecile sings is an old French lullaby, "Dodo, l'enfant, do."

House Servant's Directory, or, A Monitor for Private Families by Robert Roberts

Roberts was an African-American butler who worked for Christopher Gore, governor and senator from Massachusetts. His book was first published in 1827 by Munroe and Francis of Boston. The book proved quite popular, for it went into two more printings. According to the description on the cover, the book provides "Hints on the Arrangement and Performance of Servants' Work" with rules for everything from setting tables to conducting "large and small parties" to cleaning "patent and common" lamps.